CLUTCH (

WHE

TIED U   ...NSEL

Dame Ngaio Marsh was born in New Zealand in 1895 and died in February 1982. She wrote over 30 detective novels and many of her stories have theatrical settings, for Ngaio Marsh's real passion was the theatre. Both actress and producer, she almost single-handedly revived the New Zealand public's interest in the theatre. It was for this work that she received what she called her 'damery' in 1966.

'The finest writer in the English language of the pure, classical puzzle whodunit. Among the crime queens, Ngaio Marsh stands out as an Empress.'   *The Sun*

'Ngaio Marsh transforms the detective story from a mere puzzle into a novel.'   *Daily Express*

'Her work is as nearly flawless as makes no odds. Character, plot, wit, good writing, and sound technique.'   *Sunday Times*

'She writes better than Christie!'   *New York Times*

'Brilliantly readable . . . first class detection.'   *Observer*

'Still, quite simply, the greatest exponent of the classical English detective story.'   *Daily Telegraph*

'Read just one of Ngaio Marsh's novels and you've got to read them all . . . '   *Daily Mail*

BY THE SAME AUTHOR

NGAIO MARSH

Clutch of Constables

When in Rome

Tied Up in Tinsel

AND

Chapter and Verse

HARPER

HARPER

an imprint of HarperCollins*Publishers*
77-85 Fulham Palace Road
Hammersmith, London W6 8JB
www.harpercollins.co.uk

This omnibus edition 2009
1

Clutch of Constables first published in Great Britain by Collins 1968
When In Rome first published in Great Britain by Collins 1970
Tied Up In Tinsel first published in Great Britain by Collins 1972
Chapter and Verse first published in Great Britain in
Death on the Air and Other Stories by HarperCollins*Publishers* 1995

Ngaio Marsh asserts the moral right to
be identified as the author of these works

ISBN 978 0 00 732877 2
Printed and bound in Great Britain by
Clays Ltd, St Ives plc

Mixed Sources
Product group from well-managed
forests and other controlled sources
www.fsc.org   Cert no. SW-COC-1806
© 1996 Forest Stewardship Council

FSC is a non-profit international organisation established to promote the
responsible management of the world's forests. Products carrying the FSC
label are independently certified to assure consumers that they come
from forests that are managed to meet the social, economic and
ecological needs of present and future generations.

Find out more about HarperCollins and the environment at
www.harpercollins.co.uk/green

CONTENTS

Clutch of Constables

*For Audrey and Guy
with love*

Contents

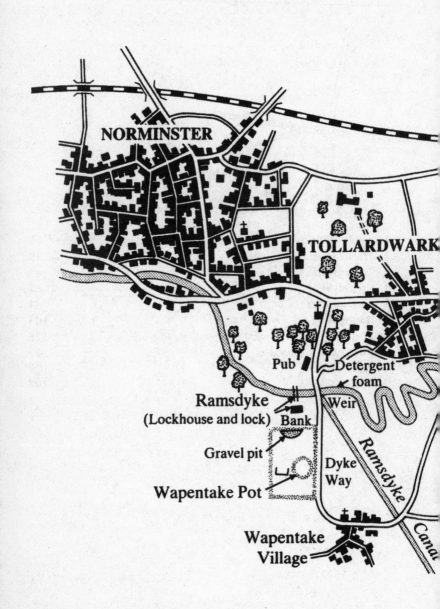

NORMINSTER

TOLLARDWARK

Pub

Detergent
foam

Ramsdyke
(Lockhouse and lock)   Bank

Weir

Gravel pit

Dyke
Way

Ramsdyke

Wapentake Pot

Wapentake
Village

Canal

Cast of Characters

Passenger List M.V. Zodiac
Mrs Roderick Alleyn
Miss Hazel Rickerby-Carrick
Mr Caley Bard
Mr Stanley Pollock
Dr Francis Natouche MD
Mr Earl J. Hewson
Miss Sally-Lou Hewson
The Rev J. de B. Lazenby

Ship's Company M. V. Zodiac

James Tretheway	*Skipper*
Mrs Tretheway	*Cook and Stewardess*
Tom Tretheway	*Boy*

Persons in or about Tollardwark

Jno. Bagg	*Licensed Dealer*
Mrs Bagg	*His mother*
Mr and Mrs John Smith	*A ton-up combo*

Police

Superintendent Albert Tillottson	*Tollardwark Constabulary*
PC Cape	*Tollardwark Constabulary*
Superintendent R. Bonney	*Longminster Constabulary*
Sundry Constables	*County police forces*
Superintendent Alleyn	*CID London*
Inspector Fox	*CID London*
Detective-Sergeant Bailey	*CID London*
Detective-Sergeant Thompson	*CID London*

CHAPTER 1

Apply Within

'There was nothing fancy about the Jampot,' Alleyn said. 'The word "Jobs" is entirely appropriate to his activities. He planned carefully, left as little as possible to chance, took a satisfaction in his work and accepted, without dwelling upon them, the occupational hazards which it involved. Retention or abolishment of capital punishment made no difference at all to his professional behaviour: I daresay he looks upon the murders that he did in fact perform, as tiresome and regrettable necessities.

'His talents were appropriate to his employment. They included manual dexterity, a passion for accuracy, a really exceptional intelligence of mathematical precision and a useful imagination offset by a complete blank where nervous anxiety might be expected. Above all he was a superb mimic. Mimics are born not made. From his childhood the Jampot showed an uncanny talent in reflecting not only the mannerisms, speech habits and social behaviour of an extraordinary diversity of persons but of knowing, apparently by instinct, how they would react to given circumstances. Small wonder,' Alleyn said, 'that he led us up the garden path for so long. He was a masterpiece.'

He looked round his audience. Six rows of sharp-cropped heads. Were the dumb-looking ones as dumb as their wrinkled foreheads, lacklustre eyes and slackish mouths seemed to suggest? Was the forward-leaning one in the second row, who had come up from the uniformed branch with an outstanding report, as good as his promise? Protectors of the people, Alleyn thought. If only the people would recognize them as such. He went on.

'I've chosen the Jampot for your consideration,' he said, 'because he's a kind of bonus in crime. He combines in himself the ingredients that you find singly in other homicides and hands you the lot in a mixed grill. His real name, believe it or not, is Foljambe.'

The forward-leaning, sandy-coloured recruit gave a laugh which he stifled. Several of his companions grinned doubtfully and wiped their mouths. Two looked startled and the rest uneasy.

'At all events,' Alleyn said, 'that's what he says it is and as he hasn't got any other name, Foljambe let the Jampot be.

'He was born in Johannesburg, received a good education and is said to have read medicine for two years but would appear to have been from birth what used to be known as a "wrong-un". His nickname was given him by his South African associates in crime and has been adopted by the police on both sides of the Atlantic. In Paris, I understand he is known as Le Folichon or "the frisky bloke".

'I'd like to pick up his story at the time of his highly ingenious escape from gaol which took place on the 7th May the year before last in Bolivia . . .'

One or two of his hearers wrote this down. He was giving an address by invitation to a ten-week course at the Police College.

'By an outlandish coincidence,' Alleyn said and his deep voice took on the note of continuous narrative, 'I was personally involved in this affair: by personally, I mean, as a private individual as well as a policeman. It so happened that my wife – '

I

'– above all it must be said of this most distinguished exhibition, that while in scope it is retrospective it is by no means definitive. The painter, one feels, above all her contemporaries, will continue to explore and penetrate: for her own and our sustained enjoyment.'

The painter in question muttered: 'O Lord, O Lord,' and laid aside the morning paper as stealthily as if she had stolen it. She left the dining-room, paid her bill, arranged to pick up her luggage in time to catch the London train and went for a stroll.

Her hotel was not far from the river. Summer sunshine defined alike ranks of unbudgingly Victorian mercantile buildings broken at irregular intervals by vast up-ended waffle-irons. Gothic spires, and a ham-fisted Town Hall poked up through the early mist. She turned her back on them and made downhill for the river.

As she drew near to it the character of the streets changed. They grew narrower and were cobbled. She passed a rope-walk and a shop called 'Rutherfords, Riverview Chandlers', a bakery smelling of new bread, a pawnbroker's and a second-hand machine-parts shop. The river itself now glinted through gaps in the buildings and at the end of passages. When she finally came within full view of it she thought it beautiful. Not picturesque or grandiloquent but alive and positive, curving in and out of the city with historical authority. It was, she thought, a thing in its own right and the streets and wharves that attended upon it belonged to it and to themselves. 'Wharf Lane' she read, and took her way down it to the front. Rivercraft of all kinds were moored along the foreshore.

Half-way down the lane she came upon the offices of The Pleasure Craft and Riverage Company. In their window were faded notices of sailing dates and various kinds of cruises. While she was reading these a man in shirt sleeves, looking larger than life in the confined space, edged his way towards the window and attached to its surface with sticky paper, a freshly-written card.

He caught sight of her, gave her a tentative smile and backed out of the window.

She read the card.

'M.V. *Zodiac*. Last minute cancellation.
A single-berth cabin is available for
this day's sailing. Apply within.'

Placed about the window were photographs of M.V. *Zodiac* in
transit and of the places she visited. In the background hung a map of
the river and the canals that articulated with it: Ramsdyke. Bullsdyke.
Crossdyke. A five day cruise from Norminster to Longminster and
back was offered. Passengers slept and ate on board. The countryside,
said a pamphlet that lay on the floor, was rich in historical associations. Someone with a taste for fanciful phrases had added: 'For Five
Days you Step out of Time.'

She had had a gruelling summer, working for her one-man show
and was due in a few weeks to see it launched in Paris and afterwards
New York. Her husband was in America and her son was taking a
course at Grenoble. She thought of the long train journey south, the
gritty arrival, the summer stifle of London and the empty stuffy
house. It seemed to her, afterwards, that she behaved like a child in
a fairytale. She opened the door and as she did so she heard something say within her head: 'For five days I step out of time.'

II

'There is,' wrote Miss Rickerby-Carrick, 'no bottom, none, to my
unquenchable infamy.'

She glanced absently at the tip of her propelling pencil and, in
falsetto, cleared her throat.

'For instance,' she wrote, 'let us examine my philanthropy. Or
rather, since I have no distaste for colloquialism, my dogoodery. No!'
she exclaimed aloud, 'That won't wash. That is a vile phrase,
Dogoodery is a vile phrase.' She paused again, greatly put out by the
suspicion that these observations were not entirely original. She
stared about her and caught the eye of a thin lady in dark blue linen
who, like herself, sat on her own suitcase.

' "Dogoodery",' Miss Rickerby-Carrick repeated. 'Is that a facetious word? Do you find it so?'

'Well – it depends, I suppose, on the context.'

'You look startled.'

'Do I?' said Troy Alleyn, looking startled indeed. 'Sorry. I was a thousand miles away.'

'I wish *I* were. Or no,' amended Miss Rickerby-Carrick. 'Wrong again. Correction. I wish I were a thousand miles away from *me*. From myself. No kidding,' she added. 'To try out another colloquialism.'

She wrote again in her book.

Her companion looked attentively at her and might have been said, after her own fashion, also to make notes. She saw a figure, not exactly of fun, but of confusion. There was no co-ordination. The claret-coloured suit, the disheartened jumper, above all the knitted jockey-cap, all looked to have been thrown at their wearer and fortuitously to have stuck. She had a strange trick with her mouth, letting it fly apart over her teeth and turn up at the corners so that she seemed to grin when in fact she did nothing of the sort. The hand that clutched her propelling pencil was arthritic.

Overhead, clouds bowled slowly across a midsummer sky. A light wind fiddled with the river and one or two small boats bumped at their moorings. The pleasure craft *Zodiac* had not appeared but was due at noon.

'My name,' said Miss Rickerby-Carrick, 'is Rickerby-Carrick. Hazel. "Spinster of this parish". What's yours?'

'Alleyn.'

'Mrs?'

'Yes.' After a moment's hesitation Troy, since it was obviously expected of her, uncomfortably added her first name. 'Agatha,' she mumbled.

'Agatharallen,' said Miss Rickerby-Carrick sharply. 'That's funny. I thought you must be K. G. Z. Andropulos, Cabin 7.'

'The cabin *was* taken by somebody called Andropulos, I believe, but the booking was cancelled at the last moment. This morning, in fact. I happened to be here on – on business and I saw it advertised in the Company's window, so I took it,' said Troy, 'on impulse.'

'Just like that. Fancy.' A longish pause followed. 'So we're ship-mates? "Water-wanderers?" ' Miss Rickerby-Carrick concluded, quoting the brochure.

'In the *Zodiac*? Yes,' Troy agreed and hoped she sounded friendly enough. Miss Rickerby-Carrick crinkled her eyes and stripped her teeth. 'Jolly good show,' she said. She gazed at Troy for some time and then returned to her writing. An affluent-looking car drove half-way down the cobbled passage. Its uniformed driver got out, walked to the quay, looked superciliously at nothing in particular, returned, spoke through the rear window to an indistinguishable occupant and resumed his place at the wheel.

'When I examine in depth the motives by which I am activated,' wrote Miss Rickerby-Carrick in her book. 'I am appalled. For instance. I have a reputation, within my circle (admittedly a limited one) for niceness, for kindness, for charity. I adore my reputation. People come to me in their trouble. They cast themselves upon my bosom and weep. I love it. I'm awfully good at being good. I think to myself that they must all tell each other how good I am. "Hay Rickerby-Carrick," I know they say, "She's *so good.*" And so I am. I *am.* I put myself out in order to keep up my reputation. I make sacrifices. I am unselfish in buses, upstanding in tubes and I relinquish my places in queues. I visit the aged, I comfort the bereaved and if they don't like it they can lump it. I am filled with amazement when I think about my niceness. O misery, misery, misery me,' she wrote with enormous relish.

Two drops fell upon her open notebook. She gave a loud, succulent and complacent sniff.

Troy thought: 'Will she go on like this for five days? Is she dotty? O God, has she got a cold!'

'Sorry,' said Miss Rickerby-Carrick. 'I've god a bid of cold. Dur,' she added making a catarrhal clicking sound and allowing her mouth to fall slightly open. Troy began to wonder if there was a good train to London before evening.

'You wonder,' said Miss Rickerby-Carrick in a thick voice, 'why I sit on my suitcase and write. I have lately taken to a diary. My self-propelling confessional, *I* call it.'

'Do you?' Troy said helplessly.

Down the cobbled lane walked a pleasant-looking man in an ancient knickerbocker suit of Donegal tweed and a cloth cap. He carried, beside a rucksack, a square box on a shoulder-strap and a canvas-covered object that might, Troy thought, almost be a grossly misshapen tennis racquet. He took off his cap when he saw the ladies and kept it off. He was of a sandy complexion with a not unattractive cast in one of his blue eyes, a freckled countenance and a tentative smile.

'Good morning,' he said. 'We must be fellow-travellers.'

Troy agreed. Miss Rickerby-Carrick, blurred about the eyes and nose, nodded, smiled and sniffed. She was an industrious nodder.

'No signs of the *Zodiac* as yet,' said the newcomer. 'Dear me,' he added, 'that's a pit-fall of a joke isn't it? We shall all be making it as punctually as the tides, I daresay.' Miss Rickerby-Carrick after a moment's thought, was consumed with laughter. He looked briefly at her and attentively at Troy. 'My name's Caley Bard,' he said.

'I'm Troy Alleyn and this is Miss Rickerby-Carrick.'

'You said you were Agatha,' Miss Rickerby-Carrick pointed out. 'You said Agatharallen,' and Troy felt herself blushing.

'So I am,' she muttered, 'the other's just a sort of a joke – my husband – ' her voice died away. She was now extremely conscious of Mr Bard's scrutiny and particularly aware of its dwelling speculatively on the veteran paintbox at her feet. All he said, however, was, 'Dear me,' in a donnish tone. When she looked her apprehension he tipped her a wink. This was disconcerting.

She was relieved by the arrival on an apocalyptic motorbicycle of a young man and his girl. The noonday sun pricked at their metal studs and turned the surface of their leather suits and calf-high boots into toffee. From under crash helmets, hair, veiled in oil and dust, fell unevenly to their shoulders. Their machine belched past the stationary chauffeur-driven car and came to a halt. They put their booted feet to the ground and lounged, chewing, against their bicycle. 'There is nothing,' Troy thought, 'as insolent as a gum-chewing face,' and at the same time she itched to make a sharp, black drawing of the riders.

'Do you suppose – ?' she ventured in a low voice.

'I hardly think water-wandering would present a very alluring prospect,' Mr Bard rejoined.

'In any case, they have no luggage.'

'They may not need any. They may bed down as they are.'

'Oh, do you think so? All those steel knobs.'

'There is that, of course,' Mr Bard agreed.

The young people lit cigarettes, inhaled deeply, stared at nothing and exhaled vapour. They had not spoken.

Miss Rickerby-Carrick gazed raptly at them and then wrote in her book.

' – "two of our Young Independents", ' she noted. 'Is it to gladiators that one should compare them? Would they like it if one did? Would I be able to get on with them? Would they like me? Would they find me sympatica or is it sympatico? Alas, there I go again. Incorrigible, hopeless old Me!'

She stabbed down an ejaculation mark, clicked off her pencil with an air of quizzical finality, and said to Troy: 'How did you get here? I came by bus: from good old Brummers.'

'I drove,' Mr Bard said. 'From London and put up at a pub. Got here last night.'

'I did too,' said Troy. 'But I came by train.'

'There's a London train that connects this morning,' Miss Rickerby-Carrick observed. 'Arrives 11.45.'

'I know. But I – there was – I had an engagement,' Troy mumbled.

'Such as going to the pictures?' Mr Bard airily suggested to nobody in particular. 'Something of that sort?' Troy looked at him but he was staring absently at the river. '*I* went to the pictures,' he said. 'But not last night. This morning. Lovely.'

'The *pictures*!' Miss Rickerby-Carrick exclaimed. 'This morning! Do you mean the cinema?'

But before Mr Bard could explain himself if indeed he intended to do so, two taxis, one after the other, came down the cobbled lane and discharged their passengers.

'There! The London train must be in,' Miss Rickerby-Carrick observed with an air of triumph.

The first to alight was an undistinguished man of about forty. Under a belted raincoat he wore a pinstriped suit which, revealed, would surely prove abominable. His shirt was mauve and his tie a brightish pink. His hair was cut short back-and-sides. He had a knobbly face and pale eyes. As he approached, carrying his fibre suitcase and wearing a jaunty air, Troy noticed that he limped, swinging a built-up boot. 'Morning all,' he said. 'Lovely day, innit?'

Troy and Mr Bard agreed and Miss Rickerby-Carrick repeated: 'Lovely! Lovely!' on an ecstatic note.

'Pollock's the name,' said the new arrival, easily. 'Stan.' They murmured.

Mr Bard introduced himself and the ladies. Mr Pollock responded with sideway wags of his head.

'That's the ticket,' he said. 'No deception practised.'

Miss Rickerby-Carrick said: '*Isn't* this going to be *fun*,' in a wildish tone that modulated into one of astonishment. Her gaze had shifted to the passenger from the second taxi who, with his back to the group, was settling his fare. He was exceedingly tall and very well-dressed at High Establishment level. Indeed his hat, houndstooth checked overcoat and impeccable brogues were in such a grand conservative style that it surprised – it almost shocked – Troy to observe that he seemed to be wearing black gloves like a Dickensian undertaker. Some yards distant, his bell-like voice rang out enormously. 'Thank you. Good morning to you. Good morning.'

He lifted his suitcase and turned. His hat tilted a little forward: the brim shadowed his face but could not be seen to do so as the face itself was darker than a shadow: the latest arrival was a coloured man.

Miss Rickerby-Carrick gave out an ejaculation. Mr Bard after the briefest glance continued talking to Troy. Mr Pollock stared, faintly whistled and then turned aside with a shuttered face. The motorcyclists for some private reason broke into ungentle laughter.

The newcomer advanced, lifted his hat generally and moved through the group to the wharf's edge where he stood looking upstream towards the bend in the river: an incongruous but impressive and elegant figure against a broken background of rivercraft, sliding water and buildings advertising themselves in a confusion of signs.

Troy said quickly: 'That makes five of us, doesn't it? Three more to come.'

'One of whom occupies that very affluent-looking car, no doubt,' said Mr Bard. 'I tried to peer in as I came past but an open newspaper defeated me.'

'Male or female, did you gather?'

'Oh the former, the former. A large manicured hand. The chauffeur is one of the stony kind. Now what is your guess? We have a choice of two from our passenger list, haven't we? Which do you think?' He just indicated the figure down by the river. 'Dr Natouche? Mr J. de B. Lazenby? Which is which?'

'I plump for J. de B. L. in the car,' Troy said. 'It sounds so magnificent.'

'Do you? No: my fancy lies in the contrary field. I put Dr Natouche in the car. A specialist in some esoteric upper reaches of the more impenetrable branches of medicine. An astronomical consulting fee. And I fetch our friend on the wharf from Barbados. He owns a string of hotels and is called Jasper de Brabazon Lazenby. Shall we have a bet on it?'

'Well,' Troy said, 'propose your bet.'

'If I win you have a drink with me before luncheon. If you win, I pay for the drinks.'

'Now then!' Troy exclaimed.

Mr Bard gave a little inward laugh.

'We shall see,' he said. 'I think that I might – ' He smiled at Troy and without completing his sentence walked down to the quay.

'Are you,' Troy could just hear him say, 'joining us? I'm sure you must be.'

'In the *Zodiac*?' the great voice replied. 'Yes. I am a passenger.'

'Shall we introduce ourselves?'

The others all strained to hear the exchange of names.

'Natouche.'

'Dr Natouche?'

'Quite so.'

Mr Bard sketched the very vaguest and least of bows in Troy's direction.

'I'm Caley Bard,' he said.

'Ah. I too have seen the passenger list. Good morning, sir.'

'Do,' said Caley Bard, 'come and meet the others. We have been getting to know each other.'

'Thank you. If you wish.'

They turned together. Mr Bard was a tall man but Dr Natouche diminished him. Behind them the river, crinkled by a breeze and dappled with discs of sunlight, played tricks with the two approaching figures. It exaggerated their size, rimmed them in a pulsing nimbus and distorted their movement. As they drew nearer, the pale man and the dark, Troy, bemused by this dazzle, thought: 'There is no reason in the wide world why I should feel apprehensive. It will be all right unless Mr Pollock is bloody-minded or the Rickerby-Carrick hideously effusive. It must be all right.' She glanced up the lane and there were the cyclists, stock-still except for their jaws: staring, staring.

She held out her hand to Dr Natouche who was formal and bowed slightly over it. His head, uncovered, showed grey close-cut fuzz above the temples. His skin was not perfectly black but warmly dark with grape-coloured shadows. The bone structure of his face was exquisite.

'Mrs Alleyn,' said Dr Natouche.

Miss Rickerby-Carrick was, as Troy had feared she would be, excessive. She shook Dr Natouche's hand up and down and laughed madly: 'Oh – ho – ho,' she laughed, 'how perfectly splendid.'

Mr Pollock kept his hands in his pockets and limped aside thus avoiding an introduction.

Since there seemed to be nothing else to talk about Troy hurriedly asked Dr Natouche if he had come by the London train. He said he had driven up from Liverpool, added a few generalities, gave her a smile and a slight inclination of his head, returned to the river and walked for some little distance along the wharves.

'Innit marvellous?' Mr Pollock asked of nobody in particular. 'They don't tell you so you can't complain.'

'They?' wondered Miss Rickerby-Carrick. 'Tell you? I don't understand?'

'When you book in.' He jerked his head towards Dr Natouche. 'What to expect.'

'Oh, but you *mustn't*!' she whispered. 'You *mustn't* feel like that. Truly.'

'Meant to be class, this carry-on? Right? That's what they tell you. Right? First class. Luxury accommodation. Not my idea of it. Not with that type of company. If I'd known one of that lot was included I wouldn't have come at it. Straight, I wouldn't.'

'How very odd of you,' said Mr Bard lightly.

'That's your opinion,' Mr Pollock angrily rejoined. He turned towards Troy, hoping perhaps for an ally. 'I reckon it's an insult to the ladies,' he said.

'Oh, go along with you,' Troy returned as good-naturedly as she could manage, 'it's nothing of the sort. Is it, Miss Rickerby-Carrick?'

'Oh *no*. No. Indeed, no.'

'I know what I'm talking about,' Mr Pollock loudly asserted. Troy looked nervously at the distant figure on the riverage. 'I own property. Once that sort settles in a district – look – it's a slum. Easy as that.'

'Mr Pollock, this man is a doctor,' Troy said.

'You're joking? Doctor? Of what?'

'Of medicine,' Mr Bard said. 'You should consult your passenger list, my dear fellow. He's an MD.'

'You can tell people you're anything,' Mr Pollock darkly declared. 'Anything. I could tell them I was a bloody earl. Pardon the French, I'm sure.' He glared at Troy who was giggling. The shadow of a grin crept into his expression. 'Not that they'd credit it,' he added. 'But still.'

The young man on the motorcycle sounded a derisive call on his siren. '*Taa* t'–ta ta ta. *Ta-Taa*.' He and his girlfriend were looking towards the bend in the river.

A rivercraft had come into view. She was painted a dazzling white. A scarlet and green houseflag was mounted at her bows and the red ensign at her stern. Sunlight splashed her brass-work, red curtains glowed behind her saloon windows. As she drew towards her moorings her name could be seen, painted in gold letters along her bows.

M.V. *Zodiac*.

The clock in a church tower above the river struck twelve.

'Here she is,' Mr Bard said. 'Dead on time.'

III

The *Zodiac* berthed and was made fast very smartly by a lad of about fifteen. Her skipper left the wheelhouse and said goodbye to his passengers who could be heard to thank him, saying they wished the voyage had been longer. They passed through the waiting group. A woman, catching Troy's eye said: 'You're going to love it.' And a man remarked to his wife: 'Well, back to earth, worse luck,' with what seemed almost excessive regret after a five day jaunt.

When they had all gone the new passengers moved down to the *Zodiac* and were greeted by the skipper. He was a pleasant-looking fellow, very neat in his white duck shirt and dark blue trousers and tie. He wore the orthodox peaked cap.

'You'd all like to come aboard,' he said. 'Tom!' The boy began to collect the luggage and pile it on the deck. The skipper offered a hand to the ladies. Miss Rickerby-Carrick made rather heavy-going of this business. 'Dear me!' she said, 'Oh. Oh, thank you,' and leapt prodigiously.

She had a trick of clutching with her left hand at her dun-coloured jumper: almost, Troy thought, as if she carried her money in a bag round her neck and wanted continuously to assure herself it was still there.

From amidships and hard-by the wheelhouse the passengers descended, by way of a steep little flight of steps and a half-gate of the loosebox kind, into the saloon. From there a further downward flight ended in a passage through the cabin quarters. Left of this companion-way a hatch from the saloon offered a bird's-eye view into the cuddy which was at lower-deck level. Down there a blonde woman assembled dishes of cold meats and salads. She wore a starched apron over a black cotton dress. Her hair, pale as straw, was drawn back from a central parting into a lustrous knob. As Troy looked down at it the woman turned and tilted her head. She smiled dazzlingly and said: 'Good morning. Lunch in half an hour. The bar will be open in a few minutes.' The bar, Troy saw, was on the port side of the saloon, near the entry.

The boy came down with Troy's suitcase and paintbox. He said: 'This way, please,' and she followed him to the lower deck and to her cabin.

No. 7 was the third on the starboard side, and was exactly twice the size of its bunk. It had a cupboard, a washbasin and a porthole near the ceiling. The counterpane and curtains were cherry-red and in a glass on the bedside shelf there was a red geranium mixed with a handful of fern and hedgerow flowers. This pleased Troy greatly. The boy put her suitcase on the bunk and her paintbox under it. For some reason she felt diffident about tipping him. She hesitated but he didn't. He gave her a smile that was the very print of the woman's and was gone. 'He's her son,' thought Troy, 'and perhaps they're a family. Perhaps the Skipper's his father.'

She unpacked her suitcase and stowed it under her bunk, washed her hands and was about to return to the saloon when, hearing voices outside, she knelt on her bunk and looked through the porthole. It was at dockside level and there, quite close at hand, were the shiny leggings and polished boots of the smart chauffeur, his brown breeches and his gloved hands each holding a suitcase. They moved out of sight, towards the boarding plank, no doubt, and were followed by shoes and clerical grey trousers. These legs paused and formed a truncated triangular frame through which Troy saw, as if in an artfully directed film, the distant black-leathered cyclists, still glinting, chewing and staring in the cobbled lane. She had the oddest notion that they stared at her, though that, as she told herself, was ridiculous. They had just been joined by the boy from the *Zodiac* when all of them were blotted out by a taxi that shot into her field of vision and halted. The framing legs moved away. The door of the taxi began to open but Troy's attention was abstracted by a loud rap on her cabin door. She sat down hurriedly on her bunk and said: 'Come in.' Miss Rickerby-Carrick's active face appeared round the door.

'I say,' she said. 'Bliss! A shower and *two* loos! *Aren't* we lucky!'

Before Troy could reply she had withdrawn. There were sounds within the craft of new arrivals.

'Thank you very much . . . Er – here – ' the voice was lowered to an indistinguishable murmur. A second voice said: 'Thank you, sir.' A door was shut. Boots tramped up the companion-way and across the deck overhead. 'The chauffeur,' Troy thought, 'and Mr. J. de B. Lazenby.' She waited for a moment listening to the movements of the other passengers. There was a further confusion of arrival and a bump of luggage. A woman's voice said: 'That's correct, stooard, we do have quite a bit of photographic equipment. I guess I'll use Number 3 as a regular stateroom and Number 6 can accommodate my brother and the overflow. OK? OK, Earl?'

'Sure. Sure.'

The cabin forward of Troy's was No. 6. She heard sounds of the bestowal of property and a number of warnings as to its fragility, all given with evident good humour. The man's voice said repeatedly: 'Sure. Sure. Fine. Fine.' There was an unsuccessful attempt to tip the boy. 'Thanks all the same,' Troy heard him say. He departed. There followed a silence and an ejaculation from the lady. 'Do you look like I feel?' and the man's answer: 'Forget it. We couldn't know.'

Troy consulted her passenger list. Mr Earl J. and Miss Sally-Lou Hewson had arrived. She stowed away her baggage and then went up to the saloon.

They were all there except the three latest arrivals. Dr Natouche sat by himself reading a newspaper with a glass of beer to hand. Miss Rickerby-Carrick, in conversation with Mr Pollock, occupied a seat that ran round the forward end of the saloon under the windows. Mr Caley Bard who evidently had been waiting for Troy, at once reminded her that she was to have a drink with him. 'Mrs Tretheway,' he said, 'mixes a superb Martini.'

She was behind the little bar, displayed in the classic manner within a frame of bottles and glasses many of which were splintered by sunlight. She herself had a kind of local iridescence: she looked superb. Mr Pollock kept glancing at her with a half-smile on his lips and then turning away again. Miss Rickerby-Carrick gazed at her with a kind of anguished wonder. Mr Bard expressed his appreciation in what Troy was to learn was a very characteristic manner.

'The Bar at the Folies Bergère may as well shut up shop,' he said to Troy. 'Manet would have changed his drinking habits. You, by the way, could show him where he gets off.' And he gave Troy a little bow and a very knowing smile. 'You ought to have a go,' he suggested. 'Don't,' she said hurriedly. 'Please.' He laughed and leant across the bar to pay for their drinks. Mrs Tretheway gave Troy a woman-to-woman look that included her fabulous smile.

Even Dr Natouche lowered his paper and contemplated Mrs Tretheway with gravity for several seconds.

At the back of the bar hung a framed legend, rather shakily typed.

THE SIGNS OF THE ZODIAC
The Hunt of the Heavenly Host begins
With the Ram, the Bull and the Heavenly Twins.
The Crab is followed by the Lion
The Virgin and the Scales,
The Scorpion, Archer and He-Goat,
The Man that carries the Watering-pot
And the Fish with the Glittering Tails.

'Isn't that charming?' Mr Bard asked Troy. 'Don't you think so?'
'The magic of the proper name,' Troy agreed. 'Especially those names. It always does the trick, doesn't it?'

Mrs Tretheway said, 'A chap that cruised with us gave it to me. He said it was out of some kid's book.'

'It's got the right kind of dream-sound for that,' Troy said. She thought she would like to make a picture of the Signs and put the rhyme in the middle. Perhaps before the cruise was over –

'To make it rhyme,' Mrs Tretheway pointed out, 'you have to say "pote". "The Man that carries the Watering-pote".'

She pushed their drinks across the bar. The back of her hand brushed Mr Bard's fingers.

'You'll join us, I hope,' he said.

'Another time, thanks all the same. I've got to look after your lunch. It's cold – what do they call it – smorgasbord, for today. If everybody would help themselves when they're ready.'

She went over to the hatch into the cuddy. Tom, the boy, had gone below and handed up the dishes to his mother who set them out on the tables that had been pushed together and covered with a white cloth.

'Whenever you're ready,' Mrs Tretheway repeated. 'Please help yourselves,' and returned to the bar where she jangled a handbell.

Without consulting Troy, Mr Bard ordered two more dry Martinis. This was not Troy's favourite drink and in any case the first had been extremely strong.

'No, really, thank you,' she said. '*Not* for me. I'm for my lunch.'

'Well,' he said. 'P'rhaps you're right. We'll postpone until dinner time. Let moderation be our cry.'

It now occurred to Troy that Mr Bard was making a dead set at her. Gratifying though this might or might not be, it did not fit in with her plan for a five days' anonymous dawdle along the British Inland Waterways. Mr Bard, it was evident, had twigged Troy. He had this morning visited her one-man show for the opening of which, last evening, she had come up from London. He had been cunning enough to realize that she wanted to remain unrecognized. Evidently he was disposed to torment her about this and to set up a kind of alliance on the strength of it. Mr Bard was a tease.

There was a place beside Dr Natouche at the end of a circular seat that ran under the forward windows of the saloon. Troy helped herself to cold meat and salad and sat beside him. He half-rose and made her a little bow. 'I hope you are pleased with the accommodation,' he said. 'I find it perfectly satisfactory.'

There was an extraordinary quality in Dr Natouche, Troy suddenly decided. It was a quality that made one intensely aware of him, as if with the awareness induced by some drug: aware of his thin, charcoal wrist emerging from a white silk cuff, of the movements of his body under his clothes, of his quiet breathing, of his smell which was of wood: cedarwood or even sandalwood.

He had neatly folded his newspaper and laid it beside his plate. Troy, glancing at it, saw herself having her hand shaken by the Personage who had opened her show. Was it possible that Dr Natouche had not recognized this photograph? 'I really don't know,' she thought, 'why I fuss about it. If I were a film star it would be something to take-on about but who cares for painters? The truth of the matter is,' Troy thought, 'I never know what to say when people who don't paint talk to me about my painting. I get creaky with shyness and hear myself mumbling and am idiotic.'

Dr Natouche, however, did not talk about painting. He talked about the weather and the days to come and he sounded a little like one of The Pleasure Craft and Riverage Company's pamphlets. 'There will be a great deal of historic interest,' he said, calmly.

He had moved away from Troy to give her plenty of room. She was as conscious of the distance between them as if she had measured it in inches.

'All the arrangements are charming,' concluded Dr Natouche.

Mr and Miss Hewson now appeared. They seemed to be the dead norm of unpretentious American tourists. Miss Hewson was fairish, shortish and compact in shape. Her brother was tall, thin and bespectacled and wore a hearing-aid. They both looked hygienic and practical.

'Well, now,' Miss Hewson said, 'if we aren't just the slowest things to settle. Pardon us, folks.'

Mrs Tretheway from behind the bar introduced them to the assembled company and in a pleasant, sensible fashion they repeated each name as they heard it while the British murmured and smiled. Dr Natouche reciprocated in this ritual and Troy wondered if he too was an American but could hear no trace of it in his voice. West Indian? African? Pakistan?

'One to come,' Miss Rickerby-Carrick presently announced, excitedly tossing salad into her mouth. 'You're not the last.' She had been talking energetically to the Hewsons who looked dazed and baffled. She indicated a copy of the passenger list that had been put on the table. Troy had already noticed that the name K.G.Z. Andropulos had been struck out opposite Cabin 7 and that her own had not been substituted. Mr Bard with one of his off-beat glances at her, now reached out for the card and made good this omission. 'We may as well,' he said, 'be all shipshape and Bristol fashion.' Troy saw that he had spelt her surname correctly but obligingly prefaced it merely by the initials A.T. She couldn't help giving him a look in return and he tipped her another of his squinny winks.

Miss Rickerby-Carrick began playfully to whisper: 'What do you think? Shall we guess? What will he be?' She pointed to Mr J. de B. Lazenby's name on the card and looked archly round the company.

They were spared the necessity of reply by the entrance of Mr Lazenby himself.

In a way, Troy felt, it was something of an anti-climax. Mr Lazenby was a clergyman.

It was also a surprise. One did not, somehow, associate the clergy, except in the upper reaches of their hierarchy, with expensive cars and uniformed chauffeurs. Mr Lazenby gave out no particular air of affluence. He was tall, rather pink and thinly crested and he wore dark glasses, an immaculate clerical grey suit, a blue pullover and the regulation dog-collar.

Mrs Tretheway from behind the bar, where to Troy's fancy, she had become a kind of oracle, pronounced his name and added sensibly that he would no doubt find out in due course who everybody was.

'Surely, surely,' said Mr Lazenby in a slightly antipodean, faintly parsonic voice.

'But,' cried Miss Rickerby-Carrick, 'it doesn't say in the passenger list. It doesn't say Rev . . . Now, why is that?'

'I expect,' said Mr Lazenby who was helping himself to luncheon, 'it was because I applied for my reservation by letter. From Melbourne. I didn't, I think, declare my cloth.'

He smiled at her, composed himself, bent his head for a moment, scratched a miniature cross on his jumper and sat down by Mr Pollock. 'This looks delicious,' he said.

'Very tasty,' said Mr Pollock woodenly and helped himself to pickles.

Luncheon went forward in little desultory gusts of conversation. Items of information were exchanged. The Hewsons had come up from the Tabard Inn at Stratford-upon-Avon where on Saturday night they had seen a performance of *Macbeth* which they had thought peculiar. Mr Lazenby had been staying with the Bishop of Norminster. Mr Pollock had caught the London train in Birmingham where he had lodged at the Osborn Hotel. Dr Natouche and Miss Rickerby-Carrick had come from their respective homes. Miss Hewson guessed that she and her brother were not the only non-Britishers aboard, addressing her remark to Mr Lazenby but angling, Troy thought, for a reaction from Dr Natouche who did not, however, respond. Mr Lazenby expounded to the Hewsons on Australia and the Commonwealth. He also turned slightly towards Dr Natouche though it was impossible to see, so dark were his spectacles, whether he really looked at him.

'Well, now,' Miss Hewson said, 'I just don't get this Commonwealth. It's the British Commonwealth but you're not a Britisher and you got the British Queen but you don't go around saying you're a monarchy. I guess the distinctions are too refined for my crass American appreciation. What do you say, dear?' she asked Mr Hewson.

'Pardon me, dear?'

Miss Hewson articulated carefully into her brother's hearing-aid and he began to look honest-to-God and dryly humorous.

Miss Rickerby-Carrick broke into the conversation with confused cries of regret for the loss of Empire and of admiration for the Monarchy. 'I know one's not meant to talk like this,' she said with conspiratorial glances at Troy, Mr Pollock and Mr Bard. 'But sometimes one can't help it. I mean I'm *absolutely all* for freedom and civil rights and integ – ' she broke off with an air of someone whose conversation has bolted with her, turned very red and madly leant towards Dr Natouche. 'Do forgive me,' she gabbled. 'I mean, of course, I don't know. I mean, am I right in supposing – ?'

Dr Natouche folded his hands, waited a moment and then said: 'Are you wondering if I am a British subject? I am. As you see, I belong to a minority group. I practise in Liverpool.' His voice was superbly tranquil and his manner entirely withdrawn.

The silence that followed his little speech was broken by the Skipper who came crabwise down the companion-way.

'Well, ladies and gentlemen,' he said. 'I hope you are comfortably settled. We'll be on our way in a few minutes. You will find a certain amount of information in the brochures supplied. We don't go in for mikes and loudspeakers in the *Zodiac* but I'm very much at your service to answer questions if I can. The weather forecast is good although at this time of year we sometimes get the Creeper, which is a local name for River fog. It usually comes up at night and can be heavy. During the afternoon we follow the upper reaches of The River through low-lying country to Ramsdyke Lock. We wind about and about quite a lot which some people find confusing. You may have noticed, by the way, that in these parts we don't talk about The River by name. To the locals it's always just The River. It was over this country that Archbishop Langton chased King John. But long before that the Romans made the Ramsdyke canal as an addition to The River itself. The waterways were busy in Roman times. We take a little while going through the lock at Ramsdyke and you might fancy a stroll up the field and a look at a hollow alongside the Dyke Way. The wapentake courts were held there in Plantagenet times. Forerunners of our Judges' Circuits. You can't miss the wapentake hollow. Matter of five minutes' walk. Thank you.'

He gave a crisp little nod and returned to the upper deck. An appreciative murmur broke out among the passengers.

'Come,' Mr Bard exclaimed. 'Here's a sensible and heartening start. A handful of nice little facts and a fillip to the imagination. Splendid. Mrs Alleyn, you have finished your luncheon. Do come on deck and witness the departure.'

'I think we should all go up,' Troy said.

'Oh ra-*ther*!' cried Miss Rickerby-Carrick. 'Come on, chaps!'

She blew her nose vigorously and made a dash for the companion-way. There was a printed warning at the top: 'Please note deeper step' but she disregarded it, plunged headlong through the half-door at the top and could be heard floundering about with startled cries on the other side. Troy overheard Mr Hewson say to Miss Hewson: 'To me she seems kind of fabulous,' and Miss Hewson reply: 'Maybe she's one of the Queen's Beasts' and they both looked dryly humorous. Illogically Troy felt irritated with them and exasperated by Miss Rickerby-Carrick who was clearly going to get on everybody's nerves. Mr Pollock for instance, after contemplating her precipitate exit, muttered: 'Isn't it marvellous!' and Mr Bard, for Troy's benefit, briefly cast up his eyes and followed the others to the upper deck. Mr Lazenby, who was still at his luncheon, waved his fork to indicate that he would follow later.

Dr Natouche rose and looked out of the saloon windows at the wharf. Troy thought: 'How *very* tall he is.' Taller, she decided, than her husband, who was over six feet. 'He's waiting,' she thought, 'for all of us to go up first,' and she found herself standing by him.

'Have you ever done this before, Dr Natouche?' she asked. 'Taken a waterways cruise?'

'No,' he said. 'Never before. It is a new experience.'

'For me too. I came on an impulse.'

'Indeed? You felt the need of a break perhaps after the strain of your public activities.'

'Yes,' Troy agreed, unaccountably pleased that he did, after all, know of her show and had recognized her. Without so much as noticing that she felt none of her usual awkwardness she said: 'They *are* a bit of a hurdle, these solemn affairs.'

Dr Natouche said: 'Some of your works are very beautiful. It gave me great pleasure in London to see them.'

'Did it? I'm glad.'

'They are casting off, if that is the right phrase. Would you like to go up?'

Troy went up on deck. Tom, the boy, had loosed the mooring lines and laid them out smartly. The Skipper was at the wheel. The *Zodiac*'s engines throbbed. She moved astern, away from her wharf and out into the main stream.

The motorcyclists were still in the lane. Troy saw young Tom signal, not very openly, to them and they slightly raised their hands in return. The girl straddled her seat, the boy kicked and their engine broke out in pandemonium. The machine, curved, belched and racketed up the lane out of sight.

Dr Natouche appeared and then Mr Lazenby. The eight passengers stood along the rails and watched the riverbanks take on a new

perspective and become remote. Spires and waffle-irons, glass boxes,
mansard roofs and the squat cupola of the Norminster Town Hall
were now merely there to be stared at with detachment. They shifted about, very slowly, and looked over one another's shoulders and
grew smaller. The *Zodiac*, now in mid-stream, set her course for
Ramsdyke Lock.

CHAPTER 2

The Wapentake

'He had been operating,' Alleyn said, 'in a very big way in the Middle East. All among the drug barons with one of whom he fell out and who is thought to have grassed on him. From drugs he turned to the Old Master racket and was certainly behind several very big jobs in Paris. Getting certificates for good fakes from galleries and the widows of celebrated painters. He then crossed to New York where he worked off the fruits of this ploy until Interpol began to make interested noises. By the way, it may be noted that at this juncture he had not got beyond a Blue Circular which means of course – '

The boots of the intelligent-looking sandy man in the second row scraped the floor. He made a slight gesture and looked eager.

'I see you know,' Alleyn said.

'Ay, sir, I do. A Blue International Circular signifies that Interpol cannot place the identity of the creeminal.'

'That's it. However, they were getting warmer and in 1965 the Jampot found it necessary to transfer to Bolivia where for once he went too far and was put in gaol. Something to do with masquerading in female attire with criminal intent. From there, as I've said, he escaped, in May of last year, and sometime later arrived with an efficiently cooked-up passport in a Spanish freighter in England. At that juncture the Yard had no specific charge against him although he featured heavily in the discussions we were holding in San Francisco. He must have already been in touch with the British group he subsequently directed, and one of them booked him in for a late summer cruise in the *Zodiac*. The object of this manoeuvre will declare itself as we go along.

'At this point I'd like you to take particular note of a disadvantage under which the Jampot laboured. In doing this I am indulging in hindsight. At the time we are speaking about we had no clear indication of what he looked like and our only photograph was a heavily bearded job supplied by the Bolivian police. The ears are hidden by flowing locks, the mouth by a luxuriant moustache and the jaw and chin by rich and carefully tended whiskers.

'We now know, of course, that there was, in his appearance, something that set him apart, that made him physically speaking, an odd man out. Need I,' Alleyn asked, 'remind you what this was – ?'

The intelligent-looking man seated in the second row made a slight gesture. 'Exactly,' Alleyn said and enlarged upon it to the class.

'I'm able,' he went on, 'to give you a pretty full account of this apparently blameless little cruise because my wife wrote at some length about it. In her first letter she told me – '

I

'And there you are.' Troy wrote. 'All done on the spur of the moment and I think I'm going to be glad I saw that notice in The Pleasure Craft Company's office window.

'It's always been you that writes in cabins and on trains and in hotel bedrooms and me that sits at the receiving end and now here we are, both at it. The only thing I mind is not getting your letters for the next five days. I'll post this at Ramsdyke Lock and with a bit of luck it should reach you in New York when I'm at Longminster on the turning point of my little journey. At that rate it'll travel about two thousand times as fast as I do so whar's your relativity, noo? I'm writing it on my knee from a deck chair. I can't tell you how oddly time behaves on The River, how fantastically remote we are from the country that lies so close on either hand. There go the cars and lorries, streaking along main arteries and over bridges and there are the sound-breakers belching away overhead but they belong to another world. Truly.

'Our world is watery: details of eddies and reeds and wet banks. Beyond it things move in a very rum and baffling kind of way. You know how hopeless I am about direction. Well, what goes on over there beyond our banks, completely flummuckses me. There's a group of vast power-houses that has spent the greater part of the afternoon slowly moving from one half of our world to the other. They retire over our horizon on the port side and just as one thinks that's the last of *them*: there they are moving in on the starboard. Sometimes we approach them and sometimes we retreat and at one dramatic phase we sailed close-by and there were Lilliputians half-way up one of them, being busy. Yes: OK darling, I know rivers wind.

'Apart from the power-houses the country beyond The River is about as empty as anywhere in England: flat, flat, flat and according to the Skipper almost hammered so by the passage of history. Red roses and white. Cavaliers and Roundheads. Priests and barons. The Percies of the North. The Jockeys of Norfolk. The lot: all galumphing over the landscape through the centuries. Did you know that Constable stayed here one summer and painted? Church spires turn up with minimal villages and of course, the locks. Do you remember

the lock in *Our Mutual Friend*: a great slippery drowning-box? I keep
thinking of it although the weirs are more noisily alarming.

'It seems we are going towards the sea in our devious fashion and
so we sink in locks.

'As for the company: I've tried to introduce them to you. We're
no more oddly-assorted, I suppose, than any other eight people that
might take it into their heads to spend five days out of time on The
River. Apart from Miss Rickerby-Carrick who sends me up the wall
(you know how *beastly* I am about ostentatious colds-in-the-head)
and Dr Natouche who is black, there's nothing at all remarkable
about us.

'I'm not the only one who finds poor Miss R-C. difficult. Her
sledge-hammer tact crashes over Dr N like a shower of brickbats, so
anxious is she to be unracial. I saw him flinch two minutes ago
under a frontal assault. Mr Bard said just now that a peep into her
subconscious would be enough to send him round more bends than
the *Zodiac* negotiates in a summer season. If only she'd just pipe
down every now and then. But no, she doesn't know how to. She
has a bosom friend in Birmingham called – incredibly I forget what
– Mavis something – upon whom we get incessant bulletins. What
Mavis thinks, what she says, how she reacts, how she has recovered
(with set-backs) from Her Operation (coyly left unspecified). We all,
I am sure, now dread the introduction of the phrase: "My special
chum, Mavis." All the same, I don't think she's a stupid woman. Just
an inksey-tinksey bit dotty. The Americans clearly think her as crazy
as a coot but typically British. This is maddening. She keeps a diary
and keeps is the operative word: she carries it about with her and
jots. I am ashamed to say it arouses my curiosity. *What* can she be
writing in it? How odious I sound.

'I don't like Mr Pollock much. He is so very sharp and pale and he
so obviously thinks us fools (I mean Mr Bard and me and, of course,
poor Miss R-C.) for not sharing his dislike of coloured people. Of
course one does see that if they sing calypsos all night in the no
doubt ghastly tenements he exorbitantly lets to them and if they roar
insults and improper suggestions at non-black teenagers, it doesn't
send up the tone. But don't non-black tenants ever send the tone
down, for pity's sake? And what on earth has all this got to do with
Dr Natouche whose tone is superb? I consider that one of the worst

features of the whole black-white thing is that nobody can say: "I don't much like black people" as they might say: "I don't like the Southern Scot or the Welsh or antipodeans or the Midland English or Americans or the League of British Loyalists or *The Readers' Digest*." I happen to be attracted to the dark-skinned (Dr Natouche is remarkably attractive) but until people who are or who are not attracted can say so unselfconsciously it'll go on being a muddle. I find it hard to be civil to Mr Pollock when he makes his common little racial gestures.

'He's not alone in his antipathy. Antipathy? I suppose that's the right word but I almost wrote "fear". It seems to me that Pollock and the Hewsons and even Mr Lazenby, for all his parsonic forbearance, eye Dr Natouche with something very like fear.

'We are about to enter our second lock – the Ramsdyke, I think. More later.

'*Later* (about 30 minutes). Ramsdyke. An incident. We were all on deck and the lock people and our Tom were doing their things with paddles and gates and all, and I noticed on the far bank from the lockhouse a nice lane, a pub, some wonderful elms, a ford and a pond. I called out to nobody in particular:

' "Oh, look – The place is swarming with Constables! Everywhere you look. A perfect clutch of them!"

'Rory, it was as if someone had plopped a dirty great weight overboard into the lock. Everybody went dead still and listened. At least – this is hard to describe – *someone* did in particular but I don't know which because nobody moved. Then Dr Natouche in mild surprise said: "The Police, Mrs Alleyn? Where? I don't see them," and I explained and he, for the first time, gave a wonderful roar of laughter. Pollock gaped at me, Caley Bard said he'd thought for a moment his sins had caught up with him, Mr Lazenby said what a droll mistake to be sure and the Hewsons looked baffled. Miss Rickerby-C. (her friends call her, for God's sake, Hay) waited for the penny to drop and then laughed like a hyena. I still don't know which of them (or whether it was more than one of them) went so very quiet and still and what's more I got the idiotic notion that my explanation had been for – someone – more disturbing than the original remark. And on top of all this, I can *not* get rid of the feeling that I'm involved in some kind of performance. Like one of those dreams actors say they get when they find themselves on an unknown stage where a play they've never heard of is in action.

'Silly? Or not silly? Rum? Or not rum?

'I'll write again at Tollardwark. The show looked all right: well hung and lit. The Gallery bought the black and pink thing and seven smaller ones sold the first night. Paris on the 31st and New York in November. Darling, if, and only if, you have a moment I *would* be glad if you could bear to call at the Guggenheim just to say – '

II

Troy enjoyed coming into the locks. Ramsdyke, as she observed in her letter, was a charming one: a seemly house, a modest plot, the tow-path, a bridge over The River and the Ramsdyke itself, a neat wet line, Roman-ruled across the fens. On the farther side was the 'Constable' view and farther downstream a weir. The *Zodiac* moved quietly into the lock but before she sank with its waters Troy jumped ashore, posted her letter and followed the direction indicated by the Skipper's tattooed arm and pointed finger. He called after her 'Twenty minutes' and she waved her understanding, crossed the tow-path, and climbed a grassy embankment.

She came into a field bordered by sod and stone walls and, on the left, beyond the wall, by what seemed to be a narrow road leading down to the bridge. This was the Dyke Way of the brochures. Troy remembered that it came from the village of Wapentake, which her map showed as lying about a mile and a half from the lock. She walked up the field. It rose gently and showed, above its crest, trees and a distant spire.

The air smelt of earth and grass and, delicately, of wood-smoke. It seemed lovely to Troy. She felt a great uplift of spirit and was so pre-occupied with her own happiness that she came upon the meeting place of the wapentake, just where the Skipper had said it would be, before she was aware of it.

It was a circular hollow, sometimes called, the brochure said, a Pot, and it was lined with grass, mosses and fern. Here the Plantagenet knights-of-the-shire had sat at their fortnightly Hundreds, dealing out justice as they saw it in those days and as the growing laws directed them. Troy wondered if, when the list was a heavy one, they stayed on into the evening and night and if torches were lit.

Below the wapentake hollow and quite close to the lock, another, but a comparatively recent depression had been cut into the hillside: perhaps to get a load of gravel of which there seemed to be a quantity in the soil, or perhaps by archaeological amateurs. An overhanging shelf above this excavation had been roughly shored up by poles with an old door for roof. The wood had weathered and looked to be rotting. 'A bit of an eyesore,' thought Troy.

She went into the wapentake and sat there, and fancied she felt beneath her some indication of a kind of bench that must have been chopped out of the soil, she supposed, seven centuries ago. 'I'm an ignoramus about history,' Troy thought, 'but I do like to feel it in my bones,' and she peopled the wapentake with heads like carven effigies, with robes in the colours of stained glass and with glints of polished steel.

She began to wonder if it would be possible to make a very formalized drawing – dark and thronged with seated, lawgiving shapes. A puff of warm air moved the grass and the hair of her head and up the sloping field came Dr Natouche.

He was bareheaded and had changed his tweed jacket for a yellow sweater. When he saw Troy he checked and stood still, formidable because of his height and colour against the mild background of the waterways. Troy waved to him. 'Come up,' she called. 'Here's the wapentake.'

'Thank you.'

He came up quickly, entered the hollow and looked about him. 'I have read the excellent account in our little book,' he said. 'So here they sat, those old chaps.' The colloquialism came oddly from him.

'You sit here, too,' Troy suggested, wanting to see his head and his torso, in its yellow sweater, against the moss and fern.

He did so, squaring himself and resting his hands on his knees. His teeth and the whites of his eyes were high accents in the picture he presented for Troy. 'You ask for the illustration of an incongruity,' he said.

'You would be nice to paint. Do you really feel incongruous? I mean is this sort of thing quite foreign to you?'

'Not altogether. No.'

They said nothing for a time and Troy did not think there was any awkwardness in their silence.

A lark sang madly overhead and the sound of quiet voices floated up from the lock. Above the embankment they could see the top of *Zodiac*'s wheelhouse. Now it began very slowly to sink. They heard Miss Rickerby-Carrick shout and laugh.

A motorcycle engine crescendoed out of the distance, clattered and exploded down the lane and then reduced its speed and noise and stopped.

'One would think it was those two again,' said Troy.

Dr Natouche rose. 'It is,' he said, 'I can see them. Actually, it is those two. They are raising their hands.'

'How extraordinary,' she said idly. 'Why should they turn up?'

'They may be staying in the district. We haven't come very far, you know.'

'I keep forgetting. One's values change on The River.'

Troy broke off a fern frond and turned it between her fingers. Dr Natouche sat down again.

'My father was an Ethiopian,' he said presently. 'He came to this country with a Mission fifty years ago and married an Englishwoman. I was born and educated in England.'

'Have you never been to your own country?'

'Once. But I was alien there. And like my father, I married an Englishwoman. I am a widower. My wife died two months ago.'

'Was that why you came on this cruise?'

'We were to have come together.'

'I see,' Troy said.

'She would have enjoyed it. It was something we could have done,' he said.

'Have you found many difficulties about being as you are? Black?'

'Of course. How sensible of you to ask, Mrs Alleyn. One knows everybody thinks such questions.'

'Well,' Troy said, 'I'm glad it was all right to ask.'

'I am perfectly at ease with you,' Dr Natouche stated rather, Troy felt, as he might have told a patient there was nothing the matter with her and really almost arousing a comparable pleasure. 'Perfectly,' he repeated after a pause: 'I don't think, Mrs Alleyn, you could ever say anything to me that would change that condition.'

Miss Rickerby-Carrick appeared at the top of the embankment. 'Hoo-hoo!' she shouted. 'What's it like up there?'

'Very pleasant,' Troy said.

'Jolly good.'

She floundered up the field towards them, blowing her nose as she came. Troy was suddenly very sorry for her. Were there, she asked herself, in Birmingham, where Miss Rickerby-Carrick lived, people, apart from Mavis, who actually welcomed her company?

Dr Natouche fetched a sigh and stood up. 'I see a gate over there into the lane,' he said. 'I think there is time to walk back that way if you would care to do so.'

'You go,' Troy muttered. 'I'd better wait for her.'

'Really? Very well.'

He stayed for a moment or two, politely greeted Miss Rickerby-Carrick and then strode away.

'*Isn't* he a dear?' Miss Rickerby-Carrick panted. '*Don't* you feel he's somebody awfully special?'

'He seems a nice man,' Troy answered and try as she might, she couldn't help flattening her voice.

'I do think we all ought to make a special effort. I get awfully worked-up about it. When people go on like Mr Pollock, you know. I tackled Mr Pollock about his attitude. I do that, you know, I do tackle people. I said: "Just because he's got another pigmentation," I said, "why should you think he's different." They're *not* different. You do agree, don't you?'

'No,' Troy said. 'I don't. They are different. Profoundly.'

'Oh! How *can* you say so?'

'Because I think it's true. They are different in depth from Anglo-Saxons. So are Slavs. So are Latins.'

'Oh! If you mean like *that*,' she said, and broke into ungainly laughter. 'Oh, I see. Oh, yes. Then you *do* agree that we should make a special effort.'

'Look, Miss Rickerby-Carrick – '

'I say, do call me Hay.'

'Yes – well – thank you. I was going to say that I don't think Dr Natouche would enjoy special efforts. Really, I don't.'

'*You* seem to get on with him like a house on fire,' Miss Rickerby-Carrick pointed out discontentedly.

'Do I? Well, I find him an interesting man.'

'There you are, you see!' she cried, proclaiming some completely inscrutable triumph, and a longish silence ensued.

They heard the motorcycle start up and cross the bridge and listened to the diminishment of sound as it made off in the direction of Norminster.

One by one the other passengers straggled up the field. Mr Pollock behind the rest, swinging his built-up boot. The Hewsons were all set-about with cameras while Caley Bard had a box slung from his shoulder and carried a lepidopterist's net.

So *that*, Troy thought, was what it was. When everybody was assembled the Hewsons took photographs of the wapentake by itself and with their fellow-travellers sitting self-consciously round it. Mr Lazenby compared it without, Troy felt, perceptible validity, to an aboriginal place of assembly in the Australian outback. Mr Pollock read his brochure and then stared with a faint look of disgust at the original.

Caley Bard joined Troy. 'So this is where you lit off to,' he murmured. 'I got bailed up by that extraordinary lady. She wants to get up a let's-be-sweet-to-Natouche movement.'

'I know. What did you say?'

'I said that as far as I am concerned, I consider I'm as sweet to Natouche as he can readily stomach. Now, tell me all about the wapentake. I'm allergic to leaflets and I've forgotten what the Skipper said. Speak up, do.'

Troy did not bother to react to this piece of cheek. She said: 'So you're a lepidopterist?'

'That's right. An amateur. Do you find it a sinister hobby? It has rather a sinister reputation, I fear. There was that terrifying film and then didn't somebody in *The Hound of the Baskervilles* flit about Dartmoor with a deceiving net and killing-bottle?'

'There's Nabokov on the credit side.'

'True. But *you* don't fancy it, all the same,' he said. 'That I can see, very clearly.'

'I like them better alive and on the wing. Did you notice those two motorcyclists? They seem to be haunting us.'

'Friends of young Tom, it appears. They come from Tollard-wark where we stay tonight. Did you know it's pronounced Toll'ark? It will take us an hour or more to get there by water but by road it's only a short walk from Ramsdyke. There's confusion for you!'

'I wouldn't want to walk: I've settled into the River-time-space-dimension.'

'Yes, I suppose it would be rather spoiling to break out of it. Hallo, that'll be for us.'

The *Zodiac* had given three short hoots. They returned hurriedly and found her waiting downstream from the lock.

There was a weir at Ramsdyke, standing off on their port side. Below the green slide of the fall, the whole surface of the river was smothered in foam: foam in islands and in pinnacles, iridescent foam that twinkled and glinted in the late afternoon sunlight, that shredded away from its own crests, floated like gossamer and broke into nothing.

'Oh!' cried Miss Rickerby-Carrick in ecstasy. '*Isn't* it lovely! Oh, *do* look! Look, look, *look*!' she insisted, first to one and then to another of her fellow-passengers. 'Who would have thought our quiet old river could froth up and behave like a fairytale? Like a dream isn't it? *Isn't* it?'

'More like washing-day I'm afraid, Miss Rickerby-Carrick,' said Mrs Tretheway looking over the half-door. 'It's detergent. There's a factory beyond those trees. Tea is ready in the saloon,' she added.

'Oh, *no*!' Miss Rickerby-Carrick lamented. A flying wisp of detergent settled on her nose. 'Oh, *dear*!' she said crossly and went down to the saloon, followed by the others.

'How true it is,' Caley Bard remarked, 'that beauty is in the Eye of the Beholder.'

He spoke to Troy but Dr Natouche, who was behind her, answered him.

'Surely,' Dr Natouche said, 'not so much in the eye as in the mind. I remember that on a walk – through a wood, you know – I looked into a dell and saw, deep down, an astonishing spot of scarlet. I thought: Ah! A superb fungus secretly devouring the earth and the air. You know? One of those savage fungi that one thinks of as devils? I went down to look more closely at it and found it was a discarded fish-tin with a red label. Was it the less beautiful for my discovery?'

He had turned to Troy. 'Not to my way of looking,' she said. 'It was a good colour and it had made its effect.'

'We are back aren't we,' Caley Bard said, 'at that old Florentine person with the bubucular nose. We are to assume that the painter doted on every blackhead, crevasse and bump.'

'Yes,' Troy said. 'You are.'

'So that if a dead something – a fish or a cat – popped up through that foam, for instance, and its colour and shape made a pleasing mélange with its surroundings, it would be a paintable subject and therefore beautiful?'

'You take,' she said dryly, 'the very words from my mouth.'

Mr Bard looked at her mouth for a second or two.

'And what satisfaction,' he said under his breath, 'is there in that?' He turned away and Troy thought, almost at once, that she must have misheard him.

Miss Rickerby-Carrick flapped into the conversation like a wet sheet. 'Oh *don't* stop. Go on. Do, do, go on. I don't want to lose a word of this,' she cried. 'Because it makes a point that I'm most awfully keen on. Beauty is everywhere. In everything,' she shouted and swept her arm past Mr Lazenby's spectacles. ' "Beauty is Truth; Truth, Beauty",' she quoted. 'That's all we need to know.'

'That's a very, very profound observation, Miss Rickerby-Carrick,' Mr Hewson observed kindly.

'I just don't go along with it,' his sister said. 'I've seen a whole lot of Truth that wasn't beautiful. A whole heap of it.'

Mr Pollock, who had been utterly silent for a very long time now heaved an enormous sigh and as if infected by his gloom the other passengers also fell silent.

Somebody – Mr Lazenby? – had left the morning's newspaper on the settle, the paper in which her own photograph had appeared. Troy, who did not eat with her tea, picked it up and seeing nothing to interest her, idly turned over a page.

'Man found strangled.

'The body of a man who had been strangled was found at 8 p.m. last night in a flat in Cyprus Street, Soho. He is believed to have been a picture-dealer and the police who are making inquiries give his name as K.G.Z. Andropulos.'

The passenger list was still on the table. Troy looked at the name Caley Bard had crossed out in favour of her own.

She rose with so abrupt a movement that one or two of her companions glanced up at her. She dropped the newspaper on the seat and went down to her cabin. After some thought, she said to herself: 'If nobody has read it there's no reason why I should point it out. It's a horrible bit of news.'

And then she thought that if, as seemed probable, the paragraph had in fact not been noticed, it might be as well to get rid of the paper, the more especially since she would like to repress her own photograph before it went into general circulation. She could imagine Miss Rickerby-Carrick's ejaculations: 'And there you both are, you and the murdered man who was to have your berth. Fancy!' She hunted out her sketchbook and returned to the saloon.

The newspaper was nowhere to be seen.

III

Troy waited for a minute or two in the saloon to collect her thoughts. Her fellow-passengers were still at tea and apparently quite undisturbed. She went up on deck. The Skipper was at the wheel.

'Everything all right, Mrs Alleyn?' he asked.

'Yes, thank you. Yes. Everything,' said Troy and found herself a chair.

Most of the detergent foam had been left behind by now. The *Zodiac* sailed towards evening through clear waters, low fields and occasional groups of trees.

Troy began to draw the Signs of the Zodiac, placing them in a ring and giving them a wonderfully strange character. Mrs Tretheway's rhyme could go in the middle and later on there would be washes of colour.

She was vaguely aware of a sudden burst of conversation in the saloon. After a time a shadow fell across her hand and there was Caley Bard again. Troy didn't look up. He moved to the opposite side and stood with his back towards her, leaning on the taffrail.

'I'm afraid,' he said presently, 'that they've rumbled you. Lazenby spotted the photograph in this morning's paper. I wouldn't have told them.'

'I believe you.'

'The Rickerby-Carrick is stimulated, I fear.'

'Hell.'

'And the Hewsons are gratified because they've read an article about you in *Life Magazine* so they know you're OK and famous. They just can't think how they missed recognizing you.'

'Too bad.'

'Pollock, surprisingly, seemed to be not unaware of your great distinction. Lazenby himself says you are regarded in Australia as being the equal of Drysdale and Dobell.'

'Nice of him.'

'There's this about it; you'll be able to do what you are doing now, without everybody exclaiming and breathing down your neck. Or I hope you will.'

'I won't be doing anything that matters,' Troy mumbled.

'How extraordinary!' he said lightly.

'What?'

'That you should be so shy about your work. You!'

'Well, I can't help it. Do pipe down like a good chap.'

She heard him chuckle and drag a deck chair into position. Presently she smelt his pipe. 'Evidently,' she thought, 'they haven't spotted the Andropulos bit in the paper.' She considered this for a moment and then added: 'Or have they?'

The River now described a series of loops so extreme, and so close together that the landscape seemed to turn about the *Zodiac* like a diorama. Wapentake church spire advanced and retreated and set to partners with a taller spire in the market town of Tollardwark which they approached with the utmost slyness, now leaving it astern and now coming round a bend and making straight for it. The water darkened with the changing sky. Along its banks and in its backwaters and eddies the creatures that belonged to The River began to come out on their evening business: water-rats, voles, toads and leaping fish as well as the insects: dragonflies in particular. Once, looking up from her drawing, Troy caught sight of a pair of ears against the sky and thought: 'There goes Wat, the hare.' A company of ducks in close formation paddled past the *Zodiac*. Where trees stood along the banks the air pulsated with high, formless, reiterative bird-chattering.

Troy thought: 'Cleopatra on the River Cydnus wasn't given more things to hear and look at.'

At intervals she stopped drawing in order to observe, but the Signs of the Zodiac grew under her hand. She amused herself by mentally allotting one to each of her fellow-passengers. The Hewsons, of course, belonged to the Heavenly Twins and Mr Pollock, because his club foot affected his gait, would be the Crab. Miss Rickerby-Carrick might be assigned to Taurus because she ran like a Bull at every Gate, but almost certainly, thought Troy, Virgo was entirely appropriate. So she gave a pair of bovine horns to the rampaging motorcyclist. Because of a certain sting in the tail of many of his observations, she decided upon Scorpio for Caley Bard. And Mr Lazenby? Well: he seemed to be extremely ill-sighted, his dark spectacles gave him a blind look like Justice, and Justice carries Scales. Libra for him. As for Dr Natouche, he must be a splendour in the firmament: Sagittarius the Archer with open shoulders and stretched bow. She began to draw The Archer in his image. Mrs Tretheway didn't seem to fit anywhere except perhaps, as they had a sexy connotation, under the Fish with the Glittering Tails. She observed the Skipper at his wheel, noted the ripple of muscles under his immaculate shirt and the close-clipped curly poll beneath his cap. The excessive masculinity, she decided, belonged to the Ram and Tom-of-all-work could be the Man who carried the Watering-pot. And having run out of passengers she raised one of the Lion's eyebrows and thus gave him a look of her husband. 'Which leaves me for the Goat,' thought Troy, 'and very suitable too, I daresay.'

One by one the passengers, with the exception of Dr Natouche, came on deck. In their several fashions and with varying degrees of success, they displayed tact towards Troy. The Hewsons smiled at each other and retired, with brochures and *Readers' Digests*, to their chairs. Mr Lazenby turned his dark spectacles towards Troy, nodded three times and passed majestically by. Mr Pollock behaved as if she wasn't there until he was behind her and then, she clearly sensed, had a good long stare over her shoulder at what she was doing.

Miss Rickerby-Carrick was wonderful. When she had floundered, with her customary difficulty, through the half-door at the top of the companion-way, she paused to converse with the Skipper but as she talked to him she rolled her eyes round until they could take in Troy. Presently she left him and archly biting her underlip advanced on tip-toe. She bent and whispered, close to Troy's ear: 'Don't put me in it,' and so passed on gaily to her deck chair.

The general set-up having now become quietly ridiculous, Troy swung round to find Mr Pollock close behind her.

His eyes were half-closed and he looked at her drawing, unmistakably with the air of someone who knew. For a moment they faced each other. He turned away, swinging his heavy foot.

Caley Bard, with a startling note of anger in his voice, said: 'Have you been given an invitation to a Private View, Mr Pollock?'

A silence followed. At last Mr Pollock said in a stifled voice: 'It's very nice. Lovely,' and retired to the far end of the deck.

Troy shut her sketchbook and with a view to papering over what seemed to be some kind of crisis, made conversation with everybody about the landscape.

The *Zodiac* reached Tollard Lock at 6.15 and tied up for the night.

CHAPTER 3

Tollardwark

'At that time,' Alleyn said, 'I was on my way to Chicago and from there to San Francisco. We were setting up a joint plan of action with USA to cope with an international blow-up in the art-forgery world. We were pretty certain, though not positive, that the Jampot was well in the phoney picture trade and that the same group was combining it with a two-way drug racket. My wife's letters to me from her river cruise missed me in New York and were forwarded to Chicago and thence to San Francisco.

'On reading them I put through a call to the Yard.'

I

Monday.
Tollardwark.
10.15 *p.m.*

'. . . This will probably arrive with the letter I posted this morning at Ramsdyke. I'm writing in my cabin having returned from Tollardwark where we spend our first night and I'm going to try and set out the sequence of events as you would do it – economically but in detail. I'm almost certain that when they are looked at as a whole they will be seen to add up to nothing in particular.

'Indeed, I only tell you about these silly little incidents, my darling, because I know you won't make superior noises, and because in a cock-eyed sort of way I suppose they may be said to tie in with what you're up to at the moment. I know, very well, that they may amount to nothing.

'You remember the silly game people used to play: making up alphabetical rhymes of impending disaster? "T is for Tiger decidedly plumper. What's that in his mouth? Oh it's Agatha's jumper."

'There are moments on this otherwise enchanting jaunt when *your* Agatha almost catches the sound of something champing in the jungle.

'It really began tonight at Tollardwark – '

II

They had berthed on the outskirts of the little market town and after dinner the passengers explored it. Troy sensed frontal attacks from Miss Rickerby-Carrick and possibly Caley Bard so, having a plan of her own, she slipped away early. There was an office on the wharf with a telephone booth at the disposal of the passengers. As it was open and nobody seemed to be about, she went straight in.

There was one thing about that number, Troy thought, you did get through quickly. In seconds she was saying: 'Is Inspector Fox in the office? Could I speak to him? It's Mrs Roderick Alleyn,' and almost immediately: 'Br'er Fox? Troy Alleyn. Listen. I expect you all know, but in case you don't: It's about the Soho thing in this morning's paper. The man was to have been a passenger in the – ' She got it out as tidily and succinctly as she could, but she had only given the briefest outline when he cut in.

'Now, that's very kind of you, Mrs Alleyn,' the familiar paddy voice said. 'That's very interesting. I happen to be working on that job. And you're speaking from Tollardwark? And you've got the vacant cabin? And you're talking from a phone box? From where?. . . I see . . . Yes.' A pause. 'Yes. We heard yesterday from New York and he's having a very pleasant time.'

'*What?*' Troy ejaculated. 'Who? You mean Rory?'

'That's right, Mrs Alleyn. Very nice indeed to have heard from you. We'll let you know, of course, if there's any change of plan. I think it might be as well if you didn't say very much at your end,' Mr Fox blandly continued. 'I expect I'm being unduly cautious, indeed I'm sure I am, but if you can do so without drawing attention to it, I wonder if you could drop in at our place in Tollardwark in about half an hour or so? It could be, if necessary, to ask if that fur you lost at your exhibition has been found. Very nice to hear from you. My godson well? Goodbye, then.'

Troy hung up abruptly and turned. Through the obscured-glass door panel which had a hole in one corner, she saw a distorted figure move quickly backwards. She came out and found Mr Lazenby standing by the outside entrance.

'You've finished your call, Mrs Alleyn?' he jovially asked. 'Good-oh. I'll just make mine then. Bishopscourt at Norminster. I spent the week there and this will let me off my bread-and-butter stint. You don't know the Bishop, I suppose? Of Norminster? No? Wonderfully hospitable old boy. Gave the dim Aussie parson a memorable time. Car, chauffeur, the lot. Going to explore?'

Yes, Troy said, she thought she would explore. Mr Lazenby replied that he understood from the Bishop that the parish church was most interesting. And he went into the telephone booth.

Troy, strangely perturbed, walked up a narrow, cobbled street into the market square of Tollardwark.

She found it enchanting. It had none of the self-consciousness that settles upon too many carefully preserved places in the Home Counties, although, so the *Zodiac* brochure said, it had in fact been lovingly rescued from the clumsy botching of Victorian meddlers. But no care, added the brochure, could replace in their niches the delicate heads, hands, leaves and curlicues knocked off by Cromwell's clean-living wreckers. But the fourteenth-century inn had been wakened from neglect, a monstrous weather-cock removed from the crest of the Eleanor Cross and Lady Godiva's endowed church of St Crispin-in-the-Fields was in good heart. As if to prove this, it being practice-night for the bell-ringers, cascades of orderly rumpus were shaken out of the belfry as Troy crossed the square.

There were not many people about. She felt some hesitation in asking her way to the police station. She walked round the square and at intervals caught sight of her fellow-passengers. There, down a very dark alley were Mr and Miss Hewson, peering in at an unlit Tudor window in a darkened shop. Mr Pollock was in the act of disappearing round a corner near the church where, moving backwards through a lychgate, was Miss Rickerby-Carrick. It struck Troy that the whole set had an air of *commedia dell' arte* about them and that the Market Square might be their painted backdrop. She was again plagued by the vague feeling that somewhere, somehow a masquerade of sorts was being acted out and that she was involved in it. 'The people of the *Zodiac*,' she thought, 'all moving in their courses and I with them, but for the life of me I don't know where we're going.'

She suspected that Caley Bard had thought it would be pleasant if they explored Tollardwark together and she was not surprised to see him across the square, turning, with a disconsolate air, into the Northumberland Arms. She would have enjoyed his company, other things being equal. She had almost completed her walk round the Market Square and wondered which of the few passers-by she should accost when she came to the last of the entrances into the square and looking down it, she saw the familiar blue lamp.

The door swung-to behind her, shutting out the voices of the bells, and she was in another world smelling of linoleum, disinfectant and uniforms. The Sergeant on duty said at once: 'Mrs Alleyn would it be? I thought so. The Superintendent's expecting you, Mrs Alleyn. 'I'll just – oh, here you are, sir. Mrs Alleyn.'

He was the predictable large, hard-muscled man just beginning to run to overweight, with extremely bright eyes and a sort of occupational joviality about him.

He shook Troy warmly by the hand. 'Tillottson,' he said. 'Nice to meet you, Mrs Alleyn,' and took her into his office.

'Very pleased,' said Superintendent Tillottson, 'to meet Roderick Alleyn's good lady. His textbook's known as the Scourge of the Service in these parts and I wouldn't mind if you passed that on to him.'

He laughed very heartily at this joke, placed the palms of his hands on his desk and said: 'Yes. Well now, I've been talking to Mr Fox at Head Office, Mrs Alleyn, and he suggested it might be quite an idea if we had a little chat. So, if it's not putting you to too much trouble – '

He led Troy, very adroitly, through the past eight hours and she was surprised that he should be so particular as to details. Evidently he was aware of this reaction because when she had finished he said he supposed she would like to know what it was all about and proceeded to give her a neat report.

'This character, this K.G.Z. Andropulos, was mixed up in quite a bit of trouble: trouble to the Yard, Mrs Alleyn, before and after the Yard got alongside him. He was, as you may have supposed, of Greek origin and he's been involved in quite a number of lines: a bit of drug-running here, a bit of receiving there, some interest in the antique lay, a picture-dealing business in Cyprus Street, Soho, above which he lived in the flat where his body was found yesterday evening. He wasn't what you'd call a key-figure but he became useful to the Yard by turning informer from spite having fallen out with a much bigger man than himself. A very big man indeed in the international underworld, as people like to call it, a character called Foljambe and known as the Jampot, in whom we are very, very interested.'

'I've heard about *him*,' Troy said. 'From Rory.'

'I'll be bound. Now, it's a guinea to a gooseberry, to our way of thinking, that this leading character – this Jampot – is behind the business in Cyprus Street and therefore the Department is more than ordinarily concerned to get to the bottom of it and anything that connects with Andropulos, however slightly, has to be followed up.'

'Even to Cabin 7 in the rivercraft *Zodiac*?'

'That's right. We'd like to know, d'you see, Mrs Alleyn, just why this chap Andropulos took the freakish notion to book himself in and when he did it. And, very particularly, we'd like to know whether any of the other passengers had any kind of link with him. Now Teddy Fox – '

'*Who!*' Troy exclaimed.

'Inspector Fox, Mrs Alleyn. He and I were in the uniformed branch together. Edward Walter Fox, he is.'

'I suppose I knew,' Troy mused. 'Yes, of course I knew. We always call him Br'er Fox. He's a great friend.'

'So I understood. Yes. Well, he's a wee bit concerned about you going with this lot in the *Zodiac*. He's wondering what the Chief-Super – your good man, Mrs Alleyn – would make of it. He's on his way to this conference in Chicago and Ted Fox wonders if he shouldn't try and talk to him.'

'Oh, *no!*' Troy ejaculated. 'Surely not.'

'Well now, frankly it seems a bit far-fetched to me but there it is. Ted Fox cut you short, in a manner of speaking, when you rang him from the Waterways office down there and he did so on the general principle that you can't be too careful on the public phone. He's a careful sort of character himself, as you probably know, and, by gum, he's thorough.'

'He is, indeed.'

'Yes. That's so. Yes. Now Ted's just been called out of London, following a line on the Andropulos business. It may take him across the Channel. In the meantime he's asked me to keep an eye on *your* little affair. So what we'd like to do is take a wee look at the passenger list. In the meantime I just wonder about these two incidents you've mentioned. Now, what are they? First of all you get the impression that someone, you're not sure who, got a fright or a shock or a peculiar reaction when you said there were Constables all over the place. And second: you see this bit about Andropulos in the paper, you drop the paper on the seat and go to your cabin. You get the idea it might be pleasanter for all concerned not to spread the information that an intended passenger has been murdered. You go back for the purpose of confiscating the paper and find it's disappeared. Right? Yes. Now, for the first of these incidents, I just wonder if it wouldn't be natural for any little gathering of passengers waiting in a quiet lock in peaceful surroundings to get a bit of a jolt when somebody suddenly says there are police personnel all over the place.

Swarming, I think you said was the expression you used. And clutch. Swarming with a clutch of Constables. *You* meaning the artist. *They* assuming the police.'

'Well – yes. But they didn't all exclaim at once. They didn't all say: "Where, where, what do you mean, policemen?" or things like that. Miss Rickerby-Carrick did and I think Miss Hewson did a bit and I rather fancy Mr Caley Bard said something like: "What *can* you mean?" But I felt terribly strongly that someone had had a shock. I – Oh,' Troy said impatiently, 'how silly that sounds! Pay no attention to it. Really.'

'Shall we take a wee look at the second item, then? The disappearance of the newspaper? Isn't it possible, Mrs Alleyn, that one of them saw you were put out and when you went to your cabin picked up the paper to see what could have upset you? And found the paragraph? And had the same reaction as you did: don't put it about in case it upsets people? Or maybe, *didn't* notice your reaction but read the paragraph and thought it'd be nice if you didn't know you'd got a cabin that was to have been given to a murder victim? Or they might all have come to that conclusion? Or, the simplest of all, the staff might just have tidied the paper away?'

'I feel remarkably foolish,' Troy said. 'How right you are. I wish I'd shut up about it and not bothered poor Br'er Fox.'

'Oh no,' Tillottson said quickly. 'Not at all. No. We're very glad to have this bit about the booking of Cabin 7. Very glad indeed. We'd very much like to know why Andropulos fancied a waterways cruise. Of course we'd have learnt about it before long but it can't be too soon for us and we're much obliged to you.'

'Mr Tillottson, you don't think, do you, that any of them could have had anything to do with that man? Andropulos? Why should they have?'

Tillottson looked fixedly at the top of his desk. 'No,' he said after a pause. 'No reason at all. You stay at Toll'ark tonight, don't you? Yes. Crossdyke tomorrow? And the following day and night at Longminster? Right? And I've got the passenger list from you and just to please Mr Fox we'll let him have it and also do a wee bit of inquiring at our end. The clerical gentleman's been staying with the Bishop at Norminster, you say? And he's an Australian? Fine. And the lady with the double name comes from Birmingham? Mr S.H. Caley Bard lives in London, SW3 and collects butterflies. And – er – this Mr Pollock's a Londoner but he came up from Birmingham where he stayed, you said – ? Yes, ta. The Osborn. And the Americans were at the Tabard at Stratford. Just a tick, if you don't mind.'

He went to the door and said: 'Sarge. Rickerby-Carrick. Hazel: Miss. Birmingham. Natouche: Doctor. G.F. Liverpool. S.H. Caley Bard, SW3. London. Pollock, Saturday and Sunday, Osborn Hotel, Birmingham. Hewson. Americans. Two. Tabard. Stratford. Yes. Check, will you?'

'I mustn't keep you,' Troy said and stood up.

'If you don't mind waiting, Mrs Alleyn. Just another tick.'

He consulted a directory and dialled a number. 'Bishopscourt?' he said. 'Yes. Toll'ark Police Station here. Sorry to trouble you, but we've had an Australian passport handed in at our office. Name of Bollinger. I understand an Australian gentleman – oh. Oh, yes? Lazenby? All last week? I see. Not his, then. Very sorry to trouble you. Thank you.'

He hung up, beamed at Troy and asked if she could give him any help as to the place of origin of the remaining passengers. She had heard the Hewsons speak of Apollo, Kansas and of a Hotel Balmoral in the Cromwell Road, and she rather fancied Caley Bard did tutorial cramming work. Mr Stanley P.K. Pollock was a Cockney and owned property in London: where, she had no idea. The Superintendent made notes and the Sergeant came in to say he'd checked his items and they were all OK. Dr Natouche had been in his present practice in Liverpool for about seven years. He had appeared for the police in a road fatality case last week and had been called in at the site of another one last Sunday. Miss Rickerby-Carrick was a well-known member of a voluntary social workers' organization. The other passengers had all been where they had said they had been. The Superintendent said there you were, you see, for what it was worth. As Troy shook hands with him he said there was a police station in the village of Crossdyke, a mile from Crossdyke Lock, and if, before tomorrow night, anything at all out of the way occurred he'd be very glad if she'd drop in at the station and give him a call or, if he was free, he might pop over himself in case she did look in.

'Don't,' said Mr Tillottson apparently as an afterthought, 'if I may make a suggestion, begin thinking everybody's behaving suspiciously,

Mrs Alleyn. It'd be rather easy to do that and it'd spoil your holiday. Going to take a look round Toll'ark? I'm afraid I've used up some of your time. Goodnight, then, and much obliged, I do assure you.'

Troy went out into the street. The church bells had stopped ringing and the town was quiet. So quiet that she quite jumped when some distance away a motorcycle engine started up explosively. It belched and puttered with a now familiar diminuendo into the distance and into silence.

'But I suppose,' Troy thought, 'all these infernal machines sound exactly alike.'

III

Evening was now advanced in Tollardwark. The Market Square had filled with shadow and only the top of St Crispin's tower caught a fugitive glint of day. Footsteps sounded loud and hollow in the darkling streets and the voices of the few people who were abroad underlined rather than diminished the sense of emptiness. Some of the shop windows had all-night lamps in them but most were unlit and their contents hard to distinguish.

Troy loved to be in a strange town at nightfall. She would have chosen always to arrive, anywhere, at dusk. None of the other passengers was in sight and she supposed they had gone back to the *Zodiac*. Except Caley Bard, perhaps, who might still be taking out his sightseeing in the Northumberland Arms which glowed with classic geniality behind its red-curtained windows. The church windows also glowed – with kaleidoscopic richness.

She crossed the square, went through the lychgate up a short path and entered the west porch. There were the usual notices about parish meetings and restoration funds and the usual collection boxes. When she passed into the church itself she saw that it was beautiful: a soaring place with a feeling of certainty and aliveness not always to be found in churches.

They were saying compline by candlelight to a tiny congregation amongst whom Troy spotted the backs of Miss Rickerby-Carrick's and Mr Lazenby's heads. As she slipped into a pew at the rear of the nave, a disembodied alto voice admonished its handful of listeners.

'Be sober, be vigilant:' said the lonely voice, 'because your adversary the devil, as a roaring lion, walketh about seeking whom he may devour.'

She waited until almost the end and then slipped away as unobtrusively as she had come. 'If it were all true,' she thought, 'and if the devil really was out and about in the streets of Tollardwark! What a thing *that* would be to be sure!'

She chose to return down a different street from the one she had come up by. It was very narrow, indeed an alleyway rather than a street, and roughly cobbled. She saw a glimmer of The River at the bottom and knew she couldn't lose her way. At first she passed between old adjoining houses, one or two of them being half-timbered with overhanging upper stories. There was an echo, here, she thought, of her own steps. After a minute or two she stopped to listen. The other footfall stopped too but was it an echo or was someone else abroad in the alley? She looked behind her but it was now quite dark and she could see nobody. So she went on again, walking a little faster, and the echo, if it had been an echo, did not follow her.

Perhaps this was because the houses had thinned out and there were open places on either side as if buildings had been demolished. The alley seemed unconscionably long. The moon rose. Instead of being one of general darkness the picture was now, Troy thought, set out in ink and luminous paint: it glittered with light and swam with shadows and through it The River ran like quicksilver. The downhill slope was steep and Troy walked still faster. She made out the ramshackle shape of a house or shed at the bottom where the alley ended in another lane that stretched along the river-front.

The footfalls began again, some way behind her now but coming nearer and certainly not an echo.

Her way might have been up-hill rather than down so senselessly hard-fetched was her heartbeat.

She had reminded herself of Mr Tillottson's injunction and had resisted an impulse to break into a run when she came to the building at the bottom of the alley. As she did this two persons moved out of the shadow into her path. Troy caught back her breath in a single cry.

'Gee, Mrs Alleyn, is that you?' Miss Hewson said. 'Earl, it's Mrs Alleyn!'

'Why, so it is,' agreed her brother. 'So it is. Hallo, there, Mrs Alleyn. Kind of murky down here, isn't it? I guess the progressive elements in Tollardwark haven't caught up with street-lighting. Still in the linkman phase.'

'Golly,' Troy said, 'you made me jump.'

They broke into an apology. If they had known it was Troy they would have hailed her as she approached. Miss Hewson herself was nervous in the dark and wouldn't stir without Brother. Miss Hewson, Mr Hewson said, was a crazy hunter after old-time souvenirs and this place looked like it was some kind of trash shop and yard and nothing would do but they must try and peer in at the windows. And, interjected his sister, they had made out a number of delectable objects. The cutest kind of work-box on legs. Heaps of portfolios. And then – it was the darn'dest thing – their flashlamp had gone dead on them.

'It's old pictures,' Miss Hewson cried, 'that I just can't keep my hands off, Mrs Alleyn. Prints. Illustrations from Victorian publications. Those cute little girls with kittens and nosegays? Military pieces? Know what I mean?'

'Sis makes screens,' Mr Hewson explained tolerantly. 'Real pretty, too. I guess, back home, she's gotten to be famous for her screens.'

'Listen to you!' his sister exclaimed, 'talking about my screens to Mrs Alleyn!'

Troy, whose heart had stopped behaving like a water-ram, said she too admired Victorian screens and reminded the Hewsons that they would be able to explore Tollardwark on the return trip. 'I guess Sis'll be heading for this antique joint,' Mr Hewson said, 'before we're tied up. Come on, now, girls, why don't we go?'

He had taken their arms when the footsteps broke out again, quite near at hand. Mr Hewson swung his ladies round to face them.

An invisible man strode towards them through the dark: a set of pale garments and shoes without face or hands. Miss Hewson let out a sharp little scream but Troy exclaimed: 'Dr Natouche!'

'I am so sorry,' the great voice boomed. 'I have alarmed you. I would have called out back there before the moon rose but did not know if you were a stranger or not. I waited for you to get away from me. Then, just now, I heard your voice. I am so very sorry.'

'No harm done I guess, Doctor,' Mr Hewson said stiffly.

'Of course not,' Troy said. 'I was in the same case as you, Dr Natouche. I wondered about calling out and then thought you might be an affronted local inhabitant or a sinister prowler.'

Dr Natouche had produced a pocket torch no bigger than a giant pencil. 'The moon has risen,' he said, 'but it's dark down here.'

The light darted about like a firefly and for a moment a name flashed out: 'Jno. Bagg: licensed dealer,' on a small dilapidated sign above a door.

'Well,' Miss Hewson said to her brother. 'C'mon. Let's go.'

He took her arm again and turned invitingly to Troy. 'We can't walk four-abreast,' Troy said. 'You two lead the way.'

They did so and she fell in beside Dr Natouche.

The bottom lane turned out to be treacherous underfoot. Some kind of slippery lichen or river-weed had crept over the cobblestones. Miss Hewson slithered, clung to her brother and let out a yelp that flushed a company of ducks who raised their own rumpus and left indignantly by water.

The Hewsons exclaimed upon the vagaries of nature and stumbled on. Troy slipped and was stayed up expertly by Dr Natouche.

'I think perhaps you should take my arm,' he said. 'My shoes seem to be unaffected. We have chosen a bad way home.'

His arm felt professional: steady and very hard. He moved with perfect ease as his forefathers might have moved, Troy thought, barefoot across some unimaginable landscape. When she slipped, as she did once or twice, his hand closed for a moment about her forearm and she saw his long fingers pressed into the white sleeve.

The surface of the lane improved but she felt it would be uncivil to withdraw her arm at once. Dr Natouche spoke placidly of the beauties of Tollardwark. He talked, Troy thought indulgently, rather like the ship's brochure. She experienced a great contentment. What on earth, she thought gaily, have I been fussing about: I'm loving my cruise.

Miss Hewson turned to look back at Troy, peered, hesitated, and said: 'OK, Mrs Alleyn?'

'Grand, thank you.'

'There's the *Zodiac*,' Mr Hewson said. 'Girls – we're home.'

She looked welcoming indeed, with her riding lights and glowing red-curtained windows. 'Lovely!' Troy said light-heartedly. Dr Natouche's arm contracted very slightly and then relaxed and withdrew, closely observed by the Hewsons. Mr Hewson handed the ladies aboard and accompanied them down to the saloon which was deserted.

Miss Hewson carefully lowering her voice said cosily: 'Now, dear, I hope you were not too much embarrassed: we couldn't do one thing, could we, Earl?' She may have seen a look of astonishment in Troy's face. 'Of course,' she added, 'we don't just know how you Britishers feel – '

'I don't feel anything,' Troy said inaccurately. 'I don't know what you mean.'

'Well!' Mr Hewson said, 'You don't aim to tell us, Mrs Alleyn, that there's no distinction made in Britain? Now, only last week I was reading – '

'I'm sure you were, Mr Hewson, but honestly, we don't all behave like that. Or believe like that. Really.'

'Is that so?' he said. 'Is – that so? You wait awhile, Mrs Alleyn. You wait until you've a comparable problem. You haven't seen anything yet. Not a thing.'

'I guess we'll just leave it, dear,' Miss Hewson said. 'Am I looking forward to my bed! Boy, oh boy!'

'We'll say goodnight then, Mrs Alleyn,' Mr Hewson said rather stiffly. 'It's a privilege to make your acquaintance.'

Troy found herself saying goodnight with much more effusiveness than she normally displayed and this, she supposed, was because she wanted everything to be pleasant in the *Zodiac*. The Hewsons seemed to cheer up very much at these signs of cordiality and went to bed saying that it took all sorts to make a world.

Troy waited for a moment and then climbed the little companionway and looked over the half-door.

Dr Natouche stood at the after-end of the deck looking, it appeared, at the silhouette of Tollardwark against the night-sky. He has a gift, Troy thought, for isolating himself in space.

'Goodnight, Dr Natouche,' she said, quietly.

'Goodnight. Goodnight, Mrs Alleyn,' he returned, speaking as low as his enormous voice permitted. It was as if he played softly on a drum.

Troy wrote a letter to her husband which she would post before they left Tollard Lock in the morning and it was almost midnight when she had finished it.

What a long, long day, she thought as she climbed into her bed.

IV

She fell asleep within half a minute and was fathoms deep when noises lugged her to the surface. On the way up she dreamed of sawmills, of road-drills and of dentists. As she awoke her dream persisted: the rhythmic hullabaloo was close at hand, behind her head, coming in at her porthole – everywhere. Her cabin was suffused in moonlight reflected off the river. It looked like a sanctuary for peace itself but on the other side of the wall Miss Rickerby-Carrick in Cabin 8 snored with a virtuosity that exceeded anything Troy had ever heard before. The pandemonium she released no more resembled normal snoring than the '1812 Overture' resembles the 'Harmonious Blacksmith'. It was monstrous. It was insupportable.

Troy lay in a sort of incredulous panic, half-giggling, half-appalled as whistles succeeded snorts, and plosives followed upon whistles. A door on the far side of the passage angrily banged. She thought it was Caley Bard's. Then Mr Hewson, in Cabin 6 on Troy's left, thudded out of bed, crossed the passage to his sister's room and knocked.

'Sis! Hey Sis!' Troy heard him wail. 'For Pete's sake! *Sis!*' Troy reached out and opened her own door a crack.

Evidently, Miss Hewson was awake. Brother and sister consulted piteously together in the passage. Troy heard Miss Hewson say: 'OK, dear. OK. Go right ahead. Rouse her up. But don't bring me into it.'

Another door, No. 5, Troy thought, had been opened and the admonitory sound 'Ssh!' was sharply projected into the passage. The same door was then smartly shut. Mr Lazenby. Finally Mr Pollock unmistakably erupted into the mêlée.

'Does everybody *mind*!' Mr Pollock asked in a fury. 'Do me a favour, ladies and gents. I got the funny habit of liking to sleep at night!' A pause, sumptuously filled by Miss Rickerby-Carrick! 'Gawd!' Mr Pollock said. 'Has it been offered to the Zoo?'

Troy suddenly thumped the wall.

Miss Rickerby-Carrick trumpeted, said 'Wh-a-a?' and fell silent. After perhaps thirty wary, listening seconds her fellow-passengers returned to their beds and as she remained tacit, all, presumably, went to sleep.

Troy again slept deeply for what seemed to her to be a very long time and was sickeningly roused by Miss Rickerby-Carrick herself, standing like the first Mrs Rochester beside her bed and looking, Troy felt, not dissimilar. Her cold was heavy on her.

'*Dear* Mrs Alleyn,' Miss Rickerby-Carrick whispered. 'Do, do, do forgive me. I'm so dreadfully sorry but I simply can *not* get off! Hour after hour and *wide* awake. I – I had a shock. In Tollardwark. I can't tell you – at least – I – might. Tomorrow. But I can't sleep and I can't find my pills. I can – not – lay my hands upon my pills. Have you by any chance an aspirin? I feel so dreadful, waking you, but I get quite frantic when I can't sleep – I – I've had a shock. I've had an awful shock.'

Troy said: 'It's all right. Yes. I've got some aspirin. Would you turn on the light?'

When she had done this, Miss Rickerby-Carrick came back to the bed and leant over Troy. She wore a dull magenta dressing-gown; dark blue pyjamas. Something depended from her not very delicious neck. It swung forward and hit Troy on the nose.

'*Oh*, I'm so sorry. I *am* so sorry.'

'It's all right. If you'll just let me up, I'll find the aspirins.' While Troy did this Miss Rickerby-Carrick whispered indefatigably. 'You'll wonder what it is. That thing. I'll tell you. It's a romantic story, no denying it. Never leaves me. You'll be surprised,' the strange whisper gustily confided. 'No kidding. An heirloom. Honestly. My grandfather – surgeon – Czar – Fabergé. I promise you!' Troy had found the aspirin.

'Here they are. I really think you shouldn't tell people about it, you know.'

'Oh – but *you*!'

'I wouldn't – really. Why don't you put it in safe-keeping?'

'You're talking like the insurance people.'

'I can well believe it.'

'It's my *Luck*,' said Miss Rickerby-Carrick. 'That's how I feel about it. I can't be without my Luck. I did try once, and immediately fell down a flight of concrete steps. There, now!'

'Well, I wouldn't talk about it if I were you.'

'That's what Miss Hewson said.'

'For Heaven's sake!' Troy exclaimed and gave up.

'Well, she's awfully interested in antiques.'

'Have you shown it to her?'

She nodded coyly, wagging her ungainly head up and down and biting her lower lip. 'You'll never guess,' she said, 'what it *is*. The design I mean. Talk about coincidence!' She put her face close to Troy's and whispered. 'In diamonds and emeralds and rubies. The Signs of the Zodiac. Now!'

'Hadn't you better go to bed?' Troy asked wearily.

Miss Rickerby-Carrick stared fixedly at her and then bolted.

When Mrs Tretheway at eight o'clock brought her a cup of tea, Troy felt as if the incidents of the night had been part of her dreams. At breakfast Mr Pollock and the Hewsons had a muttering session about Miss Rickerby-Carrick, Caley Bard openly asked Troy if she was keen on 'Eine Kleine Nacht Musik' and Mr Lazenby told him not to be naughty. As usual Dr Natouche took no part in this general, if furtive, conversation. Miss Rickerby-Carrick herself retired at mid-morning to a corner of the deck where, snuffling dreadfully and looking greatly perturbed, she kept up her diary.

The *Zodiac* cruised tranquilly through the morning. After luncheon Mr Lazenby occasioned some surprise by appearing in a bathing slip, blowing up an inflatable mattress and sunbathing on deck. 'Once an Aussie, always an Aussie,' he observed. Mr and Miss Hewson were so far encouraged as to change into Hawaiian shorts and floral tops. Dr Natouche had already appeared in immaculate blue linen and Caley Bard in conservative slacks and cotton shirt. Troy settled at a table in the saloon, finished her drawing and treated it to a lovely blush of aquarelle-crayons which she had bought for fun and because they were easy to carry. Each of the Signs now bore a crazy resemblance to the person she had assigned to it. Caley Bard's slew-eyed glance looked out of the Scorpion's head. Virgo was a kind of ethereal whiff of what Miss Rickerby-Carrick might have been. The Hewsons, *stylisés*, put their heads together for the Twins. Mr Lazenby, naked, blindfold and in elegant retreat, displayed the Scales. Something about the stalked eyes of the Crab quoted Mr Pollock's rather prominent stare. Mrs Tretheway, translated into classic splendour, presented the Fish on a celestial platter. The Ram had a steering wheel between his hoofs and the boy, Tom – Aquarius, carried water in a ship's bucket. Troy's short dark locks tumbled about the brow of the Goat, while her husband glanced ironically through the Lion's mask. The Bull, vainglorious, rode his motorbike. Splendidly alone, the dark Archer drew his bow. Troy was amused with her picture but sighed at the thought of doing the lettering.

The Hewsons, passing through the saloon, devoured by curiosity and swathed in tact, asked if they might have a peep. This led to everybody, except Dr Natouche, gathering round her.

'Just see what you've done with children's chalks and a drop of ink!' Caley Bard exclaimed. 'What magic!' He gave a little crowing sound, burst out laughing and looked round at his fellow-passengers. 'Do you see!' he cried. 'Do you see what she's done?'

After some reflection they did, each recognizing the others more readily than him – or her self. It appeared that Troy had been lucky in three of her choices. The Hewsons were, in fact, twins and, by an extraordinarily felicitous chance, had been born under Gemini while Miss Rickerby-Carrick confessed, with mantling cheeks and conscious looks, as Caley Bard afterwards put it, to Virgo. She still seemed frightened and stared fixedly at Troy.

'Natouche,' Caley Bard called up the companion-way, 'you must come down and see this.'

He came down at once. Troy gave him the drawing and for the second time heard his laugh. 'It is beautiful and it is comical,' he said presently and handed it back to Troy. 'I know, of course, that one must not frivolously compare the work of one great artist with another but may I say that Erni is perhaps your only contemporary who would have approached the subject like this.'

'Very perceptive of you,' said Caley Bard.

'I want to put the rhyme in the middle,' Troy said, 'but my lettering's hopeless: it takes ages to do and is awful when it's finished. I suppose nobody here would do a nice neo-classic job of lettering?'

'I would,' said Mr Pollock.

He was close behind Troy, staring over her arm at the drawing. 'I – ' he paused and, most unaccountably, Troy was revisited by yesterday's impression of an impending crisis. 'I started in that business,' Pollock said and there seemed to be a note of apology in his voice. 'Commercial art. You know? Gave it up for real estate. I – if you show me what you'd like – the type of lettering – I'll give satisfaction.'

He was looking at the drawing with the oddest expression in his barrow-boy face: sharp, appreciative and somehow – what? – shamefaced? Or – could Mr Pollock possibly be frightened?

Troy said, cordially. 'Will you really? Thank you so much. It just wants to be a sort of Garamond face. A bit fantasticated if you like.'

Dr Natouche had a book in his hand with the dust-jacket titled in Garamond. 'That sort of thing,' Troy said pointing to it.

Mr Pollock looked reluctantly but sharply at it and then bent over the drawing. 'I could do that,' he said. 'I don't know anything about fantasticate,' and added under his breath something that sounded like: 'I can copy anything.'

Mr Lazenby said loudly: 'You're very sure of yourself, Mr Pollock, aren't you?' and Caley Bard ejaculated: 'Honestly, Pollock, how you dare!'

There followed a brief silence. Pollock mumbled: 'Only a suggestion, isn't it? No need to take it up, is there?'

'I'd be very glad to take it up,' Troy said. 'There you are: it's all yours.'

She moved away from the table and after a moment's hesitation he sat down at it.

Troy went up on deck where she was soon joined by Caley Bard.

'You didn't half snub that little man,' she said.

'He irritates me. And he's a damn' sight too cool about your work.'

'Oh come!'

'Yes, he is. Breathing down your neck. My God, you're *you*. You're "Troy". How he dares!'

'Do come off it.'

'Have you noticed how rude he is to Natouche?'

'Well, that – yes. But you know I really think direct antagonism must be more supportable than the "don't let's be beastly" line.'

'See the Rickerby-Carrick?'

'If you like. Yes.'

'You know,' he said, 'if you weren't a passenger in the good ship *Zodiac* I think I'd rat.'

'Nonsense.'

'It's not. Where did you get to last night?'

'I had a telephone call to make.'

'It couldn't have taken you all evening.'

Remembering Fox's suggestion Troy, who was a poor liar, lied. 'It was about a fur I left at the gallery. I had to go to the police station.'

'And then?'

'I went to the church.'

'You'd much better have come on a one-pub-crawl with me,' he grumbled. 'Will you dine tomorrow night in Longminster?'

Before Troy could reply, Miss Rickerby-Carrick, looking scared, came up from below, attired in her magenta wrapper. Her legs were bare and her arthritic toes emerged like roots from her sandals. She wore dark glasses and a panama hat and she carried her Li-lo and her diary. She paused by the wheelhouse for her usual chat with the Skipper, continued on her way and to Troy's extreme mortification avoided her and Bard with the kind of tact that breaks the sound-barrier, bestowing on them as she passed an understanding smile. She disappeared behind a stack of chairs covered by a tarpaulin, at the far end of the deck.

Troy said: 'Not true, is she? Just a myth?'

'What's she writing?'

'A journal. She calls it her self-propelling confessional.'

'Would you like to read it?'

'Isn't it awful – but, yes, I can't say I wouldn't fancy a little peep.'

'How about tomorrow night? Dinner ashore, boys, and hey for the rollicking bun.'

'Could we decide a bit later?'

'In case something more interesting turns up, you cautious beast.'

'Not altogether that.'

'Well – what?'

'We don't know what everybody will be doing,' Troy said feebly and then: 'I know. Why don't we ask Dr Natouche to come?'

'We shall do nothing of the sort and I must say I think that's a pretty cool suggestion. I invite you to dine, tête-à-tête and – '

Miss Rickerby-Carrick screamed.

It was a positive, abrupt and piercing scream and it brought everybody on deck.

She was leaning over the after-taffrail, her wrapper in wild dis-array. She gesticulated and exclaimed and made strange grimaces.

'My diary! Oh stop! Oh please! My diary!' cried Miss Rickerby-Carrick.

Somehow or another she had dropped it overboard. She made confused statements to the effect that she had been observing the depths, had leant over too far, had lost her grip. She lamented with catarrhal extravagance, she pointed aft where indeed the diary was to be seen, open and fairly rapidly submerging. Her nose and eyes ran copiously.

The Tretheways behaved with the greatest address. The Skipper put the *Zodiac* into slow-astern, Tom produced a kind of long-handled curved hook used for clearing river-weed and Mrs Tretheway, placidity itself, emerged from below and attempted to calm Miss Rickerby-Carrick.

The engine was switched off and the craft, on her own momen-tum came alongside Miss Rickerby-Carrick's diary. Tom climbed over the taffrail, held to it with his left hand and with his right, prepared to angle.

'But no!' screamed Miss Rickerby-Carrick. 'Not with that thing! You'll destroy it! Don't, don't, don't! Oh please. Oh please.'

'Stone the crows!' Mr Lazenby astonishingly ejaculated. With an air of hardy resignation he rose from his Li-lo, turned his back on the company, removed his spectacles and placed them on the deck. He then climbed over the taffrail and neatly dived into The River.

Miss Rickerby-Carrick screamed again, the other passengers ejac-ulated and, with the precision of naval ratings, lined the port side to gaze at Mr Lazenby. He was submerged but quickly re-appeared with his long hair plastered over his eyes and the diary in his hand.

The Skipper instructed him to go ashore and walk a couple of chains downstream where it was deep enough for the *Zodiac* to come alongside. He did so, holding the diary clear of the water. He climbed the bank and squatted there, shaking the book gently and separating and turning over the leaves. His hair hung to one side like a caricature of a Carnaby Street fringe, completely obscuring the left eye.

Miss Rickerby-Carrick began to give out plaintive little cries inter-spersed with gusts of apologetic laughter and incoherent remarks upon the waterproof nature of her self-propelling pen. She could not wait for Mr Lazenby to come aboard but leant out at a dangerous angle to receive the book from him. The little lump of leather, Troy saw, still dangled from her neck.

'Oh ho, ho!' she laughed, 'my poor old confidante. Alas, alas!'

She thanked Mr Lazenby with incoherent effusion and begged him not to catch cold. He reassured her, accepted his dark glasses from Troy who had rescued them and turned aside to put them on. When he faced them all again it really seemed as if in some off-beat fashion and without benefit of dog-collar, he had resumed his canonicals. He even made a little parsonic noise: 'N'yer I'll just get out of my wet bathers,' he said. 'There's not the same heat in the English sun: not like Bondi.' And retired below.

'Well!' said Caley Bard. 'Who says the Church is effete?'

There was a general appreciative murmur in which Troy did not join.

Had she or had she not seen for a fractional moment, in Mr Lazenby's left hand, a piece of wet paper with the marks of a propelling pencil across it?

While Troy still mused over this, Miss Rickerby-Carrick who squatted on the deck examining with plaintive cries the ruin of her journal, suddenly exclaimed with much greater emphasis.

The others broke off and looked at her with that particular kind of patient endurance that she so pathetically inspired.

This time, however, there was something in her face that none of them had seen before: a look, not of anxiety or excitement but, for a second or two Troy could have sworn, of sheer panic. The dun skin had bleached under its freckles and round the jawline. The busy mouth was flaccid. She stared at her open diary. Her hands trembled. She shut the drenched book and steadied them by clutching it.

Miss Hewson said: 'Miss Rickerby-Carrick, are you OK?'

She nodded once or twice, scrambled to her feet and incontinently bolted across the deck and down the companion-way to the cabins.

'And *now*,' Troy said to herself. 'What about *that* one? Am I still imagining?'

Again she had sensed a kind of stillness, of immense constraint and again she was unable to tell from whom it emanated.

'Like it or lump it,' Troy thought, 'Superintendent Tillottson's going to hear about that lot and we'll see what he makes of it. In the meantime – '

In the meantime, she went to her cabin and wrote another letter to her husband.

Half an hour later the *Zodiac* tied up for the afternoon and night at Crossdyke.

CHAPTER 4

Crossdyke

'As I told you,' Alleyn said. 'I rang up the Yard from San Francisco. Inspector Fox, who was handling the Andropulos Case, was away, but after inquiries I got through to Superintendent Tillottson at Tollardwark. He gave me details of his talks with my wife. One detail worried me a good deal more than it did him.'

Alleyn caught the inevitable glint of appreciation from the man in the second row.

'Exactly,' he said. 'As a result I talked to the Yard again and was told there was no doubt that Foljambe had got himself to England and that he was lying doggo. Information received suggested that Andropulos had tried a spot of blackmail and had been fool enough to imply that he'd grass on the Jampot if the latter didn't come across with something handsome. Andropulos had in fact talked to one of our chaps in the way they do when they can't make up their minds to tell us something really useful. It was pretty obvious he was hinting at the Jampot.

'So he was murdered for his pains.

'The method used had been that of sudden and violent pressure on the carotids from behind and that method carries the Jampot's signature. It is sometimes preceded by a karate chop which would probably do the trick anyway, but it's his little fancy to make assurance double-sure.'

The Scot in the second row gave a smirk to indicate his recognition of the quotation. 'If I'm not careful,' Alleyn thought, 'I'll be playing up to that chap.'

'There had,' he said, 'been two other homicides, one in Ismalia and one in Paris where undoubtedly Foljambe had been the expert. But not a hope of cracking down on him. The latest line suggested that he had lit off for France. An envelope of the sort used by a well-known travel-agency had been dropped on the floor near Andropulos's body and it had a note of the price of tickets and times of departure from London scribbled on the back. It had, as was afterwards realized, been planted by the Jampot and had successfully decoyed Mr Fox across the Channel. A typical stroke. I've already talked about his talent – it amounts to genius – for type-casting himself. I don't think I mentioned that when he likes to turn it on he has a strong attraction for many, but not all, women. His ear for dialects of every description is phenomenal, of course, but he not only speaks whatever it may be – Oxbridge, superior grammar, Australasian, barrow-boy or Bronx, but he really seems to think along the appropriate wave-lengths. Rather as an actor gets behind the thought-pattern of the character he plays. He can act stupid, by the way, like nobody's business. He is no doubt a great loss to the stage. He is gregarious, which you'd think would be risky and he has a number of unexpected, off-beat skills that occasionally come in very handy indeed.

'Well: you'll appreciate the situation. Take a look at it. Andropulos has been murdered, almost certainly by the Jampot and the Jampot's at large. Andropulos, scarcely a candidate, one would have thought, for the blameless delights of British Inland Waterways was to have been a passenger in the *Zodiac*. My wife now has his cabin. There's no logical reason in the wide world why his murderer should be her fellow-passenger: indeed the idea at first sight is ludicrous, and yet and yet – my wife tells me that her innocent remark about "Constables" seemed to cast an extraordinary gloom upon someone or other in the party, that the newspaper report of Andropulos's murder has been suppressed by someone in the *Zodiac*, that she's pretty sure an Australian padre who wears dark glasses and conceals his right eye has purloined a page of a farcical spinster's diary, that she half-suspects him of listening-in to her telephone conversation with Mr Fox and that she herself can't escape a feeling of impending disaster. And there's one other feature of this unlikely set-up that, however idiotically, strikes me as being more disturbing than all the rest put together. I wonder if any of you – '

But the man in the second row already had his hand up.

'Exactly,' Alleyn said when the phenomenon had delivered himself of the correct answer in a strong Scots accent. 'Quite so. And you might remember that I am five thousand odd miles away in San Francisco on an extremely important conference.

'What the hell do I do?'

After a moment's thought the hand went up again.

'All right, all right,' Alleyn said. '*You* tell *me*.'

I

Hazel Rickerby-Carrick sat in her cabin turning over with difficulty the disastrous pages of her diary.

They were not actually pulp; they were stuck together, buckled, blistered and disfigured. They had half-parted company with the spine and the red covers had leaked into them. The writing, however, had not been irrevocably lost.

She separated the entries for the previous day and for that afternoon.

'I'm at it again,' she read dismally. 'Trying too hard, as usual. It goes down all right with Mavis, of course, but not with these people: not with Troy Alleyn. If only I'd realized who she was from the first! Or if only I'd heard she was going to be next door in Cabin 7: I could have gone to the Exhibition. I could have talked about her pictures. Of course, I don't pretend to know anything about – ' Here she had had second thoughts and had abstained from completing the aphorism. She separated the sopping page from its successor using a nail-file as a sort of slice. She began to read the final entry. It was for that afternoon, before the diary went overboard.

' – I'm going to write it down. I've got my diary with me: here, now. I'm lying on my Li-lo on deck (at the "blunt end"!!!) behind a pile of chairs covered with a tarpaulin. I'm having a sun-tan. I suppose I'm a goose to be so shy. In this day and age! What one *sees*! And of course it's much healthier and anyway the body is beautiful: *beautiful*. Only mine isn't so very. What I'm going to write now, happened last night. In Tollardwark. It was so frightful and so strange and I don't know what I ought to do about it. I think what I'll do is I'll tell Troy Alleyn. She can't say it's not extraordinary because it is.

'I'd come out of church and I was going back to the *Zodiac*. I was wearing what the Hewsons call "sneakers". Rubber soles. And that dark maroon jersey thing so I suppose I was unnoticed because it was awfully dark. Absolutely pitchers. Well, I'd got a pebble or something in my left "sneaker" and it hurt so I went into a dark shop-entry where I could lean against a door and take it off. And it was while I was there that those others came down the street. I would have hailed them: I was just going to do it when they stopped. I didn't recognize the voices at once because they spoke very low. In fact the one of them who whispered, I *never* recognized. But the others! Could they have said what I'm sure they did? The *first words* froze me. But literally. *Froze* me. I was *riveted*. Horror-stricken. I can hear them now. It – '

She had reached the bottom of the page. She picked at it gingerly, slid the nail-file under it, crumpled it and turned it.

The following pages containing her last entry were gone.

The inner margins where they were bound together had to some extent escaped a complete soaking. She could see by the fragments that remained that they had been pulled away. 'But after all, that's nothing to go by,' she thought, 'because when he dived, Mr Lazenby may have grabbed. The book was open. It was open and lying on its face when it sank. That's it. That's got to be it.'

Miss Rickerby-Carrick remained perfectly still for some minutes. Once or twice she passed her arthritic fingers across her eyes and brow almost as if she tried to exorcize some devil of muddlement within.

'He's a clergyman,' she thought, 'a clergyman! He's been staying with a bishop. I could ask him. Why not? What could he say? Or do? But I'll ask Troy Alleyn. She'll jolly well have to listen. It'll interest her. Her *husband*!' she suddenly remembered. 'Her husband's a famous detective. I *ought* to tell Troy Alleyn: and then she may like me to call her Troy. We may get quite chummy,' thought poor Hazel Rickerby-Carrick without very much conviction.

She put the saturated diary open on her bedside shelf where a ray of afternoon sunlight reached it through the porthole.

A nervous weakness had come upon her. She suffered a terrible sense of constraint as if not only her head was iron-bound but as if the tiny cabin contracted about her. 'I shan't sleep in here,' she thought. 'I shan't get a wink or if I do there'll be beastly dreams and I'll make noises and they'll hate me.' And as she fossicked in an already chaotic drawer for Troy's aspirin she was visited by her great idea. She would sleep on deck. She would wait until the others had settled down and then she would take her Li-lo from its jolly old hidey-hole behind the tarpaulin and blow it up and sleep, as she phrased it to herself, 'under the wide and starry sky'. And perhaps – perhaps.

'I've always been one to go straight at a thing and tackle it,' she thought and finding Troy's aspirins with the top off inside her sponge-bag, she took a couple, lay on her bunk and made several disastrous plans.

II

For Troy, the evening at Crossdyke began farcically. The passengers were given an early dinner to enable them to explore the village and the nearby ruin of a hunting lodge where King John had stayed during his misguided antics in the north.

Troy who had the beginning of a squeamish headache hoped to get a still earlier start than she had achieved at Tollardwark and to make her call at the police station before any of her fellow-passengers appeared on the scene. Her story of the lost fur was now currency in the ship and would explain the visit if explanation was needed but she hoped to avoid making one.

Throughout dinner Miss Rickerby-Carrick gazed intently at Troy who found herself greatly put-out by this attention: the more so because what her husband once described as her King-Size Bowels of Compassion had been roused by Miss Rickerby-Carrick. The more exasperating she became the more infuriatingly succulent her cold, the more embarrassingly fixed her regard, the sorrier Troy felt for her and the less she desired her company. Either, she thought, the wretched woman was doing a sort of dismal lion-hunt, or, hideous notion, had developed a *schwarm* for Troy herself. Or was it possible, she suddenly wondered, that this extraordinary lady had something of moment to communicate.

Miss Rickerby-Carrick commanded rather less tact than a bull-dozer and it must be clear, Troy thought, to everybody in the saloon that a happening was on the brew.

Determined to look anywhere but at her tormentor, Troy caught the ironical, skew-eyed glance of Caley Bard. He winked and she lowered her gaze. Mr Pollock stared with distaste at Miss Rickerby-Carrick and the Hewsons caught each other's glances and assumed a mask-like air of detachment. Mr Lazenby and Dr Natouche swopped bits of medieval information about the ruins.

Troy went straight on deck when she had finished her dinner and was about to go ashore when up came Miss Rickerby-Carrick from below, hailing her in a curious kind of soft-pedalled shout.

'Mrs Alleyn! I say! Mrs Alleyn!'

Troy paused.

'Look!' said Miss Rickerby-Carrick coming close to her and whispering. 'I – are you going up to the village? Can I come with you? I've got something – ' she looked over her shoulder and up and down the deck though she must have known as well as Troy that the others were all below. 'I want to ask your advice. It's awfully important. Really. I promise,' she whispered.

'Well – yes. All right, if you really think – '

'*Please*. I'll just get my cardi. I won't be a tick. Only as far as the village. Before the others start – it's awfully important. Honest injun. *Please*.'

She advanced her crazy-looking face so close that Troy took an involuntary step backward.

'Be kind!' Miss Rickerby-Carrick whispered. 'Let me tell you. Let me!'

She stood before Troy: a grotesque, a dreadfully vulnerable person. And the worst of it was, Troy thought, she herself was now so far caught up in a web of intangible misgivings that she could not know, could not trust herself to judge, whether the panic she thought she saw in those watery eyes was a mere reflection of the ill-defined anxiety which was building itself up around her own very real delight in the little cruise of the *Zodiac*. Or whether Miss Rickerby-Carrick's unmistakable *schwarm* was about to break out in a big way.

'Oh please!' she repeated, 'for God's sake! Please.'

'Well, of course,' Troy said, helplessly. 'Of course.'

'Oh, you *are* a darling,' exclaimed Miss Rickerby-Carrick and bolted for the companion-way.

She collided with Mr Pollock and there was much confusion and incoherent apology before she retired below and he emerged on deck.

He had brought back to Troy the Signs of the Zodiac with the lettering completed. It was beautifully done, right in scale and manner and execution and Troy told him so warmly. He said in his flat voice with its swallowed consonants and plummy vowels that she need think nothing of it, the obligation was all his and he hung about in his odd way offering a few scraps of disjointed information to the effect that he'd gone from the signwriting into the printing trade but there hadn't been any money in that. He made remarks that faded out after one or two words and gave curious little sounds that were either self-conscious laughs or coughs.

'Do you paint?' Troy asked. 'As well as this? Or draw?'

He hastened to assure her that he did not. 'Me? A flippin' awtist? Do you mind!'

'I thought from the way you looked at this thing – '

'Then you thought wrong,' he said with an unexpected slap of rudeness.

Troy stared at him and he reddened. 'Pardon my French,' he said, 'I'm naturally crude. I do not paint. I just take a fancy to look.'

'Fair enough,' Troy said pacifically.

He gave her a shamefaced grin and said oh well he supposed he'd better do something about the nightlife of Crossdyke. As he was evidently first going below Troy asked him to keep the drawing for the time being.

He paused at the companion-way for Miss Rickerby-Carrick. She erupted with monotonous precipitancy through the half-door, saw Mr Pollock who had the Zodiac drawing open in his hands, looked at it as if it was a bomb and hurried on to Troy.

'Do let's go,' she said. 'Do come on.'

They took their long strides from the gunwale to the bank, a simple exercise inevitably made complex by Miss Rickerby-Carrick, who, when she had recovered herself, seized Troy's arm and began to gabble.

'At once. I'll tell you at once before anyone can stop me. It's about – about – ' She drove her free hand through her dishevelled hair and began distractedly to whisper and stammer quite incomprehensibly.

' – about last evening – And – And – Oh God! – And – '

'About *what*?'

'And – wait – And – '

But it was not to be. She had taken a deep breath, screwed up her eyes and opened her mouth, almost as if she were about to sneeze, when they were hailed from the rear.

'Hi! Wait a bit! What are you two up to?'

It was Mr Lazenby. He leapt nimbly ashore and came alongside Troy. 'We can't have these exclusive ladies' excursions,' he said roguishly. 'You'll have to put up with a mere man as far as the village.'

Troy looked up at him and he shook a playful finger at her. 'He's rescued me,' she thought and with what she herself felt to be a perverse change of mood suddenly wanted to hear Miss Rickerby-Carrick's confidences. 'Perhaps,' Troy thought, 'she'll tell us both.'

But she didn't. By means of sundry hard-fingered squeezes and tweaks she conveyed her chagrin. At the same time Mr Lazenby went through much the same routine with Troy's left arm and she began to feel like Alice between the Queens.

She produced, once more, her story of the lost fur and said she was going to inquire at the local police station.

'I suppose,' Miss Rickerby-Carrick observed, 'they make great efforts for you. Because – I mean – your husband – and everything.'

'Ah!' Mr Lazenby archly mocked. 'How right you are! Police protection every inch of the way. Big drama. You heard her say yesterday, Miss Rickerby-Carrick. The landscape's swarming with Constables.'

The hand within Troy's right arm began to tremble. 'She meant the painter,' whispered Miss Rickerby-Carrick.

'That's only her cunning. She's sly as you make 'em, you may depend upon it. We're none of us safe.'

The fingers on Troy's right arm became more agitated while those on her left gave it a brief conspiratorial squeeze. 'Arms,' Troy thought. 'Last night Dr Natouche and tonight, these two, and I'm not the sort to link arms.' But she was aware that while these contacts were merely irksome, last night's had both disturbed and reassured her.

She freed herself as casually as she could and talking disjointedly they walked into the village where they were overtaken by Caley Bard, complete with butterfly net and collector's box. All desire for the Rickerby-Carrick disclosures had left Troy. She scarcely listened to madly divergent spurts of information: '. . . my friend, Mavis . . . you would love her . . . such a brilliant brain . . . art . . . science . . . butterflies even, Mr Bard . . . though not for me – Lamborine – . . . my friend, Mavis . . . Highlands . . . *how* I wish she was here . . . Mavis . . .'

The undisciplined voice gushed and dwindled, gabbled and halted. Troy had an almost overwhelming urge to be alone with her headache.

They came up with the cottage police station. A small car and a motorcycle stood outside.

'Shall we wait for you?' Bard asked. 'Or not?'

'Not, please, I may be quite a time. They'll probably want to telephone about it. As a matter of fact,' Troy said, 'I believe when I've finished here I'll just go back to the *Zodiac*. For some reason I've got a bit of a headache.'

It was an understatement. Her headache was ripening. She was subject to occasional abrupt onsets of migraine and even now a thing like a starburst pulsed in one corner of her field of vision and her temples had begun to throb.

'You *poor* darling,' cried Miss Rickerby-Carrick. 'Shall I come back with you. Would you like a sleeping-pill? Miss Hewson's got some. She's given me two for tonight. Shall I wait for you? Yes?'

'But *of course* we'll wait,' Mr Lazenby fluted.

Caley Bard said that he was sure Troy would rather be left to herself and proposed that he and Mr Lazenby and Miss Rickerby-Carrick should explore the village together and then he would teach them how to lepidopterize. Troy felt this was a truly noble action.

'Don't let those bobbies worry you,' he said. 'Take care of yourself, do. Hope you recover your morsel of mink.'

'Thank you,' Troy said and tried to convey her sense of obligation without alerting Miss Rickerby-Carrick whose mouth was stretched in an anxious grin. She parted with them and went into the police station where at once time slipped a cog and she was back in last evening for there was Superintendent Tillottson blandly remarking that he had just popped over from Toll'ark in case there had been any developments. She told him (speaking against the beat of her headache and with the sick dazzle in her vision making nonsense of his face) about Mr Lazenby and the page from the diary and about the odd behaviour of Mr Pollock and Miss Rickerby-Carrick. And again, on describing them, these items shrank into insignificance.

Mr Tillottson with his hands in his pockets, sitting easily on the corner of the local Sergeant's desk said with great geniality that there didn't seem to be much in any of *that* lot did there, and she agreed, longing to be rid of the whole thing and in bed.

'Yerse,' Mr Tillottson said. 'So that's the story.' And he added with the air of making conversation: 'And this chap Lazenby had his hair all over his right eye like a hippy? Funny idea in a clergyman. But it was wet, of course.'

'Over his left eye,' Troy corrected as a sharp stab of pain shot through her own.

'His *left* eye, was it?' said Mr Tillottson casually. 'Yes. Fancy. And you never got a look at it. The eye I mean?'

'Well, no. He turned his back when he put on his dark spectacles.'

'P'raps he's got some kind of disfigurement,' Mr Tillottson airily speculated. 'You never know, do you? Jim Tretheway's a very pleasant kind of chap, isn't he? And his wife's smashing, don't you think, Mrs Alleyn? Very nice couple the Tretheways.'

'Very,' Troy agreed and stood up to a lurching spasm of migraine.

They shook hands again and Mr Tillottson produced, apparently as an afterthought, the suggestion that she should drop in at 'their place in Longminster' where she would find Superintendent Bonney a most sympathetic person: 'a lovely chap' was how Mr Tillottson described him.

'I honestly don't think I need trouble him,' Troy said. She was beginning to feel sick.

'Just to keep in touch, Mrs Alleyn,' he said and made a little sketch plan of Longminster, marking the police station with a cross. 'Go to the point marked X,' he said facetiously. 'We may have a bit of news for you,' he playfully added. 'There's been a slight change in your good man's itinerary. We'll be pleased to let you know.'

'Rory!' Troy exclaimed. 'Is he coming back earlier?'

'I understand it's not quite settled yet, Mrs Alleyn.'

'Because if he is – '

'Oh, it wouldn't be anything you might call immediate. If you'd just look in on our chaps at Longminster we'd be much obliged. Very kind of you.'

By this time Troy could have hurled the local Sergeant's inkpot at Mr Tillottson but she took her leave with circumspection and made her way through nauseating sunbursts back to The River. Before she reached it her migraine attained its climax. She retired behind a briar bush and emerged, shaken but on the mend.

Her doctor had advanced the theory that these occasional onsets were associated with nervous tension and for the first time she began to think he might be right.

She would quite have liked to look at the ruins which were
visible from her porthole, doing their stuff against the beginning of
a spectacular sunset but the attack had left her tired and sleepy and
she settled for an early night.

There seemed to be no other passengers aboard the *Zodiac*. Troy
took a shower and afterwards knelt in her dressing-gown on the
bed and watched the darkling landscape across which, presently,
her companions began to appear. There on the rim of a hillside
rising to the ruins was Caley Bard in silhouette with his butterfly
net. He gave a ridiculous balletic leap as he made a sweep with it.
He was followed by Miss Rickerby-Carrick in full cry. Troy saw them
put their heads together over the net and thought: 'She's driving
him crackers.' At that moment Dr Natouche came down the lane
and Miss Rickerby-Carrick evidently spied him. She seemed to take
a hasty farewell of Bard and, in her precipitancy, became almost air-
borne as she plunged downhill in pursuit of the Doctor. Troy heard
her hail him.

'Doctor! Doctor Na-tooo-sh.'

He paused, turned and waited. He was incapable, Troy thought,
of looking anything but dignified. Miss Rickerby-Carrick closed in.
She displayed her usual vehemence. He listened with that doctor's
air which is always described as being grave and attentive.

'Can she be consulting him?' Troy wondered. 'Or is she perhaps
confiding in him instead of me.'

Now, she was showing him something in the palm of her hand.
Could it be a butterfly, Troy wondered. He bent his head to look at it.
Troy saw him give a little nod. They walked slowly towards the *Zodiac*
and as they approached, the great booming voice became audible.

' – your own medical man . . . something to help you . . . quite
possibly . . . indeed.'

She *is* consulting him, thought Troy.

They moved out of her field of vision and now there emerged
from the ruins the rest of the travellers: the Hewsons, Mr Lazenby
and Mr Pollock. They waved to Caley Bard and descended the hill in
single file, like cut-out figures in black paper against a fading green
sky. *Commedia dell' arte* again, Troy thought.

The evening was very warm. She lay down on her bunk. There
was little light in the cabin and she left it so, fearing that Miss

Rickerby-Carrick would call to inquire. She even locked her door, and, obscurely, felt rather mean for doing so. The need for sleep that always followed her migraines must now be satisfied and Troy began to dream of voices and of a mouselike scratching at somebody's door. It persisted, it established itself over her dream and nagged her back into wakefulness. She struggled with herself, suffered an angry spasm of conscience and finally in a sort of bemused fury, got out of bed and opened the door.

On nobody.

The passage was empty. She thought afterwards that as she opened her own door another one had quietly closed.

She waited but there was no stirring or sound anywhere and, wondering if after all she had dreamt the scratching at her door, she went back to bed and at once fell fathoms deep into oblivion that at some unidentifiable level was disturbed by the sound of an engine.

III

She half-awoke to broad daylight and the consciousness of a subdued fuss: knocking and voices, footsteps in the passage and movements next door in Cabin 8. While she lay, half-detached and half-resentful of these disturbances, there was a tap on her own door and a rattle of the handle.

Troy, now fully awake, called out, 'Sorry. Just a moment,' and unlocked her door.

Mrs Tretheway came in with tea.

'Is anything wrong?' Troy asked.

Mrs Tretheway's smile broke out in glory all over her face. 'Well,' she said, 'not to say wrong. It's how you look at it, I suppose, Mrs Alleyn. The fact is Miss Rickerby-Carrick seems to have left us.'

'*Left* us? *Gone?*'

'That's right.'

'Do you mean – ?'

'It must have been very early. Before any of us were about and our Tom was up at six.'

'But – '

'She's packed her suitcase and gone.'

'No message?'

'Well now – yes – scribbled on a bit of newspaper. "Called away. So sorry. Urgent. Will write".'

'How very extraordinary.'

'My husband reckons somebody must have come in the night. Some friend with a car or else she might have rung Toll'ark or Longminster for a taxi. The telephone booth at the lockhouse is open all night.'

'*Well*,' Troy muttered, 'she is a rum one and *no* mistake.'

Mrs Tretheway beamed. 'It may be all for the best,' she remarked. 'It's a lovely day, anyhow,' and took her departure.

When Troy arrived in the saloon she found her fellow-passengers less intrigued than might have been expected and she supposed that they had already exhausted the topic of Miss Rickerby-Carrick's flight.

Her own entrance evidently revived it a little and there was a short barrage of rather flaccid questions: had Miss Rickerby-Carrick 'said anything' to Troy? She hadn't 'said anything' to anyone else.

'Shall we rather put it,' Caley Bard remarked sourly, 'that she hadn't said anything of *interest*. Full stop. Which God knows, by and large, is only too true of all her conversation.'

'Now, Mr Bard, isn't that just a little hard on the poor girl?' Miss Hewson objected.

'I don't know why we must call her "poor",' he rejoined.

'Of course you do,' Troy said. 'One can't help thinking of her as "poor Miss Rickerby-Carrick" and that makes her all the more pitiful.'

'What a darling you are,' he said judicially.

Troy paid no attention to this. Dr Natouche who had not taken part in the conversation, looked directly at her and gave her a smile of such clear understanding that she wondered if she had blushed or turned pale.

Mr Lazenby offered one or two professional aphorisms to the effect that Miss Rickerby-Carrick was a dear soul and kindness itself. Mr Hewson looked dry and said she was just a mite excitable. Mr Pollock agreed with this. 'Talk!' he said. 'Oh dear!'

'They are all delighted,' Troy thought.

On that note she left them and went up on deck. The *Zodiac* was still at Crossdyke, moored below the lock, but Tom and his father were making their customary preparations for departure.

They had cast off and the engine had started when Troy heard the telephone ringing in the lock-keeper's office. A moment later his wife came out and ran along the tow-path towards them.

'Skipper! Hold on! Message for you.'

'OK. Thanks.'

The engine fussed and stopped and the *Zodiac* moved back a little towards the wharf. The lock-keeper came out and arched his hands round his mouth.

'Car Hire and Taxi Service, Longminster.' He called. 'Message for you, Skipper. Miss something-or-another Carrick asked them to ring. She's been called away to a sick friend. Hopes you'll understand. OK?'

'OK.'

'Ta-ta, then.'

'So long, then, Jim. Thanks.'

The Skipper returned to his wheelhouse doing 'thumbs up' to Troy on the way. The *Zodiac* moved out into mid-stream, bound for Longminster.

Dr Natouche had come on deck during this exchange. He said: 'Mrs Alleyn, may I have one word with you?'

'Yes, of course,' Troy said. 'Where? Is it private?'

'It is, rather. Perhaps if we moved aft.'

They moved aft round the tarpaulin-covered heap of extra chairs. There, lying on the deck, was an inflated, orange-coloured Li-lo mattress.

Dr Natouche, stooped, looked down at it and up at Troy. 'Miss Rickerby-Carrick slept here last night, I think,' he said.

'She did?'

'Yes. That, at least, was her intention.'

Troy waited.

'Mrs Alleyn, you will excuse me, I hope, for asking this question. You will, of course, not answer it if you do not wish. Did Miss Rickerby-Carrick speak to you after she returned to the ship last evening?'

'No. I went very early to my cabin. I'd had a go of migraine.'

'I thought you seemed to be not very well.'

'It was soon over. I think she may have – sort of scratched – at my door. I fancy she did but I was asleep and by the time I opened my door there was nobody.'

'I see. She intimated to me that she had something to tell you.'

'I know. Oh, dear!' Troy said. '*Should* I have gone to her cabin, do you think?'

'Ah, no! No. It's only that Miss Rickerby-Carrick has a very high opinion of you and I thought perhaps she intended – ' He hesitated and then said firmly. 'I think I must explain that this lady spoke to me last evening. About her insomnia. She had been given some tablets – American proprietary product – by Miss Hewson and she asked me what I thought of these tablets.'

'She offered me one.'

'Yes? I said that they were unknown to me and suggested that she should consult her own doctor if her insomnia was persistent. In view of her snoring performance on the previous night I felt it might, at least in part, be an imaginary condition. My reason for troubling you with the incident is this. I formed the opinion that Miss Rickerby-Carrick was overwrought, that she was experiencing some sort of emotional and nervous crisis. It was very noticeable – very marked. I felt some concern. You understand that she did not consult me on the score of this condition: if she had it would be improper for me to speak to you about it. I think she may have been on the point of doing so when she suddenly broke off, said something incoherent and left me.'

'Do you think she's actually – well – mentally unbalanced?'

'That is a convenient phrase without real definition. I think she is disturbed – which is another such phrase. It is because I think so that I am a little worried about this departure in the middle of the night. Unnecessarily so, I dare say.'

'You heard the telephone message, just now?'

'Yes. A friend's illness.'

'Can it,' Troy exclaimed, 'be Mavis?'

She and Dr Natouche stared speculatively at each other. She saw the wraith of a smile on his mouth.

'No. Wait a bit,' Troy went on. 'She walked up to the village with Mr Lazenby and me. My head was swinging with migraine and I scarcely listened. He might remember. Of course she talked incessantly about Mavis. I think she said Mavis is in the Highlands. I'm sure she did. Do you suppose Miss Rickerby-Carrick has shot off by taxi to the Highlands in the dead of night?'

'Perhaps only to Longminster and thence by train?'

'Who can tell! Did nobody hear anything?' Troy wondered. 'I mean, somebody must have come on board with this news and roused her up. It would be a disturbance.'

'Here? At the stern? It's far removed from our cabins.'

'Yes,' Troy said, 'but how would they *know* she was back here?'

'She told me she would take her tablet and sleep on deck.'

Troy stooped down and after a moment, picked up a blotched, red scrap of cloth.

'What's that?' she asked.

The long fingers that looked as if they had been imperfectly treated with black cork, turned it over and laid it in the pinkish palm. 'Isn't it from the cover of her diary?' Troy said.

'I believe you're right.'

He was about to drop it overboard but she said: 'No – don't.'

'No?'

'Well – only because – ' Troy gave an apologetic laugh. 'I'm a policeman's wife,' she said. 'Put it down to that.'

He took out a pocket-book and slipped the scrap of cloth into it.

'I expect we're making a song about nothing,' Troy said.

Suddenly she felt an almost overwhelming impulse to tell Dr Natouche about her misgivings and the incidents that had prompted them. She had a vivid premonition of how he would look as she confided her perplexity. His head would be courteously inclined and his expression placid and a little withdrawn – a consulting-room manner of the most reassuring kind. It really would be a great relief to confide in Dr Natouche. An opening phrase had already shaped itself in her mind when she remembered another attentive listener.

'And by-the-way, Mrs Alleyn,' Superintendent Tillottson had said in his infuriatingly bland manner, 'we won't mention this little matter to anybody, shall we? Just a routine precaution.'

So she held her tongue.

CHAPTER 5

Longminster

'I suppose one of his greatest assets,' Alleyn said, 'is his ability to instil confidence in the most unlikely people. An infuriated Bolivian policeman is supposed to have admitted that before he could stop himself he found he was telling the Jampot about his own trouble with a duodenal ulcer. This may not be a true story. If not, it was invented to illustrate the more winning facets in the Foljambe façade. The moral is: that it takes all sorts to make a thoroughly bad lot and it sometimes takes a conscientious police officer quite a long time to realize this simple fact of unsavoury life. You can't type criminals. It's just as misleading to talk about them as if they never behave out of character as it is to suppose the underworld is riddled with charmers who only cheat or kill by some kind of accident.

'Foljambe has been known to behave with perfect good-nature and also with ferocity. He is attracted by beauty at a high artistic level. His apartment in Paris is said to have been got up in the most impeccable taste. He likes money better than anything else in life and he enjoys making it by criminal practices. If he was left a million pounds it's odds on he'd continue to operate the rackets. If people got in his way he would continue to remove them.

'I've told you that my wife's letters missed me in New York and were forwarded to San Francisco. By the time they reached me her cruise in the *Zodiac* had only two nights to go. As you know I rang the Department and learnt that Mr Fox was in France, following what was hoped to be a hot line on Foljambe. I got through to Mr

84

Tillottson who in view of this development was inclined to discount the *Zodiac* altogether. I was not so inclined.

'Those of you who are married,' Alleyn said, 'will understand my position. In the Force our wives are not called upon to serve in female James-Bondage and I imagine most of you would agree that any notion of their involvement in our work would be outlandish, ludicrous and extremely unpalatable. My wife's letters, though they made very little of her misgivings, were disturbing enough for me to wish her out of the *Zodiac*. I thought of asking Tillottson to get her to ring me up but I had missed her at Crossdyke and if I waited until she reached Longminster I myself would miss my connection from San Francisco. And if, by any fantastic and most improbable chance one of her fellow-passengers in some way tied in with the Andropulos-Jampot show, the last thing we would want to do was to alert him by sending police messages to lock-keepers asking her to leave the cruise. My wife is a celebrated painter who is known, poor thing, to be married to a policeman.'

The Scot in the second row smirked.

'Well,' Alleyn said, 'in the upshot I told Tillottson I thought my present job might finish earlier than expected and I would get back as soon as I could. I would remind you that at this stage I had no knowledge of the disappearance of Miss Rickerby-Carrick. If I had heard that bit I would have taken a very much stronger line.

'As it was – '

I

There was no denying it, the cruise was much more enjoyable without Miss Rickerby-Carrick.

From Crossdyke to Longminster the sun shone upon fields, spinneys, villages and locks. It was the prettiest of journeys. Everybody seemed to expand. The Hewsons' cameras clicked busily. Mr Lazenby and Mr Pollock discovered a common interest in stamps and showed each other the contents of sad-looking envelopes. Caley Bard told Troy a great deal about butterflies but she refused, nevertheless, to look at the Death's Head he had caught last evening on Crossdyke Hill. 'Well,' he said gaily, 'don't look at it if it's going to set you against me. Why can't you be more like Hay? She said she belonged to the SPCA but lepidoptera didn't count.'

'Do you call her Hay?'

'No. Do you?'

'No, but she asked me to.'

'Stand-offish old you, as usual,' he said and for no reason at all Troy burst out laughing. Her own apprehensions and Dr Natouche's anxiety had receded in the pleasant atmosphere of the third day's cruise.

Even Dr Natouche turned out to have a hobby. He liked to make maps. If anyone as tranquil and grave as Dr Natouche could be said to exhibit coyness, he did so when questioned by Troy and Bard about his cartography. He was, he confessed, attempting a chart of their cruise: it could not be called a true chart because it was not being scientifically constructed but he hoped to make something of it when he had consulted Ordnance maps. Troy wondered if persons of Dr Natouche's complexion ever blushed and was sure, when he was persuaded to show them his little drawing, that he felt inclined to do so.

It was executed in very hard lead-pencil and was in the style of the sixteenth-century English cartographers with tiny drawings of churches and trees in their appropriate places and with extremely minute lettering.

Troy exclaimed with pleasure and said: 'That we should have two calligraphers on board! Mr Pollock, do come and look at this.'

Pollock who had been talking to the Hewsons, hesitated, and then limped over and looked at the map but not at Dr Natouche.

'Very nice,' he said and returned to the Hewsons.

Troy had made a boldish move. Pollock, since the beginning of the cruise had only just kept on the hither side of insulting Dr Natouche. He had been prevented, not by any tactics that she and Caley Bard employed but rather by the behaviour of Dr Natouche himself who skilfully avoided giving Pollock any chance to exhibit ill-will. Somehow it came about that at mealtimes Dr Natouche was as far removed as possible from Mr Pollock. On deck, Dr Natouche had conveyed himself to the area farthest aft, which Miss Rickerby-Carrick's mattress, deflated to the accompaniment of its own improper noises, by the boy Tom, had previously occupied.

So Dr Natouche had offered no opportunity for Mr Pollock to insult him and Mr Pollock had retired, as Caley Bard pointed out to Troy, upon a grumpy alliance with the Hewsons with whom he could be observed in ridiculously furtive conference, presumably about racial relations.

To these skirmishes and manoeuvres Mr Lazenby appeared to be oblivious. He swapped philatelic gossip with Mr Pollock, he discussed the tendencies of art in Australia with Troy when she was unable to escape him, and he made jovial, unimportant small-talk with Dr Natouche.

Perhaps the most effective deterrent to any overt display of racialism from Mr Pollock was an alliance he had formed with the Tretheways.

To Troy, it appeared that Mr Pollock, in common, she thought, with every other male in the *Zodiac*, was extremely conscious of Mrs Tretheway's allure. That was not surprising. What did surprise was Mrs Tretheway's fairly evident response to Mr Pollock's offering of homage. Evidently, she found him attractive but not apparently to an extent that might cause the Skipper any concern since Troy heard them all planning to meet at a pub in Longminster. They were going to have a bit of an evening, they agreed.

Troy herself was in something of a predicament. She could not, without making a ridiculous issue of it, refuse either to lunch or dine with Caley Bard in Longminster and indeed she had no particular desire to refuse since she enjoyed his company and took his cock-eyed and purely verbal advances with the liberal pinch of salt that she felt sure he expected. So she agreed to dine with him but said she had appointments during the earlier part of the day.

Somehow or another, she must yet again visit a police station and commune with Superintendent Bonney whose personality, according to Superintendent Tillottson, she would find so very congenial. She could not help but feel that the legend of the lost fur had begun to wear thin but she supposed, unless some likelier device occurred to her, that she must continue to employ it. She told Caley Bard she'd have to make a final inquiry as they'd promised to let the Longminster police know if the wretched fur turned up and she also hinted at visits to the curator of the local gallery and a picture-dealer of some importance.

'All right,' he said, 'I'll accept your feeble excuses for the day and look forward to dinner. After all you *are* famous and allowances must be made.'

'They are *not* feeble excuses,' Troy shouted. Afterwards she determined at least to call on the curator and thus partially salve her conscience. She had arrived at this stage of muddled thinking when Dr Natouche approached her with an extremely formal invitation.

'You have almost certainly made your own arrangements for today,' he said. 'In case you have not I must explain that I have invited a friend and his wife to luncheon at the Longminster Arms. He is Sir Leslie Fergus, a bio-chemist of some distinction, now dedicated to research. We were fellow-students. I would, of course, be delighted if by any fortunate chance you were able to come.'

Troy saw that, unlike Caley Bard who had cheerfully cornered and heckled her, Dr Natouche was scrupulous to leave her the easiest possible means of escape. She said at once that she would be delighted to lunch at the Longminster Arms.

'I am so pleased,' said Dr Natouche with his little bow and withdrew.

'Well!' ejaculated Caley who had unblushingly listened to this exchange. 'You *are* a sly-boots!'

'I don't know why you should say that.'

'You wouldn't lunch with me.'

'I'm dining with you,' Troy said crossly.

'Sorry,' he said. 'I'm being a bore and unfunny. I won't do it again. Thank you for dining. I hope it'll be fun and I hope your luncheon is fabulous.'

She now began to have misgivings about Caley Bard's dead set at her.

'At my age,' Troy thought, 'this sort of thing can well become ridiculous. Am I in for a tricky party, I wonder.'

The day, however, turned out to be a success.

They reached Longminster at 10.30. Mr Lazenby and Mr Pollock were going straight to the Minster itself and from there planned to follow the itinerary set out in the *Zodiac's* leaflet. The Hewsons, who had intended to join them were thrown into a state of ferment when the Skipper happened to remark that it would be half-day closing in Tollardwark on the return journey. They would arrive there at noon.

Miss Hewson broke out in lamentation. The junk shops where she was persuaded she would find the most exciting and delectable bargains! Shut! Now wasn't that just crazy planning on somebody's part? To spend the afternoon in a closed town? In vain did the Tretheways explain that the object of the stay was a visit by special bus to a historic Abbey six miles out of Tollardwark. The Hewsons said in unison that they'd seen enough abbeys to last them the rest of their lives. What they desired was a lovely long shop-crawl. Why Miss Hewson had seen four of the cutest little old shops – one in particular – she appealed to Troy to witness how excited she had been.

They went on and on until at last Caley Bard, in exasperation, suggested that as it was only a few miles by road back to Tollardwark they might like to spend the day there. Mrs Tretheway said there were buses and the road was a very attractive one, actually passing the Abbey. The Skipper said there were good car-hire services, as witness the one that had rung through with Miss Rickerby-Carrick's message.

The Hewsons went into a huffy conference from which they emerged with their chagrin somewhat abated. They settled on a car. They would spend half the day in Tollardwark and half in Longminster. One could see, Troy thought, the timeless charm of the waterways evaporating in the Hewsons' esteem. They departed, mollified and asking each other if it didn't seem kind of dopey to spend two days getting from one historic burg to another when you could take them both in between breakfast and dinner with time left over for shopping.

Caley Bard announced that he was going to have his hair cut and then go to the museum where the lepidoptera were said to be above

average. Dr Natouche told Troy that he would expect her at one
o'clock and the two men walked off together.

Troy changed into a linen suit, consulted Mr Tillottson's map and
found her way to the Longminster central police station and
Superintendent Bonney.

Afterwards she was unable to make up her mind whether or not
she had been surprised to find Mr Tillottson there.

He explained that he happened to be in Longminster on a routine
call. He did not suggest that he had timed his visit to coincide with
Troy's. He merely shook hands again with his customary geniality
and introduced her to Superintendent Bonney.

Mr Bonney was another large man but in his case seniority would
have seemed to have run to bone rather than flesh. His bones were
enormous. They were excessive behind his ears, under and above his
eyes and at his wrists. His jaws were cadaverous and when he
smiled, even his gums were knobbly. Troy would not have fallen in
with Mr Tillottson's description of his colleague as a lovely chap.

They were both very pleasant. Troy's first question was as to her
husband's return. Was there any chance, did they think, that it
might be earlier because if so –

They said, almost in unison, that Alleyn had rung through last
evening: that he would have liked to talk to her this morning but
would have missed his connection to New York. And that he hoped
he might be home early next week but that depended upon a final
conference. He sent his love, they said, beaming at her, and if she was
still uneasy she was to abandon ship. 'Perhaps a telegram from a sick
friend – ' Mr Tillottson here suggested and Troy felt a strong inclination to laugh in his face and ask him if it should be signed 'Mavis'.

She told them about Miss Rickerby-Carrick.

They listened with great attention saying: 'Yerse. Yerse.' and 'Is that
a fact?' and 'Fancy that, now.' When she had finished Mr Bonney
glanced at his desk pad where he had jotted down a note or two.

'The Longminster Car Hire and Taxi Service, eh?' he said. 'Now,
which would that be, I wonder, Bert? There's Ackroyd's and there's
Rutherford's.'

'We might make a wee check, Bob,' Mr Tillottson ventured.

'Yerse,' Mr Bonney agreed. 'We might at that.'

He made his calls while Troy, at their request, waited.

'Ackroyd's Car Hire Service? Just a little item about a telephone call. Eighty-thirty or thereabouts to Crossdyke Lockhouse. Message from a fare phoned by you to the Lock for Tretheway, Skipper, M.V. *Zodiac*. Could you check for us? Much obliged.' A pause while Mr Bonney stared without interest at Mr Tillottson and Mr Tillottson stared without interest at nothing in particular.

'I see. No note of it? Much obliged. Just before you go: Fare from Crossdyke Lock, picked up sometime during the night. Lady. Yerse. Well, *any* trips to Crossdyke? Could you check?' Another pause. 'Much obliged. Ta,' said Mr Bonney and replaced the receiver.

He repeated this conversation almost word for word on three more calls.

In each instance, it seemed, a blank.

'No trips to Crossdyke,' said Mr Bonney, 'between 6.45 last evening and 11 a.m. today.'

'Well, well,' said Mr Tillottson, 'that's quite interesting, Bob, isn't it?'

All Troy's apprehensions that with the lightened atmosphere of the morning had retired to an uneasy hinterland now returned in force.

'But that means whoever rang gave a false identity,' she said.

Mr Tillottson said it looked a wee bit like that but they'd have to check with the lock-keeper at Crossdyke. He might have mistaken the message. It might have been, he suggested, Miss Rickerby-Carrick herself saying she was hiring a car.

'That's true!' Troy agreed.

'What sort of a voice, now, would she have, Mrs Alleyn?'

'She's got a heavy cold and she sounds excitable. She gabbles and she talks in italics.'

'She wouldn't be what you'd call at all eccentric?'

'She would. Very eccentric.'

Mr Tillottson said ah, well, now, there you were, weren't you? Mr Bonney asked what age Miss Rickerby-Carrick might be and when Troy hazarded, 'fortyish', began to look complacent. Troy mentioned Mavis of Birmingham now in the Highlands and when they asked Mavis who, and where in the Highlands was obliged to say she'd forgotten. This made her feel foolish and remember some of her husband's strictures upon purveyors of information received.

'I'm sorry,' she said, 'to be so perfectly hopeless.'

They soothed her. Why should she remember these trifles? They would, said Mr Tillottson, have a wee chin-wag with the lock-keeper at Crossdyke just to get confirmation of the telephone call. They would ring the telephone department and they would make further inquiries to find out just how Miss Rickerby-Carrick got herself removed in the dead of night. If possible they would discover her destination.

Their manner strongly suggested that Troy's uneasiness rather than official concern was the motive for these inquiries.

'They think I've got a bee in my bonnet,' she told herself. 'If I wasn't Rory's wife they wouldn't be bothered with me.'

She took what she felt had now become her routine leave of Superintendents in North Country police stations and, once more reassured by Mr Tillottson, prepared to enjoy herself in Longminster.

II

She spent the rest of the morning looking at the gallery and the Minster and wandering about the city which was as beautiful as its reputation.

At noon she began to ask her way to the Longminster Arms. After a diversion into an artist-colourman's shop where she found a very nice old frame of the right size for her Signs of the Zodiac, she arrived at half past twelve. Troy was one of those people who can never manage to be unpunctual and was often obliged to go for quite extensive walks round blocks in order to be decently late or at least not indecently early.

However, she didn't mind being early for her luncheon with Dr Natouche and his friends. She tidied up and found her way into a pleasant drawing-room where there were lots of magazines.

In one of them she at once became absorbed. It printed a long extract from a book written some years ago by a white American who had had his skin pigmentation changed by what, it appeared, was a dangerous but entirely effective process. For some months this man had lived as one of themselves among the Negroes of the Deep South. The author did not divulge the nature of this transformation process and Troy found herself wondering if Dr Natouche would be able to tell what it was. Could she ask him? Remembering their conversation in the wapentake, she thought she could.

She was still pondering over this and had turned again to the article when she became aware of a presence and found that Dr Natouche stood beside her, quite close, with his gaze on the printed page.

Her diaphragm contracted with a jolt and the magazine crackled in her hands.

'I am so very sorry,' he said. 'I startled you. It was stupid of me. The carpet is thick and you were absorbed.'

He sat down opposite to her and with a look of great concern said: 'I have been unforgivably clumsy.'

'Not a bit of it,' Troy rejoined. 'I don't know why I should be so jumpy. But as you say, I *was* absorbed. Have you read this thing, Dr Natouche?'

He had lifted his finger to a waiter who approached with a perfectly blank face.

'We shall not wait for the Ferguses,' Dr Natouche said. 'You must be given a restorative. Brandy? And soda? Dry Ginger? Yes? Two, if you please and may I see the wine list?'

His manner was grand enough to wipe the blank look off any waiter's face.

When the man had gone Dr Natouche said: 'But I have not answered your question. Yes, I have read this book. It was a courageous action.'

'I wondered if you would know exactly what was done to him. The process, I mean.'

'*Your* colour is returning,' he said after a moment. 'And so, of course, did his. It was not a permanent change. No, I do not know what was done. Sir Leslie might have an idea, it is more in his line than mine. We must ask him.'

'I would have thought – '

'Yes?' he said, when she stopped short.

'You said, when we were at the wapentake, that you didn't think I could say anything to – I don't remember the exact phrase – '

'To hurt or offend me? Something like that was it? It is true.'

'I was going to ask, then, if the change of pigmentation would be enough to convince people, supposing the features were still markedly

European. And then I saw that your features, Dr Natouche, are not at all – '

'Negroid?'

'Yes. But perhaps Ethiopians – one is so ignorant.'

'You must remember I am a half-caste. My facial structures are those of my mother, I believe.'

'Yes, of course,' Troy said. 'Of course.'

The waiter brought their drinks and the wine list and menu and hard on his heels came Sir Leslie and Lady Fergus.

They were charming and the luncheon party was a success but somehow neither Troy nor her host got round to asking Sir Leslie if he could shed any light on the darkening by scientific methods of the pigmentation of the skin.

III

Troy returned to the *Zodiac*, rested, changed and was taken in a taxi by Caley Bard to dinner with champagne at another hotel.

'I'm not 'alf going it,' she thought and wondered what her husband would have to say about these jaunts.

When they had dined she and Bard walked about Longminster and finally strolled back to The River at half past ten.

The *Zodiac* was berthed romantically in a bend of The River from which one could see the Long Minster itself against the stars. The lights of the old city quavered and zig-zagged with those of other craft in the black night waters. Troy and Bard could hear quiet voices in the saloon but they loitered on the deserted deck and before she could do anything about it Bard had kissed Troy.

'You're adorable,' he said.

'Ah, get along with you. Goodnight, and thank you for a nice party.'

'Don't go away.'

'I think I must.'

'Couldn't we have a lovely, fairly delicate little affair? Please?'

'We could not,' said Troy.

'I've fallen for you in a bloody big way. Don't laugh at me.'

'I'm not. But I'm not going to pursue the matter. Don't you, either.'

'Well, I can't say you've led me on. You don't know a garden path when you see one.'

'I wouldn't say as much for you.'

'I like that! What cheek!'

'Look,' Troy said, 'who's here.'

It was the Hewsons. They had arrived on the wharf in a taxi and were hung about with strange parcels. Miss Hewson seemed to be in a state of exalted fatigue and her brother in a state of exhausted resignation.

'Boy, oh boy!' he said.

They had to be helped on board with their unwieldy freight and when this exercise had been accomplished, it seemed only decent to get them down the companion-way into the saloon. Here the other passengers were assembled and about to go to bed. They formed themselves into a sort of chain gang and by this means assembled the Hewsons' purchases on three of the tables. Newspaper was spread on the deck.

'We just ran crazy,' Miss Hewson panted. 'We just don't know what's with us when we get loose on an antique spree, do we, Earl?'

'You said it, dear,' her brother conceded.

'Where,' asked Mr Pollock, 'will you put it?' Feeling, perhaps, that his choice of words was unfortunate, he threw a frightened glance at Mr Lazenby.

'Well! Now!' Miss Hewson said. 'We don't figure we have a problem there, do we, dear? We figure if we talk pretty to the Skipper and Mrs Tretheway we might be allowed to cache it in Miss Rickerby-Carrick's stateroom. We just kind of took a calculated risk on that one didn't we, dear?'

'Sure did, honey.'

'The Tretheways,' Pollock said, 'have gone to bed.'

'Looks like we'll have to step up the calculated risk, some,' Mr Hewson said dryly.

Mr Lazenby was peering with undisguised curiosity at their booty and so were Troy and Bard. There was an inlaid rosewood box, a newspaper parcel from which horse-brasses partly emerged, a pair of carriage-lamps and, packed piecemeal into an open beer-carton, a wag-at-the-wall Victorian clock.

Propped against the table was a really filthy roll of what appeared through encrustations of mud to be a collection of prints tied together with an ancient piece of twine.

It was over this trove that Miss Hewson seemed principally to gloat. She had found it, she explained, together with their other purchases, in the yard of the junk shop where Troy had seen them that first night in Tollardwark. Something had told Miss Hewson she would draw a rich reward if she could explore that yard and sure enough, jammed into a compartment in an Edwardian sideboard, all doubled up, as they could see if they looked, there it was.

'I'm a hound when I get started,' Miss Hewson said proudly. 'I open up everything that has a door or a lid. And you know something? This guy who owns this dump allowed he never knew he had this roll. He figured it must have been in this terrible little cupboard at the time of the original purchase. And you know something? He said he didn't care if he didn't see the contents and when Earl and I opened it up he gave it a kind of weary glance and said was it worth "ten bob"? Was it worth one dollar twenty! Boy, I guess when the Ladies Handicraft Guild, back in Apollo, see the screen I get out of this lot, they'll go crazy. Now, Mrs Alleyn,' Miss Hewson continued, 'you're artistic. Well, I mean – well, you know what I mean. Now, I said to Brother, I can't wait till I show Mrs Alleyn and get me an expert opinion. I said: we go right back and show Mrs Alleyn – '

As she delivered this speech in a high gabble, Miss Hewson doubled herself up and wrestled with the twine that bound her bundle. Dust flew about and flakes of dry mud dropped on the deck. After a moment her brother produced a pocket knife and cut the twine.

The roll opened up abruptly in a cloud of dust and fell apart on the newspaper.

Scraps. Oleographs. Coloured supplements from *Pears' Annual*. Half a dozen sepia photographs, several of them torn. Four flower pieces. A collection of Edwardian prints from dressmaker's journals. Part of a child's scrapbook. Three lamentable water-colours.

Miss Hewson spread them out on the deck with cries of triumph to which she received but tepid response. Her brother sank into a chair and closed his eyes.

'Is that a painting?' Troy asked.

It had enclosed the roll and its outer surface was so encrusted with occulted dirt that the grain of the canvas was only just perceptible.

It was lying curled up on what was presumably its face. Troy stooped and turned it over.

It was a painting in oil: about 18 by 12 inches.

She knelt down and tapped its edge on the deck, releasing a further accretion of dust. She spread it out.

'Anything?' asked Bard, leaning down.

'I don't know.'

'Shall I get a damp cloth or something?'

'Yes, do. If the Hewsons don't mind.'

Miss Hewson was in ecstasies over a Victorian scrap depicting an innocent child surrounded by rosebuds. She said: 'Sure, sure. Go right ahead.' Mr Hewson was asleep.

Troy wiped the little painting over with an exquisite handkerchief her husband had bought her in Bruges. Trees. A bridge. A scrap of golden sky.

'Exhibit I. My very, very own face-flannel,' said Bard, squatting beside her. 'Devotion could go no further. I have added (Exhibit 2) a smear of my very, very own soap. It's called Spruce.'

The whole landscape slowly emerged: defaced here and there by dirt and scars in the surface, but not, after all, in bad condition.

In the foreground: water – and a lane that turned back into the middle-distance. A pond and a ford. A child in a vermilion dress with a hay-rake. In the middle-distance, trees that reflected in countless leafy mirrors, the late afternoon sun. In the background: a rising field, a spire, a generous and glowing sky.

'It's sunk,' Troy muttered. 'We could oil it out.'

'What does that mean?'

'Wait a bit. Dry the surface, can you?'

She went to her cabin and came back with linseed oil on a bit of paint-rag. 'This won't do any harm,' she said. 'Have you got the surface dry? Good. Now then.'

And in a minute the little picture was clearer and cleaner and speaking bravely for itself.

' "Constables",' Caley Bard quoted lightly, ' "all over the place". Or did you say "swarming".'

Troy looked steadily at him for a moment and then returned to her oiling. Presently she gave a little exclamation and at the same moment Dr Natouche's great voice boomed out: 'It is a picture of Ramsdyke. That is the lock and the lane and, see, there is the ford and the church spire above the hill.'

The others, who had been clustered round Miss Hewson's treasures on the table, all came to look at the painting.

Troy said: 'Shall we put it in a better light?'

They made way for her. She stood on the window seat and held the painting close to a wall lamp. She examined the back of the canvas and then the face again.

'It's a good picture,' Mr Lazenby pronounced. 'Old-fashioned of course. Early Victorian. But it certainly looks a nice bit of work, don't you think, Mrs Alleyn?'

'Yes,' Troy said. 'Yes. It does. Very nice.'

She got down from the seat.

'Miss Hewson,' she said, 'I was in the gallery here this morning. They've got a Constable. One of his big, celebrated worked-up pieces. I think you should let an expert see this thing because – well because as Mr Lazenby says it's a very good work of its period and because it might have been painted by the same hand and because – well, if you look closely you will see – it is signed in precisely the same manner.'

IV

'For pity's sake,' Troy said, 'don't take my word for anything. I'm not an expert. I can't tell, for instance, how old the actual canvas may be though I do know it's not contemporary and I do know it's the way he signed his major works. "John Constable. R.A.f." and the date, 1830, which, I *think*, was soon after he became an R.A. The thing may be a copy of an original Constable. I don't think there's an established work of his that has Ramsdyke Lock as its subject. That doesn't say he didn't paint Ramsdyke Lock when he was in these parts.'

'And it doesn't say,' Mr Lazenby added, 'that this isn't the Ramsdyke Lock he painted.'

Miss Hewson, who seemed never to have heard of Constable until Troy made her remark at Ramsdyke, now became madly excited. She pointed out the excellencies of the picture and how you could just fancy yourself walking up that little old-world lane into the sunset.

Mr Hewson woke up and after listening, in his dead-pan, honest-to-God, dehydrated manner to his sister's ravings asked Troy what, supposing this item was in fact the genuine product of this guy, it might be worth in real money.

Troy said she didn't know – a great deal. Thousands of pounds. It depended upon the present demand for Constables.

'But don't for Heaven's sake go by anything I say. As for forgeries, I am reminded – ' She stopped. 'I suppose it doesn't really apply,' she said. 'You'd hardly expect to find an elaborate forgery in a junk-shop yard at Tollardwark, would you?'

'But you were going to tell us a story,' Bard said. 'Mayn't we have it?'

'It was only that Rory, my husband, had a case quite recently in which a young man, just for the hell of it, forged an Elizabethan glove and did it so well that the top experts were diddled.'

'As you say, Mrs Alleyn,' said Mr Lazenby, 'it doesn't really apply. But about forgeries. I always ask myself – '

They were off on an argument that can be depended upon to ruffle more tempers in quicker time than most others. If a forgery was 'that good' it could take in the top experts, why wasn't it just as good in every respect as the work of the painter to whom it was falsely attributed?

To and fro went the declarations and aphorisms. Caley Bard was civilized under the heading of 'the total œuvre', Mr Hewson said, wryly and obscurely, that every man had his price, Mr Lazenby upheld a professional view: the forgery was worthless because it was based upon a lie and clerical overtones informed his antipodean delivery. Mr Pollock's manner was, as usual, a little off-beat. Several times, he interjected: 'Oy, chum, half a tick – ' only to subside in apparent embarrassment when given the floor. Miss Hewson merely stated, as if informed by an oracle, that she just *knoo* she'd got a genuine old master.

Dr Natouche excused himself and went below.

And Troy looked at the little picture and was visited once again by the notion that she was involved in some kind of masquerade, that the play, if there was a play, moved towards its climax, if there was a climax, that the tension, if indeed there was any tension, among her fellow-passengers, had been exacerbated by the twist of some carefully concealed screw.

She looked up. Mr Lazenby's dark glasses were turned on her, Mr Pollock's somewhat prominent eyes looked into hers and quickly away, Miss Hewson smiled ever so widely at her and Mr Hewson's dead-pan grin seemed to be plastered over his mouth like a gag.

Troy said goodnight to them all and went to bed.

The *Zodiac* left for the return journey before any of the passengers were up.

They had a long morning's cruise, passing through Crossdyke and arriving at Tollardwark at noon.

That evening the Hewsons, Mr Pollock and Mr Lazenby played Scrabble. Dr Natouche wrote letters and Caley Bard suggested a walk but Troy said that she too had letters to write. He pulled a face at her and settled with a book.

Troy supposed that Superintendent Tillottson was in Tollardwark and wondered if he expected her to call. She saw no reason to do so and was sick of confiding nebulous and unconvincing sensations. Nothing of interest to Mr Tillottson, she thought, had occurred over the past thirty-six hours. He could hardly become alerted by the discovery of a possible 'Constable': indeed he could be confidently expected if told about it to regard her with weary tolerance. Still less could she hope to interest him in her own fanciful reactions to an unprovable impression of some kind of conspiracy.

He had promised to let her know by a message to Tollard Lock if there was further news of Alleyn's return. No, there was really no need at all to call on Superintendent Tillottson.

She wrote a couple of short letters to save her face with Caley and at about half past nine went ashore to post them at the box outside the lockhouse.

The night was warm and still and the air full of pleasant scents from the lock-keeper's garden: stocks, tobacco flowers, newly watered earth and at the back of these the cold dank smell of The River. These scents, she thought, made up one of the three elements of night; the next was composed of things that were to be seen before the moon rose: ambiguous pools of darkness, lighted windows, stars, the shapes of trees and the dim whiteness of a bench hard by their moorings. Troy sat there for a time to listen to the third element of night: an owl somewhere in a spinney downstream, the low, intermittent colloquy of moving water, indefinable stirrings, the small flutters and bumps made by flying insects and the homely sound of people talking quietly in the lockhouse and in the saloon of the *Zodiac*.

A door opened and the three Tretheways who had been spending the evening with the lock-keeper's family, exchanged goodnights and crunched down the gravel path towards Troy.

'Lovely evening, Mrs Alleyn,' Mrs Tretheway said. The Skipper asked if she was enjoying the cool air and as an afterthought added: 'Telegram from Miss Rickerby-Carrick, by the way, Mrs Alleyn. From Carlisle.'

'Oh!' Troy cried, 'I *am* glad. Is she all right?'

'Seems so. Er – what *does* she say exactly, dear? Just a minute.'

A rustle of paper. Torchlight darted about the Tretheways' faces and settled on a yellow telegram in a brown hand. ' "Sorry abrupt departure collected by mutual friends car urgent great friend seriously ill Inverness awfully sad missing cruise cheerio everybody Hay Rickerby-Carrick".'

'There! *She's* quite all right, you see,' Mrs Tretheway said comfortably. 'It's the friend. Just like they said on the phone at Crossdyke.'

'So it wasn't a taxi firm that rang through to Crossdyke,' Troy pointed out. 'It must have been her friends in the car.'

'Unless they were in a taxi and asked the office to ring. Anyway,' Mrs Tretheway repeated, 'it's quite all right.'

'Yes. It must be.' Troy said.

But when she was in bed that night she couldn't help thinking there was still something that didn't quite satisfy her about the departure of Miss Rickerby-Carrick.

'Tomorrow,' she thought, 'I'll ask Dr Natouche what he thinks.'

Before she went to sleep she found herself listening for the sound she had heard – where? At Tollardwark? At Crossdyke? She wasn't sure – the distant sound of a motorbicycle. And although there was no such sound to be heard that night she actually dreamt she had heard it.

V

Troy thought: 'Tomorrow we step back into time.' The return journey had taken on something of the character of a recurrent dream: spires, fens, individual trees, locks; even a clod of tufted earth that had fallen away from a bank and was half drowned or a broken branch that dipped into the stream and moved with its flow: these were familiar landmarks that they might have passed, not once, but many times before.

At four in the afternoon the *Zodiac* entered the straight reach of The River below Ramsdyke Lock. Already, drifts of detergent foam had begun to float past her. Wisps of it melted on her deck. Ahead of her the passengers could see an unbroken whiteness that veiled The River like an imponderable counterpane. They could hear the voice of Ramsdyke weir and see a foaming pother where the corrupted fall met the lower reach.

Troy leant on the starboard taffrail and watched their entry into this frothy region. She remembered how she and Dr Natouche and Caley Bard and Hazel Rickerby-Carrick had discussed reality and beauty. Fragments of conversation drifted across her recollection. She could almost re-hear the voices.

'– in the Eye of the Beholder – '
'– a fish tin with a red label. Was it the less beautiful – '
'– if a dead something popped up through that foam – '
'– a dead something – '
'– a dead something – '
'– a fish – a cat – '
'– through that foam – '
'– a dead something – '

Hazel Rickerby-Carrick's face, idiotically bloated, looked up: not at Troy, not at anything. Her mouth, drawn into an outlandish rictus, grinned through discoloured froth. She bobbed and bumped against the starboard side. And what terrible disaster had corrupted her river-weed hair and distended her blown cheeks?

The taffrail shot upwards and the trees with it. The voice of the weir exploded with a crack in Troy's head and nothing whatever followed it. Nothing.

CHAPTER 6

Ramsdyke

'From this point,' Alleyn said, 'the several elements, if I can put it like that, converge.

'The discovery of this woman's body suddenly threw a complex of apparently unrelated incidents into an integrated whole. You grind away at routine, you collect a vast amount of data ninety-percent of which is useless and then – something happens and Bingo – the other ten-percent sits up like Jacky and Bob's your uncle.'

He paused, having astonished himself by this intemperate excursion into jokeyness. He met broad grins from his audience and a startled glance from the man in the second row.

' "O God, your only jig-maker",' thought Alleyn and resumed in a more orthodox style.

'It struck me that there might be some interest – possibly some value – in putting this case before you as it appeared to my wife and as she put it to the county police and in her letters to me. And I wonder if at this juncture you feel you could sort out the evidential wheat from the chaff.

'What, in fact, do you think we ought to have concentrated upon when Inspector Fox and I finally arrived on the scene?'

Alleyn fancied he could detect a certain resentment in the rest of the class when the man in the second row put up his hand.

I

Troy could hear an enormous unlocalized voice in an echo chamber. It approached and enveloped her. It was unalarming.

She emerged with a sickening upward lurch from somewhere that had been like death and for an unappreciable interval was flooded by a delicious surge of recovery. She felt grateful and opened her eyes.

A black face and white teeth were close before her. A recognizable arm supported her.

'You fainted. You are all right. Don't worry.'

'I never faint.'

'No?'

Fingers on her wrist.

'Why did it happen, I wonder,' said Dr Natouche. 'When you feel more like yourself we will make you comfortable. Will you try a little water?'

Her head was supported. A rim of cold glass pressed her underlip.

'Here are Miss Hewson and Mrs Tretheway, to help you.'

Their faces swam towards her and steadied.

Everything had steadied. The passengers stared at her with the greatest concern. Six faces behind Dr Natouche and Mrs Tretheway: Miss Hewson with the look of a startled bun, her brother with his hearing-aid and slanted head, Mr Lazenby's black glasses, Mr Pollock's ophthalmic stare, like close-ups in a suspense film. And beyond them the Skipper at the wheel.

'Feeling better, honey?' asked Miss Hewson, and then: 'Don't look that way, dear. What is it? What's happened?'

'She's frightened,' said Mrs Tretheway.

'Oh God, God, God!' Troy said and her voice sounded in her own ears like that of a stranger. 'Oh God, I've remembered.'

She turned and clung to Dr Natouche, 'They must stop,' she stammered. 'Stop. Make them stop. It's Hazel Rickerby-Carrick. There. Back there. In The River.'

They broke into commotion. Caley Bard shouted: 'You heard what she said. Skipper!'

The *Zodiac* stopped.

Caley Bard knelt beside her. 'All right, my dear!' he said. 'We've stopped. Don't be frightened. Don't worry. We'll attend to it.' And to Dr Natouche: 'Can't we take her down?'

'I think so. Mrs Alleyn, if we help you, do you think you can manage the stairs? It will be best. We will take it very steadily.'

'I'm all right,' Troy said. 'Please don't worry. I'm perfectly all right. It's not me. Didn't you hear what I said? Back there – in The River.'

'Yes, yes. The Captain is attending to it!'

'*Attending* to it!' An ungainly laugh bubbled in Troy's throat. 'To *that*! I should hope so! Look, don't fuss about me. I'm all right.'

But when they helped her to her feet she was very shaky. Dr Natouche went backwards before her down the companion-way and Caley Bard came behind. The two women followed making horrified comments.

In the passage her knees gave way. Dr Natouche carried her into her cabin and put her on her bunk as deftly as if she was a child. The others crowded in the doorway.

'I'm all right,' she kept repeating. 'It's ridiculous, all this. No – please.'

He covered her with the cherry-red blanket and said to Mrs Tretheway: 'A hot-water bottle and tea would not be amiss.'

The ladies bustled away in confusion. He stooped his great body over Troy: 'You're shocked, Mrs Alleyn. I hope you will let me advise you.'

Troy began to tell them what she had seen. She took a firm hold of herself and spoke lucidly and slowly as if they were stupid men.

'You must tell the police,' Troy said. 'At once. At once.'

Caley Bard said: 'Yes, of course. I'm sure the Skipper will know what to do.'

'Tell him. It mustn't be – lost – it mustn't be – ' she clenched her hands under the blanket. 'Superintendent Tillottson at Tollardwark. Tell the Skipper.'

'I'll tell him,' Dr Natouche offered and Caley Bard said: 'There now! Don't fuss. And do, like a good girl, stop bossing.'

Troy caught the familiar bantering tone and was comforted by it. She and Bard exchanged pallid grins.

'I'll be off,' he said.

Dr Natouche said: 'And I. I may be wanted. I think you should stay where you are, Mrs Alleyn.'

He had moved away when Troy, to her own astonishment, heard herself say. 'Dr Natouche!' and when he turned with his calmly polite air, 'I – I should like to consult you, please, when you are free. Professionally.'

'Of course,' he said. 'In the meantime these ladies will take care of you.'

They did. They ministered with hot-water bottles and with scalding tea. Troy only now realized that she was shivering like a puppy.

Miss Hewson was full of consolatory phrases and horrified speculation.

'Gee,' she gabbled, 'isn't this just awful? That poor girl and all of us asleep in our beds. What do you figure, Mrs Tretheway? She was kind of sudden in her reflexes wasn't she? Now, could it add up this way? She was upset by this news about her girlfriend and she got up and dressed and packed her grip and wrote her little note on the newspaper and lit off for for wherever she fixed to meet up with her friends and in the dark she – '

Miss Hewson stopped as if jerked to a halt by her listeners' incredulity.

'Well – gee – well, maybe not,' she said. 'OK, OK. Maybe not.'

Mrs. Tretheway said: 'I don't fancy we do any good by wondering. Not till they know more. Whatever way it turns out, and it looks to me to be a proper mess, it'll bring nothing but worry to us in the Zodiac: I know that much.'

She took the empty cup from Troy. 'You'd best be left quiet,' she said. 'We'll look in and see how you prosper.'

When they had gone Troy lay still and listened. The shivering had stopped. She felt at once drowsy, and horrified that she should be so.

By looking up slantways through her open porthole she could see a tree top. It remained where it was for the most part, only sliding out of its place and returning as the Zodiac moved with The River. She heard footfalls overhead and subdued voices and after an undefined interval, a police siren. It came nearer and stopped. More and heavier steps on deck. More and newer voices, very subdued. This continued for some time. She half-dozed, half-woke.

She was roused by something outside that jarred against the port wall of the *Zodiac* and by the clunk of oars in their rowlocks and the dip and drip of the blades.

'Easy as you go, then,' said a voice very close at hand. 'Shove off a bit.' The top of a helmet moved across the porthole. 'That's right. Just a wee bit over. Hold her at that, now. Careful now.'

Superintendent Tillottson. On the job.

Troy knew with terrible accuracy what was being done on the other side of the cabin wall. She was transfixed in her own vision and hag-ridden by a sick idea that there was some obligation upon her to stand on her bunk and look down into nightmare. She knew this idea was a fantasy but she was deadly afraid that she would obey its compulsion.

'All right. Give way and easy. Easy as you go.'

'I can't.'

'What? *What?*'

'It's foul of something.'

'Here. Hold on.'

'Look there, Super. Look.'

'All right, all right. Hold steady again and I'll see.'

'What is it, then?'

'A line. Cord. Round the waist and made fast to something.'

'Will we cut it?'

'Wait while I try a wee haul. *Hold steady*, I said. Now then.'

An interval with heavy breathing.

'Coming up. Here she comes.'

'*Suitcase?*'

'That's right. Now. Bear a hand to ship it. It's bloody heavy. God, don't do that, man. We don't want any more disfigurement.'

A splash and then a thud.

'Fair enough. Now, you can give way. Signal the ambulance, Sarge. Handsomely, now.'

The rhythmic clunk, dip and drip: receding.

Troy thought with horror: 'They're towing her. It's *Our Mutual Friend* again. Through the detergent foam. They'll lift her out, dripping foam, and put her on a stretcher and into an ambulance and drive her away. There'll be an autopsy and an inquest and I'll have to say what I saw and, please God, Rory will be back.'

The *Zodiac* trembled. Trees and blue sky with a wisp of cloud, moved across the porthole. For a minute or so they were under way and then she felt the slight familiar shock when the craft came up to her mooring.

Miss Hewson opened the door and looked in. She held a little bottle rather coyly between thumb and forefinger and put her head on one side like her brother.

'Wide awake?' she said. 'I guess so. Now, look what I've brought!'

She tiptoed the one short pace between the door and the bunk and stooped. Her face really was like a bun, Troy thought, with currants for eyes and holes for nostrils and a bit of candy-peel for a mouth. She shrank back a little from Miss Hewson's face.

'I just knew how you'd be. All keyed-up like nobody's business. And I brought you my Trankwitones. You needn't feel any hesitation about using them, dear. They're recommended by pretty well every darn' doctor in the States and they just act – '

The voice droned on. Miss Hewson was pouring water into Troy's glass.

'Miss Hewson, you're terribly kind but I don't need anything like that. Really. I'm perfectly all right now and very much ashamed of myself.'

'Now, listen dear – '

'No, truly. Thank you *very* much but I'd rather not.'

'You know something? Mama's going to get real tough with baby – '

'But, Miss Hewson, I promise you I don't want – '

'May I come in?' said Dr Natouche.

Miss Hewson turned sharply and for a moment they faced each other.

'I think,' he said, and it was the first time Troy had heard him speak to her, 'that Mrs Alleyn is in no need of sedation, Miss Hewson.'

'Well, I'm surely not aiming – I just thought if she could get a little sleep – I – '

'That was very kind but there is no necessity for sedation.'

'Well – I certainly wouldn't want to – '

'I'm sure you wouldn't. If I may just have a word with my patient.'

'Your patient! Pardon me. I was not aware – well, pardon me, *Doctor*,' said Miss Hewson with a spurt of venom in her voice and slammed the door on her exit.

Troy said hurriedly: 'I want to talk to you. It's about what we discussed before. About Miss Rickerby-Carrick. Dr Natouche, have you seen – '

'Yes,' he said. 'They asked me to make an examination – a very superficial examination, of course.'

'I could hear them: outside there. I could hear what they found. She's been murdered, hasn't she? Hasn't she?'

He leant over the bunk and shut the porthole. He drew up the little stool and sat on it, leaning towards her. 'I think,' he said as softly as his huge voice permitted, 'we should be careful.' His fingers closed professionally on Troy's wrist.

'You could lock the door,' she said.

'So I could.' He did so and turned back to her.

'Until the autopsy,' he murmured, 'it will be impossible to say whether she was drowned or not. Externally, in most respects, it would appear that she was. It can be argued, and no doubt it will be argued, that she committed suicide by weighting her suitcase and tying it to herself and perhaps throwing herself into The River from the weir bridge.'

'If that was so, what becomes of the telephone call and the telegram from Carlisle?'

'I cannot think of any answer consistent with suicide.'

'Murder, then?'

'It would seem so.'

'I am going to tell you something. It's complicated and a bit nebulous but I want to tell you. First of all – my cabin. You know it was booked – '

'To somebody called Andropulos? I saw the paragraph in the paper. I did not speak of it as I thought it would be unpleasant for you.'

'Did any of the others?'

'Not to my knowledge.'

'I'll make this as quick and as clear as I can – it has to do with a case of my husband's. There's a man called Foljambe – '

A crisp knock on her door and Superintendent Tillottson's voice: 'Mrs Alleyn? Tillotson here. May I come in.'

Troy and Dr Natouche stared at each other. She whispered: 'He'll have to,' and called out: 'Come in, Mr Tillottson.' At the same time Dr Natouche opened the door.

Suddenly the little cabin was crammed with enormous men. Superintendent Tillottson and Doctor Natouche were both over six feet tall and comparably broad. She began to introduce these mammoths to each other and then realized they had been introduced already in hideous formality by Hazel Rickerby-Carrick. She could not help looking at Mr Tillottson's large pink hands which were a little puckered as if he had been doing the washing. She was very glad he did not offer one to her, after his hearty fashion, for shaking.

She said: 'Dr Natouche is looking after me on account of my making a perfect ass of myself.'

Mr Tillottson said, with a sort of wide spread of blandness, that this was very nice. Dr Natouche then advised Troy to take things easy and left them.

Troy pushed back the red blanket, sat up on her bunk, put her feet on the deck and ran her fingers through her short hair. 'Well, Mr Tillottson,' she said, 'what about this one?'

II

With the exception of Chief-Inspector Fox for whom she had a deep affection, Troy did not meet her husband's colleagues with any regularity. Sometimes Alleyn would bring a few of them in for drinks and two or three times a year the Alleyns had easy-going evenings when their house, like Troy's cabin in the *Zodiac*, was full of enormous men talking shop.

From these encounters she had, she thought, learnt to recognize certain occupational characteristics among officers of the Criminal Investigation Department.

They were men who, day in, day out, worked in an atmosphere of intense hostility. They were, they would have said, without illusions and unless a built-in scepticism, by definition includes a degree of illusion, she supposed they were right. Some of them, she thought, had retained a kind of basic compassion: they were shocked by certain crimes and angered by others. They honestly saw themselves as guardians of the peace however disillusioned they might be as to the character of the beings they protected. Some regarded modern psychiatric theories about crime with massive contempt. Others seemed to look upon the men and women they hunted with a kind of sardonic affection and would strike up what passed for friendships with them. Many of them, like Fox, were of a very kindly disposition yet, as Alleyn once said of them, if pity entered far into the hunter his occupation was gone. And he had quoted Mark Antony who talked about 'pity choked with custom of fell deeds'. Some of the men she met were bitter and with reason, about public attitudes towards the police. 'A character comes and robs their till or does their old Mum or interferes with their kid sister,' Mr Fox once remarked, 'and they're all over you. Next day they're among the pigeons in Trafalgar Square advising the gang our chaps are trying to deal with to put in the boot. You could say it's a lonely sort of job.'

Very few of Alleyn's colleagues, Troy thought, were natural bullies but it was to be expected that the Service would occasionally attract such men and that its disciplines would sometimes fail to control them.

At which point in her consideration of the genus of CID Troy was invariably brought up short by the reflection that her husband fitted into none of these categories. And she would give up generalization as a bad job.

Now, however, she found herself trying to place Superintendent Tillottson and was unable to do so.

How tough was Mr Tillottson? How intelligent? How impenetrable? And what on earth did he now make of the cruise of the *Zodiac*? If he carried on in his usual way, ironing-out her remarks into a featureless expanse of words, she would feel like hitting him.

So. 'What do you make of this one?' she asked and heard his 'Well, now, Mrs Alleyn – ' before he said it.

'Well, now, Mrs Alleyn,' said Mr Tillottson and she cut in.

'Has she been murdered? Or can't you say until after the autopsy?'

'We can't say,' he admitted, looking wary, 'until after the inquest. Not on – er – on – er – '

'The external appearance of her body?'

'That is so, Mrs Alleyn. That is correct, yes.'

'Have you heard that last night the Skipper got a telegram purporting to come from her? From Carlisle? Intimating she was on her way to the Highlands?'

'We have that information, Mrs Alleyn. Yes.'

'Well, then?'

Mr Tillottson coined a phrase: 'It's quite a little problem.' he said.

'You,' Troy said with feeling, 'are telling me.' She indicated the stool. 'Do sit down, Mr Tillottson,' she said.

He thanked her and did so, obliterating the stool.

'I suppose,' she continued. 'You want a statement from me, don't you?'

He became cautiously playful. 'I see you know all about routine, Mrs Alleyn. Well, yes, if you've no objection, just a wee statement. Seeing you, as you might say – '

'Discovered the body?'

'That is so, Mrs Alleyn.'

Troy said rapidly: 'I was on deck on the port side at the after-end, I think you call it. I leant on the rail and looked at the water which was covered with detergent foam. We were, I suppose, about two chains below Ramsdyke weir and turning towards the lock. I saw it – I saw her face – through the foam. At first I only thought – I thought – '

'I'm sure it was very unpleasant.'

She felt that to concede this understatement would be to give ground before Mr Tillottson.

'I thought it was something else: a trick of light and colour. And then the foam broke and I saw. That's all really. I don't think I called out. I'm not sure. Very stupidly, I fainted. Mr Tillottson,' Troy hurried on, 'we know she left the *Zodiac* some time during the night before last at Crossdyke. She slept on deck, that night.'

'Yes?' he asked quickly. 'On deck? Sure?'

'Didn't you know?'

'I haven't had the opportunity as yet, to get what you'd call the full picture.'

'No, of course not. She told Dr Natouche she meant to sleep on deck. She complained of insomnia. And I think she must have done so because he and I found a bit of cloth from the cover of her diary – you know I told you how it went overboard – on her Li-lo mattress.'

'Not necessarily left there during the night, though, would you say?'

'Perhaps not. It was discoloured. I think Dr Natouche has kept it.'

'*Has* he? Now why would the doctor do that, I wonder.'

'Because I asked him to.'

'You *did*!'

'We were both a bit worried about her. Well, *you* know *I* was, don't you? I told you.'

Mr Tillottson at once looked guarded. 'That's so, Mrs Alleyn,' he said. 'You did mention it. Yerse.'

'There's one thing I want you to tell me. I daresay I've got no business to pester you but I hope you won't mind too much.'

'Well, of course not. Naturally not, I'm sure.'

'It's just this. If it is found to be homicide you won't will you, entertain any idea of her having been set upon by thugs when she went ashore in the night? That can't be the case, possibly, can it?'

'We always like to keep an open mind.'

'Yes, but you can't, can you, keep an open mind about that one? Because if she was killed by some unknown thug, who on earth sent the telegram from Carlisle?'

'We'll have to get you in the Force, Mrs Alleyn. I can see that,' he joked uneasily.

'I know I'm being a bore.'

'Not at all.'

'But you see,' Troy couldn't resist adding, 'it's because of all those silly little things I told you about at the police stations. They don't sound quite so foolish, now. Or do they?'

'Er – no. No. You may be quite sure, Mrs Alleyn, that we won't neglect any detail, however small.'

'Of course. I know.'

'I might just mention, Mrs Alleyn, that since we had our last chat we've re-checked on the whereabouts of the passengers over last weekend. They're OK. The Hewson couple were in Stratford-upon-Avon. Mr Pollock did stay in Birmingham. Dr Natouche *was* in Liverpool, and – '

'But – that's all before the cruise began!'

'Yerse,' he said and seemed to be in two minds what to say next. 'Still,' he said, 'as far as it goes, there it is,' and left it at that.

'Please, Mr Tillottson, there's only one more thing. Had she – did you find anything round her neck. A cord or tape with a sort of little bundle on it. Sewn up, I fancy, in chamois leather?'

'No,' he said sharply. 'Nothing like that. Did she wear something of that nature?'

'Yes,' Troy said. 'She did. It was – I know this sounds fantastic but it's what she told me – it was an extremely valuable Fabergé jewel representing the Signs of the Zodiac and given to her grandfather who was a surgeon, by, believe it or not, the Czar of Russia. She told me she never took it off. Except one supposes when she – ' Troy stopped short.

'Did she talk about it to anyone else, Mrs Alleyn?'

'I understood she'd told Miss Hewson about it.'

'There you are! The foolishness of some ladies.'

'I know.'

'Well, now,' he said. 'This is interesting. This is quite interesting, Mrs Alleyn.'

'You're thinking of motive.'

'We have to think of everything,' he sighed portentously. 'Everything.'

'I suppose,' Troy said, 'you've looked in her suitcase.'

She thought how preposterous it was that she should be asking the question and said to herself: 'If it wasn't for Rory, he'd have slapped me back long ago.'

He said: 'That would be routine procedure, wouldn't it, Mrs Alleyn?'

'You were alongside this cabin when you – when you – were in that boat. The porthole was open. I heard about the suitcase.'

He glanced with something like irritation at the porthole.

'There's nothing of the nature of the object you describe in the suitcase,' he said and stood up with an air of finality. 'I expect you'll appreciate, Mrs Alleyn, that we'll ask for signed statements from all the personnel in this craft.'

'Yes, of course.'

'I've suggested they assemble in the saloon upstairs for a preliminary interview. You're feeling quite yourself again – ?'

'Quite, thank you.'

'That's fine. In about five minutes, then?'

'Certainly.'

When he had gone, softly closing the door behind him, Troy tidied herself up. The face that looked out of her glass was pretty white and her hand was not perfectly steady but she was all right. She straightened the red blanket and turned to the washbasin. The tumbler had been half-filled with water and placed on the shelf. Beside it were two capsules.

Trankwitones, no doubt.

Persistent woman: Miss Hewson.

Never in her life, Troy thought, had she felt lonelier. Never had she wished more heartily for her husband's return.

She believed she knew now for certain, what had happened to Hazel Rickerby-Carrick. She had been murdered and her murderer was aboard the *Zodiac*.

'But,' she thought, 'it may stop there. She told Miss Hewson about the jewel and Miss Hewson may well have told – who? Her brother almost certainly and perhaps Mr Pollock with whom they seem to be pretty thick. Or the Tretheways? For the matter of that, every man and woman of us may know about the thing and the ones like Dr Natouche and Caley Bard and me may simply have used discretion and held their tongues.

'And then it might follow that some single one of us,' she thought, 'tried to steal the jewel when she was asleep on deck and she woke and would have screamed and given him – or her – away and so she got her quietus. But after that – ? Here's a nightmarish sort of thing – after that how did poor Hazel get to Ramsdyke weir seven miles or more upstream?'

She remembered that Miss Rickerby-Carrick had been presented with some of Miss Hewson's Trankwitones and that Dr Natouche had said they were unknown to him.

Now. Was there any reason to suppose that the case didn't stop there but reached out all round itself like a spider to draw in Andropulos and behind Andropulos, the shadowy figure of Foljambe? The Jampot? The ultra-clever one?

Was it too fantastic, *now*, to think the Jampot might be on board? And if he was? Well, Troy thought, she couldn't for the life of her name her fancy. Figures, recalled by a professional memory, swam before her mind's eye, each in its way outlandish – black patch, deaf ear, club foot and with a sort of mental giggle she thought: 'If it's Caley I've been kissed by a triple murderer and Rory can put *that* on his needles and knit it.'

At this point Mrs Tretheway's little bell that she rang for meal-times, tinkled incisively. Troy opened the door and heard Tillottson's paddy voice and a general stir as of an arrival. While she listened, trying to interpret these sounds, the cabin door on her left opened and Mr Lazenby came out. He turned and stood on her threshold and they were face-to-face. Even as close to him as she was now Troy could make nothing of the eyes behind the dark glasses and this circumstance lent his face an obviously sinister look as if he were a character out of an early Hitchcock film.

'You are better?' he asked. 'I was about to inquire, I'm afraid you were very much upset and distressed. As indeed we all are. Oh, *terribly* distressed. Poor soul! Poor quaint, kindly soul! It's hard to believe she's gone.'

'I don't find it so,' Troy snapped.

She saw his lips settle in a rather sharp line. There was a further subdued commotion somewhere on deck. Troy listened for a second. A new voice sounded and her heart began to thud against her ribs.

'If a poor parson may make a suggestion, Mrs Alleyn,' Mr Lazenby said and seemed to peer at her. 'I think perhaps you should leave the *Zodiac*. You have had a great shock. You look – ' The bell rang again. He turned his head sharply and the spectacles moved. For a fraction of a second Troy caught a glimpse of the left eye-socket behind its dark window. There was no eye in it.

And then she heard a very deep voice at the head of the companion-way.

Without thought or conscious effort she was past Mr Lazenby, out of the cabin, up the stairs and into her husband's arms.

III

Of course it was an extraordinary situation. She could think: 'how extraordinary' even while her delight in his return sang so loudly it was enough to deafen her to anything else.

There had been some sort of explanation at large – introductions even – to whoever had been in the saloon followed by a retreat with

Alleyn to her cabin. She remembered afterwards that they had encountered Mr Lazenby in the passage.

Now they sat, side by side, on her bunk and she thought she could cope with Catastrophe itself.

He put his arm round her and swore briefly but violently, asking her what the bloody hell she thought she was doing and giving her a number of hasty but well-planted embraces. This she found satisfactory. He then said they couldn't sit down here on their bottoms all day and invited her to relate as quickly as possible anything she thought he ought to know.

'I've heard your extraordinary spinster's been found in The River and that you were the first to see her. Tillottson seems to think it's a case of foul play. Otherwise I know nothing beyond what you wrote in your letters. Look at you. You're as white as a sheet. Troy, my darling.'

'It only happened a couple of hours ago, you might remember. Don't fuss. Rory, there's so much to tell and I'm meant to be upstairs being grilled with the others.'

'To hell with that. No. Wait a bit. I think we must listen to Tillottson in action. I've thrown him into a fine old tizzy, anyway, by turning up. Tell me quickly, then: what's happened since you posted your last letter at Tollardwark?'

'All right. Listen.'

She told him about the diary going overboard, the behaviour of Mr Lazenby, the disappearance of Hazel Rickerby-Carrick, her sense of growing tension and Miss Hewson's discovery of the 'Constable'.

'There are a lot of other little things that seemed odd to me but those are the landmarks.'

'We'll have the whole saga in detail later on. You've put me far enough in the picture for the moment. Come on. Let's give Tillottson a treat. I've arranged to sit in.'

So they went upstairs. There were the other passengers in an uneasy row on the semi-circular bench at the end of the saloon: the Hewsons, Mr Pollock, Mr Lazenby, Caley Bard and, a little apart as always, Dr Natouche. The Tretheways were grouped together near the bar.

Facing the passengers at a dining table were Superintendent Tillottson and a uniformed Sergeant.

Troy sat by Dr Natouche who, with Caley Bard, rose at her approach. Alleyn stayed at the other end of the saloon. The *Zodiac* was tied up alongside the wapentake side of The River, below Ramsdyke Lock and the shapeless thunder of the weir could be distinctly heard. Scurries of detergent foam were blown past the open windows.

It was easy to see that Mr Tillottson suffered from a deep embarrassment. He looked at Troy and cleared his throat, he turned and nodded portentously to Alleyn. His neck turned red and he pursed up his lips to show that the situation was child's play to him.

'Yerse, well now,' Mr Tillottson said. 'I think if you don't mind, ladies and gentlemen, we'll just have a wee re-cap. I'll go over the information we have produced about this unfortunate lady and I'll be obliged if you'll correct me if I go wrong.'

The Sergeant pushed his book across. Mr Tillottson put on a pair of spectacles and began to summarize, consulting the notes from time to time.

It was very soon clear to Troy that he refreshed his memory, not only from the Sergeant's notes on what the passengers had divulged but also from the information she had given him on her three visits to police stations. Particularly was this apparent when he outlined the circumstances of Hazel Rickerby-Carrick's disappearance. Troy sensed her companions' surprise at Mr Tillottson's omniscience. How, they must surely be asking themselves, had he found time to make so many inquiries? Or would they merely put it all down to the expeditious methods of our county police?

She glanced quickly at Alleyn and saw one eyebrow go up.

Mr Tillottson himself evidently realized his mistake. His résumé became a trifle scrambled and ended abruptly.

'Well now,' he said. 'Ladies and gentlemen, since we are all agreed that as far as they go, these are the facts I won't trouble you any more just now except to say that I hope you will all complete your cruise as planned. The craft will proceed shortly to a mooring above Ramsdyke Lock where she will tie up for the night and she will return to Norminster at about eleven o'clock tomorrow morning. I'm afraid I shall have to ask you to remain within reach for the inquest which will probably be held the following day. In Norminster. If there is any trouble about securing accommodation, my department will be glad to assist.'

Upon this the Hewsons broke into vehement expostulation, complaining that they were on a tight schedule and were due next evening, to make a connection for Perth, Scotland.

Caley Bard said that with any luck they might meet up with Mavis and everybody but Troy and Dr Natouche looked shocked. Miss Hewson said if that was a specimen of British humour she did not, for her part, appreciate it and Mr Hewson said he did not find himself in stitches either.

Mr Lazenby asked if – since all their accounts of the affair agreed – it would not be acceptable for them to be represented at the inquest by (as it were) a spokesman and it was clear that he did not cast himself for this role. He had important appointments with ecclesiastical big-wigs in London and was loath to forgo them. He developed antipodean-type resentment and began to speak of the reactionary conduct of pom policemen. He said: 'Good on you,' to the Hewsons and formed an alliance.

Caley Bard said it was an unconscionable bore but one didn't, after all, fish corpses out of the waterways every day of the week and he would resign himself to the ruling. He grew less popular with every word he uttered.

Mr Pollock whined. He wanted to know why they couldn't sign a joint statement, for God's sake, and then bugger off if the ladies would excuse the expression.

Everybody except Caley Bard, Troy and Alleyn looked scandalized and Mr Lazenby expostulated.

Dr Natouche asked if, since his practice was within reasonable driving distance of Norminster, he might be summoned from thence. He realized, of course, that as he had made the preliminary examination he would be required to give evidence under that heading.

Mr Tillottson glanced at Alleyn and then said he thought that would be quite in order.

He now asked to see the passports of Mr Lazenby and the Hewsons and they were produced, Mr Lazenby taking the opportunity to complain about the treatment of Australian visitors at British Customs. Mr Tillottson said the passports would be returned and shifted his feet about as a preface to rising.

It was now that Mr Lazenby suddenly said: 'I'm puzzled.' And Troy thought 'Here we go.'

'I'd like to ask,' he said, and he seemed to be looking at her, 'just how the police have come by some of their information. When did the Superintendent find the opportunity to make the necessary inquiries? To the best of my belief, from the time he got here until this present moment, the Superintendent has been on The River or here in this boat. If you don't object, Superintendent, I think this calls for an explanation. Just to keep the record straight.'

'Blimey, chum, you're right!' Mr Pollock exclaimed and the Hewsons broke into a little paean of agreement. They all stared at Troy.

Mr Tillottson made an almost instant recovery. He looked straight before him and said that he happened to receive information about Miss Rickerby-Carrick's mode of departure and had thought it unusual enough to warrant a routine inquiry.

And from whom, if the Superintendent didn't mind, Mr Lazenby persisted, had he received this information.

Troy heard herself, as if it were with somebody else's voice, saying: 'It was from me. I think you all know I called at the police station at Tollardwark. I happened in the course of conversation to say something about Miss Rickerby-Carrick's unexpected departure.'

'Quite so,' said Mr Tillottson. 'That is correct.'

'And I imagine,' Caley Bard said angrily, 'you have no objections to that perfectly reasonable explanation, Mr Lazenby.'

'Certainly not. By no means. One only wanted to know.'

'And now one does know one may as well pipe down.'

'There's no call to take that tone,' Mr Pollock said. 'We didn't mean anything personal.'

'Then what the hell did you mean?'

'Gentlemen!' Mr Tillottson almost shouted and they subsided. 'A statement,' he said, 'will be typed on the lines of your information. You will be asked to look it over and if you find it correct, to sign it. I have only one other remark to make, ladies and gentlemen. As you have already been informed, we have Superintendent Alleyn, CID with us. Mr Alleyn came, you might say, on unofficial business.' Here Mr Tillottson ducked his head at Troy, 'But I don't have to tell him we'll be very glad of his advice in a matter which I'm sure everybody wants to see cleared up to the satisfaction of all concerned. Thank you.'

Having wound himself into a cocoon of generalities Mr Tillottson added that as the afternoon was rather close he was sure they would all like a breath of air. Upon this hint the passengers retired above. Troy after a look from Alleyn went with them. She noticed that Dr Natouche remained below.

It seemed to her that the Hewsons and Mr Lazenby and Mr Pollock were in two minds as to what attitude they would adopt towards her. After a short and uncomfortable silence, Mr Lazenby settled this problem by bearing down upon her with his widest smile.

'Happy now, Mrs Alleyn?' he fluted. 'I'll bet! And I must say, without, I hope, being uncharitable, we all ought to congratulate ourselves on your husband's arrival. Really,' Mr Lazenby said, looking – or seeming to look – about him, 'it would almost seem that he was Sent.'

It was from this moment, that Troy began to suspect Mr Lazenby, in spite of the Bishop of Norminster, of not being a clergyman.

He had sparked off a popularity poll in favour of Troy. Miss Hewson said that maybe she wasn't qualified to speak but she certainly did not know what was with this cop and for her money the sooner Alleyn set up a regular investigation the better she'd feel and Mr Pollock hurriedly agreed.

Caley Bard watched this demonstration with a scarcely veiled expression of glee. He strolled over to Troy and said: 'We don't know yet, though, or do we, if the celebrated husband *is* going to act.'

'I'm sure *I* don't,' she said. 'They have to be asked. They don't just waltz in because they happen to be on the spot.'

'I suppose you're enchanted to see him.'

'Of course I am.'

'That monumental creature seemed to indicate a collaboration, didn't you think?'

'Well, yes. But it'd all be by arrangement with head office.'

'Hallo,' he said, 'we're going through the lock.'

'Thank God!' Troy ejaculated.

It would be something – it would be a great deal – to get out of that region of polluted foam. Troy had been unable to look at The River since she came on deck.

They slipped into the clear dark waters, the sluice-gates were shut, the paddles set, and the familiar slow ascent began. She moved to the after-end of the *Zodiac* and Caley Bard joined her there.

'I don't know if it has occurred to you,' he said, 'that everybody is cutting dead the obvious inference.'

'Inference?'

'Well – question if you prefer. Aren't we all asking ourselves whether the ebullient Hay has been made away with?'

After a pause, Troy said: 'I suppose so.'

'Well, of course we are. We'd be certifiable if we didn't. Do you mind talking about it?'

'I think it's worse not to do so.'

'I couldn't agree more. Have you heard what they found?'

'In The River?'

'Yes.'

'I *did* hear a good deal. In my cabin.'

'I was on deck. I saw.'

'How horrible,' said Troy.

But she was not as deeply horrified as she might have been because her attention was riveted by a pair of large, neat and highly polished boots and decent iron-grey trousers on the rim of the lock above her. They looked familiar. She tilted her head back and was rewarded by a worm's-eye view in violent perspective of the edge of a jacket, the modest swell of a stomach, the underneath of a massive chin, a pair of nostrils and the brim of a hat.

As the *Zodiac* quietly rose in the lock, these items resolved themselves into an unmistakable whole.

'Well,' Troy thought, 'this settles it. It's a case,' and when she found herself sufficiently elevated to do so without absurd contortion, she addressed herself to the person now revealed.

'Hallo, Br'er Fox,' she said.

IV

'What was *said*,' Fox explained, 'was this. Tillottson's asked for us to come in. He rang the Department on finding the body. The AC said that as you've been in on this Jampot thing from the time it came our way, the only sensible course is for you to follow it up. Regardless, as it were. And I've been shot up here by plane to act as your support and to let you know how things stand on my file.

Which is a nice way of saying how big a bloody fool I've been made to look by this expert.'

'But who says this is a Jampot affair, may I ask?' Alleyn crossly interjected.

'The AC works it out that this job up here, this river job, ought properly to be regarded as a possible lead on Foljambe. On account of the Andropulos connection. Having been made a monkey of,' Fox added with feeling, 'by a faked-up false scent to Paris, I don't say I reacted with enthusiasm to his theories but you have to look at these things with what I've heard you call a disparate eye.'

'I entirely agree. And that, under the circumstances is something I cannot be expected to do. Look here, Fox. Here's Troy, one of a group of people who, if this woman was murdered, and I'll bet she was, come into the field of police investigation: right?'

'The AC says it'll be nicer for you to be here with her.'

'That be damned! What? Me? Needle my wife? Give her the old one-two treatment if she doesn't provide all the answers? *Nicer?*'

'It won't,' Fox said, 'be as bad as that now, will it?'

'I can't tell you how much I dislike having her mixed up in any of our shows. I came here to get her out of it. Not to take on a bloody homicide job.'

'I know that. It's a natural reaction,' Mr Fox said. 'Both of you being what you are.'

'I don't know what you mean by that.'

'Suppose you didn't take the case, Mr Alleyn. What's the drill on that one? Somebody else comes up from the Yard and you hand him the file. And is his face red! He goes ahead and you clear out leaving Mrs Alleyn here to get through the routine as best she can.'

'You know damn' well that's grotesque.'

'Well, Mr Alleyn, the alternative's not to your fancy either, is it?'

'If you put it like that the only thing that remains for me to do is to retire in a hurry and to hell with the pension.'

'Oh, now! Come, come!'

'All right. *All* right. I'm unreasonable under this heading and we both know it.'

Fox mildly contemplated his superior officer. 'I can see it's awkward,' he said. 'It's not what we'd choose. You're thinking about her position and how it'll appear to others and what say the Press get on to it, I daresay. But if you ask me it won't be so bad. It's only until the inquest.'

'And in the meantime what's the form? We've issued orders that they're all to stay in that damned boat tonight, one of them almost certainly being the Rickerby-Carrick's murderer and just possibly the toughest proposition in homicide on either side of the Atlantic. I can't withdraw my wife and insist on keeping the others there. Well, can I? Can I?'

'It might be awkward,' said Fox. 'But you could.'

They fell silent and as people do when they come to a blank wall in a conversation, stared vaguely about them. A lark sang, a faint breeze lifted the long grass and in the excavation below the wapentake, sand and gravel fell with a whisper of sound from the grassy overhang.

'That's very dangerous,' Fox said absently. 'That place. Kids might get in there. If they interfered with those props, anything could happen.' He stood up, eased his legs and looked down at The River. It was masked by a rising mist.

The *Zodiac* was moored for the night some distance above Ramsdyke Lock. The passengers were having their dinner, Mr Tillottson and his sergeant being provided for at an extra table. Alleyn had had a moment or two with Troy and had suggested that she might slip away and join them if an opportunity presented itself. If, however, she could not do so without attracting a lot of attention she was to go early to bed and lock her door. He would come to her later and she was to unlock it to nobody else. To which she had replied: 'Well, naturally,' and he had said she knew damned well what he meant and they had broken into highly inappropriate laughter. He and Fox had then walked up to the wapentake where at least they were able to converse above a mutter.

'There is,' Alleyn said, 'a vacant cabin, of course. Now.'

'That's right.'

'I tell you what, Fox. We'll have a word with the Skipper and take it over. We'll search and we'll need a warrant.'

'I picked one up on my way from the beak at Tollardwark. He didn't altogether see it but changed his mind when I talked about the Foljambe connection.'

'As well he might. One of us could doss down in the cabin for the night if there's any chance of a bit of kip which is not likely. It'd be a safety measure.'

'You,' said Fox, 'if it suits. I've dumped a homicide bag at the Ramsdyke Arms.'

'Tillottson kept his head and had the cabin locked. He says it's full of junk. We'll get the key off him. Look who's here.'

It was Troy, coming into the field from Dyke Way by the top gate. Alleyn thought: 'I wonder how rare it is for a man's heart to behave as mine does at the unexpected sight of his wife.'

Fox said: 'I'll nip along to the pub, shall I, and settle for my room and bring back your kit and something to eat. Then you can relieve Tillottson and start on the cabin. Will I ring the Yard and get the boys sent up?'

'Yes,' Alleyn said. 'Yes. Better do that. Thank you, Br'er Fox.' By 'the boys' Br'er Fox meant Sergeants Bailey and Thompson, finger-print and photograph experts, who normally worked with Alleyn.

'We'll need a patrol,' Alleyn said, 'along The River from Tollard Lock to where she was found and we'll have to make a complete and no doubt fruitless search of the tow-path and surroundings. You'd bet-ter get on to that, Fox. Take the Sergeant with you. Particular atten-tion to the moorings at Crossdyke and the area round Ramsdyke weir.'

'Right, I'll be off, then.'

He started up the hill towards Troy looking, as always, exactly what he was. An incongruous figure was Mr Fox in that still medieval landscape. They met and spoke and Fox moved on to the gate.

Alleyn watched Troy come down the hill and went out of the wapentake to meet her.

'They've all gone ashore,' she said, 'I *think* to talk about me. Except Dr Natouche who's putting finishing touches to his map. They're sitting in a huddle in the middle-distance of the view that inspired my original remark about Constables. I expect you must push on with routine mustn't you? What haven't I told you that you ought to know? Should I fill you in, as Miss Hewson would say, on some of the details?'

'Yes, darling, fill me in, do. I'll ask questions, shall I? It might be quickest. And you add anything – anything at all – that you think might be, however remotely, to the point. Shall we go?'

'Fire ahead,' said Troy.

During this process Troy's answers became more and more staccato and her face grew progressively whiter. Alleyn watched her with an attentiveness that she wondered if she dreaded and knew that she loved. She answered his final question and said in a voice that sounded shrilly in her own ears: 'There. Now you know as much as I do. See.'

'What is it?' he asked. 'Tell me.'

'She scratched on my door,' Troy said. 'And when I opened it she'd gone away. She wanted to tell me something and I let Mr Lazenby rescue me because I had a migraine and because she was such a bore. She was unhappy and who can tell what might have been the outcome if I'd let her confide? Who can tell *that*?'

'I *think* I can. I don't believe – and I promise you this – I don't believe it would have made the smallest difference to what happened to her. And I'll promise you as well, that if it turns out otherwise I shall say so.'

'I can't forgive myself.'

'Yes, you can. Is one never to run away from a bore for fear she'll be murdered?'

'Oh Rory.'

'All right, darling. I know. And I tell you what – I'm glad you had your migraine and I'm bloody glad she didn't talk to you. Now, then. Better?'

'A bit.'

'Good. One more question. That junk shop in Tollardwark where you encountered the Hewsons. Did you notice the name of the street?'

'I think it was Ferry Lane.'

'You wouldn't know the name of the shop?'

'No,' Troy said doubtfully. 'It was so dark. I don't think I saw. But – wait a bit – yes: on a very dilapidated little sign in Dr Natouche's torchlight. "Jno. Bagg: Licensed Dealer".'

'Good. And it was there they made their haul?'

'That's right. They went back there from Longminster. Yesterday.'

'Do you think it might be a Constable?'

'I've no idea. It's in his manner and it's extremely well painted.'

'What was the general reaction to the find?'

'The Hewsons are going to show it to an expert. If it's genuine I think they plan to come back and scour the district for more. I rather fancy Lazenby's got the same idea.'

'And you've doubts about him being a parson?'

'Yes. I don't know why.'

'No eye in the left socket?'

'It was only a glimpse but I think so. Rory – ?'

'Yes?'

'The man who killed Andropulos – Foljambe – the Jampot. Do you know what he looks like?'

'Not really. We've got a photograph but Santa Claus isn't more heavily bearded and his hair, which looks fairish, covers his ears. It was taken over two years ago and is not a credit to the Bolivian photographer. He had both his eyes then but we *have* heard indirectly that he received some sort of injury after he escaped and lay doggo with it for a time. One report was that it was facial and another that it wasn't. There was a third rumour thought to have originated in the South that he'd undergone an operation to change his appearance but none of this stuff was dependable. We think it likely that there is some sort of physical abnormality.'

'Please tell me, Rory. *Please*. Do you think he's on board?'

And because Alleyn didn't at once protest, she said: 'You do. Don't you? Why?'

'Before I got here, I would have said there was no solid reason to suppose it. On your letters and on general circumstances. Now, I'm less sure.'

'Is it because of – have you seen . . . ?'

'The body? Yes, it's largely because of that.'

'Then – what – ?'

'We'll have to wait for the autopsy. I don't think they'll find she drowned, Troy. I think she was killed in precisely the same way as Andropulos was killed. And I think it was done by the Jampot.'

CHAPTER 7

Routine

' – And so,' Alleyn said, 'we set up the appropriate routine and went to work in the usual way. Tillottson was under-staffed – the familiar story – but he was able to let us have half a dozen uniformed men. He and the Super at Longminster – Mr Bonney – did all they could to co-operate. But once we'd caught that whiff of the Jampot it became essentially our job with strong European and American connections.

'We did a big line with Interpol and the appropriate countries but although they were dead keen they weren't all that much of a help. Throughout his lamentable career the Jampot had only made one blunder: and that, as far as we could ferret it out, was because an associate at the Bolivian end of his drug racket had grassed. The associate was found dead by quick attack from behind on the carotids: the method that Foljambe had certainly employed in Paris and was later to employ upon the wretched Andropulos. But for reasons about which the Bolivian police were uncommonly cagey, the Jampot was not accused by them of murder but of smuggling. Bribery is a little word we are not supposed to use when in communication with our brothers in anti-crime.

'It's worth noticing that whereas other big-shots in his world employ their staffs of salaried killers the Jampot believes in the do-it-yourself kit and is unique in this as in many other respects.

'Apart from routine field-work the immediate task, as I saw it, was to lay out the bits of information as provided by my wife and try to discover which fitted and which were extraneous. I suggest that you treat yourselves to the same exercise.'

The man in the second row could almost be seen to lay back his ears.

'We found nothing to help us on deck,' continued Alleyn. 'Her mattress had been deflated and stowed away and so had her blankets and the deck had been hosed down in the normal course of routine.

'But the tow-path and adjacent terrain turned up a show of colour. At the Crossdyke end, and you'll remember it was during the night at Crossdyke that the murdered woman disappeared, Mr Fox's party found on the riverbank at the site of the *Zodiac*'s moorings, a number of indentations, made either by a woman's cuban heel or those of the kind of "gear" boots currently fashionable in Carnaby Street. They overlapped and their general type and characteristics suggested that the wearer had moved forwards with ease and then backwards under a heavy load. Here's a blow-up of Detective-Sergeant Thompson's photographs.

'There had either been some attempt to flatten these marks or else a heavy object had been dragged across them at right angles to the riverbank.

'The tow-path was too hard to offer anything useful, and the path from there up to the road was tar-sealed and provided nothing. Nor did a muddy track along the waterfront. If the heels had gone that way we would certainly have picked them up so the main road must have been the route. Mr Fox, who is probably the most meticulous clue-hound in the Force, had a long hard look at the road. Here are some blown-up shots of what he found. Footprints. A patch of oil on the verge under a hedgerow not far from the moorings. Accompanying tyre marks suggest that a motorbike had been parked there for some time. He found identical tracks on the road above Ramsdyke. At Crossdyke on an overhanging hawthorn twig – look at this close-up – there was a scrap of a dark blue synthetic material corresponding in colour and type with deceased's pyjamas.

'Right. Question now arose: if deceased came this way was she alive or dead at the time of transit? Yes, Carmichael?'

The man in the second row passed his paddle of a hand over the back of his sandy head.

'Sir,' he said. 'It would appear from the character of the footprints, the marks on the bank, the evidence at the braeside and the
wee wispies of cloth, that the leddy was at the least of it, unconscious and carried from the craft to the bike. Further than that, sir, I
would not care to venture.'

The rest of the class stirred irritably.

'By and large,' Alleyn said, 'you would be right. To continue – '

I

Alleyn and Troy returned together to the *Zodiac*. They found Dr Natouche reading on deck and the other passengers distantly visible in a seated group on the far hillside above the ford.

Natouche glanced up for a moment at Troy. She walked towards him and he stood up.

'Rory,' Troy said, 'you've not heard how good Dr Natouche has been. He gave me a lovely lunch at Longminster and he was as kind as could be when I passed out this afternoon.'

Alleyn said: 'We're lucky, on all counts, to have you on board.'

'I have been privileged,' he replied with his little bow.

'I've told him,' Troy said, 'how uneasy you were when she disappeared and how we talked it over.'

'It was not, of course, that I feared that any violence would be done to her. There was no reason to suppose that. It was because I thought her disturbed.'

'To the point,' Alleyn said, 'where she might do violence upon herself?'

Dr Natouche folded his hands and looked at them. 'No,' he said. 'Not specifically. But she was, I thought, in a very unstable condition: a condition that is not incompatible with suicidal intention.'

'Yes,' Alleyn said. 'I see. Oh dear.'

'You find something wrong, Mr Alleyn?'

'No, no. Not wrong. It's just that I seem to hear you giving that opinion in the witness box.'

'For the defence?' he asked calmly.

'For the defence.'

'Well,' said Dr Natouche, 'I daresay I should be obliged to qualify it under cross-examination. While I am about it, may I give you another opinion? I think your wife would be better away from the *Zodiac*. She has had a most unpleasant shock, she is subject to migraine and I think she is finding the prospect of staying in the ship a little hard to face.'

'No, no,' Troy said. 'Not at all. Not now.'

'You mean not now your husband is here. Of course. But I think he will be very much occupied. You must forgive me for my persistence but – why not a room at the inn in Ramsdyke? Or even in Norminster? It is not far.'

'I couldn't agree more,' Alleyn said, 'but there are difficulties. If my wife is given leave – '

'Some of us may also demand it? If you will allow me I'll suggest that she should go immediately and I'll say that as her medical adviser, I insisted.'

'Rory – would it be easier? It would, wouldn't it? For you? For both of us?'

'Yes, darling, it would.'

'Well, then?'

She saw Alleyn give Natouche one utterly non-committal look of which the doctor appeared to be perfectly unaware. 'I think you are right,' Alleyn said. 'I have been in two minds about it but I think you are right. How far is it by road to Norminster?'

'Six miles and three-eighths,' Natouche said.

'How very well-informed!'

'Dr Natouche is a map-maker,' Troy said. 'You must see what he's doing.'

'Love to,' Alleyn agreed politely. 'Where did you stay in Norminster, Troy? The Percy, was it?'

'Yes.'

'All right?'

'Perfectly.'

'I'll ring it up from the lockhouse. If they've got a room I'll send for a taxi. We'll obey doctor's orders.'

'All right. But – '

'What?'

'I'll feel as if I'm ratting. So will they.'

'Let them.'

'All right.'

'Would you go down and pack, then?'

'Yes. All right.' They could say nothing to each other, Troy thought, but 'all right'.

She went down to her cabin.

Natouche said: 'I hope you didn't mind my making this sugges-tion. Your wife commands an unusual degree of self-discipline, I think, but she really has had as much as she should be asked to take. I may say that some of the passengers would not be inclined to make matters any easier for her if she stayed.'

'No?'

'They are, I think, a little suspicious of the lost fur.'

'I can't blame them,' Alleyn said dryly.

'Perhaps,' Natouche continued, 'I should say this. If you find, as I think you will, that Miss Rickerby-Carrick was murdered I fully realize that I come into the field of suspects. Of course I do. I only mention this in case you should think that I try to put myself in an exclusive position by speaking as a doctor in respect of your wife.'

'Do you suppose,' Alleyn asked carefully, 'that any of the others think it may be a case of homicide?'

'They do not confide in me, but I should undoubtedly think so. Yes.'

'And they suspect that they will come into the field of inquiry?'

'They would be extremely stupid if they did not expect to do so,' he said. 'And by and large I don't find they are stupid people. Although at least three of them will certainly begin to suspect me of killing Miss Rickerby-Carrick.'

'Why?'

'Briefly: because I am an Ethiopian and they would prefer that I, rather than a white member of the company, should be found guilty.'

Alleyn listened to the huge voice, looked at the impassive face and wondered if this was a manifestation of inverted racialism or of sober judgment.

'I hope you're mistaken,' he said.

'And so, of course, do I,' said Dr Natouche.

'By the way, Troy tells me you found a scrap of material on deck.'

'Ah, yes. You would like to see it? It's here.'

He took out his pocket-book and extracted an envelope. 'Shall I show you where it was?' he asked.

'Please.'

They went to the after-end of the deck.

'The mattress was inflated,' Natouche explained, 'and lying where it had been when she used it. Mrs Alleyn noticed this fragment. It was caught under the edge of the pillow pocket. You will see that it is stained, presumably with river water. It seemed to me that Miss Rickerby-Carrick had probably taken her diary with her when she came up here to bed and that this piece of the cover, if it is that, became detached. The book was of course, saturated. I noted the cloth of its cover was torn when Lazenby rescued it. Your wife thought we should keep the fragment.'

'Yes, she told me. Thank you. I must get on with my unlovely job. I am very much obliged to you, Dr Natouche, for having taken care of Troy.'

'Please! I was most honoured that she placed a little confidence in me. I think,' he added, 'that I shall stroll up to the wapentake. If you'll excuse me.'

Alleyn watched him take an easy stride from the gunwale of the *Zodiac* to the grassy bank and noticed the perfect co-ordination of movement and the suggestion of unusual strength. Alleyn was visited by an odd notion: 'Suppose' he thought, 'he just went on. Suppose he became an Ethiopian in a canary-coloured sweater striding over historic English fens and out of our field of inquiry. Ah well, he's extremely conspicuous, after all.'

He looked downstream towards the weir and could see Fox and the local sergeant moving about the tow-path. Fox stooped over a wayside patch of bramble and presently righted himself with an air that Alleyn even at that distance, recognized as one of mild satisfaction. He turned, saw Alleyn and raised a hand, thumb up.

Alleyn went ashore, telephoned the Percy Hotel at Norminster, booked a room and ordered a taxi for Troy. When he returned to the *Zodiac* he found it deserted except for Troy who had packed her bags and was waiting for him in her cabin.

Half an hour later he put her in her taxi and she drove away from Ramsdyke. Her fellow-passengers, except for Dr Natouche, were sitting round an outdoor table at the pub. The Hewsons, Mr Lazenby and Mr Pollock had their heads together. Caley Bard slouched back dejectedly in his chair and gazed into a beer pot.

She asked the driver to stop and got out. As she approached the men stood up, Caley Bard at once, the others rather mulishly.

Troy said: 'I've been kicked out. Rory thinks I'll be an embarrassment to the Force if I stay and I think he's got something so I'm going to Norminster.'

Nobody spoke.

'I would rather have stayed,' she said, 'but I do see the point and I hope very much that all of you do, too. Wives are not meant to muscle-in on police routine.'

Caley Bard put his arm across her shoulders and gave her a little shake. 'Of course we do,' he said. 'Don't be a donkey. Off you go to Norminster and good riddance.'

'Well!' Troy said, 'that *is* handsome of you.'

Mr Lazenby said: 'This is the course I suggested, if you remember, Mrs Alleyn. I said I thought you would be well advised to leave the *Zodiac*.'

'So you did,' Troy agreed.

'For *your* sake, you know. For your sake.'

'For whatever reason, you were right.'

Pollock said something under his breath to Mr Hewson who received it with a wry grin that Troy found rather more disagreeable than a shouted insult would have been. Miss Hewson laughed.

'Well,' Troy said. 'We'll all meet, I suppose. At the inquest. I just felt I'd like to explain. Goodbye.'

She went back to the taxi. Caley Bard caught her up. 'I don't know if your old man thinks this is a case of murder,' he said, 'but you can take it from me I'd cheerfully lay that lot out. For God's sake don't let it hurt you. It's not worth a second thought.'

'No,' Troy said. 'Of course not. Goodbye.'

The car drove through the Constable landscape up the hill. When they got to the crest they found a policeman on duty at the entry to the main road. Troy looked back. There, down below, was The River with the *Zodiac* at her moorings. Fox had moved from the weir and Alleyn and Tillottson had met him. They seemed to examine something that Fox held in his hand. As if he felt her gaze upon him, Alleyn lifted his head and, across the Constable picture, they looked at each other and waved their hands.

Above The River on the far side was the wapentake and alone in its hollow like a resident deity sat a figure in a yellow sweater with a black face and hands.

It would be getting dark soon and the passengers would stroll back to the ship. For the last time they would go to bed in their cabins. The River and trees and fields would send up their night-time voices and scents and the countryside after its quiet habit, move into night. The seasonal mist which the Skipper had told them was called locally, The Creeper, had increased and already The River looked like a stream of hot water threading the low country.

How strange, Troy thought, as they drove away that she should so sharply regret leaving The River. For a moment she entertained a notion that because of the violence that threaded its history there was something unremarkable, even appropriate, in the latest affront to The River. Poor Hazel Rickerby-Carrick, she thought, has joined a long line of drowned faces and tumbled limbs: Plantagenets and Frenchmen, Lancastrians and Yorkists, cropped, wigged and ring-leted heads: bloated and desecrated bodies. They had drenched the fields and fed The River. The landscape had drawn them into itself and perhaps grown richer for them.

'I shall come back to the waterways,' Troy thought. She and Alleyn and their son and his best girl might hire a longboat and cruise, not here, not between Tollardwark and Ramsdyke, but farther south or west where there was no detergent on the face of the waters. But it was extremely odd all the same, that she should want to do so.

II

While Fox and Tillottson stooped over footprints on the bank at Crossdyke and Sergeants Bailey and Thompson sped northwards, Alleyn explored the contents of Miss Rickerby-Carrick's cabin.

The passengers were still up at the pub and if Dr Natouche had returned he had not come below. The Tretheways were sitting in a family huddle near the bar. Out in the darkling landscape the Creeper rose stealthily and police constables patrolled the exits from Ramsdyke into the main roads and the tow-path near the *Zodiac*.

The cabin, of course, had been swept out and the berth stripped of its bed-clothes. The Hewsons had made use of it not only for their purchases but for their camera equipment and some of their luggage.

Alleyn found that their cameras – they had three – were loaded with partially used film. They were expensive models, one of them being equipped with a phenomenally powerful lens of the sort used by geologists when recording rock-faces.

Their booty from Tollardwark was bestowed along the floor, most of it in a beer-carton; the prints and scraps had been re-rolled, pretty roughly, into a bundle tied up with the original string.

The painting of Ramsdyke Lock was laid between sheets of newspaper in an empty suitcase.

He took it out and put it on the bunk.

Troy and Caley Bard had made a fairly thorough job of their cleaning and oiling but there were still some signs of dirt caught under the edge of brush strokes, but not, he thought, incorporated in the paint. It was a glowing picture and as Troy had said, it was well-painted. Alleyn was not an expert in picture forgery but he knew that the processes were refined, elaborate and highly scientific, involving in the case of seventeenth-century reproductions the use of specially manufactured pigments, of phenol-formaldehyde and an essential oil, of baking and of old paintings scraped down to the ground layer. With nineteenth-century forgeries these techniques might not be necessary. Alleyn knew that extremely indifferent forgeries had deceived the widows and close associates of celebrated painters and even tolerable authorities. He had heard talk of 'studio sweepings' and arguments that not every casual, unsigned authentic sketch bore the over-all painterly 'signature' of the master. One much-practised trick, of course, was to paint the forgery over an old work. An X-ray would show if this had been done.

Outside, presenting itself for comparison, was the subject of the picture: Ramsdyke Lock, the pond, the ford, the winding lane, the hazy distance. Nothing could be handier, he thought, and he did in fact compare them.

He made an interesting discovery.

The trees in the picture were in the right places, they were elms, they enclosed the middle-distance just as the real elms did in the now darkling landscape outside. Undoubtedly, it was a picture of Ramsdyke Lock.

But they were not precisely the same elms.

The masses of foliage, painted with all the acute observation of Constable's school, were of a different relationship, one to another. Would this merely go to show that, when the picture was painted the trees were a great deal smaller? No, he thought not. These *were* smaller but the major branches sprang from their trunks at different intervals. But might not this be a deliberate alteration made by the artist for reasons of composition? He remembered Troy saying that the painter has as much right to prune or transplant a tree as the clot who had planted it in the wrong place.

All the same . . .

Voices and footfalls on the upper deck announced the return of the passengers. Alleyn restored the painting to its suitcase and the suitcase to its position against the wall. He opened the cabin door, shut his working-kit, took out his pocket-lens, squatted at the head of the bunk and waited.

Not for long. The passengers came below: Mr Lazenby first. He paused, looked in and fluted: 'Busy, Superintendent?'

'Routine, sir.'

'Ah! Routine!' Lazenby playfully echoed. That's what you folk always say, isn't it, Superintendent? Routine!'

'I sometimes think it's all we ever do, Mr Lazenby.'

'Really? Well, I suppose I mustn't ask what it's all about. Poor girl. Poor girl. She was not a happy girl, Mr Alleyn.'

'No?'

'Emotionally unstable. A type that we parsons are all too familiar with, you know. Starved of true, worthwhile relationships, I suspect, and at a difficult, a trying time of life. Poor girl.'

'Do I take it, you believe this to be a case of suicide, Mr Lazenby?'

'I have grave misgivings that it may be so.'

'And the messages received after her death?'

'I don't profess to have any profound knowledge of these matters, Superintendent, but *as* a parson, they *do* come my way. These poor souls can behave very strangely, you know. She might even have arranged the messages, hoping to create a storm of interest in herself.'

'That's a very interesting suggestion, sir.'

'I throw it out,' Mr Lazenby said with a modest gesture, 'for what it's worth. I mustn't be curious,' he added, 'but – you hope to find some – er help – in here? Out of, as it were, Routine?'

'We'd be glad to know whether or not she returned to her cabin during the night,' Alleyn said. 'But, to tell you the truth, there's nothing to show, either way.'

'Well,' said Mr Lazenby, 'good on you, anyhow. I'll leave you to it.'

'Thank you, sir,' Alleyn said, and when Mr Lazenby had gone, whistled, almost inaudibly, the tune of 'Yes, we have no bananas', which for some reason seemed to express his mood.

He was disturbed, almost immediately, by the arrival of the Hewsons and Mr Pollock.

Miss Hewson came first. She checked in the open doorway and looked, as far as an inexpressive face allowed her to do so, absolutely furious. Alleyn rose.

'Pardon *me*. I *had* gotten an impression that this stateroom had been allocated to our personal use,' said Miss Hewson.

Alleyn said he was sure she would find that nothing had been disturbed.

Mr Hewson, looking over his sister's shoulder like a gaunt familiar spirit said he guessed that wasn't the point and Mr Pollock, obscured, could be heard to say something about search-warrants.

Alleyn repeated his story. Without committing himself in so many words he contrived to suggest that his mind was running along the lines of suicide as indicated by Mr Lazenby. He sensed an easing off in antagonism among his hearers. The time had come for what Troy was in the habit of referring to as his unbridled comehithery, which was unfair of Troy. He talked about the Hewsons' find and said his wife had told him it might well prove to be an important Constable.

He said, untruthfully, that he had had no police experience in the realms of art-forgery. He believed, he said, and he had, in fact, been told by a top man, that it was most important for the canvas to be untouched until the experts looked at it. He wasn't sure that his wife and Mr Bard hadn't been naughty to oil the surface.

He would love to see the picture. He said if he could afford it he would be a collector. He had the mania. He gushed.

As soon as he broached the matter of the picture Alleyn was quite sure that the Hewsons did not want him to see it. They listened to him and eyed him and said next to nothing. Mr Pollock, still in the background, hung off and on and could be heard to mutter.

Finally, Alleyn fired point-blank. 'Do show me your "Constable",' he said. 'I'm longing to see it.'

Miss Hewson with every appearance of the deepest reluctance seemed to be about to move into the cabin when her brother suddenly ejaculated –

'Now, isn't this just too bad! Sis, what do you know!'

From the glance she shot at him, Alleyn would have thought that she hadn't the remotest idea what he was driving at. She said nothing.

Mr Hewson turned to Alleyn with a very wide smile.

'Just too bad,' he repeated. 'Just one of those darn' things! It sure would've been a privilege to have your opinion, Superintendent, but you know what? We packaged up that problem picture and mailed it right back to our London address not more'n half an hour before we quit Crossdyke.'

'Did you really? I *am* disappointed,' said Alleyn.

III

'Funny way to carry on,' said Tillottson.

'So funny that I've taken it upon myself to lock the cabin door, keep the key and make sure there is not a duplicate. And if the Hewsons don't fancy that one they can lump it. What's more I'm going to rouse up Mr Jno. Bagg, licensed dealer of Tollardwark. I think you'd better come, too, Bert,' said Alleyn who had arrived at Mr Tillottson's first name by way of Fox.

'*Him!* Why?'

'I'll explain on the way. Warn them at the lock, will you, Bert, to hold anything from the *Zodiac* that's handed in for posting. After all, they could pick that lock. And tell your chaps to watch like lynxes for anything to go overboard. It's too big,' he added, 'for them to shove it down the loo and if they dropped it out of a porthole I think it'd float. But tell your chaps to watch. We'll take your car, shall we?'

They left the mist-shrouded *Zodiac* and drove up the lane through the Constable landscape. When they reached the intersection a policeman on a motorcycle saluted.

'My chap,' Tillottson said.

'Yes. I'm still uneasy, though. You're sure this specimen can't break for the open country and lie doggo?'

'I've got three chaps on the intersections and two down at the lock. No one'll get off that boat tonight: I'll guarantee it.'

'I suppose not. All right. Press on,' Alleyn said.

The evening had begun to close in when they reached Tollardwark and Ferry Lane. They left their car in the Market Square and followed Troy's route downhill to the premises of Jno. Bagg.

'Pretty tumbledown dump,' Tillottson said. 'But he's honest enough as dealers go. Not a local man. Southerner. Previous owner died and this chap Jo Bagg, bought the show as it stood. We've nothing against him in Records. He's a rum character, though, is Jo Bagg.'

The premises consisted of a cottage, a lean-to and a yard, which was partly sheltered by a sort of ramshackle cloister pieced together from scrap iron and linoleum. The yard gate was locked. Through it Alleyn saw copious *disjecta membra* of Mr Bagg's operations. A shop window in the cottage wall dingily faced the lane. It was into this window that Troy had found the Hewsons peering last Monday night.

Tillottson said. 'He'll be in bed as like as not. They go to bed early in these parts.'

'Stir him up,' Alleyn rejoined and jerked at a cord that dangled from a hole near the door. A bell jangled inside. No response. 'Up you get,' Alleyn muttered and jerked again. Tillottson banged on the door.

'If you lads don't want to be given in charge,' bawled a voice within, 'you better 'op it. Go on. Get out of it. I'll murder you one of these nights, see if I don't.'

'It's me, Jo,' Tillottson shouted through the keyhole. 'Tillottson. Police. Spare us a moment, will you?'

'*Who?*'

'Tillottson: Toll'ark Police.'

Silence. A light was turned on somewhere behind the dirty window. They heard shuffling steps and the elaborate unchaining and unbolting of the door which was finally dragged open with a screech to reveal a small, dirty man wearing pyjamas and an unspeakable overcoat.

'What's it all about?' he complained. 'I'm going to bed. What's the idea?'

'We won't keep you, Jo. If we can just come in for half a sec.'

He muttered and stood aside. 'In there, then,' he said and dragged and banged the door shut. 'In the shop.'

They walked into what passed for a shop: a low room crammed to its ceiling and so ill-lit that nothing came out into the open or declared itself in its character of table, hat-rack or mouldering chair. Rather, everything lurked in menacing anonymity and it really was going too far in the macabre for Jno. Bagg to suspend a doll from one of the rafters by a cord round its broken neck.

'This,' said Mr Tillottson, 'is Superintendent Alleyn of the CID, Jo. He wonders if you can help him.'

''Ere,' said Mr Bagg, 'that's a type of remark I never expected to have thrown at me on me own premises. Help the police. We all know what that one leads to.'

'No, you don't, Jo. Listen, Jo – '

Alleyn intervened. 'Mr Bagg,' he said, 'you can take my word for it there is no question of anything being held against you in any way whatever. I'll come to the point at once. We are anxious to trace the origin of a picture which was sold by you yesterday to an American lady and her brother. We have reason to believe – '

'Don't you start making out I'm a fence. Don't you come at that one, mister. Me! A fence – !'

'I don't for one moment suggest you're anything of the sort. Do pay attention like a good chap. I have reason to believe that this picture may have been dumped on your premises and I want to find out if that could be so.'

'Dumped! You joking?'

'Not at all. Now, listen. The picture, as you will remember, was in a bundle of old prints and scraps and the lady found it when she opened the door of a cupboard in your yard. The bundle was rolled up and tied with string and very dirty. It looked as if it hadn't been touched for donkey's years. You told the lady you didn't know you had it and you sold it to her unexamined for ten bob and nobody's complaining or blaming you or suspecting you of anything.'

'Are you telling me,' Mr Bagg said with a change of manner, 'that she struck it lucky? Is that the lay?'

'It may be a valuable painting and it may be a forgery.'

'I'll be damned!'

'Now, all I want to know, and I hope you'll see your way to telling me, is whether, on thinking it over, you can remember seeing the roll of prints in that cupboard before yesterday.'

'What I meantersay, no. No, I can't. No.'

'Had you never opened the cupboard, or sideboard is it, since you bought it?'

'No. I can't say fairer than that, mister, can I? No. Not me, I never.'

'May I look at it?'

He grumbled a little but finally led them out to his yard where the very dregs of his collection mouldered. The sideboard was a vast Edwardian piece executed in pitchpine with the cupboard in the middle. Alleyn tried the door which had warped and only opened to a hard wrench and a screech that compared favourably with that of the front door.

'She was nosey,' Mr Bagg offered. 'Had to open everything she saw. Had a job with that one. Still nothing would do – nosey.'

'And there it was.'

'That's correct, mister. There it was. And there it wasn't if you can understand, three days before.'

'*What?*'

'Which I won't deceive you, mister. While my old woman was looking over the stock out here, Monday, she opened that cupboard and she mentions the same to me when them two Yanks had gone and she says it wasn't there then.'

'Why couldn't you tell us at once, Jo?' Mr Tillottson asked more in resignation than in anger.

'You arst, you know you did, or this gentleman which is all one, arst if *I* never opened the cupboard and I answered truthfully that I never. Now then!'

'All right, Jo, all right. That's all we wanted to know.'

'Not quite,' Alleyn said. 'I wonder, Mr Bagg, if you've any idea of how the bundle could have got there. Have you anybody working for you? A boy?'

'Boy! Don't mention Boy to me. Runaway knockers and ringers, the lot of them. I wouldn't have Boys on me property, not if *they* paid *me*.'

'Is the gate from this yard to the road unlocked during the day?'

'Yes, it is unlocked. To oblige.'

'Have many people been in over the last two days, would you say?'

Not many, it appeared. His customers, as a general rule came into the shop. All the stuff in the yard was of a size or worthlessness that made it unpilferable. It was evident that anybody with a mind to it could wander round the yard without Mr Bagg being aware of their presence. Under persuasion he recalled one or two locals who had drifted in and bought nothing. Alleyn delicately suggested that perhaps Mrs Bagg – ?

'Mrs Bagg,' said Mr Bagg, 'is in bed and asleep which game to rouse her, I am not. No more would you be if you knew how she can shape up.'

'But if your wife – '

'Wife? Do me a favour! She's my mum.'

'Oh.'

As if to confirm the general trend of thought a female voice like a saw screamed from inside the cottage that its owner wanted to know what the hell Mr Bagg thought he was doing creating a nuisance in the middle of the night.

'There you are,' he said. 'Now, see what you done.' He approached a window at the rear of the cottage and tapped on it. 'It's me,' he mumbled. 'It's not the middle of the night, Mum, it's early. It's Mr Tillottson of the Police, Mum, and a gentleman friend. They was inquiring about them Yanks what bought that stuff.'

'I can't hear you. Police! Did you say Police? 'Ere! Come round 'ere this instant-moment, Jo Bagg, and explain yerself: *Police.*'

'I better go,' he said and re-entered the cottage.

'The old lady,' Mr Tillottson said, 'is a wee bit difficult.'

'So it would seem.'

'They make out she's nearly a hundred.'

'But she's got the stamina?'

'My oath!'

The Baggs were in conversation beyond the window but at a subdued level and nothing could be made of it. When Mr Bagg re-emerged he spoke in a whisper.

'Do me a favour, gents,' he whispered. 'Move away.'

They withdrew into the shop and from thence to the front door.

'She's deaf,' Mr Bagg said, 'but there are times when you wouldn't credit it. She don't know anything about nothing but she worked it out that if this picture you mention is a valuable antique it's been taken off us by false pretences and we ought to get it back.'

'Oh.'

'That's the view she takes. And so,' Mr Bagg added loyally, 'do I. Now!'

'I dare say you do,' Mr Tillottson readily conceded. 'Very natural. And she's no ideas about how it got there?'

'No more nor the Holy Saints in Heaven, and she's a Catholic,' Mr Bagg said unexpectedly.

'Well, we'll bid you goodnight, Jo. Unless Mr Alleyn has anything further?'

'Not at the moment, thank you Mr Bagg.'

Mr Bagg wrenched open the front door to the inevitable screech which was at once echoed from the back bedroom.

'You ask them Police,' screamed old Mrs Bagg, 'why they don't do something about them motorbiking Beasts instead of making night hijjus on their own accounts.'

'What motorbiking beasts?' Alleyn suddenly yelled into the darkness.

'You know. And if you don't you ought to. Back-firing up and down the streets at all hours and hanging round up to no good. Jo! Show them out and get to bed.'

'Yes, Mum.'

'And another thing,' invisibly screamed Mrs Bagg. 'What was them two Americans doing nosey-parkering about the place last-week-was a-month-back, taking photers and never letting-on they was the same as before.'

Alleyn set himself to bawl again and thought better of it. 'What does she mean?' he asked Mr Bagg.

'You don't have to notice,' he said. 'But it's correct, all right. They been here before, see, taking photographs and Mum recognized them. She wouldn't have made nothink of it only for suspecting they done us.'

'When were they here? Where did they stay?'

'In the spring. May. Late April: I wouldn't know. But it was them all right. They made out, when I says weren't they here before, they was that taken with the place they come back for more.'

'You're sure about this?'

'Don't be funny,' Mr Bagg said. 'Course I'm sure. This way, for Gawd's sake.'

They went out. Mr Bagg had re-addressed himself to the door when Alleyn said: 'Can you tell us anything about these motor-cyclists?'

'Them? Couple of mods. Staying up at the Star in Chantry Street. Tearing about the country all hours and disturbing people. Tuesday evening Mum 'eard something in our yard and caught the chap nosing round. Looking for old chain he said, but she didn't fancy him. She took against him very strong, did Mum, and anyway we ain't got no old chain. *Chain!*'

'Why,' began Mr Tillottson on a note of anguish, 'didn't you mention – '

'I never give it a thought. You can't think of everything.'

'Nor you can,' Alleyn hurriedly intervened. 'But now you have thought, can you tell us what drew Mrs Bagg's attention to the chap in the yard?'

'Like I said, she 'eard something.'

'What, though?'

'Some sort of screech. I 'eard it too.'

'You did!'

'But I was engaged with a customer,' Mr Bagg said majestically, 'in my shop.'

'Could the screech have been made by the door in the sideboard?'

Mr Bagg peered into Alleyn's face as if into that of an oracle. 'Mister,' he said, 'it not only could but it did.' He took thought and burst into protestation.

'Look,' he said. 'I want an explanation. If I been done I want to know how I been done. If I been in possession of a valuable article and sold this article for a gift without being fully informed I want to get it back, fair and proper. Now.'

They left him discontentedly pursuing this thought but not loudly enough to arouse the curiosity of old Mrs Bagg. The door shrieked and slammed and they heard the bolts shoot home on the inside.

'Star Inn,' Alleyn said as they got in the car but when they reached the inn it was to find that the motorbicyclists had paid their bill the previous evening and set off for an unknown destination. They had registered as Mr and Mrs John Smith.

IV

The motorbicycle had been parked in a dampish yard behind the pub and the tyre-tracks were easy enough to pick up. Alleyn took measurements, made a sketch of the prints and had them covered, pending the arrival of Bailey and Thompson. He thought that when they examined Fox's find under the hedgerow above Crossdyke they would find an exact correspondence. An outside man at the Star remembered the make of vehicle – Route-Rocket – but nobody could give the number.

Alleyn telephoned Troy at the Percy Arms in Norminster and asked her if by any chance she could recall it.

She sat on the edge of her bed with the receiver at her ear and tried to summon up her draughtsman's memory of the scene on the quay at Norminster last Monday morning. Miss Rickerby-Carrick squatted on her suitcase, writing. Caley Bard and Dr Natouche were down by The River. Pollock limped off in a sulk. The Bishop's car was in the lane with Lazenby inside. The two riders lounged against their machine, their oiled heads and black leather gear softly glistening in the sun. She had wanted to draw them, booted legs, easy, insolent pose, gum-chewing faces, gloved hands. And the machine. She screwed her memory to the sticking point, waited and then heard her own voice.

'I think,' said her voice, 'it was XKL-460.'

'Now, there!' Alleyn exclaimed. 'See what a girl I've got! Thank you, my love, and goodnight.' He hung up. 'All right,' he said. 'We set up a general call. They'll be God knows where by now but they've got to be somewhere and by God we'll fetch them in.'

He, Fox and Tillottson were in the superintendent's office at the Tollardwark police station where, on Monday night, Troy had first encountered Mr Tillottson. The sergeant set up the call. In a matter of minutes all divisions throughout the country and all police personnel were alerted for a Route-Rocket, XKL-460, black, with either one or two riders, mod-types, leather clothes, dark, long hair, calf-boots. Retain for questioning and report in.

'And by now,' Fox observed, 'they've repainted their bike, cut their hair and gone into rompers.'

'Always the little sunbeam,' Alleyn muttered, absently. He had covered a table in the office with newspaper and now very carefully they laid upon it an old-fashioned hide suitcase, saturated with river water, blotched, disreputable, with one end of its handle detached from its ring. A length of cord had been firmly knotted through both rings.

'We opened it,' Tillottson said, 'and checked the contents as they lay. We left them for a doing-over and re-closed the lot. You can see what happened. The other end of the cord was secured round her waist. The slack had been passed two or three times under the handle and round the case. When the handle came away at one end the slack paid out and instead of being anchored on the river bed, the body rose to the surface but remained fastened to the weighted case. As it was when we recovered it.'

'Yes,' Alleyn agreed. 'You can see where the turns of rope bit into the leather.'

Fox, who was bent over the cord, said: 'Clothes-line. Did they pinch it or had they got it?' and sighed heavily. 'We'll inquire,' he said.

'They might have had it,' Tillottson said. 'In their kit, you know. Easily they might. Or what-say,' he added, brightening, 'they picked it up in Jo's yard? How's that?'

'That might or might not argue premeditation,' Alleyn said. 'For the moment it can wait. We'd better take another look inside.'

The case was unlocked but fastened with strong old-fashioned hasps and a strap. The saturated leather was slimy to the touch. He opened and laid back the lid.

A jumble of clothes that had been stuffed into the case. Three pairs of shoes which spoke with dreadful eloquence of the feet that had distorted them. A seedy comb and hairbrush with straggles of grey hairs still engaged in them.

'And the whole lot stowed away in a hurry and not by her. No hope of prints, he's a damn' sight too fly for that, but we'll have to try. Hallo, what's here?'

Five stones of varying sizes. A half-brick. Two handfuls of gravel. Underneath all these, a sponge-bag containing a half-empty bottle of aspirins (Troy's, thought Alleyn) a tooth brush and a tube of paste and, in a state of disintegration, Hazel Rickerby-Carrick's 'self-pro-pelling confessional'.

'The diary,' Alleyn said. 'And to misuse a nastily appropriate line: "lift it up tenderly, treat it with care". You never know: it may turn out to be a guide-book.'

CHAPTER 8

Routine Continued

'At this point,' Alleyn said, 'I'm going to jump the gun and show you a photograph of post-mortem marks across the back at waist level and diagonally across the shoulder-blades of the body. Here are her wrists, similarly scarred. These marks were classed as having been inflicted after death. As you see they have all the characteristics of post-mortem scarring. What do they suggest? Yes?'

'The cord, sir,' ventured Carmichael in the second row. 'The cord that attached the bawdy to the suitcase.'

'I'm afraid that's not quite accurate. These grooves are narrow and deep and only appear on the back. Now look at this. That's the cord, laid beside the marks. You can see it tallies. So far you are right, Carmichael. But you see that the higher marks cross each other in the form of an X with a line underneath. Have another shot. What are they?'

From somewhere towards the back a doubtful voice uttered the word 'flagellation' and followed it with an apologetic little cough. Someone else made the noise 'gatcha' upon which there was a muffled guffaw.

'You'll have to do better than that,' Alleyn said. 'However: to press on with Mr Fox's investigations. He found nothing else of interest at the Crossdyke end and moved to the stretch of river below Ramsdyke weir where the body was found. Above Ramsdyke near the hollow called Wapentake Pot, the road from Crossdyke and Tollardwark was undergoing repairs. There were loose stones and rubble. It crosses Dyke Way and Dyke Way leads down to a bridge over The River where the Roman canal joins it. Downstream from here is the weir with its own bridge, a narrow affair with a single handrail. It's here that the effluent from a factory enters the mainstream and brews a great mass of detergent foam over the lower reaches.

'The weir bridge is narrow, green, wet and slithery with foam blown back from the fall. It is approached from the road by concrete steps and a cinder path.

'Along this path, Mr Fox again found a thread or two of dark blue synthetic caught on a bramble. Here's the photograph. And I may tell you that a close search of the pyjamas revealed a triangular gap that matched the fragment from Crossdyke. Classic stuff.

'The path is bordered on one side by a very old wall from which a number of bricks had worked loose.

'Now for the weir bridge. Nearly three days had passed between the night she disappeared and our work on it. A pretty dense film of detergent had been blown back and it was a particularly awkward job to examine it without destroying any evidence there might be. However, there was a notice warning people that it was dangerous to use the bridge and the lock-keeper said he didn't think anyone had been on it for at least a week.

'Mr Fox found some evidence of recent gloved hand-holds on the rail. No prints were obtainable. For a distance of about twelve feet from the bank the actual footway looked to be less thickly encrusted than the remaining stretch of the bridge. Mr Fox reckoned that there was a sort of family resemblance between the appearance of the bridge and the drag over the heel prints on the bank at Crossdyke. Here are Thompson's blow-ups for comparison. You can see how bad, from our point of view, the conditions were on the bridge.

'Now, out of all this, what sort of picture do you begin to get. Yes? All right, Carmichael?'

Carmichael rose, fixed Alleyn with his blue stare and delivered.

'To re-cap, sir,' Carmichael began ominously. 'As a wur-r-r-king hypothesis, it could be argued that the bawdy of the deceased had been passed from the deck of the vessel into the possession of the persons who received it and that it had maybe been drawped and dragged in the process, sir, thus pairtially obleeterating the heel prints. Furthermore it could be reasonably deduced, sir, that the bawdy was transported by means of the motorbike to Ramsdyke where it was conveyed by hand to the weir bridge, dragged some twelve feet along it and consigned to the watter.'

He stopped, cleared his throat and raised his hand: 'As a rider to the above, sir, and proceeding out of it,' he said. 'A suitcase, being the personal property of deceased, and packed with her effects, was removed from her cabin and transferred by the means already detailed, *with* the bawdy, *to* the said weir and there, weighted with stones and gravel and a half-brick, attached to the bawdy by the cord produced. The bawdy and the suitcase were then as detailed consigned to the watter.'

He resumed his seat and gave Alleyn a modest smile.

'Yes, Carmichael, yes,' Alleyn said, 'and what about the post-mortem marks of the cord?'

Carmichael rose again.

'For want of an alternative,' he said with the utmost complacency, 'I would assume as a wurrking premiss, sir, that the deed bawdy was lashed to the person of the cyclist thus rendering the spurious appearance of a pillion-rider.'

'Revolting as the picture you conjure up may be,' Alleyn said. 'I'm afraid you're right, Carmichael.'

'Shall we say *deed* right, sir?' Carmichael suggested with an odiously pawky grin.

'We shall do nothing of the sort, Carmichael. Sit down.'

I

'It's a horrid picture that begins to emerge, isn't it?' Alleyn said as he eased the diary out of the sponge-bag and laid it with elaborate care on a folded towel. 'The body is lashed to the cyclist's back and over it is dragged the dull magenta gown, hiding the cord. The arms are pulled round his waist and the wrists tied. The head, one must suppose, lolls forward on the rider's shoulder.

'And if anyone was abroad in the night on the road from Crossdyke to Ramsdyke they might have seen an antic show: a man on a Route-Rocket with what seemed to be either a very affectionate or a very drunken rider on his pillion: a rider whose head lolled and jerked preposterously and who seemed to be glued to his back.'

'What about the suitcase?' asked Tillottson.

'Made fast. It's not weighted at this stage. The stones were collected at the weir.'

'Roadside heap,' Fox put in. 'Loose brick. Shingle. We've got all that.'

'Exactly, Br'er Fox. Fish out a sponge from my bag, would you?'

Fox did so. Alleyn pressed it over the surfaces of the diary, mopping up the water that seeped out. 'It's when he gets to Ramsdyke,' he went on, 'that the cyclist's toughest job begins. Presumably he's single-handed. He has to dismount, carry his burden, a ghastly pick-a-back, presumably, down to the weir. He unlooses and dumps it, returns for the case, puts in the stones and shingle, humps the case to the body, adds a loose half-brick, ties the body to the case and pushes both of them far enough along the footbridge to topple them into the weir.'

'Do I,' Fox blandly inquired, 'hear the little word conjecture?'

'If you do you can shut up about it. But you don't hear it all that clearly, old boy. Find me another theory that fits the facts and I'll eat the dust.'

'I won't give you the satisfaction, Mr Alleyn.'

'Find something to slide under the diary, will you? I want to turn it over. A stiff card will do. Good. Here we go. Now, the sponge again. Yes. Well, from here, the sinister cyclist and his moll begin to set-up their disappearing act. All we know is that they had paid their bill at the Star and that they lit off some time that night or early next morning. Presumably with a fabulous Fabergé bibelot representing the Signs of the Zodiac in their possession.'

'Hi!' Tillottson ejaculated. 'D'you reckon?'

'This really *is* conjecture,' Alleyn said. 'But I don't mind betting we do *not* find the damned jewel on board the *Zodiac*.'

'River bed? Swept off the body, like?'

'I don't see him leaving it on the body, you know.'

'I suppose not. No.'

'It may have been the motive,' Fox said. 'If it's all that fabulous.'

'Or it may have been a particularly lush extra: a kind of bonus in the general scheme of awards.'

Tillottson said: 'You don't lean to the notion that this cyclist character – '

'Call him Smith,' Fox suggested sourly. 'I'll bet nobody else ever has.'

'This Smith, then. You don't fancy he did the killing?'

'No,' Alleyn said. 'I don't. I think she was killed on board the *Zodiac*. I think the body was handed over to Smith together with the suitcase and probably the Fabergé jewel. Now, dare we take a look inside this diary.'

It had deteriorated since poor Hazel Rickerby-Carrick had examined it after its first immersion. The block of pages had parted company with the spine and had broken into sections. The binding was pulpy and the paper softened.

'Should we dry it out first?' Fox asked.

'I'll try one gingerly fiddle. Got a broadish knife in the station?'

Tillotson produced a bread knife. With infinite caution Alleyn introduced it into the diary at the place where the condition of the edges suggested a division between the much used and still unused sections. He followed the knife blade up with a wider piece of card and finally turned the top section back.

Blotched, mottled, in places blistered and in others torn, it was still for the most part legible.

'Waterproof ink,' Alleyn said. 'God bless the self-propelling pencil.'

And like the writer, when she sat in her cabin on the last day of her life, Alleyn read the final entry in her diary.

'*I'm at it again. Trying too hard, as usual –* '

And like her, having read it, he turned the page and drew a blank.

II

'So there it is,' Alleyn said. 'She writes that she returned from compline at St Crispin-in-the-Fields to the motor-vessel *Zodiac*. She doesn't say by what road but as Troy followed the same procedure and returned by Ferry Lane and did not encounter her, it may be that she took a different route.'

'She could,' Tillottson said. 'Easily. Weyland Street, it'd have to be.'

'All right. She was wearing rubber-sole shoes. At some stage in her return trip she retired into a dark shop-entry to remove a pebble or something from one of her sneakers. From this position, she overheard a conversation between two or more – from the context I would think more – people that, quote, "froze" and "riveted" her. One of the voices, it was a whisper, she failed to identify. The other – or others – she no doubt revealed on the subsequent page which has been torn out of the diary. Now. My wife has told me that after Lazenby rescued the diary she thought she saw, for a fractional moment, paper with writing on it, clutched in his left hand. That evening at Crossdyke, Miss Rickerby-Carrick, who was in a state of violent excitement, intimated that she wanted urgently to confide in Troy, to ask her advice. No doubt she would have done so but Troy got a migraine and instead of exploring Crossdyke went early to bed. Miss R-C. joined the others and inspected the ruins and was shown how to catch butterflies by Caley Bard. Troy, who was feeling better, saw this episode through her porthole.

'She also saw Miss Rickerby-Carrick peel off from the main party, run down the hill and excitedly latch on to Dr. Natouche who was walking down the lane. She seemed to show him something that she held in the palm of her hand. Troy couldn't see what it was.'

'That's interesting,' said Fox.

'Dr Natouche has subsequently told Troy that she asked him about some sort of tranquillizer pill she'd been given by Miss Hewson. He did not, I think, actually say that she showed him this pill when they were in the lane: Troy simply supposes that was what it was.'

'Might it,' Tillottson ventured, 'have been this what-you-call-it – furbished jewel?'

'Fah-ber-zhay,' murmured Mr Fox who spoke French. 'And she wore that round her neck on a cord, Bert.'

'Yes.'

'Well,' Alleyn said, leaving it, 'that night she disappeared and in my opinion, that night, very late, she was murdered.

'The next day, Natouche told Troy he was concerned about Miss Rickerby-Carrick. He didn't say in so many words that he thought she might commit suicide but Troy got the impression that he did in fact fear it.

'I'll round up the rest of the bits and pieces gleaned by my wife, most of which, but I think not all, you have already heard, Tillottson.'

'Er – well – yerse.'

'Here they are, piecemeal. Pollock started life as a commercial artist and changed to real estate. He does a beautiful job of lettering when told exactly what's wanted.

'Natouche makes pretty maps.

'Miss Hewson was shown the Fabergé bibelot by its owner.

'Miss Hewson seems to be very keen on handing out pills.

'The Hewsons were disproportionately annoyed when they heard that the return visit to Tollardwark would be on early-closing day. They hired a car from Longminster to do their shop-crawl in Tollardwark and on that trip bought their stuff at Jo Bagg's in Ferry Lane.

'In their loot was an oil painting, purporting to be a signed Constable. Hewson said they'd posted it on to their address in London but I saw it in one of their suitcases.

'The cyclists watched the *Zodiac* sail from Norminster and re-appeared that evening at Ramsdyke. Troy thought she heard them – but says of course she might be wrong – during the night in Tollardwark.

'Mrs Bagg complains about cyclists hanging round their yard on Tuesday. A screech, as of the cupboard door, attracted her attention.

'The Baggs say the roll of prints was not in the cupboard a few days before the Hewsons found it there.

'Lazenby is a one-eyed man and conceals the condition. Troy, who can give no valid reason, thinks he's not a parson, an opinion that evidently is not shared by the Bishop of Norminster who had him to stay and sent him in the episcopal car to the *Zodiac*. He says he's an Australian. We send his prints and a description to the Australian police. We also send the Hewsons' over to the FB in New York.'

Fox made a note of it.

'The Hewsons,' Alleyn continued, 'are expensively equipped photographers.

'Pollock irritates Caley Bard. Miss Rickerby-Carrick irritates everybody. Caley Bard irritates the Hewsons, Pollock, and possibly, Lazenby.

'Pollock and the Hewsons are racially prejudiced against Natouche. Bard and Lazenby are not.

'A preliminary examination of the body in question supports the theory that she was killed by an attack from behind on the carotids.

'Andropulos would have been a passenger in the *Zodiac* if Foljambe hadn't killed him – by sudden and violent pressure from behind on the carotids.'

Alleyn broke off, stared absently at the diary, waited for a moment and then said: 'Some of these items are certainly of the first importance, others may be of none at all. Taken as a whole do you think they point to any one general conclusion?'

'Yes,' Fox said. 'I do. I certainly do.'

'What?' Tillottson asked.

'Conspiracy.'

'I agree with you,' said Alleyn. 'Between whom?'

'You mean – what's the gang?'

'Yes.'

'Ah. Now.' Fox dragged his great palm across his mouth. 'Why don't we say it?' he asked.

'Say what? That the real question is not only one of conspiracy but of who's running the show? And more particularly: is it the Jampot?'

'That's right. That's it. *Cherchez*,' said Mr Fox with his customary care, '*le Folichon. Ou*,' he added, '*le Pot à Confiture*, which is what they're beginning to call him in the Sûreté.'

'You made your mark, evidently, in Paris.'

'Not so's you'd notice,' Fox said heavily. 'But let it pass. Yes, Mr Alleyn. I reckon it's the Jampot on this job.'

'Why,' Tillottson asked, 'are you so sure, Teddy?'

'Well, take a look at it, Bert. Take a look at the lot Mr Alleyn's just handed us. Three items point to it, you know, now don't they?'

'Yerse,' Mr Tillottson concurred after a long pause. 'I get you. Yerse.'

Alleyn was bent over the diary. His long forefinger touched the rag of paper that was the remnant of the last entry. He slipped his nail under it and disclosed another and then another torn marginal strip still caught in the binding. 'Three pages gone,' he said, 'and it's not unreasonable to suppose they would have told us what she overheard from her dark entry in Tollardwark. Wrenched out in a hurry, and, I suppose, either burnt or thrown overboard. The latter almost certainly. They were wet and pulpy. Torn out whether purposely or accidentally, and into The River with *them*.'

'That'll be the story,' Fox agreed heavily. 'And the inference is – by Lazenby.'

'*If* Troy's right. She's not certain.'

Mr Tillottson who had been in a hard, abstracted stare since his last utterance now said: 'So it's a field of five – six if you count the Skipper and that'd be plain ridiculous. I've known Jim Tretheway these five years, decent wee man.'

'He's not all that wee,' Fox said mildly.

'The Doctor, Mr Bard, Mr Hewson, the Reverend and Pollock. And if you're right one of them's the toughest proposition in what they call the international crime world. You wouldn't credit it, though, would you? Here!' Mr Tillottson said, struck by a new thought. 'You wouldn't entertain the idea of the whole boiling being in cahoots, would you? If so: why? Why go river-cruising if they're a pack of villains in a great big international racket. Not for kicks you'd think, now, would you?'

'Of the lot that remains on board, excluding the Tretheways,' Alleyn said, 'I incline to think there's only one non-villain. I'll give you my reasons, such as they are, and I fully admit they wouldn't take first prize in the inescapable logic stakes. But still. Here they are.'

His colleagues listened in massive silence. Fox sighed heavily when he had finished. 'And that,' he said, 'followed out, leaves us with only one guess for the identity of the Jampot. Or does it?'

'I think it does. If, if, if and it's a hell of a big if.'

'I'll back it,' Fox said. 'What's our next bit of toil.'

'We don't wait for the report on the PM. I think, Br'er Fox, we cut in and use our search-warrant. What's the time? Five past nine. If they've gone to bed it's just too bad. Back to Ramsdyke Lock with us. Did you pick up a bit of nosh, by the way?'

'Pickle and beef sandwiches and a couple of half-pints.'

'We'll sink them on the trip. Hark bloody forrard away.'

III

If events do, as some would have us believe, stamp an intangible print upon their surroundings, this phenomenon is not instantaneous. Murder doesn't scream instantly from the walls of a room that may be drenched in blood. Clean the room up and it is just a room again. If violence of behaviour or of emotion does, in fact, project itself upon its immediate surroundings, like light upon photographic film, the process seems to be cumulative rather than immediate. It may be a long time after the event that people begin to think: this is an unhappy house. Or room. Or place. Or craft.

The saloon in that most pleasant of water-wanderers, the *Zodiac*, wore its usual after-dark aspect. Its cherry-coloured window-curtains were drawn and its lamps were lit. It was cosy. The more so, perhaps, because the river mist known as the Creeper had now shut the craft off from her surroundings.

The six remaining passengers occupied themselves in much the same way as they had done before Hazel Rickerby-Carrick disappeared in the night. The Hewsons, Mr Lazenby and Mr Pollock played Scrabble. Caley Bard read. Dr Natouche, a little removed, as always, put some finishing touches to his map of the The River. Behind the bar, Mrs Tretheway read a magazine. The Skipper was ashore and the boy Tom was in bed.

Troy's Zodiac picture with its vivid impersonations of the passengers was now framed and had replaced its begetter above the bar. There they all were, preposterously masquerading as Heavenly bodies, skipping round Mr Pollock's impeccable lettering.

The Hunt of the Heavenly Host begins
With the Ram, the Bull and the Heavenly Twins.
The Crab is followed by the Lion
The Virgin and the Scales,
The Scorpion, Archer and He-Goat,
The Man that carries the Watering-pot
And the Fish with the Glittering Tails.

The Virgin was gone for good and the Goat, as Troy had thought of herself, was removed to Norminster but there, Alleyn thought, were all the others, mildly employed, with a killer and a single detached person among them.

When Alleyn and Fox arrived in the saloon, the Scrabble players became quieter still. Miss Hewson's forefinger, pushing a lettered tile into place, stopped and remained, pointed down, like an admonitory digit on a monument. Pollock's head, bent over the Scrabble-board, was not raised though his eyes were and looked at Alleyn from under his brows, showing rims of white. Lazenby, who had been attending to the score, let his pencil remain in suspended action. Hewson, pipe gripped in teeth, held the head of a match against the box but did not strike it.

For a few seconds this picture was presented like an unheralded still at the cinema; then it animated as if there had been no hitch in its mild progression.

'I'm sorry,' Alleyn said, 'that we have to make nuisances of ourselves again but there it is. In police work it's a case of set a nuisance to catch a nuisance.'

'Well!' Caley Bard ejaculated. 'I must say that as reassuring remarks go, I don't think much of that one. If it was meant to reassure.'

'It was meant as a sort of apology,' Alleyn said, 'but I see your point. Please don't let us disturb anybody. We've come to tidy up a loose end of routine and I'm afraid we shall have to ask you all to be very patient and stay out of your cabins until we've done so. We won't be long about it, I hope.'

After a considerable silence Mr Hewson predictably said: 'Yeah?' and leant back in his chair with his thumbs in the arm-holes of his waistcoat. He turned his left ear with its hearing-aid towards Alleyn.

'Stay out of our cabins,' he quoted with what seemed to be intended as a parody of Alleyn's voice. 'Is that so? Now, would that be a kind of polite indication of a search, Superintendent?'

'I'm glad it sounded polite,' Alleyn rejoined cheerfully. 'Yes. It would.'

'You got a warrant?' Pollock asked.

'Yes, indeed. Would you like to see it?'

'Of course we don't want to see it,' Caley Bard wearily interjected. 'Don't be an ass, Pollock.'

Pollock muttered: 'I'm within my rights, aren't I?'

Alleyn said: 'Miss Hewson, I'll start with your cabin, if that suits you, and as soon as I've finished, you will be free to use it. At the same time Inspector Fox will take a look at yours, Mr Hewson.'

'A second look,' Mr Hewson sourly amended.

'That's right,' Alleyn said. 'So it is. A formality, you might call it.'

'You might,' Mr Hewson conceded. 'I wouldn't.'

Miss Hewson said: 'Gee, Earl, if I hadn't clean forgotten! Gee, how crazy can you get? Look, Mr Alleyn: look, Superintendent, I got to "fess up" right now, about that problem-picture. There's been a kind of misunderstanding between Brother and me. *He* calculated *I'd* sent it off and *I* calculated *he* had.'

'Just the darndest thing,' Mr Hewson put in with a savage glance at his sister.

'Certainly is,' she agreed. 'And so what do you know? There it is just exactly where it's been all this time. In the bottom of a grip in my stateroom.'

'Fancy,' said Alleyn. 'I shall enjoy taking a second look. Last time I saw it, it was in an otherwise empty case in the deceased's cabin, which, by the way, I locked.'

A fairly long silence was decorated with a stifled giggle from Caley Bard.

Miss Hewson said breathlessly: 'Well, pardon me, again. I guess I'm kind of nervously exhausted. I meant to say the spare cabin.'

Mr Hewson said angrily, 'OK. OK. So it wasn't posted. So we acted like it was. Why? I'll tell you precisely why, Superintendent. This picture's a work of art. Ask your lady-wife. And this work of art maybe was executed by this guy Constable which would make it a very, very interesting proposition commercially. And we paid out real money, real British money, if that's not a contradiction in terms, for this work of art and we don't appreciate the idea of having it removed from our possession by anybody. Repeat: anybody. Period. Cops or whoever. Period. So whadda-we-do?' Mr Hewson asked at large and answered himself with perhaps a slight loss of countenance. 'We anticipate,' he said, 'the event. We make like this picture's already on its way.'

'And so I'm sure it would be,' Alleyn said cheerfully, 'if it wasn't for a large and conspicuous constable on duty outside the Ramsdyke Lock post-office.'

Mr Hewson's face became slightly pink but his gaze which was directed at Alleyn did not shift. His sister coughed with refinement, said: 'Pardon me,' and looked terrified.

'You can't win,' Mr Pollock observed to nobody in particular and added after a moment's reflection: 'It's disgusting.'

'If we're not going to keep you up till all hours,' Alleyn said, 'we'd better begin. Anybody really want to see the search-warrant, by the way?'

'I certainly do,' Mr Hewson announced. 'It may be a very crude notion but I certainly do want that thing.'

'But not at all,' Alleyn rejoined. 'Very sensible of you. Here it is.'

Fox displayed the warrant and the Hewsons and Mr Pollock looked upon it with distaste. Mr Lazenby said generally that it was a fair go and he had no complaints. Caley Bard tipped Alleyn one of his cock-eyed winks but offered no comment and Dr Natouche interrupted his work on the map to produce the key of his cabin and lay it on the table. This action seemed to rattle everybody but Caley Bard who merely remarked that his own cabin was unlocked.

'Thank you so much,' Alleyn said. 'We do carry one or two of those open-sesame jobs but this will be quicker.' He picked up the key. 'Any more?' he asked.

'You know something?' Mr Hewson said. 'If you hadn't gotten those other honest-to-God cops around I'd say you were some kind of phoney laugh with the pay-off line left out.'

'You would?' Alleyn said absently. 'Sorry. There's no joke anywhere that I can see, I promise you that.'

It turned out that the only other locked cabin apart from Natouche's and the Hewsons' was Mr Pollock's. He handed over his key with as bad a grace as he could muster, turned his back on the company and sucked his teeth.

Before he left, Alleyn walked over to the corner table where Dr Natouche still concerned himself with his map of the waterways. He drew back, rested his dark hands and looked placidly at what he had done. 'I am an amateur of maps,' he said, perhaps by way of excuse.

If this was a true example of his work he was right. The chart with its little tentative insets and its meticulous lettering was indeed the work of a devoted amateur. It was so fine and so detailed that it almost needed a lens to examine it. Alleyn followed the line of The River to Longminster. There he saw, predictably, the Minster itself but there, too, was an inn-sign and beside it a thin, gallant and carefully drawn female figure with a dark cropped head.

He looked down at Dr Natouche's head with its own short-cropped fuzz and at the darkish scalp beneath. The two men did not speak to each other.

Alleyn and Fox embarked on their search.

They found the 'Constable' still in place, took possession of it, moved into Miss Hewson's cabin and methodically emptied the drawers and luggage.

'Funny,' Mr Fox remarked, laying out a rather dreary nightgown with infinite care upon Miss Hewson's bed. 'I always expect American ladies' lingerie to be more *troublante* than this type of stuff.'

Alleyn stared at him. 'I am speechless,' he said.

'Why do you make out they were so anxious we wouldn't get a look at that picture?'

'You tell me.'

'Well,' Fox said. 'I've been trying to set up a working theory. Suppose it was all on the level. Suppose this picture was in the cupboard when this Jo Bagg bought the sideboard.'

'Which it wasn't, if his story's right.'

'Quite so. Suppose, then, it'd been on the premises and somebody shoved it in the cupboard and the Baggs hadn't taken any notice of it and suppose the Hewsons just happened to pick it up like they said and pay for it all fair and above board. In that case what's wrong with letting us have a look at it? They showed it off willingly enough last night, by all accounts. *He* kind of hinted they were afraid we might confiscate. They *may* have been looking at British telly exports in the States, of course, and taken some fanciful notion of how we go to work but personally I didn't think their yarn stood up.'

'I agree. Playing it by ear, they were, I don't mind betting.'

'All right, then. Why? People only go on in that style because they've got something to hide. What would they have to hide about this picture? I can only think of one answer. What about you, Mr Alleyn?'

'That it's a racket and they're in on it.'

'Just so. The thing's a forgery and they know it. From that it's a short step to supposing Jo Bagg never had it. The Hewsons brought it with them and planted it in the cupboard when the Baggs weren't looking.'

'I don't think so, Br'er Fox. Not from the account Bagg gave of the sale.'

'No? I wasn't there, of course, when he gave it,' Fox admitted.

'How do you like the possibility of the motorcyclists planting it? They were hanging about Bagg's yard on Tuesday and the screech of the cupboard door seems to have drawn old Mrs B.'s baleful attention to them.'

'Could be. Could well be. Come to that, they might be salting the district with carefully planted forgeries.'

'They might, at that. Look at these, Fox.'

Alleyn had drawn out of a pocket in Miss Hewson's dressing-case, a folder of colour photographs and film. He laid the prints out on the lid of the suitcase. Three of them were of Ramsdyke Lock. He put the painting on the deck beside them.

'Same thing,' Fox said.

'Yes. Taken from precisely the same spot and by the look of the trees, in spring. Presumably on the previous visit that old Mrs Bagg went on about. But look. There's that difference we noticed.'

'The trees. Yes. Yes. In the painting they're smaller and – well – different.'

'Very thorough. Wouldn't do, you see, to have them as they are now. They had to go back to the Constable era. I wouldn't mind betting,' Alleyn said. 'That those trees have been copied from an actual Constable or a reproduction of one.'

'Who by?'

Alleyn didn't reply at once. He restored the photographs to the dressing-case and after another long look at the picture, rolled it carefully and tied it up. 'We'll take possession of this,' he said, 'and thus justify the Hewsons' worst forebodings. I'll write a receipt. Everything in order here? We'll move on, Br'er Fox, to the other locked cabin: I simply can't wait to call, in his absence, on Mr Pollock.'

IV

Thompson and Bailey had arrived. They went quietly round the cabins collecting prints from tooth glasses and were then to move to the sites of the motorbicycle traces. Tillottson was in his station in Tollardwark hoping for news of the cyclists and, optimistically, for reports from America and Australia to come through London. Meanwhile the appropriate department was setting up an exhaustive check on the deceased and on the two passengers, Natouche and Caley Bard, who lived in England. Caley had given a London address and his occupation as: 'Crammer of ill-digested raw-material into the maws of unwilling adolescents.' In other words, he was a freelance coach to a tutorial firm of considerable repute.

Troy was in bed and asleep at the Percy Arms in Norminster and Alleyn and Fox had completed their search of the cabins.

'A poor, thin time we've had of it,' Alleyn said. 'Except for that one small thing.'

'The Pollock exhibit?'

'That's right.'

In Mr Pollock's cabin they had found in the breast pocket of his deplorable suit a plastic wallet containing a print of the Hewson photograph of Ramsdyke Lock and several envelopes displaying trial sketches for the words with which he had subsequently embellished Troy's picture. He had evidently taken a lot of trouble over them, interrupting himself from time to time to doodle. It was his doodling that Alleyn had found interesting.

'Very neat, very detailed, very meticulous,' he had muttered. 'Not the doodles of a non-draughtsman. No. I wonder what the psychiatric experts have to say under this heading. Someone ought to write a monograph: "Doodling and the Unconscious" or: "How to – ".' And he had broken off in the middle of the sentence to stare at the last of Mr Pollock's trial efforts. He held it out to Fox to examine.

'The Crab is Followed – ' Mr Pollock had printed and then repeated, with slight changes, several of the letters. But down one side of the envelope he had made a really elaborate doodle.

It was a drawing of a tree, for all the world twin to the elm that overhung the village pond in Miss Hewson's oil painting.

'Very careless,' Alleyn had said as he put it in his pocket. 'I'm surprised at him.'

When they returned to the saloon they found the Hewsons, and Mr Pollock and Mr Lazenby, still up and still playing Scrabble. Caley Bard and Dr Natouche were reading. Mrs Tretheway had gone to bed.

Bailey and Thompson passed through, carrying their gear. The passengers watched them in silence.

When they had gone Alleyn said: 'We've done our stuff down there and the cabins are all yours. I'm very sorry if we've kept you up too late. Here are the keys.' He laid them on the table. 'And here,' he said, holding up the rolled canvas, 'is your picture, Miss Hewson. We would like to take charge of it for a short time, if you please. I'll give you this receipt. I assure you the canvas will come to no harm.'

Miss Hewson had turned, as Fox liked to say, as white as a turnip and really her skin did have something of the aspect of that unlovely root. She looked from Alleyn to her brother and then wildly round the group of passengers as if appealing against some terrible decision. She rose to her feet, pulled at her underlip with uncertain fingers and had actually made a curious little whining sound when her brother said: 'Take it easy, Sis. You don't have to act this way. It's OK: take it easy.'

Mr Hewson had very large, pale hands. Alleyn saw his left hand clench and his right hand close round his sister's forearm. She gave a short cry of pain, sank back in her chair and shot what seemed to be a look of terror at her brother.

'My sister's a super-sensitive girl, Superintendent,' Mr Hewson said. 'She gets nervous very, very easy.'

'I hope there is no occasion for her to do so now,' Alleyn said. 'I understand this is not your first visit to this district, Mr Hewson. You were here in the spring, weren't you?'

Dr Natouche lowered his book and for the first time seemed to listen to what was being said; Caley Bard gave an exclamation of surprise. Miss Hewson mouthed inaudibly and fingered her arm and Mr Lazenby said, 'Really? Is that so? Your second visit to The River? I didn't realize,' as if they were all making polite conversation.

'That is so,' Mr Hewson said. 'A flying visit. We were captivated and settled to return.'

'When did you book your passages in the *Zodiac*?' Alleyn asked.

A silence, broken at last by Mr Hewson.

'Pardon me, I should have put that a little differently, I guess. We made our reservations before we left the States. I should have said we were enchanted to learn when we got here that the *Zodiac* cruise would cover this same territory.'

'On your previous visit, did you take many photographs?'

'Some. Yes, sir: quite some.'

'Including several shots here at Ramsdyke, of exactly the same subject as the one in this picture?'

Mr Hewson said: 'Maybe. I wouldn't remember off hand. We certainly do get around to taking plenty of pictures.'

'Have you seen this particular photograph, Mr Pollock?'

Mr Pollock lounged back in his seat, put his hands in his trouser pockets and assumed a look of cagey impertinence with which Alleyn was very familiar.

'Couldn't say, I'm sure,' he said.

'Surely you'd remember. The photograph that is taken from the same place as the painting?'

'Haven't the vaguest.'

'You mean you haven't seen it?'

'Know what?' Mr Pollock said. 'I don't get all this stuff about photos. It doesn't mean a thing to me. It's silly.'

Mr Pollock's tree doodle and the Hewsons' photograph of Ramsdyke Lock dropped on the table in front of him.

'These were in the pocket of your suit.'

'What of it?'

'The drawing is a replica of a tree in the painting.'

'Fancy that.'

'When did you make this drawing?'

For the first time he hesitated but said at last. 'After I seen the picture. It's kind of recollection. I was doodling.'

'While you practised your lettering?'

'That's right. *No!*' he said quickly. 'After.'

'It would have to be after, wouldn't it? Because you'd done the lettering on the Zodiac drawing before you saw the picture. A day or more before. Hadn't you?'

'That's your idea: I didn't say so.'

'Mr Pollock: I suggest that your first answer is the true one. I suggest that you did in fact "doodle" this very accurate drawing when you were practising your lettering a couple of days ago and that you did it, subconsciously or not, out of your knowledge of the picture. Your very vivid and accurate recollection of the picture with which you were already as familiar as if – ' Alleyn paused. Mr Pollock had gone very still. ' – as if you yourself had painted it,' said Alleyn.

Dr Natouche rose, murmured, 'Excuse me, please,' and went up on deck.

'You don't have to insult me,' Pollock said, 'in front of that nigger.'

Caley Bard walked over and looked at him as if he was something nasty he'd caught in his butterfly net.

'You *bloody* little tit,' he said. 'Will you shut up, you perfectly bloody little tit?'

Pollock stared at him with a kind of shrinking defiance that was extremely unpleasant to see.

'Sorry,' Caley said to Alleyn and returned to his seat.

' – as if you yourself had painted it,' Alleyn repeated. 'Did you paint it, Mr Pollock?'

'No. And that's it. No.'

And that *was* it as far as Mr Pollock was concerned. He might have gone stone deaf and blind for all the response he made to anything else that was said to him.

'It's very hot in here,' said Mr Lazenby.

It was indeed. The summer night had grown sultry. There were rumours of thunder in the air and sheet-lightning made occasional irrelevant gestures somewhere a long way beyond Norminster.

Mr Lazenby pulled the curtain back from one of the windows and exposed a white blank. The Creeper had risen.

'Very close,' Mr Lazenby said and ran his finger under his dog-collar. 'I think,' said he in his slightly parsonic, slightly Australian accents, 'that we're entitled to an explanation, Superintendent. We've all experienced a big shock, you know. We've found ourselves alongside a terrible tragedy in the death and subsequent discovery of this poor girl. I'm sure there's not one of us doesn't want to see the whole thing cleared up and settled. If you reckon all this business about a painting picked up in a yard has something to do with the death of the poor girl, well: good on you. Go ahead. But, fair dinkum. I don't myself see how there can be the remotest connection.'

'With which observation,' Mr Hewson said loudly, 'I certainly concur. Yes, *sir*.'

'The connection,' Alleyn said, 'if there is one, will I hope declare itself as the investigation develops. In the meantime, if you don't mind, we'll push along with preliminaries. Will you cast your minds back to Monday night when you all explored Toll'ark?'

The group at the table eyed him warily. From behind his book Caley said: 'OK. I've cast mine, such as it is, back.'

'Good. What did you do in Toll'ark?'

'Thwarted of my original intention which was to ask your wife if she'd explore the antiquities with me, I sat in the Northumberland Arms drinking mild-and-bitter and listening to the dullest brand of Mummerset-type gossip it would be possible to conceive. When the pub closed I returned, more pensive than pickled, to our gallant craft.'

'By which route?'

'By a precipitous, rather smelly and cobbled alley laughingly called Something Street – wait – It was on a shop wall. I've got it. Weyland Street.'

'Meet any of the other passengers?'

'I don't think so. Did we?' Caley asked them.

They slightly shook their heads.

'You, Mr Lazenby, attended compline in the church. Did you return alone to the *Zodiac*?'

'No,' he said easily. 'Not all the way. I ran into Stan and we went back together. Didn't we, Stan?'

Mr Pollock, answering to his first name, nodded glumly.

'We know that Mr and Miss Hewson, followed by my wife and then by Dr Natouche returned to The River by way of Ferry Lane where they all met, outside Bagg's second-hand premises. We also know,' Alleyn said, 'that Miss Rickerby-Carrick returned alone, presumably not by Ferry Lane. As Weyland Street is the only other direct road down to The River it seems probable that she took that way home. Did either of you see her?'

'No,' Pollock said instantly and very loudly.

'No,' Lazenby agreed.

'Mr Lazenby,' Alleyn said, taking a sudden and outrageous risk, 'what did you do with the papers you tore out of Miss Rickerby-Carrick's diary?'

A gust of misted air moved the curtain over an open window on the starboard side and the trees above Ramsdyke Lock soughed and were silent again.

'I don't think that's a very nice way of talking,' said Mr Lazenby.

Miss Hewson had begun quietly to cry.

'There are ways and ways of putting things,' Mr Lazenby continued, 'and that way was offensive.'

'Why?' Alleyn asked. 'Do you say you didn't tear them out?'

'By a mishap, I may have done something of the sort. Naturally. I rescued the diary from a watery grave,' he said, attempting some kind of irony.

'Which was more than anybody did for its owner,' Caley Bard remarked. They looked at him with consternation.

'It was a very, very prompt and praiseworthy undertaking,' said Mr Hewson stuffily. 'She was very, very grateful to the Reverend. It was the Action of a Man. Yes, sir. A Man.'

'As we could see for ourselves,' Caley remarked and bowed slightly to Mr Lazenby.

'It was nothing, really,' Mr Lazenby protested. 'I'm a Sydneysider, don't forget and I *was* in my bathers.'

'As I have already indicated,' Caley said.

'The pages,' Alleyn said, 'were in your left hand when you sat on the bank just before the *Zodiac* picked you up. You had turned the leaves of the diary over while you waited.'

Mr Pollock broke his self-imposed silence. 'Anybody like to make a guess where all this information came from?' he asked. 'Marvellous, isn't it? Quite a family affair.'

'Shut up,' Caley said and turned to Alleyn. 'You're right, of course, about this. I remember – I expect we all do – that the Padre had got a loose page in his hand. But, Alleyn, I do think there's a very obvious explanation – the one that he has in fact given you. The damn' diary was soaked to a sop and probably disintegrated in his hands.'

'It's not in quite as bad shape as that.'

'Well – all right. But it *had* opened in the water, you know. And when he grabbed it, surely he might have loosened a couple of pages or more.'

'But,' Alleyn said mildly, 'I haven't for a moment suggested anything else. I only asked Mr Lazenby what he did with the loose page or pages.'

'Mr Bard is right. I did not tear them out. They came out.'

'Cometer pieces in 'is 'ands, like,' Caley explained.

'Very funny,' said Mr Pollock. 'I don't think.'

'I do not know,' Mr Lazenby announced with hauteur, 'what I did with any pieces of pulpy paper that may or may not have come away in my hand. I remember nothing about it.'

'Did you read them?'

'That suggestion, Superintendent, is unworthy of you.'

Alleyn said: 'Last Monday night on your way to the *Zodiac* you and Mr Pollock stopped near a dark entry in Weyland Street. What did you talk about?'

And now, he saw with satisfaction, they were unmistakably rattled. 'They're asking themselves,' he thought, 'just how much I am bluffing. They know Troy couldn't have told me about this one. They're asking themselves where I could have picked it up and the only answer is the Rickerby-Carrick diary. I'll stake my oath, Lazenby read whatever was on the missing pages and Pollock knows about it. What's more they probably know the diary was in the suit-case and that we must have seen it. They're dead scared we've found something which I wish to hell we had. If they're as fly as I believe they are, there's only one line for them to take and I hope they don't take it.'

They took it, however. 'I'm not making any more bloody state-ments,' Mr Pollock suddenly shouted, 'till I've seen a lawyer and that's my advice to all and sundry.'

'Dead right,' Mr Lazenby applauded. 'Good on you.' And feeling perhaps that his style was inappropriate, he added, 'We shall be absolutely within our rights to adopt this attitude. In my opinion it is entirely proper for us to do so.'

'Reverend Lazenby,' Mr Hewson said with fervour, 'you said it. Boy, you certainly said it.'

Miss Hewson, who had been furtively dabbing at her eyes and nose gave a shatteringly profound sob.

'Ah, for Pete's sake, Sis,' said Hewson.

'No! No! No!' she cried out on a note of real terror. 'Don't touch me. I'm not staying here. I'm going to my room. I'm going to bed.'

'Do,' Alleyn said politely. 'Why not take one of your own pills?'

She caught her breath, stared at him and then blundered down the companion-way to the lower deck.

'Poor girl,' said Mr Lazenby. 'Poor dear girl.'

'There's one other question,' Alleyn said. 'In view of your decision of a moment ago you may not feel inclined to answer it. Unless –?' he smiled at Caley Bard.

'At the moment,' Caley said, 'I'm not sending for my solicitor or taking vows of silence.'

'Good. Well, then, here it is. Miss Rickerby-Carrick wore on a cord round her neck, an extremely valuable jewel. She told Miss Hewson and my wife about it. It has not been found.'

'Washed off ?' Caley suggested.

'Possible, of course. If necessary we'll search the river bed.'

Caley thought for a moment. 'Look,' he then said. 'She was a pretty scatty individual. I gather she was sleeping on deck or trying to sleep. She said she suffered from insomnia. My God, if she did it was fully orchestrated but that's by the way. Suppose in the dead of night she *was* awake and suppose she took a hike along the tow-path in her navy pi-jams and her magenta gown with her bit of Fabergé tat around her neck? Grotesque it may sound but it would be entirely in character.'

'How,' Alleyn said, 'do you know it was Fabergé, Mr Bard?'

'Because, for God's sake, she told me. When we thundered about the Crossdyke ruins, butterfly hunting. I dare say she told everybody. She was scatty as a hen, poor wretch.'

'Well?'

'Well, and suppose she met an unsavoury character who grabbed the bauble and when she cut up rough, throttled her and shoved her in the river?'

'First collecting her suitcase from her cabin in the Zodiac?'

'Damn!' said Caley. 'You would bring that up wouldn't you.'

'All the same,' Alleyn said, turning to the group round the table, 'we can't overlook the possibility of interference of some sort from outside.'

'Like who?' Hewson demanded.

'Like, for instance, a motorcyclist and his girl who seem to have rather haunted the course of the *Zodiac*. Do you all know who I mean?'

Silence.

'Oh *really*!' Caley exclaimed, 'this is too much! Of course we all know who you mean. They've turned up from time to time like prologues to the omens coming on in an early Cocteau film.' He addressed his fellow-passengers. 'We've seen them, we've remarked upon them, why the hell shouldn't we say so?'

They stirred uneasily. Lazenby said: 'You're right, of course, Mr Bard. No reason at all. A couple of young mods – we used to call them bodgies in Aussie – with I dare say no harm in them. They seem to be cobbers of young Tom's.'

'Have any of you ever spoken to them?'

Nobody answered.

'You better ask the coloured gentleman,' Hewson said and Alleyn thought he heard a note of fear in his voice.

'Dr Natouche has spoken to them, you think?'

'I don't think. I know. The first day when we went through the lock here. They were on the bridge and he came down the road from this helluva whatsit in the hillside. These two hobos shouted something and he walked up to them and said something and they kinda laughed and kicked up their machine and roared off.'

'Where were you?'

'Me? Walking up the hill with the mob.'

Hewson shifted his position slightly and continued, with considerable finesse, to emphasize the already richly offensive tone of his behaviour. 'Mrs Alleyn,' he said, 'was in the whatsit with the deceased. She'd been there for quite some time before the deceased got there. So'd he. Natouche. Yes, sir. Quite some time.'

This was said so objectionably that Alleyn felt the short hair rise on the back of his scalp. Fox, who had performed his usual trick of making his bulk inconspicuous while he took notes, let out a slight exclamation and at once stifled it.

Hewson, after a look at Alleyn's face said in a great hurry: 'Don't get me wrong. Take it easy. Hell, Superintendent, I didn't mean a thing.'

Alleyn raised his eyebrows at Fox who soundlessly formed the word 'Tom?' and went below. Alleyn climbed the companion-way leading to the upper deck and looked over the half-door. Dr Natouche leant on the port taffrail. He was wreathed in mist. His hands were clasped and his head bent as if he stared at them.

'Dr Natouche, can I trouble you again for a moment?'

'Certainly. Shall I come down?'

'If you please.'

When he had come down, blinking a little in the light, Alleyn, watching Pollock and the Hewsons and Lazenby, was reminded of Troy's first letter. These passengers, she had written, eyed Natouche with something that seemed very like fear.

He asked Natouche what had passed between him and the motorcyclists. He waited for a moment or two and then said the young man had asked him if he was a passenger in the *Zodiac*. He thought from his manner that the question was intended as a covert insult of some sort, Dr Natouche said tranquilly, but he had answered that he was and the girl had burst out laughing.

'I walked away,' he said, 'and the young man gave one of those cries – I think they are known as catcalls. It was not an unusual incident.'

'Can you remember them clearly? They sound sufficiently objectionable to be remembered.'

'They were dressed in black leather. The man was rather older than one expected. They both had long, very dark hair falling from their helmets to their shoulders. The man's hair was oily. He had a broad face, small, deep-set eyes and a slightly prognathic jaw. The girl was sallow. She had large eyes and an outbreak of acne on her chin.'

Pollock made his standard remark. 'Isn't it marvellous?' and gave his little sneering laugh.

'Thank you,' Alleyn said. 'That's very useful.'

Pollock now took action. He got up from the table, lounged across the saloon and stood with his hands in his pockets and his head on one side, quite close to Natouche.

''Ere,' he said. 'You! "Doctor". What's the big idea?'

'I don't understand you. I'm sorry.'

'You don't? I think you do. I see you talking to the ton-up combo and I never took the impression they was slinging off at you. I think that's just your story like you lot always trot out: "Oh, dear, aren't they all insultin' to us noble martyrs". I took a different impression. I took the impression you knew them two before. See?'

'You are mistaken.'

Alleyn said: 'Did anyone else get such an impression?'

Hewson said: 'Yeah, I guess I did. Yeah, sure I did.'

'Mr Lazenby?'

'I'm very loath to jump to conclusions. I'm not prepared to say positively. I must confess – '

'Well?'

'We were some way away, Superintendent, on the wapentake slope. I don't think an impression at that distance has much value. But – well, yes I thought – vaguely, you know – that perhaps the Doctor had found some friends. Only a vague idea.'

'Mr Bard? What about you?'

Caley Bard drove his fingers through his hair and swore under his breath. He then said 'I agree that any impression one may have taken at that remove is absolutely valueless. We could hear nothing that was said. Dr Natouche's explanation fits as well as any other.'

'If he never seen them before how's he remember all this stuff about jaws and pimples?' Pollock demanded. 'After half a minute! Not likely!'

'But I fancy,' Alleyn said, 'that in common with all the rest of you, Dr Natouche had ample opportunity to observe them at Norminster on the morning you embarked.'

'Here!' Pollock shouted. 'What price this for a theory? What price him and them knocked it up between them? What price they did the clobbering and he handled the suitcase? Now then!'

He stared in front of him, sneering vaingloriously and contriving at the same time to look frightened. Natouche's face was closed like a wall.

'I thought,' Caley said to Pollock, 'you'd settled to keep your mouth shut until you got a solicitor. Why the devil can't you follow your own advice and belt up?'

'Here, 'ere, 'ere!'

Fox returned with young Tom who, tousled with sleep and naked to the waist, looked very young indeed and rather frightened.

'Sorry to knock you up like this, Tom,' Alleyn said. 'Mr Fox will have told you what it's all about.'

Tom nodded.

'We just want to know if you can tell us anything about the ton-up couple. Friends of yours?'

Tom showed the whites of his eyes and said not to say friends exactly. He shifted his feet, curled his toes, looked everywhere but at Alleyn and answered in monosyllables. The passengers listened avidly. Alleyn wondered if he was wise to conduct this one-sided interview in front of them and thought that on the whole, it would probably pay off. He extracted, by slow degrees, that Tom had hob-nobbed with the ton-up pair some time ago in a coffee-bar in Norminster. When? He couldn't say exactly. Some time back. Early in the cruising season? Yes. Early on. He hadn't seen them again until this cruise. Names? He wouldn't know the surnames. The chap got called Pluggy and his girlfriend was Glenys. Did they live in the district? He didn't think so. He couldn't say where they lived.

This was heavy going. Caley sighed and took up his book. Dr Natouche had the air of politely attending a function that did not interest him. Pollock bit his nails. Lazenby assumed a tolerant smile and Hewson stared at Tom with glazed intensity.

Alleyn said: 'Did they talk to you first or did you make up to them? In the coffee-bar?'

'They did,' Tom mumbled. 'They wanted to know about places.'

'What sort of places?'

'Along The River. Back of The River.'

'Just any old places?'

No. It appeared, not quite that. They were interested in the second-hand trade. They wanted to know where there were junk shops or yards or used-parts dumps. Yes, he'd told them about Jo Bagg.

The passengers shifted their feet.

By a tortuous process something like a coherent story began to emerge. Alleyn thought he recognized the symptoms. The ton-ups had been adventurous figures to young Tom. They had a buccaneering air about them. They were cool. They were with it. They had flattered him. Troy had noticed when the *Zodiac* sailed, something furtive in their exchange of signals. Alleyn asked Tom abruptly what his parents thought of the acquaintanceship. He flushed scarlet and muttered indistinguishably. They bad, it seemed, not approved. The Skipper's attitude to ton-ups was evidently regrettably square. Alleyn gathered that he had asked Tom if he hadn't got something better to do than hang round the moorings with a couple of freaks.

'Did they ever ask you to talk about any of the passengers?'

Tom was silent.

'This is important, Tom,' Alleyn said. 'You know what's happened, don't you? You know why we're here?'

He nodded.

'You wouldn't want to see someone wrongfully accused, would you?'

He shook his head.

'Did they talk about any of the passengers?'

Tom's dark eyes slewed round until they looked at Dr Natouche and then at the floor.

'Did they talk about Dr Natouche?'

He nodded again.

'What did they say?'

'They – They said to – give him a message.'

'What message? Come along. As far as you can remember it, in their own words: what message?'

Tom, looking as if he was about to cry, blurted out. 'They said to tell him from them he could – '

'Could what?'

A stream of obscenity quoted in the broken voice of an adolescent boy, jetted into the quiet decency of the little saloon.

'You asked,' Tom said miserably. 'You asked. I can't help it. It's what they said. They don't like – they don't like – ' He jerked his head at Natouche.

'Very well,' Alleyn said. 'We'll leave it at that.' He turned to Natouche. 'I take it,' he said, 'the message was not delivered?'

'No.'

'I should bloody well hope not,' said Caley Bard.

'Did they talk about any of the other passengers?' Alleyn pursued.

At Norminster they had asked, it appeared, about Troy. Only, Tom said, twisting himself about in a quite astonishing manner, only who she was and when she booked her passage.

'Did you know the answer?'

He knew she'd booked a cancellation that morning. He didn't know then – Here Tom boggled and shuffled and was finally induced to say he didn't know until later that she was the celebrated painter or who her husband was.

'And Miss Rickerby-Carrick – did they talk about her?'

Only, Tom mumbled, to say she was some barmy old tart.

'When did you last see them?'

This provoked another unhappy reaction. The dark, uncertain face whitened, the lips opened and moved but no sound came from them. Tom looked as if for tuppence he'd bolt.

Caley said: 'This is getting a bit tough, Alleyn, isn't it?' and Pollock at once began to talk about police methods. 'This is nothing,' he said. 'Nothing to what goes on in the cells. Don't you answer 'im, kid. Don't give 'im the satisfaction. They can't make you. Don't put yourself in wrong.'

Tom turned aside, ducked his head into the crook of his arms and gave way to ungainly tears. There were sounds of indignation from the passengers.

The Skipper had returned. His voice could be heard on deck and in a moment he came nimbly down the companion-way followed by the Sergeant from Tollardwark.

The Skipper looked at his son. 'What's all this?' he asked.

Tom raised a tear-blubbered face, tried to say something and incontinently bolted to the lower deck.

Alleyn said: 'I'll have a word with you about this in a moment, Skipper,' and turned to the Sergeant.

'What is it?'

'Message from the Super at Toll'ark, sir.' He looked at the assembly and produced a note which he handed to Alleyn.

'Motorbike couple picked up near Pontefract. Bringing them to Tollardwark at once. With article of jewellery.'

CHAPTER 9

The Creeper

'I pause here,' Alleyn said, 'to draw your attention to a matter of technique.

'You'll have noticed that at this point I questioned the passengers in a group instead of following the more orthodox line of seeing them separately, taking notes and getting a signed statement. This was admittedly a risky thing to do and I didn't take that risk without hesitation. You see, by now we were sure we had a case of conspiracy on our hands and I felt that, interviewed separately, they would have time to concoct some kind of consistent tarradiddle whereas, if we caught them all together and on the hop, they would have to improvise and in doing so might give themselves away. We felt certain they were under orders from Foljambe and that Foljambe was one of them, and Mr Fox and I had a pretty good notion which. You will, I dare say, have a pretty good notion yourselves.'

Carmichael, in the second row, showed signs of becoming active.

'I won't, however,' Alleyn said, 'ask what they are. We're not playing a guessing game, or are we? Well – never mind. I'll press on.

'In due course, we came, as you will hear, to a point in the investigation where we could draw only one conclusion. The "alibis", to call them so, for the earlier case would be established in that suspects of given names would be proved to be in given places at given times. The only conclusion, as I hope you will see as the case develops, could be that one of these suspects was operating under what might be called the double identity lay. This is, in fact, what Foljambe was doing. He had adopted, for purposes of the cruise, the identity of another and a living person whom he knew to be out of England. This meant that in the event of an inquiry the police would check this person's background, see that it was impeccable, look up his address, find that he was away, make further inquiries and discover he could not possibly be fitted into the Foljambe file. And so turn elsewhere for a culprit. It is an extremely risky but not unusual gimmick and is only effective for a short time but the Jampot is a tip-and-run expert and had decided to give it a go. Bear this in mind as we go on.

'We come now to the point when the investigation went grievously, indeed tragically, wrong and it went wrong because a police officer neglected a fundamental rule. Police officers, like the rest of mankind, are vulnerable creatures and like the rest of mankind they sometimes slip up. In this case a simple, basic rule of procedure was ignored. The chap who ignored it was a middle-aged provincial PC, not all that familiar with the type of job in hand and not as alert as he needed to be. He had his dim moment and the result was a death that could have been avoided. I don't mind telling you it still, as people say, haunts me. There's one such case at least in the lives of most investigating officers and sooner or later every man jack of you is liable to encounter it. Ours is a job, let's face it, for which one has to grow an extra skin. In some of us, under constant irritation this becomes a rhinoceros hide. We are not a starry-eyed lot. But at the risk of getting right off the track – a most undesirable proceeding – I would like to say this. You won't be any the worse at your job if you can keep your humanity. If you lose it altogether you'll be, in my opinion, better out of the Force because with it you'll have lost your sense of values and that's a dire thing to befall any policeman.

'Sorry. I'll push on. Following the signal about the motorbike pair, Mr Fox and I returned in the Yard car to Tollardwark. But first of all I talked to the Skipper – '

I

'Now get this straight,' Alleyn said. 'I'm not suggesting the boy's implicated in any way whatever. I am suggesting that they've appealed to his imagination and to the instinct for rebellion that rumbles in any normal chap of Tom's age. Now, after what's happened, he's scared. He knows something but he won't talk. I'm not going to sit him down and grill him. I don't want to and I haven't time. If you can get him to tell you whether he saw or spoke to or knows anything about, this precious pair *after* he saw them on the bridge here at Ramsdyke on Monday afternoon: well, it may help us and it may not. We've caught them in possession of a valuable jewel which when last seen was slung round Miss Rickerby-Carrick's neck. That's the picture, Skipper, and as far as Tom's concerned it's over to you.'

'I told him. I told him to keep clear of that lot. If I thought it'd do any good I'd belt him.'

'Would you? He's left school, hasn't he? What does he do week in week out? Norminster to Longminster and back with a trick at the wheel if he's in luck on the straight reaches? What did you do at his age, Skipper?'

'Me?' The Skipper shot a look at Alleyn. 'I shipped cabin boy aboard a Singapore tramp. All right, I get the point. I'll talk to him.'

Alleyn walked to the starboard side and looked at The River.

It almost seemed as if the field of detergent foam that had closed over Hazel Rickerby-Carrick had supernaturally climbed the weir, invested the upper reaches and closed in upon the *Zodiac*. 'Is this what you call the Creeper?' Alleyn said.

'That's right. You get her at this time of year. Very low-lying country from Norminster to Crossdyke.'

'Thick,' Fox said. 'Fog, more like.'

'And will be more so before dawn. She's making.'

'We'll push on,' Alleyn said. 'You know the drill, don't you, Skipper? As soon as they're all in bed put your craft in the lock and empty the lock. Give them a bit of time to settle. Watch for their lights to go out. It's twenty to eleven. You won't have long to wait.'

'It is OK with the Authority, isn't it? I wouldn't want – '

'Perfectly. It's all fixed.'

'A man could scramble out of it, you know.'

'Yes, but only with a certain amount of trouble. It wouldn't be so simple in this fog, whereas at her moorings it would be extremely easy to jump or, if necessary, swim. It'll confine the escape area, in effect. You'll be relieved as soon as possible after first light. We're very much in your debt over this, Skipper. Thank you for helping. Goodnight.'

With Fox and the constable he went ashore. The Skipper removed the gangplank.

'Goodnight, then,' said the Skipper softly.

The Creeper had already begun to move about the tow-path and condense on a green hedge near the lockhouse. It was threading gently into the trees and making wraiths of those that could be seen. The night smelt dank. Small sounds were exaggerated and everything was damp to the touch.

'Damn,' Alleyn whispered. 'We don't want this. Where's that chap – oh, there you are.'

The considerable bulk of Tillottson's PC on duty, loomed out of a drift of mist.

'Sir,' said the shape.

'You know what you've got to do, don't you? Nobody to leave the *Zodiac*.'

'Yes, sir.'

'Where's your nearest support?'

'T'other bank, sir.'

'And then?'

'This side, up beyond Wapentake Pot at th' crossroads. T'other side, sir, above pub at main road crossing.'

'Yes. Well, you'd better keep well down by the craft, with this mist rising. The Skipper's putting her in the lock before long. If there's an attempt you should be able to spot it. If anyone tries to come ashore, order them back and if they try to bolt, get them.'

'Sir.'

'Watch it, now.'

'Sir.'

'A dull-sounding chap,' Alleyn muttered.

They climbed up to the road and crossed the main bridge below the lock to the left bank. The formless voice of the weir obliterated other sounds. Blown flecks of detergent mingled with the rising mist.

'We'll have a bloody tiresome drive back to Toll'ark, if this is the form. Where's that car? And where – oh – here you are.'

Thompson and Bailey loomed up. They'd completed their job along the riverside and were told to come back to Tollardwark. The London police car gave a discreet hoot and turned on its fog lamps. They piled into it. Alleyn called up Tollardwark on the sound system and spoke to Tillottson.

'They won't talk,' Tillottson said. 'Not a peep out of them.'

'We're on our way. I hope. Over and out.'

The local man gave them a lead on his motorbike. When they reached the crest of the hill they found the mist had not risen to that level. The man at the crossroads flashed his torch, they turned into the main road and in eight minutes arrived once again at Tollardwark.

In the office where Troy had first encountered Mr Tillottson, he sat behind his desk with a telephone receiver at his ear and a note pad under his hand. He repeated everything that was said to him, partly, it seemed for accuracy's sake and partly for Alleyn's information.

'Ta,' he said and signalled to Alleyn, 'Yes, ta. Mind repeating that? Description tallies with that of "Dinky Dickson", con man 1964. Sus. drug contact Kings Cross, Sydney. Place of origin unknown but claims to be Australian. Believed to be – Here! What's that? Oh! Oh, I get you! Unfrocked clergyman. Australian police got nothing on him since May '67 when heavy sus. drug racket but no hard proof. Very plausible type. Ta. And the US lot? Two hundred and seven left-ear-deficients on FB records. No Hewsons. Might be Deafy Ed Moran, big-time fix, heroin, Chicago, undercover picture-dealing. Expatriated Briton but speaks with strong US accent. Sister works with him; homely, middle-aged, usually known as Sis. No convictions since 1960 but heavy sus., Foljambe – here, wait a sec. This is important – heavy sus., Foljambe – accomplice. Message ends. Ta. What about Pollock, then? Anything come through? Pardon?'

Mr Tillottson's pen hovered anxiously. 'Pardon?' he repeated. 'Oh. Wait a wee, till I get it down. One time commercial artist. No present known occupation but owns property, is in the money and living well. Nothing in Records? OK? And the other two? Natouche and Bard? Nothing. What's that? Yes, we've got that stuff about his practice in Liverpool. What? Laurenson and Busby, London? Tutorial Service? Spends his vacations chasing butterflies. Known to *who*? British Lepi – Oh. Given his name to *what*? Spell it out. L.A.P.A.Z.B.A.R.D.I.I. What's that when it's at home? A *butterfly*? Ta. Yes. Yes. Mr Alleyn's come in. I'll tell him, then. Thanks.'

Alleyn said: 'Don't hang up. Let me have a word.' He took the receiver. 'Alleyn here,' he said. 'Look, I heard all that but I'd like men to call immediately at all the addresses. Yes. Liverpool, too. Yes, I know. Yes, but nevertheless – right. And ring us back, will you? Yes.'

He hung up. 'Well, Bert,' he said, 'what have you got in your back parlour? Let's take a look, shall we?'

'Better see this first, hadn't you?'

Tillottson unlocked a wall safe and from it took an object like a miniature pudding tied up in chamois leather and attached to a cord. 'I haven't opened it,' he said.

Alleyn opened it, cautiously. 'Good God!' he said.

There it lay, on a police officer's desk in an English market town: an exotic if ever there was one: a turquoise enamel ovoid, starred with diamonds and girt with twelve minuscule figures decked out in emeralds and rubies and pearls, all dancing in order round their jewelled firmament. Aries, Taurus, Gemini – . 'The old gang' Alleyn said. 'It's an Easter egg by Fabergé, Fox, and the gift of an Emperor. And now – what a descent! – we've got to try it for dabs.' He looked at Thompson and Bailey. 'Job for you,' he said.

'Do you mean to say she charged about the place with this thing hung round her neck!' Fox exclaimed. 'It must be worth a fortune. And it's uncommonly pretty,' he added. 'Uncommonly so.'

'That, unless we're on the wrong track altogether, is what the Jampot thought. Go ahead, you two. Dabs and pictures.'

They were about to leave the room when the telephone rang. Tillottson answered it. 'You'd better report to Mr Alleyn,' he said. 'Hold on.' He held out the receiver. 'PM result,' he said.

Alleyn listened. 'Thank you,' he said. 'What we expected.' He hung up. 'She didn't drown, Fox. Pressure on the carotids and vagus nerve. The mixture as before and straight from the Jampot. All right, Bert. Show us your captives.'

They were in the little charge-room, lounging back on a couple of office chairs and chewing gum. They were as Natouche had described them and their behaviour was completely predictable: the quarter sneer, the drooped eyelid, the hunched shoulder and the perpetual complacent chew. The girl, Alleyn thought, looking at her hands, was frightened: the man hid his hands in his pockets and betrayed nothing but his own insolence.

'They've been charged,' Tillottson said, 'with theft. They won't make a statement.'

Alleyn said to the young man: 'I'm going to put questions to you. You've been taken into custody and found to be in possession of a jewel belonging to a lady into whose death we are inquiring. Driving licence?' He looked at Tillotson who slightly nodded. The young man, sketching boredom and impertinence in equal parts, raised his eyebrows, dipped his fingers into a pocket and threw a licence on the table. He opened his mouth, accelerated his chewing and resumed his former pose.

The licence was made out in the name of Albert Bernard Smith and seemed to be in order. It gave an address in Soho.

'This will be checked. The night before last,' Alleyn said, 'you were on the tow-path at Crossdyke alongside the *Zodiac* wearing those boots. You had parked your bicycle under a hedge on the left-hand side of the road above the lock. Later that night you were here at Ramsdyke. You arrived here, with a passenger. Not:' he looked at the girl, 'this lady. You carried your passenger – a dead weight – ' For two seconds the slightly prognathic jaw noticed by Dr Natouche, stopped champing. The girl suddenly re-crossed her legs.

' – a dead weight,' Alleyn repeated, 'down to the weir. Her pyjamas caught on a briar. You did what you'd been instructed to do and then picked up your present companion and made off for Carlisle where you arrived yesterday in time to send a telegram to the Skipper of the *Zodiac*. It was signed Hay Rickerby-Carrick which is not much like Albert Bernard Smith. Having executed this commission you turned south and were picked up by the police at Pontefract.'

The young man yawned widely, displaying the wad of gum on his tongue. He stretched his arms. The girl gave a scary giggle and clapped her hand over her mouth.

'You've been so busy,' Alleyn said, 'on your northern jaunt that you can't have heard the news. The body has been found and the woman was murdered. I shall now repeat the usual warning which you've already had from Superintendent Tillottson. At the moment you are being held for theft.'

The young man, now very white about the side whiskers, heard the usual warning with a sneer that seemed to have come unstuck. The girl watched him.

'Any statement?'

For the first time the young man spoke. His voice was strongly Cockney.

'You can contact Mr C.D.E. Struthers,' he said. 'I'm not talking.'

Mr C.D.E. Struthers was an extremely adroit London solicitor whose practice was confined, profitably, to top-level experts in mayhem.

'Really?' Alleyn said. 'And who's going to pay for that?'

'Mention my name.'

'If I knew it, I would be delighted to do so. Good evening to you.'

When the couple had swaggered unconvincingly to the cells Tillottson said: ' "Smith" they may be, but not for my money.'

'Ah,' Fox agreed. 'They'd have done the virtuous indignation stuff if they were.'

'Well, Smith or Montmorency,' Alleyn said, 'we'd better let them talk to Mr C.D.E. Struthers. He may wish them on to one of his legal brethren in the North or he may come up here himself. It's a matter of prestige.'

'How d'you mean? Prestige?' asked Tillottson.

'The other name for it is Foljambe. Get your Sergeant here to trace the licence will you, Bert? And a description to Records. And Dabs.'

'Yes, OK. I'll see to it.'

But before he could do so the Sergeant himself appeared looking perturbed.

'Call for you, sir,' he said to Alleyn. 'PC Cape on duty at Ramsdyke Lock. Very urgent.'

'What the hell's this,' Alleyn said. But when he heard the voice, he guessed.

'I'm reporting at once, sir,' gabbled PC Cape. 'I'm very sorry, sir, but there's been a slip-up, sir. In the fog, sir.'

'Who?'

'The lady, sir. The American lady.'

'What do you mean – slip-up?'

'She's gone, sir.'

II

Six minutes with their siren wailing brought them back to Ramsdyke. Tillottson kept up an uninterrupted flow of anathemas against his PC Cape. Alleyn and Fox said little, knowing that nothing they could offer would solace him. There was still no fog to speak of on the main road but when they turned off into the lane above Ramsdyke Lock they looked down on a vague uniform pallor of the sort that fills the valleys in a Japanese landscape. Their fog lamps isolated them in a moving confinement that closed as they descended.

'A likely night for it,' Tillottson kept repeating. 'My Gawd, a likely night.'

He was driving his own car with Alleyn and Fox as passengers. The London CID car followed with a driver, a local constable and Sergeants Thompson and Bailey who had been pressed in as an emergency measure.

Sirens could be heard without definition as to place or distance. Road blocks and search parties from Longminster, Norminster and Crossdyke were being established about the landscape.

With that dramatic suddenness created by fog, a constable flashing an amber torchlight stood in their path. 'Well?' Tillottson said, leaning out of the window.

'This is as far as you can drive, sir.'

'Where's Cape?'

' T'other side, sir.'

They got out. Close on their left hand the fog-masked weir kept up its anonymous thunder. They followed the constable along the tow-path to the flight of steps that led up to the main bridge.

'All right,' Tillottson said. 'Get back to your point.'

As they groped their way over the bridge a car crept past them filled with revellers engaged in doleful song.

The constable stepped into its path and waved his torch.

'Hullo-'ullo-'ullo,' shouted the driver. 'Anything wrong, Officer?'

'Just a minute, if you please, sir.'

'Our Breath is as the Breath of Spring,' someone in the back seat sang dismally.

'May I see your licence, sir?'

When this formality was completed Alleyn and Tillottson moved in. Had they, Alleyn asked, seen a solitary woman? They replied merrily that they'd had no such luck and emitted wolf-like whistles. Alleyn said: 'If we weren't so busy we'd have something to say to you. As it is, will you pull yourselves together, proceed on your silly journey, stop if you see a solitary woman, and address her decently. If she's got a strong American accent, offer her a lift, behave yourselves and drive her to the nearest police stop or police station, whichever comes first. Do you understand?'

'Er – yes. Righty-jolly-ho. Fair enough,' said the driver, taken aback as much by Alleyn's manner and voice as by what he said. The passengers had become very quiet.

'Repeat it, if you please.'

He did.

'Thank you. Drive carefully. We've got your number. Goodnight.'

They crawled away.

Bailey and Thompson and their driver loomed up and the whole party inched along until they found the top of a flight of steps going down to the lock.

'What can have got into her?' Fox mused, not for the first time.

'Fear,' said Alleyn. 'She was terrified. She's tried to do a bolt. *And* succeeded, blast it. The Skipper must have delayed – hallo, here we are. That's the roof of the lockhouse down there. Come on and for God's sake don't let's have any falling into the lock. Easy as we go, now.'

They felt their way down the steps to the tow-path.

'*Cape!*' Tillottson shouted in a terrible voice.

'Here, sir.'

He was wretchedly waiting where he had been told to wait: between the lock and the lockhouse. The fog down here was dense indeed and they were upon him almost before they saw him. He seemed to be standing to attention and expecting the worst.

'Ever heard of a Misconduct Form?' Tillottson ominously began.

'Sir.'

'Superintendent Alleyn's got something to say to you.'

'Sir.'

Alleyn said: 'What happened, Cape?'

There had, he said, been a commotion on board the *Zodiac*. He couldn't see anything much because of the Creeper but he heard the Skipper's voice asking what was wrong and a woman taking on a fair treat, shrieking: 'Let me go. Let me go.' He went down to the moorings and called out: 'What seems to be wrong there?' but as far as he could make out the happening was on the far side. And then one of the gentlemen on board came round the deck and asked PC Cape where he was and said he'd better come on board and get things under control like. He could hardly see a thing except that there was a gap between the edge and the gunwale. He couldn't see the gentleman either but said he had a very loud voice.

'Go on.'

The loud voice said he could jump for it and as he could just make out enough for that he did jump and came aboard in a flounder and nearly lost his helmet. Alleyn gathered that a sort of blind search had set in under circumstances of the greatest possible confusion. Cape had proceeded with outstretched arms doing a breast stroke action, to the starboard side which was the farthest removed from the tow-path. He had bumped into a number of persons and had loudly demanded that everybody should keep calm.

A strange disordered mêlée now took place in the greatest possible confusion. Presently it occurred to Cape that the woman's voice could no longer be heard. He had got alongside the Skipper and they had, between them, rounded up the passengers and herded them into the saloon where after a good deal of milling about and counting of heads, Miss Hewson's head was found to be missing.

By this time the policemen on the pub side of The River had become alerted and started to cross the bridge.

Cape and the Skipper went through the cabins and searched the craft. All available lights were switched on but were not much help on deck where the fog was now of the pea-soup variety.

Caley Bard and Dr Natouche bore a hand and the Skipper had evidently behaved very sensibly. When it was certain that Miss Hewson was not in the *Zodiac*, Cape got himself ashore and blew his whistle. He and his colleague now met, poked uselessly about in the fog and settled that while Cape got through to Tollardwark his mate should alert by walkie-talkie the other men on duty in the vicinity.

Alleyn said: 'Very well. Where's the *Zodiac*?'

'The *boat*, sir?' Cape ejaculated. 'I beg pardon, sir?'

'Where's the bloody *lock*, for pity's sake.'

'The lock, sir?'

'Find the lockhouse and stay by it, all of you.'

Alleyn inched along the tow-path. A lighted window loomed up on his left. The lockhouse. He faced right, stood still, listened and peered down into a blanket.

'Hallo? *Zodiac*?' he said very quietly.

'Hallo,' said a muted voice below his feet.

'Skipper?'

'That's right.'

'Show a light, can you?'

A yellow globe swam into being far below.

'You did it, then? You and Tom?'

'And the Lock himself. Talk about stable-doors! It was a job in this muck but here we are.'

'All present?'

'Except for her.'

'Sure?'

'Dead sure.'

'No idea, of course, which way she went?'

'No idea.'

'And Mrs Tretheway's sleeping at the lockhouse?'

'Yes.'

'Good. You're very quiet down there.'

'They've gone to bed. I waited for it.'

'Do they know where they are?'

'Not when I saw them. They will.'

'They could scramble up and out, of course.'

'They're in their cabins and they can't get ashore from there. Have to come up on deck and young Tom and I are keeping watch.'

'Splendid. Stay put till you hear from us, won't you?'

'Don't make it too long,' the voice murmured.

'Do our best. Goodnight.'

Alleyn returned to the lockhouse. He and the other six men were admitted by the keeper and crowded into the parlour.

'Well,' Alleyn said. 'Search we must. Any chance of this lifting?'

Not before dawn, most likely, said the lock-keeper but you never knew. If a wind got up, she'd shift.

'It's essentially a river mist, isn't it?' Alleyn said. 'Miss Hewson may still be milling round in it or lying doggo. If she managed to get above it she'll be on the move. All we can do is follow the usual procedure.' He looked at the Tollardwark constable. 'You'd better keep within hailing distance of Mr Tillottson, Mr Fox and me. You've got radar and we haven't. We're going to find our way up to the wapentake. Br'er Fox, would you work out to my right. Bert, if you'd keep going beyond that and take the driver out on your own right wing. Bailey and Thompson, you take the left wing. Near the roadside hedge if you could see it. She may be anywhere: under the hedge in the Wapentake Pot or a quarter of a mile away. As little noise and talk as possible. The rest of this unspeakable terrain we leave to the men already alerted.'

He looked at the wretched Cape.

'Oh, yes. You,' he said. 'You move up the hill on my left.' And to the two remaining men: 'And you watch the *Zodiac*. She's in the lock and the lock's at its lowest. Nobody can leap ashore in seconds but that doesn't say they can't make it.'

Tillottson said: 'The *Zodiac*? In the lock?'

'Yes,' Alleyn said. He looked at the keeper who was grinning. 'By arrangement. Like it or lump it with any luck and a good watch they're there till we want them. Come on.'

II

Seven hours ago he and Fox had climbed this hill and Troy, a little later, had come to them in the wapentake. Four days ago Troy and the other passengers had met there and Troy had sat in the Wapentake Pot and talked with Dr Natouche.

Alleyn tried to recall the lie of the land. This was the first grassy slope under his feet, now, and ahead of him must be the tufted embankment below the wapentake field. He had begun to think he must have veered and now walked parallel with the embankment when it rose at his feet. He climbed it and could hear the others breathe and the soft thud of their feet. They used torches to show their whereabouts. The insignificant yellow discs floated and bobbed, giving an occasional glimpse of a leg or coat or a few inches of earth and grass.

The ascent felt steeper and more uneven under these blindfold conditions than it had in the afternoon. They had only climbed a few paces when, suddenly and inconsequently there was less mist. It drifted and eddied and thinned out and now they waded rather than swam through it and appeared to each other as familiar phantoms.

'Clearing,' Fox murmured.

Alleyn sniffed. 'Rum!' he said, 'I seem to smell dust.'

The hillside was before them, living its own life under the stars. A blackness vaguely defined the wapentake itself. Alleyn moved his torchlight slowly across to his right and gave a stifled exclamation.

'Come in on this, all of you,' he said.

Their lights met at a dishevelment of earth, gravel and pieces of half-buried timber.

'It's that old digging,' Fox exclaimed. 'I said it wasn't safe. It's caved in.'

'Come in, all of you.'

The seven men collected round him and used their torchlights. The crazy structure had collapsed. A fang of broken timber stuck out of the rubble and the edge of an old door that had supported an overhanging roof of earth now showed beneath a landslide of earth and gravel.

Alleyn said: 'And there's still a smell of dust in the air. Don't go nearer, any of you. Stay where you are. Give me all the light you can raise. Here.'

Their lights concentrated round his on a patch of ground near his feet and came to a halt again at the edge of the rubble.

'Bailey,' Alleyn said.

Bailey and he knelt together, their heads bowed devoutly over slurs, indentations and flattened grass.

'Here's a good one. A patch of bare soil. Take a look at this,' Alleyn said. Bailey took a long hard look.

'Fair enough,' he said. 'She was wearing them and there's another pair in her cabin.'

'American type, low-heeled walking jobs.'

'That's right, sir.'

'Good Gawd!' Tillottson loudly exclaimed. 'She went in there to hide and – Good Gawd!'

But Alleyn and Bailey paid no attention to Tillottson and Fox said: 'Wait on, Bert.'

The wapentake field had turned towards a rising moon and was illuminated. The mist had now retired upon its source and wound like a cottonwool snake between the riverbanks. The landscape had changed and lightened.

Alleyn had thrown off his overcoat and was working at the rubble with his gloved hands.

'Bear a hand,' he said. 'We're too late but bear a hand.'

The other men joined him. They mounted their torches where they shone on the rubble and went hard to work.

'Very painstaking,' Alleyn grunted. 'But not quite painstaking enough. Something – a stone, a bit of broken wood from the rubble – something – has been scuffed over the ground. Prints of the woman's shoes have been left. Right up to where the rubble has lapped over them and pointing towards the excavation. But the surrounding patches of soil have been scuffed. We are meant to think what you thought, Bert.'

Superintendent Tillottson peered sideways at PC Cape as if longing for a better view.

'You hear that?' he said. 'You understand what's been said? You know what you've allowed to be done, you disgusting chap?'

Alleyn said: 'All right, Cape, you'll have to take what's coming, won't you?'

He squatted back on his heels. 'This is no good,' he said and turned to the two constables: 'Go down to the lockhouse and get spades. There's not a hope, now, but we've got to act as if there was. And bring something – pieces of wood – galvanized iron – anything to cover these prints. Quick as you can. Thompson, have you got a flash? All right. Go ahead.'

Sergeant Thompson moved in with the hand-held camera he used in emergencies. His light flashed intermittently. The wretched Cape and his opposite number thundered downhill.

'We'd better continue to go through the motions,' Alleyn said: 'As I recollect there were two props. One may have been used to knock away the other. He'd have a second or two to jump clear. Or there may have been a spare timber lying around.'

Fox said: 'What's the form, Mr Alleyn? About that lot down there in the lock? There's nobody missing?' He jerked his head at the rubble. 'Apart from her?'

'The Skipper says not but we'll have to see them. Look Bert, will you go down there? Ring your local police surgeon. My compliments and he'll be needed again, with the ambulance and the usual equipment. Give him the story and tell him it's suspected homicide. Then get yourself aboard the *Zodiac*. We won't raise her until we've checked and then only when we can muster a closer guard. We've got a tough little clutch of villains down there and the big double-barrel himself.'

'I'll go, then. And if they *are* all there?'

'Call off the general search and bring the men in to Ramsdyke.'

'See you in a wee while, then,' Tillottson said.

Bailey and Thompson went back to the car to fetch their heavy gear and Alleyn and Fox were left together: a tall elegant figure and a large thickset one incongruously moonlit in the wapentake field and scraping like dogs with their forepaws at gravelly rubble.

'This is quite a big case,' Fox remarked.

'You are the king of meiosis. Take an international triple murderer fresh from his latest kill, and pen him up with his associates in a pleasure craft at the bottom of a lock. Flavour with at least three innocent beings and leave to explode. And you call it quite a big case.'

'I suppose,' Fox said, disregarding this, 'it was all done under – ' He stopped short. 'How do you work it out?' he said. 'A put-up job, the whole thing? What?'

'She was blowing up for trouble when we had that last interview. She may have threatened to grass on them. Perhaps, the Jampot saw how she shaped up, and offered to get her away. Or – ,' Alleyn panted as he shifted a largish boulder, 'or she may simply have bolted. Whichever way it was, she raised a rumpus – screeching and on-going. When that ass Cape flung himself aboard, off she lit in the fog, pursued I don't mind betting by the Jampot. In a matter of minutes they were over the embankment and into the pit. And that was it.'

'I like that one best.'

'It has a Foljambe smack about it, you think?'

'Suppose,' Fox said, 'she's not here. Suppose she and who-ever-it-was came up here this afternoon and she poked into this excavation and came out again and it collapsed later?'

'No prints to suggest a return. And why did whoever-it-was try to obliterate his own prints?'

'There's that, of course. And you make out that while the commotion in the *Zodiac* still continued he went straight back and was all present and correct when that silly chump Cape and the Skipper started counting heads in the saloon?'

'That's it.'

They worked for some time in silence.

'I don't know,' Fox said presently. 'I don't somehow feel too certain she's here.'

'Don't you?' Alleyn said with a change of voice.

Fox let out an oath and drew back his hand.

From under a counterpane of soil that might have been withdrawn by a sleeping hand, a foot stuck up, rigid in its well-made American walking shoe.

The two constables came up the hill, swinging a lantern and carrying shovels. Bailey and Thompson returned with their gear. In a very little while they had uncovered Miss Hewson. Her print dress was up round her neck and contained her arms. Her body and legs clad in their sensible undergarments were shockingly displayed and so was her face: open eyes and open mouth filled with sandy soil and the cheekbones cut about with gravel.

'But not congested,' Fox said and added loudly: 'That's not a suffocated face. Is it?'

'Oh, no,' Alleyn said. 'No. Did you expect it would be, Br'er Fox? It's hopeless but we'll try artificial respiration.'

One of the local men took off his helmet and knelt down.

'The old carotid job?' Fox mused.

'That's what I expect. We'll see what the doctor says.'

Fox made a movement of his head towards the hidden *Zodiac*.

'Not, of course – him?'

'No. No. And yet – After all, why not? Why not, indeed.' He thought for a moment. 'Perhaps better not,' he said and turned to Bailey and Thompson. 'The lot,' he said. 'Get going.'

He and Fox moved to where the roof had originally overhung the excavation. Here they looked down on the whole subsidence. Tiny runnels of friable soil trickled and started at their footfall. They found no footprints or traces of obliteration.

Alleyn said: 'I think you'd better take over here, Br'er Fox, if you will. Meet the doctor when he comes and when he's finished bring him down to the lock.'

As he went down the hill Thompson's flashlamp blinked and blinked again.

The River was still misted but when Alleyn looked into the lock, there was the roof of the *Zodiac*'s wheelhouse, her deck and the tarpaulin cover, the top of a helmet, shoulders, a stomach and a pair of regulation boots.

Light from the saloon shone on the wet walls of the lock. He could hear voices.

'Hallo,' he said. The constable looked up and saluted. He was the man who had been on duty by the pub.

'There's a ladder at the lockhouse, sir,' he said.

'I'll drop, thank you.'

He managed this feat and for what turned out to be the last time, met the *Zodiac* passengers in the *Zodiac* saloon.

IV

They were in what Fox liked to call *déshabillé* and looking none the better for it with the exception of Dr Natouche who wore a dressing-gown of sombre grandeur, scarlet kid slippers and a scarf that bore witness as did none of his other garments, to an exotic taste for colour. He was, indeed, himself an exotic, sitting apart at a corner table, upright, black and without expression. Troy would have liked to paint him, Alleyn thought, as he was now. What a pity she couldn't.

The Skipper also sat apart, looking watchful. Mr Tillottson was back at his former table and the passengers were in the semi-circular seat under the windows. Hewson at once began a heated protest. His sister! Where was his sister! What was the meaning of all this! Did Alleyn realize that he and his sister were American citizens and as such were entitled to protest to their Ambassador in London? Did he appreciate –

Alleyn let it run for a minute and then clamped down.

'I think,' he said, 'that we do have a rough idea of the situation, Mr Hewson. We're in touch with the Federal Bureau in New York. They've been very helpful.'

Hewson changed colour, opened his mouth and shut it again.

Alleyn said: 'Do you really not know where your sister has gone?'

'I know,' he said, 'she's been real scared by you guys acting like you thought – ' he stopped, got to his feet and looked from Tillottson to Alleyn. 'Say, what is all this?' he said. 'What's with you guys? What's happened to Sis?' He fumbled with his hearing-aid and thrust his deaf ear towards Alleyn. 'C'mon,' he said. 'C'mon. Give, can't you?'

Alleyn said clearly, 'Something very bad, I'm afraid.'

'Like what? Hell, can't you talk like it makes sense? What's happened?' And then, it seemed with flat incredulity, he said: 'Are you telling me she's dead? Sis? Dead? Are you telling me that?'

Lazenby walked over to Hewson and put his arm across his shoulders: 'Hold hard, old man,' he fluted. 'Stick it out, boy. Steady. Steady.'

Hewson looked at him. 'You make me sick,' he said. 'Christ Almighty, you make me sick to my stomach.' He turned on Alleyn. 'Where?' he said. 'What was it? What happened?'

Alleyn told him where she had been found. He listened with his head slanted and his face screwed up as if he still had difficulty in hearing.

'Smothered,' he said. 'Smothered, huh?'

Alleyn said nothing. There was an immense stillness in the saloon as if everybody waited for a climax.

'Why don't you all say something?' Hewson suddenly demanded. 'Sitting round like you were dumb-bells. God damn you. Say something.'

'What can we say?' Caley Bard murmured. 'There's nothing we can say.'

'*You*,' Hewson said. And as if he had to find some object upon which to focus an undefined misery and resentment he leant forward and shook his finger at Caley Bard. 'You sit around!' he stammered.

'You act like nothing mattered! For Pete's sake, what sort of a monster do you figure *you* are?'

'I'm sorry,' Caley said.

'Pardon me?' Hewson shouted angrily with his hand cupped round his ear. 'What's that? Pardon?'

'I'm sorry,' Caley shouted in return.

'Sorry? *Sorry*, hell! He says he's sorry!'

Pollock intervened. 'There you are,' he said. 'That's what happens. That's the way our wonderful police get to work. Scare the daylights out of some poor woman so she scarpers and gets herself smothered in a gravel-pit. All in the day's work.'

'In our opinion,' Alleyn said, 'Miss Hewson was not smothered in the gravel pit. She was buried there.'

'My dear Superintendent – ' Lazenby exclaimed, 'what *do* you mean by that? That's a shocking statement.'

'We think that she was murdered in the same way as Miss Rickerby-Carrick was murdered on Tuesday night and a man called Andropulos was murdered last Saturday. And we think it highly probable that one of you is responsible.'

'Do you know,' Caley said, 'I had a strong premonition you were going to say that. But *why*? Why should you suppose one of *us* – ? I mean we're a cross-section of middle-class people from four different countries of origin who have never met before. We none of us knew that unfortunate eccentric before she, to speak frankly, bored the pants off us in the *Zodiac*. With the exception of her brother we'd none of us ever set eyes on Miss Hewson. Earlier tonight, Alleyn, you seemed to be suggesting there was some kind of conspiracy at work among us. All this carry-on about people being overheard muttering together in a side street in Tollardwark. And then you started a line about Miss Rickerby-Carrick having been robbed of a Fabergé bibelot. And what's the strength of the bit about Pollock and his doodles? I must apologize,' Caley said with a change of tone. 'I didn't mean to address the meeting at such length, but really, Alleyn, when you coolly announce that one of us is a murderer it's bloody frightening and I for one want to know what it's all about.'

Alleyn waited for a little and then said: 'Yes. Of course. I'm sure you do. Under ordinary conditions it wouldn't be proper for me to tell you but in several ways this is an extraordinary case and I propose to be a damn' sight more candid than I dare say I ought to be.'

'I'm glad to hear it,' Caley said wryly.

Alleyn said, 'Here goes, then. Conspiracy? Yes. We think there is a conspiracy at work in the *Zodiac* and we think all but one of the passengers is involved. Murder? Yes. We think one of you is a murderer and hope to prove it. His name? Foljambe, alias the Jampot. At present, however, known by the name of another person. And his record? International bad lot with at least five homicides to his discredit.'

The silence that followed was broken by Pollock. 'You must be barmy,' he said.

'Conspiracy,' Alleyn went on. 'Briefly, it involves the painting by you, Mr Pollock, of extremely accomplished Constable forgeries. The general idea, we think, went something like this. You made the forgeries. Your young friends on the motorbike, working under Foljambe's orders, were to plant them about this countryside where Constable once painted. The general principle of "salting" the non-existent mine. The first discovery by Mr and Miss Hewson (if that is their name) in Bagg's yard was to be given exactly the right amount of publicity. If necessary the circumstances surrounding the lucky find would be authenticated by Bagg himself, by my wife and Miss Rickerby-Carrick and the only other unimplicated passenger. There was to be an immediate bogus hunt throughout the countryside by: *a*) Mr Lazenby better known in the Antipodes, we incline to believe, as Dinky Dickson: *b*) Mr and Miss Hewson or Ed and Sally-Lou Moran as the case may be, and *c*) – ineffable cheek – by you yourself, Mr Pollock, in hot pursuit of your own forgeries.'

'You got to be dreaming,' said Mr Pollock.

'The result of this treasure-hunt would be – surprise! surprise! – a tidy haul of "Constables" and a general melting away of the conspirators to sell them in the highest market. The whole operation was, we believe, in the nature of a trial run, observed by the key figures and designed for expansion, with appropriate modifications, into world-wide operations.'

'All of this,' said Lazenby breathlessly, 'is untrue. It is wickedly and scandalously untrue.'

'Meanwhile,' Alleyn continued, 'the terrain would have been thoroughly explored for the subsequent disposal (or we don't know anything about our Jampot) of hard drugs by means of what is laughingly known in the racket as aerial top-dressing. The collectors would be at large among a swarm of Constable-seekers and would be accepted by the locals, with however marked a degree of exasperation, as such.'

'How do you like this fella? Do we have to sit around and take this?' Mr Hewson asked of no one in particular.

'You haven't got much choice, have you?' Caley Bard said. And to Alleyn: 'Go on, please.'

'Almost from the first things went askew. I again draw your attention to Mr K. G. Z. Andropulos who was to be a passenger in Cabin 7. He was a bit of wreckage from Greece who had a picture-dealing shop in Soho which may have been intended as a dispersal point for some of the forgeries. He turned nark on Foljambe, madly tried a spot of blackmail, and was murdered, exactly in the same way as the women. By the Jampot himself, about thirty-eight hours before he embarked in the *Zodiac*.'

The three men broke into simultaneous ejaculations. Alleyn raised his hand.

'We'll come to alibis,' he said, 'in due course. They have been checked.'

'All I can say,' Caley said, 'is Thank God and perhaps I'm being premature, at that.'

'Yes, and perhaps you bloody well are,' Pollock burst out. 'Sitting there, like Jacky. How do we know – '

'You don't,' Caley said. 'So shut up.' He turned to Alleyn. 'But about this – about Miss Hewson. Why, to begin with, are you so sure there's been foul play?'

Alleyn said: 'We are waiting for an official medical opinion. In the meantime, since we have a doctor among us, I think I shall ask him to describe the post-mortem appearances of suffocation by earth and gravel. As opposed to those following an attack from behind involving abrupt and violent pressure on the carotid arteries.'

'Ah *no*!' Caley cried out. 'Alleyn, I mean – *surely*!' He looked at Hewson who leant on the table, his face in his hands. 'I mean,' Caley repeated. 'I mean – well – there *are* decencies.'

'As far as possible,' Alleyn rejoined, 'we try to observe them. Mr Hewson will be asked to identify. He may prefer to know, if he doesn't know already, what to expect.'

'*Know!*' Hewson sobbed behind his fingers. '*Know*. My God, how should I know!'

'You *all* want to know, I gather, why we believe Miss Hewson was murdered. Our opinion rests to a considerable extent on post-mortem appearances. Dr Natouche?'

It was a long time since they had heard that voice. He had been there, sitting apart in his splendid gown and scarlet slippers. They had shot uneasy, resentful or curious glances at him but nobody had spoken to him and he had not uttered.

He said: 'You have sent for your police consultant. It would be improper for me to give an opinion.'

'Even in the interest of justice?'

'It is not clear to me how justice would be served by my intervention.'

'If you consider for a moment, it may become clear.'

'I think not, Superintendent.'

'Will you at least tell us if you would expect to find a difference between post-mortem appearances in these two cases?'

A long silence before Dr Natouche said: 'Possibly.'

'In the case of an attack on the carotids you would expect to find external post-mortem marks on the areas attacked?'

'Superintendent, I have told you I prefer not to give an opinion. The external appearances from suffocation vary enormously. I have – ' He waited for some seconds and then spoke very strongly. 'I have never seen a case of death from a murderous assault on the carotids. My opinion would be valueless,' said Dr Natouche.

Pollock cried out shrilly: 'You'd know how to *do* it, though, wouldn't you? *Wouldn't you?*'

Hewson lowered his hands and stared at Natouche.

'Any medical man,' Natouche said, 'would know technically, what death by such means involved. I must decline to discuss it.'

'I don't like this,' Lazenby said, turning his dark glasses on the doctor. 'I don't like this, at all. It's not honest. It's not a fair go. You've been asked a straight question, Doctor, and you refuse to give a straight answer.'

'On the contrary.'

'Well,' Alleyn said, 'let's take another look at the situation. Before she left the *Zodiac*, Miss Hewson was in distress. She was heard by the constable on duty at the lock to scream, to break into a hysterical demonstration and to cry out repeatedly: "Let me go. Let me go!" Is that agreed?'

Hewson said: 'Sure! Sure, she was hysterical. Sure, she wanted to escape. What sort of deal had she had for Christ's sake! Police standing her up like she was involved in this phoney art racket. A corpse fished outa The River and everyone talking about homicide. Sure, she was scared. She was real scared. She was desperate. I didn't want to leave her up here but she acted like crazy and said why couldn't I let her alone. So I did. I left her right here in the saloon and I went to bed.'

'You were the last then, to go down?'

'Well – the Padre and Stan and I – we went together.'

'And Dr Natouche? Did he go down?'

'No, sir. He went up on deck. He went up soon as Sis began to act nervous. Pretty queer it seemed to me: go out into that doggone fog but that's what he did and that's where he went.'

'I would like to get a clear picture, if "clear" is the word, of where you all were and what happened after she was left here in the saloon.'

They all began to speak at once and incontinently stopped. Alleyn looked at Caley Bard.

'Let's have your version,' he said.

'I wish you luck of it,' Caley rejoined. 'For what it's worth I'll – well, I'll have a stab. I'd gone to bed: at least I'd gone to my cabin and undressed and was having a look at some butterflies I caught on the cruise. I heard – ' he looked at Lazenby, Hewson and Pollock ' – these three come down and go to the loo and their cabins and so on. They all have to go past my door, I being in Cabin I. They were talking in the passage, I remember. I didn't notice what they said: I was spreading a specimen I picked up at Crossdyke. Subconsciously though, I suppose I must have recognized their voices.'

'Yes?'

'All of a sudden a hell of a rumpus broke loose, up topside. Sorry, Hewson, I might have put that better. I heard, in fact, Miss Hewson scream "Let me go". Two or three times, I think. I heard a kind of thudding in the saloon here, above my head. And then, naturally, a general reaction.'

'What sort of general reaction?'

'Doors opening and slamming. Hewson calling out for his sister, Lazenby and Pollock shouting to each other and a stampede upstairs. I'm afraid,' Caley said with what could only be described as an arch glance out of his curious eyes, 'I did *not* hurtle into the lists. Not then and there. You see, Alleyn, we had, to quote an extremist, supped rather full of horrors and, to be quite honest, my immediate reaction was to think: "Oh, *no*! Not *again*!" Meaning it in a general sense, you understand.'

'So – what did you do?'

'In effect, listened to what seemed to be an increasing hubbub, had a bit of an argument with what passes for my conscience and finally, I'm afraid more than reluctantly, went up topside myself.'

Where you found?'

'Damn' all that could be distinguished. Everybody milling about in the fog and asking everybody else what the hell they were doing and where was Miss Hewson.'

'Can you say how many persons you could distinguish?'

He thought for a moment. 'Well – yes. I suppose – I got a general idea. But it couldn't be less reliable. I heard – these three men again – calling out to each other and I heard the Skipper warn people not to go overboard, I remember Lazenby called out that he thought we ought to leave Miss Hewson alone and that she would get over it best by herself. And Hewson said he couldn't leave her. And Pollock, you were milling round asking what the police thought they were doing. So I yelled for the police – it seemed a reasonable thing to do – and a great bumbling copper landed on the deck like a whale.'

Nobody looked, now, at the motionless figure behind the corner table.

'Do I gather,' Alleyn said, 'that at no stage did you hear Dr Natouche's voice? Or hear him come down to his cabin?'

Caley was silent.

'I did, then,' Pollock said. 'I heard him just before she began to call out "Let me go". He was with her. He *said* something to her. I'll swear to that. Gawd knows what he did.'

'Did anyone hear Dr Natouche after they heard Miss Hewson for the last time?'

As if they were giving responses in some disreputable litany, Pollock, Hewson and Lazenby loudly said 'No.'

'Skipper?'

The Skipper laid his workaday hands out on his knees and frowned at them. 'I can't say I did. I was forrard in my cabin and in bed when it started up. I shifted into this rig and came along. They were on deck and someone was bawling for the police. Not her. A man. Mr Bard, if he says so. She'd gone. I never heard the doctor at any stage and I didn't bump into him like I did the others.'

'Yeah, and do you know why, mate?' Pollock said. 'Because he wasn't there. Because he'd followed her and done bloody murder on her up the hill. Because he's not a bloody doctor but a bloody murderer. Now!'

Alleyn moved to face Dr Natouche. Tillottson, who had been taking notes walked to the foot of the companion-way. At the head of it the constable could be seen beyond the half-door.

Dr Natouche had risen.

'Do you want to make a statement?' Alleyn asked and knew that they all waited for the well-worn sequel. But already the enormous voice had begun.

'I am alone,' it said, 'and must defend myself. When these men who accuse me had gone to their cabins I was, as Mr Hewson has said, on deck. The mist or fog was dense and I could see nothing but a few feet of deck and the glow of the lockhouse windows and that only very faintly. The night was oppressive and damp. I was about to go back when Miss Hewson came very quickly up the stairway, crying out and weeping and in a condition of advanced hysteria. She ran into me and would have fallen. I took her by the arms and tried to calm her. She became violent and screamed "Let me go" several times. Since I frightened her – she was I believe allergic to people of my colour – I did let her go and she stumbled across the deck and was hidden by the fog. I thought she might injure herself. I drew nearer but she heard me and screamed again: "Let me go". By that time these gentlemen were approaching. They came up on deck calling to her and plunging about in the fog. I waited unseen until I heard the Captain's voice and then, since obviously there was nothing I could do, I went below and to bed. I remained in my cabin until the arrival of your colleagues.'

He waited for a moment. 'That is all,' he said and sat down.

Alleyn had the impression, an obscene and grotesque one, of Lazenby, Pollock and Hewson running together and coagulating into a corporate blob of enormity. They did actually move towards each other. They stood close and watched Natouche.

Caley Bard said: 'I'm sorry. I'm terribly sorry but I can't accept that. It's just not true. It can't be true.'

The group of three moved very slightly. Pollock gave a little hiss of satisfaction. Lazenby said: 'Ah!' and Hewson: 'Even *he* sees that,' as if Caley were an implacable enemy.

'Why can't it be true?' Alleyn said.

Caley walked up to Natouche and looked steadily at him.

'Because,' he said, 'I never left the top of the companion-way. I stood there, listening to the hullabaloo and not knowing what to do. I stayed there until after the Skipper arrived and after the constable came on board. He – ' he moved his head at Natouche – 'Well, look at him. The size of him. He never passed me or went down the companion-way. Never. He wasn't there.'

Natouche's arms rose naked from the sleeves of his gown, his hands curled above his head and his teeth were bared. He looked like an effigy, carved from ebony. Before the curled hands could do their work, Alleyn and Tillottson grabbed him. They lurched against the bar. Troy's Signs of the Zodiac fell from their firmament and Hewson screamed: 'Get him! Get him! Get him!'

Above the uproar, voices shouted on deck. A rival commotion had broken out and even as Alleyn and Tillottson screwed the great arms behind the heavy back, somebody came tumbling down the companion-way, followed by Inspector Fox and two deeply perturbed constables.

He was a Dickensian little man: bald, bespectacled and irritated. He contemplated the outlandish scene with distaste and cried in a shrillish voice:

'Once and for all, I demand to know the meaning of this masquerade.'

Fox arrived at his side and, seeing his principal engaged in strenuous activity, lent his aid. Natouche no longer struggled. He looked at the men who had subdued him as if he himself was in the ascendant.

Alleyn moved away from him and confronted the little man. 'May I have your name, sir,' he said.

'My name!' the little man ejaculated. '*My name!* Certainly you may have my name, sir. My name, sir, is Caley Bard.'

CHAPTER 10

Closed File

'And that,' Alleyn said, laying down his file, 'was virtually the end of the Jampot. He is now, together with his chums, serving a life sentence and good behaviour is not likely to release him in the foreseeable future. I understand he finds it particularly irksome not to be able to lepidopterize on Dartmoor where, as we know from Sir Arthur Conan Doyle, there are butterflies. Or perhaps none of you has read *The Hound of the Baskervilles*. All right, Carmichael, I dare say you have.

'A little time before Foljambe arrived in England the real Caley Bard, who is a gifted amateur of the net and killing-bottle, had advertised in *The Times* for a fellow-lepidopterist who would share expenses on a butterfly hunt in South America. Foljambe's agents in England – Messrs. Dinky Dickson alias the Reverend Mr Lazenby and Stanley Pollock – noted this circumstance. Further discreet inquiries satisfied them that Mr Bard had left for a protracted visit to South America, that he was something of a recluse and had private means fortified by occasional coaching in mathematics for tutorial organizations. So it was decided that the mantle of Lepidoptery should descend upon the Jampot's shoulders, lepidoptery was his hobby as a schoolboy and he knew enough to pass muster with a casual enthusiast. If, by an outlandish chance, he had encountered an expert or an acquaintance of his original he would have exclaimed: "Me? oh, no, not *that* Caley Bard. I wish I were!" or words to that effect. The only thing they hadn't anticipated was that the real Caley Bard should return, two months before his time, having picked up an unpleasant bug in the country beyond La Paz.

'So that when, at my suggestion, one of our chaps called at the address they found the house occupied by an extremely irate little man whom they promptly flew by helicopter to Tollardwark for what I am obliged to call a confrontation.

'There was, of course, no doubt about his identity and guilt, once we had established alibis for the others in the Andropulos business. However, he did make a mistake. He talked about Miss Rickerby-Carrick's bit of Fabergé before he should have known it was anything of the sort. A rare thing, though, for him to slip up. He's a brilliant villain.

'He presented himself to my wife in exactly the light best calculated to produce a tolerant and amused acceptance. She was not likely, as he realized, to succumb to his well-tested but, to a man, inexplicable charms but she found him companionable and entertaining. I am told that a swivel-eye is, to many people, sexually alluring. The Jampot's swivel-eye was the result of a punch-up, or a jab-up, with a rival gang in Santa Cruz. He subsequently underwent a bit of very efficient plastic surgery. Lazenby – Dickson to you – had lost *his* eye, by the way, in the Second World War where he was an Australian army chaplain until they found him out. He was born in the West Indies, went to a European mission-school and had in fact been ordained and unfrocked. He had no difficulty at all in passing himself off to the Bishop of Norminster who was very cross about it.

'That, more or less, is it. I'll be glad to answer questions.'

Carmichael's instant boots had already scraped the floor when Alleyn caught the eye of a quiet-looking type in the back row.

'Yes?' he said. 'Something?'

'Sir. I would like to ask, sir, if the missing pages from the diary ever came to hand?'

'No. We searched, of course, but it was a hopeless job. Lazenby probably reduced them to pulp and put them down the lavatory.'

'Sir. Having read them when he sat on the bank, sir, and torn them out as a consequence?'

'That's it. Before the trial he ratted in the hope of reducing his sentence and will live in terror of the Jampot for the rest of his days.

He told us the missing pages contained an account of the conversation Miss Rickerby-Carrick overheard in Tollardwark. Between – '

Carmichael's boots became agitated.

' – between,' Alleyn loudly went on, 'Foljambe, Lazenby and Pollock. About – all right, Carmichael, all right. You tell us.'

'About your leddy-wife maybe,' Carmichael said, 'sir. And maybe they touched on the matter of the planted picture, sir. And their liaison with cyclists, and so on and so forth.'

'Perhaps. But according to the wretched Lazenby it was mostly about Andropulos. When Miss Rickerby-Carrick tried to confide in my wife, she was very agitated. She kept saying "And – And – " and "Oh God. Wait". I think – we shall never know, of course – she was trying to remember his name. Lazenby intervened as the Jampot did when Pollock became altogether too interested in my wife's drawing and altogether too ready to assist. The Jampot let it appear that he resented Pollock's over-familiarity. So he did, but not for reasons of gallantry.'

Carmichael resumed his seat.

'Any more? Yes?' It was the same man in the back row.

'I was wondering, sir, exactly what did happen on the night in question. At Crossdyke, sir?'

'The autopsy showed Miss Rickerby-Carrick had taken a pretty massive barbiturate. One of Miss Hewson's pills no doubt. She slept on deck at the after-end behind a heap of chairs covered by a tarpaulin. Foljambe's cabin, No. I, was next to the companion-way. When all was quiet he went up through the saloon to the deck and, because she knew too much, killed her, took the Fabergé jewel and handed it and the body over to the cyclist – his name by the way *is* Smith – who had been ordered to wait ashore for it and was given his instructions. My wife remembered that, at sometime in the night, she had heard the motorbike engine. Yes?'

A man in the third row said, 'Sir: Did they all know, sir? About the murder, sir. Except the doctor?'

'According to Lazenby (I'll still call him that) not beforehand. When Lazenby told Foljambe about the diary Foljambe merely said he would deal with the situation and ordered Lazenby to keep his mouth shut, which he did. No doubt in the sequel they all knew or guessed. But he was not a confiding type, even with his closest associates.'

'And – the way they carried on, sir. Bickering and all that among themselves. Was that a put-up show, then, sir?'

'Ah!' Alleyn said. 'That's what my wife asked me the next night in Norminster.'

I

'It was all a put-up job, then?' Troy asked. 'The way Caley – he – I still think of him as that – the way he blazed away at Pollock and the way those three seemed to dislike and fight shy of him and abuse him – well – the whole inter-relationship as it was displayed to us? All an act?'

'My love, yes.'

'But, Hewson's distress over his sister – ' she turned to Dr Natouche. 'You said he was distressed, didn't you?'

'I thought so, certainly.'

'He was distressed all right and he was deadly frightened into the bargain,' Alleyn grunted and after a moment he said: 'You were among counterfeiters, darling, and very expert hands at that. Do fill up your glass, Natouche.'

'Thank you. I suppose,' Dr Natouche said, 'they looked upon me as a sort of windfall. They could all combine to throw suspicion upon me. Bard was particularly adroit. I must apologize, by the way, for losing my temper. It was when he lied about my going below during the uproar. He knew perfectly well that I went below. We ran into each other at the stairhead. When he lied I behaved like the savage they all thought me.' He turned to Troy. 'I am glad you did not see it,' he said.

Alleyn remembered the uplifted ebony arms, the curved hands and the naked fury of the face and he thought Troy might have seen an element in Dr Natouche's rage that he would never suspect her of finding.

In some sort echoing, as she often did, Alleyn's thoughts about her, she said to Dr Natouche. 'You must say at once – you will, please, won't you? – if it's an unwelcome suggestion, but some day, when you can spare the time, will you let me paint you?'

'If you look closely,' he said with an air of astonishment, 'you may be able to see that I am blushing.'

They finished their dinner and talked for a time and then Troy and Alleyn walked with Dr Natouche to the garage where he had left his car. The inquest was over and he was driving back to Liverpool that night. By a sort of tacit consent they did not discuss the sequel.

It was a sultry night and very still with a hint of thunder in the air. But there was no mist. They came to the top of Wharf Lane and looked down at The River. There was the *Zodiac*, quietly riding at her moorings with her cherry-coloured curtains glowing companionably. And there, on the right, were the offices of The Pleasure Craft and Riverage Company. Troy fancied she could make out a card stuck to the window and crossed the lane to see.

'They've forgotten to take it down,' she said and the men read it.

> M.V. *Zodiac*. Last minute cancellation.
> A single-berth cabin is available for
> this day's sailing. Apply within.

When in Rome

Contents

Cast of Characters

Patrons of Mr Sebastian Mailer's conducted tour

Mr Barnaby Grant — *Author of Simon in Latium*

The Baron and Baroness Van der Veghel

Miss Sophy Jason — *Writer of children's stories*

Lady Braceley

The Hon. Kenneth Dorne — *Her nephew*

Major Hamilton Sweet

Superintendent Roderick Alleyn — *CID London*

Officers of the Roman Police Department

Il Questore Valdarno

Il Vice-Questore Bergarmi

Sundry members of the Questura

Dominicans in charge at S. Tommaso in Pallaria

Father Denys

Brother Dominic

Mr Sebastian Mailer — *Il Cicerone Conducted Tours*

Giovanni Vecchi — *His assistant*

Violetta — *A postcard vendor*

Marco — *A restaurateur*

A British Consul

Signor Pace — *A travel agent*

A Porter and sundry waiters

CHAPTER 1

Barnaby in Rome

Barnaby Grant looked at the Etruscan Bride and Bridegroom who reclined so easily on their sarcophagal couch and wondered why they had died so young and whether, as in Verona, they had died together. Their gentle lips, he thought, brushed with amusement, might easily tilt into the arrowhead smile of Apollo and Hermes. How fulfilled they were and how enigmatically alike. What signal did she give with her largish hands? How touchingly *his* hand hovered above her shoulder.

' – from Cerveteri,' said a guide rapidly. 'Five hundred and thirty years before Christ.'

'Christ!' said a tourist on a note of exhaustion.

The party moved on. Grant stayed behind for a time and then, certain that he desired to see no more that morning, left the Villa Giulia and took a taxi to the Piazza Colonna for a glass of beer.

II

As he sat at a kerbside table in the Piazza Colonna, Barnaby thought of the Etruscan smile and listened to thunder.

The heavens boomed largely above the noon traffic but whatever lightning there might be was not evident, being masked by a black canopy of low and swollen cloud. At any moment, thought Barnaby, Marcus Aurelius's Column will prick it and like 'a foul bumbard' it will shed its liquor! And then what a scene!

Before him on the table stood a glass and a bottle of beer. His mackintosh was folded over the back of his chair and on the ground, leaning against his leg, was a locked attaché case. Every so often his left hand dropped to the case and fingered it. Refreshed by this contact his mouth would take on an easier look and he would blink slowly and push away the lock of black hair that overhung his forehead.

A bit of a swine, this one, he thought. It's been a bit of a swine.

A heavy rumbling again broke out overhead. Thunder on the left, Barnaby thought. The gods are cross with us.

He refilled his glass and looked about him.

The kerbside caffè had been crowded but now, under threat of a downpour, many customers had left and the waiters had tipped over their chairs. The tables on either side of his own, however, were still occupied: that on his right by three lowering young men whose calloused hands jealously enclosed their glasses and whose slow eyes looked sideways at their surroundings. Countrymen, Grant thought, who would have been easier in a less consequential setting and would be shocked by the amount of their bill. On his left sat a Roman couple in love. Forbidden by law to kiss in public, they gazed, clung hand-to-hand, and exchanged trembling smiles. The young man extended his forefinger and traced the unmarred excellence of his girl's lips. They responded, quivering. Barnaby could not help watching the lovers. They were unaware of him and indeed of everything else around them, but on the first visible and livid flash of lightning, they were taken out of themselves and turned their faces towards him.

It was at this moment, appropriately as he was later to consider, that he saw, framed by their separated heads, the distant figure of an Englishman.

He knew at once that the man was English. Perhaps it was his clothes. Or, more specifically, his jacket. It was shabby and out-of-date but it had been made from West Country tweed though not, perhaps, for its present wearer. And then – the tie. Frayed and faded, grease-spotted and lumpish: there it was, scarcely recognizable, but if you were so minded, august. For the rest, his garments were dingy and nondescript. His hat, a rusty black felt, was obviously Italian. It was pulled forward and cast a shadow down to the bridge of the nose, over a face of which the most noticeable feature was its extreme pallor. The mouth, however, was red and rather full-lipped. So dark had the noonday turned that without that brief flash, Barnaby could scarcely have seen the shadowed eyes. He felt an odd little shock within himself when he realized they were very light in colour and were fixed on him. A great crack of thunder banged out overhead. The black canopy burst and fell out of the sky in a deluge.

There was a stampede. Barnaby snatched up his raincoat, struggled into it and dragged the hood over his head. He had not paid his bill and groped for his pocket-book. The three countrymen blundered towards him and there was some sort of collision between them and the young couple. The young man broke into loud quarrelsome expostulation. Barnaby could find nothing smaller than a thousand-lire note. He turned away, looked round for a waiter and found that they had all retreated under the canvas awning. His own man saw him, made a grand-opera gesture of despair, and turned his back.

'*Aspetti,*' Barnaby shouted in phrase-book Italian waving his thousand-lire note. '*Quanto devo pagare?*'

The waiter placed his hands together as if in prayer and turned up his eyes.

'*Basta!*'

' – *lasci passare* – '

'*Se ne vada ora* – '

'*Non desidero parlarle.*'

'*Non l'ho fatto io* –'

'*Vattene!*'

'*Sciocchezze!*'

The row between the lover and the countrymen was heating up. They now screamed into each other's faces behind Barnaby's back. The waiter indicated, with a multiple gesture, the heavens, the rain, his own defencelessness.

Barnaby thought: After all, I'm the one with a raincoat. Somebody crashed into his back and sent him spread-eagled across his table.

A scene of the utmost confusion followed accompanied by flashes of lightning, immediate thunder-claps and torrents of rain. Barnaby was winded and bruised. A piece of glass had cut the palm of his hand and his nose also bled. The combatants had disappeared but his waiter, now equipped with an enormous orange-and-red umbrella, babbled over him and made ineffectual dabs at his hand. The other waiters, clustered beneath the awning, rendered a chorus to the action. '*Poverino!*' they exclaimed. 'What a misfortune!'

Barnaby recovered an upright posture. With one hand he dragged a handkerchief from the pocket of his raincoat and clapped it to his face. In the other he extended to the waiter his bloodied and rain-sopped thousand-lire note.

'Here,' he said in his basic Italian. 'Keep the change. I require a taxi.'

The waiter ejaculated with evident pleasure. Barnaby sat down abruptly on a chair that had become a bird-bath. The waiter ludicrously inserted his umbrella into a socket in the middle of the table, said something incomprehensible, turned up the collar of his white jacket and bolted into the interior. To telephone, Barnaby hoped, for a taxi.

The Piazza Colonna was rain-possessed. A huge weight of water flooded the street and pavements and spurted off the roofs of cars as if another multiple Roman fountain had been born. Motorists stared through blurred glass and past jigging windscreen-wipers at the world outside. Except for isolated, scurrying wayfarers, the pavements were emptied. Barnaby Grant, huddled, alone and ridiculous under his orange-and-red umbrella, staunched his bloody nose. He attracted a certain incredulous attention. The waiter had disappeared and his comrades had got up among themselves one of those inscrutable Italian conversations that appear to be quarrels but very often end in backslaps and roars of laughter. Barnaby never could form the slightest notion of how long he had sat under the umbrella before he made his hideous discovery, before his left arm dangled from his shoulder and his left hand encountered – nothing.

As if it had a separate entity the hand explored, discovered only the leg of his chair, widened its search and found – nothing.

He remembered afterwards that he had been afraid to get into touch with his hand, to duck his head and look down and find a puddle of water, the iron foot of his chair-leg and again – nothing.

The experience that followed could, he afterwards supposed, be compared to the popular belief about drowning. In that an impossible flood of thoughts crowded his brain. He thought, for instance, of how long it had taken him to write his book, of his knowledge that undoubtedly it was the best thing he had done, perhaps would ever do. He remembered his agent had once suggested that it was dangerous to write in longhand with no duplication. He remembered how isolated he was in Rome with virtually no Italian, and how he hadn't bothered to use his introductions. He thought inaccurately of – who? Was it Sir Isaac Newton? 'O, Diamond, Diamond, you little know what you have done!' Above all he thought of the ineffable, the unthinkable, the atrocious boredom of what must now ensue: the awful prospect of taking steps as opposed to the numb desolation of his loss: the rock-bottom horror of the event itself which had caused a thing like a water-ram to pound in his thorax. A classic phrase stood up in his thoughts: 'I am undone.' And he almost cried it aloud.

Here, now, was the waiter, smirking and triumphant, and here at the kerbside, a horse-carriage with a great umbrella protecting the seats and a wary-looking driver with some sort of tarpaulin over his head.

Grant attempted to indicate his loss. He pointed to where his attaché case had been, he grimaced, he gesticulated. He groped for his phrase-book and thumbed through it. '*Ho perduto,*' he said. '*Ho perduto mia valigia.* Have you got it? My case? *Non trovo. Valigia.*'

The waiter exclaimed and idiotically looked under the table and round about the flooded surroundings. He then bolted into cover and stood there gazing at Barnaby and shrugging with every inch of his person.

Barnaby thought: This is it. This is the worst thing that has ever happened to me.

The driver of the horse-carriage hailed him mellifluously and seemed to implore him to make up his mind. He looked at the desolation around him and got into the carriage.

'*Consolato Britannico,*' Grant shouted. 'O God! *Consolato Britannico.*'

III

'Now look here,' the Consul had said, as if Barnaby Grant required the information, 'this is a bad business, you know. It's a bad business.'

'You, my dear Consul, are telling me.'

'Quite so. Quite so. Now, we'll have to see what we can do, won't we? My wife,' he added, 'is a great fan of yours. She'll be quite concerned when she hears of this. She's a bit of an egg-head,' he had jokingly confided.

Barnaby had not replied. He contemplated his fellow-Briton over a handful of lint kindly provided by the consular staff and rested his bandaged left hand upon his knee.

'Well, of course,' the Consul continued argumentatively, 'properly speaking it's a matter for the police. Though I must say – however, if you'll wait a moment I'll just put a call through. I've got a personal contact – nothing like approaching at the right level, is there? Now, then.'

After a number of delays there had been a long and virtually incomprehensible conversation during which Barnaby fancied he was being described as Great Britain's most celebrated novelist. With many pauses to refer to Barnaby himself, the Consul related at dictation speed the details of the affair and when that was over showered a number of grateful compliments into the telephone – '*E stato molto gentile – Grazie, Molto grazie, Signore,*' which even poor Barnaby could understand.

The Consul replaced the receiver and pulled a grimace. 'Not much joy from *that* quarter,' he said. Barnaby swallowed and felt sick.

He was assured that everything that could be done, would be done, but, the Consul pointed out, they hadn't much to go on, had they? Still, he added more brightly, there was always the chance that Barnaby might be blackmailed.

'*Blackmailed?*'

'Well, you see, whoever took the case probably expected, if not a haul of valuables, or cash, something in the nature of documents for the recovery of which a reward would be offered and a haggling basis thus set up. *Blackmail,*' said the Consul, 'was not, of course, the right word. *Ransom* would be more appropriate. Although . . . ' He was a man of broken sentences and he left this one suspended in an atmosphere of extreme discomfort.

'Then I should advertise and offer a reward?'

'Certainly. Certainly. We'll get something worked out. We'll just give my secretary the details in English and she'll translate and see to the insertions.'

'I'm being a trouble,' said the wretched Barnaby.

'We're used to it,' the Consul sighed. 'Your name and London address were on the manuscript, you said, but the case was locked. Not, of course, that *that* amounts to anything.'

'I suppose not.'

'You are staying at – ?'

'The Pensione Gallico.'

'Ah yes. Have you the telephone number?'

'Yes – I think so – somewhere about me.'

Barnaby fished distractedly in his breast pocket, pulled out his note-case, passport and two envelopes which fell on the desk, face downwards. He had scribbled the Pensione Gallico address and telephone number on the back of one of them.

'That's it,' he said and slid the envelope across to the Consul, who was already observant of its august crest.

'Ah – yes. Thank you.' He gave a little laugh. 'Done your duty and signed the book, I see,' he said.

'What? Oh – that. Well, no, actually,' Barnaby mumbled. 'It's – er – some sort of luncheon. Tomorrow. I mustn't take up any more of your time. I'm enormously grateful.'

The Consul, beaming and expanding, stretched his arm across the desk and made a fin of his hand. 'No, no, no. Very glad you came to us. I feel pretty confident, all things considered. *Nil desperandum,* you know, *nil desperandum.* Rise above!'

But it wasn't possible to rise very far above his loss as two days trickled by and there was no response to advertisements and nothing came of a long language-haltered interview with a beautiful representative of the Questura. He attended his Embassy luncheon and tried to react appropriately to ambassadorial commiseration and concern. But for most of the time he sat on the roof-garden of the Pensione Gallico among potted geraniums and flights of swallows. His bedroom had a french window opening on to a neglected corner of this garden and there he waited and listened in agony for every telephone call within. From time to time he half-faced the awful notion of re-writing the hundred thousand words of his novel but the prospect made him physically as well as emotionally sick as he turned away from it.

Every so often he experienced the sensation of an abrupt descent in an infernal lift. He started out of fits of sleep into a waking nightmare.

He told himself he should write to his agent and to his publisher but the mere thought of doing so tasted as acrid as bile and he sat and listened for the telephone instead.

On the third morning a heat wave came upon Rome. The roof-garden was like a furnace. He was alone in his corner with an uneaten brioche, a pot of honey and three wasps. He was given over to a sort of fretful lassitude and finally to a condition that he supposed must be that of Despair itself. 'What I need,' he told himself on a wave of nausea, 'is a bloody good cry on somebody's bloody bosom.'

One of the two waiters came out.

'*Finito?*' he sang, as usual. And then, when Barnaby gave his punctual assent, seemed to indicate that he should come indoors. At first he thought the waiter was suggesting that it was too hot where he was and then that for some reason the manageress wanted to see him.

And then, as a sudden jolt of hope shook him, he saw a fattish man with a jacket hooked over his shoulders come out of the house door and advance towards him. He was between Barnaby and the sun and appeared fantastic, black and insubstantial but at once Barnaby recognized him.

His reactions were chaotic. He saw the man as if between the inclined heads of two lovers, and to the accompaniment of thunder and lightning. And whether the sensation that flooded him was one solely of terrified relief, or of a kind of blessed anticlimax he could never determine. He merely wondered, when the man advanced into the shade and drew an attaché case from under his jacket, if he himself was going to faint.

'Mr Barnaby Grant?' asked the man. 'I think you will be pleased to see me, will you not?'

IV

They escaped from the Gallico which seemed to be over-run with housemaids to a very small caffè in a shaded by-way off the Piazza Navona, a short walk away. His companion had suggested it. 'Unless, of course,' he said archly, 'you prefer something smarter – like the Colonna, for instance,' and Barnaby had shuddered. He took his attaché case with him and, at his guest's suggestion, unlocked it. There, in two looseleaf folders, lay his book, enclosed by giant-sized rubber bands. The last letter from his agent still lay on top, just as he had left it.

He had rather wildly offered his guest champagne cocktails, cognac, wine – anything – but when reminded that it was not yet ten o'clock in the morning settled for coffee. 'Well then,' he said, 'at a more appropriate hour – you will let me – and in the meantime I must – well – of course.'

He slid his hand inside his jacket. His heart still thumped at it like a fist.

'You are thinking of the reward so generously offered,' said his companion. 'But, please – no. No. It is out of the question. To have been of service even on so insignificant a scale to Barnaby Grant – that really is a golden reward. Believe me.'

Barnaby had not expected this and he at once felt he had committed a gigantic error in taste. He had been misled, he supposed, by general appearances: not only by the shabby alpaca jacket that had replaced the English tweed and like it was hooked over the shoulders, displaying a dingy open shirt with worn cuffs, nor by the black-green hat or the really lamentable shoes but by something indefinable in the man himself. I wish, he thought, I could take an instant liking to him. I owe him that, at the least.

And as his companion talked Barnaby found himself engaged in the occupational habit of the novelist: he dwelt on the bullet head, close cropped like an American schoolboy's, and the mouse-coloured sparse fringe. He noted the extreme pallor of the skin, its appearance of softness and fine texture like a woman's: the unexpected fullness and rich colour of the mouth and those large pale eyes that had looked so fixedly into his in the Piazza Colonna. The voice and speech? High but muted, it had no discernible accent but carried a suggestion of careful phrasing. Perhaps English was no longer the habitual language. His choice of words was pedantic as if he had memorized his sentences for a public address.

His hands were plump and delicate and the nails bitten to the quick.

His name was Sebastian Mailer.

'You wonder, of course,' he was saying, 'why you have been subjected to this no doubt agonizing delay. You would like to know the circumstances?'

'Very much.'

'I can't hope that you noticed me the other morning in Piazza Colonna.'

'But yes. I remember you very well.'

'Perhaps I stared. You see, I recognized you at once from the photographs on your book-jacket. I must tell you I am a most avid admirer, Mr Grant.'

Barnaby murmured.

'I am also, which is more to the point, what might be described as "an old Roman hand". I have lived here for many years and have acquired some knowledge of Roman society at a number of levels. Including the lowest. You see I am frank.'

'Why not?'

'Why not indeed! My motives in what I imagine some of our compatriots would call muck-raking, are aesthetic and I think I may say philosophical, but with that I must not trouble you. It will do well enough if I tell you that at the same time as I recognized you I also recognized a despicable person known to the Roman riff-raff as – I translate – "Feather-fingers". He was stationed at a short distance from you and behind your back. His eyes were fastened upon your attaché case.'

'God!'

'Indeed, yes. Now, you will recollect that the incipient thunderstorm broke abruptly and that with the downpour and subsequent confusion a fracas arose between some of the occupants of tables adjacent to your own.'

'Yes.'

'And that you received a violent blow in the back that knocked you across your table.'

'So it did,' Barnaby agreed.

'Of course you thought that you had been struck by one of the contestants but this was not so. The character I have brought to your notice took advantage of the mêlée, darted forward, delivered the blow with his shoulder, snatched up your case and bolted. It was an admirably timed manoeuvre and executed with the greatest speed and precision. The contestants continued to shout at each other and I, my dear Mr Grant, gave chase.'

He sipped his coffee, made a small inclination, an acknowledgement perhaps of Barnaby's passionate attention.

'It was a long pursuit,' Mailer continued. 'But I clung to his trail and – is the phrase "ran him to earth"? It *is*. Thank you. I ran him to earth, then, in what purveyors of sensational fiction would describe as "a certain caffè in such-and-such a little street not a thousand miles from – " etc., etc. – perhaps my phraseology is somewhat dated. In plain terms I caught up with him at his habitual haunt, and by means with which I shall not trouble you, recovered your attaché case.'

'On the same day,' Barnaby couldn't help asking, 'that I lost it?'

'Ah! As the cornered victim of an interrogation always says: I am glad you asked that question. Mr Grant, with any less distinguished person I would have come armed with a plausible prevarication. With you, I cannot adopt this measure. I did not return your case before because –'

He paused, smiling very slightly, and without removing his gaze from Barnaby's face, pushed up the shirt-sleeve of his left arm which was white-skinned and hairless. He rested it palm upwards on the table and slid it towards Barnaby.

'You can see for yourself,' he said. 'They look rather like mosquito bites, do they not. But I'm sure you will recognize them for what they are. Do you?'

'I – I think I do.'

'Quite. I have acquired an addiction for cocaine. Rather "square" of me, isn't it? I really must change, one of these days, to something groovier. You see I am conversant with the jargon. But I digress. I am ashamed to say that after my encounter with "Feather-fingers", I found myself greatly shaken. No doubt my constitution has been somewhat undermined by my unfortunate proclivity. I am not a robust man. I called upon my – the accepted term is, I believe, fix – and, in short, I rather exceeded my usual allowance and have been out of circulation until this morning. I cannot, of course, hope that you will forgive me.'

Barnaby gave himself a breathing space and then – he was a generous man – said: 'I'm so bloody thankful to have it back I feel nothing but gratitude, I promise you. After all, the case was locked and you were not to know – '

'Oh but I was! I guessed. When I came to myself I guessed. The weight, for one thing. And the way it shifted, you know, inside. And then, of course, I saw your advertisement: "containing manuscript of value only to owner". So I cannot lay that flattering unction to my soul, Mr Grant.'

He produced a dubious handkerchief and wiped his neck and face with it. The little caffè was on the shady side of the street but Mr Mailer sweated excessively.

'Will you have some more coffee?'

'Thank you. You are very kind. Most kind.'

The coffee seemed to revive him. He held the cup in his two plump, soiled hands and looked at Barnaby over the top.

'I feel so deeply in your debt,' Barnaby said. 'Is there nothing I can do – ?'

'You will think me unbearably fulsome – I have, I believe, become rather Latinized in my style, but I assure you the mere fact of meeting you and in some small manner – '

This conversation, Barnaby thought, is going round in circles. 'Well,' he said, 'you must dine with me. Let's make a time, shall we?'

But Mr Mailer, now squeezing his palms together, was evidently on the edge of speech and presently achieved it. After a multitude of deprecating parentheses he at last confessed that he himself had written a book.

He had been at it for three years: the present version was his fourth. Through bitter experience, Barnaby knew what was coming and knew, also, that he must accept his fate. The all-too-familiar phrases were being delivered '. . . value, enormously, your opinion . . .' '. . . glance through it' '. . . advice from such an authority . . .' '. . . interest a publisher. . .'

'I'll read it, of course,' Barnaby said. 'Have you brought it with you?'

Mr Mailer, it emerged, was sitting on it. By some adroit and nimble sleight-of-hand, he had passed it under his rump while Barnaby was intent upon his recovered property. He now drew it out, wrapped in a dampish Roman news-sheet and, with trembling fingers, uncovered it. A manuscript, closely written in an Italianate script, but not, Barnaby rejoiced to see, bulky. Perhaps forty thousand words, perhaps, with any luck, less.

'Neither a novel nor a novella in length, I'm afraid,' said its author, 'but so it has befallen and as such I abide by it.'

Barnaby looked up quickly. Mr Mailer's mouth had compressed and lifted at the corners. Not so difficult, after all, Barnaby thought.

'I hope,' said Mr Mailer, 'my handwriting does not present undue difficulties. I cannot afford a typist.'

'It seems very clear.'

'If so, it will not take more than a few hours of your time. Perhaps in two days or so I may – ? But I mustn't be clamorous.'

Barnaby thought: And I must do this handsomely. He said: 'Look, I've a suggestion. Dine with me the day after tomorrow and I'll tell you what I think.'

'How kind you are! I am overwhelmed. But, please, you must allow me – if you don't object to – well to somewhere – quite modest – like this, for example. There is a little trattoria, as you see. Their *fettuccini* – really very good and their wine quite respectable. The manager is a friend of mine and will take care of us.'

'It sounds admirable and by all means let us come here but it shall be my party, Mr Mailer, if you please. You shall order our dinner. I am in your hands.'

'Indeed? Really? Then I must speak with him beforehand.'

On this understanding they parted.

At the Pensione Gallico Barnaby told everybody he encountered: the manageress, the two waiters, even the chambermaid who had little or no English, of the recovery of his manuscript. Some of them understood him and some did not. All rejoiced. He rang up the Consulate which was loud in felicitations. He paid for his advertisements.

When all this had been accomplished he re-read such bits of his book as he had felt needed to be re-written, skipping from one part to another.

It crossed his mind that his dominant reaction to the events of the past three days was now one of anticlimax: All that agony and – back to normal, he thought and turned a page.

In a groove between the sheets held by their looseleaf binder he noticed a smear and, on opening the manuscript more widely, found a slight deposit of something that looked like cigarette ash. He had given up smoking two years ago.

V

On second thoughts (and after a close examination of the lock on his case) he reminded himself that the lady who did for him in London was a chain-smoker and excessively curious and that his manuscript often lay open on his table. This reflection comforted him and he was able to work on his book and, in the siesta, to read Mr Mailer's near-novella with tolerable composure.

'Angelo in August
by
Sebastian Mailer.'

It wasn't bad. A bit jewelled. A bit fancy. Indecent in parts but probably not within the meaning of the act. And considering it was a fourth draft, more than a bit careless: words omitted: repetitions, redundancies. Barnaby wondered if cocaine could be held responsible for these lapses. But he'd seen many a worse in print and if Mr Mailer could cook up one or two shorter jobs to fill out a volume he might very well find a publisher for it.

He was struck by an amusing coincidence and when, at the appointed time, they met for dinner, he spoke of it to Mr Mailer.

'By the way,' he said, refilling Mr Mailer's glass, 'you have introduced a secondary theme which is actually the ground-swell of my own book.'

'Oh no!' his guest ejaculated, and then: 'But we are told, aren't we, that there are only – how many is it? three? – four? – basic themes?'

'And that all subject matter can be traced to one or another of them? Yes. This is only a detail in your story, and you don't develop it. Indeed, I feel it's extraneous and might well be dropped. The suggestion is *not*,' Barnaby added, 'prompted by professional jealousy,' and they both laughed, Mr Mailer a great deal louder than Barnaby. He evidently repeated the joke in Italian to some acquaintances of his whom he had greeted on their arrival and had presented to Barnaby. They sat at the next table and were much diverted. Taking advantage of the appropriate moment, they drank Barnaby's health.

The dinner, altogether, was a great success. The food was excellent, the wine acceptable, the proprietor attentive and the *mise-en-scène* congenial. Down the narrowest of alleyways they looked into the Piazza Navona, and saw the water-god Il Moro in combat with his Fish, superbly lit. They could almost hear the splash of his fountains above the multiple voice of Rome at night. Groups of youths moved elegantly about Navona and arrogant girls thrust bosoms like those of figureheads at the eddying crowds. The midsummer night pulsed with its own beauty. Barnaby felt within himself an excitement that rose from a more potent ferment than their gentle wine could induce. He was exalted.

He leant back in his chair, fetched a deep breath, caught Mr Mailer's eye and laughed. 'I feel,' he said, 'as if I had only just arrived in Rome.'

'And perhaps as if the night had only just begun?'

'Something of the sort.'

'Adventure?' Mailer hinted.

Perhaps, after all, the wine had not been so gentle. There was an uncertainty about what he saw when he looked at Mailer, as if a new personality emerged. He really had got *very* rum eyes, thought Barnaby, tolerantly.

'An adventure?' the voice insisted. 'May I help you, I wonder? A cicerone?'

May I help you? Barnaby thought. He might be a shop-assistant. But he stretched himself a little and heard himself say lightly: 'Well – in what way?'

'In any way,' Mailer murmured. 'Really, in any way at all. I'm versatile.'

'Oh,' Barnaby said. 'I'm very orthodox, you know. The largest Square,' he added and thought the addition brilliantly funny, 'in Rome.'

'Then, if you will allow me – '

The proprietor was there with his bill. Barnaby thought that the little trattoria had become very quiet but when he looked round he saw that all the patrons were still there and behaving quite normally. He had some difficulty in finding the right notes but Mr Mailer helped him and Barnaby begged him to give a generous tip.

'Very good indeed,' Barnaby said to the proprietor, 'I shall return.' They shook hands warmly.

And then Barnaby, with Mr Mailer at his elbow, walked into narrow streets past glowing windows and pitch-dark entries, through groups of people who shouted and by-ways that were silent into what was, for him, an entirely different Rome.

CHAPTER 2

An Expedition is Arranged

Barnaby had no further encounter with Sebastian Mailer until the following spring when he returned to Rome after seeing his book launched with much éclat in London. His Pensione Gallico could not take him for the first days so he stayed at a small hotel not far from it in Old Rome.

On his second morning he went down to the foyer to ask about his mail but finding a crowd of incoming tourists milling round the desk, sat down to wait on a chair just inside the entrance.

He opened his paper but did not read it, finding his attention sufficiently occupied by the tourists who had evidently arrived *en masse:* particularly by two persons who kept a little apart from their companions but seemed to be of the same party nevertheless.

They were a remarkable pair, both very tall and heavily built with high shoulders and a surprisingly light gait. He supposed them to be husband and wife but they were oddly alike, having perhaps developed a marital resemblance. Their faces were large, the wife's being emphasized by a rounded jaw and the husband's by a short chin-beard that left his mouth exposed. They both had full, prominent eyes. He was very attentive to her, holding her arm and occasionally her big hand in his own enormous one and looking into her face. He was dressed in blue cotton shirt, jacket and shorts. Her clothes, Barnaby thought, were probably very 'good' though they sat but lumpishly on her ungainly person.

They were in some sort of difficulty and consulted a document without seeming to derive any consolation from it. There was a large map of Rome on the wall: they moved in front of it and searched it anxiously, exchanging baffled glances.

A fresh bevy of tourists moved between these people and Barnaby and for perhaps two minutes hid them from him. Then a guide arrived and herded the tourists off exposing the strange pair again to Barnaby's gaze.

They were no longer alone. Mr Mailer was with them.

His back was turned to Barnaby but there was no doubt about who it was. He was dressed as he had been on that first morning in the Piazza Colonna and there was something about the cut of his jib that was unmistakable.

Barnaby felt an overwhelming disinclination to meet him again. His memory of the Roman night spent under Mr Mailer's ciceronage was blurred and confused but specific enough to give him an extremely uneasy impression of having gone much too far. He preferred not to recall it and he positively shuddered at the mere thought of a renewal. Barnaby was not a prig but he did draw a line.

He was about to get up and try a quick getaway through the revolving doors when Mailer made a half turn towards him. He jerked up his newspaper and hoped he had done so in time.

This is a preposterous situation, he thought behind his shield. I don't know what's the matter with me. It's extraordinary. I've done nothing really to make me feel like this but in some inexplicable way I do feel – he searched in his mind for a word and could only produce one that was palpably ridiculous – contaminated.

He couldn't help rather wishing that there was a jalousie in his newspaper through which he could observe Mr Mailer and the two strangers and he disliked himself for so wishing. It was as if any thought of Mailer involved a kind of furtiveness in himself and since normally he was direct in his dealings, the reaction was disagreeable to him.

All the same he couldn't resist moving his paper a fraction to one side so that he could bring the group into his left eye's field of vision.

There they were. Mailer's back was still turned towards Barnaby. He was evidently talking with some emphasis and had engaged the rapt attention of the large couple. They gazed at him with the utmost deference. Suddenly both of them smiled.

A familiar smile. It took Barnaby a moment or two to place it and then he realized with quite a shock that it was the smile of the

Etruscan terra-cottas in the Villa Giulia: the smile of Hermes and
Apollo, the closed smile that sharpens the mouth like an arrowhead
and – cruel, tranquil or worldly, whichever it may be – is always
enigmatic. Intensely lively, it is as knowledgeable as the smile of the
dead.

It faded on the mouths of his couple but didn't quite vanish so
that now, thought Barnaby, they had become the Bride and Groom
of the Villa Giulia sarcophagus and really the man's gently protective air furthered the resemblance. How *very* odd, Barnaby
thought. Fascinated, he forgot about Sebastian Mailer and lowered
his newspaper.

He hadn't noticed that above the map in the wall there hung a
tilted looking-glass. Some trick of light from the revolving doors
flashed across it. He glanced up and there, again between the heads
of lovers, was Mr Mailer, looking straight into his eyes.

His reaction was indefensible. He got up quickly and left the
hotel.

He couldn't account for it. He walked round Navona telling
himself how atrociously he had behaved. Without the man I have
just cut, he reminded himself, the crowning event of my career
wouldn't have happened. I would still be trying to re-write my most
important book and very likely I would fail. I owe everything to
him! What on earth had moved him, then, to behave atrociously?
Was he so ashamed of that Roman night that he couldn't bear to be
reminded of it? He supposed it must be that but at the same time he
knew that there had been a greater compulsion.

He disliked Mr Mailer. He disliked him very much indeed. And in
some incomprehensible fashion he was afraid of him.

He walked right round the great Piazza before he came to his decision. He would, if possible, undo the damage. He would go back to
the hotel and if Mr Mailer was no longer there he would seek him
out at the trattoria where they had dined. Mailer was an habitué and
his address might be known to the proprietor. I'll do that! thought
Barnaby.

He had never taken more distasteful action. As he entered by the
revolving doors into the hotel foyer he found that all the tourists had
gone but that Mr Mailer was still in conference with the 'Etruscan'
couple.

He saw Barnaby at once and set his gaze on him without giving the smallest sign of recognition. He had been speaking to the 'Etruscans' and he went on speaking to them but with his eyes fixed on Barnaby's. Barnaby thought: Now *he's* cut *me* dead, and serve me bloody well right, and he walked steadily towards them.

As he drew near he heard Mr Mailer say:

'Rome *is* so bewildering, is it not? Even after many visits? Perhaps I may be able to help you? A cicerone?'

'Mr Mailer?' Barnaby heard himself say. 'I wonder if you remember me. Barnaby Grant.'

'I remember you very well, Mr Grant.'

Silence.

Well, he thought, I'll get on with it, and said: 'I saw your reflection just now in that glass. I can't imagine why I didn't know you at once and can only plead a chronic absence of mind. When I was half-way round Navona the penny dropped and I came back in the hope that you would still be here.' He turned to the 'Etruscans'. 'Please forgive me,' said the wretched Barnaby, 'I'm interrupting.'

Simultaneously they made deprecating noises and then the man, his whole face enlivened by that arrowhead smile, exclaimed: 'But I am right! I cannot be mistaken! This is *the* Mr Barnaby Grant.' He appealed to Mr Mailer. 'I *am* right, am I not?' His wife made a little crooning sound.

Mr Mailer said: 'Indeed, yes. May I introduce: The Baron and Baroness Van der Veghel.'

They shook hands eagerly and were voluble. They had read all the books, both in Dutch (they were by birth Hollanders) and in English (they were citizens of the world) had his last (surely his greatest?) work actually with them – *there* was a coincidence! They turned to Mr Mailer. He, of course, had read it?

'Indeed, yes,' he said exactly as he had said it before. 'Every word. I was completely riveted.'

He had used such an odd inflexion that Barnaby, already on edge, looked nervously at him but their companions were in full spate and interrupted each other in a recital of the excellencies of Barnaby's works.

It would not be true to say that Mr Mailer listened to their raptures sardonically. He merely listened. His detachment was an acute embarrassment to Barnaby Grant. When it had all died down: the predictable hope that he would join them for drinks – they were staying in the hotel – the reiterated assurances that his work had meant so much to them, the apologies that they were intruding and the tactful withdrawal, had all been executed, Barnaby found himself alone with Sebastian Mailer.

'I am not surprised,' Mr Mailer said, 'that you were disinclined to renew our acquaintance, Mr Grant. I, on the contrary, have sought you out. Perhaps we may move to somewhere a little more private? There is a writing-room, I think. Shall we –'

For the rest of his life Barnaby would be sickened by the memory of that commonplace little room with its pseudo Empire furniture, its floral carpet and the false tapestry on its wall: a mass-produced tapestry, popular in small hotels, depicting the fall of Icarus.

'I shall come straight to the point,' Mr Mailer said. 'Always best, don't you agree?'

He did precisely that. Sitting rather primly on a gilt-legged chair, his soft hands folded together and his mumbled thumbs gently revolving round each other, Mr Mailer set about blackmailing Barnaby Grant.

II

All this happened a fortnight before the morning when Sophy Jason saw her suddenly bereaved friend off at the Leonardo da Vinci Airport. She returned by bus to Rome and to the roof-garden of the Pensione Gallico where, ten months ago, Barnaby Grant had received Sebastian Mailer. Here she took stock of her situation.

She was twenty-three years old, worked for a firm of London publishers and had begun to make her way as a children's author. This was her first visit to Rome. She and the bereaved friend were to have spent their summer holidays together in Italy.

They had not made out a hard-and-fast itinerary but had snowed themselves under with brochures, read the indispensable Miss Georgina Masson and wandered in a trance about the streets and monuments. The friend's so-abruptly-deceased father had a large interest in a printing works near Turin and had arranged for the girls to draw most generously upon the firm's Roman office for funds. They had been given business and personal letters of introduction. Together, they had been in rapture: alone, Sophy felt strange but fundamentally exhilarated. To be under her own steam – and in Rome! She had Titian hair, large eyes and a generous mouth and had already found it advisable to stand with her back to the wall in crowded lifts and indeed wherever two or more Roman gentlemen were gathered together at close quarters. 'Quarters', as she had remarked to her friend, being the operative word.

I must make a plan or two, of sorts, she told herself but the boxes on the roof-garden were full of spring flowers, the air shook with voices, traffic, footsteps and the endearing clop of hooves on cobble-stones. Should she blue a couple of thousand lire and take a carriage to the Spanish Steps? Should she walk and walk until bullets and live coals began to assemble on the soles of her feet? What to do?

Really, I *ought* to make a plan, thought crazy Sophy and then – here she was, feckless and blissful, walking down the Corso in she knew not what direction. Before long she was contentedly lost.

Sophy bought herself gloves, pink sun-glasses, espadrilles and a pair of footpads, which she put on, there and then, greatly to her comfort. Leaving the store she noticed a little bureau set up near the entrance. 'DO,' it urged in English on a large banner, 'let US be your Guide to Rome.'

A dark, savage-looking girl sat scornfully behind the counter, doing her nails.

Sophy read some of the notices and glanced at already familiar brochures. She was about to leave when a smaller card caught her eye. It advertised in printed Italianate script: 'Il Cicerone, personally conducted excursions. Something different!' it exclaimed. 'Not too exhausting, sophisticated visits to some of the least-publicized and most fascinating places in Rome. Under the learned and highly individual guidance of Mr Sebastian Mailer. Dinner at a most exclusive restaurant and further unconventional expeditions by arrangement.

'*Guest of honour:* The distinguished British Author, Mr Barnaby Grant, has graciously consented to accompany the excursions from April 23rd until May 7th. Sundays included.'

Sophy was astounded. Barnaby Grant was the biggest of all big guns in her publisher's armoury of authors. His new and most important novel, set in Rome and called *Simon in Latium* had been their prestige event and the best-seller of the year. Already bookshops here were full of the Italian translation.

Sophy had offered Barnaby Grant drinks at a deafening cocktail party given by her publishing house and she had once been introduced to him by her immediate boss. She had formed her own idea of him and it did not accommodate the thought of his traipsing round Rome with a clutch of sightseers. She supposed he must be very highly paid for it and found the thought disagreeable. In any case could so small a concern as this appeared to be, afford the sort of payment Barnaby Grant would command? Perhaps, she thought, suddenly inspired, he's a chum of this learned and highly individual Mr Sebastian Mailer.

She was still gazing absent-mindedly at the notice when she became aware of a man at her elbow. She had the impression that he must have been there for some time and that he had been staring at her. He continued to stare and she thought: Oh blast! What a bore you are.

'Do forgive me,' said the man removing his greenish black hat. 'Please don't think me impertinent. My name is Sebastian Mailer. You had noticed my little announcement I believe.'

The girl behind the counter glanced at him. She had painted her nails and now disdainfully twiddled them in the air. Sophy faced Mr Mailer.

'Yes,' she said. 'I had.'

He made her a little bow. 'I must not intrude. Please!' and moved away.

Sophy said: 'Not at all,' and because she felt that she had made a silly assumption, added: 'I was so interested to see Barnaby Grant's name on your card.'

'I am indeed fortunate,' Mr Mailer rejoined, 'am I not? Perhaps you would care – but excuse me. One moment. *Would* you mind?'

He said something in Italian to the savage girl who opened a drawer, extracted what seemed to be a book of vouchers and cast it on the counter.

Mr Mailer inspected it. 'Ah yes,' he said. 'Others, also, would seem to be interested. We are fully booked, I see.'

At once Sophy felt an acute disappointment. Of all things now, she wanted to join one of Mr Mailer's highly sophisticated tours. 'Your numbers are strictly limited, are they?' she asked.

'It is an essential feature.' He was preoccupied with his vouchers.

'Might there be a cancellation?'

'I beg your pardon? You were saying?'

'A cancellation?'

'Ah. Quite. Well – possibly. You feel you would like to join one of my expeditions.'

'Very much,' Sophy said and supposed that it must be so.

He pursed up his full mouth and thumbed over his vouchers. 'Ah,' he said. 'As it falls out! There is a cancellation I see. Saturday, the twenty-sixth. Our first tour. The afternoon and evening. But before you make a decision I'm sure you would like to know about cost. Allow me.'

He produced a folder and turned aside in a gentlemanly manner while Sophy examined it. The itinerary was given and the name of the restaurant where the party would dine. In the evening they would take a carriage drive and then visit a nightclub. The overall charge made Sophy blink. It was enormous.

'I *know*,' Mr Mailer tactfully assured her. 'But there are many much, much less expensive tours than mine. The Signorina here would be pleased to inform you.'

Obviously he didn't give a damn whether she went or stayed away. This attitude roused a devil of recklessness in Sophy. After all, mad though it seemed, she *could* manage it.

'I shall be very glad to take the cancellation,' she said and even to herself her voice sounded both prim and defiant.

He said something further in Italian to the girl, raised his hat, murmured, 'Then – *arrivederci*' to Sophy, and left her to cope.

'You paya to me,' said the girl ferociously and when Sophy had done so, presented her with a ticket and a cackle of inexplicable laughter. Sophy laughed jauntily if senselessly in return, desiring, as always, to be friendly with all and sundry.

She continued to walk about Rome and to anticipate with feelings she would have been quite unable to define, Saturday, the twenty-sixth of April.

III

'I must say,' Lady Braceley murmured, 'you don't seem to be enjoying yourself very madly. I never saw such a glum face.'

'I'm sorry, Auntie Sonia. I don't mean to look glum. Honestly, I couldn't be more grateful.'

'Oh,' she said, dismissing it, 'grateful! I just hoped that we might have a nice, gay time together in Rome.'

'I'm sorry,' he repeated.

'You're so – odd. Restless. And you don't look at all well, either. What have you been doing with yourself?'

'Nothing.'

'On the tiles, I suppose.'

'I'll be all right. Really.'

'Perhaps you shouldn't have pranced out of Perugia like that.'

'I couldn't have been more bored with Perugia. Students can be such an unutterable drag. And after Franky and I broke up – you know.'

'All the same your parents or lawyers or the Lord Chancellor or whoever it is will probably be livid with me. For not ordering you back.'

'Does it matter? And anyway – my parents! We know, with all respect to your horrible brother, darling, that the longer his boy-child keeps out of his life the better he likes it.'

'Kenneth – darling!'

'As for Mummy – *what's* the name of that dipso-bin she's moved into? I keep forgetting.'

'Kenneth!'

'So come off it, angel. We're not still in the 'twenties, you know.'

They looked thoughtfully at each other.

His aunt said: 'Were you a very bad lot in Perugia, Kenneth?'

'No worse than a dozen others.'

'What *sort* of lot? What did you do?'

'Oh,' Kenneth said, 'this and that. Fun things.' He became self-suffused with charm. 'You're much too young to be told,' he said. 'What a fabulous dress. Did you get it from that amazing lady?'

'Do you like it? Yes, I did. Astronomical.'

'And looks it.'

His aunt eyed herself over. 'It had better,' she muttered.

'Oh lord!' Kenneth said discontentedly and dropped into a chair. 'Sorry! It must be the weather or something.'

'To tell you the truth I'm slightly edgy myself. Think of something delicious and outrageous we can do, darling. What is there?'

Kenneth had folded his hands across the lower half of his face like a yashmak. His large and melting brown eyes looked over the top at his aunt. There was a kind of fitful affectation in everything he did: he tried-on his mannerisms and discarded them as fretfully as his aunt tried-on her hats.

'Sweetie,' he said. 'There *is* a thing.'

'Well – what? I can't hear you when you talk behind your fingers.'

He made a triangular hole with them and spoke through that. 'I know a little man,' he said.

'What little man? Where?'

'In Perugia and now here.'

'What about him?'

'He's rather a clever little man. Well, not so little, actually.'

'Kenneth, don't go on like that. It's maddening: it's infuriating.' And then suddenly:

'In Perugia. Did you – did you – *smoke* – ?'

'There's no need for the hushed tones, darling. You've been handed the usual nonsense, I see.'

'Then you *did*?'

'Of course,' he said impatiently and, after a pause, changed his attitude. He clasped his hands round his knee and tilted his head on one side. 'You're so fabulous,' he said. 'I can tell you anything. As if you were my generation. Aren't we wonderful? Both of us?'

'Are we? Kenneth – what's it like?'

'Pot? Do you really want to know?'

'I'm asking, aren't I?'

'Dire the first time and quite fun if you persevere. Kid-stuff really. All the fuss is about nothing.'

'It's done at – at parties, isn't it?'

'That's right, lovey. Want to try?'

'It's not habit-forming. Is it?'

'Of course it's not. It's nothing. It's OK as far as it goes. You don't get hooked. Not on pot. You'd better meet my little man. Try a little trip. In point of fact I *could* arrange a *fabulous* trip. Madly groovy. You'd adore it. All sorts of gorgeous gents. Super exotic pad. The lot.'

She looked at him through her impossible lashes: a girl's look that did a kind of injury to her face.

'I might,' she said.

'Only thing – it's top bracket for expense. All-time-high and worth it. One needs lots of lovely lolly and I haven't – surprise, surprise – got a morsel.'

'Kenneth!'

'In fact if my rich aunt hadn't invited me I would have been out on my little pink ear. Don't pitch into me, I don't think I can take it.'

They stared at each other. They were very much alike: two versions of the same disastrous image.

'I understand you,' Kenneth said. 'You know that, don't you? I'm a sponge, OK? But I'm not just a sponge. I give back something. Right?' He waited for a moment and when she didn't answer, shouted, 'Don't I? *Don't* I?'

'Be quiet. Yes. Yes, of course you do. Yes.'

'We're two of a kind, right?'

'Yes. I said so, didn't I. Never mind, darling. Look in my bag. I don't know how much I've got.'

'God, you're wonderful! I – I'll go out straight away. I – I'll – I'll get it – ' his mouth twisted ' – fixed. We'll have such a – what did that old burnt-out Egyptian bag call it? – or her boyfriend? – gaudy night? – won't we?'

Her note-case shook in his hand. 'There isn't much here,' he said.

'Isn't there?' she said. 'They'll cash a cheque downstairs. I'll write one. You'd better have something in hand.'

When he had gone she went into her bedroom, sat in front of her glass and examined the precarious mask she still presented to the world.

Kenneth, yawning and sweating, went in febrile search of Mr Sebastian Mailer.

IV

'It's the familiar story,' the tall man said. He uncrossed his legs, rose in one movement, and stood, relaxed, before his companion who, taken by surprise, made a laborious business of getting to his feet.

'The big boys,' said the tall man, 'keep one jump ahead while their henchmen occasionally trip over our wires. Not often enough, however.'

'Excuse me, my dear colleague. Our wires?'

'Sorry. I meant: we do sometimes catch up with the secondary villains but their principals continue to evade us.'

'Regrettably!'

'In this case the biggest boy of all is undoubtedly Otto Ziegfeldt who, at the moment, has retired to a phoney castle in the Lebanon. We can't get him. Yet. But this person, here in Rome, is a key man.'

'I am most anxious that his activities be arrested. We all know, my dear colleague, that Palermo has most regrettably been a transit port. And also Corsica. But that he should have extended his activities to Naples and, it seems, to Rome! No, assure yourself you shall have every assistance.'

'I'm most grateful to you, Signor Questore. The Yard was anxious that we should have this talk.'

'*Please!* Believe me, the greatest pleasure,' said Il Questore Valdarno. He had a resonant voice and grand-opera appearance. His eyes melted and he gave out an impression of romantic melancholy. Even his jokes wore an air of impending disaster. His position in the Roman police force corresponded, as far as his visitor had been able to work it out, with that of a Chief Constable.

'We are all so much honoured, my dear Superintendent,' he continued. 'Anything that we can do to further the already cordial relationship between our own Force and your most distinguished Yard.'

'You are very kind. Of course, the whole problem of the drug traffic, as we both know, is predominantly an Interpol affair but as in this instance we are rather closely tied up with them – '

'Perfectly,' agreed Valdarno, many times nodding his head.

'– and since this person is, presumably, a British subject – '

The Questore made a large involved gesture of deprecation: 'Of course!'

' – in the event of his being arrested the question of extradition might arise.'

'I assure you,' said the Questore, making a joke, 'we shall not try to deprive you!'

His visitor laughed obligingly and extended his hand. The Questore took it and with his own left hand dealt him the buffet with which Latin gentlemen endorse their friendly relationships. He insisted on coming to the magnificent entrance.

In the street a smallish group of young men carrying a few inflammatory placards shouted one or two insults. A group of police, gorgeously arrayed, pinched out their cigarettes and moved towards the demonstrators who cat-called and bolted a short way down the street. The police immediately stopped and relit their cigarettes.

'How foolish,' observed the Questore in Italian, 'and yet after all, not to be ignored. It is all a great nuisance. You will seek out this person, my dear colleague?'

'I think so. His sightseeing activities seem to offer the best approach. I shall enrol myself for one of them.'

'Ah-ah! You are a droll! You are a great droll.'

'No. I assure you. *Arrivederci.*'

'Goodbye. Such a pleasure. Goodbye.'

Having finally come to the end of a conversation that had been conducted in equal parts of Italian and English, they parted on the best of terms.

The demonstrators made some desultory comments upon the tall Englishman as he walked past them. One of them called out, 'Ullo, gooda-day!' in a squeaking voice, another shouted. 'Rhodesia! *Imperialismo!*' and raised a cat-call but a third remarked *'Molto elegante'* in a loud voice and apparently without sardonic intention.

Rome sparkled in the spring morning. The swallows had arrived, the markets were full of flowers, young greens and kaleidoscopic cheap-jackery. Dramatic façades presented themselves suddenly to the astonished gaze, lovely courtyards and galleries floated in shadow and little piazzas talked with the voices of their own fountains. Behind magnificent doorways the ages offered their history lessons in layers. Like the achievements of a Roman pastrycook, thought the tall man irreverently: modern, renaissance, classic, mithraic, each under another in one gorgeous, stratified edifice. It would be an enchantment to walk up to the Palatine Hill where the air would smell freshly of young grass and a kind of peace and order would come upon the rich encrustations of time.

Instead he must look for a tourist bureau either in the streets or at the extremely grand hotel he had been treated to by his Department in London. He approached it by the way of the Via Condotti and presently came upon a window filled with blown-up photographs of Rome. The agency was a distinguished one and their London office well-known to him.

He turned into an impressive interior, remarked that its décor was undisturbed by racks of brochures and approached an exquisite but far from effete young man who seemed to be in charge.

'Good morning, sir,' said the young man in excellent English. 'May I help you?'

'I hope so,' he rejoined cheerfully. 'I'm in Rome for a few days. I don't want to spend them on a series of blanket-tours covering the maximum amount of Sights in the minimum amount of time. I have seen as much as I can take of celebrated big-boomers. What I would like now is to do something leisurely and civilized that leads one a little off the beaten way of viewing and yet is really – well, really *of* Rome and not, historically speaking, beside the point. I'm afraid I put that very badly.'

'But not at all,' said the young man looking hard at him. 'I understand perfectly. A personal courier might be the answer but this is the busy season, sir, and I'm afraid we've nobody free for at least a fortnight whom I could really recommend.'

'Somebody told me about something called Il Cicerone. Small parties under the guidance of a – I'm not sure if I've got his name right – Sebastian Something? Do you know?'

The young man looked still more fixedly at him and said: 'It's odd – really, it's quite a coincidence, sir, that you should mention Il Cicerone. A week ago I could have told you very little about it. Except, perhaps, that it wasn't likely to be a distinguished affair. Indeed – ' he hesitated and then said – 'please forgive me, sir. I've been at our London office for the past three years and I can't help thinking that I've had the pleasure of looking after you before. Or at least of seeing you. I hope you don't mind,' the young man said in a rush. 'I trust you will not think this insufferable cheek: I haven't mastered my Anglo-Saxon attitudes, I'm afraid.'

'You've mastered the language, at least.'

'Oh – that! After an English university and so on, I should hope so.'

' – and have an excellent memory.'

'Well, sir, you are not the sort of person who is all that readily forgotten. Perhaps, then, I am correct in thinking – ?'

'You came into the general manager's office in Jermyn Street while I was there. Some two years ago. You were in the room for about three minutes: during which time you give me a piece of very handy information.'

The young man executed an involved and extremely Italianate gesture that ended up with a smart slap on his own forehead.

'Ah-ah-ah! *Mamma mia!* How could I be such an ass!' he exclaimed.

'It all comes back to you?' observed the tall man drily.

'But completely. All!' He fell away a step and contemplated his visitor with an air of the deepest respect.

'Good,' said the visitor, unmoved by this scrutiny. 'Now about the Il Cicerone thing – '

'It is entirely for recreation, sir, that you inquire?'

'Why not?'

'Indeed! Of course! I merely wondered – '

'Come on. What did you wonder?'

'If perhaps there might be a professional aspect.'

'And why did you wonder that? Look, Signor Pace – that *is* your name, isn't it?'

'Your own memory, sir, is superb.'

'Signor Pace. Is there, perhaps, something about this enterprise, or about the person who controls it that makes you think I might be interested in it – or him – for other than sightseeing reasons?'

The young man became pink in the face, gazed at his clasped hands, glanced round the bureau which was empty of other people and finally said, 'The cicerone in question, Signore – a Mr Sebastian Mailer – is a person of a certain, or perhaps I should say, *uncertain* reputation. Nothing specific you understand, but there are – ' he agitated his fingers ' – suggestions. Rome is a great place for suggestions.'

'Yes?'

'I remarked that it was quite a coincidence you should inquire about him. That is because he was here earlier today. Not for the first time.

He asked to be put on our books some weeks ago but his reputation, his appearance – everything – did not recommend his venture to us and we declined. Then, this morning as a new inducement he brings us his list of patrons. It was quite astonishing, Signore, this list.'

'May I see it?'

'We still have not accepted him. I – I don't quite – '

'Signor Pace, your guess was a good one. My interest in this person is professional.'

'Ah!'

'But I am most anxious to appear simply as a tourist. I remember that in London your chief spoke very highly indeed of your discretion and promise – a promise that is evidently being fulfilled.'

'You are kind enough to say so, sir.'

'I realize that I can't get a booking with Il Cicerone through you but perhaps you can tell me – '

'I can arrange it with another agency and will be delighted to do so. As for the list of patrons: under the circumstances, I think, there is no reason why I should not show it to you. Will you come into the office, if you please. While you examine it I will attend to your booking.'

The list Signor Pace produced was a day-by-day record of people who had put themselves down for Il Cicerone expeditions. It was prefaced by a general announcement that made his visitor blink: 'Under the distinguished patronage of the celebrated author, Mr Barnaby Grant.'

'This *is* coming it strong!'

'Is it not?' Signor Pace said, busily dialling. 'I cannot imagine how it has been achieved. Although – ' he broke off and addressed himself elegantly to the telephone. *'Pronto. Chi parla?'* – and, as an aside: 'Look at the patronage, Signore. On the first day, Saturday, the twenty-sixth, for instance.'

Here it was, neatly set out in the Italianate script.

Lady Braceley.	London
The Hon. Kenneth Dorne.	London
Baron and Baroness Van der Veghel.	Geneva
Major Hamilton Sweet.	London
Miss Sophy Jason.	London
'Mr Barnaby Grant (Guest of Honour).	London

After further discussion, Signor Pace broke out in a cascade of thanks and compliments and covered the mouthpiece. 'All is arranged,' he cried. 'For whichever tour you prefer.'

'Without hesitation – the first one. Saturday, the twenty-sixth.'

This, evidently, was settled. Signor Pace hung up and swung round in his chair. 'An interesting list, is it not? Lady Braceley – what *chic*!'

'You may call it that.'

'Well, Signore! A certain reputation, perhaps. What is called the "jet set". But from the point of view of the tourist-trade – extremely *chic*. Great éclat. We always arrange her travel. There is, of course, immense wealth.'

'Quite so. The alimony alone.'

'Well, Signore.'

'And the Hon. Kenneth Dorne?'

'I understand, her nephew.'

'And the Van der Veghels?'

'I am dumb. They have not come our way. Nor have Miss Jason and Major Sweet. But, Signore, the remarkable feature, the really astonishing, as one says, turn-up for the book, is the inclusion of Mr Barnaby Grant. And what is meant, I ask myself, by Guest of Honour?'

' "Prime Attraction", I imagine.'

'Of course! But for him to consent! To lend his enormous prestige to such a very dim enterprise. And, we must admit, it appears evident that the gimmick has worked.'

'I wouldn't have thought Lady Braceley was a natural taker for the intellectual bait.'

'Signore, he is impressive, he is handsome, he is famous, he is prestigious – Am I correct in saying "prestigious"?'

'It really means he's a bit of a conjuror. And so, of course, in a sense, he is.'

'And therefore to be acquired by Lady Braceley. Or, at least, considered.'

'You may be right. I understand she's staying at my hotel. I heard her name at the desk.'

'Her nephew, Mr Dorne, is her guest.'

'Fortunate youth! Perhaps. By the way, what are the charges for these jaunts?'

'In the top bracket and, at that, exceedingly high. I would have said impertinently so but, as you see, he is getting the response. One can only hope the patrons are satisfied.'

'In any case you have given me the opportunity to form an opinion. I'm extremely obliged to you.'

'But, please! Come,' said the jaunty Signor Pace, 'let us make our addition to the list.'

He gaily drew it towards him and at the bottom wrote his addition.

'You see!' he cried in playful triumph. 'I remembered everything! The rank! The spelling!'

'If you don't mind, we'll forget about the rank and the spelling.'

The visitor drew a line through the word 'Superintendent' and another through the letter 'y', so that the entry read:

'R. Allen, London.'

CHAPTER 3

Saturday, the Twenty-sixth

It became fairly clear from the outset why Mr Sebastian Mailer made extravagant charges for his expeditions.

At three-thirty in the afternoon two superb Lancias arrived at the rendezvous near the Church of the Trinity and therefore within a very short distance of the hotel where three of Mr Mailer's prospects were staying.

From here, as they assembled, his seven guests looked down at April azaleas flaring on the Spanish Steps and at Rome suddenly laid out before them in a wide gesture. There was a sense of opulence and of excitement in the air.

Alleyn got there before the appointed time and saw the cars draw up. They had small labels in their windows: 'Il Cicerone'. Out of one of them stepped a dark man of romantic appearance whom he at once recognized as Barnaby Grant and out of the other the person he had come to see: Sebastian Mailer. He was smartened up since Barnaby Grant's last encounter with him and was dressed in a black suit of some material that might have been alpaca. This, together with a pair of clumping black shoes gave him a dubiously priestly look and made Alleyn think of Corvo and wonder if he might turn out to be such another. The white silk shirt was clean and the black bow tie looked new. He now wore a black beret on his cropped head and no longer had the appearance of an Englishman.

Alleyn kept his distance among a group of sightseers who milled about taking photographs. He saw that while Sebastian Mailer, half-smiling, talked vivaciously, Grant seemed to make little or no response.

He had his back to Alleyn who thought the nape of his neck looked indignant. It looks, Alleyn thought, like the neck of a learner-driver seen from the rear. Rigid, cross and apprehensive.

A young woman approached the cars, spotted Mailer and made towards him. She had a glowing air about her as if Rome had a little gone to her head. Miss Sophy Jason, Alleyn said to himself. He saw her look quickly at Barnaby Grant. Mailer pulled slightly at his beret, made a little bow and introduced her. The girl's manner was shy, Alleyn thought, but not at all gauche: rather charming, in fact. Nevertheless she said something to Grant that seemed to disconcert him. He glared at her, replied very shortly and turned away. The girl blushed painfully.

This brief tableau was broken by the arrival of two over-sized persons hung about with canvas satchels and expensive cameras: a man and a woman. The Van der Veghels, Alleyn concluded and, like Barnaby Grant before him, was struck by their resemblance to each other and their strangely archaic faces. They were well-dressed in a non-with-it sort of way: both of them in linen and both wearing out-size shoes with great rubber-studded soles and canvas tops. They wore sensibly shady hats and identical sun-glasses with pink frames. They were eager in their greetings and evidently had met Grant before. What great hands and feet you have, Baron and Baroness, thought Alleyn.

Lady Braceley and her nephew were still to come. No doubt it would be entirely in character for them to keep the party waiting. He decided it was time for him to present himself and did so, ticket in hand.

Mailer had the kind of voice Alleyn had expected: a rather fluting alto. He was a bad colour and his hands were slightly tremulous. But he filled his role very competently: there was the correct degree of suavity and assurance, the suggestion that everything was to be executed at the highest level.

'So glad you are joining us, Mr Allen,' said Sebastian Mailer. 'Do come and meet the others, won't you? May I introduce – '

The Baron and Baroness were cordial. Grant looked hard at him, nodded with what seemed to be an uneasy blend of reluctance and good manners, and asked him if he knew Rome well.

'Virtually, not at all,' Alleyn said. 'I've never been here for more than three or four days at a time and I'm not a systematic sightseer.'

'No?'

'No. I want things to occur and I'm afraid spend far too much time sitting at a caffè table waiting for them to do so which of course they don't. But who knows? One of these days the heavens may open and big drama descend upon me.'

Alleyn was afterwards to regard this as the major fluke-remark of his career. At the moment he was merely astonished to see what an odd response it drew from Barnaby Grant. He changed colour, threw an apprehensive glance at Alleyn, opened his mouth, shut it and finally said 'Oh,' without any expression at all.

'But today,' Alleyn said, 'I hope to improve my condition. Do we, by any chance, visit one of your Simon's haunts? That would be a wonderful idea.'

Again Grant seemed to be about to speak and again he boggled. After a sufficiently awkward pause he said: 'There's some idea of it. Mailer will explain. Excuse me, will you.'

He turned away. All right, Alleyn thought. But if you hate it as much as all this, why the hell do you do it?

He moved on to Sophy Jason, who was standing apart and seemed to be glad of his company. We're all too old for her, Alleyn thought. Perhaps the nephew of Lady Braceley will meet the case but one doubts it. He engaged Sophy in conversation and thought her a nice intelligent girl with a generous allowance of charm. She looked splendid against the background of azaleas, Rome and a pontifical sky.

Before long Sophy found herself telling Alleyn about her suddenly-bereaved friend, about this being her first visit to Rome, about the fortunate accident of the cancellation and finally about her job. It really was extraordinary, she suddenly reflected, how much she was confiding to this quiet and attentive stranger. She felt herself blushing. 'I can't imagine why I'm gabbling away like this!' she exclaimed.

'It's obliging of you to talk to me,' Alleyn said. 'I've just been, not exactly slapped back but slightly edged off by the Guest of Honour.'

'Nothing to what I was!' Sophy ejaculated. 'I'm still cringing.'

'But – isn't he one of your publisher's authors?'

'He's our great double-barrel. I was dumb enough to remind him that I had been presented by my boss. He took the news like a dose of poison.'

'How very odd of him.'

'It was really a bit of a facer. He'd seemed so unfierce and amiable on the earlier occasion and has the reputation in the firm of being a lamb. Aren't we rather slow getting off our mark? Mr Mailer is looking at his watch.'

'Major Sweet's twenty minutes late and so are Lady Braceley and the Hon. Kenneth Dorne. They're staying at the – ' He broke off. 'Here, I fancy, they come.'

And here, in fact, they came and there was Mr Mailer, his beret completely off, advancing with a winning and proprietary air towards them.

Alleyn wondered what first impression they made on Sophy Jason. For all her poise and obvious intelligence he doubted if the like of Sonia Braceley had ever come her way. Alleyn knew quite a lot about Sonia Braceley. She began life as the Hon. Sonia Dorne and was the daughter of a beer-baron whose children, by and large, had turned out disastrously. Alleyn had actually met her, many years ago, when visiting his Ambassadorial elder brother George at one of his official Residences. Even then she had what his brother, whom Alleyn tolerantly regarded as a bit of an ass, alluded to as 'a certain reputation'. With the passage of time, this reputation had consolidated. 'She has experienced everything,' Sir George had weightily quipped, 'except poverty.'

Seeing her now it was easy to believe it. It's the legs, Alleyn thought. More than the precariously maintained mask or the flabby underarm or the traitorous neck. It's the legs. Although the stockings are tight as a skin they look as if they should hang loose about these brittle spindle-shanks and how hazardously she's balanced on her golden kid sandals. It's the legs.

But the face was not too good either. Even if one discounted the ruches under the eyes and the eyes themselves, there was still that dreadfully slack mouth. It was painted the fashionable livid colour but declared itself as unmistakably as if it had been scarlet: the mouth of an elderly Maenad.

Her nephew bore some slight resemblance to her. Alleyn remembered that his father, the second Lord Dorne, had been rapidly divorced by two wives and that the third, Kenneth's mother, had been, as George would have said, 'put away'. Not much of a start, Alleyn thought, compassionately, and wondered if the old remedy of 'live on a quid-a-day and earn it,' would have done anything for Kenneth Dorne.

As they advanced, he noticed that the young man watched Mailer with an air that seemed to be made up of anxiety, furtiveness and perhaps subservience. He was restless, pallid, yellow and damp about the brow. When Mailer introduced him and he offered his hand it proved to be clammy as to the palm and tremulous. Rather unexpectedly, he had a camera slung from his shoulder.

His aunt also shook hands. Within the doeskin glove the fingers contracted, momentarily retained their clasp and slowly withdrew. Lady Braceley looked fixedly into Alleyn's eyes. So she still, he thought, appalled, gives it a go.

She said: 'Isn't this *fun*?' Her voice was beautiful.

Mailer was at her elbow with Grant in tow: 'Lady Braceley, may I present? Our guest of honour – Mr Barnaby Grant.'

She said: 'Do you know you're the sole reason for my coming to this party? Kenneth, with a team of wild horses, wouldn't have bullied me into sightseeing at this ghastly hour. *You're* my "sight".'

'I don't know,' Grant said rapidly, 'how I'm meant to answer that. Except that I'm sure you'll find the Church of S. Tommaso in Pallaria much more rewarding.'

'Is that where we're going? Is it a *ruin*?' she asked, opening her devastated eyes very wide and drawling out the word. 'I can't tell you how I hate roo-ins.'

There was perhaps one second's silence and then Grant said: 'It's not exactly that. It's – well, you'll see when we get there.'

'Does it come in your book? I've read your book – that Simon one – which is a great compliment if you only knew it because you don't write my sort of book at all. Don't be huffy. I adored this one although I haven't a clue, really, what it's about. You shall explain it to me. Kenneth tried, didn't you, darling, but he was even more muddling than the book. Mr Allen, come over here and tell me – have *you* read the last Barnaby Grant and if you have, did you know what it was about?'

Alleyn was spared the task of finding an answer to this by the intervention of Sebastian Mailer who rather feverishly provided the kind of raillery that seemed to be invited and got little reward for his pains. When he archly said: 'Lady Braceley, you're being very naughty. I'm quite sure you didn't miss the last delicate nuance of *Simon in Tuscany*,' she merely said 'What?' and walked away before he could repeat his remark.

It was now the turn of the Baron and Baroness. Lady Braceley received the introduction vaguely. 'Aren't we going to start?' she asked Alleyn and Grant. 'Don't you rather hate hanging about? Such a bore, don't you think? Who's missing?'

Upon this cool inquiry, Sebastian Mailer explained that Major Sweet was joining them at the basilica and proceeded to outline the programme for the afternoon. They would drive round the Colosseum and the Forum and would then visit the basilica of S. Tommaso in Pallaria which, as they all knew, was the setting for the great central scene in Mr Barnaby Grant's immensely successful novel, *Simon in Latium*. He had prevailed upon the distinguished author, Mr Mailer went on, to say a few words about the basilica in its relation to his book which, as they would hear from him, was largely inspired by it.

Throughout this exposition Barnaby Grant, Alleyn noticed, seemed to suffer the most exquisite embarrassment. He stared at the ground, hunched his shoulders, made as if to walk away and, catching perhaps a heightened note in Mr Mailer's voice, thought better of this and remained, wretchedly it appeared, where he was.

Mr Mailer concluded by saying that as the afternoon was deliciously clement they would end it with a picnic tea on the Palatine Hill. The guests would then be driven to their hotels to relax and change for dinner and would be called for at nine o'clock.

He now distributed the guests. He, with Lady Braceley, Alleyn and Barnaby Grant would take one car; the Van der Veghels, Sophy Jason and Kenneth Dorne would take the other. The driver of the second car was introduced. 'Giovanni is fluent in English,' said Mr Mailer, 'and learned in the antiquities. He will discourse upon matters of interest en route. Come, ladies and gentlemen,' said Mr Mailer, 'let us embark. *Pronto!*'

II

The four arches that lead into the porch of S. Tommaso in Pallaria are of modest proportion and their pillars, which in classic times adorned some pagan temple, are slender and worn. The convolvulus tendrils that their carver twined about them have broken in many places but the work is so delicate that the stone seems to tremble. In the most shadowed corner of the porch sat a woman with a tray of postcards. She wore a black headscarf pulled forward over her face and a black cotton dress. She shouted something, perhaps at Mr Mailer. Her voice was strident which may have caused her remark to sound like an insult. He paid no attention to it.

He collected his party about him and looked at his watch. 'Major Sweet,' he said, 'is late. We shall not wait for him but before we go in I should like to give you, very shortly, some idea of this extraordinary monument. In the fourth century before Christ – '

From the dark interior there erupted an angry gentleman who shouted as he came.

'Damned disgusting lot of hanky-panky,' shouted this gentleman. 'What the hell – ' He pulled up short on seeing the group and narrowed his blazing eyes in order to focus upon it.

He had a savage white moustache and looked like an improbable revival of an Edwardian warrior. 'Are you Mailer?' he shouted. 'Sweet,' he added, in explanation.

'Major Sweet, may I – '

'You're forty-three minutes late. Forty-three minutes!'

'Unfortunately – '

'Spare me,' begged Major Sweet, 'the specious excuses. There is no adequate explanation for unpunctuality.'

Lady Braceley moved in. '*All* my fault, Major,' she said. 'I kept everybody waiting and I've no excuses: I never have and I always do. I dare say you'd call it "ladies' privilege", wouldn't you? Or would you?'

Major Sweet turned his blue glare upon her for two or three seconds. He then yapped 'How do you do' and seemed to wait for further developments.

Mr Mailer with perfect suavity performed the introductions. Major Sweet acknowledged them by making slight bows to the ladies and an ejaculation of sorts to the men. 'Hyah,' he said.

'Well,' said Mr Mailer. 'To resume. When we are inside the basilica I shall hand over to our most distinguished guest of honour. But perhaps beforehand a very brief historical note may be of service.'

He was succinct and adequate, Sophy grudgingly admitted. The basilica of San Tommaso, he said, was one of a group of monuments in Rome where the visitors could walk downwards through the centuries into Mithraic time. At the top level, here where they now stood, was the twelfth-century basilica which in a moment they would enter. Beneath it, was the excavated third-century church which it had replaced. 'And below that – imagine it – ' said Mr Mailer, 'there has lain sleeping for over eighteen hundred years a house of the Flavian period: a classic "gentleman's residence" with its own private chapel dedicated to the god Mithras.' He paused and Sophy, though she regarded him with the most profound distaste, thought: He's interested in what he's talking about. He knows his stuff. He's enjoying himself.

Mr Mailer went on to describe briefly the enormous task of nineteenth-century excavation that had so gradually disclosed first, the earlier basilica and then, deep down beneath it, the pagan household. 'Rome has risen, hereabout, sixty feet since those times,' he ended. 'Does that surprise you? It does me, every time I think of it.'

'It doesn't me,' Major Sweet announced. 'Nothing surprises me. Except human gullibility,' he added darkly. 'However!'

Mr Mailer shot him an uneasy glance. Sophy gave a little snort of suppressed amusement and caught Barnaby Grant looking at her with something like appreciation. Lady Braceley, paying no attention to what was said, let her ravaged eyes turn from one man's face to another. The Van der Veghels, standing close together, listened intently. Kenneth Dorne, Sophy noticed, was restless and anxious-looking. He shuffled his feet and dabbed at his face with his handkerchief. And the tall man, what was his name – Allen? – stood a little apart, politely attentive and, Sophy thought, extremely observant.

'But now,' Mr Mailer said, 'shall we begin our journey into the past?'

The woman with the postcards had sidled between the group and the entrance. She had kept her face down and it was still shadowed by her black headscarf. She muttered, almost inaudibly, *'Cartoline?*

Posta-carda?' edging towards Sebastian Mailer. He said generally to his company, 'There are better inside. Pay no attention,' and moved forward to pass the woman.

With extraordinary swiftness she pushed back her headscarf, thrust her face up at him and whispered: *'Brutto! Farabutto! Traditore!'* and added what seemed to be a stream of abuse. Her eyes burned. Her lips were retracted in a grin and then pursed together. She's going to spit in his face, thought Sophy in alarm and so she was, but Mr Mailer was too smart for her. He dodged and she spat after him and stood her ground with the air of a grand-opera virago. She even gave a hoarse screech of eldritch laughter. Mr Mailer entered the basilica. His discomfited flock divided round the postcard-seller and slunk after him.

'Kenneth, darling,' Lady Braceley muttered. 'Honestly! *Not* one's idea of a gay little trip!'

Sophy found herself between Barnaby Grant and Alleyn. 'Was that lady,' Alleyn asked Grant, 'put in as an extra touch of atmosphere? Does she recur, or was she a colourful accident?'

Grant said, 'I don't know anything about her. Mad, I should think. Ghastly old bag, wasn't she?' and Sophy thought: Yes, but he hasn't answered the question.

She said to Alleyn, 'Would you suppose that all that carry-on, if translated into Anglo-Saxon terms, would amount to no more than a cool glance and an indrawn breath?'

Grant looked across Alleyn at her, and said with a kind of eagerness, 'Oh, rather! You have to make allowances for their sense of drama.'

'Rather excessive in this instance,' she said coolly, giving, she said to herself, snub for snub. Grant moved round and said hurriedly, 'I know who you are, now. I didn't before. We met at Koster Press didn't we?' Koster Press was the name of his publisher's house in London.

'For a moment,' Sophy said and then: 'Oh, but how lovely!'

They were in the basilica.

It glowed sumptuously as if it generated its own light. It was alive with colour: 'mediterranean' red, clear pinks, blues and greens; ivory and crimson marble, tingling gold mosaic. And dominant in this concourse of colour the great vermilion that cries out in the backgrounds of Rome and Pompeii.

Sophy moved away from the group and stared with delight at this enchantment. Grant, who had been left with Alleyn, abruptly joined her.

'I've got to talk about this,' he muttered. 'I wish to God I hadn't.'

She looked briefly at him. 'Then why do it?' said Sophy.

'You think that was an affectation. I'm sorry.'

'Really, it couldn't matter less what I think.'

'You needn't be so snappish.'

They stared at each other in astonishment.

'I can't make this out,' Grant said unexpectedly. 'I don't know you,' and Sophy in a panic, stammered, 'It's nothing. It's none of my business. I'm sorry I snapped.'

'Not at all.'

'And now,' fluted Sebastian Mailer, 'I hand over to my most distinguished colleague, Mr Grant.'

Grant made Sophy an extremely stuffy little bow and moved out to face his audience.

Once he was launched he too did his stuff well and with considerable charm, which was more than could be said for Mr Mailer. For one thing, Sophy conceded, Grant looked a lot nicer. His bony face was really rather beautifully shaped and actually had a carved, medieval appearance that went handsomely with its surroundings. He led them farther into the glowing church. There were two or three other groups of sightseers but, compared with the traffic in most celebrated monuments, these were few.

Grant explained that even in this, the most recent of the three levels of San Tommaso, there was a great richness of time sequences. When in the twelfth century the ancient church below it was filled in, its treasures, including pieces from the pagan household underneath it, were brought up into this new basilica so that now classical, medieval and renaissance works mingled. 'They've kept company,' Grant said, 'for a long time and have grown together in the process. You can see how well they suit each other.'

'It happens on the domestic level too,' Alleyn said, 'don't you think? In houses that have belonged to the same family for many generations? There's a sort of consonance of differences.'

'Exactly so,' Grant agreed with a quick look at him. 'Shall we move on?'

A wave of scent announced the arrival of Lady Braceley at Alleyn's elbow. 'What a marvellous way of putting it,' she murmured. 'How clever you are.'

The doeskin glove with its skeletal enclosure touched his arm. She tipped her head on one side and was looking up at him. Sophy, watching, thought a shutter had come down over his face and indeed Alleyn suffered a wave of revulsion and pity and a recognition of despair. I'd give a hell of a lot, he thought, to be shot of this lady.

Sebastian Mailer had come up on the far side of Lady Braceley. He murmured something that Alleyn couldn't catch. Grant was talking again. The hand was withdrawn from Alleyn's arm and the pair turned away and moved out of sight behind the junction of two pilasters. Now, Alleyn speculated, was Mailer doing a rescue job or had he something particular and confidential to say to Lady Braceley?

Grant led his party into the centre of the nave and through the enclosed *schola cantorum,* saying, Sophy thought, neither too much nor too little but everything well. She herself was caught up in wonder at the great golden bowl-shaped mosaic of the apse. Acanthus and vine twined tenderly together to enclose little groups of everyday persons going about their medieval business. The Cross, dominant though it was, seemed to have grown out of some pre-Christian tree. 'I shall say nothing about the apse,' Grant said. 'It speaks for itself.'

Mailer and Lady Braceley had re-appeared. She sat down on a choir bench and whether by some accident of lighting or because she was overtaken by one of those waves of exhaustion that unexpectedly fall upon the old, she looked as if she had shrunk within her own precarious façade. Only for a moment, however. She straightened her back and beckoned her nephew who fidgeted about on the edge of the group, half-attentive and half-impatient. He joined her and they whispered together, he yawning and fidgeting, she apparently in some agitation.

The party moved on round the basilica. The Van der Veghels took photographs and asked a great many questions. They were laboriously well-informed in Roman antiquities. Presently the Baron, with an arch look, began to inquire about the particular features that appeared so vividly in Grant's novel. Were they not standing, at this very moment, in the place where his characters assembled? Might one not follow, precisely, in the steps they had taken during that wonderful climactic scene?

'O-o-oah!' cried the Baroness running her voice up and down a chromatic scale of enthusiasm. 'It will be so farskinating. Yes?'

Grant reacted to this plea as he had to earlier conversations: with a kind of curbed distaste. He gave Sophy and Alleyn one each of his sharp glances, darted a look of something like pure hatred at Sebastian Mailer and suggested confusedly, that an author seldom reproduced in scrupulous detail, an actual *mise-en-scène* any more than he used unadulterated human material. 'I don't mean I didn't start off with San Tommaso,' he shot out at Sophy. 'Of course I did. But I gave it another name and altered it to my purpose.'

'As you had every right to do,' Sophy said boldly and Alleyn thought the two of them were united for the moment in their common field of activity.

'Yes, but do *show* us,' Lady Braceley urged. 'Don't be beastly. *Show* us. You promised. You know you did.'

Kenneth Dorne said, 'Isn't that why we came? Or not? I thought you were to be the great attraction.'

He had approached Grant and stood in an attitude of some elegance, his left arm extended along one of the closure-slabs of the *schola*, his right hand on his hip. It was not a blatant pose but it was explicit nevertheless and at least one aspect of Kenneth was now revealed. He looked at Grant and widened his eyes. 'Is it all a sell-out?' he asked. 'Or have I made a muddle? Or am I merely being impertinent?'

A rabid oath, instantly stifled, burst from Major Sweet. He shouted, 'I beg your pardon,' and glared at a wall-painting of the Foolish Virgins.

'Oh dear,' Kenneth said, still to Grant. 'Now the Major's cross. What *have* I said?' He yawned again and dabbed at his face with his handkerchief.

Grant gave him a comprehensive look. 'Nothing to the purpose,' he said shortly and walked away. Mr Mailer hurried into the breach.

'Naughty!' he tossed at Kenneth and then, vindicating Grant to his disconcerted customers, told them he was unbelievably modest.

Lady Braceley eagerly supported this view as did the Van der Veghels. Grant cut short their plaudits by adopting, with a great effort, it seemed to Alleyn, a brisk and business-like air and by resuming his exposition.

'Of course,' he said, 'if you'd really like to see the equivalent places to those in the book I'll be delighted to point them out, although I imagine if you've read it they declare themselves pretty obviously. There, in the right-hand aisle, for instance, is the picture so much admired by Simon and, I may add, by me. Doubting Saint Thomas, himself, by Masolino da Panicale. Look at those pinks and the "Pompeian" red.'

'Fabulous!' Kenneth restlessly offered. 'Psychedelic, aren't they?'

Grant disregarded this. He said to Sophy, 'He's so *very* doubtful, isn't he? Head on one side, lips pursed up and those gimlet fingers! How right that enormous hospital in London was to adopt him: he's the very pith and marrow of the scientific man, don't you think?'

Sebastian Mailer gave a shrill little cackle of appreciation: perhaps of surprise.

'While we are in this aisle of the basilica,' Grant said, leading them along it for a short distance, 'you may like to see something that I'm afraid I did adopt holus-bolus.'

He showed them a railed enclosure, about six feet by three in size. They collected round it with little cries of recognition.

It encompassed an open rectangular hole like the mouth of a well. Fixed to the rails was a notice saying in five languages, that climbing them was strictly forbidden.

'Listen,' Grant said. 'Can you hear?'

They stood still. Into the silence came the desultory voices of other sightseers moving about the basilica: the voice of a guide out in the atrium, footfalls on marble and a distant rumour of the Roman streets. 'Listen,' Grant repeated and presently from under their feet, scarcely recognizable at first but soon declaring itself, rose the sound of running water, a steady, colloquial voice, complex and unbroken.

'The Cloaca Maxima?' Major Sweet demanded.

'A pure stream leading into it,' Grant rejoined. 'More than sixty feet below us. If you lean over the rail you may be able to see that there is an equivalent opening immediately beneath this one, in the floor of the earlier church. Yet another thirty feet below, out of sight unless someone uses a torch, is a third opening and far down *that*, if a torch is lowered, it's possible to see the stream that we can hear. You may remember that Simon dropped a pebble from here and that it fell down through the centuries into the hidden waters.'

The Van der Veghels broke into excited comment.

Grant, they warmly informed him, had based the whole complex of imagery in his book upon this exciting phenomenon. 'As the deeper reaches of Simon's personality were explored – ' on and on they went, explaining the work to its author. Alleyn, who admired the book, thought that they were probably right but laid far too much insistence on an essentially delicate process of thought.

Grant fairly successfully repressed whatever embarrassment he felt. Suddenly the Baron and Baroness burst out in simultaneous laughter and cries of apology. How ridiculous! How impertinent! Really, what could have possessed them!

Throughout this incident, Major Sweet had contemplated the Van der Veghels with raised eyebrows and a slight snarl. Sophy, stifling a dreadful urge to giggle, found herself observed by Alleyn and Grant, while Lady Braceley turned her huge, deadened lamps from one man to another, eager to respond to whatever mood she might fancy she detected.

Kenneth leant far over the rail and peered into the depths. 'I'm looking down through the centuries,' he announced. His voice was distorted as if he spoke into an enormous megaphone. 'Boom! Boom!' he shouted and was echoed far below. *'Ghost beneath: Swear,'* he boomed, and then: 'Oh God!' He straightened up and was seen to have turned a sickly white. 'I'd forgotten,' he said. 'I'm allergic to heights. What a revolting place.'

'Shall we move on?' said Grant.

Sebastian Mailer led the way to a vestibule where there was the usual shop for postcards, trinkets and colour slides. Here he produced tickets of admission into the lower regions of San Tommaso.

III

The first descent was by way of two flights of stone stairs with a landing between. The air was fresh and dry and smelt only of stone. On the landing was a map of the underground regions and Mailer drew their attention to it. 'There's another one down below,' he said. 'Later on, some of you may like to explore. You can't really get lost: if you think you are, keep on going up any stairs you meet and sooner or later you'll find yourself here. These are very beautiful, aren't they?'

He drew their attention to two lovely pillars laced about with convolvulus tendrils. 'Pagan,' Mr Mailer crooned, 'gloriously pagan. Uplifted from their harmonious resting place in the Flavian house below. By industrious servants of the Vatican. There are ways and ways of looking at the Church's appropriations are there not?'

Major Sweet astonished his companions by awarding this remark a snort of endorsement and approval.

Mr Mailer smiled and continued.

'Before we descend – look, ladies and gentlemen, behind you.'

They turned. In two niches of the opposite wall were terra-cotta sculptures: one a male, ringleted and smiling, the other a tall woman with a broken child in her arms. They were superbly lit from below and seemed to have, at that instant, sprung to life.

'Apollo, it is thought,' Mr Mailer said, 'and perhaps Athena. Etruscan, of course. But the archaic smiles are Greek. The Greeks, you know, despised the Etruscans for their cruelty in battle and there are people who read cruelty into these smiles, transposed to Etruscan mouths.' He turned to Grant: 'You, I believe – ' he began and stopped. Grant was staring at the Van der Veghels with an intensity that communicated itself to the rest of the party.

They stood side by side admiring the sculptures. Their likeness, already noticed by Grant, to the Etruscan terra-cottas of the Villa Giulia startlingly declared itself here. It was as if their faces were glasses in which Apollo and Athena smiled at their own images. Sharp arrowhead smiles, full eyes and that almost uncanny liveliness – the lot, thought Alleyn.

It was obvious that all the company had been struck by this resemblance, except, perhaps, Lady Braceley who was uninterested in the Van der Veghels. But nobody ventured to remark on it apart from Sebastian Mailer who, with an extraordinary smirk, murmured as if to himself: 'How *very* remarkable. *Both.*'

The Van der Veghels, busy with flashlights, appeared not to hear him and Alleyn very much doubted if any of the others did. Barnaby

Grant was already leading them down a further flight of steps into a church that for fifteen hundred years had lain buried.

In excavating it a number of walls, arches and pillars had been introduced to support the new basilica above it. The ancient church apart from the original apse, was now a place of rather low, narrow passages, of deep shadows and of echoes. Clearly heard, whenever they all kept still, was the voice of the subterranean stream. At intervals these regions were most skilfully lit so that strange faces with large eyes floated out of the dark: wall-paintings that had been preserved in their long sleep by close-packed earth.

'The air,' Barnaby Grant said, 'has done them no good. They are slowly fading.'

'They enjoyed being stifled,' Sebastian Mailer said from somewhere in the rear. He gave out a little whinnying sound.

'More than I do,' Lady Braceley said. 'It's horribly stuffy down here, isn't it?'

'There are plenty of vents,' Major Sweet said. 'The air is noticeably fresh, Lady Braceley.'

'I don't think so,' she complained. 'I don't think I'm enjoying this part, Major. I don't think I want – ' She screamed.

They had turned a corner and come face to face with a nude, white man wearing a crown of leaves in his curls. He had full, staring eyes and again the archaic smile. His right arm stretched towards them.

'Auntie darling, what *are* you on about!' Kenneth said. 'He's fabulous. Who is he, Seb?'

'Apollo again. Apollo shines bright in the Mithraic mystery. He was raised up from below by recent excavators to garnish the Galalian corridors.'

'Damn highfalutin' poppycock,' Major Sweet remarked. It was impossible to make out in what camp he belonged. So Kenneth, Alleyn noted, calls Mailer 'Seb'. Quick work!

'And they are still digging?' the Baron asked Grant as they moved on. 'The Apollo had not risen when your Simon came to S. Tommaso? He is then a contemporary resurrection?'

'A latter-day Lazarus,' fluted Mr Mailer. 'But how *much* more attractive!'

Somewhere in the dark Kenneth echoed his giggle.

Sophy, who was between Alleyn and Grant, said under her breath, 'I wish they wouldn't,' and Grant made a sound of agreement that seemed to be echoed by Major Sweet.

They continued along the cloister of the old church.

It was now that Baron Van der Veghel developed a playful streak. Holding his camera at the ready and humming a little air, he outstripped the party, turned a corner and disappeared into shadow.

Mr Mailer, at this juncture, was in full spate. 'We approach another Etruscan piece,' he said. 'Thought to be Mercury. One comes upon it rather suddenly: on the left.'

It was indeed a sudden encounter. The Mercury was in a deep recess: an entrance, perhaps to some lost passage. He was less strongly lit than the Apollo but the glinting smile was sharp enough. When they came up with him, a second head rose over his shoulders and smirked at them. A flashlight wiped it out and the echoes rang with Baron Van der Veghel's uninhibited laughter. Lady Braceley gave another scream.

'It's too much,' she cried. 'No. It's too much!'

But the elephantine Van der Veghels, in merry pin, had frisked ahead. Major Sweet let fly anathema upon all practical jokers and the party moved on.

The voice of the subterranean stream grew louder. They turned another corner and came upon another railed well. Grant invited them to look up and there, directly overhead, was the under-mouth of the one they had already examined in the basilica.

'But what were they *for*,' Major Sweet demanded. 'What's the idea? Grant?' he added quickly, apparently to forestall any comment from Mr Mailer.

'Perhaps,' Grant said, 'for drainage. There's evidence that at some stage of the excavations seepage and even flooding occurred.'

'Hah,' said the Major.

The Baroness leant over the rail of the well and peered down.

'Gerrit!' she exclaimed. 'L-oo-ook! There is the sarcophagus! Where Simon sat and meditated!' Her voice, which had something of the reedy quality of a schoolboy's, ran up and down the scale. 'See! Down there! Belo-oow.' Her husband's flashlight briefly explored her vast stern as he gaily snapped her. Heedless, she leant far over the railing.

'Be careful, my darlink!' urged her husband. 'Mathilde! Not so far! Wait till we descend.'

He hauled her back. She was greatly excited and they laughed together.

Alleyn and Sophy approached the well-railing and looked downwards. The area below was illuminated from some unseen source and the end of a stone sarcophagus was clearly visible. From their bird's eye position they could see that the stone lid was heavily carved.

As they looked, a shadow, much distorted, moved across the wall behind it, disappeared, and was there again, turning this way and that.

Sophy cried out: 'Look! It's – it's that woman!' But it had gone.

'What woman?' Grant asked, behind her.

'The one with the shawl over her head. The postcard-seller. Down there.'

'Did you see her?' Mr Mailer asked quickly.

'I saw her shadow.'

'My dear Miss Jason! Her shadow! There are a thousand Roman women with scarves over their heads who could cast the same shadow.'

'I'm sure not. I'm sure it was she. It looked as if – as if – she wanted to hide.'

'I agree,' Alleyn said.

'Violetta is not permitted to enter the basilica, I assure you. You saw the shadow of someone in another party, of course. Now – let us follow Mr Grant down into the temple of Mithras. He has much to relate.'

They had completed their circuit of the cloisters and entered a passage leading to a spiral iron stairway. The ceiling was lower here and the passage narrow. Grant and Mailer led the way and the others trailed behind them. The head of the little procession had reached the stairhead when Lady Braceley suddenly announced that she couldn't go on.

'I'm frightfully sorry,' she said, 'but I want to go back. I'm afraid you'll think it too dreary of me but I can't, I can't, *I can't* stay in this awful place another moment. You must take me back, Kenneth. I didn't know it'd be like this. I've never been able to endure shut up places. At once. *Kenneth! Where are you! Kenneth!'*

But he wasn't with them. Her voice flung distorted echoes about the hollows and passages. 'Where's he gone?' she cried out and the whole region replied ' – gone – on – on.'

Mailer had taken her by the arm. 'It's all right, Lady Braceley. I assure you. It's perfectly all right. Kenneth went back to photograph the Apollo. In five minutes I will find him for you. Don't distress yourself. No doubt I'll meet him on his way here.'

'I won't wait for him. Why's he suddenly taking photographs? I gave him a camera costing the earth and he never uses it. I won't wait for him, I'll go now. *Now.*'

The Baron and Baroness swarmed gigantically about her making consoling noises. She thrust them aside and made for Grant, Major Sweet and Alleyn who were standing together. 'Please! *Please!*' she implored and after a quick look round, latched with great determination on to the Major. 'Please take me away!' she implored. 'Please do.'

'My dear lady,' Major Sweet began in tones more consistent with 'My good woman' – 'My dear lady, there's no occasion for hysteria. Yes – well, of course, if you insist. Be glad to. No doubt,' said the Major hopefully, 'we'll meet your nephew on our way.'

Clinging to him, she appealed to Grant and Alleyn. 'I know you think me too hopeless and silly,' she said. 'Don't you?'

'Not at all,' Alleyn said politely and Grant muttered something that might have been 'claustrophobia'.

Mr Mailer said to the Major: 'There's a continuation of this stairway that goes up into the basilica. If you'll take Lady Braceley that way I'll go back and find Mr Dorne and send him to her.'

Lady Braceley said, 'It's maddening of him. *Honestly!*'

Sophy said, 'Would you like me to come with you, Lady Braceley?'

'Oh no,' she said. 'No. Thank you. Too kind but – ' her voice trailed away. She still gazed at Alleyn and Grant. She wants an entourage, Sophy thought.

'Well,' Major Sweet said crossly. 'Shall we go?'

He piloted her towards the upper flight of the spiral stairway. 'I'll come back,' he shouted, 'as soon as that young fellow presents himself. Hope he's quick about it.'

'You'll carry on, won't you?' Mr Mailer said to Grant.

'Very well.'

Grant, Alleyn and Sophy embarked on the downward flight. They could hear Lady Braceley's heels receding up the iron treads together

with the duller clank of Major Sweet's studded brogues. Behind them
the Van der Veghels shouted excitedly to each other.

'It is only,' roared the Baroness, 'that I do not wish to miss a word,
my darlink, that he may let fall upon us.'

'Then on! Go and I will join you. One more picture of the
Mercury. Joost one!' cried the Baron.

She assented and immediately fell some distance down the iron
stairs. A cry of dismay rose from her husband.

'Mathilde! You are fallen.'

'That is so.'

'You are hurt.'

'Not. I am uninjured. What a joke.'

'On, then.'

'So.'

The descending spiral made some two or three turns. The sound
of running water grew louder. They arrived at a short passage. Grant
led them along it into a sort of ante-room.

'This is the insula,' he said. 'You might call it a group of flats. It
was built for a Roman family or families somewhere about the
middle of the first century. They were not, of course, Christians. You
will see in a moment how they worshipped their god. Come into the
Triclinium. Which is also the Mithraeum.'

He motioned them into a cave-like chamber. The roof was vaulted
and studded with small stones. Massive stone benches ran along the
sides and in the centre was an altar.

Grant said, 'You know about the Mithraic cult. There's no need
for me – '

'Please! But *please*,' implored the Baroness. 'We would like so
much! Everythink! Please!'

Alleyn heard Grant say 'Oh God!' under his breath and saw him
look, almost as if he asked for her support, at Sophy Jason.

And, for her part, Sophy received this appeal with a ripple of
warmth that bewildered her.

'Only if he wants to,' she said.

But Grant, momentarily shutting his eyes, embarked on his task.
The Baroness, all eyes and teeth, hung upon his every word. Presently
she reached out an imploring hand and whispered, 'Excuse! Forgive
me. But for my husband to miss this is too much. I call for him.' She

did so with a voice that would have done credit to Brunnhilde. He came downstairs punctually and nimbly and in response to her finger on her lips, fell at once into a receptive attitude.

Grant caught Sophy's eye, scowled at her, momentarily shut his own eyes, and, in an uneven voice told them about the cult of the god Mithras. It was, he said, a singularly noble religion and persisted, literally underground, after other pagan forms of worship had been abolished in Christian Rome.

'The god Mithras,' he said, and although at first he used formal, guide-book phrases, he spoke so directly to Sophy that they might have been alone together, 'the god Mithras was born of a rock. He was worshipped in many parts of the ancient world including England and was, above all, a god of light. Hence his association with Apollo who commanded him to kill the Bull which is the symbol of fertility. In this task he was helped by a Dog and a Snake but a Scorpion double-crossed him and spilled the bull's blood from which all life was created. And in that way evil was let loose upon mankind.'

'Yet another expulsion from Eden?' Sophy said.

'Sort of. Strange, isn't it? As if blind fingers groped about some impenetrable, basic design.'

'Curse of mankind!' Major Sweet proclaimed.

He had rejoined the party unnoticed and startled them by this eruption. 'Religions,' he announced, 'bally-hoo! The lot of them! Scoundrels!'

'Do you think so?' Grant asked mildly. 'Mithras doesn't seem so bad, on the whole. His was a gentle cult for those days. His worship was Mystery and the initiates passed through seven degrees. It was tough going. They underwent lustral purification, long abstinence and most severe deprivation. Women had no part of it. You wouldn't have been allowed,' he told Sophy, 'to enter this place, still less to touch the altar. Come and look at it.'

'You make me feel I shouldn't.'

'Ah, no!' cried the Baroness. 'We must not be superstitious, Miss Jason. Let us look, because it is very beautiful, see, and most interestink.'

The altar was half-way down the Mithraeum. The slaughter of the Bull was indeed very beautifully carved on one face and the apotheosis of Mithras assisted by Apollo on another.

To Grant's evident dismay Baron Van der Veghel had produced out of his vast canvas satchel, a copy of *Simon*.

'We must,' he announced, 'hear again the wonderful passage. See, Mr Grant, here is the book. Will the author not read it for us? How this English Simon finds in himself some equivalent to the Mithraic powers. Yes?'

'Ah no!' Grant ejaculated. 'Please!' He looked quickly about and beyond the group of six listeners as if to assure himself that there were no more. 'That's *not* in the bargain,' he said. 'Really.' And Alleyn saw him redden. 'In any case,' said Grant, 'I read abominably. Come and look at Mithras himself.'

And at the far end of the chamber, there was the god in a grotto, being born out of a stony matrix: a sturdy person with a Phrygian cap on his long curls and a plumpish body: neither child nor man.

Alleyn said, 'They made sacrifices, didn't they? In here.'

'Of course. On the altar,' Grant said quickly. 'Can you imagine! A torch-lit scene, it would be, and the light would flicker across those stone benches and across the faces of initiates, attenuated and wan from their ordeal. The altar fire raises a quivering column of heat, the sacrificial bull is lugged in: perhaps they hear it bellowing in the passages. There is a passage, you know, running right round the chamber. Probably the bull appears from a doorway behind Mithras. Perhaps it's garlanded. The acolytes drag it in and the priest receives it. Its head is pulled back, the neck exposed and the knife plunged in. The reek of fresh blood and the stench of the burnt offering fills the Mithraeum. I suppose there are chanted hymns.'

Sophy said drily, 'You gave us to understand that the Mithraic cult was a thoroughly nice and, did you say, gentle religion.'

'It was highly moral and comparatively gentle. Loyalty and fidelity were the ultimate virtues. Sacrifice was a necessary ingredient.'

'Same idea,' Major Sweet predictably announced, 'behind the whole boiling. Sacrifice. Blood. Flesh. Cannibalism. More refinement in one lot, more brutality in another. Essentially the same.'

'You don't think,' Alleyn mildly suggested, 'that this might indicate pot-shots at some fundamental truth?'

'Only fundamental truth it indicates – humans are carnivores,' shouted the Major in triumph. 'Yak-yak-yak,' he added and was understood to be laughing.

'It is so unfortunate,' said Baron Van der Veghel, 'that Lady Braceley and Mr Dorne are missing all this. And where is Mr Mailer?'

'Did you see them?' Alleyn asked Major Sweet.

'I did not. I put *her* in the – what d'you call it? Garden? Courtyard?'

'Atrium?'

'Whatever it is. On the bench. She didn't much like it, but still . . . Silly woman.'

'What about young Dorne?' Alleyn said.

'Didn't see 'im. Frightful specimen.'

'And Mailer?'

'No. Damn casual treatment, I call it. What do we do now?'

Grant said with that air of disengagement that clung about him so persistently: 'I understand it was thought that you might like to look round here under your own steam for a few minutes. We can meet again here, or if you prefer it up above in the atrium. I'll stay here for ten minutes in case there's anything you want to ask and then I'll go and wait in the atrium. We'll probably meet on the way and in any case you can't get lost. There are "out" notices everywhere. I'm sure Mailer – '

He broke off. Somebody was approaching down the iron stairway.

'Here he is,' Grant said.

But it was only Kenneth Dorne.

He had sounded to be in a hurry and made a precipitate entry but when he came out of the shadows and saw the others he halted and slouched towards them. His camera dangled from his hand. It struck Sophy that he was, in some unsatisfactory way, assuaged and comforted.

'Hullo,' he said. 'Where's my aunt?'

Grant informed him. He said 'Oh dear!' and giggled.

'Hadn't you better take a look at her?' Major Sweet asked.

'What?'

'Your aunt. She's up top. In the garden.'

'May she flourish,' Kenneth said, 'like the Green Bay Tree. Dear Major.'

Major Sweet contemplated him for one or two seconds. 'Words,' he then said, 'fail me.'

'Well,' Kenneth rejoined, 'thank God for that.'

This produced a kind of verbal stalemate.

It was broken by the Van der Veghels. They had, they excitedly explained, hoped so much (ah, *so* much, interpolated the Baroness), that Mr Grant would be persuaded to read aloud the Mithraic passage from *Simon* in its inspirational environment. As everybody saw, they had brought their copy – was it too much, even, to ask for a signature? – to that end. They understood, none better, the celebrated Anglo-Saxon reticence. But after all, the terms of the brochure, not of course to be insisted upon *au pied de la lettre*, had encouraged them to believe . . .

They went on along these lines with a sort of antiphonal reproachfulness and Grant's face, even in that dim light, could be seen to grow redder and redder. At last he turned helplessly to Sophy, who muttered, 'Hadn't you better?' and was strangely gratified when he said at once and at large, 'If you really want it, of course. I didn't mean to be disobliging. It's only that I'll feel such an ass.'

The Van der Veghels broke into delighted laughter and the Baron developed a more extravagant flight of fancy. They would take a photograph; a group at the centre of which would be Grant, reading aloud. In the background, the god Mithras himself would preside over the work he had inspired. This extraordinary variant on Victorian group-photography was put into operation after a playful argument between the Van der Veghels about their active and passive roles. Finally they agreed that the Baroness would take the first picture and she went excitedly into action. The wretched Grant, with open book, was placed upon an obscure stone protrusion to the left of Mithras. Alleyn on his one hand and Sophy, who was beginning to get the giggles, on the other. Behind Sophy posed Major Sweet and behind Alleyn, Kenneth Dorne.

'And you, Gerrit, my darlink,' the Baroness instructed her husband, 'because you are so big, yes? at the rear.'

'Afterwards we exchange,' he urged.

'So.'

'And all to concentrate upon the open page.'

'Ach. So.'

Major Sweet, always unpredictable, took a serious view of this business. 'How,' he objected, 'are we to concentrate on something we can scarcely see?'

And indeed, it was well-urged. The head of the little god, like the altar and all the other effigies in these regions, was cleverly lit from a concealed niche but his surroundings were deep in shadow, none more so than the area in which the group was deployed. The Van der Veghels explained that all would be revealed by the flashlamp. Their great desire was that the god should be incorporated in the group and to this end a little make-believe was to be excused. Grant's discomfiture had become so evident that Alleyn and Sophy Jason, simultaneously but without consultation, decided upon a note of high comedy.

'I see,' Alleyn suddenly offered. 'Even if we can't see it, we're all to gaze upon the book? Fair enough. And I expect Mr Grant knows the passage by heart. Perhaps he could recite it for us in the dark.'

'I can do nothing of the sort, damn you,' Grant said warmly. The Baroness explained. Afterwards they would move into a more luminous spot and Grant would then, without subterfuge, read the appropriate passage.

In the meantime, the Baroness reiterated, would they all concentrate upon the almost imperceptible page.

After a good deal of falling about in the dark the group assembled. 'Would it be pretty,' Alleyn suggested, 'if Miss Jason were to point out a passage in the book and I were to place my arm about the author's shoulders, eagerly seeking to read it?'

'*What* a good suggestion,' Sophy cried. 'And Major Sweet could perhaps bend over on the other side.'

'Delighted, I'm sure,' said the Major with alacrity and did bend very closely over Sophy. 'Damn good idea, what,' he whistled into her ear.

'It recalls,' Alleyn said, 'Tchekov reading aloud to Stanislavsky and the Moscow Arts players.'

This observation was received with loud applause from the Baroness. Sophy and Alleyn crowded up to Grant.

'You shall suffer for this,' Grant said between his teeth. 'Both of you.'

'On the book, on the book, all on the book!' gaily chanted the Baroness. 'Nobody to move. Gerrit, you must step a little back and Mr Dorne, are you there, please?'

'Oh God, yes, I'm here.'

'Good. Good. And so, all are ready? Freeze, please. I shoot.'

The camera clicked but the darkness was uninterrupted. The Baroness who had uttered what was no doubt a strong expletive in her own language now followed it up with a reproach to her husband. 'What did I tell you, my darlink! They are useless these local bulps. No! Do not answer. Do not move. I have another in my pocket. Not to move anybody, please, or speak. I find it.'

Sophy giggled. Major Sweet immediately groped for her waist.

'Serve you bloody well right,' whispered Grant to Sophy. He had detected this manoeuvre. From somewhere not far away but beyond the Mithraeum there came the sound, distorted as all sounds were in that region, by echoes, as of a high-pitched voice.

There followed a seemingly interminable interval broken after a time by a distant thud as of a heavy door being shut. The Baroness fiddled and muttered. Kenneth detached himself from the group and took a flashlight shot of the god. He was urged back into position and at last the Baroness was ready.

'Please. Please. Attention. Freeze, please. Again, I shoot.'

This time the light flashed, they were all blinded and the Baroness gave out loud cries of satisfaction and insisted upon taking two more. Against mounting impatience the group was then re-formed with the Baroness replacing her husband and over-hanging Major Sweet like some primitive earth-mother. The Baron had better luck with his flashlamp and all was accomplished.

'Although,' he said, 'it would have been nicer to have included our cicerone, would it not?'

'Must say he's taking his time,' Major Sweet grumbled. 'Damned odd sort of behaviour if you ask me.'

But Kenneth pointed out that Sebastian Mailer was probably keeping his aunt company in the atrium. 'After all,' he said to Grant, 'he handed over to you, didn't he?'

Grant, under pressure from the Van der Veghels, now moved into the area of light and with every sign of extreme reluctance read the Mithraic passage from *Simon* to this most strangely assorted audience. He read rapidly and badly in an uninflected voice but something of the character of his writing survived the treatment.

'– Nothing had changed. The dumpy god with Phrygian cap, icing-sugar ringlets, broken arms and phallus rose from his matrix of stony female breasts. A rather plebeian god one might have said, but in his presence fat little Simon's ears heaved with the soundless roar of a sacrificial bull, his throat and the back of his nose were stung by blood that nineteen centuries ago had boiled over white-hot stone, and his eyes watered in the reek of burning entrails. He trembled and was immeasurably gratified.'

The reading continued in jerks to the end of the appropriate passage. Grant shut the book with a clap, passed it like a hot potato to the Baroness and hitched his shoulders against obligatory murmurs from his audience. These evaporated into an uneasy silence.

Sophy felt oppressed. For the first time claustrophobia threatened her. The roof seemed lower, the walls closer, the regions beyond them very much quieter as if the group had been deserted, imprisoned almost so many fathoms deep in the ground. For tuppence, she thought, I could do a bolt like Lady Braceley.

Grant repeated his suggestion that the others might like to explore and that he himself would remain for ten minutes in the Mithraeum in case anyone preferred to rejoin him there before returning to the upper world. He reminded them that there were side openings and an end one, leading into surrounding passages, and the insula.

Kenneth Dorne said he would go up and take a look at his aunt. He seemed to be more relaxed and showed a tendency to laugh at nothing in particular. 'Your reading was m-a-a-r-vellous,' he said to Grant and smiled from ear to ear. 'I adore your Simon.' He laughed immoderately and left by the main entrance. Major Sweet said he would take a look-see round and rejoin them above. 'I have,' he threatened 'a bone to pick with Mailer. Extraordinary behaviour.' He stared at Sophy. 'Thinking of looking round at all?' he invited.

'I think I'll stay put for a moment,' she said. She did not at all fancy roaming in a Mithraic gloaming with the Major.

Alleyn said he, too, would find his own way back and the Van der Veghels who had been photographing each other against the sacrificial altar decided to join him, not, Sophy thought, entirely to his delight.

Major Sweet left by one of the side doors. Alleyn disappeared behind the god, enthusiastically followed by the Van der Veghels. They could be heard ejaculating in some distant region. Their voices died and there was no more sound except, Sophy fancied, the cold babble of that subterranean stream.

'Come and sit down,' Grant said.

She joined him on one of the stone benches.

'Are you feeling a bit oppressed?'

'Sort of.'

'Shall I take you up? There's no need to stay. That lot are all right under their own steam. Say the word.'

'How kind,' Sophy primly rejoined, 'but, thank you, no. I'm not all that put out. It's only – '

'Well?'

'I've got a theory about walls.'

'*Walls?*'

'Surfaces. Any surfaces.'

'Do explain yourself.'

'You'll be profoundly unimpressed.'

'One never knows. Try me.'

'Mightn't surfaces – wood, stone, cloth, anything you like – have a kind of physical sensitivity we don't know about? Something like the coating on photographic film? So that they retain impressions of happenings that have been exposed to them. And mightn't some people have an element in their physical make-up – their chemical or electronic arrangements or whatever – that is responsive to this and aware of it?'

'As if other people were colour-blind and only they saw red?'

'That's the idea.'

'That would dispose rather neatly of ghosts, wouldn't it?'

'It wouldn't be only the visual images the surfaces retained. It'd be emotions too.'

'Do you find your idea an alarming one?'

'Disturbing, rather.'

'Well – yes.'

'I wonder if it might fit in with your Simon.'

'Ah,' ejaculated Grant, 'don't remind me of that, for God's sake!'

'I'm sorry,' Sophy said, taken aback by his violence.

He got up, walked away and with his back turned to her said rapidly, 'All right, why don't you say it! If I object so strongly to all this show-off, why the hell do I do it? That's what you're thinking, isn't it? Come on. *Isn't it?*

'If I am it's no business of mine. And anyway I *did* say it. Up above.' She caught her breath. 'It seems ages ago,' said Sophy. 'Ages.'

'We've dropped through some twenty centuries, after all. And I'm sorry to have been so bloody rude.'

'Think nothing of it,' Sophy said. She looked up at the sharply lit head of Mithras. 'He is not very formidable after all. Plump and placid, really, wouldn't you say? Isn't it odd, though, how those blank eyes seem to stare? You'd swear they had pupils. Do you suppose – '

She cried out. The god had gone. Absolute darkness had closed down upon them like a velvet shutter.

'It's all right,' Grant said. 'Don't worry. They do it as a warning for closing time. It'll go on again in a second.'

'Thank the Lord for that. It's – it's so completely black. One might be blind.'

' "All dark and comfortless"?'

'That's from *Lear,* isn't it? Not exactly a reassuring quotation, if I may say so.'

'Where are you?'

'Here.'

In a distant region there was a rumour of voices: distorted, flung about some remote passage. Grant's hand closed on Sophy's arm. The god came into being again, staring placidly at nothing.

'There you are,' Grant said. 'Come on. We'll climb back into contemporary Rome, shall we?'

'Please.'

He moved his hand up her arm and they embarked on the return journey.

Through the insula, a left turn and then straight towards the iron stairway passing a cloistral passage out of which came the perpetual voice of water. Up the iron stairway. Through the second basilica, past Mercury, and Apollo, and then up the last flight of stone steps towards the light, and here was the little shop: quite normal and bright.

The people in charge of the postcard and holy trinket stalls, a monk and two youths, were shutting them up. They looked sharply at Grant and Sophy.

'No more,' Grant said to them. 'We are the last.'

They bowed.

'There's no hurry,' he told Sophy. 'The upper basilica stays open until sunset.'

'Where will the others be?'

'Probably in the atrium.'

But the little garden was quite deserted and the basilica almost so. The last belated sightseers were hurrying away through the main entrance.

'He's mustered them outside,' Grant said. 'Look – there they are. Come on.'

And there, in the outer porch where they had originally assembled, were Mr Mailer's guests in a dissatisfied huddle: the Van der Veghels, the Major, Lady Braceley, Kenneth and, removed from them, Alleyn. The two sumptuous cars were drawn up in the roadway.

Grant and Alleyn simultaneously demanded of each other: 'Where's Mailer?' and then, with scarcely a pause: 'Haven't *you* seen him?'

But nobody, it transpired, had seen Mr Mailer.

CHAPTER 4

Absence of Mr Mailer

'Not since he slouched off to find *you*,' Major Sweet shouted, glaring at Kenneth. 'Down below, there.'

'Find *me*,' Kenneth said indifferently. 'I don't know what you're talking about. I haven't seen him.'

Alleyn said, 'He went back to find you when you returned to photograph the Apollo.'

'He must have changed his mind then. Last I saw of him was – you know – it was – you know, it was just before I went back to Apollo.'

Kenneth's voice dragged strangely. He gave an aimless little giggle, closed his eyes and reopened them sluggishly. By the light of day, Alleyn saw that the pupils had contracted. 'Yes, that's right,' Kenneth drawled, 'I remember. It was then.'

'And he didn't follow you and Lady Braceley, Major Sweet?'

'I imagined that to be perfectly obvious, sir. He did not.'

'And he didn't join you, Lady Braceley, in the atrium?'

'If that's the rather dismal little garden where the gallant major dumped me,' she said, 'the answer is no. Mr Mailer didn't join me there or anywhere else. I don't know why,' she added, widening her terrible eyes at Alleyn, 'but that sounds vaguely improper, don't you think?'

Major Sweet, red in the face, said unconvincingly that he had understood Lady Braceley would prefer to be alone in the atrium.

'That,' she said, 'would have rather depended on what was offering as an alternative.'

'I must say – ' he began in a fluster but Alleyn interrupted him.

'Would you stay where you are, all of you,' Alleyn said. And to Grant, 'You're in charge, aren't you? Be a good chap and see they stay put, will you?'

He was gone – back into the church.

'By God, that's pretty cool I must say,' fumed the Major. 'Ordering people about, damn it, like some blasted policeman. Who the devil does he think he is!'

'I fancy,' Grant said, 'we'd better do as he suggests.'

'Why?'

'Because,' Grant said with a half-smile at Sophy, 'he seems to have what Kent recognized in *Lear*.'

'What the hell's that?'

'Authority.'

'How right you are,' said Sophy.

'I think he's gorgeous,' Lady Braceley agreed, 'too compulsive and masterful.'

A long and uneasy silence followed this appraisal.

'But what's he *doing*?' Kenneth suddenly asked. 'Where's he gone?'

'I'm blasted well going to find out,' the Major announced.

As he was about to carry out this threat, Alleyn was seen, returning quickly, through the basilica.

Before Major Sweet could launch, as he clearly intended to do, a frontal attack, Alleyn said:

'Do forgive me, all of you. I'm afraid I was insufferably bossy but I thought it as well to go back and ask at the shop if Mr Mailer had come through.'

'All right, all right,' said the Major. 'Had he?'

'They say not.'

'They might not have noticed him,' Grant offered.

'It's possible, of course, but they know him by sight and say they were waiting for him to go out. They check the numbers of tickets for the lower regions in order to guard against shutting someone in.'

'What's he doing, skulking down there?' the Major demanded. 'I call it a damn poor show. Leaving us high and dry.' He attacked Grant. 'Look here, Grant, you're on the strength here, aren't you? Part of the organization, whatever it is.'

'Absolutely not. I've nothing to do with it. Or him,' Grant added under his breath.

'My dear fellow, your name appears in their literature.'

'In a purely honorary capacity.'

'I suppose,' Kenneth said, 'it's publicity for you, isn't it?'

'I'm not in need – ' Grant began and then turned white. 'Isn't all this beside the point?' he asked Alleyn.

'I'd have thought so. The people in charge have gone down to find him. There's a complete system of fluorescent lighting kept for maintenance, excavation and emergencies. If he's there they'll find him.'

'He may have been taken ill or something,' Sophy hazarded.

'That is so, that is so,' cried the Van der Veghels like some rudimentary chorus. They often spoke in unison. 'He is of a sickly appearance,' the Baroness added. 'And sweats a great deal,' said her husband, clinching the proposition.

The two drivers now crossed the road. Giovanni, the one who spoke English and acted as an assistant guide, invited the ladies and gentlemen to take their seats in the cars. Alleyn asked if they had seen Mr Mailer. The drivers put their heads on one side and raised their hands and shoulders. No.

'Perhaps,' Lady Braceley said in an exhausted voice, 'he's fallen down those horrid-awful stairs. Poorest Mr Mailer. Do you know, I think I will sit in the car. I'm no good at standing about on my gilded pins.'

She swivelled one of her collective stares between Grant, Alleyn and the Baron and got into the car, finding a moment to smile into the face of Giovanni as he opened the door. Established, she leant out of the window. 'The offer of a cigarette,' she said, 'would be met in the spirit in which it was made.'

But only Kenneth, it seemed, could oblige and did so, leaning his face down to his aunt's as he offered his lighter. They spoke together, scarcely moving their lips and for a moment or two looked alike.

Grant muttered to Alleyn, 'This is a bloody rum turn-up for the books, isn't it?' 'Rum enough, yes.'

Sophy said, 'Of course, they'll find him, won't they? I mean they must.'

'You were together, weren't you, after the rest of us left?'

'Yes,' they said.

'And returned together?'

'Of course,' Grant said. 'You saw us. Why?'

'You were the last out by some moments. You didn't hear anything? Mailer's wearing rather heavy shoes. They made quite a noise, I noticed, on the iron steps.'

No, they said. They hadn't heard a thing.

'I think I'll go back, Grant. Care to come?'

'Back? You mean – down below again?'

'If necessary.'

'I'll come,' Grant said, 'as far as the office – the shop. I'm not madly keen to traipse round the nether regions after Mailer. If he's there the staff'll find him.'

'All right. But don't you think something ought to be done about this lot?'

'Look here,' Grant said angrily, 'I've already said I accept no responsibility for this turn-out. Or for anyone in it – ' his voice wavered and he glanced at Sophy. 'Except Miss Jason who's on her own.'

'I'm all right,' Sophy said airily and to Alleyn, 'What should we do? Can you suggest anything?'

'Suppose you all carry on with your picnic on the Palatine Hill? The drivers will take you there. The one that speaks English – Giovanni – seems to be a sort of second-in-command. I'm sure he'll take over. No doubt they'll unpack hampers and lay on the charm: they're wonderful at that. I'll unearth Mailer and if he's all right we'll follow you up. It'll be a lovely evening on the Palatine Hill.'

'What do you think?' Sophy asked Grant.

'It's as good an idea as any other.' He turned to Alleyn. 'Sorry to be bloody-minded,' he said. 'Shall we go back in there, then?'

'On second thoughts I won't bother you. If you wouldn't mind fixing things with Giovanni – I suggest that even if I don't re-appear with Mailer in hand, you carry on with the programme. The alfresco tea, then back to your hotels and the cars will pick you all up again at nine o'clock. You're at the Gallico, aren't you? You might be very kind and just make a note of where the others are staying. There I go, bossing again. Never mind.'

He gave Sophy a little bow and as Major Sweet bore down upon them, neatly side-stepped him and returned to the basilica.

'I'll be damned,' said Barnaby Grant.

'I dare say,' Sophy said. 'But all the same you'll do it. It's like what you said.'

'*What* did I say, smarty-pants?'

'He's got authority.'

II

When Alleyn got back to the vestibule he found the shop still in process of closure. An iron lattice gate with a formidable padlock shut off the entrance to the lower regions. S. Tommaso in Pallaria, like its sister basilica, S. Clemente, is in the care of Irish Dominicans. The monk in charge – Father Denys, it transpired – spoke with a superb brogue. Like so many Irishmen in exile, he had the air of slightly putting it on as if he played his own part in some pseudo-Hibernian comedy. He greeted Alleyn like an old acquaintance.

'Ah, it's yourself again,' he said. 'And I have no news for you. This fellow Mailer's not below. We've had the full power of the lighting on and it's enough to dazzle the eyes out of your head. I'm after looking beneath with these two young chaps – ' he indicated his assistants. 'We made a great hunt of it, every nook and cranny. He's not there, at all, no doubt of it.'

'How very odd,' Alleyn said. 'He's in charge of our party, you know. What can have happened to him?'

'Well, now, it's a strange occurrence and no mistake. I can only suggest he must have slipped through here at a great pace when we were all occupied and never noticed 'um. Though that's not an easy thing to credit, for as I've mentioned we keep a tally ever since a Scandinavian lady twisted a fetlock and got herself locked in five years ago and she screeching all night to no avail and discovered clean demented, poor soul, in the morning. And another thing. Your party was the only one beneath, for the one or two odd visitors had come out before you arrived. So he would have been on his own and the more noticeable for it.'

'I don't want to make a nuisance of myself, Father, and I don't for a moment suggest your search wasn't thorough but would you mind if I – '

'I would not but I can't permit it. It's the rule of the place, d'ye see. No visitors beneath under any pretext after closure.'

'Yes, I see. Then I wonder – is there a telephone I could use?'

'There is and welcome. In here. You can go, now,' he said over his shoulder to his assistants and repeated it in Italian.

He opened a door into a store-cupboard, pointed to a telephone and switched on a light.

There wasn't much room or air when the door was shut. Alleyn backed gingerly into an open box of holy trinkets, eased himself into a crouch supported by the edge of a shelf, examined his memory and dialled the resulting number.

Il Questore Valdarno had not left his office. He listened to Alleyn's story with an animation that was almost tangible but with few interruptions. When Alleyn had finished Valdarno said in English: 'He has run.'

'Run?'

'Flown. He has recognized you and decamped.'

'They seemed pretty sure, here, that he couldn't have got past them.'

'Ah, ah, ah,' said the Questore contemptuously, 'who are they? a monk and two pale shop boys. Against this expert! Pah! He has run away at the double-up behind the show-cases.'

'Speaking of postcards, there was a savage elderly postcard lady in the entrance who made a scene with Mailer.'

'A scene? How?'

'Yelling abuse at him. It was not in the sort of Italian we learnt in my Diplomatic days but the general drift was invective and fury.'

Alleyn could almost hear the Questore's shrug.

'He has done something to annoy her, perhaps,' he suggested in his melancholy voice.

'She spat at him.'

'Ah,' sighed the Questore. 'He had irritated her.'

'No doubt,' Alleyn faintly agreed. 'She's called Violetta,' he added.

'Why do you concern yourself with this woman, my dear colleague?'

'Well, if I understood her at all, she threatened to kill him.'

'Evidently a short-tempered woman. Some of these street-vendors are in fact badly-behaved persons.'

'I thought he was greatly disturbed by the encounter. He made light of it but he turned very white.'

'Ah.' There was a brief silence. 'She sells postcards outside S. Tommaso?'

'Yes. One of our party thought she saw her shadow on the wall of a passage down in the Mithraeum.'

'They are not permitted to enter.'

'So I gathered.'

'I will have inquiries made. I will also have the airports, omnibus and railway stations watched. I feel there is a strong probability Mailer has recognized you and will attempt an escape.'

'I am deeply obliged to you, Signor Questore.'

'Please!'

'But I confess the chances of his recognizing me – we have never met – do seem a bit thin.'

'Some contact of his, an English contact, may have seen you and informed him. It is most possible.'

'Yes,' Alleyn said, 'it's possible of course.'

'We shall see. In the meantime, my dear Superintendent, may I have a little speech with this Dominican?'

'I'll call him.'

'And we keep in close touch, isn't it?'

'Of course.'

'With my compliments, then,' said Il Questore Valdarno sadly.

Alleyn returned to the shop and delivered his message.

'Il Questore Valdarno, is it?' said Father Denys. 'You didn't let on this was a pollis affair but it doesn't surprise me at all. Wait, now, and I'll talk to 'um.'

He did so in voluble Italian and returned looking perturbed. 'It's a queer business,' he said, 'and I don't say I fancy the turn it's taking. He wants to send in some of his fellows to search below and is going to talk to my Superior about it. I told 'um we'd overlooked every inch of the place but that doesn't satisfy the man. He says will I tell you you're welcome to join in. Eight sharp in the morning.'

'Not tonight?'

'Ah, why would it be tonight and himself if he's below, which he's not, locked up like a fish in a tin.' Father Denys looked pretty sharply at Alleyn. 'You're not the cut of a policeman, yourself,' he said. 'None of my business, of course.'

'Do I look like a harmless visitor? I hope I do. Tell me, do you know anything about the woman called Violetta who sells postcards here?'

Father Denys clapped his hand to his forehead. 'Violetta, is it!' he ejaculated. 'A terrible pest, that one, God forgive me, for she's touched in her wits, poor creature. Sure, this other business put her clean out of my mind. Come into the atrium till I tell you. We'll lock up this place.'

He did lock up the vestibule and pretty securely, too, fetching a great key out of a pocket in his habit. Nobody else had that one or a key to the iron grille he said, except Brother Dominic who opened up in the morning.

The basilica was now deserted and the time six o'clock. All the bells in Rome rang the Ave Maria and Father Denys took time off to observe it. He then led the way into the atrium and settled beside Alleyn on a stone bench, warm with the westering sun. He was a cosy man and enjoyed a gossip.

Violetta, he said, had sold postcards in the entrance to S. Tommaso for some months. She was a Sicilian of dubious origins, was not as old as Alleyn may have supposed and when she first appeared carried upon her the remnants of ferocious good looks. Her story, which she never ceased to pour out, was that her husband had deserted her and in doing so had betrayed her to the police.

'For doing what?' Alleyn asked.

'Ah, she never lets on exactly. Something to do with passing prohibited articles. Likely enough stolen, though she makes out she'd no notion what mischief was in it till the pollis came down upon her and destroyed her. She's very wild in her conversation and the saints themselves wouldn't know which was fact and which was fantasy.'

She had behaved herself reasonably well, however, reserving her outbursts for the Dominicans and sticking to her legal postcard-vending territory until about two days ago when he had found her squatting in a corner of the porch letting out the most frightful animadversions in a hissing torrent and shaking her fists. She literally foamed at the mouth and was quite incoherent, but after Father Denys had rebuked her for blasphemy and, Alleyn gathered, sorted her out in a pretty big way, she became slightly more comprehensible. Her rage, it emerged, had been directed at a person who had visited the Sacristy to discuss arrangements for sightseeing trips by a newly-formed enterprise called –

'Don't tell me,' Alleyn said as Father Denys paused for dramatic effect. 'Let me guess. Called "Il Cicerone".'

'Right for you.'

'In the person of Mr Sebastian Mailer?'

'Right again,' cried Father Denys, clapping his hands together. 'And the poor creature's husband or if he's not he ought to be, God help him.'

III

It was past five o'clock on that very warm afternoon when two cars arrived at the Palatine Hill. The air smelt of sunny earth, grass, myrtle and resin. In lengthening shadows poppies made little scarlet exclamations and legions of acanthus marched down the contours of the hill. The skies had deepened behind broken columns and arches: the bones of classic Rome.

Giovanni, the driver, had responded with gusto to the role of guide. He said that he had no notion of what had befallen Mr Mailer but suggested that a sudden onslaught of the affliction known to tourists as Roman Tummy might have overtaken him. By its nature, Giovanni delicately reminded them, it necessitated an immediate withdrawal. He then led his party across the ruins of Domus Augustana and down a little flight of steps towards a grove of pines. Back again and here and there he led them giving names to ruins and with sweeps of his arms laying Rome at their feet.

Sophy looked and dreamed and ached with pleasure and did not listen very closely to Giovanni. She was suddenly tired and vaguely happy. Barnaby Grant walked beside her in companionable silence, the Van der Veghels thundered about with cries of appreciation, a thousand inquiries and much photography. Lady Braceley, arm-in-arm with Kenneth and the reluctant Major, trailed and hobbled in the rear and could be heard faintly lamenting the rough going.

'I've a low saturation point for sights,' Sophy remarked. 'Or rather for information about sights. I stop listening.'

'Well,' Grant said kindly, 'at least you admit it.'

'I'd have you know it doesn't mean that I'm insensible to all this.'

'All right. I didn't suppose you were.'

'On the contrary. I'm knocked dumb. Or nearly dumb,' Sophy amended. 'You may say: *visually* speechless.'

He looked at her with amusement. 'I dare say you're hungry,' he offered.

'And I dare say you're right,' she agreed in surprise. 'Thirsty, anyway.'

'Look, we're settling for our tea.'

They had come to a terrain called the Belvedere and looked beyond the tops of a pine grove to the monstrous splendour of the Colosseum. Spires, roofs, gardens, an obelisk, insubstantial in the late afternoon haze, swam into the distance and dissolved against the Alban Hills.

Giovanni and his assistant, having found a place by a fallen column, spread rugs and cloths and opened hampers.

It was, as Sophy said, an exquisite snack: delicate little sandwiches of smoked salmon and caviare: Roman and Neapolitan pastries, fruit and a chilled white wine. There was also, surprisingly, whisky and soda. And tea for anybody who preferred it as Sophy herself did, iced with lemon, and very fragrant.

What a rum little lot we are, she thought indulgently. A light breath of air brought a stronger whiff of myrtle and pine needles with it and momentarily lifted her hair from her forehead. She found that Grant looked fixedly at her and she said hurriedly: 'We none of us seem to be worrying about poor Mr Mailer, do we?'

He made a sharp movement of his hands. 'No doubt our authoritative friend has coped,' he said.

Major Sweet, having eaten very heartily and made smart work of two whiskies and soda, appeared to be in a mollified condition. He said: 'Most extraordinary chap. My opinion.' But lazily and without rancour. ''Strordinary good tea,' he added.

'*I* think,' Lady Braceley said, 'we're all getting along very nicely as we are – with Giovanni,' and gave Giovanni a sufficiently lingering glance. 'Although,' she said, 'it's a pity that other gorgeous brute's deserted us.'

'What exactly,' Kenneth asked restlessly, 'is the programme for tonight? Cars at nine – for where? Where do we dine?'

'At the Gioconda, sir,' Giovanni said.

'Good God!' the Major ejaculated. As well he might. The Gioconda is the most exclusive as it is undoubtedly the most expensive restaurant in Rome.

'Really?' Lady Braceley said. Then I must make up my quarrel with Marco. We had a row about tables last week. He turfed out a Mexican attaché or somebody thought to be rather grand, and gave his table to me. There was almost an international incident. I told him I hated that sort of thing. Actually it was too naughty of him.'

This time,' Kenneth said, 'darling Auntie, you'll find yourself with a set dinner at a back table near the service door. If I know anything about escorted tours.'

'Excuse me, but no, sir,' Giovanni said. 'This is not such an arrangement. The service is in all ways as for the best. You will order, if you please, what you wish.'

'And pay for it?' Kenneth asked rudely.

'On the contrary, sir, no. I will attend to the settlement.' He turned to Grant. 'When you are ready to leave, sir,' he said, 'will you please ask your waiter to send for me? I will make the tipping also but of course if any of you is inclined – ' he made an eloquent gesture. 'But it will not be necessary,' he said.

'Well!' the Major ejaculated, 'I must say this is – ah – it seems – ah – ' he boggled slightly ' – quite in order,' he said. 'What?'

The Van der Veghels eagerly concurred. 'At first,' the Baron confided to Sophy, 'my wife and I thought perhaps the charge was too much – a ridiculous amount – but Mr Mailer impressed us so greatly, and then – ' he gaily bowed to Grant ' – there was the unique opportunity to meet the creator of *Simon*. We were captured! And now, see, how nicely it develops, isn't it, providing all is well with the excellent Mailer.'

'Ah, pooh, ah pooh, ah pooh!' cried the Baroness rather as if she invoked some omnipotent Chinese. 'He will be very well, he will be up and bobbing. There will be some easy explaining and all laughing and jolly. We should not allow our pleasures to be dim by this. Not at all.'

'I must tell you,' the Baron waggishly said to Grant, 'that I have a professional as well as an aesthetic pleasure in meeting Mr Barnaby Grant. I am in the publishing trade, Mr Grant. Ah-ha, ah-ha!'

'Ah-ha, ah-ha!' confided the Baroness.

'Really?' Grant said, politely whipping up interest. 'Are you indeed!'

'The firm of Adriaan and Welker. I am the editor for our foreign productions.'

Sophy had given a little exclamation and Grant turned to her. 'This is your field,' he said, and to the Van der Veghels: 'Miss Jason is with my own publishers in London.'

There were more ejaculations and much talk of coincidence while Sophy turned over in her mind what she knew of the firm of Adriaan and Welker and afterwards as they drove away from the Palatine, confided to Grant.

'We've done a few of their juvenile and religious books in translation. They're predominantly a religious publishing firm, the biggest, I fancy, in Europe. The angle is Calvinistic and as far as children's books go, rather nauseatingly pi. The head of the firm, Welker, is said to be the fanatical king-pin of some extreme sect in Holland. As you may imagine, they do *not* publish much contemporary fiction.'

'Not, one would venture, a congenial milieu for the romping Van der Veghels.'

'Oh, I don't know,' Sophy said vaguely. 'I dare say they manage to adjust.'

'What a world-weary child!' Grant observed and shook his head at her. Sophy turned pink and fell silent.

They were in the second car with Major Sweet who was asleep. The other four had seated themselves, smartly, with Giovanni. Lady Braceley, offering the plea that she suffered from car-sickness, had placed herself in the front seat.

The horrific evening welter of Roman traffic surged, screeched and hooted through the streets. Drivers screamed at each other, removed both hands from the wheel to fold them together in sarcastic prayer at the enormities perpetrated by other drivers. Pedestrians, launching themselves into the maelstrom, made grand-opera gestures against oncoming traffic. At pavement tables, Romans read their evening papers, made love, argued vociferously, or, over folded arms, stared with portentous detachment at nothing in particular. Major Sweet lolled to and fro with his mouth open and occasionally snorted. Once he woke and said that what was wanted here was a London bobby.

'Out there,' said Grant, 'he wouldn't last three minutes.'

'Balls,' said the Major and fell asleep again. He woke when they stopped suddenly and added, 'I'm most frightfully sorry, can't think what's come over me,' and slept again immediately.

Grant found to his surprise that Sophy, too, was at the Pensione Gallico. He himself had only moved in the day before and had not yet eaten there. He asked her if he might give her a drink at Tre Scalini in Navona. 'They could pick us both up there,' he said.

'Nice idea. Thank you.'

'At half past eight then?'

He managed to make this clear to the driver.

The Major was decanted at his hotel and Sophy and Grant at the Gallico.

Grant's room was like an oven. He bathed, lay down for an hour in a state of nature and extreme perturbation and then dressed. When he was ready he sat on his bed with his head in his hands. If only, he thought, this could be the definitive movement. If only it all could stop: *now.* And the inevitable reference floated up: *'the be-all and the end-all here, but here upon this bank and shoal of time –* '

He thought of Sophy Jason, sitting on the Palatine Hill, her hair lifted from her forehead by the evening breeze and a look of pleased bewilderment in her face. A remote sort of girl, a restful girl who didn't say anything silly, he thought, and then wondered if, after all, 'restful' was quite the word for her. He leant over his window-sill and looked at the façades and roofs and distant cupolas.

The clock struck eight. A horse-carriage rattled through the cobbled street below, followed by a succession of motorbicycles and cars. In an upstairs room across the street an excited babble of voices erupted and somewhere deep inside the house a remorseless, untrained tenor burst into song. Farther along the second floor of the Pensione Gallico a window was thrown up and out looked Sophy, dressed in white.

He watched her rest her arms on the window ledge, dangle her hands and sniff the evening air. How strange it was to look at someone who was unaware of being observed. She was turned away from him and craned towards the end of their street where spray from a fountain in Navona could just be seen catching the light in a feathered arc. He watched her with a sense of guilt and pleasure. After a moment or two he said: 'Good evening.'

She was still for a moment and then slowly turned to him. 'How long have you been there?' she asked.

'No time at all. You're ready, I see. Shall we go?'

'If you like: yes, shall we?'

It was cooler out of doors. As they entered Navona the splashing of water, by its very sound, freshened the evening air. The lovely piazza sparkled, lights danced in cascades of water, glared from headlamps and glowed in Tre Scalini caffè.

'There's a table,' Grant said. 'Let's nab it, quickly.'

It was near the edge of the pavement. Their view of Navona was minimal. To Sophy this was of small matter. It suited her better to be here, hemmed in, slightly jostled, bemused, possibly bamboozled in some kind of tourist racket, than to be responding to Rome with scholarly discretion and knowledgeable good taste and a reserve which in any case she did not command.

This is magic,' she said, beaming at Grant. 'That's all. It's magic. I could drink it.'

'So you shall,' he said, 'in the only possible way,' and ordered champagne cocktails.

At first they did not have a great deal to say to each other but were not troubled by this circumstance. Grant let fall one or two remarks about Navona. 'It was a circus in classical times. Imagine all these strolling youths stripped and running their courses by torchlight or throwing the discus in the heat of the day.' And after one of their silences. 'Would you like to know that the people in the middle fountain are personifications of the Four Great Rivers? Bernini designed it and probably himself carved the horse, which is a portrait.' And later: 'The huge church was built over the site of a brothel. Poor St Agnes had her clothes taken off there and in a burst of spontaneous modesty, instantly grew quantities of luxurious and concealing hair.'

'She must have been the patron saint of Lady Godiva.'

'And of the librettists of *Hair*.'

'That's right.' Sophy drank a little more champagne cocktail. 'I suppose we really ought to be asking each other whatever could have happened to Mr Mailer,' she said.

Grant was motionless except that his left hand, resting on the table, contracted about the stem of his glass.

'Oughtn't we?' Sophy said vaguely.

'I feel no obligation to do so.'

'Nor I really. In fact, I think it's very much nicer without him. If you don't mind my saying so?'

'No,' Grant said heavily. 'No, I don't mind. Here comes the car.'

IV

When Alleyn got back to his fine hotel at ten past six he found a message asking him to telephone Il Questore Valdarno. He did so and was told with a casual air that scarcely concealed the Questore's sense of professional gratification, that his people had already traced the woman called Violetta to her lair which was in a slum. When he said they had traced her, the Questore amended, he did not mean precisely in person since she was not at home when his man called. He had, however, made rewarding inquiries among her neighbours who knew all about her war with Sebastian Mailer and said, variously, that she was his cast-off mistress, wife or shady business associate, that he had betrayed her in a big way and that she never ceased to inveigh against him. Violetta was not popular among the ladies in her street, being quarrelsome, vindictive and unpleasant to children. She was also held to poach on certain begging preserves in the district. It emerged that Mr Mailer in his salad days had abandoned Violetta in Sicily, 'Where, my dear Superintendent,' said the Questore, 'she may well have been one of his contacts in the smuggling of heroin. Palermo is a port of transit as we well know.'

'Yes, indeed.'

'All are agreed that she is a little mad.'

'Ah.'

It appeared, the Questore continued, that for an unspecified time, years perhaps, Mailer had eluded Violetta, but getting wind of his being first in Naples and then in Rome she had chased him, finally establishing herself on the postcard beat outside S. Tommaso.

'I have spoken with this Irish Dominican,' said the Questore. 'It is nonsense for him to say that no one could escape their vigilance going or coming from the places below. It is ridiculous. They sell their cards, they sell their rosaries, they add up their cashes, they visit their stores, they sleep, they talk, they say their prayers. A man of Mailer's talents would have no difficulty.'

'What about a woman of Violetta's talents?'

'Ah-ah. You speak of the shadow on the wall? While I am sure that she *could* elude the vigilance of these gentlemen, I doubt if she did so. And if she did, my dear colleague, where was she when they made their search? I have no doubt the search was thorough: of *that* they are perfectly capable and the lighting is most adequate. They know the terrain. They have been excavating there for a century. No, no, I am persuaded that Mailer recognized you and, being aware of your most formidable and brilliant record in this field, took alarm and fled.'

'Um,' Alleyn said, 'I'm not at all sure I struck terror in that undelicious breast. Mailer seemed to me to be, in a subfusc sort of way, cocksure. Not to say gloating!'

'*Scusi?* Subfusc?'

'Dim. It doesn't matter. Do you mean you think that at some moment when we were groping about in the underworld, recognition came upon him like a thunder-clap and he fled. There and then?'

'We shall see, we shall see. I spread my net. The airports, the wharves, the *stazioni.*'

Alleyn hurriedly congratulated him on all this expedition.

'But nevertheless,' Valdarno said, 'we make our examination of these premises. Tomorrow morning. It is, of course, not my practice personally to supervise such matters. Normally if a case is considered important enough one of my subordinates reports to one of my immediate staff.'

'I assure you, Signor Questore – '

'But in this case, where so much may be involved, where there are international slantings and above all, where so distinguished a colleague does us the honour – *Ecco!*'

Alleyn made appropriate noises and wondered how great a bore Valdarno really thought him.

'So tomorrow,' the Questore summed up. 'I leave my desk and I take the fields. With my subordinates. And you accompany us, is it not?'

'Thank you. I shall be glad to come.'

They whipped through the routine of valedictory compliments and hung up their receivers.

Alleyn bathed and dressed and wrote a letter to his wife.

' – so you see it's taken an odd turning. I'm supposed to be nudging up to Mailer with the object of finding out just how vital a cog he is in the heroin game and whether, through him, I can get a line on his bosses. My original ploy was to be the oblique approach, the hint, the veiled offer, the striking-up of an alliance and finally the dumping upon him of a tidy load of incriminating evidence and so catching him red-handed. And now, damn him, he disappears and I'm left with a collection of people some of whom may or may not be his fall guys. Consider, if you're not fast asleep by this time, my darling – consider the situation.

'To launch this Il Cicerone business, Mailer must have had access to very considerable funds. You can't do this sort of thing on HP. The cars, the drivers, the food and, above all, the quite phenomenal arrangement that seems to have been made with the Gioconda Restaurant who as a general rule would look upon package diners, on however exalted a scale, as the Caprice would look upon coach-loads from the Potteries. It appears that we dine *à la carte* at the best tables and drink distilled gold if they've got it in their cellars. And Mailer pays all. Well, I know we've paid him through the nose but that's another story.

'And then – this lot. This lot who've stumped up fifty quid each for the pleasure of hearing Barnaby Grant, with evident reluctance, read aloud, very badly, from his own best-seller. Next attraction: a walk round an ancient monument that's open to the public followed by tea or whatever they had on the Palatine Hill, and dinner at the Gioconda which could set them back anything up to £20 a nob if they went under their own steam, and then on to a further entertainment coyly unspecified in the brochure. Probably a very expensive strip and champagne show with possibly a pot party to follow. Or worse.

'All right. Take Lady B. She's rolling in money. One of her husbands was an Italian millionaire and she may have alimony paid out to her in Rome. She could obviously afford this show. She's rich, raffish, pretty bloody awful and all for *la dolce vita*. No doubt she's paying for the egregious Kenneth who looks to me very much as if he's hooked and may therefore turn out to be a useful lead into

Mailer's activities. I gather from something young Sophy Jason, who is an enchanter, let fall that she just suddenly decided to blue fifty quid out of the Italian funds available to her through business connections.

'The Van der Veghels are a couple of grotesques, and interest me enormously as I think they would you. Grotesques? No, not the right word. We both go for the Etruscan thing, don't we? Remember? Remember that male head, bearded and crowned with leaves in the Museo Barraco? Remember the smiling mouth, shaped, now I come to think of it, exactly like a bird in flight with the thin moustache repeating and exaggerating the curve of the lips? And the wide open eyes? What an amusing face, we thought, but it is perhaps atrociously cruel? I assure you, a portrait of the Baron Van der Veghel. But against this remember the tender and fulfilled couple of that sarcophagus in the Villa Giulia: the absolute in satisfied love? Recall the protective hand of the man. The extraordinary marital likeness, the suggestion of heaviness in the shoulders, the sense of completion. Portrait, I promise you, of the Van der Veghels. They may be Dutch by birth but blow me down flat if they're not Etruscan by descent. Or nature. Or something.

'The overall effect of the Van der Vs is, however, farcical. There's always an easy laugh to be won from broken English or, come to that, fractured French. Remember the de Maupassant story about an English girl who became increasingly boring as her command of French improved? The Baroness's lapses are always, as I'm sure beastly Kenneth would say, good for a giggle.

'I suppose their presence in the set-up is the least surprising. They're avid and merciless sightseers and photographers and their fund of enthusiasm is inexhaustible. Whether one can say the same of their fund of cash is anyone's guess.

'Major Sweet. Now, why has Major Sweet coughed up fifty quid for this sort of jaunt? On the face of it he's a caricature, a museum piece: the sort of Indian Army officer who, thirty years ago, was fair game for an easy laugh shouting Qui-hi at a native servant and saying By George, what? I find it unconvincing. He's bad-tempered, I should imagine pretty hard on the bottle, and amorous. As the young Sophy found to her discomfort in the Mithraic underworld. He's violently, aggressively and confusingly anti-religious. Religion of any kind. He lumps them all together, turns purple in the face and, deriving his impenetrable argument from the sacraments, pagan or Christian, says the whole lot are based on cannibalism. Why should he pay through the nose to explore two levels of Christianity and a Mithraic basement? Just to have a good jeer?

'Finally – Barnaby Grant. To my notion, the prime puzzle of the party. Without more ado I would say, quite seriously, that I can think of no earthly reason why he should subject himself to what is clearly the most exquisite torture, unless Mailer put the screws on him in another sense. Blackmail. It might well be one of Mailer's subsidiary interests and can tie in very comfortably with the drug racket.

'And as a *bonne-bouche* we have the antic Violetta. If you could have seen Violetta with her *"Cartoline – posta-cardas"* and harpy's face, foaming away under a black headpiece! Il Questore Valdarno can shrug her off with remarks about short-tempered postcard ladies but never trust me again if that one isn't possessed of a fury. As for Sophy Jason saying it was Violetta's shadow she saw on the wall by the stone sarcophagus, I think it's odds-on she's right. I saw it, too. It was distorted but there was the tray, the shawl and the hitched up shoulder. Clear as mud or my name's Van der Veghel.

'And I think Valdarno's right when he says Mailer could have nipped out under the noses of Father Denys and his boys. There's plenty of cover.

'But without any justification for saying so, I don't believe he did.

'On the same premise Violetta could have nipped in and I do believe *she* did. And out again?

'That too is another story.

'It's now a quarter past eight of a very warm evening. I am leaving my five-star room for the five-star cocktail bar where I rather hope to hob-nob with the Lady B. and her nephew. From there we shall be driven to La Gioconda where we shall perhaps eat quails stuffed with pâté and washed down with molten gold. At Mailer's expense? Well – allegedly.

'More of the continuing story of Anyone's Guess tomorrow. Bless you, my dear love, My – '

CHAPTER 5

Evening Out

They had dined by candlelight at a long table in the garden. Between leafy branches of trees and far below, shone Rome. It might have been its own model, laid out on a black velvet cloth and so cunningly illuminated that its great monuments glowed in their setting like jewels. At night the Colosseum is lit from within and at this distance it was no longer a ruin but seemed so much alive that a mob might have spewed through its multiple doorways, rank with the stench of the circus. It was incredibly beautiful.

Not far from their table was a fountain, moved there at some distant time from its original site down in Old Rome. At its centre lolled Neptune: smooth, luxurious and naked, idly fingering the long ringlets of his beard. He was supported by tritons and all kinds of monsters. They spouted, jetted and dribbled into basins that overflowed into each other making curtains of water-drops. The smell of water, earth and plants mingled with cigar-smoke, coffee, cosmetics and fumes of wine.

'What is all this *like*?' Sophy asked Grant. 'All this magnificence? I've never read Ouida, have you? And anyway this is not at all Victorian.'

'How about Antonioni?'

'Well – all right. But not *La Dolce Vita*. I don't think I get any whiffs of social corruption, really. Do you?'

He didn't answer and she looked across the table at Alleyn. 'Do you?' she asked him.

Alleyn's glance fell upon Lady Braceley's arm, lying as if discarded on the table. Emeralds, rubies and diamonds encircled that flaccid member, veins stood out on the back of the hand, her rings had slipped to one side and her talons – does she have false ones, he wondered, and saw that she did – made little dents in the table-cloth.

'Do *you*,' Sophy persisted, 'sniff the decadent society?' and then, evidently aware of Lady Braceley and perhaps of Kenneth, she blushed.

Sophy had the kind of complexion Jacobean poets would have praised, a rose-blush that mounted and ebbed very delicately under her skin. Her eyes shone in the candlelight and there was a nimbus round her hair. She was as fresh as a daisy.

'At the moment,' Alleyn said, smiling at her, 'not at all.'

'Good!' said Sophy and turned to Grant. 'Then I needn't feel apologetic about enjoying myself.'

'Are you liking it so much? Yes, I see you are. But why should you apologize?'

'Oh – I don't know – a streak of puritan, I suppose. My grandpa Jason was a Quaker.'

'Does he often put in an appearance?'

'Not all that often but I thought he lurked just now. "Vanity, vanity," you know, and the bit about has one any right to buy such a sumptuous evening, the world being as it is.'

'Meaning you should have spent the cash on doing good?'

'Yes. Or not spent it at all. Grandpapa Jason was also a banker.'

'Tell him to buzz off. You've done a power of good.'

'I? How? Impossible.'

'You've turned what promised to be a perfectly hellish evening into – ' Grant stopped short, waited for a moment and then leant towards her.

'Yes, well, all right,' Sophy said in a hurry. 'You needn't bother about that. Silly conversation.'

' – into something almost tolerable,' Grant said.

On the other side of the table Alleyn thought: No doubt she's very well able to take care of herself but I wouldn't have thought her one of the easy-come easy-go sort. On the contrary. I hope Grant isn't a predatory animal. He's a god in her world and a romantic-looking, ravaged sort of god, at that. Just the job to fill in the Roman foreground. Twenty years her senior, probably. He's made her blush again.

Major Sweet, at the head of the table, had ordered himself yet another cognac but nobody followed his example. The champagne bottles were upside down in the coolers and the coffee cups had been removed. Giovanni appeared, spoke to the waiter and retired with him, presumably to pay the bill. The maître-d'hôtel, Marco, swept masterfully down upon them and not for the first time inclined, smiled and murmured over Lady Braceley. She fished in her golden reticule and when he kissed her hand, left something in his own. He repeated this treatment with subtle modulations, on the Baroness, worked in a gay salute to Sophy, included the whole table in a comprehensive bow and swept away with the slightest possible oscillation of his hips.

'Quite a dish, isn't he?' Kenneth said to his aunt.

'Darling,' she replied, 'the things you say! Isn't he too frightful, Major?' She called up the table to Major Sweet, who was staring congestedly over the top of his brandy glass at Sophy.

'What!' he said. 'Oh. Ghastly.'

Kenneth laughed shrilly. 'When do we move?' he asked at large. 'Where do we go from here?'

'Now we are gay,' cried the Baroness. 'Now we dance and all is hip and nightlife. To the Cosmo, is it not?'

'Ah-ha, ah-ha, to the Cosmo!' the Baron echoed.

They beamed round the table.

'In that case,' Lady Braceley said, picking up her purse and gloves, 'I'm for the *ritirata.*'

The waiter was there in a flash to drop her fur over her shoulders.

'I too, I too,' said the Baroness and Sophy followed them out.

The Major finished his brandy. 'The Cosmo, eh?' he said. 'Trip a jolly old measure, what? Well, better make a move, I suppose – '

'No hurry,' Kenneth said. 'Auntie's best official clocking in *la ritirata* is nineteen minutes and that was when she had a plane to catch.'

The Baron was in deep consultation about tipping with the Major and Grant. Their waiter stood near the door into the restaurant. Alleyn strolled over to him.

'That was a most excellent dinner,' he said and overtipped just enough to consolidate his follow-on. 'I wonder if I may have a word with Signor Marco? I have a personal introduction to him which I would like to present. Here it is.'

It was Valdarno's card with an appropriate message written on the back. The waiter took a quick look at it and another at Alleyn and said he would see if the great man was in his office.

'I expect he is,' Alleyn said cheerfully. 'Shall we go there?'

The waiter, using his restaurant walk, hurried through the foyer into a smaller vestibule where he begged Alleyn to wait. He tapped discreetly at a door marked *Il direttore,* murmured something to the elegant young man who opened it and handed in the card. The young man was gone for a very short time and returned with a winning smile and an invitation to enter. The waiter scuttled off.

Marco's office was small but sumptuous. He advanced upon Alleyn with ceremony and a certain air of guarded cordiality.

'Good evening, again, Mr – ' he glanced at the card. 'Mr Alleyn. I hope you have dined pleasantly.' His English was extremely good. Alleyn decided to be incapable of Italian.

'Delightfully,' he said. 'A superb evening. Il Questore Valdarno told me of your genius and how right he was.'

'I am glad.'

'I think I remember you some years ago in London, Signore. At the Primavera.'

'Ah! My "salad days". Thirty-one different salads, in fact. Perhaps five are worth remembering. Can I do anything for you, Mr Alleyn? Any friend of Il Questore Valdarno – ?'

Alleyn made a quick decision.

'You can, indeed,' he said. 'If you will be so kind. I think I should tell you, Signore, that I am a colleague of the Questore's and that I am not in Rome entirely for pleasure. May I – '

He produced his own official card. Marco held it in his beautifully manicured fingers and for five seconds was perfectly motionless. 'Ah, yes,' he said at last. 'Of course. I should have remembered from my London days. There was a *cause célèbre*. Your most distinguished career. And then – surely – your brother – he was Ambassador in Rome, I think, some time ago?'

Alleyn normally reacted to remarks about his brother George by falling over backwards rather than profit by their relationship. He bowed and pressed on.

'This is an affair of some delicacy,' he said and felt as if he spoke out of an Edwardian thriller or, indeed, from No. 221B Baker Street.

'I assure you I wouldn't have troubled you if I could have avoided doing so. The fact is Il Questore Valdarno and I find ourselves in something of a quandary. It's come to our knowledge that a certain unsavoury character whose identity has hitherto been unknown is living in Rome. He has formed associations with people of the highest standing who would be appalled if they knew about him. As I think you yourself would be.'

'I? Do you suggest – ?'

'He is one of your patrons. We think it proper that you should be warned.'

If Marco had seemed, for an Italian, to be of a rather florid complexion he was so no longer. His cheeks were wan enough to make his immaculately shaven jaws look, by contrast, a cadaverous purple. There was a kind of scuffling noise behind Alleyn. He turned and saw the beautiful young man who had admitted him seated behind a table and making great play with papers.

'I didn't realize – ' Alleyn said.

'My secretary. He does not speak English,' Marco explained and added in Italian, 'Alfredo, it might be as well for you to leave us.' And still in Italian, to Alleyn: 'That will be better, will it not?'

Alleyn looked blank. 'I'm sorry,' he said and spread his hands.

'Ah, you do not speak our language?'

'Alas!'

The young man said rapidly in Italian: *'Padrone,* is it trouble? It is – ?' and Marco cut him short. 'It is nothing. You heard me. Leave us.'

When he had gone Alleyn said, 'It won't take long. The man I speak of is Mr Sebastian Mailer.'

A short pause and Marco said, 'Indeed? You are, I must conclude, certain of your ground?'

'Certain enough to bring you the information. Of course you will prefer to check with the Questore himself. I assure you, he will confirm what I've said.'

Marco inclined and made a deprecatory gesture. 'But of course, of course. You have quite taken me aback, Mr Alleyn, but I am most grateful for this warning. I shall see that Mr Mailer's appearances at La Gioconda are discontinued.'

'Forgive me, but isn't it rather unusual for La Gioconda to extend its hospitality to a tourist party?'

Marco said rapidly and smoothly, 'A normal tourist party – a "package" – would be out of the question. A set meal and a *fiasco* of wine – with little flags on the table – unthinkable! But this arrangement, as you found, is entirely different. The guests order individually, *à la carte*, as at a normal dinner-party. The circumstance of the *conto* being settled by the host – even though he is a professional host – is of little significance. I confess that when this Mailer first approached me I would not entertain the proposal but then – he showed me his list. It was a most distinguished list. Lady Braceley alone – one of the most elegant of our clientèle. And Mr Barnaby Grant – a man of the greatest distinction.'

'When *did* Mailer first approach you?'

'I believe – about a week ago.'

'So tonight was the first of these dinner-parties?'

'And the last, I assure you, if what you tell me is true.'

'You noticed, of course, that he did not appear?'

'With some surprise. But his assistant, Giovanni Vecchi, is a courier of good standing. He informed us that his principal was unwell. Am I to understand – ?'

'He may be unwell, he has undoubtedly disappeared.'

'*Disappeared?*' The colour seeped back, unevenly, into Marco's cheeks. 'You mean – ?'

'Just that. Vanished.'

'This is very confusing. Should I understand that you believe him to have – ' Marco's full lips seemed to frame and discard one or two words before they chose ' – absconded?'

'That is the Questore's theory.'

'But not yours?' he asked quickly.

'I have none.'

'I conclude, Mr Alleyn, that your attendance here tonight, which must have followed your enrolment in today's tour, is professional rather than recreational.'

'Yes,' Alleyn agreed cheerfully. 'That's about it. And now I mustn't take up any more of your time. If – and the chances I believe are remote – if Mr Mailer should put in an appearance here – ' Marco gave an ejaculation and a very slight wince ' – Il Questore Valdarno and I would be most grateful if you would say nothing to him about this discussion. Simply telephone at once to – but the number is on the Questore's card, I think.'

'The Questore,' said Marco in a hurry, 'will I am sure appreciate that any kind of unpleasantness, here, in the restaurant, would be – ' he flung up his hands.

'Unthinkable,' Alleyn filled in. 'Oh yes. It would all be done very tactfully and quite behind the scenes, you know.'

He held out his hand. Marco's was damp and exceedingly cold.

'But you think,' he persisted, 'you yourself think, isn't it, that he will not come back?'

'For what it's worth,' Alleyn agreed, 'that's my idea. Not, at any rate, of his own volition. Goodbye.'

On his way out he went to the telephone booth and rang Il Questore Valdarno, who reported that he had set up further inquiries but had no news. Mailer's flat had been found. The porter said Mailer left it at about three o'clock and had not returned. The police briefly examined the flat, which seemed to be in order.

'No signs of a sudden departure?'

'None. Yet I am still persuaded – '

'Signor Questore, may I ask you to add to the many favours you have already granted? I am not familiar with your police regulations and procedures but I understand you are less restricted than we are. Would it be possible to put a man in Mailer's flat at once and could that man answer the telephone and make a careful note of any calls, if possible tracing their origin? I think it's highly probable that Marco of La Gioconda will at this moment be trying to get him and will try again. And again.'

'*Marco!* Indeed? But – yes of course. But – '

'I have spoken to him. He was discreet but his reaction to the disappearance was interesting.'

'In what way? He was distressed?'

'Distress – yes. Not, I think, so much by Mailer's disappearance as by the thought of his return. That prospect, unless I'm very much mistaken, terrifies him.'

'I shall attend to this at once,' said Il Questore.

'If Mailer is still missing tomorrow, would you allow me to have a look at his rooms?'

'But of course. I will instruct my people.'

'You are too kind,' said Alleyn.

When he returned to the vestibule of La Gioconda he found all the party there except Lady Braceley. He noticed that Giovanni was having little conferences with the men. He spoke first with Kenneth Dorne, who responded with an air of connivance and cast furtive looks about him. Giovanni moved on to the Major who, ignoring Kenneth, listened avidly but with an affectation of indifference much at odds with the grin that twitched the corners of his mouth. Giovanni seemed to send out a call of some sort to Baron Van der Veghel, who joined them. He too listened attentively, the Etruscan smile very much in evidence. He said little and presently rejoined his wife, linked his arm in hers and stooped towards her. She put her head on one side and gazed at him. He took the tip of her nose between his fingers and gently, playfully waggled it. She beamed at him and tapped his cheek. He pulled her hand down to his mouth. Alleyn thought he had never seen a more explicit display of physical love. The Baron slightly shook his head at Giovanni, who bowed gracefully and looked at Grant, who was talking to Sophy Jason. Grant at once said quite loudly, 'No, thank you,' and Giovanni moved on to Alleyn.

'Signore,' he said. 'We go now to the Cosmo, a very elegant and exclusive nightclub where the guests will remain for as long as they wish. Perhaps until two when the Cosmo closes. That will conclude the programme for this tour. However, Signor Mailer has arranged that a further expedition is available for those who are perhaps a little curious and desire to extend their knowledge of Roman nightlife. Some drinks. A smoke. Congenial company. Boys and girls, very charming. Everything very discreet. The cars will be available without further charge but the entertainment is not included in the tour.'

'How much?' Alleyn asked.

'Signore, the fee is fifteen thousand lire.'

'Very well,' Alleyn said. 'Yes.'

'You will not be disappointed, Signore.'

'Good.'

Lady Braceley re-entered the vestibule.

'Here I am!' she cried. 'High as a kite and fit for the wide, wild way-out. Bring on the dancing girls.'

Kenneth and Giovanni went to her. Kenneth put his arm round her waist and said something under his breath.

'Of course!' she said loudly. 'Need you ask, darling? I'd adore to.' She advanced her face towards Giovanni and widened her eyes.

Giovanni bowed and gave her a look, so overtly deferential and subtly impertinent that Alleyn felt inclined either to knock him down or tell Lady Braceley what he thought of her. He saw Sophy Jason looking at her with something like horror.

'And now, ladies and gentlemen,' said Giovanni, 'to Il Cosmo.'

II

The Cosmo was a nightclub with a lavish floorshow. As soon as the party was seated, bottles of champagne were clapped down on their tables. They hadn't been there long before the members of the orchestra left their dais and walked severally to the front tables. The bass and 'cello players actually planted their instruments on the tables and plucked the strings. The fiddlers and saxophonists came as close as possible. The tympanist held his cymbals poised above the shrinking Major Sweet's head. Eight marginal nudes trimmed with tropical fruit, jolted round the floor space. 'Black lightning,' was introduced and they turned into Negresses. The noise was formidable indeed.

'Well,' Grant asked Sophy. 'Still keeping Grandpapa Jason at bay?'

'I'm not so sure he doesn't ride again.'

The uproar was such that they were obliged to shout into each other's ears. Lady Braceley was jerking her shoulders in time with the saxophonist at her table. He managed to ogle her while continuing his exertions. 'She seems,' Grant said, 'to be on the short list of *persona grata* here as well as at the Gioconda.'

'It's a bit hard to take, I find.'

'Say the word if you'd like to go. We could, you know. Or do you want to see the rest of the show?' Sophy shook her head vaguely. She tried to get her reactions into some kind of perspective. It was odd to reflect that less than twelve hours ago she had met Grant for virtually the first time. It was not the first time by many that she made an instant take but she had never before experienced so sharp an antagonism followed for no discernible reason by so complete a sense of familiarity. At one moment they had blackguarded each other to heaps and at another, not fifteen minutes later, they had gossiped away in the shrine of Mithras as if they had not only known but understood each other for years. Me, thought Sophy, and Barnaby Grant. Jolly odd when you come to think of it. It would have been quite a thing if she could put it all down to the violent antagonism that sometimes precedes an equally violent physical attraction but that was no go. Obviously they were under no compulsion to fall into each other's arms.

'If we stay,' Grant was saying, 'I can snatch you up in my arms.'

Sophy gaped at this uncanny distortion of her thoughts.

'In a cachuca, fandango, bolero or whatever,' he explained. 'On the other hand – *do* pay attention,' he said crossly. 'I'm making a dead set at you.'

'How lovely,' Sophy rejoined. 'I'm all ears.'

The rumpus subsided, the orchestra returned to its dais, the Negresses were changed back into naked pink chicks and retired. A mellifluous tenor, all eyes, teeth and sob-in-the-voice, came out and sang 'Santa Lucia' and other familiar pieces. He too moved among his audience. Lady Braceley gave him a piece of everlasting greenery from her table decorations.

He was followed by the start of the programme, a celebrated black singer of soul music. She was beautiful and disturbing and a stillness came over the Cosmo when she sang. One of her songs was about hopelessness, injury and degradation and she made of it a kind of accusation. It seemed to Sophy that her audience almost disintegrated under her attack and she thought it strange that Lady Braceley, for instance, and Kenneth, could sit and look appreciative and join so complacently in the applause.

When she had gone Grant said, 'That was remarkable, wasn't it?' Alleyn, overhearing him, said, 'Extraordinary. Do modern audiences find that the pursuit of pleasure is best satisfied by having the rug jerked from under their feet?'

'Oh,' Grant said, 'hasn't that always been so? We like to be reminded that something is rotten in the State of Denmark. It makes us feel important.'

The programme ended with a very stylish ensemble, the lights were subdued, the band insinuated itself into dance music and Grant said to Sophy, 'Come on. Whether you like it or not.'

They danced: not saying very much, but with pleasure.

Giovanni appeared and Lady Braceley danced with him. They did intricate things with great expertise.

The Van der Veghels, half-smiling, closely embraced, swayed and turned on sixpence, keeping to the darkened perimeter of the floor.

Major Sweet who had made a willing but belated attempt upon Sophy sank back in his chair, drank champagne and moodily discoursed with Alleyn. He was, Alleyn concluded, the sort of practised drinker who, while far from being sober, would remain more or less in control for a long time. 'Lovely little girl, that,' he said. 'Natural. Sweet. But plenty of spunk, mind you. Looks you bang in the eye, what?' He maundered on rather gloomily: 'Just a nice, sweet, natural little girl – as I was saying.'

'Are you going on to this other show?' Alleyn asked.

'What about yourself?' countered the Major. 'Fair's fair. No names,' he added more obscurely, 'no pack-drill that I'm aware of. Other things being equal.'

'I'm going, yes.'

'Shake,' invited the Major, extending his hand. But finding that it encountered the champagne bottle he refilled his glass. He leant across the table. 'I've seen some curious things in my time,' he confided. 'You're a broadminded man. Everyone to his own taste and it all adds up to experience. Not a word to the ladies: what they can't grieve about they won't see. How old am I? Come on. You say. How old jer say I am?'

'Sixty?'

'And ten. Allotted span, though that's all my eye. See the rest of you out tonight, my boy.' He leant forward and looked dolefully at Alleyn with unfocused eyes. 'I say,' he said. *'She's* not going on, is she?'

'Who?'

'Old Bracegirdle.'

'I believe so.'

'Gawd!'

'It's pretty steep,' Alleyn suggested. 'Fifteen thousand lire.'

'Better be good, what? I'm full of hopes,' leered the Major. 'And I don't mind telling you, old boy, I wouldn't have been within coo-ee of this show tonight in the orinry way. You know what? Flutter. Green baize. Monte. And – phew!' He made a wild gesture with both arms. 'Thas-sall: – phew!'

'A big win?'

'Phew!'

'Splendid.'

And that, Alleyn supposed, explained the Major. Or did it?

'Funny thing about Mailer, don't you think?' he asked.

'Phew!' said the Major, who seemed to be stuck with this ejaculation. ''Strordinary conduct,' he added. 'Conduct unbecoming if you ask me, but let it go.' He slumped into a moody silence for some moments and then shouted so loudly that people at the neighbouring table stared at him: 'Bloody good riddance. 'Scuse language.'

After this he seemed disinclined for conversation and Alleyn joined Kenneth Dorne.

With the departure of the soul-singer, Kenneth had slumped back into what seemed to be chronic inertia interrupted by fidgets. He made no attempt to dance but fiddled with his shirt ruffles and repeatedly looked towards the entrance as if he expected some new arrival. He gave Alleyn one of his restless, speculative glances. 'You look marvellous,' he said. 'Are you having a gay time?'

'An interesting time, at least. This sort of thing is quite out of my line. It's an experience.'

'Oh!' Kenneth said impatiently. 'This!' He shuffled his feet about. 'I thought you were terrific,' he said. 'You know. The way you managed everybody after Seb vanished. Look. Do you think he's – you know – I mean to say – what *do* you think?'

'I've no notion,' Alleyn said. 'I've never set eyes on the man before. You seem to be quite friendly with him.'

'Me?'

'You call him Seb, don't you?'

'Oh well. You know. Just one of those things. Why not?'

'You find him helpful, perhaps.'

'How d'you mean?' Kenneth said, eyeing him.

'In Rome. I rather hoped – I may be quite wrong, of course.' Alleyn broke off. 'Are you going on to this late party?' he asked.

'Of course. And I don't care how soon.'

'Really?' Alleyn said. And hoping he introduced the jargon correctly and with the right inflection, he asked, 'May one expect to meet "a scene"?'

Kenneth swept his hair from his eyes with a fingertip.

'What sort of a scene?' he said cautiously.

'A group – a – have I got it wrong? I'm not turned on – is that right? – as yet. I want to "experience". You know?'

Kenneth now undisguisedly inspected him. 'You look fabulous, of course,' he said. 'You know: way up there. But – ' He drew a rectangle with his forefinger in the air. 'Let's face it. Square, sweetheart. Square.'

'Sorry about that,' Alleyn said. 'I was depending on Mr Mailer to make the change.'

'Don't let that trouble you. Toni's terrific.'

'Toni?'

'Where we're going. Toni's Pad. It's the greatest. Groovy. You know? Grass, hard stuff, the lot. Mind you, he plays it cool. There'll be a freak-out.'

'A –?'

'A happening. Psychedelic.'

'A floorshow?'

'If you like – but way-out. Ever so trendy. Some people just go for giggles and come away. But if it sends you, which is what it's *for,* you move on to the buzz.'

'Obviously you've been there before?'

'Not to deceive you, I have. Seb took us.'

'Us?'

'Auntie came too. She's all for experience. She's fabulous – honestly. I mean it.'

With considerable effort Alleyn said casually, 'Did Seb – turn you on?'

'That's right. In Perugia. I'm thinking,' Kenneth said, 'of making the move.'

'To – ?'

'The big leap. Pothead to main-liner. Well, as a matter of fact I've had a taste. You know. Mind you, I'm not hooked. Just the odd pop. Only a fun thing.'

Alleyn looked at a face that not so long ago might have been attractive. Policemen are as wary of reading character into other people's faces as they are of betraying their thoughts in their own, but it occurred to him that if Kenneth was a less repellent colour and if he would shut his mouth instead of letting it droop open in a flaccid smirk he wouldn't be a bad-looking specimen. He might, even at this stage, be less dissolute than his general behaviour suggested. And whatever has happened or is about to happen to Mr Sebastian Mailer, Alleyn thought, it cannot be one millionth fraction of what he most richly deserves.

Kenneth broke the silence that had fallen between them.

'I say,' he said, 'it's idiotic of course but wouldn't it be a yell if after being on about Seb and Toni's Pad and all that bit, you were The Man?'

'The Man?'

'Yes. You know. A plain-clothes fuzz.'

'Do I look like it?'

'Nobody less. You look gorgeous. That might be your cunning, though, mightn't it? Still you couldn't have me busted when we're not on British soil. Or could you?'

'*I* don't know,' Alleyn said. 'Ask a policeman.'

Kenneth gave an emaciated little laugh. 'Honestly, you kill me,' he said, and after another pause: 'If it's not going too far, what *do* you do?'

'What do you think?'

'I don't know. Something frightfully high-powered and discreet. Like diplomacy. Or has that gone out with the Lord Chamberlain?'

'Has the Lord Chamberlain gone out?'

'Gone in, then. I suppose he still potters about palatial corridors with a key on his bottom.' A disturbing thought seemed to strike Kenneth. 'Oh God!' he said faintly. 'Don't tell me you *are* the Lord Chamberlain.'

'I am not the Lord Chamberlain.'

'It would have been just my luck.'

The dance band came to an inconclusive halt. Barnaby Grant and Sophy Jason returned to the table. Giovanni elegantly steered Lady Braceley to hers where the Major sat in a trance. The Van der Veghels, hand-linked, joined them.

Giovanni explained that the second driver would return Sophy, the Van der Veghels and Grant to their hotels whenever they wished and that he himself would be responsible for the other members of the party.

Alleyn noticed that Toni's Pad had not been named by Giovanni and that there had been no general, open announcement of the extra attraction. Only those rather furtive approaches to the male members of the party. And through Kenneth to Lady Braceley.

The Van der Veghels said they would like to dance a little more and then go home. Sophy and Grant agreed to this and, when the band struck up again, returned to the floor. Alleyn found himself alone with the Van der Veghels, who contentedly sipped champagne.

'I'm not much good, Baroness,' Alleyn said. 'But will you risk it?'

'Of course.'

She herself, like many big women, was very good – steady and light. 'But you dance well,' she said after a moment. 'Why do you say not so? It is this British self-deprecation we hear about?'

'It would be hard to blunder with you as one's partner.'

'Ah-ha, ah-ha, a compliment! Better and better!'

'You are not going on to this other party.'

'No. My husband thinks it would not suit us to go. He did not very much care for the style of the suggestion. It is more for the men, he said, so I tease him and say he is a big square and I am not so unsophisticated.'

'But he remains firm?'

'He remains firm. So you go?'

'I've said yes but now you alarm me.'

'No!' cried the Baroness with a sort of obligatory archness. 'That I do not believe. You are a cool one. A sophisticate. That I see very clearly.'

'Change your mind. Come and take care of me.'

This brought peals of jollity from the Baroness. She floated expertly and laughed up and down the scale and then, when he persisted, suddenly adopted an air of gravity. Her voice deepened and she explained that though she was sure Alleyn would not believe her, she and the Baron were in fact quite puritanical in their outlook. They came, she said, of Lutheran stock. They did not at all fancy, for instance, Roman nightlife as portrayed by Italian films.

Had Alleyn ever heard of the publishing firm of Adriaan and Welker? If not, she must tell him that they took a very firm stand in respect of moral tone and that the Baron, their foreign representative, upheld this attitude.

'In our books all is clean, all is honest and healthful,' she declared and elaborated upon this high standard of literary hygiene with great enthusiasm.

It was not a pose, Alleyn thought, it was an attitude of mind: the Baroness Van der Veghel (and evidently her husband, too) was a genuine pietist and, he thought, with a sidelong look at the Etruscan smile, in all probability she was possessed of the calm ruthlessness that so often accompanies a Puritanical disposition.

'My husband and I,' she said, 'are in agreement on the – I think you call it "permissive" society, do you not? In all things,' she added with stifling effrontery, 'we are in absolute accord. We are sure of ourselves. Always we are happy together and agreeing in our views. Like twins, isn't it?' and again she burst out laughing.

In her dancing, in her complacency, in her sudden bursts of high spirits she bore witness to her preposterous claims: she was a supremely contented woman, Alleyn thought; a physically satisfied woman. Intellectually and morally satisfied, too, it would appear. She turned her head and looked towards the table where her husband sat. They smiled at each other and twiddled their fingers.

'Is this your first visit to Rome?' Alleyn asked. When people dance together and there is concord in their dancing, however alien they may be in other respects, they are in physical agreement. Alleyn felt at once a kind of withdrawal in the Baroness but she answered readily that she and her husband had visited Italy and in particular, Rome, on several previous occasions. Her husband's publishing interests brought him there quite often and when it was convenient she accompanied him.

'But this time,' Alleyn mentioned, 'it is for fun?' and she agreed.

'For you also?' she asked.

'Oh absolutely,' said Alleyn and gave her an extra twirl. 'Have you made any of the Il Cicerone trips on previous visits?' he asked. Again – it was unmistakable – a withdrawal.

She said, 'I think they are of recent formink. Quite new and of the greatest fun.'

'Does it strike you as at all odd,' asked Alleyn, 'that we none of us seem to be particularly bothered about the non-appearance of our cicerone?'

He felt her massive shoulders rise. 'It is strange, perhaps,' she conceded, 'that he disappears. We hope all is well with him, do we not? That is all we can do. The tour has been satisfactory.' They moved past their table. The Baron cried, 'Good, good!' and gently clapped his enormous hands in praise of their dancing. Lady Braceley removed her gaze from Giovanni and gave them a haggard appraisal. The Major slept.

'We think,' said the Baroness, resuming their conversation, 'that there was perhaps trouble for him with the postcard woman. The Violetta.'

'She certainly made him a scene.'

'She was down there, we think. Below.'

'Did you see her?'

'No. Miss Jason saw her shadow. We thought that Mr Mailer was unhappy when she said so. He made the big pooh-pooh but he was unhappy.'

'She's a pretty frightening lady, that one.'

'She is terrible. Such hatred so nakedly shown is terrible. All hatred,' said the Baroness, deftly responding to a change of step, 'is very terrible.'

'The monk in charge had the place searched. Neither Mailer nor Violetta was found.'

'Ah. The monk,' Baroness Van der Veghel remarked and it was impossible to read anything at all into this observation. 'Possibly. Yes. It may be so.'

'I wonder,' Alleyn presently remarked, 'if anyone has ever told you how very Etruscan you are.'

'I? I am a Dutchwoman. We are Netherlanders, my husband and I.'

'I meant, if you'll forgive me, in looks. You are strikingly like the couple on that beautiful sarcophagus in the Villa Giulia.'

'My husband's is a very old Netherlands family,' she announced apparently without any intention of snubbing Alleyn but merely as a further statement of fact.

Alleyn thought he also could pursue an independent theme. 'I'm sure you won't mind my saying so,' he said, 'because they are so very attractive. They have that strong marital likeness that tells one they, too, are in perfect accord.'

She offered no comment unless her next remark could be construed as such. 'We are distantly related,' she said. 'We are in fact descended upon the distaff side from the Wittelsbachs. I am called Mathilde Jacobea after the so celebrated Countess. But it is strange, what you say, all the same. My husband believes that our family had its origins in Etruria. So perhaps,' she added playfully, 'we are backthrows. He thinks of writing a book on the subject.'

'How very interesting,' said Alleyn politely and entered upon a spinning manoeuvre of some virtuosity. It rather irritated him that she followed with perfect ease. 'Yes,' she said, confirming her own pronouncement, 'you dance well. That was most pleasant. Shall we return?'

They went back to her husband, who kissed her hand and contemplated her with his head on one side. Grant and Sophy joined them. Giovanni asked if they were ready to be driven to their hotels and on learning that they were, summoned the second driver.

Alleyn watched them leave and then, with the resignation that all policemen on duty command, addressed himself to the prospect of Toni's Pad.

III

'Pad' was not, he discovered, included in the official title. It was simply 'Toni's' and the name was not displayed on the façade. The entrance was through a wrought-iron gate, opened, after a subdued exchange with Giovanni, by a porter. Then across a paved courtyard and up five floors in a lift. Giovanni had collected fifteen thousand lire from each member of his party. He handed these amounts to someone who peered through a trap in a wall. A further door was then opened from the inside and the amenities of Toni's Pad were gradually disclosed.

They were everything and more that might be expected on a pretty elaborate scale and they catered for all tastes at predictable levels. The patrons were ushered into a pitch-dark room and seated on velvet divans round the wall. It was impossible to discover how many were there but cigarette ends pulsed in many places and the room was full of smoke. Giovanni's party seemed to be the last arrivals. They were guided to their places by someone with a small blue torchlight. Alleyn contrived to settle near the door. A voice murmured: 'A "Joint", Signore?' and a box with a single cigarette in it was displayed by the torch. Alleyn took the cigarette. Every now and then people murmured and often giggling broke out.

The freak-out was introduced by Toni himself, holding a torch under his face. He was a smooth man who seemed to be dressed in floral satin. He spoke in Italian and then haltingly in English. The name of the performance, he said, was 'Keenky Keeks'.

A mauve light flooded the central area and the show was on.

Alleyn was not given to subjective comment where police field-work was concerned but in a report that he subsequently drew up on the case-in-hand he referred to Toni's Kinky Kicks as 'infamous' and, since a more explicit description was unnecessary, he did not give one.

The performers were still in action when his fingers found the doorhandle behind a velvet curtain. He slipped out.

The porter who had admitted them was in the vestibule. He was big, heavy and lowering and lay back in a chair placed across the entrance. When he saw Alleyn he did not seem surprised. It might be supposed that rebellious stomachs were not unknown at Toni's.

'You wish to leave, Signore?' he asked in Italian and gestured towards the door. 'You go?' he added in basic English.

'No,' Alleyn said in Italian. 'No, thank you. I am looking for Signor Mailer.' He glanced at his hands, which were trembling, and thrust them in his pockets.

The man lowered his feet to the floor, gave Alleyn a pretty hard stare and got up.

'He is not here,' he said.

Alleyn withdrew his hand from his trouser pocket and looked absent-mindedly at the L.50,000 note. The porter slightly cleared his throat. 'Signor Mailer is not here this evening,' he said, 'I regret.'

'That is disappointing,' Alleyn said. 'I am very surprised. We were to meet. I had an arrangement with him: an arrangement for special accommodation. You understand?' He yawned widely and used his handkerchief.

The porter, watching him, waited for some moments. 'Perhaps he has been delayed,' he said. 'I can speak to Signor Toni on your behalf, Signore. I can arrange the accommodation.'

'Perhaps Signor Mailer will come. Perhaps I will wait a little.' He yawned again.

'There is no need. I can arrange everything.'

'You don't even know – '

'You have only to speak, Signore. Anything!'

The porter became specific. Alleyn affected restlessness and discontent. 'That's all very fine,' he said. 'But I wish to see the Padrone. It is an appointment.'

Alleyn waited for the man to contradict the term 'padrone' but he did not. He began to wheedle. Mellifluously he murmured and consoled. He could see, he said, that Alleyn was in distress. What did he need? Was it perhaps H. and C.? And the equipment? He could provide everything at once and a sympathetic couch in privacy. Or did he prefer perhaps to take his pleasure in his apartment?

Alleyn realized after a minute or two that the man was trading on his own account and had no intention of going to Toni for the cocaine and heroin he offered. Perhaps he stole from the stock in hand. He himself kept up his display of 'withdrawal' symptoms. The L.50,000 note shook in his grasp; he gaped, dabbed at his nose and mopped his neck and brow. He affected to mistrust the porter. How did he know that the porter's stuff would be of good quality? Mr Mailer's supplies were of the best: unadulterated, pure. He understood Mr Mailer was a direct importer from the Middle East. How was he to know – ?

The porter said at once that it would be from Mr Mailer's stock that he would produce the drugs. Mr Mailer was indeed an important figure in the trade. He became impatient.

'In a moment, Signore, it will be too late. The performance will end. It is true that Toni's guests will retire to other rooms and other amusements. To be frank, Signore, they will not receive the service that I can provide.'

'You guarantee that it is of Signor Mailer's supply?'

'I have said so, Signore.'

Alleyn consented. The man went into a sort of cubby-hole off the vestibule that was evidently his office. Alleyn heard a key turn. A drawer was shut. The porter returned with a sealed package neatly wrapped in glossy blue paper. The cost was exorbitant: about thirty per cent on the British black-market price. He paid and said agitatedly that he wanted to go at once. The man opened the door, took him down in the lift and let him out.

A car was drawn up in the alley and at its wheel, fast asleep, Giovanni's second-in-command. Alleyn concluded that Giovanni found himself fully occupied elsewhere.

He walked to the corner, found the name of the main street – the Via Aldo – and took his bearings. He returned to the car, woke the driver and was driven to his hotel. He maintained his withdrawal symptoms for the driver's benefit, made a muddle over finding his money and finally overtipped lavishly with a trembling hand.

After Toni's Pad the hotel vestibule might have been in the Austrian Tyrol, so healthful did its quietude, its subdued luxury, its tinkling fountains and its emptiness appear. Alleyn went to his room, bathed, and for a minute or two stood on his small balcony and looked down at Rome. Eastward there was a faint pallor in the sky. In those churches, shut like massive lids over the ancient underworld, they would soon be lighting candles for the first offices of the day. Perhaps the lay brother at S. Tommaso in Pallaria was already awake and preparing to go slap-slap in his sandals through the empty streets with a key to the underworld in his habit.

Alleyn locked the cigarette and the package of cocaine and heroin in his briefcase and, telling himself to wake at seven o'clock, went to bed and to sleep.

IV

Much earlier in the night Barnaby Grant and Sophy Jason from the top of the Pensione Gallico had also looked at Rome.

'It's not very late,' Grant had said. 'Shall we go out on the roof-garden for a minute or two? Would you like a drink?'

'I don't want any more alcohol, thank you,' Sophy said.

'I've got some oranges. We could squeeze them out and add cold water, couldn't we? Fetch your tooth mug.'

The roof-garden smelt of night-scented stocks, watered earth and fern. They made their orange drinks, pointed out the silhouettes of Rome against the sky and spoke very quietly because bedrooms opened on to the roof-garden. This gave their dialogue an air of conspiracy.

'I wish I had one of them,' Sophy said.

'I did last time I was here. That one over there with the french windows.'

'How lovely.'

'I – suppose it was.'

'Didn't you like it?'

'Something rather off-putting happened that time.'

If Sophy had asked 'what' or indeed had shown any kind of curiosity Grant would probably have fobbed her off with a vague sentence or two but she said nothing. She looked at Rome and sipped her drink.

'You have the gift of Virgilia, Sophy.'

'What was that?'

'A gracious silence.'

She didn't answer and suddenly he was telling her about the morning of the thunderstorm in the Piazza Colonna and the loss of his manuscript. She listened with horror, her fingers at her lips. '*Simon*,' she muttered. 'You lost *Simon*!' And then: 'Well – but obviously you got it back.'

'After three days' sweltering hell spent largely on this roof-garden. Yes. I got it back.' He turned away and sat in one of the little wrought-iron chairs. 'At this table, actually,' he said indistinctly.

'I wonder you can face it again.'

'You don't ask how I got it back.'

'Well – how, then?'

'Mailer – brought it here.'

'*Mailer*? Did you say *Mailer*? Sebastian Mailer?'

'That's right. Come and sit here. Please.'

She took the other chair at his table, as if, she thought, the waiter was going to bring their breakfast. 'What is it?' she asked. 'You're worried about something. Do you want to talk about it?'

'I suppose I must. To this extent, at least. Do you believe me when I tell you that at the moment I can almost wish he had never recovered the thing?'

Sophy said, after a pause, 'If you say so, I believe you, but it's a monstrous idea. For you to wish *Mailer* hadn't found it – yes. That I can imagine.'

'And this is what I meant. You're too young to remember when my first book came out. You were a child, of course.'

'*Aquarius*? Well, I was about fourteen, I think. I read it with goggling eyes and bated breath.'

'But afterwards. When you came into Koster Press? You heard about – the scandal? Well, didn't you? You can't tell me they don't still thumb it over in those august premises.'

'Yes,' Sophy said. 'I heard about the coincidence bit.'

'The *"coincidence"* bit! Did you, by God! And did you believe that I could have repeated in exact detail the central theme of a book I'd never read?'

'Certainly. That's the general opinion at Koster's.'

'It wasn't the opinion of twelve good, bloody men and true.'

'Token damages, though, weren't they? And there's a long list of proven literary coincidences. I write children's books. I found last year that I'd lifted the entire story-line of Mrs Molesworth's *Cuckoo Clock*. Actually it wasn't coincidence. My grandmother had read her copy aloud to me when I was six. I suppose it was stowed away in my subconscious and bobbed up unbeknownst. But I swear I didn't know.'

'What did you do when you found out?'

'Scrapped it. I was just in time.'

'You were lucky.'

'Does it still hurt so much?'

'Yes,' Grant said. 'Yes, my girl, it does.'

'Why, though? Because people may still believe you cribbed?'

'I suppose so – yes. The whole thing's a nightmare.'

'I'm sorry,' Sophy said. 'That's beastly for you. But I can't quite see – '

'What it's got to do with this book – and Mailer?'

'Yes.'

Grant said: 'Was it at half past three last afternoon that we met for the first time?'

'We've been thrown together. Like people in ships,' Sophy said with a practical air that was invalidated by the circumstance of her being obliged to murmur.

'Mailer kept the manuscript for three days.'

'Why?'

'He says because he flaked out. Cocaine. He showed me his arm to prove it. I don't believe it for a moment.'

'Was he waiting for a reward to be offered?'

'He wouldn't take it.'

'Amazing!' said Sophy.

'I don't think so. I don't think he's an addict. I think he's a pusher in a big way and they never are. He took me to the place they've gone on to, tonight. Toni's. It's a highly tarted-up junk and flop shop. Caters for all tastes. It's outrageous. Where was I?'

'You were going to say – '

'Why he waited three days. Because it took him that amount of time to cook up a novella with a resemblance in theme to an incident in *Simon*. He asked me to read it and give him a criticism. I'm certain *now* that he'd opened my case, read the MS and deliberately concocted this thing. It had all the characteristics, only I was too dumb to spot them. I gave him an opinion and mentioned, as an amusing coincidence, the resemblance. We were in a restaurant and he told some friends about it. Later on in that damnable evening he told other people. He made a great story of it.'

Grant stopped speaking. A belated horse-carriage clopped down the street under their garden. Much farther away a babble of Italian voices broke out, topped by a whistle, laughter and a snatch of song. A driver in Navona changed gears and revved up his engine.

'Do I begin to see,' Sophy said, 'why you put up with – this afternoon?'

'Do you begin to see!' he burst out. 'Yes, you do begin to see. You haven't heard half of it yet, but by God you do begin to see.' He brought his clenched fist down on the table with a crash and their tooth mugs clattered together.

'Pardon *me*,' said a shrill lady behind the french windows, 'but is it too much to ask for a mite of common courtesy and consideration?'

And then in an access of rage. 'If you can't keep your voices down you can belt up and get out.'

V

Morning was well-established when Giovanni and Kenneth Dorne with Lady Braceley, maintained by lateral pressure and support from the armpits and not so much propelled as lifted, crossed the foyer of the hotel and entered the lift.

Cleaning women with black-currant eyes exchanged looks with the night porter, who was preparing to go off duty. The man with the vacuum cleaner watched their progress to the lift and then joined them and, with back turned and averted glance, took them up to their floor. A chambermaid, seeing their approach, opened the door into their suite and hurried away.

They put Lady Braceley into a chair.

Kenneth fumbled in his pocket for his note-case. 'You're sure, aren't you?' he said to Giovanni. 'It's going to be OK. I mean – you know – ?'

Giovanni, indigo about the jaws but otherwise impeccable, said, 'Perfectly, Signore. I am fully in Signor Mailer's confidence.'

'Yes – but – you know? This thing about – well, about the police – did he – ?'

'I will be pleased to negotiate.'

They both looked at Lady Braceley.

'We'll have to wait,' Kenneth said. 'It'll be all right, I promise. Later. Say this afternoon when she's – you know?'

'As soon as possible. A delay is not desirable.'

'All right. All right. I know. But – see for yourself, Giovanni.'

'Signore, I have already perceived.'

'Yes. Well, in the meantime – here.'

'You are very kind,' Giovanni said, taking his dirt-money with infinite aplomb. 'I will return at two-thirty, Signore. *Arrivederci.*'

Left alone, Kenneth bit his knuckles, looked at his aunt and caught back his breath in a dry sob. Then he rang for her maid and went to his room.

VI

'You have enjoyed yourself, my beloved?' the Baron had asked the Baroness in their own language as they prepared for bed.

'Very much. The tall Englishman is a good dancer and clearly a person of some distinction. He what the English call *"funned"* me about not going on to the other place. To take care of him, he said. He is a flirt.'

'I am jealous.'

'Good-good. Almost, I wish we had decided to go.'

'Now, you tease me, my love. It is quite unthinkable that I should take you to one of these places, Mathilde. You would be insulted. I wonder that this person, Allen, suggested it.'

'He was *"funning"* me, my darling.'

'He had no business to do so on that subject.'

The Baroness turned her back to her husband, who deftly unzipped her dress and awarded her a neat little slap.

'The relief,' she said, 'is so enormous, Gerrit. I dare not believe in it. Tell me, fully, what happened.'

'In effect – nothing. As you know I hoped to negotiate. I kept the appointment. He did not. It is very strange.'

'And, for the moment at least, we are free of our anxiety?'

'I think we are free altogether, darling. I think we shall not see this Mailer again.'

'No?'

'My feeling is that he is in trouble with the police. Perhaps he was recognized. Perhaps the woman who threatened him has some hold over him. I am sure he has bolted. We shall not be troubled by him again, my poor love.'

'And our secret – our secret, Gerrit?'

'Remains our secret.'

The Baron's winged smile tilted his mouth. He opened his eyes and put his head on one side. 'And as for our financial disaster,' he said. 'It is vanished. Look.'

He unlocked a cupboard, removed from it the great satchel in which he carried his photographic equipment, unlocked that and displayed a large sealed package.

'Such a business it was,' he said, 'getting it all together. And now – back to Geneva and lock it all up again. What a farce!'

'What a farce,' she echoed obediently.

He put the satchel away, locked the cupboard, turned and opened wide his arms.

'So,' he said. 'And now – ! Come to me, my beloved.'

VII

Major Sweet was the last of his party to return to his lodging. He was taken to his room by the second driver, being in a trance-like condition from which he neither passed into oblivion nor wholly recovered. The second driver watched him make a pretty good hash of withdrawing money from his pockets and did not attempt to conceal his own chagrin when given a worse than conservative tip.

Alone, the Major was at laborious pains to retrieve the money he had dropped on the carpet. He was reduced to crawling after it like a botanist in search of some rare specimen.

Having achieved several pieces of cash and two notes he sat on the floor with his back to the bed, stared at his gleanings with astonishment and then, inconsistently, threw them over his shoulder.

He rolled over, climbed up to his bed, fell on it, removed his tie and slept.

CHAPTER 6

Re-appearance of a Postcard Vendor

At seven o'clock Alleyn obeyed his own orders and woke. He ordered breakfast, bathed, shaved and was ready for the day when the hotel office rang to say a car had called for him.

It was Il Questore Valdarno's car and in it, exuding his peculiar brand of melancholy and affability, was the Questore himself. He welcomed Alleyn and in doing so contrived to establish the awesome condescension of his being there at all. It was a long time, Alleyn understood, since the Questore had risen at this hour, a long time since his association with fieldwork had taken any form other than the august consideration of material pre-filtered by his subordinates.

Alleyn expressed, not for the first time, his deep sense of obligation.

The air was fresh, Rome sparkled, the streets swam with shoals of early workers. Above them and against a pontifical blue, giant personages in marble looked downwards, the arms frozen in benediction. Under the streets, behind façades, in still-dominant monuments the aspirations of senators, Caesars and Emperors held their ground. And nowhere more strangely, Alleyn thought, than in S. Tommaso in Pallaria.

When they arrived they were met by three of the Questore's 'people': Agenti de Questura, which Alleyn took to be the equivalent of constables, and by Father Denys and the Sacristan, Brother Dominic, a dour man who drew the key to the underworld from his habit as if it was a symbol of mortality.

Valdarno was rather high and remote with the clergy, but complaisant too, and not ungracious.

Father Denys greeted Alleyn as an old friend.

'It's yourself again, is it, and you not letting on what was your true function. Sure, I thought to myself there was something about you that was more than met the eye and here you are, they tell me, a great man in the CID.'

'I hope it was an innocent – reservation, Father.'

'Ah, well,' said Father Denys with a tolerance, Alleyn felt, reserved for heretics, 'we'll let you off this time. Now what is all this? A wild-goose chase you and the Questore are on over the head of this queer fellow. Be sure he's given us the slip and away on his own devices.'

'You're persuaded he did give you the slip, Father?'

'What else could it be? He's not beneath.' He turned to Valdarno. 'If you're ready, Signor Questore, we may proceed.'

Cleaners were busy in the upper basilica, which in common with most Latin churches, had the warm air of always being in business and ready for all comers. A Mass had been said and a small congregation of old women and early workers were on their way out. Three women and one man knelt in prayer before separate shrines. The Sacristy was open. The celebrant had concluded his after-Mass observances and was about to leave. They moved on into the vestibule and shop. Brother Dominic opened the great iron grille and he, with Valdarno, Alleyn and three attendant policemen, began their search of the underworld. Father Denys remained above, being, as he pointed out, entirely satisfied of the non-presence of Mr Mailer in the basements and having a job to do in the shop.

As they descended Brother Dominic turned on the fluorescent lighting used by the monks in their maintenance and excavation. It completely changed the atmosphere and character of the underworld, which had become a museum with no shadows and its exhibits remorselessly displayed. Nothing could reduce the liveliness, beauty and strangeness of the Etruscan terra-cottas but they no longer disconcerted.

Little heaps of rubble, tools and rope, tidily disposed, stood at entrances to passages that were still being explored. The Agenti poked into all these and re-emerged dusting their knees and shoulders.

Brother Dominic looked on with his hands in his sleeves and an expression of disfavour on his face. The Questore lost no opportunity of telling Alleyn in a stagy aside that this, undoubtedly, was merely a routine search and they might expect nothing from it.

Alleyn asked him if any results had come through from Mailer's flat and learnt that somebody had telephoned immediately after he himself had done so, that the man seemed to be in some agitation, refused to give his name and rang again several times enabling the number to be traced. It was that of La Gioconda. Marco, without a doubt.

'And the woman, Violetta?'

Certainly. Naturally the matter of the woman Violetta had been followed up. Curiously, it must be admitted, she had not returned to her lodging and so far had not been found.

'It is possible,' Valdarno said, 'that they are together.'

'You think so?'

'One cannot tell. She may be implicated. He may have informed her of your identity and frightened her into taking flight. This is mere speculation, my dear Superintendent, and I know your views. I have read your book. In English, I have read it.'

'Well, I'll break my rule and indulge in a bit of speculation on my own account. It occurs to me there is another possible explanation for their double disappearance.'

'Indeed? Please tell me of it.'

Alleyn did so. Valdarno stared straight in front of him and nursed his splendid moustache. When Alleyn had finished, he turned an incredulous gaze upon him and then decided to be arch. He shook his finger at Alleyn. 'Ah-ah-ah, you pull my leg,' he said.

'I don't, you know.'

'No? Well,' said the Questore, thinking it over, 'we shall see. Yet I fear,' he added, giving Alleyn a comradely clap on the shoulder, 'that we shall see – nothing in particular.'

They moved laboriously onwards and down. To the church on the second level. To the first smiling Apollo and the tall woman with the broken child, to the white Apollo with a crown of leaves, to the Mercury behind whom Baron Van der Veghel had so playfully hidden. The men flashed torchlights into the recesses and niches. Alleyn looked into them a little more closely. Behind the white Apollo he found a screwed-up piece of glossy blue paper which he retrieved and wrapped in his handkerchief, sharply observed by Valdarno, to whom he scrupulously confided his reasons for doing so. Behind the Mercury he found a sealing tab from an undeveloped film, left there no doubt by Baron Van der Veghel when he played his little joke and frightened Lady Braceley into fits.

On to the railed hole in the floor of the second-level cloister where Baroness Van der Veghel had peered into the underworld and where Sophy Jason and Alleyn, also looking down, had seen the shadow of a woman they took to be Violetta.

Alleyn reminded Valdarno of this and invited him to stand where Sophy had stood while he himself looked over the Questore's shoulder. There was no lighting down below and they stared into a void.

'You see, Signor Questore, we are looking straight down into the well-head on the bottom level. And there to the right is the end of the sarcophagus with the carved lid. You can, I think, just make it out. I wonder – could one of your men go down there and switch on the normal lighting? Or perhaps –' He turned with diffidence to the Dominican. 'I wonder,' he said, 'if you would mind going down, Brother Dominic? Would you? You are familiar with the switches and we are not. If we could just have the same lighting as there was yesterday? And if you would be very kind and move between the source of light and the well. We'd be most grateful.'

Brother Dominic waited for so long, staring in front of him, that Alleyn began to wonder if he had taken some vow of silence. However, he suddenly said 'I will' in a loud voice.

'That's very kind of you. And – I hope I'm not asking for something that is not permitted – would you have your hood over your head?'

'What for would I be doing that?' asked Brother Dominic in a sudden access of communication.

'It's just to lend a touch of verisimilitude,' Alleyn began, and to his astonishment Brother Dominic instantly replied, ' "To an otherwise bald and unconvincing narrative"?'

'Bless you, Brother Dominic. You'll do it?'

'I will,' Brother Dominic repeated, and stalked off.

'These holy fathers!' Valdarno tolerantly observed. 'The one talks to distraction and the other has half a tongue. What is it you wish to demonstrate?'

'Only, in some sort, how the shadow appeared to us.'

'Ah, the shadow. You insist on the shadow?'

'Humour me.'

'My dear colleague, why else am I here? I am all attention.'

So they leant over the railing, stared into the depths and became aware of the now familiar burble of subterranean water.

'Almost,' Alleyn said, 'you can persuade yourself that you see a glint of it in the well – almost but not quite. Yesterday I really thought I did.'

'Some trick of the light.'

'I suppose so. And pat on his cue, there goes Brother Dominic.'

A concealed lamp had been switched on. The lid of the sarcophagus, the wall behind it and the railings round the well all sprang into existence. Their view from immediately above was one of bizarre shadows and ambiguous shapes, of exaggerated perspectives and detail. It might have been an illustration from some Victorian thriller: a story of Mystery and Imagination.

As if to underline this suggestion of the macabre a new shadow moved into the picture: that of a hooded form. It fell across the sarcophagus, mounted the wall, grew gigantic and vanished.

'Distorted,' Alleyn said, 'grotesque, even, but quite sharply defined, wasn't it? Unmistakably a monk. One could even see that the hands were concealed in the sleeves. Brother Dominic, obliging, in fact. The shadow Miss Jason and I saw yesterday was equally well-defined. One saw that the left shoulder was markedly higher than the right, that the figure was a woman's and even that she carried some tray-like object slung round her neck. It was, I am persuaded, Signor Questore, the shadow of Violetta and her postcards.'

'Well, my friend, I do not argue with you. I will take it as a working hypothesis that Violetta escaped the vigilance of the good fathers and came down here. Why? Perhaps with the intention of pursuing her quarrel with Mailer. Perhaps and perhaps. Perhaps,' the Questore continued with a sardonic inflection, 'she frightened him and that is why he ran away. Or even – as you have hinted – but come – shall we continue?'

Alleyn leant over the well-rails and called out. 'Thank you, Brother Dominic. That was excellent. We are coming down.'

He had a resonant voice and it roused a concourse of echoes: '–down–ow–ow–ow–n–n.'

They descended the circular iron stairway, walking along the narrow passage and found Brother Dominic, motionless beside the well-head. The scene was lit as it had been yesterday afternoon.

Alleyn stood by the well-head and looked up. The opening above his head showed as a brilliant square of light and far above that, the opening into the basilica. As he watched, Father Denys's head appeared at the top level, peering into the depths. If Father Denys, like Violetta, was given to spitting, Alleyn thought, he would spit straight in my eye.

'Are you all right, beneath?' asked Father Denys and his voice seemed to come from nowhere in particular.

'We are,' boomed Brother Dominic without moving. The head was withdrawn.

'Before we turn on the fluorescent light,' Alleyn said, 'shall we check on the movements of the woman in the shawl? Brother Dominic, I take it that just now you walked from the foot of the iron stair where you turned on the usual lighting, down the passage and across the light itself to where you now stand?'

'I did,' said Brother Dominic.

'And so must she, one would think?'

'Of course,' said Valdarno.

'It wasn't quite the same, though. Violetta's shadow – we are accepting Violetta as a working hypothesis – came from the right as Brother Dominic's did and, like his, crossed to the left. But there was a sequel. It re-appeared, darting into view, lying across the sarcophagus and up the wall. It paused. It turned this way and that, and then shot off to the right. The suggestion, a vivid one, was of a furtive person looking for a hiding-place. Miss Jason thought so, too.'

'Did Mailer comment?'

'He pooh-poohed the idea of it being Violetta and changed the subject.' Alleyn looked about him. 'If we extend the "working hypothesis" which, by the way, Signor Questore, is a nice alternative to the hateful word "conjecture", we must allow that there are plenty of places where she *could* hide. Look what a black shadow the sarcophagus throws, for instance.'

Alleyn had a torch and now used it. He flashed it along the well-rails, which turned out to be makeshift construction of roughly finished wood.

'You would like the working lights, Signore?' said one of the men.

But the darting beam paused and sharpened its focus. Alleyn stooped and peered at the rail.

'There's a thread of some material caught here,' he said. 'Yes, may we have the lights, please?'

The man went back down the passage, his retreating footfalls loud on the stone floor.

The torchlight moved away from the rails, played across the lid of the sarcophagus, caused little carved garlands to leap up in strong relief, found the edge of the lid. Stopped.

'Look here.'

Valdarno used his torch and the other two men came forward with theirs. As they closed in the pool of light contracted and intensified.

The lid of the sarcophagus was not perfectly closed. Something black protruded and from the protrusion dangled three strands of wool.

'*Dio mio!*' whispered the Questore.

Alleyn said, 'Brother Dominic, we must remove the lid.'

'Do so.'

The two men slid it a little to one side, tilted it and with a grating noise, let it slide down at an angle. The edge of the lid hit the floor with a heavy and resounding thud, like the shutting of a monstrous door.

The torchlights fastened on Violetta's face.

Her thickened eyes stared sightlessly into theirs. Her tongue was thrust out as if to insult them.

Valdarno's torch clattered on the stone floor.

The long silence was broken by a voice: uninflected, deep, rapid. Brother Dominic prayed aloud for the dead.

II

A consultation was held in the vestibule. The church was shut and the iron grille into the underworld locked, awaiting the arrival of Valdarno's Squadra Omicidi. It was strange, Alleyn found, to hear the familiar orders being laid on by somebody else in another language.

Valdarno was business-like and succinct. An ambulance and a doctor were sent for, the doctor being, as far as Alleyn could make out, the equivalent of a Home Office pathologist. The guard at all points of departure from Rome was to be instantly stepped up. Toni's premises were to be searched and the staff examined. Mailer's apartment was to be occupied in such a way that if he returned he would walk into a trap. Violetta's known associates were to be closely questioned.

Alleyn listened, approved and said nothing.

Having set up this operational scheme, the Questore turned his deceptively languishing gaze upon Alleyn.

'*Ecco!*' he said. 'Forgive me, my friend, if I have been precipitate. This was routine. Now we collaborate and you shall tell me how we proceed.'

'Far be it from me,' Alleyn rejoined in the nearest Italian equivalent to this idiom that he could at the moment concoct, 'to do anything of the sort. May we continue in English?'

'Of course,' cried the Questore in that language.

'I suppose,' Alleyn said, 'that now you have so efficiently set up the appropriate action we should return to the persons who were nearest to the crime at the time it was committed.'

'Of course. I was about to say so. And so,' Valdarno archly pointed out, 'you interview yourself, isn't it?'

'Among others. Or perhaps I may put myself in your hands. How would you set about me, Signor Questore?'

Valdarno joined his fingertips and laid them across his mouth. 'In the first place,' he said, 'it is important to ascertain the movements of this Mailer. I would ask that as far as possible you trace them. When you last saw him, for example.'

'The classic question. When the party was near the iron stairway on the middle level. We were about to go down to the Mithraic household on the lowest level when Lady Braceley said she was nervous and wanted to return to the top. She asked for her nephew to take her up but we found that he was not with us. Mailer said he had returned to photograph the statue of Apollo and that he would fetch him. Lady Braceley wouldn't wait and in the upshot Major Sweet took her up to the basilica garden – the atrium – and rejoined us later. When they left us Mailer set off along the passage, ostensibly to retrieve Kenneth Dorne. The rest

of us – the Van der Veghels, Miss Jason and I, with Barnaby Grant
as guide, went down the iron stair to the Mithraeum. We had been
there perhaps eight minutes when Major Sweet made himself
known – I put it like that because at this point he spoke. He may
have actually returned un-noticed before he spoke. The place is
full of shadows. It was some five or six minutes later that Kenneth
Dorne appeared, asking for his aunt.'

'So Mailer had not met this Dorne after all?'

'Apparently not, but there is some evidence –'

'Ah! I had forgotten. But on the face of it no one had seen Mailer
after he walked down the passage?'

'On the face of it – nobody.'

'We must question these people.'

'I agree with you,' said Alleyn.

For some seconds the Questore fixed his mournful gaze upon
Alleyn.

'It must be done with tact,' he said. 'They are persons of some
consequence. There could be undesirable developments. All but
two,' he added, 'are British citizens.'

Alleyn waited.

'In fact,' said Valdarno, 'it appears to me, my Superintendent, that
there is no longer any cause for you to preserve your anonymity.'

'I haven't thought that one out but – no, I suppose you're right.'

One of the Agenti came in.

'The Squadra Omicidi, Signor Questore, the ambulance, Vice-
Questore and the doctor.'

'Very well. Bring them.'

When the man had gone Valdarno said, 'I have, of course, sent for
the officer who would normally conduct this inquiry, Il
Vice-Questore Bergarmi. It would not be fitting for me to engage
myself in my subordinate's duties. But in view of extraordinary
circumstances and international implications I shall not entirely
dissociate myself. Besides,' he added with a totally unexpected flash
of candour, 'I am enjoying myself prodigiously.'

For Alleyn the confrontation at close quarters with a strangled
woman had not triggered off an upsurge of pleasure. However, he
said something vague about fieldwork as an antidote to the desk.
Valdarno developed his theme.

'My suggestion,' he said, 'is this and you shall tell me if I am faulty. I propose to invite these people to my office where they will be received with *ceremoniale*. There will be no hint of compulsion but on the contrary a glass of wine. I present you in your professional role. I explain a little but not too much. I implore their help and I then push them over to you.'

'Thank you. It will, don't you feel, be a little difficult to sustain the interview at this level? I mean, on his own admission to me, Kenneth Dorne has been introduced to soft and then to hard drugs by Mailer. And so, after last night, I believe, has Lady Braceley. And I'm perfectly certain Mailer exercised some sort of pull over Barnaby Grant. Nothing short of blackmail, it seems to me, would have induced Grant to take on the role of prime attraction in yesterday's conducted tour.'

'In which case he, at least, will be glad to help in bringing about the arrest of Mailer.'

'Not if it means publicity of a very damaging kind.'

'But my dear colleague, will you not assure them that the matter at issue is murder and nothing else? Nothing, as you say, personal.'

'I think,' Alleyn said drily, 'that they are not so simple as to swallow that one.'

The Questore hitched his shoulders and spread his hands. 'They can be assured,' he threw out, 'of our discretion.'

Alleyn said: 'What's Mailer's nationality – has he taken out Italian citizenship?'

'That can be ascertained. You are thinking, of course, of extradition.'

'Am I?' Alleyn muttered absently. *'Am* I?'

The doctor, the ambulance men, the Questore's subordinate, Vice-Questore Bergarmi and the Roman version of a homicide squad now arrived with their appropriate gear: cameras, tripods, lamps, cases, a stretcher and a canvas sheet; routine props in the international crime show.

The men were solemnly presented. Alleyn supposed Bergarmi to be the opposite number in rank of a detective-inspector.

They were given their instructions. Everyone was immensely deferential to Il Questore Valdarno and, since it was clearly indicated, to Alleyn. The grille was unlocked and the new arrivals went below.

'We shall not accompany them,' Valdarno said. 'It is not necessary. It would be inappropriate. In due course they will report themselves. After all, one does not need a medical officer to tell one when
a woman has been strangled.'

Alleyn thought: I've got to tread delicately here. This is going to
be tricky.

He said, 'When your photographer has taken his pictures I would
be very glad to have another look round, if I might. Particularly at
the top railing round the well. Before that fragment of material,
whatever it is, is removed. May I?'

'But of course. You find some significance in this fragment? The
rail has a rough surface, many, many persons have brushed past it
and grasped it. I saw that you examined the area closely after the
lights were on. What did you see? What was this material?'

'Some kind of black stuff. It's the position that I find interesting.
The rail is about five by two inches. It is indeed rough on the inside
surface and it is on the inside surface near the lower edge that this
scrap of material has been caught.'

After a considerable pause Valdarno said, 'This is perhaps a little
curious but, I would suggest, not of great moment. Some person has
leant over the rail, lolling his arms down, peering into the depths
and – ' he stopped, frowned and then said, 'by all means go down,
my friend, and examine the area as you require. You have my full
authority.'

'How very kind,' Alleyn said and took immediate advantage of
the offer.

He went below and found Valdarno's 'people' very active in the
familiar routine under Bergarmi. Violetta had been photographed *in
situ* and was now transferred to the stretcher where the surgeon
hung over her terrible face. The lid of the sarcophagus was being
treated by a fingerprint officer. Alleyn didn't for a moment suppose
that they would find anything. Bergarmi received his principal's card
with elaborate courtesy and little enthusiasm.

Alleyn had his own and very particular little camera. While
Bergarmi and his staff were fully extended in other directions, he
took three quick shots of the inner-side rails. He then returned to
the basilica. He told Valdarno what he had done and said that
he would now take advantage of his kind offer and visit Mailer's

apartment. Valdarno instructed one of his drivers to take him there and, having shaken hands elaborately for the second time in an hour, they parted.

Mailer's apartment was in a side street behind the Pantheon. It was reached through a little run-down courtyard and up the first flight of a narrow outdoor stairway. Valdarno's man on duty let Alleyn in and, after a look at the all-powerful card, left him to his own devices.

The rooms, there were three of them, struck Alleyn as being on their way up. One or two new and lusciously upholstered armchairs, a fine desk, a sumptuous divan, and on Mr Mailer's bed, a heavily embroidered and rather repellent velvet cover, all pointed to affluence. A dilapidated kitchenette, murky bathroom and blistered walls suggested that it was of recent origin. The bookshelves contained a comprehensive line in high-camp pornography, some of it extremely expensive, and a selection of mere pornography, all of it cheap and excessively nasty. Signor Valdarno's man was whiling away his vigil in a sample of the latter kind.

Alleyn asked him if the contents of the desk had been examined. He said Vice-Questore Bergarmi had intimated that he would attend to it later on if Mailer did not return.

'He has not returned,' Alleyn said. 'I will look at it. You, perhaps, would prefer to telephone Il Questore Valdarno before I do so.'

This did the trick. The man returned to his book and Alleyn tackled the desk. The only lock that gave him any trouble was that of a concealed cupboard at the back of the knee-hole and it was in this cupboard, finally, that he struck oil: a neatly kept ledger: a sort of diary-cum-reference book. Here, at intervals, opposite a date, was a tick with one, or sometimes two letters beside it. Alleyn consulted his own notebook and found that these entries tallied with those connected with suspected shipments of heroin from Izmir to Naples and thence, via Corsica, to Marseilles. He came to a date a little over a year ago and found: *'Ang. in Aug.* B.G.' and four days later: 'B.G. *S. in L.'* This he thought very rum indeed, until, in a drawer of the desk he found a manuscript entitled *Angelo in August.* He returned to the ledger.

Nothing of interest until he came to an entry for May of the previous year. 'V. der V. Confirmed. Wait.' From now on there appeared at intervals entries of large sums of money with no explanation but bearing a relationship to the dates of shipment. He plodded on. The Agente yawned over his book. Entries for the current year. 'Perugia. K.D. L. 100,000.' Several entries under K.D. After that: merely a note of the first and subsequent Il Cicerone tours.

Alleyn completed his search of the desk. He found in a locked cash box a number of letters that clearly indicated Mr Mailer's activities in the blackmailing line and one in a language that he did not know but took to be Dutch. This he copied out and then photographed, together with several entries in the diary. It was now half past eleven. He sighed, said good morning to the Agente and set out for Valdarno's office, reflecting that he had probably just completed a bare-faced piece of malfeasance but not in the least regretting it.

III

At noon Mr Mailer's unhappy band of pilgrims assembled in the Questore Valdarno's sumptuous office.

Lady Braceley, Kenneth Dorne and Major Sweet all bore shattering witness to the extravagances of the previous night. The Van der Veghels looked astonished, Barnaby Grant anxious and Sophy Jason shocked. They sat in a semi-circle on imitation renaissance chairs of great splendour and little ease while Valdarno caused wine to be handed round on a lordly tray. Lady Braceley, Kenneth Dorne and Major Sweet, turned sickly glances upon it and declined. The rest of the party sipped uncomfortably while the Questore addressed them at length.

Alleyn sat a little apart from the others who, as the Questore proceeded, eyed him with increasing consternation.

Without much elaboration, Valdarno told them of the discovery of Violetta's body and remarked upon Sebastian Mailer's continued non-appearance. He sat behind his magnificent desk. Alleyn noticed that the centre drawer was half-open and that it contained paper. The Questore had placed his folded hands negligently across the drawer but as he warmed to his theme he forgot himself and gestured freely. His audience shifted uneasily. Major Sweet, rousing himself, said that he'd known from the first that there was something fishy about the fellow Mailer. Nobody followed this up.

'My Lady, Ladies and Gentlemen,' the Questore concluded, 'you will, I am sure, perceive that it is important for this Mr Mailer to be traced. I speak from the highest authority when I assure you of our great concern that none of you should be unduly inconvenienced and that your visit to Rome, we hope a pleasurable one, should not be in any way – ' he paused and glanced into the drawer of his desk ' – diminished,' he said, 'by this unfortunate occurrence.'

He made the slight mistake of absent-mindedly closing the drawer with his thumb. Otherwise, Alleyn thought, he had managed beautifully.

Major Sweet said, 'Very civil, I'm sure. Do what we can.' The Van der Veghels and Sophy said, 'Of course,' Lady Braceley looked vaguely about her. 'No, but *really*!' she said. 'I mean, how too off-putting and peculiar.' She opened her cigarette case but made a sad botch of helping herself. Her hands jerked, cigarettes shot about the floor.

'*Excellenza!*' the Questore ejaculated. '*Scusi!* Allow me!' He leapt to his feet.

'No! No! Please! Kenneth! Too stupid of me. No!'

Kenneth gathered the cigarettes, pushed them back into the case and with some difficulty lit the one that shook between his lips. They all looked away from Lady Braceley and Kenneth.

Grant said loudly, 'You haven't actually told us so, but I suppose I am right in thinking you suspect Mailer of this murder?'

Kenneth Dorne gave out a noise somewhere between a laugh and a snort.

The Questore made one of his more ornate gestures. 'One must not be precipitate,' he said. 'Let us say, Mr Grant, that we feel he may – '

' "*Help the police in their investigation*",' Kenneth said, 'that's got a familiar ring about it! "Inspector or Superintendent Flookamapush says he's anxious to trace Mr Sebastian Mailer who the police believe may help – " '

He broke off, staring at Alleyn. 'My *God*!' he said and got to his feet. 'I was right! My *God*. I remember, now. I knew I'd seen that fabulous face before. My God, you *are* a policeman!'

He turned to the others. 'He's a bloody policeman,' he said. 'He's the detective they're always writing up in the papers. "Handsome" something – what is it? – yes – by God – "Handsome Alleyn".' He pointed to Alleyn. 'He's no tourist, he's a spy. Last night. At Toni's. Spying. That's what he was doing.'

Alleyn watched all the heads turn in his direction and all the shutters come down. I'm back in business, he thought.

He stood up. 'Mr Dorne,' he said, 'has beaten us to the post by one second. I think the Questore was about to explain.'

The Questore did explain, with one or two significant evasions and a couple of downright lies that Alleyn would have avoided. He said that the highly distinguished Superintendent was on holiday but had made a courtesy call at police headquarters in Rome, that he had expressed a wish to remain incognito which the Questore had of course respected. It was by pure accident, he lied, that Alleyn had joined in the Cicerone tour but when Mailer disappeared he had felt it his duty to report the circumstance. For which the Questore and his subordinates were greatly obliged to him.

Here he paused. Of his audience Sophy and the Van der Veghels looked perfectly satisfied. The others exhibited distrust and scepticism in varying degrees.

The Questore continued. In view of the death of this unfortunate woman, and because Mr Mailer was a British subject, he had asked Superintendent Alleyn to assist, which he had most graciously consented to do. The Questore felt sure that the Superintendent's fellow-countrymen would greatly prefer the few enquiries to be under his guidance. In any case, he ended, the proceedings would probably be very short and there would be no radical interference in their holidays. He bowed to the Van der Veghels and added that he hoped they, also, would find themselves in agreement with this plan.

'But, of course,' the Baron said. 'It is a satisfactory and intelligent suggestion. A crime has been committed. It is our duty to assist. At the same time I am glad of your assurance that we shall not be detained for very long. After all,' and he bowed to Alleyn, 'we are also, on vacation.'

With many mellifluous assurances the Questore begged them to withdraw to a room which had been placed at Alleyn's disposal.

It was less sumptuous than the first office but more than sufficient for the purpose. There was a desk for Alleyn and extra chairs were brought in for the seven travellers. He noticed that Barnaby Grant was quick to place himself next to Sophy Jason, that Major Sweet was fractionally less bleary-eyed than he had been, that Lady Braceley had better luck with a new cigarette and in controlling the tremor that was nevertheless still in evidence. Kenneth, fidgety and resentful, looked out of the corner of his eye at Alleyn and clearly was not much mollified by the official pronouncement.

Alleyn's chief concern was to avoid sounding like a replay of the Valdarno disc.

'This is both a tragic and an absurd situation,' he said, 'and I don't really know what you'll be making of it. Cutting it down to size it amounts to this. An unfortunate woman has been murdered and a rather strange individual of presumed British nationality has disappeared. We seem to be the last people to have seen him and the police, obviously, want to get statements from all of us. Signor Valdarno is much too grand a personage to handle the case: he's the equivalent in rank of our Chief Constable or perhaps Assistant Commissioner. His man in charge doesn't speak English and because I'm a cop he's asked me to sort it out. I hope that's all right with all of you. I could hardly refuse, could I?'

'You might have told us about your job,' Major Sweet said resentfully.

'But why? You haven't told us about yours.'

The Major reddened.

'Look,' Alleyn said. 'Let's get it over shall we? The sooner the better, surely.'

'Certainly,' Sophy Jason said. 'By all means, let's.'

Grant said, 'Oh, by all means,' in a wooden voice, and Lady Braceley and Kenneth made plaintive sounds of acceptance.

'Ach, yes' cried the Baroness. 'No more delays, isn't it? Already our plans for today look silly. Instead of fountinks at the Villa d'Este here is a stuffed room. Come! On!'

Thus encouraged, Alleyn set about his task. His situation was an odd one, removed as he was from immediate reliance upon the CID and from the sense of being an integral part of its structure. This was an 'away match' and presented its own problems, not the least of which was to define his area of investigation. Originally this had simply been that which covered Mailer's presumed activities in the international drug racket and possible association with the key figure – the fabulous Otto Ziegfeldt. Now, with the discovery of Violetta, staring and frightful, in a stone coffin that had held who could guess what classic bones and flesh, the case had spilled into a wider and more ambiguous affair. The handling of it became very tricky indeed.

He began: 'I think we'd better settle the question of when each of us last saw Sebastian Mailer. For my part, it was when we were on the middle level and just after Major Sweet and Lady Braceley had left to go up to the atrium. Mr Grant, Miss Jason and the Baron and Baroness were with me and we all went down to the Mithraic dwelling together. Major Sweet and Mr Dorne joined us there separately, some five to ten – or fifteen minutes later. May I begin by asking you, Lady Braceley, if you saw anything of Mailer or of Violetta after you left us?'

Not only, Alleyn thought, was she in the grip of a formidable hangover but she was completely nonplussed at finding herself in a situation that could not be adjusted to a nineteen-twentyish formula for triteness. She turned her lacklustre gaze from one man to another, ran her tongue round her lips and said, 'No. No, of course I didn't. No.'

'And you, Major? On your way down? Did you see either of them?'

'I did not.'

'You stayed for a minute of two with Lady Braceley and then came down to the Mithraeum?'

'Yes.'

'And met nobody on the way.'

'Nobody.'

Alleyn said casually, 'There must at that time have been besides yourself, three persons at large between the top level – the basilica, and the bottom one – the Mithraeum. Mailer himself, Violetta and Mr Kenneth Dorne. You neither saw nor heard any of them?'

'Certainly not.'

'Mr Dorne, when exactly did you leave us?'

'I haven't the faintest idea.'

'Perhaps,' Alleyn said with undiminished good humour, 'we can help you. You were with us in the middle level cloisters when Mailer made his joke about Apollo being a latter-day Lazarus.'

'How do you know?'

'Because you giggled at it.'

'Marvellous,' said Kenneth.

'It was not a nice joke,' the Baroness said. 'We did not find it amusink, did we, Gerrit?'

'No, my dear.'

'It was a silly one.'

'So.'

'You think it funnier perhaps,' Kenneth said, 'to dodge behind terra-cotta busts and bounce out at old – at highly-strung people. It takes all sorts to raise a laugh.'

'You were not there, Mr Dorne,' said the Baron. 'You had left the party. We had crossed the nave of the early church and you did not come with us. How did you know I bounced?'

'I heard of it,' Kenneth said loftily, 'from my aunt.'

Alleyn plodded on. 'We understood from Mailer that you had gone back to photograph the Apollo. Is that right?'

'Certainly.'

'And you did photograph it?'

Kenneth slid his feet about and after a pretty long pause said, 'As it happened, no. I'd run out of film.' He pulled out his packet of cigarettes and found it was empty.

'No, you hadn't,' shouted Major Sweet. 'You hadn't done any such thing. You took a photograph of Mithras when we were all poodlefaking round Grant and his book.'

Grant most unexpectedly, burst out laughing.

'There's such a thing,' Kenneth said breathlessly, 'as putting in a new film, Major Sweet.'

'Well, yes,' said Alleyn. 'Of course there is. Tell me, did Mailer rejoin you while you were not photographing Apollo?'

This time the pause was an uncomfortably long one. Major Sweet appeared to take the opportunity to have a nap. He shut his eyes, lowered his chin and presently opened his mouth.

At last: 'No,' Kenneth said loudly. 'No. He didn't turn up.'

' "Turn up?" You were expecting him, then?'

'No, I wasn't. Why the hell do you suppose I was? I wasn't expecting him and I didn't see him.' The cigarette packet dropped from his fingers. *"What's that?'* he demanded.

Alleyn had taken a folded handkerchief from his pocket. He opened it to display a crumpled piece of glossy blue paper.

'Do you recognize it?' he asked.

'No!'

Alleyn reached out a long arm, retrieved the cigarette packet from the floor and dropped in on the desk.

He said, 'I was given two boxes wrapped in similar paper to this at Toni's Pad last night.'

'I'm afraid,' Kenneth said whitely, 'my only comment to that is: "So, dear Mr Superintendent Alleyn, what?"'

'In one of them there were eight tablets of heroin. Each I would guess, containing one-sixth of a grain. In the other, an equal amount of cocaine in powder form. Mr Mailer's very own merchandise, I was informed.'

The Van der Veghels broke into scandalized ejaculations, first in their own language and then in English.

'You didn't throw this paper behind the statue of Apollo, Mr Dorne?'

'No. *Christ!'* Kenneth screamed out. 'What the hell is all this? What idiot stuff are you trying to sell me? All right, so this was an H. and C. wrapping. And how many people go through Saint what's-his-name's every day? What about the old woman? For all you know she may have peddled it. To anyone. Why, for God's sake, pick on me?'

'Kenneth – darling – no. Please. No!'

'Partly,' Alleyn said, 'because up to that time you had exhibited withdrawal symptoms but on your arrival in the Mithraeum appeared to be relieved of them.'

'No!'

'We needn't labour the point. If necessary, we can take finger-prints.' He pointed to the paper, and to the empty cigarette packet. 'And in any case, last night you were perfectly frank about your experiments with drugs. You told me that Mailer introduced you to them. Why are you kicking up such a dust now?'

'I didn't know who you were.'

'I'm not going to run you in here, in Rome, for making a mess of yourself with drugs, you silly chap. I simply want to know if, for whatever reason, you met Mailer by the statue of Apollo in the middle level at S. Tommaso.'

'Kenneth – *no*!'

'Auntie, do you *mind*! I've told him – no, no, *no.*'

'Very well. We'll go on. You returned to photograph Apollo, found you had used up the film in your camera, continued on down to the bottom level and joined us in the Mithraeum. At what stage did you put a new film in your camera?'

'I don't remember.'

'Where is the old film?'

'In my pocket, for God's sake. In my room.'

'You didn't encounter Major Sweet either although he must have been on his way down, just ahead of you.'

'No.'

'You passed the Apollo, Major, on your way down?'

'I suppose so. Can't say I remember. Must have, of course.'

'Not necessarily. The cloisters run right round the old church at the middle level. If you'd turned right instead of left when you reached that level you would have come by a shorter route, and without passing Apollo, to the passage leading to the iron stairway.'

'I could have but I didn't.'

'Odd!' Alleyn said. 'And neither of you had sight, sound or smell of Mailer and Violetta?' Silence.

'With the exception of Lady Braceley we all came together in the Mithraeum and were there for, I suppose, at least fifteen minutes while the Baroness and Baron and Mr Dorne took photographs and Mr Grant read to us. Then we found our several ways back to the top. You left first, Mr Dorne, by the main entrance.'

'You're so right. And I went up by the shortest route and I met nobody and heard nothing and I joined my aunt in the garden.'

'Quite so. I went back with the Baron and Baroness. We left the Mithraeum by a doorway behind the figure of the god, turned right twice and followed the cloister, if that's what it should be called, passing the well and the sarcophagus and arriving finally at the passage to the iron stairway.' He turned to the Van der Veghels. 'You agree?'

'Certainly,' said the Baroness. 'That was the way. Stoppink some-times to examine – ' She broke off and turned in agitation to her husband, laying her hands on his arm. She spoke to him in their own language, her voice trembling. He stooped over her, solicitous and concerned, gathered her hands in his and said gently: 'In

English, my dear, should we not? Let me explain.' He turned to Alleyn. 'My wife is disturbed and unhappy,' he said. 'She has remembered, as no doubt you will remember, Mr Alleyn – or, no! You had already turned into the passage, I think. But my wife took a photograph of the sarcophagus.'

'It is so dreadful to think,' the Baroness lamented. 'Imagink! This wretched woman – her body – it may have been – no, Gerrit, it is dreadful.'

'On the contrary, Baroness,' Alleyn said. 'It may be of great assistance to the investigation. Of course, one understands that the implications are distasteful – '

'Distasteful!'

'Well – macabre – dreadful, if you like. But your photograph may at least prove that the sarcophagus had not been interfered with at that juncture.'

'It had not. You yourself must have seen – '

'In that lighting it looked perfectly all right but a flashlamp might bring out some abnormality, you know.'

'What was it like,' Grant said, 'when you examined it, as I gather you did, with Valdarno?'

'There was – a slight displacement,' Alleyn said. 'If the Baroness's photograph shows none it will establish that the murder was committed after we left the Mithraeum.'

'And after we had all left the building?' Grant asked.

'Not quite that, perhaps, but it might come to that. May we just define the rest of the party's movements. Yours, for instance.'

'I had offered to stay in the Mithraeum in case anybody wanted information about the rest of the insula. Miss Jason remained with me for, I suppose, ten minutes or so and we then made our way up by the shortest route: the main exit from the Mithraeum, through the ante-chamber and then down the short passage to the stairway. We didn't pass the well and sarcophagus, of course, and we met nobody.'

'Hear anybody? Voices?'

'No. I don't think so.'

'Wait a bit,' Sophy said.

'Yes, Miss Jason?'

'I don't suppose it matters but she appealed to Grant. 'Do you remember? Just as we were leaving the Mithraeum there was a sound of voices. All mixed up and booming because of the echo.'

'Was there? I've forgotten.'

'Men's or women's voices?' Alleyn asked.

'They were so distorted it's hard to say. A man's I think and perhaps a woman's: perhaps yours and Baroness Van der Veghel's on your way up the stairs. Or Baron Van der Veghel's. Or all three.'

'Might be,' Alleyn said. 'Which way did you go back, Major Sweet?'

'Ah, 'um. I pottered round a bit. Had another look at the well and if you ask me whether the lid of the sarcophagus was out of position I can only say if it was I didn't notice it. I – ah – I went up into the nave of the old church. Matter of fact, while I was there I heard you and – ah – the Van der Veghels in the cloisters. Taking photographs.'

That is so,' said the Baroness. 'I took the head of Mercury.'

'You were still at it when I went on up the stone stairs. Took my time. Didn't see the woman. Or Mailer. My opinion, he wasn't there, anywhere in the premises. Sure of it.'

'Why?' Alleyn asked.

'To be perfectly honest because if the fellow had been there I'd have found him. I thought it damned peculiar him not turning up like that, leaving us cold after taking a whacking great fee off us. So I thought: if the blighter's hanging about somewhere I'm going to dig him out. And I didn't.'

'I really can't believe,' said Grant, 'that you could have made anything remotely resembling a thorough search, Major Sweet. In that short time? In that light? And with all those side passages and excavations? No!'

'That is so,' said the Baron. 'That is undoubtedly so.'

'I resent that, sir,' said the Major and blew out his cheeks.

The Baron paid no attention to him. 'Mr Alleyn,' he said. 'Surely it is not impossible that this Mailer was hiding down there, perhaps already with the body of the woman he had murdered, and that he waited until we had gone before putting it – where it was found. Mr Alleyn – what do you say? Is it possible?'

'I think it's possible, Baron, yes. But when, in that case, did he make his escape?'

'Perhaps he's still there,' Kenneth suggested, and gave his little whinnying laugh.

'I have thought of that,' the Baron said, disregarding Kenneth. 'I have thought that perhaps he waited until the good fathers made their search. That he hid himself somewhere near the top and while they looked elsewhere, contrived to elude them and again hid himself in the basilica until we had driven away and then made his escape. I do not know. Perhaps it is an absurd suggestion but – he is gone, after all.'

'I think,' Lady Braceley said, 'it's a very clever suggestion.' And she actually summoned up the wreck of an arch glance for the Baron, who bowed and looked horrified.

'To sum up,' Alleyn said, 'if that's not a laughable phrase in the context. None of us saw Mailer or Violetta after Mailer left us, ostensibly to join Mr Dorne at the statue of Apollo in the cloisters of the old church at the middle level of S. Tommaso.'

Sophy had given a little ejaculation.

'Yes, Miss Jason? You've thought of something?'

'Only just. It may be – it probably is – nothing. But it was during the group-photograph episode.'

'Yes?'

There was a noise somewhere outside the Mithraeum. Not far away, I'd have thought, but all mixed up and distorted by echoes. A woman's voice, I think, and then it was – well, kind of cut off. And then – later – a kind of thud. At the time I supposed somebody – somewhere – had shut a very heavy door.'

'I remember!' the Baron ejaculated. 'I remember perfectly! It was when I took my picture of the group.'

'Yes? You do?' Sophy said. 'A kind of bang – thumping noise?'

'Exactly.'

'Like a door?'

'A very heavy door.'

'Yes,' Alleyn agreed, 'it did sound rather like that, didn't it?'

'But,' Sophy said, turning white, 'there aren't any heavy doors down there that I can remember.' She appealed to Grant. 'Are there?'

'No. No doors,' he said.

'So I wonder if it was something else – something being dropped, for instance. Not from a great height. Just a little way. But something very heavy.'

'Like a stone lid?' Alleyn suggested.

Sophy nodded.

CHAPTER 7

Afternoon

When Alleyn asked the travellers not to leave Rome for the present there was a great outcry from Lady Braceley and Major Sweet. The Major talked noisily about his rights as a British subject. Lady Braceley lamented and referred to persons in high places to whom she commanded immediate access. She was silenced at last by her nephew, who muttered and cajoled. She shed tears which she dexterously manipulated with the folded edge of her handkerchief.

The Major seemed to be sensibly influenced by the information that additional expenses would be met. He subsided into a sullen and wary acquiescence.

Grant, Sophy and the Van der Veghels were temperate in their reactions. What, as the Baroness rhetorically and vaguely asked, could one do against Fate? Her husband, at a more realistic level, said that while it was inconvenient, it was at the same time obligatory upon them to remain *in situ* if circumstances seemed to require their presence.

Grant said impatiently that he had intended to stay in Rome anyway and Sophy said her holiday extended over the next four weeks. While she had made vague plans for Perugia and Florence she was perfectly ready to postpone them.

They broke up at half past one. The travellers, with the exception of Grant and Sophy, availed themselves of the large car provided by Valdarno. Alleyn had a brief talk with the Questore and with appropriate regrets declined an invitation for luncheon. He had, he said, to write a report.

When he finally emerged from the building he found Grant and Sophy waiting for him.

'I want to talk to you,' Grant said.

'By all means. Will you have lunch with me?' Alleyn made a bow to Sophy. 'Both of you? Do.'

'Not me,' Sophy said. 'I'm only a hanger-on.'

'You're nothing of the sort,' Grant contradicted.

'Well, whatever I am, I've got a date for lunch. So – thank you, Mr Alleyn – but I must be off.'

And before they could do anything to stop her she had in fact darted across the street and stopped a taxi.

'A lady of incisive action,' Alleyn remarked.

'She is indeed.'

'Here's another cab. Shall we go?'

They lunched at Alleyn's hotel. He caught himself wondering if to Grant the occasion seemed like a rendering in another key of his no doubt habitual acceptance of expense-account hospitality.

Alleyn was a good host. He made neither too much nor too little of the business of ordering and when that was done, talked about the difficulties of adjusting oneself to Rome and the dangers of a surfeit of sightseeing. He asked Grant if he'd had to do a great deal of research for *Simon in Latium*.

'Of course,' Alleyn said, 'it's bloody cheek to say so, but it always seemed to me that a novelist who has set his book in a foreign environment is, in some sort, like an investigating officer. I mean, in my job one is for ever having to "get up" information, to take in all sorts of details – technical, occupational, indigenous, whatever you like – in surroundings that are quite outside one's experience. It's a matter of mugging up.'

'It certainly was in the case of *Simon in Latium*.'

'You must have stayed in Rome for some time, surely?'

'Two months,' Grant said, shortly. He laid down his knife and fork. 'As a matter of fact it's about that – in a way – that I want to talk to you.'

'Do you? Fair enough. Now?'

Grant thought for a moment or two. 'It's a poor compliment to a superb luncheon but – now, if you please.'

So he told Alleyn how Sebastian Mailer found his manuscript and about the sequel.

'I think I know *now* how he'd worked the whole job. When he found the MS he got his idea. He picked the lock of my case and read the book. He spent three days concocting his *Angelo in August*. He didn't make it blatantly like *Simon*. Just introduced my major theme as a minor one. Enough to make me talk about it in front of his revolting chums.

'He took me on a night-crawl, fetching up at the place you went to last night – Toni's. I don't remember much about the later part of the experience but enough to make me wish I'd forgotten the lot. Apparently I talked about the "resemblance" at the restaurant we went to – Il Eremo it's called – and to some American chum of his who would be delighted to blow it to the Press.

'I went back to England. The book came out and three weeks ago I returned to Rome, as he knew I would. I ran into him and he took me into a ghastly little parlour in the Van der Veghels' hotel and blackmailed me. He was quite shameless. He practically said, in so many words, that he'd rehashed his story so that now it was blatantly like mine and that he had witnesses from – that night – to say I'd talked about the resemblance when I was drunk. One of them, he said, was the Roman correspondent for the *News of the World* and would make a big splash with the story. Oh yes!' Grant said when Alleyn opened his mouth. 'Oh yes. I know. Why didn't I tell him to go to hell? You may not remember – why should you? – what happened over my first book.'

'I remember.'

'And so would a great many other people. Nobody except my publishers and a few friends believed that bloody business was a coincidence. The case would be hauled into the light again. All the filthy show re-hashed and me established as a shameless plagiarist. I may be a louse but I couldn't face it.'

'What did he ask?'

'That's the point. Not so much, in a way. Just that I took on these unspeakable tours.'

'It wouldn't have stopped there, you know. He was easing you in. Why did you decide to tell me all this?'

'It's just got too much. I told Sophy about it and she suggested I tell you. After the meeting was over and we waited outside. It's an extraordinary thing,' Grant said, 'I met that girl yesterday. It's by no means a quick take, she's not that sort. And yet . . . Well,' Grant said, giving it up, 'there you are. You tell us your main interest in him is as a drug-runner. He turns out to be a murderer. I daresay it's only of academic interest that he happens to be a blackmailer as well.'

'Oh, everything is grist that comes to our grubby little mill,' Alleyn said. 'I'm in a damn tricky sort of position myself, you know. I've learnt this morning that the Roman police have found out Mailer's definitely a British subject. That, in a vague way, keeps me in the picture but with a shift of emphasis: my masters sent me here on the drug-running lay and I find myself landed with the presumptive murder of an Italian.'

'So your presence in yesterday's ongoings was not accidental?'

'No. Not.'

'I may as well tell you, Alleyn, I'm not as keen as mustard for you to catch Mailer.'

'I suppose not. You're afraid, aren't you, that if he's brought to trial he'll blow the story of your alleged plagiarism?'

'All right. Yes. I am. I don't expect you to understand. The police,' Grant said savagely, 'are not exactly famous for their sympathy with the arts.'

'On the other hand they are acquainted with a tendency on the part of the general public, artistic or otherwise, to separate what is laughingly called justice from the concept of enlightened self-interest.'

'I imagine,' Grant said after a sufficient pause, 'that my face could scarcely be redder.'

'Don't give it another thought. As for your fear of a phoney exposure, I think I can promise you it is absolutely groundless.'

'You can? You really can do that?'

'I believe so. I'd take long odds on it.'

'I suppose the whole thing, from the police point of view, is entirely beside the point.'

'You may put it like that,' Alleyn said. 'How about a liqueur with our coffee?'

II

The next two days went by without incident. Mr Mailer's guests followed, Alleyn presumed, their own inclinations. He himself wrote up a detailed report on the case and sent a précis of it to his masters. He had three indeterminate conversations with Valdarno and put a call through to London asking for detailed reports on Lady Braceley and Kenneth Dorne and a check through the Army lists on Major Hamilton Sweet. He also asked for the appropriate branch to make inquiries through the Dutch authorities about the Van der Veghels.

On the third day Rome was engulfed in a heat wave. Pavements, walls and the sky itself quivered under its onslaught and the high saints extended their stone arms above the city in a shimmer that resembled movement. Alleyn lunched in the hotel and spent a good deal of time wondering how Fox was prospering in London.

The Latin siesta is a civilized habit. At its best it puts the sweltering heat of the day behind insect-proof barriers, gives people a rest from excitedly haranguing each other and causes a lull in the nervous activity of the streets.

For Alleyn the siesta was not a blessing. Trained to do with less sleep than most persons require and, when necessary, to catch what he could get in cat-naps and short periods of oblivion, he found the three odd hours of disengagement an irritant rather than a tranquillizer.

He stripped, slept soundly for an hour, took a shower and, freshly dressed, went out into the street.

Rome was under a haze and the Spanish Steps were deserted. No ambiguous youths displayed on their accepted beat. Flowers blazed under protective canvas or drooped where the sun had found them. All the shops down in the Via Condotti were shut and so was the travel agency where Alleyn had booked his tour.

He walked down the steps: not quite the only person abroad in the heat of the day. Ahead of him at intervals were a belated shop-girl, a workman, an old woman and – having apparently come from the hotel – Giovanni Vecchi! Alleyn took cover behind an awning. Giovanni went on down the steps and into the Via Condotti. Alleyn followed cautiously. Giovanni stopped.

Alleyn's instant sidestep into the entrance of a closed shop was a reflex action. He watched Giovanni between two handbags in the corner window. Giovanni glanced quickly up and down the street, and then at his watch. A taxi appeared, stopped at a house almost opposite the shop and discharged its fare. Giovanni hailed it and came back to meet it.

Alleyn moved farther into the doorway and turned his back. He heard Giovanni say 'Il Eremo' and name the street.

The door slammed, the taxi rattled off and Alleyn, looking in vain for another, set off at a gruelling pace for Navona.

Arriving there some ten minutes later, he made his way down an alley smelling of cooking oil and garlic.

There it was: the little trattoria with kerbside caffè where a year ago Mailer and Grant had dined together. The door into the restaurant was shut and the blinds were drawn. Chairs had been tipped forward over the outside tables. The place at first sight seemed to be quite deserted.

As Alleyn drew cautiously nearer, however, he saw that two men were seated at a table in a shadowed corner under the awning and that one of them was Giovanni. They had their backs towards him but there was no mistaking Giovanni's companion.

It was Major Sweet.

Alleyn had arrived at a yard belonging to a junk shop of the humbler sort. Bad pictures, false renaissance chairs, one or two restored pieces ruined by a deluge of cheap varnish. A large dilapidated screen. He moved into the shelter of the screen and surveyed Major Sweet and Giovanni through the hinged gap between two leaves.

Major Sweet, from the rear, looked quite unlike himself: there was something about his back and the forward tilt of his head that suggested extreme alertness. A slight movement and his cheek, the end of his moustache and his right eye came into view. The eye was cocked backwards: the eye of a watchful man. Giovanni leant towards the Major and talked. No Italian can talk without hands and Giovanni's were active but, as it were, within a restricted field. The Major folded his arms and seemed to wait.

Could he, Alleyn wondered, be arranging with Giovanni for a further instalment of the other night's excesses? Somehow the two of them didn't look quite like that. They looked, he thought, as if they drove some other kind of bargain and he hoped he wasn't being too fanciful about them.

He saw that by delicate manoeuvring he could cross the yard,
edge up to a bin with a polyglot collection of papers under a tall
cupboard and thus bring himself much nearer to the caffè. He did so,
slid a disreputable but large map out of the bin and held it in front
of him in case they suddenly came his way. Lucky, he thought, that
he'd changed his shoes and trousers.

They spoke in English. Their voices dropped and rose and he
caught only fragments of what they said, as if a volume control were
being turned up and down by some irresponsible hand.

'. . . waste of time talking . . . you better understand, Vecchi . . .
danger. Ziegfeldt . . .'

'. . . are you mad? How many times I tell you . . . instructions . . .'

'. . . search . . . police . . .'

'. . . OK, Signore. So they search and find nothing . . . I have
made . . . "arrangements" . . .'

'. . . *arrangements*. Try that on Alleyn and see what . . . Different . . .
Take it from me . . . I *can* do it. And I will. Unless . . .'

'. . . drunk . . .'

'. . . nothing to do with it. Not so drunk I didn't know . . . It's a
fair offer. Make it right for me or . . .'

'You dare not.'

'Don't you believe it. Look here . . . if I report . . . Ziegfeldt . . .'

'*Taci!*'

'Shut up.'

A savage-sounding but muted exchange followed. Finally
Giovanni gave a sharp ejaculation. Chair legs grated on the
pavement. A palm was slapped down on the table. Alleyn, greatly
stimulated, squatted behind the ruin of a velvet chair and heard
them go past. Their footsteps died away and he came out of cover.
Somewhere behind a shuttered window a man yawned vocally and
prodigiously. Farther along the street a door opened. A youth in
singlet and trousers lounged out, scratching his armpits. A woman
inside the trattoria called with an operatic flourish, 'Mar–cel–lo.'

The siesta was over.

It was a long time since Alleyn had 'kept observation' on anybody
and like Il Questore Valdarno, he didn't altogether object to an
unexpected return to fieldwork.

It was not an easy job. The streets were still sparsely populated and offered little cover. He watched and waited until his men had walked about two hundred yards, saw them part company and decided to follow the Major who had turned into a side alley in that part of Old Rome devoted to the sale of 'antiques'.

Here in the dealers' occupational litter it was easier going and by the time they had emerged from the region Alleyn was close behind the Major, who was headed, he realized, in the direction of his small hotel where they had deposited him in the early hours of the morning.

All that for nothing, thought Alleyn.

The Major entered the hotel. Alleyn followed as far as the glass door, watched him go to the reception-desk, collect a key and move away, presumably to a lift.

Alleyn went in, entered a telephone booth opposite the lift and rang up Valdarno as he had arranged to do at this hour. He gave the Questore a succinct account of the afternoon's work.

'This Major, hah? This Sweet? Not quite as one supposed, hah?' said the Questore.

'So it would seem.'

'What is your interpretation?'

'I got a very fragmentary impression, you know. But it points, don't you think, to Major Sweet's connection with Ziegfeldt and in a greater or less degree with the Mailer enterprise?'

'Undoubtedly. As for the premises – this Toni's – Bergarmi conducted a search yesterday afternoon.'

'And found –?'

'Nothing. There was evidence of hurried proceedings but no more.'

'The stuff they sold me was in a very small office near the main entrance.'

'It is empty of everything but a cashbox, ledger and telephone directory. There is no lead at all so far as Mailer is concerned. We are satisfied he has not left Rome. As you know, I set a watch of the most exhaustive, immediately after you telephoned.'

If Alleyn felt less sanguine than the Questore under this heading he did not say so.

'I think,' Valdarno was saying, 'we tug in this Giovanni Vecchi. I think we have little talks with him. You say he spoke of "arrangements". What arrangements do you suppose?'

'Hard to say,' Alleyn cautiously replied. 'I seemed to smell bribery. Of a particular kind.'

There was a longish silence. He thought that perhaps it would be tactful not to mention Major Sweet's remark about himself.

'And your next move, my dear colleague?'

'Perhaps while your people have their little talk with Giovanni Vecchi, I have one with Major Sweet. And after that, Signor Questore, I'm afraid I'm going to suggest that perhaps – a close watch on the Major?'

'Where are you?'

'At his hotel. The Benvenuto.'

'That will be done. There is,' Valdarno confessed, 'some confusion. On the one hand we have the trade in illicit drugs which is your concern. On the other the murder of Violetta which is also ours. And Mailer who is the key figure in both. One asks oneself: is there a further interlockment? With the travellers? Apart, of course, from their reluctance to become involved in any publicity arising out of our proceedings. Otherwise, between the murder and these seven travellers there is no connection?'

'I wouldn't say that,' Alleyn said. 'Oh, my dear Signor Questore, I wouldn't say that, you know. Not by a long chalk.'

When he had explained this point-of-view he hung up the receiver and took counsel with himself. At last, by no means sure that he was doing the right thing, he went to the reception desk and sent up his name to Major Sweet.

III

It was hard to believe that this was the same man who, half an hour ago, had muttered away with Giovanni. The Major was right back on the form that Alleyn had suspected from the first to be synthetic. There he sat in his impeccable squarish light-weight suit, wearing an RA tie, a signet ring, brown brogues polished like chestnuts and the evidence of a mighty hangover in his bloodshot eyes. The hangover, at least, was not assumed. Perhaps none of it was assumed. Perhaps the Major was all he seemed to be and all of it gone to the bad.

'Glad you looked in, Alleyn,' he said. 'I hoped to have a word with you.'

'Really?'

'Only to say that if I can be of use I'll be delighted. Realize you're in a difficult position. Treading on foreign protocol corns, what? Don't suppose there's much I can do but such as I am – here I am. Services ought to stick together, what?'

'You're a Gunner, I see.'

'*Was*, old man. *Was*. Retired list now but still good for a spell of duty, I hope.' He gave a sly comradely laugh. 'In spite of the other night. Mustn't judge me by that, you know. Bad show. Rather fun once in a while, though, what?'

'You're not a regular patron of Mr Mailer's then?'

A fractional pause, before Major Sweet said, 'Of *Mailer's*? Oh, see what you mean. Or do I? Can't stomach the feller, actually. Picked him for a wrong 'un straight off. Still, I must say that show was well-run even if I did look on the wine when it was red, but let that go.'

'I wasn't talking about alcohol. I meant hard drugs. Heroin. Cocaine.'

'I say, look here! You're not telling me they've been pushing that rot-gut at Toni's Pad! I mean regularly.'

'And you're not telling me you didn't know.'

The Major took an appreciably longer pause before he said with quiet dignity, 'That was uncalled for.'

'I would have thought it was obvious enough.'

'Not to me, sir. Hold on, though. Wait a bit. You're referring to that ghastly youth: Dorne. Sorry I spoke. Good lord, yes, I knew what *he* was up to, of course. You brought it all out next morning. Very neatly done if I may say so, though as a matter of fact I dozed off a bit. Didn't get the hang of all that was said.'

'This isn't your first visit to Rome, is it?'

'Oh no. No. I was here on active service in 1943. And once or twice since. Never got hold of the lingo.'

'How long have you known Giovanni Vecchi?'

The beetroot ran out of the Major's carefully shaven jaw leaving the plum behind but only in this respect could he be said to change countenance. 'Giovanni how much?' he said. 'Oh. You mean the courier fellow.'

'Yes. The courier fellow. He's in the drug business with Mailer.'

'Good lord, you don't say so!'

'I do, you know. They're tied up,' Alleyn said, mentally taking a deep breath, 'with Otto Ziegfeldt.'

'Who's he?' asked the Major in a perfectly toneless voice. 'Some dago?'

'He's the biggest of the drug barons.'

'You don't tell me.'

'I don't think I need to, do I?'

'What you need to do,' said the Major and his voice jumped half an octave, 'is explain yourself. I'm getting sick of this.'

'Ziegfeldt imports morphine from Turkey. The usual route, by diverse means, is from Izmir via Sicily to the USA. During the past year, however, an alternative route has developed: to Naples by a Lebanese shipping line and thence by Italian coastal traders to Marseilles, where it is converted to heroin. Ziegfeldt established an agent in Naples whose job was to arrange and supervise the trans-shipments. We believe this man to have been Sebastian Mailer.'

Alleyn waited for a moment. They sat in the deserted smoking-room of the hotel. It smelt of furniture polish and curtains and was entirely without character. Major Sweet rested his elbow on the arm of his uncomfortable chair and his cheek on his hand. He might have been given over to some aimless meditation.

'It appears,' Alleyn said, 'that at one time Mailer was married to the woman Violetta. Probably she acted for him in some minor capacity. Subsequently he deserted her.'

'Now,' said the Major into the palm of his hand, 'you're talking. Threatened to expose him.'

'Very likely.'

'Killed her.'

'Highly probable.'

'There you are, then.'

'Ziegfeldt doesn't at all care for agents who help themselves to goods in transit and then set up on their own account.'

'Dare say not.'

'He has them, as a general practice, bumped off. By another agent. He sets a spy upon them. Sometimes the spy is too greedy. He extorts a pay-off from – say – Giovanni? On consideration that he will not betray Giovanni and Mailer to his master. And then, unless he is very clever indeed, he is found out by his master and he too gets bumped off.'

A little bead of sweat trickled down Sweet's forehead and got hung up in his eyebrow.

'The Gunners were not in Italy in 1943. They arrived in '44,' said Alleyn. 'Where do you buy your ties?'

' – slip of the tongue, 'forty-four.'

'All right,' Alleyn said and stood up. 'How many times can a man double-cross,' he asked of nobody in particular, 'before he loses count? What's your price?'

Sweet raised his head and stared at him.

'I wouldn't try to bolt either. You know your own business best, of course, but Otto Ziegfeldt has a long arm. So, for a matter of fact, have Interpol and even the London Police Force.'

Sweet dabbed his mouth and forehead with a neatly folded hand-kerchief. 'You're making a mistake,' he said. 'You're on the wrong track.'

'I heard you talking to Giovanni Vecchi in the Eremo caffè at a quarter to four this afternoon.'

A very singular noise came from somewhere inside the massive throat. For the first time Sweet looked fixedly at Alleyn. He mouthed rather than said: 'I don't know what you're talking about.'

'I have the advantage of you, there. I do know what you and Vecchi were talking about. Come,' Alleyn said. 'You'll do yourself no good by keeping this up. Understand me. I'm here in Rome to find out what I can about Otto Ziegfeldt's operations. I'm not here to run in his lesser agents unless by doing so I can carry my job a step further.' He thought for a moment and then said, 'And of course, unless such an agent commits some action that in itself warrants his immediate arrest. I think I know what you've been up to. I think you've been sent by Ziegfeldt to spy upon Mailer and Giovanni Vecchi and report on their side-activities in Italy. I think you've double-crossed Ziegfeldt and played along with Mailer and Giovanni and now Mailer's disappeared you're afraid he may put you away with Ziegfeldt. I think you threatened to betray Giovanni to Ziegfeldt unless he pays you off in a big way. And I think you plan to clear up and get out while the going's good. You haven't a hope. You're in a pretty ugly situation, one way and another, aren't you? The safest thing for you, after all, might be for the Roman police to lock you up. The Roman streets won't be too healthy for you.'

'What do you want?'

'A complete list of Ziegfeldt's agents and a full account of his *modus operandi* between Izmir and the USA. Step by step. With particular respect to Mailer.'

'I can't. I don't know. I – I'm not – I'm not as deeply committed – '

'Or trusted? Perhaps not. But you're fairly far in or you wouldn't have been given your present job.'

'I can't do it, Alleyn.'

'Giovanni is being questioned.'

'Give me time.'

'No.'

'I want a drink.'

'You may have a drink. Shall we go to your room?'

'All right,' said Sweet. 'All right, God damn you, all right.'

IV

When Alleyn got back to his hotel he found a note from Lady Braceley under his door and a message that 'Fox' had rung from London and would ring again at six. The time was now 5.15. Lady Braceley wrote a large, mad hand that spilled all over the paper.

'Must see you,' said the note. 'Terribly urgent. Desperate. Please, *please* come to this apartment as soon as possible. If you see K. *say nothing*. S.B.'

'This,' Alleyn said to himself, 'is going to be the bottom. Bullying a phoney Major is a pastoral symphony compared to the tune Lady B.'s going to call.'

He tore up the note and went to the apartment.

She received him, predictably, on a chaise-longue, wearing a gold lamé trouser suit. A hard-featured maid let him in and withdrew, presumably into the bedroom.

Lady Braceley swung her feet to the floor and held out her hands. 'Oh God!' she said. 'You've come. Oh bless you, bless you, bless you.'

'Not at all,' Alleyn said, and glanced at the bedroom door.

'It's all right. Swiss. Doesn't speak a word of English.'

'What is it, Lady Braceley? Why do you want to see me?'

'It's in deadly confidence. *Deadly*. If Kenneth knew I was telling you I don't know what he'd say to me. But I just can't take this sort of thing. It kills me. He won't come in. He knows I always rest until six and then he always rings first. We're safe.'

'Perhaps you'll explain – '

'Of course. It's just that I'm so nervous and upset. I don't know *what* you're going to say.'

'Nor,' Alleyn said lightly, 'do I. Until I hear what it's all about.'

'It's about him. Kenneth. And me. It's – oh, he's been so naughty and stupid, I can't *think* what possessed him. And now – if you *knew* where he's landed us.'

'What has he done?'

'I don't follow it all. Well, first of all he behaved very badly in Perugia. He got into a wild set and ran out of money, it appears, and – oh, I don't know – sold something he hadn't paid for. And that wretched murderer Mailer got him out of it. Or said he had. And then – when we were in that ghastly church, Mailer spoke to me about it and said the police – the *police* – were making a fuss and unless he could "satisfy" them it would all come out and Kenneth would be – imagine it! – arrested. He wanted £500 paid into some bank somewhere. All I had to do was to write an open cheque and he would – what's the word – negotiate the whole thing and we could forget it.'

'Did you write this cheque?'

'Not there and then. He said he would hold the police off for two days and call for the cheque at midday today. And then, of course, there was this thing about his disappearing and all the murder horror. And then Giovanni – you know? – rather sweet, or so I thought. Giovanni said he knew all about it and he would arrange everything only now it would be more expensive. And he came in here after lunch today and said the situation was more difficult than he had understood from Mailer and he would want £800 in lire or it might be easier if I let him have some jewellery instead. And I've got rather a famous tiara thing my second husband gave me only it's in the bank here. And quite a lot of rings. He seemed to know all about my jewellery.'

'Did you give him anything?'

'Yes. I did. I gave him my diamond and emerald sunburst. It's insured for £900, I think. I've never really liked it frightfully. But still – '

'Lady Braceley, why are you telling me all this?'

'Because,' she said, 'I'm frightened. I'm just frightened. I'm out of my depth. Kenneth behaves so oddly and, clearly, he's got himself into the most hideous mess. And although I'm awfully fond of him I don't think it's fair to land me in it, too. And I can't cope. I feel desperately ill. That place – I don't know whether you – anyway they gave me something to turn me on and it wasn't anything like they tell you it'll be. It was too awful. Mr Alleyn, please, *please* be kind and help me.'

She wept and chattered and dabbed at him with her awful claws. In a moment, he thought, she'll take off into the full hysteria bit.

'You're ill,' he said. 'Is there anything I can get you?'

'Over there. In the drinks place. Tablets. And brandy.'

He found them and poured out a moderate amount of brandy. She made a sad botch of shaking out three tablets. He had to help her. 'Are you sure you should take three?' he asked. She nodded, crouched over her hand, gulped and swallowed the brandy. 'Tranquillizers,' she said. 'Prescription.'

For a minute or so she sat with her eyes closed, shivering. 'I'm sorry. Do have a drink,' she offered in a travesty of her social voice.

He paid no attention to this. When she had opened her eyes and found her handkerchief he said, 'I'll do what I can. I think it's unlikely that your nephew is in danger of arrest. I'll find out about it. In the meantime you mustn't think of giving anything else to Giovanni. He is blackmailing you and he will certainly not carry out any negotiations with the police. But I don't think he will come. It's highly possible that he himself is under arrest. I'll leave you now but before I go tell me one thing. Your nephew did meet Mailer that afternoon by the statue of Apollo, didn't he?'

'I think so.'

'To collect his drugs?'

'I think so.'

'For any other purpose, do you know? Did he tell you?'

'I – think – he'd seen Mailer talking to me and he'd seen I was upset. And – I think he wanted to find out if – if – '

'If you'd agreed to pay up?' She nodded.

'When your nephew appears,' Alleyn said grimly, 'will you tell him I want to see him? I will be in my room, 149, for the next hour. And I think, Lady Braceley, you should go to bed. Shall I call your maid?'

'She'll come.'

She was gazing at him now with an intensity that appalled him. She suddenly burst into an incoherent babble of thanks and since there seemed no hope of stemming the flood, he left her, still talking, and returned to his room.

V

Inspector Fox came through, loud and clear at six o'clock. The department had been expeditious in collecting information about the travellers. The Dutch Embassy and the London representative of Messrs Adriaan and Welker had confirmed the Van der Veghels' account of themselves: an ancient family, a strict Lutheran background conforming with the evangelical policy of the firm.

'Very strict in their attitudes,' Fox said. 'Puritanical, you might say. The lady I talked to in their London office is one of the modern sort. Groovy. She said that the Baron's a very different type from his father who was what they call a "sport". In both senses. A bit of a lad. Edwardian playboy type and notorious in his day. She said there are some very funny stories they tell in the firm about the Baron coming face to face with himself and cutting himself dead. She said they live very quietly. In Geneva mostly. The Baroness writes some kind of religious tales for kids but she never accompanies him to The Hague and is thought to be delicate.'

Fox enlarged cosily upon his theme. Believed to be distantly related to her husband, the Baroness, it was understood, belonged to an expatriate branch of the family. The nature of the Baron's work for the firm obliged them to live abroad. A highly respected and unblemished record.

Lady Braceley: 'Nothing in our way, really,' said Fox, 'unless you count a 1937 Ascot weekend scandal. She was an unwilling witness. Recently, just the usual stuff about elderly ladies in the jet set. Do you want the list of husbands?'

'She'd love to tell me herself but – all right. In case.'

He took them down.

'The nephew's different,' said Fox. 'He's a naughty boy. Sacked from his school for pot-parties and sex. Three convictions for speeding. Got off on a charge of manslaughter but only just. Accident resulting from high jinks at what was called a "gay pad".'

'Press on, Br'er Fox.'

'This Sweet, Hamilton. Major. There's no Major Hamilton Sweet in the Royal Artillery or any other Army lists for the given period. So we looked up recent cases of False Pretences and Fraud, Army Officers, masquerading as. Less popular than it used to be.'

'See British possessions, armed forces, for the use of. Dwindling.'

'That's right. Well, anyway we looked. And came up with James Stanley Hamilton who answers to your description. Three fraudulent company affairs and two Revenue charges involving drugs. Known to have left the country. Wanted.'

'That, as they say in the late-night imported serials, figures. Thank you, Br'er Fox.'

'You mentioned Mr Barnaby Grant and Miss Sophy Jason. Nothing apart from what you know. You seem to be in a funny sort of *milieu*, Mr Alleyn,' said Fox who spoke French, '*n'est-ce pas?*'

'It gets funnier every second. *Mille remerciements, Frère Renard*, and why the hell aren't you speaking Italian? Goodnight to you.'

Bergarmi rang up to say the Questore had told him to report. They had pulled in Giovanni Vecchi but had not persuaded him to talk. Bergarmi thought Giovanni might be hiding Mailer and almost certainly knew where he was, but had no hard facts to support what seemed to be merely a hunch. They would continue to hold Vecchi. Alleyn again reflected upon the apparently wide divergences between Italian and British police procedure. He asked Bergarmi if he had made any inquiries as to Kenneth Dorne's activities in Perugia. Bergarmi had done so and found that a complaint had been made to the police by a jeweller about a cigarette case but the man had been repaid and the charge withdrawn. There had been no further developments.

'I thought as much,' Alleyn said.

He then told Bergarmi of his interview with Sweet. 'I've got a list of Ziegfeldt's top agents from him,' he said. 'I think it's genuine. He's been playing the double-agent between Ziegfeldt and Mailer and now he's got very cold feet.'

Bergarmi said he would have the Major watched. An arrest at this juncture would probably prove unfruitful but under obvious supervision he might crack and do something revealing: clearly Bergarmi now regarded the Major as his most fruitful source of information. He added that with the material Alleyn had obtained, no doubt his mission in Rome had been accomplished. There was no mistaking the satisfaction in Bergarmi's voice. Alleyn said that you might put it like that, he supposed, and they rang off.

As he intended to dine in the hotel, he changed into a dinner-jacket. At half past seven Kenneth Dorne came to see him. His manner slithered about between resentment, shamefacedness and sheer funk.

Alleyn ran through Kenneth's record as supplied by Fox and asked him if it was substantially correct. Kenneth said he supposed so. 'Anyway,' he said, 'you've made up your mind so there's no point in saying it's not.'

'None whatever.'

'Very well, then. What's the object in my coming here?'

'Briefly: this. I want to know what happened between you and Mailer by the Apollo, the other day. No,' Alleyn said and lifted a hand, 'don't lie again. You'll do yourself a lot of damage if you persist. You met him by arrangement to collect your supply of heroin and cocaine. But you also wanted to find out whether he'd been successful in blackmailing Lady Braceley on your behalf. Perhaps that's a harsh way of putting it but it's substantially what happened. You had got yourself into trouble in Perugia, Mailer had purported to get you out of it. Knowing your talent for sponging on your aunt, he came again with completely false stories of police activity and the necessity for bribery on a large scale. He told you, no doubt, that Lady Braceley had promised to comply. Do you deny any of this?'

'No comment,' said Kenneth.

'My sole concern is to get a statement from you about your parting with Mailer and where he went – in what direction – when he left

you. Your wits,' Alleyn said, 'are not so befuddled with narcotics that
you don't understand me. This man has not only made a fool of you
and robbed your aunt. He has murdered an old woman. I suppose you
know the penalty for comforting and abetting a murderer.'

'Is this Roman law?' Kenneth sneered in a shaking voice.

'You're a British subject. So is Mailer. You don't want him caught,
do you? You're afraid of exposure.'

'No!'

'Then tell me where he went when he left you.' At first Alleyn
thought Kenneth was going to break down, then that he was going
to refuse, but he did neither of these things. He gazed dolefully at
Alleyn for several seconds and appeared to gain some kind of initia-
tive. He folded his white hands over his mouth, bit softly at his
fingers and put his head on one side. At last he talked and, having
begun, seemed to find a release in doing so.

He said that when Mailer had fixed him up with his supply of
heroin and cocaine he had 'had himself a pop'. He carried his own
syringe and Mailer, guessing he would be avid for it, had provided
him with an ampoule of water and helped him. He adjusted the
tourniquet, using Kenneth's scarf for the purpose. 'Seb,' Kenneth
said, 'is fabulous – you know – it's not easy till you get the knack.
Finding the right spot. So he cooked up and fixed me, there and
then, and I felt fantastic. He said I'd better carry on with the party.'

They had walked together round the end of the old church and
arrived at the iron stairway. Mailer had gone down the stairway into
the insula with Kenneth but instead of entering the Mithraeum had
continued along the cloister in the direction of the well.

Kenneth, saturated, Alleyn gathered, in a rising flood of well-
being, had paused at the entry into the Mithraeum and idly watched
Mailer. Having got so far in his narrative he ran the tip of his tongue
round his lips and, eyeing Alleyn with what actually seemed to be a
kind of relish, said:

'Surprise, surprise.'

'What do you mean?'

'I saw it. Again. The same as what the Jason dolly saw. You know.
The shadow.'

'Violetta's.'

'Across the thing. You know. The sarcophagus.'

'Then you saw her?'

'No, I didn't. I suppose he was between. I don't know. I was high. There's a kind of buttress thing juts out. Anyway I was high.'

'So high, perhaps, that you imagined the whole thing.'

'*No*,' Kenneth said loudly. '*No*.'

'And then?'

'I went into that marvellous place. The temple or whatever. There you were. All of you. On about the god. And the great grinning Baroness lining us up for a team-photograph. And all the time,' Kenneth said excitedly, 'all the time just round the corner, Seb was strangling the postcard woman. Wouldn't it send you!' He burst out laughing.

Alleyn looked at him. 'You can't always have been as bad as this,' he said. 'Or are you simply a born, stupid, unalterable monster? How big a hand has Mailer taken with his H. and C. and his thoughtful ever-ready ampoule of distilled water in the making of the product?'

Kenneth's smile still hung about his mouth even as he began to whimper.

'Shut up,' Alleyn said mildly. 'Don't do that. Pull yourself together if you can.'

'I'm a spoilt boy. I know that. I never had a chance. I was spoilt.'

'How old are you?'

'Twenty-three. Someone like you could have helped me. Truly.'

'Did you get any idea of why Mailer didn't go into the Mithraeum with you? Was he expecting to meet the woman?'

'No. No, I'm sure he wasn't,' Kenneth said eagerly, gazing at Alleyn. 'I'm telling the truth,' he added with a dreadful imitation of a chidden little boy. 'I'm trying to be good. And I'll tell you something else. To show.'

'Go on.'

'He told me why he wouldn't come in.'

'Why?'

'He had a date. With someone else.'

'Who?'

'He didn't say. I'd tell you if I knew. He didn't say. But he had a date. Down there in that place. He told me.'

The telephone rang.

When Alleyn answered it he received an oddly familiar sensation: an open silence broken by the distant and hollow closure of a door, a suggestion of space and emptiness. He was not altogether surprised when a rich voice asked: 'Would this be Mr Alleyn?'

'It would, Father.'

'You mentioned this morning where you were to be found. Are you alone, now?'

'No.'

'No. Well, we'll say no more under that heading. I've called upon you, Mr Alleyn, in preference to anybody else, on account of a matter that has arisen. It may be no great matter and it may be all to the contrary.'

'Yes?'

'If it's not putting too much upon you I'd be very greatly obliged if you'd be kind enough to look in at the basilica.'

'Of course. Is it –?'

'Well now, it may be. It may be and then again it may not and to tell you the truth I'm loath to call down a great concourse of the pollis upon me and then it turning out to be a rat.'

'A rat, Father Denys?'

'Or rats. The latter is more like it. Over the head of the strength.'

'The strength, did you say?'

'I did that. The strength of the aroma.'

'I'll be with you,' Alleyn said, 'in fifteen minutes.'

His professional homicide kit was in the bottom of his wardrobe. He took it with him.

CHAPTER 8

Return of Sebastian Mailer

S. Tommaso in Pallaria looked different after sunset. Its façade was dark against a darkening sky and its windows only faintly illuminated from within. Its entrance where Violetta had cursed Sebastian Mailer was quite given over to shadows and its doors were shut.

Alleyn was wondering how he would get in when Father Denys moved out of the shadows.

'Good evening and God bless you,' he said.

He opened a little pass-door in the great entry and led the way in.

The smell of incense and hot candles seemed more noticeable in the dark. Galaxies of small flaming spearheads burned motionless before the saints. A ruby lamp glowed above the high altar. It was a place fully occupied within itself. A positive place.

Brother Dominic came out of the Sacristy and they walked into the vestibule with its shrouded stalls. The lights were on in there and it felt stuffy.

'It's like enough a fool's errand I've brought you on and you maybe not eaten yet,' said Father Denys. 'I may tell you it's not been done without the authority of my Superior.'

'I'm entirely at your service, Father.'

'Thank you, my son. We've had this sort of trouble before, d'ye see, over the head of the excavations and all. Rat trouble. Though Brother Dominic's been after them in a very big way and it was our belief they were exterminated. And wouldn't we look the fools if we'd stirred up Signor Bergarmi and his body of men and they fully occupied with their task?'

'Shall we have a look where the trouble seems to be?'

'A look is it? A smell, more likely. But come along, come along.'

As he made that downward journey for the third time, it seemed to Alleyn that in its quiet way it was one of the strangest he had ever taken. A monk, a lay-brother and himself, descending, if one cared to be fanciful, through a vertical section of the past.

When they reached the cloisters on the second level, Brother Dominic, who had not yet uttered, turned on the fluorescent lights and back into their immovable liveliness sprang the Apollo and the Mercury.

Down the iron spiral: two pairs of sandals and one pair of leather soles with the ever-mounting sound of flowing water. The bottom level and a right turn. This was where Kenneth Dorne had parted company with Sebastian Mailer. On their left was the little ante-room into the Mithraeum. Ahead – the lights came on – ahead, the sarcophagus and the railed well.

They walked towards them.

The lid had not been replaced. It stood on its side, leaning against the empty stone coffin where Violetta had been urgently housed.

Father Denys put his hand on Alleyn's arm.

'Now,' he said and they stopped.

'Yes,' Alleyn said.

It declared itself: sweetish, intolerable, unmistakable.

He went on alone, leant over the top rail where he had found a fragment of cloth and looked into the well, using the torch they had given him.

It showed walls in a sharp perspective and at the bottom an indefinable darkness.

'The other day,' he said, 'when I looked down, there was a sort of glint. I took it to be a chance flicker of light on the moving stream.'

'It could be that.'

'What is there – down below?'

'The remains of a stone grille. As old,' Father Denys said, 'as the place itself. Which is seventeen hundred years. We've lowered a light and it revealed nothing that you could call of any consequence but it was too far beneath to be of any great help.'

'The grille is above the surface of the stream?'

'It is. A few inches at the downstream end of the well. And it's the remains only. A fragment you may say.'

'Could something have been carried down by the stream and got caught up in it?'

'It's never been known in the history of this place. The water is pure. Every so often we let down a wee tin and haul up a sample for the testing. There's never been the hint of contamination in it.'

'Can one get down there?'

'Well, now – '

'I think I can see footholds and – yes – '

Brother Dominic spoke. 'You can,' he said.

'Aren't there iron pegs?'

'There are.'

'And they rotten no doubt,' Father Denys urged, 'and falling out like old teeth at the first handling.'

'Have you a rope, Father?'

'Sure, we have them for the excavations. You're not thinking – '

'I'll go down if you'll give me a hand.'

'Dominic, let you fetch a rope.'

'And a head-lamp and overalls,' Brother Dominic ennumerated with a glance at Alleyn's impeccable suit. 'We have them all got. I'll fetch them, Father.'

'Do so.'

'It's unwholesome here,' Father Denys said when Brother Dominic had gone. 'Let us move away for the time being.'

They entered the Mithraeum. Father Denys had switched on the lighting used in visiting hours. The altar glowed. At the far end, the god, lit from beneath, stared out of blank eyes at nothing. They sat on one of the stone benches where in the second century his initiates had sat, wan with their ordeal, their blanched faces painted by the altar fires.

Alleyn thought he would like to ask Father Denys what he made of the Mithraic Cult but when he turned to speak to him found that he was withdrawn into himself. His hands were pressed together and his lips moved.

Alleyn waited for a minute and then, hearing the returning slap of sandals in the cloister, went quickly out by the doorway behind the god. This was the passage by which he and the Van der Veghels had left the Mithraeum. It was very dark indeed and the Baroness had exclaimed at it.

Two right turns brought him back into sight of the well and there was Brother Dominic with ropes, an old-fashioned head-lamp of the sort miners use, a suit of workmen's overalls and a peculiar woolly cap.

'I'm obliged to you, Brother Dominic,' said Alleyn.

'Let you put them on.'

Alleyn did so. Brother Dominic fussed about him. He fixed the head-lamp and with great efficiency made fast one end of the rope round Alleyn's chest and under his shoulders.

Alleyn transferred a minuscule camera from his homicide kit to the pocket of his overalls. After looking about for a minute, Brother Dominic asked Alleyn to help him place the lid of the sarcophagus at right angles across the coffin. It was massive but Brother Dominic was a strong man and made little of it. He passed the slack of the rope twice round the lid, crossing it in the manner of sailors when they wear a rope in lowering a heavy load.

'We could take your weight neat between us,' he said, 'but this will be the better way. Where's Father?'

'In the Mithraeum. Saying his prayers, I think.'

'He would be that.'

'Here he is.'

Father Denys returned looking anxious. 'I hope we are right about this,' he said. 'Are you sure it's safe, now, Dominic?'

'I am, Father.'

'Mr Alleyn, would you not let me place a – a handkerchief over your – eh?'

He hovered anxiously and finally did tie his own large cotton handkerchief over Alleyn's nose and mouth.

The two Dominicans tucked back their sleeves, wetted their palms and took up the rope, Brother Dominic on Alleyn's side of the sarcophagus lid and Father Denys on the far side, close to the turn.

'That's splendid,' Alleyn said. 'I hope I won't have to trouble you. Here I go.'

'God bless you,' they said in their practical way.

He had another look at the wall. The iron pegs went down at fairly regular intervals on either side of one corner. The well itself was six feet by three. Alleyn ducked under the bottom rail, straddled the corner with his back to the well, knelt, took his weight on his forearms, wriggled backwards and groped downwards with his right foot.

'Easy now, easy,' said both the Dominicans. He looked up at Brother Dominic's sandalled feet, at his habit and into his long-lipped Irish face. 'I have you held,' said Brother Dominic and gave a little strain on the rope to show that it was so.

Alleyn's right foot found a peg and rested on it. He tested it, letting himself down little by little. He felt a gritting sensation and a slight movement under his foot but the peg took his weight.

'Seems OK,' he said through Father Denys's handkerchief.

He didn't look up again. His hands, one after the other, relinquished the edge and closed, right and then left, round pegs. One of them tilted, jarred and ground its way out of its centuries-old housing. It was loose in his hand and he let it fall. So long, it seemed, before he heard it hit the water. Now he had only one handhold and his feet but the rope sustained him. He continued down. His face was close to the angle made by the walls and he must be careful lest he knock his head-lamp against stone. It cast a circle of light that made sharp and intimate the pitted surface of the rock. Details of colour, irregularities and growths of some minute lichen passed upwards through the light as he himself so carefully sank.

Already the region above seemed remote and the voices of the Dominicans disembodied. His world was now filled with the sound of running water. He would have smelt water, he thought, if it had not been for that other growing and deadly smell. How far had he gone? Why hadn't he asked Brother Dominic for the actual depth of the well? Thirty feet? More? Would the iron pegs have rusted and rotted in the damper air?

The peg under his left foot gave way. He shouted a warning and his voice reverberated and mingled with Brother Dominic's reply. Then his right foot slipped. He hung by his hands and by the rope. 'Lower away,' he called, released his hold, dangled and dropped in short jerks fending himself clear of the two walls. The voice of the stream was all about him.

A sudden icy cold shock to his feet came as a surprise. They were carried aside. At the same moment he saw and grabbed two pegs at shoulder level. 'Hold it! Hold it! I'm there.'

He was lowered another inch before the rope took up. He scrab-
bled with his feet against the pressure of the stream. The backs of his
legs hit against something hard and firm. He explored with his feet,
lifted them clear of the water and found in a moment with a kind of
astonishment that he was standing on bars that pressed into his feet.

The grille.

A broken grille, the monks had said.

The surface of the stream must be almost level with the bottom of
the well and about an inch below the grille which projected from its
wall. Supporting himself in the angle of the walls, Alleyn contrived
to turn himself about so that he now faced outwards. His head-lamp
showed the two opposite walls. He leant back into the angle, braced
himself and shouted, 'Slack off a little.'

'Slack off, it is,' said the disembodied voice.

He leant forward precariously as the rope gave, shouted 'Hold it!'
and lowered his head so that his lamp illuminated the swift-flowing
black waters, the fragment of grille that he stood upon and his
drenched feet, planted apart and close to its broken fangs.

And between his feet? A third foot ensnared upside down in the
broken fangs: a foot in a black leather shoe.

II

His return to the surface was a bit of a nightmare. Superintendents
of the CID, while they like to keep well above average in physical fit-
ness and have behind them a gruelling and comprehensive training
to this end, are not in the habit of half-scrambling and half-dangling
on the end of a rope in a well. Alleyn's palms burnt, his joints were
banged against rock walls, and once he got a knock on the back of
his head that lit up stars and made him dizzy. Sometimes he walked
horizontally up the wall while the monks hauled in. They do these
things better, he reflected, in crime films.

When he had finally been landed, the three of them sat on the
floor and breathed hard: as odd a little group, it occurred to Alleyn,
as might be imagined.

'You were superb,' he said. 'Thank you.'

'Ah, sure, it was nothing at all,' Father Denys panted. 'Aren't we used to this type of thing in the excavating? It's yourself should have the praise.'

They shared that peculiar sense of fellowship and gratification which is the reward of such exercises.

'Well,' Alleyn said. 'I'm afraid you'll have to ring the Questura, Father. Our man's down there and he's dead.'

'The man Mailer?' Father Denys said when they had crossed themselves. 'God have mercy on his soul.'

'Amen,' said Brother Dominic.

'What's the way of it, Mr Alleyn?'

'As I see it, he probably fell through the well head-first and straight into the stream, missing the broken grille, which, by the way, only extends a few inches from the wall. The stream swept him under the grille, but one foot, the right, was trapped between two of the broken fangs. And there he is, held in the current.'

'How are you sure it's himself?'

'By the shoe and the trouser-leg and because – ' Alleyn hesitated.

'What are you trying to tell us?'

'It was just possible to see his face.'

'There's a terrible thing for you! And so drowned?'

'That,' Alleyn said, 'will no doubt appear in due course.'

'Are you telling us there's been – what are you telling us? – a double murder?'

'It depends upon what you mean by that, Father.'

'I mean does someone have that sin upon his soul to have killed Violetta and Sebastian Mailer, the both of them?'

'Or did Mailer kill Violetta and was then himself killed?'

'Either way, there's a terrible thing!' Father Denys repeated. 'God forgive us all. A fearful, fearful thing.'

'And I do think we should ring the Vice-Questore.'

'Bergarmi, is it? Yes, yes, yes. We'll do so.'

On the return journey, now so very familiar, they passed by the well-head on the middle level. Alleyn stopped and looked at the railings. As in the basilica, they were made of more finished wood than those in the insula. Four stout rails, well polished, about ten inches apart.

'Have you ever had any trouble in the past? Any accidents?'
Alleyn asked.

Never, they said. Children were not allowed unaccompanied
anywhere in the building and people obeyed the notice not to climb
the railings.

'Just a moment, Father.'

Alleyn walked over to the well. 'Somebody's ignored the notice,'
he said and pointed to two adjacent marks across the top of the
lowest rail. 'Somebody who likes brown polish on the under-instep
of his shoes. Wait a moment, Father, will you?'

He squatted painfully by the rails and used his torch. The smears
of brown polish were smudged across with equidistant tracks almost
as if somebody had tried to erase them with an india rubber.

'If you don't mind,' he said, 'I've got a fancy to take a shot of this.'
And did so with his particular little camera.

'Will you look at that, now!' exclaimed Father Denys.

'It won't amount to a row of beans, as likely as not. Shall we go
on?'

Back in the vestibule he rang up the Questura and got through
to Bergarmi. He had to go warily. As he expected, the Vice-Questore
immediately said that the Dominicans should have reported the
trouble to him. Alleyn made the most of Father Denys's reluctance
to bother the police with what might well turn out to be the trivial
matter of a couple of dead rats. Bergarmi gave this a sardonic
reception, muttering *'Topi, topi,'* as if he used an incredulous slang
equivalent of 'Rats!' This Alleyn felt to be a little unfair, but he
pressed on with his report.

'You'll have a difficult job getting the body out,' he said, 'but of
course you have all the resources and the expertise.'

'You have communicated this matter, Superintendent Alleyn, to
Il Questore Valdarno?'

'No. I thought best to report at once to you.'

This went down much better. 'In which respect,' Bergarmi
conceded, 'you have acted with propriety. We shall deal with this
matter immediately. The whole complexion of the affair alters. I
myself will inform Il Questore. In the meantime I will speak, if you
please, with the Padre.'

While Father Denys talked volubly with Bergarmi, Alleyn washed his hands in a cubby-hole, found them to be rather more knocked about than he had realized, changed back into his own clothes and took stock of the situation.

The complexion had indeed changed. What, he sourly asked himself, was the position of a British investigator in Rome when a British subject of criminal propensities had almost certainly been murdered, possibly by another Briton, not impossibly by a Dutchman, not quite inconceivably by an Italian, on property administered by an Irish order of Dominican monks?

This is one, he thought, to be played entirely by ear and I very much wish I was shot of it.

He had an egg-shaped lump on the back of his head. He was bruised, sore, and even a bit shaky, which made him angry with himself. I could do with black coffee, he thought.

Father Denys came back, caught sight of Alleyn's hands and immediately produced a first-aid box. He insisted on putting dressings over the raw patches.

'You'd be the better for a touch of the cratur,' he said, 'and we've nothing of the kind to offer. There's a caffè over the way. Go there, now, and take a drop of something. The pollis will be a while yet for that fellow Bergarmi is all for getting on to the Questore before he stirs himself. Are you all right, now?'

'I'm fine but I think it's a marvellous suggestion.'

'Away with you.'

The caffè was a short distance down the street: a very modest affair with a scatter of workaday patrons who looked curiously at him. He had coffee and brandy and forced himself to eat a couple of large buns that turned out to be delicious.

Well, he thought, it was on the cards. From the beginning it was on the cards and I'm glad I said as much to Valdarno.

He began a careful re-think. Suppose, he thought, as a starting point, we accept that the noise we heard while the Baroness was setting up that ludicrous group-photograph was, in fact, the sound of the sarcophagus lid thumping down on its edge, and I must say it sounded exactly like it. This would mean presumably that Violetta had just been killed and was about to be safely stowed. By

Mailer? If by Mailer, then he himself survived to be killed, again presumably – no, almost certainly – before we all reassembled. The only members of the party who were alone were Sweet and young Dorne who found their way up independently, and Lady B. who was parked in the atrium.

The Van der Veghels were with me. Sophy Jason was with Barnaby Grant. *We* met nobody on our way up and *they* say as much for themselves.

Query. If Mailer killed Violetta while we were all having our photographs taken, why did he – not a robust man – go through the elaborate and physically exhausting job of putting the body in the sarcophagus and replacing the lid instead of doing what was subsequently done to him – dispatching it down the well?

I have no answer.

On the other hand, suppose one person killed both of them. Why? I am dumb, but suppose it was so? Why, for pity's sake, make a sarcophagus job of Violetta and a well job of Mailer? Just for the hell of it?

But. But, suppose, on the third hand, Mailer killed Violetta and hadn't time to do anything further about it before he himself was knocked off and pushed down the well? How will this fadge? Rather better, I fancy. And why does his killer take the trouble to box Violetta up? That's an easier one. Much easier.

I suppose there's a fourth hand. We approach Indian god status. Suppose Violetta killed Mailer and heaved him overboard and was then – no, that I refuse to entertain.

How long were we all boxed up together under the blank eyes of Mithras? Sweet arrived first and about five minutes later, young Dorne. Then there was the business of the photographs. The discussion, the groping and the grouping. Sophy and I being funnymen and Grant cursing us. He had just said 'Serve you bloody well right' to Sophy, who was having trouble with the Major, when the lid, if it was the lid, thudded. After that came the failure of the flashlight, the interminable wait while the Baroness set herself up again. At least ten minutes, I would think. Then Dorne took his photo of Mithras. Then the Baroness loosed off, this time successfully. Then she took two more shots, not without further re-arrangements and palaver. Another four minutes? All of that. And finally the Baron changed places with the Baroness and blazed away on his own account. Then Grant read his piece. Another five minutes. And then the party broke up. After that Dorne and Sweet are again odd men out. So it looks as if we were all together in that bloody basement for about twenty-five minutes, give or take the odd five. So everybody's got an alibi for the salient time. Everybody? No. No, not quite. Not . . . Sit still, my soul. Hold on to your hats, boys –

A great rumpus of sirens broke out in the distance, drew rapidly nearer and exploded into the little street. The police. The Squadra Omicidi in strength. Three large cars and a van, eight Agenti and four practical-looking characters in overalls.

Alleyn paid his bill and returned to the church, stiffer now about the shoulders and ribs and painful as to the head, but in other respects his own man again.

A large amount of equipment was being unloaded: two pairs of waders, ropes, pullies, an extension ladder, a winch, a stretcher. Il Vice-Questore Bergarmi watched the operation with an air of tetchy disdain. He greeted Alleyn ceremoniously and with a fine salute.

Patrons from the little caffè, some groups of youths and a car or two quickly collected and were bossed about by two of the Agenti who were otherwise unoccupied. Brother Dominic came out, surveyed the assembly, and opened the main doors.

'Il Questore Valdarno, Signor Alleyn,' said Bergarmi fairly stiffly, 'sends his compliments. He wishes me to express his hopes that you will continue to interest yourself in our investigations.'

'I am very much obliged to him,' Alleyn replied, groping about in his Italian for the correct phrases, 'and will be glad to do so without, I trust, making a nuisance of myself.'

'Mente affalto,' Bergarmi replied. Which was as much, Alleyn thought, as to say 'Don't let that worry you,' or even, 'Forget it.' Somehow it sounded a good deal less cordial.

It was after ten o'clock when Bergarmi's men landed Sebastian Mailer's body in the insula.

It lay on a stretcher not far from the sarcophagus, an inconsequential sequel to a flabby, fat man. It wore a ghastly resemblance to Violetta. This was because Mr Mailer, also, had been strangled.

His body had been knocked about; both before and after death, said the medical man – presumably a police surgeon – called in to make an immediate examination. His face had been scored by fangs of the broken grille. There was a heavy livid mark across the neck quite apart from the typical stigmata of manual strangulation. Alleyn watched the routine procedure and spoke when he was spoken to. There was a certain hauteur in the attitude of the investigating officers.

'We shall, of course, perform an autopsy,' said the doctor. 'He was a man of full habit. No doubt we shall find he was killed not so very long after he had eaten. *Ecco!* We find certain manifestations. You may cover the cadaver.' They did so. 'And remove it,' added the doctor. 'Unless, of course – ' he bowed to Alleyn who had moved forward ' – the Signor Superintendent wishes – ?'

Alleyn said, 'Thank you. I am sure, gentlemen, you have already taken every possible photograph required for the investigation, but unfortunately, as we all know, under such difficult conditions there can be accidents. When I found the body I did get a shot of it *in situ.'* He produced his very special minuscule camera. 'It seems to have survived a rather rough passage,' he said. 'If by any chance you would like a print I shall of course be delighted to give you one.'

He knew at once by a certain momentary stillness that no photographs had been taken down below by the recovery team. He hurried on. 'Perhaps I may be allowed to finish my film and then – a further favour. Signor Bergarmi – perhaps your laboratories would be kind enough to develop it.'

'Of course, Signore. Our pleasure.'

'You are very good,' Alleyn said and instantly whipped back the sheet and took four photographs of Mailer, deceased, with special attention to the right foot. He then removed the cassette and handed it with a bow to Bergarmi.

The body was re-shrouded and taken away.

Bergarmi said irritably that this was a bad evening for such an event. Student demonstrations had broken out in Navona and its surrounding district and threatened to become serious. The Agenti were fully equipped. A mammoth demonstration was planned for the morrow and the police expected it to be the worst yet. He must get this job through as quickly as possible. He suggested that nothing further could be done at the moment but that in view of the grossly altered circumstances his chief would be glad if Alleyn would wait on him in the morning at 9.30. It seemed advisable to call the seven travellers together again. Bergarmi's officers would attend to this. A car was at Alleyn's disposal. No doubt he would like to go home.

They shook hands.

When Alleyn left he passed Father Denys, who came as near to tipping him a wink as lay within the dignity of his office.

III

Sophy Jason and Barnaby Grant met for breakfast on the roof-garden. The morning sparkled freshly and was not yet too hot for comfort. From the direction of Navona there came vague sounds of singing, a discordant band and the rumour of a crowd. A detachment of police marched down their street. The waiter was full of confused chatter about riots. It seemed unreal to Sophy and Barnaby.

They talked of the blameless pleasures of the previous evening when they had walked about Roman streets until they tired and had then taken a carriage-drive fraught with the inescapable romanticism of such exercise. Finally, after a glass of wine in Navona, they had strolled home. When they said goodnight Grant had kissed Sophy for the first time. She had taken this thoughtfully with a nod as if to say 'Well, yes, I suppose so,' had blushed unexpectedly and left him in a hurry. If they could have read each other's thoughts they would been surprised to find that they were so nearly identical. Each, in fact, speculated upon immediate as opposed to past emotions under like circumstances and each, with a kind of apprehensive delight, recognized an essential difference.

Sophy had arrived first for breakfast and had sat down determined to sort herself out in a big way but instead had idly dreamed until Grant's arrival set up a commotion under her ribs. This was quickly replaced by a renewed sense of companionship unfolding like a flower in the morning air. 'How happy I am,' each of them thought. 'I am delighted.'

In this frame of mind they discussed the coming day and speculated about the outcome of the Violetta affair and the probability of Mr Mailer being a murderer.

'I suppose it's awful,' Sophy said, 'not to be madly horrified but truth to tell I'm not much more appalled than I would be if I'd read it in the papers.'

'I'll go one worse than you. In a way I'm rather obliged to him.'

'Honestly! What can you mean?'

'You're still hanging about in Rome instead of flouncing off to Assisi or Florence or wherever.'

'That,' Sophy said, 'is probably a remark in execrable taste although I must say I relished it.'

'Sophy,' said Grant, 'you're a sweetie. Blow me down flat if you're not.'

He reached out his hand and at that moment the waiter came out on the roof-garden.

Now it was Grant who experienced a jolt under the diaphragm. Here he had sat, and so, precisely here, had the waiter appeared, on that morning over a year ago when Sebastian Mailer was announced.

'What's the matter?' Sophy asked.

'Nothing. Why?'

'You looked – odd.'

'Did I? What is it?' he asked the waiter.

It was the Baron Van der Veghel hoping Mr Grant was free.

'Ask him to join us, please.'

Sophy stood up.

'Don't you dare,' Grant said. 'Sit down.'

'Yes, but – well, anyway, you shut up.'

'Siddown.'

'I'll be damned if I do,' said Sophy, and did.

The Baron arrived: large, concerned and doubtful. He begged their forgiveness for so early a call and supposed that, like him, they had received a great shock. This led to some momentary confusion until, gazing at them with those wide-open eyes of his, he said, 'But surely you must know?' and finding they did not, flatly told them.

'The man Mailer,' he said, 'has been murdered. He has been found at the bottom of the well.'

At that moment all the clocks in Rome began to strike nine and Sophy was appalled to hear a voice in her head saying: *'Ding, dong bell. Mailer's in the well.'*

'No doubt,' the Baron said, 'you will receive a message. As we did. This of course, changes everything. My wife is so much upset. We have found where is a Protestant church and I have taken her there for some comfort. My wife is a most sensitive subject. She senses,' the Baron explained, 'that there has been a great evil amongst us. That there is still this evil. As I do. How can one escape such a feeling?'

'Not very readily,' Grant conceded, 'particularly now when I suppose we are all much more heavily involved.'

The Baron glanced anxiously at Sophy. 'Perhaps,' he said, 'we should – '

'Well, of course we're involved, Baron,' she said.

Clearly, the Baron held that ladies were to be protected. He goes through life, she thought, tenderly building protective walls round that huge, comical sex-pot of his and he's got plenty of concern left over for extramural sympathy. Who says the age of chivalry is dead? He's rather a dear, is the Baron. But beneath her amusement, flowing under it and chilling it, ran a trickle of consciousness: I'm involved in a murder, thought Sophy.

She had lost track of the Baron's further remarks but gathered that he had felt the need for discussion with another man. Having left the Baroness to pursue whatever Spartan devotions accorded with her need, he had settled upon Grant as a confidant.

Deeply perturbed though she was, Sophy couldn't help feeling an indulgent amusement at the behaviour of the two men. It was so exclusively masculine. They had moved away to the far side of the garden. Grant, with his hands in his pockets, stared between his feet and then lifted his head and contemplated the horizon. The Baron folded his arms, frowned portentously, and raised his eyebrows almost to the roots of his hair. They both pursed their lips, muttered, nodded. There were long pauses.

How different, Sophy thought, from the behaviour of women. We would exclaim, gaze at each other, gabble, ejaculate, tell each other how we felt and talk about instinctive revulsion and how we'd always known, right along, that there was *something*.

And she suddenly thought it would be satisfactory to have such a talk with the Baroness, though not on any account with Lady Braceley.

They turned back to her, rather like doctors after a consultation.

'We have been saying, Miss Jason,' said the Baron, 'that as far as we ourselves are concerned there can be only slight formalities. Since we were in company from the time he left us, both in the Mithraeum and when we returned (you with Mr Grant and my wife and I with Mr Alleyn) until we all met in the church portion, we cannot be thought of either as witnesses or as – as – '

'Suspects?' Sophy said.

'So. You are right to be frank, my dear young lady,' said the Baron, looking at Sophy with solemn and perhaps rather shocked approval.

Grant said, 'Well, of course she is. Let's all be frank about it, for heaven's sake. Mailer was a bad lot and somebody has killed him. I don't suppose any of us condones the taking of life under any circumstances whatever, and it is, of course, horrible to think of the explosion of hatred, or alternatively the calculated manoeuvring, that led to his death. But one can scarcely be expected to mourn for him.' He looked very hard at Sophy. 'I don't,' he said. 'And I won't pretend I do. It's a bad man out of the way.'

The Baron waited for a moment and said very quietly, 'You speak, Mr Grant, with conviction. Why do you say so positively that this was a bad man?'

Grant had gone very white but he answered without hesitation. 'I have first-hand knowledge,' he said. 'He was a blackmailer. He blackmailed me. Alleyn knows this and so does Sophy. And if me, why not others?'

'Why not?' Van der Veghel said. 'Why not, indeed!' He hit himself on the chest and Sophy wondered why the gesture was not ridiculous. 'I too,' he said. 'I who speak to you. I too.' He waited for a moment. 'It has been a great relief to me to say this,' he said. 'A great relief. I shall not regret it, I think.'

'Well,' Grant said, 'it's lucky we are provided with alibis. I suppose a lot of people would say we have spoken like fools.'

'It is appropriate sometimes to be a fool. The belief of former times that there is God's wisdom in the utterances of fools was founded in truth,' the Baron proclaimed. 'No. I do not regret.'

A silence fell between them and into it there was insinuated the sound of a distant crowd – shrilling of whistles. A police-car shot down the street with its siren blasting.

'And now, my dear Baron,' said Grant, 'having to some extent bared our respective bosoms, perhaps we had better, with Sophy's permission, consider our joint situation.'

'With the greatest pleasure,' said the Baron politely.

IV

Alleyn found a change in the atmosphere of Il Questore Valdarno's splendid office and in the attitude of Valdarno himself. It was not that he was exactly less cordial but rather that he was more formally so. He was very formal indeed and overpoweringly polite. He was also worried and preoccupied and was constantly interrupted by telephone calls. Apparently the demonstrations were hotting up in Navona.

Valdarno made it perfectly clear that the discovery of Mailer's body altered the whole complexion of the case: that while he had no intention of excluding Alleyn from the investigation and hoped he would find some interest in the proceedings, they would be absolutely in the hands of the Roman Questura, which, he added, with an unconvincing air of voicing an afterthought, was under the direct control of the Minister of the Interior. Valdarno was very urbane. Alleyn had his own line of urbanity and retired behind it, and between them, he thought, they got exactly nowhere.

Valdarno thanked Alleyn with ceremony for having gone down the well and for being so kind as to photograph the body *in situ*. He contrived to suggest that this proceeding had, on the whole, been unnecessary if infinitely obliging.

The travellers, he said, were summoned to appear at 10.30. Conversation languished but revived with the arrival of Bergarmi who had the results of the post-mortems. Violetta had been hit on the back of the head and manually strangled. Mailer had probably been knocked out before being strangled and dropped down the well, though the bruise on his jaw might have been caused by a blow against the rails or the wall on his way down. The fragment of material Alleyn had found on the inner side of the top rail matched the black alpaca of his jacket and there was a corresponding tear in the sleeve.

At this point Valdarmo, with stately punctilio, said to Bergarmi that they must acknowledge at once that Signor Alleyn had advanced the theory of Mailer's possible disappearance down the well and that he himself had accepted it. They both bowed, huffily, to Alleyn.

'It is of the first importance,' Valdarno continued, 'to establish whether the sound which was heard by these persons when they were in the Mithraeum was in fact the sound made by the lid of the sarcophagus falling upon its edge to the floor where, it is conjectured, it remained, propped against the casket while the body of the woman was disposed of. Your opinion, Signore, is that it was so?'

'Yes,' Alleyn said. 'You will remember that when we removed the lid it made a considerable noise. Two minutes or more before that, we heard a confused sound that might have been that of a woman's voice. It was greatly distorted by echo and stopped abruptly.'

'Screaming?'

'No.'

'One would expect the woman Violetta to scream.'

'Perhaps not, do you think, if she was there unlawfully? When she abused Mailer on the earlier occasion she didn't scream: she whispered. I got the impression of one of those harridan-voices that have worn out and can no longer scream.'

Valdarno surveyed Bergarmi. 'You realize what all this implies, no doubt?'

'Certainly, Signor Questore.'

'Well?'

'That if this was the woman Violetta and if the sound was the sound of the sarcophagus lid and if the person Mailer killed the woman Violetta and was himself killed soon afterwards – ' here Bergarmi took a breath ' – then, Signor Questore, the field of suspects is confined to such persons as were unaccompanied after the party left the Mithraeum. These were the Major Sweet, the Baronessa Braceley, the nephew Dorne.'

'Very well.'

'And that in fact the field of suspects remains the same,' Bergarmi said, fighting his way out, 'whether the woman Violetta was killed by the person Mailer or by the killer of the person Mailer.'

Valdarno turned to Alleyn and spread his hands.

'*Ecco!*' he said. 'You agree?'

'A masterly survey,' Alleyn said. 'There is – if I may? – just one
question I would like to ask.'

'Ah?'

'Do we know where Giovanni Vecchi was?'

'Vecchi?'

'Yes,' Alleyn said apologetically. 'He was by the cars when we
came out of the basilica but he might have been inside while we
were in the nether regions. He wouldn't attract notice, would he? I
mean he's a regular courier and must often hang about the premises
while his customers are below. Part of the scenery, as it were.'

Valdarno gazed in his melancholy way at nothing in particular.
'What,' he asked Bergarmi, 'has the man Vecchi said?'

'Signor Questore – nothing.'

'Still nothing?'

'He is obstinate.'

'Has he been informed of Mailer's death?'

'Last night, Signor Questore.'

'His reaction?'

Bergarmi's shoulders rose to his ears, his eyebrows to the roots of
his hair and his pupils into his head.

'Again nothing. A little pale, perhaps. I believe him to be
nervous.'

'He must be examined as to his movements at the time of the
crimes. The priests must be questioned.'

'Of course, Signor Questore,' said Bergarmi, who had not looked
at Alleyn.

'Send for him.'

'Certainly, Signor Questore. At once.'

Valdarno waved a hand at his telephone and Bergarmi hurried to it.

An Agente came in and saluted.

'The tourists, Signor Questore,' he said.

'Very well. All of them?'

'Not yet, Signor Questore. The English *nobildonna* and her nephew.
The English writer. The Signorina. The Olandese and his wife.'

'Admit them,' said Valdarno, with all the grandeur of a
Shakespearean monarch.

And in they came: that now familiar and so oddly assorted
company.

Alleyn stood up and so did Valdarno, who bowed with the utmost formality. He said, merely, 'Ladies and Gentlemen,' and motioned them to their seats.

Lady Braceley, who was dressed, with an over-developed sense of occasion, in black, ignored this invitation. She advanced upon Valdarno and held out her hand at the kissing level. He took it and kissed his thumb.

'*Baronessa,*' he said.

'Too shattering,' she lamented. 'I can't believe it. That's all. I simply can *not* believe it.'

'Unfortunately it is true. Please! Be seated.'

The Agente hastened to push a chair into the back of her knees. She sat abruptly, gazed at Valdarno and shook her head slowly from side to side. The others regarded her with dismay. The Van der Veghels exchanged brief, incredulous glances. Kenneth made a discontented noise.

Bergarmi finished his orders on the telephone and seated himself at a little distance from the administrative desk.

'We shall not wait for the assembly to complete itself,' said Valdarno. He explained, loftily, that under the normal and correct form of procedure the interview would be in charge of his Vice-Questore but that as this would necessitate an interpreter he proposed to conduct it himself.

Alleyn thought that little time was saved by this departure as Il Questore continually interrupted the proceedings with translations into Italian from which Bergarmi took notes.

The ground that had been so laboriously traversed before was traversed again and nothing new came out except a rising impatience and anxiety on the part of the subjects. When Kenneth tried to raise an objection he was reminded, icily, that with the discovery of Mailer's body they were all much more deeply involved. Both Kenneth and his aunt looked terrified and said nothing.

Il Questore ploughed majestically on. He had arrived at the point of the departure from the Mithraeum when Grant, who had become increasingly and obviously restive, suddenly interrupted him.

'Look here,' he said, 'I'm very sorry but I simply cannot see the point of all this reiteration. Surely by now it's abundantly clear that whether the noise we heard was or was not this bloody lid, it would have been quite impossible for the Baron, the Baroness, Alleyn, Miss Jason or me to have killed this man. I imagine that you don't entertain the idea of a conspiracy and if you don't, you have irrefutable proof that none of us was ever, throughout the whole trip, alone.'

'This may be so, Signor Grant. Nevertheless, statements must be taken – '

'All right, my dear man, all right. And they have been taken. And what are we left with, for pity's sake?'

He looked at Alleyn, who raised an eyebrow at him and very slightly shook his head.

'We're left,' Grant said, raising his voice, 'as far as the touring party is concerned with a field of three. Lady Braceley in the atrium. I'm sorry, Lady Braceley, but there you were and I'm sure nobody supposes you left it. Dorne – '

'No!' Kenneth whispered. 'No! Don't you dare. Don't dare!'

' – Dorne on his way up – and alone.'

' – and who else – who else? Go on. *Who else?*'

' – and Major Sweet, who seems to be taking an unconscionable time getting to this meeting – '

There,' Kenneth chattered. There! You see? What I always said. I said – '

'And heaven knows what intruder from outside,' Grant ended. 'As far as I can see, you've no absolute proof that some complete outsider didn't lie in wait down there for Mailer, kill him and make a getaway. That's all. I've spoken out of order and I don't regret it.'

Valdarno had begun, 'Mr Grant, I must insist – ' when his telephone rang. He gestured angrily at Bergarmi, who lifted the receiver. A spate of Italian broke out at the other end. Bergarmi ejaculated and answered so rapidly that Alleyn could only just make out what he said. He picked up something like ' – insufferable incompetence. At once. All of you. You hear me! All!' He clapped the receiver down and turned to Valdarno.

'They have lost him,' he said. 'Buffoons! Idiots! Lunatics! He has given them the slip.'

'Vecchi?'

'Vecchi! No, Signor Questore, no. Sweet. Major Sweet.'

CHAPTER 9

Death in the Morning

He made his getaway during the riots.

After Alleyn left him on the previous afternoon he had begun to keep watch from behind his window-blind on a man in the street below. The man had changed three times, the second to last being a short, swarthy fellow wearing a green hat. Sweet could not be sure if these watchers were police agents or spies employed by Giovanni. The latter would be infinitely more dangerous.

He had eaten in his room, giving it out that he was unwell and had managed to keep on the safe side of the whisky-bottle although, as evening came on, he had taken more than most men could stand.

Once when he was not looking into the street, he made a tiny fire of paper in an ashtray. Two larger papers he tore into fragments and put down the lavatory across the landing. But he had never carried much really incriminating stuff about with him and these were soon disposed of.

When it grew dark he did not turn on his light but still watched. The man in the green hat was at no pains to make himself inconspicuous. Often, he looked directly at the window so that, although Sweet knew this was not possible, he felt as if they stared into each other's eyes. When the man's relief came – he arrived on a motorbicycle – they pointed out the window to each other.

The lavatory was at the back of the landing. He had stood on the seat and looked through the window louvres. Yes, sure enough, there was another man, watching the rear of the hotel.

When he got down he saw he had left marks of the shoe-polish on the seat. He had always been particular about his shoes, liking the arches of their soles to be attended to. He wiped away the marks.

If they were Agenti down there, it meant that Alleyn had told the police and they had decided he should be kept under observation. And if, as Alleyn had suggested, Giovanni was under arrest? He might still have managed to lay this on. And if he had done that, then things looked black indeed.

At eleven o'clock he was still watching and being watched. At five past eleven the telephone on the landing rang and went on ringing. He heard the man in the next room groan and go out. He was prepared for the bang on his own door and the slam of the neighbouring one. He answered the telephone. It was somebody speaking basic English for the Vice-Questore Bergarmi. The travellers were required to report next morning at the office where they had formerly been interviewed. At 10.30.

He waited for two or three seconds while he ran the tip of his tongue over his trim little moustache. His hand slithered on the receiver.

'Jolly good,' he said. 'Can do.'

'I beg your pardon, Signore? You said?'

'I'll be there.'

'Thank you.'

'Wait a bit. Hold on.'

'Have you found Mailer?'

A pause. A consultation in Italian.

'Hullo? Are you there?'

'Yes, Signore, Mailer has been found.'

'Oh.'

'His body has been found. He has been murdered.'

He should have said something. He shouldn't have hung up the receiver without a word. Too late now.

He lay on his bed and tried to think. The hours went by and sometimes he dozed but he always came to with a jerk and returned to look down into the street. The brief quietude of the small hours came over Rome and then, with the first light, the gradual return of traffic. Presently there were movements within the hotel.

At eight o'clock he heard a vacuum cleaner whining in the passage. He got up, shaved, packed a small overnight bag and then sat looking at nothing and unable to think coherently.

At 9.30 the biggest student demonstrations of the year began. The point of assembly was Navona but as they increased in violence the crowds overflowed and erupted into the narrow street below. A gang of youths ran down it manhandling parked cars into a herringbone pattern. He could see bald-heads among them, urging them on. He began to make frantic preparations. Still watching the street, he struggled into his overcoat. There was a scarf in the pocket. He wound it over his mouth. Then he found a tweed hat he hadn't worn since he arrived. He checked that he had his passport and money in his pockets and took up the overnight bag. There was now a great deal of noise in the street. A group of students milled round the watcher's motor-bicycle. They had opened the tank and then set fire to the petrol. Six or seven of them swarmed about the man. A fight broke out.

He heard windows opening and voices in the other rooms exclaiming.

The landing and stairs were deserted.

When he reached the street the bicycle was in flames. The crowd manhandled the owner. He struggled, caught sight of Sweet, and yelled.

Sweet dodged and ran. He was hustled and thrust aside and finally caught up in a general stampede down the street and into the main thoroughfare. Here he took to his heels and ran, disregarded, until he was winded.

There was a traffic block at an intersection. He saw an empty taxi in midstream, got to it, wrenched open the door and fell in. The driver shouted angrily at him. He pulled out his wallet and showed a L. 10,000 note, *'Stazione!'*

The traffic moved and the cars behind set up a great hooting. The driver gestured, seemed to refuse but finally moved with the stream, still shouting incomprehensibly.

Then Sweet heard the siren.

The police-car was some way behind them but the traffic between made way for it. Sweet and the driver saw each other in the rear-vision glass. Sweet pounded with both fists on the driver's back. 'On!' he screamed. *'Go on!'*

The taxi screeched to a halt as the man crammed on his brakes. The police-car drew alongside and Sweet hurled himself through the opposite door.

For a moment he showed up in the sea of traffic: a well-dressed man in an English overcoat and tweed hat. Then he went down under an oncoming van.

II

'He is not expected,' Bergarmi said, 'to recover consciousness.'

Since Sweet's escape had been reported, less than half an hour had elapsed. During that interval, while Valdarno and his Vice-Questore were still at blast-off potential, Giovanni had been brought in. He was unshaven, pale and dishevelled, and had looked round the group of tourists as if he saw them for the first time. When his glance fell on Lady Braceley he half-closed his eyes, smirked and bowed. She had not looked at him.

He was questioned by Bergarmi with occasional interjections from Valdarno. This time there was no translation and only Alleyn knew what was said. The travellers leant forward in their chairs and strained and frowned as if they were physically rather than intellectually deaf. It was difficult, indeed, to think of any good reason why their presence was supposed to be desirable. Unless, Alleyn thought, we are to become bilingual again and some sort of confrontation is envisaged.

The official manner with Giovanni was formidable. Bergarmi shot out the questions. Valdarno folded his arms, scowled and occasionally threw in a demand if not a threat. Giovanni alternately sulked and expostulated. A good deal of what went on, Alleyn reflected, would be meat and drink to defending counsel in Great Britain. The examination was twice interrupted by reports of further violence in the street and the Questore flung orders into the telephone with the precision of a souped-up computer. Alleyn could not escape the feeling that they all three greatly relished running through this virtuoso performance before their baffled and uncomprehending audience.

After a prolonged skirmish leading nowhere in particular Giovanni suddenly flung out his arms, made a complicated acknowledgement of his own stainless integrity, and intimated that he was prepared to come clean.

This turned out to be the overstatement of the day. What he was prepared to do, and did, was to accuse Major Sweet of murdering Sebastian Mailer. He said that while he himself was innocent of all knowledge of Mailer's side activities and had merely acted in good faith as a top-class courier for Il Cicerone, it had come to his knowledge that there was some kind of hanky-panky going on between Mailer and Sweet.

'Something told me it was so,' said Giovanni. 'I have an instinct in such matters.'

'For "instinct",' Il Questore said, 'read "experience".' Bergarmi laughed rather in the manner of deferential junior counsel.

'And what steps,' Valdarno asked nastily, 'did this instinct prompt you to take?' He glanced at Alleyn.

Giovanni said he had observed, when Violetta attacked Mailer in the portico, that Sweet watched with a certain eagerness. He became even more interested in Sweet. When the party went below he strolled into the basilica and said a prayer to S. Tommaso for whom he had a devotion. Major Sweet, he said in parenthesis, was an atheist and made several abominable remarks about the holy saints.

'His remarks are unimportant. Continue.'

Giovanni was still in the basilica when Major Sweet returned with Lady Braceley, he said, and slid his eyes in her direction. Sweet's behaviour was peculiar and far from polite. He planted her in the atrium and hastened to return below. Giovanni, filled, if he was to be believed, with nameless misgiving, had gone to the top well-head in the basilica and looked down – to his astonishment upon Major Sweet who (against the holy fathers' regulations) had mounted the rails of the well-head directly underneath and seemed to strain over the top and peer into the Mithraic insula below. There was something extraordinarily furtive about the way he finally climbed down and darted out of sight.

'This is nothing,' said Valdarno, flicking it away with his fingers.

'Ah,' said Giovanni, 'but wait.' Wait, as he had, for the return of the party. First to arrive was Signor Dorne, who went immediately to his aunt in the atrium. And then, alone, the Major. White. Trembling. Agitated. A terrible expression in the eyes. He had passed

Giovanni without seeing him and staggered into the porch. Giovanni had gone to him, had asked him if he was unwell. He had cursed Giovanni and asked him what the hell he meant and told him to get out. Giovanni had gone to his car and from there had seen the Major fortify himself from a pocket flask. His recovery was rapid. When the others appeared he was in full command of himself.

'At the time, Signor Questore, I was at a loss to understand – but now, now I understand. Signor Questore, I,' said Giovanni, slapping his chest and shaking his finger and making his point with the greatest virtuosity, 'had looked upon the face of a murderer.'

And it was at this point that the telephone had rung. Bergarmi answered it, received the news of Sweet's catastrophe and informed his Superior.

'He is not expected,' he said, 'to recover consciousness.'

And while we're on the subject of facial expression, Alleyn thought, if ever I've seen incredulous delight flash up in anybody's face it's now. And the face is Giovanni's.

III

Five minutes later came the information that Hamilton Sweet had died without speaking.

Valdarno unbent so far as to convey this news to the travellers. And again relief, decently restrained, was in the air. Barnaby Grant probably voiced the majority's reaction when he said, 'For God's sake don't let's go through the motions. He was a disastrous specimen and now it seems he was a murderer. It's beastly but it's over. Better for them – all three of them – by a long chalk and for everybody else that it should be.'

Alleyn saw Sophy look steadily at Grant for a moment and then frowningly at her own clenched hands. The Baron made sounds of agreement, but his wife, disconcertingly, broke into protest.

'Ah no, ah no!' cried the Baroness. 'We cannot so coldly dismiss! Here is tragedy! Here is Nemesis! Behind this dénouement what horror is not lurkink?' She appealed from one to another of the hearers and finally to her husband. Her eyes filled with tears. 'No, Gerrit, no! It is dreadful to think,' she said. 'The Violetta and this

Mailer and the Sweet: between them was such hatred! Such evil! So close to us! I am sick to think of it.'

'Never mind, my darling. It is gone. They are gone.'

He comforted her in their own language, gently patting one of her large hands between his own two enormous ones as if to warm it. He looked round at the others with that winged smile inviting them to indulge a childish distress. They responded awkwardly.

Valdarno said that they would all perceive, no doubt, that the affair now wore an entirely different complexion. It would be improper, until legal pronouncements had been made and the case formally wound up, for him to make a categorical pronouncement but he felt, nevertheless, that as representative of the Minister for the Interior he might assure them they would not be unduly troubled by further proceedings. They would be asked to sign a statement as to their unfortunate experience. Possibly they would be required to give formal evidence and should hold themselves in readiness to do so. And now, perhaps, they would be kind enough to wait in the next room while Vice-Questore Bergarmi prepared a statement. He greatly regretted –

He continued in this strain for a few more rounded periods and then they all stood up and responded as best they could to a ceremonial leave-taking.

Alleyn remained behind.

'If it would save trouble, Signor Questore,' he said, 'I'm at your service – you'll want an English transcription of this statement, for instance. And perhaps – as I was there, you know – ?'

'You are very kind,' Valdarno began, and broke off to deal with yet another report of violence. Bergarmi had gone to some inner office and for a moment or two Alleyn and Giovanni were confronted. The Questore's back was turned to them as he apostrophized the telephone.

'You too,' Alleyn said, 'will no doubt sign a statement, will you not?'

'But certainly, Signore. On my conscience and before the saints. It is my duty.'

'Will it include an account of your talk with Major Sweet yesterday afternoon, at the Eremo?'

Giovanni, snakelike, retracted his head. Almost, Alleyn thought, you could hear him hiss. He half-closed his eyes and whispered disgustingly.

For the hundredth time that morning Valdarno shouted, '*E molto seccante! Presto!*' He clapped down the receiver, spread his hands for Alleyn's benefit, and caught sight of Giovanni. 'You! Vecchi! You are required to make a written statement.'

'Of course, Signor Questore,' Giovanni said. The intercom buzzed. Valdarno took another call.

An officer came in and removed Giovanni, who darted a look at Il Questore's back and as he passed Alleyn rapidly mimed a spit into his face. The officer barked at him and pushed him out. Violetta, thought Alleyn, would not have stopped short at pantomime.

'These students!' cried Valdarno, leaving the telephone. 'What do they suppose they achieve? Now, they burn up Vespa motorcycles. Why? Possibly they are other students' Vespas. Again, why? You were speaking of the signed statement. I would be greatly obliged if you would combine with Bergarmi.' The buzzer sounded. '*Basta!*' shouted Il Questore and answered it.

Alleyn joined Bergarmi, who received him with a strange blend of huffishness and relief. He had written out a résumé in Italian, based on his own notes of the now desperately familiar experiences of the travellers in the depths of S. Tommaso. Alleyn found this accurate and put it into English. 'Would you like a check of the translation by a third person, Signor Vice-Questore?' he asked. Bergarmi made deprecatory noises. 'After all,' he said, 'it is no longer of the first importance, all this. Giovanni Vecchi's evidence and the fact that this – ' he slapped the statement ' – does nothing to contradict it and, above all, Sweet's attempt to escape, are sufficient, for our purpose. The case is virtually closed.'

Alleyn pushed his translation across the table. 'There is just one thing I'd like to suggest.'

'Yes? And that is?'

'The Van der Veghels took photographs in the Mithraeum and the insula. Flashlights. Two by the Baroness and one by the Baron. Kenneth Dorne also took one. After that, when we were returning, the Baroness photographed the sarcophagus. I thought you might like to produce these photographs.'

'Ah. Thank you. The sarcophagus, yes. Yes. That might be interesting.'

'If it shows the piece of shawl?'

'Quite so. It would limit the time. To some extent that is true. It would show that the woman Violetta was murdered before you all left the Mithraeum. By Mailer, of course. There can be no doubt, by Mailer. It would not help us – not that we need this evidence – to fix a precise time for Sweet's attack upon Mailer. We have, my dear Signor Super,' said Bergarmi with evident pleasure in discovering this new mode of address, 'motive. From your own investigation of Sweet.' Alleyn made a wry face. 'Intent. As evidenced in suspicious behaviour noted by Vecchi. Opportunity. Apart from Signor Dorne and his Aunt Baroness (this latter being a ludicrous notion), he is the only one with opportunity.'

'With the greatest respect – the only one?'

'Signore?'

'Well,' Alleyn said apologetically, 'it's just that I wonder if Giovanni was speaking all of the truth all of the time.'

After a considerable pause Bergarmi said, 'I find no occasion to doubt it.' And after an even longer pause: 'He had no motive, no cause to attack Mailer.'

'He had every reason, though, to attack Sweet. But don't give it another thought.'

Alleyn's translation was typed, with copies, by a brisk bilingual clerk. During this period Bergarmi was rather ostentatiously busy. When the transcription was ready he and Alleyn went to the lesser office where for the second and last time the travellers were assembled. At Bergarmi's request Alleyn handed out the copies.

'I find this a correct summary of our joint statements,' Alleyn said, 'and am prepared to sign it. What about everyone else?'

Lady Braceley, who was doing her face, said with an unexpected flight of fancy: 'I'd sign my soul to the devil if he'd get me out of here.' She turned her raffish and disastrous gaze upon Alleyn. 'You're being too wonderful,' she predictably informed him.

He said, 'Lady Braceley, I wonder – simply out of curiosity, you know – whether you noticed anything at all odd in Sweet's manner when he took you up to the atrium. Did you?'

He thought she might seize the chance to tell all how responsive she was to atmosphere and how she had sensed that something was wrong, or possibly come out with some really damaging bit of information. All she said, however, was: 'I just thought him a bloody rude, common little man.' And after a moment's thought: 'And I'll eat my hat if he was ever in the Gunners.' She waited again for a moment and then said, 'All the same, it's quite something, isn't it, to have been trotted about by a murderer, however uncivil? My dear, we'll dine on it: Kenny and I. Won't we, darling?'

Her nephew looked up at her and gave a sort of restless acknowledgement. 'I just don't go with all this carry-on,' he complained.

'I *know*, darling. Too confusing. Three dead people in as many days, you might say. Still, it's a wonderful relief to be in the clear oneself.' She contemplated Bergarmi, smiling at him with her head on one side. 'He really *doesn't* speak English, does he? He's not making a nonsense of us?'

Bergarmi muttered to Alleyn, 'What is she saying? Does she object to signing? Why is she smiling at me?'

'She doesn't object. Perhaps she has taken a fancy to you, Signor Vice-Questore.'

'*Mamma mia!*'

Alleyn suggested that if they were all satisfied they would sign and Lady Braceley instantly did so, making no pretence of reading the statement. The Van der Veghels were extremely particular and examined each point with anxious care and frequent consultations. Barnaby Grant and Sophy Jason read the typescript with professional concentration. Then they all signed. Bergarmi told them, through Alleyn, that they were free to go. They would be notified if their presence at the inquest was required. He bowed, thanked them and departed with the papers.

The six travellers rose, collected themselves and prepared, with evident signs of relief, to go their ways.

Sophy and Barnaby Grant left together and the Van der Veghels followed them.

Lady Braceley with her eye on Alleyn showed signs of lingering.

Kenneth had lounged over to the door and stood there, watching Alleyn with his customary furtive, sidelong air. 'So that would appear to be that,' he threw out.

'You remember,' Alleyn said, 'you took a photograph of Mithras when we were all down there?'

'That's right.'

'Have you had it developed?'

'No.'

'Is it in black-and-white or colour?'

'Black-and-white,' Kenneth mumbled. 'It's meant to be better for the architecture and statues bit.'

'Mine are being developed by the police expert, here. They'll only take a couple of hours. Would you like me to get yours done at the same time?'

'The film's not finished. Thank you very much, though.'

Lady Braceley said, 'No, but do let Mr Alleyn get it done, darling. You can't have many left. You never stopped clicking all through that extraordinary picnic on the what-not hill. And you must admit it will have a kind of grisly interest. Not that *I'll* be in the one Mr Alleyn's talking about, you know – the bowels of the earth. Do give it to him.'

'It's still in my camera.'

'And your camera's in the car. Whip down and get it.'

'Darling Auntie – it'll wait. Need we fuss?'

'Yes,' she said pettishly, 'we need. Go *on*, darling!' He slouched off.

'Don't come all the way back,' Alleyn called after him. 'I'll collect it down there. I won't be a moment.'

'Sweet of you,' Lady Braceley said, and kissed her hand. 'We'll wait.'

When they had gone Alleyn went out to the lift landing and found the Van der Veghels busily assembling the massive photographic gear without which they seemed unable to move. He reminded the Baroness of the photographs she had taken in the Mithraic insula and offered to have the police develop the film.

'I think,' he said 'that the police would still be very glad to see the shot you took of the sarcophagus, Baroness. I told them I'd ask you for it.'

'You may have it. I do not want it. I cannot bear to think of it. Gerrit, my darlink, please give it to him. We wish for no souvenirs of that terrible day. Ach, no! No!'

'Now, now, now,' the Baron gently chided. 'There is no need for such a fuss-pot. I have it here. One moment only and I produce it.'

But there was quite a lot to be done in the way of unbuckling and poking in their great rucksacks, and all to no avail.

Suddenly the Baroness gave a little scream and clapped her hand to her forehead.

'But I am mad!' she cried. 'I forget next my own head.'

'How?'

'It was the young Dorne. Yesterday we arrange he takes it with his own development.'

'So,' said the Baron. 'What a nonsense,' and began with perfect good humour to re-assemble the contents of his rucksack.

'He hasn't done anything about it,' Alleyn said. 'If I may, I'll collect your film with his.'

'Good, good,' agreed the Baron.

Alleyn said aside to him, 'You're sure you don't want it?'

He shook his head, pursed his lips and frowned like a nanny.

'No, no, no,' he murmured. 'You see how it is. My wife prefers – no. Although,' he added rather wistfully, 'there *are* some pictures – our little group, for instance. But never mind.'

'I'll let you know how it comes out,' Alleyn said.

They went down in the lift together. He wondered if, long after the case of Sebastian Mailer had faded out of most people's memories, he and the Van der Veghels would meet somewhere. The Baroness had cheered up. They were off on a coach trip to the water-gardens at the Villa d'Este. He walked with them to the main entrance. She went ahead with that singularly buoyant tread that made Alleyn think of the gait of some kind of huge and antique bird: a moa, perhaps.

'My wife,' said the Baron fondly regarding her, 'has the wise simplicity of the classic age. She is a most remarkable woman.' And dropping his voice, he added to himself rather than to Alleyn, 'And to my mind, very beautiful.'

'You are a fortunate man.'

'That, also, is my opinion.'

'Baron, will you have a drink with me? At about six o'clock? I will be able to show you your photographs. Since they would distress the Baroness I don't ask you to bring her with you.'

'Thank you,' he said. 'I shall be delighted. You are very considerate,' and, shifting his rucksack on his massive shoulders, he called: 'Mathilde, not so fast! Wait! I am coming.'

And he, also with springing gait, sped nimbly after his wife. They went down the street together, head and shoulders above the other pedestrians, elastically bobbing up and down and eagerly talking.

Kenneth Dorne sat at the wheel of a white sports-car with his aunt beside him. It occurred to Alleyn that they might have been served up neat by an over-zealous casting department as type-material for yet another *Dolce Vita*. Kenneth had one of the ridiculous 'trendy' caps on his head, a raspberry-coloured affair with a little peak. He was very white and his forehead glistened.

'Here we are,' cried Lady Braceley, 'and here's the film. Such a fuss! Come and have drinks with us this evening. I suppose it's frightful of one, isn't it, but one can't help a feeling of relief. I mean that poisonous Giovanni terrifying one. And all lies. Kenneth knows that I told you. So, don't you think a little celebration? Or don't you?'

Kenneth stared at Alleyn with a pretty ghastly half-grin. His lips moved. Alleyn leant forward. 'What am I to do?' Kenneth mouthed.

Alleyn said aloud, 'I'm afraid I'm booked for this evening.' And to Kenneth, 'You don't look well. I should see a doctor if I were you. May I have the film?'

He handed it over. The carton was damp.

'I think you've got the Baroness's film too, haven't you?'

'Oh God, have I? Yes, of course. Where the hell – Here!'

He took it out of the glove-box and handed it over.

'*Can* we give you a lift?' Lady Braceley asked with the utmost concern. 'Do let us give you a lift.'

'Thank you, no. I've a job to do here.'

The sports-car shot dangerously into the traffic.

Alleyn went back into the building.

He sought out Bergarmi and got the name and working address of their photographic expert. Bergarmi rang the man up and arranged for the films to be developed immediately.

He offered to accompany Alleyn to the photographic laboratory and when they got there expanded on his own attitude.

'I have looked in,' Bergarmi said, 'to see our own photographs. A matter of routine, really. The case against Sweet is perfectly established by Giovanni Vecchi's evidence alone. He now admits that he was aware of a liaison of some sort between Sweet and

Mailer and will swear that he heard Mailer threaten Sweet with exposure.'

'I see,' Alleyn said, 'exposure of what? And to whom?'

'Giovanni believes, Signore, that Mailer was aware of Sweet's criminal record in England and threatened to expose his identity to you whom he had recognized.'

'Very neat flashes of hindsight from Giovanni,' said Alleyn drily. 'I don't believe a word of it. Do you?'

'Well, Signore, that is his guess! His evidence of fact I accept entirely. The important point is that Sweet was in danger, for whatever reason, and that the threat came from Mailer. Who, of course, had discovered that Sweet was sent to spy upon him by Ziegfeldt. It is a familiar story, Signor Super, is it not? The cross and the double-cross. The simple solution so often the true one. The circumstance of Mailer being a *ricattatore* and of his extorting money from tourists has no real bearing on his murder, though Sweet may have hoped it would confuse the issue.' Bergarmi's quick glance played over Alleyn. 'You are in doubt, Signor Super, are you not?' he asked.

'Pay no attention to me,' Alleyn said. 'I'm a foreigner, Signor Vice-Questore, and I should not try to fit Giovanni into an English criminal mould. You know your types and I do not.'

'Well, Signore,' said Bergarmi, smiling all over his face, 'you have the great modesty to say so.'

The photographic expert came in. 'They are ready, Signor Vice-Questore.'

'Ecco!' said Bergarmi, clapping Alleyn on the shoulder. 'The pictures. Shall we examine?'

They were still submerged in their fixative solution along benches in the developing-room. The Questore's photographs: Violetta in the sarcophagus with her tongue out. Violetta on the stretcher in the mortuary. Mailer's jaw. Details. Alleyn's photographs of Mailer, of a scrap of alpaca caught in a rail, of Mailer's foot, sole uppermost, caught in the fangs of the grille, of boot polish on another rail. Of various papers found in Mailer's apartment. Regulation shots that would fetch up in the police records.

And now, unexpectedly, views of Rome. Conventional shots of familiar subjects always with the same large, faintly smiling figure somewhere in the foreground or the middle distance. The Baron looking waggish with his head on one side, throwing a penny into the Trevi Fountain. The Baron looking magisterial in the Forum, pontifical before the Vatican and martial underneath Marcus Aurelius. And finally a shot taken by a third person of the Van der Veghels' heads in profile with rather an Egyptian flavour, hers behind his. They even had the same large ears with heavy lobes, he noticed.

And then – nothing. A faint remnant of the Baron at the head of the Spanish Steps heavily obscured by white fog. After that – nothing. Blankness.

'It is a pity,' said the photographic expert, 'there has been a misfortune. Light has been admitted.'

'So I see,' Alleyn said.

'I think,' Bergarmi pointed out, 'you mentioned, did you not, that there was difficulty with the Baroness's camera in the Mithraeum?'

'The flashlamp failed. Once. It worked the second time.'

'There is a fault, evidently, in the camera. Or in the removal of the film. Light,' the expert reiterated, 'has been admitted.'

'So,' Bergarmi said, 'we have no record of the sarcophagus. It is of secondary interest after all.'

'Yes,' Alleyn said. 'It is. After all. And as for the group by the statue of Mithras – '

'Ah, Signore,' said the expert. 'Here the news is better. We have the film marked Dorne. Here, Signore.'

Kenneth's photographs were reasonably good. They at once disproved his story of using the last of his film before meeting Mailer at the Apollo and of replacing it on his way to the Mithraeum. Here in order were snapshots taken in Perugia. Two of these showed Kenneth himself, *en travesti* in a garden surrounded by very dubious-looking friends, one of whom had taken off his clothes and seemed to be posing as a statue.

'*Molto sofisticato,*' said Bergarmi.

Next came pictures of Kenneth's aunt outside their hotel and of the travellers assembling near the Spanish Steps. Midway in the sequence was the picture of the god Mithras.

Kenneth had stood far enough away from his subject to include in the foreground the Baroness, fussing with her camera, and beyond her the group. Alleyn and Sophy grinned on either side of the

furiously embarrassed Grant and there was Sweet very clearly groping for Sophy's waist. They had the startled and rigid look of persons
in darkness transfixed by a flashlight. The details of the wall behind
them, their own gigantic shadows and the plump god with his
Phrygian cap, his smile and his blankly staring eyes, all stood out in
the greatest clarity. Kenneth had taken no other photographs in S.
Tommaso. The rest of his film had been used up on the Palatine Hill.

Alleyn waited for the films and prints to dry. Bergarmi pleaded
pressure of work and said he would leave him to it.

As he was about to go Alleyn said, 'You know, Signor
Vice-Questore, there is one item in this case that I find extremely
intriguing.'

'Yes? And it is – ?'

'This. Why on earth should Mailer, a flabby man, go to all the
exertion and waste a great deal of time in stowing Violetta in the
sarcophagus when he might so easily and quickly have tipped her
down the well?'

Bergarmi gazed at him in silence for some moments.

'I have no answer,' he said. 'There is, of course, an answer but I
cannot at the moment produce it. Forgive me, I am late.'

When he had gone Alleyn muttered, 'I can. Blow me down flat if
I can't.'

It was ten to three when he got back to his hotel.

He wrote up his report, arranged a meeting with Interpol and
took counsel with himself.

His mission, such as it was, was accomplished. He had got most of
the information he had been told to get. He had run the Mailer case
down to its grass roots and had forced Sweet to give him the most
useful list yet obtained of key figures in the biggest of the drug rackets.

And Mailer and Sweet were dead.

Professionally speaking, their deaths were none of his business.
They were strictly over to the Roman Questura, to Valdarno and
Bergarmi and their boys, and very ably they were being handled.
And yet . . .

He was greatly troubled.

At half past five he laid out all the photographs on his bed. He took
a paper from his file. The writing on it was in his own hand. He looked
at it for a long time and then folded it and put it in his pocket.

At six o'clock Kenneth Dorne rang up and asked apparently in some agitation if he could come and collect his film.

'Not now. I'm engaged,' Alleyn said, 'at least until seven.' He waited a moment and then said, 'You may ring again at eight.'

'Have – have they turned out all right? The photos?'

'Yours are perfectly clear. Why?'

'Is something wrong with hers – the Baroness's?'

'It's fogged.'

'Well, that's not my fault, is it? Look: I want to talk to you. Please.'

'At eight.'

'I see. Well I – yes – well, thank you. I'll ring again at eight.'

'Do that.'

At half past six the office called to say that the Baron Van der Veghel had arrived. Alleyn asked them to send him up.

He opened his door and when he heard the lift whine, went into the corridor. Out came a waiter ushering the Baron, who greeted Alleyn from afar and springingly advanced with outstretched hand.

'I hope you don't mind my bringing you up here,' Alleyn said. 'I thought we wanted a reasonable amount of privacy and the rooms down below are like a five-star Bedlam at this hour. Do come in. What will you drink? They make quite a pleasant cold brandy-punch. Or would you rather stick to the classics?'

The Baron chose brandy-punch and while it was coming enlarged upon their visit to the water-gardens at the Villa d'Este. 'We have been there before, of course,' he said, 'but with each visit the wonder grows. My wife said today that now she summons up, always at the same vista, a scarlet cardinal and his guests. She sees them through the mists of the fountains.'

'She has second sight,' Alleyn said lightly. Seeing the Baron was puzzled, he explained.

'Ach – no. No, we do not believe such phenomena. No, it is her imagination which is so very vivid. She is most sensitive to her surroundings but she does not see ghosts, Mr Alleyn.'

The drinks arrived. Alleyn attended to them and then said, 'Would you like to look at your photographs? I'm afraid you will be disappointed.'

He had left all the prints except Kenneth's on the bed.

When the Baron saw Violetta and Mailer, which he did at once, he said, 'Oh, no! This is too horrible! Please!'

'I'm so sorry,' Alleyn said and swept them away. 'Here are your wife's photographs. The early ones, you see, are very good. It is when we come to S. Tommaso that the trouble begins.'

'I cannot understand this,' the Baron said. He stooped, peered at them and took them up, one by one. 'My wife's camera is in good condition: it has never happened before. The film was correctly rolled off before it was removed. Where are the negatives?'

'Here they are.'

He held them in turn up to the light. 'I am sorry,' he said. 'And I confess I am puzzled. Forgive me, but – the man who processed the film – you said he was a police photographer?'

'I honestly don't think for a moment that he was careless.'

'My wife,' said the Baron, 'will be relieved after all. She wanted no record of the visit to that place.'

'No.'

'But I am sorry. You wished for the photograph of the sarcophagus, I believe.'

'The police attach little importance to it. But there is, after all, a record of the group in the Mithraeum.'

He dropped Kenneth's print on the bed.

The Baron stooped over it.

The room was quiet. The windows were shut and the great composite voice of Rome was not obtrusive. A flight of swallows flashed past almost too rapidly for recognition.

'Yes,' said the Baron. He straightened up and looked at Alleyn. 'It is a clear picture,' he said. 'Isn't it?'

The Baron sat down with his back to the windows. He drank a little of his cold brandy-punch. 'This is an excellent concoction,' he said. 'I am enjoying it.'

'Good. I wonder if you would do me a favour.'

'A favour? But certainly, if it is possible.'

'I have a copy of a letter. It's written in a language that I don't know. I think it may be in Dutch. Will you look at it for me?'

'Of course.'

Alleyn gave it to him. 'You will see,' he said, 'that the original was written – typed, actually – on the letter-paper of your publishing firm – of Adriaan and Welker. Will you read it?'

There was a long silence and then the Baron said, 'You ask me here to drink with you. You show me – these things. Why do you behave in this way? Perhaps you have a microphone concealed in the room and a tape-recorder, as in some ridiculous crime film?'

'No. I am not acting for the police. My job here is finished. No doubt I should have taken this letter to them but they will find the original when they search Mailer's rooms. I doubt if they will take very much interest in it, but of course I have not read it and may be wrong. They know very well that he was a blackmailer. I have seen that your wife's name appears in the letter. I am behaving reprehensibly in this matter, I dare say, but I don't think you have any reason to throw your brandy-punch in my face, Baron. It was offered in what may fairly be called good faith.'

The Baron moved slightly. The light from the window crossed his face and in a moment the white Apollo, the glancing Mercury, the faintly smiling Husband of the Villa Giulia seemed in turn to look through his mask. 'I must believe you,' he said. 'What else can I do?'

'If you like you can go away leaving me to deal with – for example – Kenneth Dorne and his photography.'

'Whatever I do,' said the Baron, 'it is clear that I put myself in your hands. I have no choice, I think.'

He got up and walked about the room, still with some trace of elasticity in his tread. At last he said, 'It seems to me there would be little point in my refusing to give you the content of this letter since you tell me, and I believe you, that the original is extant. You can get a translation easily enough. In effect it appears that someone – you will have seen the name – calling himself Silas J. Sebastian had written to my firm asking if they could give him any information about my wife. Apparently the writer had said he represented an American magazine and was organizing a series of articles on the incursions into the business world of persons of the old nobilities. From the point of view of their wives. The writer, it appears, went on to say that he had a personal interest in my wife as he believed they were distantly related. Evidently he asked for my wife's maiden name. This letter is an answer to their inquiry.'

'Yes?'

'It says – ' The Baron seemed to flinch from his intention. He shut his eyes for a moment and then examined the letter as if he saw it for the first time. Presently in an extraordinarily prim voice that seemed not to belong to him he said: 'In accordance with my standing instructions it states that the Baroness Van der Veghel is a permanent invalid and lives in retirement.'

'When did you first encounter Sebastian Mailer?'

'Eighteen months ago. In Geneva.'

'And a few weeks later he wrote his letter. He didn't trouble to find himself an entirely dissimilar pseudonym.'

'No doubt he felt sure of himself.'

'After all,' Alleyn said, 'this letter might be a standard reply to choke off boring inquiries.'

'He did not think so. He pursued the matter,' said the Baron. 'He extended his investigations.'

'To – ?'

'I regret: I must decline to answer.'

'Very well. Let us accept that he found his material. Will you tell me this much? When you met him again, in Rome, the other day, had you any idea – ?'

'*None!* My God, none! Not until – '

'Until?'

'A week before the – before S. Tommaso.'

'And then the blackmailing process began?'

'Yes.'

'Were you prepared to pay?'

'Mr Alleyn, I had no choice. I flew to Geneva and obtained the money in notes of small denomination.'

'You presented a brave front,' Alleyn said, 'on that expedition. You and your wife. So much enthusiasm for the antiquated! Such *joie de vivre*!'

The Baron Van der Veghel looked steadily at Alleyn for some few moments and then he said, 'You yourself have a distinguished and brilliant wife, I think? We have admired her work very greatly. She is a superb painter.'

Alleyn said nothing.

'You must know, then, Mr Alleyn, that a preoccupation with the arts is not to be tampered with – my English is unable to explain me, I think – it is not to be cut off and turned on like taps. Beauty and, for us, antique beauty in especial – is absolute. No misfortune or anxiety can colour our feeling for it. When we see it we salute it and are greatly moved. The day before yesterday at S. Tommaso I was furnished with the money demanded of me as a price of silence. I was prepared to hand it over. The decision had been taken. I have to confess that a lightness of spirit came over me and a kind of relief. The beauty of the Etruscan works in that underworld did much to enhance this feeling.'

'And also it was advisable, wasn't it, to keep up appearances?'

'That, too,' said the Baron steadily. 'I admit. That too. But it was not difficult. There were the Etruscans to support me. I may tell you that I believe our family, which is of great antiquity, arose in classical times in the lands between the Tiber and the Arno.'

'Your wife told me so. Did you hand over the money?'

'No. There was no opportunity. As you know, he had gone.'

'A further and very understandable relief.'

'Of course.'

'You were not his only victim in that party you know.'

'So I believe.'

Alleyn took his glass. 'Let me give you a drink.'

'It will not increase my indiscretion,' said the Baron. 'But thank you.'

When Alleyn had given it to him he said, 'You may not believe me when I say that it would solace me if I could tell you what it was that he had discovered. I cannot. But on my honour I wish that I could. I wish it with all my heart, Mr Alleyn.'

'Let us take it as read.'

Alleyn collected the Baroness's photographs, prints and negatives. 'You will take these, won't you?' he said. 'There is nothing in the earlier ones to distress your wife.' He gave them to him. The picture in profile of the Van der Veghels' heads was on top.

'It's a striking picture,' Alleyn said lightly, 'Isn't it?'

The Baron stared at it and then looked up at him.

'We think alike, too,' he said. 'My wife and I. You may have noticed it.'

'Yes,' said Alleyn. 'I noticed.'

'When such a bond occurs, and I think it occurs very seldom, it cannot be – I am lost for the English word.'

'Gainsaid?'

'Perhaps. It cannot be interrupted. You have it in your literature. In your *Wutherink Heights* you have it.'

It was not easy, Alleyn thought, to clothe the Van der Veghels in the mantles of Heathcliff and Cathy, but all the same, it was not altogether a ludicrous association.

The Baron finished his drink and with a well-managed air of briskness, lightly slapped his knees and stood up.

'And now I go,' he said. 'It is unlikely we meet again, unless at whatever formalities the authorities may require of us. I believe that I am your debtor, Mr Alleyn, to – to an indefinable extent. You would not wish me to say more, I think.'

'Not another syllable.'

'As I supposed. May we – ?'

For the only time during their brief acquaintance Alleyn saw the Baron Van der Veghel really uncertain of himself. He looked at his enormous hand and then doubtfully at Alleyn.

'But of course,' Alleyn said and his own hand was briefly engulfed. 'I am truly grateful,' said the Baron.

Alleyn watched him go, bouncily as ever, to the lift.

By and large, he thought to himself, that was the nicest murderer I have met.

CHAPTER 10

When in Rome

'The case was clinched,' Alleyn wrote, 'when I saw young Dorne's snapshot. No Baron.

'It'd been a possibility all along. While we were lined up in that preposterous group scarcely able to see each other he hadn't spoken. *She* talked to *him*. When she told him to stand farther back and not to speak he wasn't there. While she fussed about hunting for her second flashlamp – and of course the first dud was a put-up affair – he was off by the passage behind that smirking little god. He had his date with Mailer. He had to hand over the money. Mailer was to dispose of it – in the car I expect – and had stayed behind for that purpose.

'At the moment when we all heard Violetta's voice, Van der Veghel was in the passage. I don't believe he witnessed the murder. I think he came upon Mailer with Violetta dead at his feet. I think Mailer bolted and Van der Veghel chased him up the iron stairs to the next landing. There was a struggle. Mailer was knocked out and throttled and tipped over the well-head. The body fell like a plummet into the well below and in doing so a coat sleeve brushed the inner side of the rail and was torn.

'Van der Veghel climbed the rail at the upper well in order to look down and discover whether his victim had, in fact, made a straight fall into the depths. In doing so the rubber studs on his shoes scored through the brown boot polish that may well have been left there by the abominable Sweet on his way back from dumping Lady B. in the atrium. His brogues were polished underneath the instep, *à la* the

414

batman he never had. Sweet may have caught sight of Violetta or Mailer or both and snooped.

'My contention is that Van der Veghel, when he looked down, saw that Mailer's body had gone and that Violetta's lay where Mailer had left it. He returned and he stowed it in the sarcophagus, deliberately leaving a bit of her shawl exposed.

'He wanted Violetta to be found.

'He wanted the police to know Mailer had killed her. He wanted them to believe Mailer had bolted with her death on his head.

'The whole business would, as one says, take less time to happen than it has taken to set it down. Eight minutes at the most, I'd say, and the Baroness was a great deal longer than that, setting up her group, fiddling and faddling, changing her "bulps", taking a second shot. He was back, on his nimble rubber-studded shoes, well in time to take his own shots of the group. When he removed the film from the Baroness's camera, he was careful to expose the greater part of it. He didn't know about young Dorne's shot.

'And the Baroness? I could have driven him harder here. I could have forced him to confirm what I believe to be her part in the performance. I think she knew they were being blackmailed by Mailer and I think her husband asked her to hold up the proceedings while he kept his assignation and paid over the cash. I don't believe she knows he killed Mailer and I don't believe it would make a scrap of difference to their passionate, their overwhelming union if she did.

'And finally – the material for blackmail? Troy, my darling, the chances of distantly related persons bearing a startling physical resemblance to each other are not impossible. But they *are* extremely remote. In our job we are taught that the ear gives one of the most valuable proofs of identification. The Van der Veghels' ears are, if not identical as near as damn it, and very, very strange, great ears they are.

'Fox, with his genius for inspiring gossip, has gleaned from a London representative of Adriaan and Welker that the late Baron was what he describes as a bit of a lad with a European reputation as such. The Baroness is said to belong to an expatriate branch of the family. She doesn't accompany her husband on his visits to The Hague and is understood to be an invalid. She! The Baroness! An invalid!

'I've gone on about their strangeness, haven't I? Their resemblance, not only to each other but to the Etruscan antiquities to which they are so much attracted? I see them as larger than life: classical figures springing about behind, of all things, a nonconformist façade. And I think that very probably they are half-siblings.

'None of this would be provable in a court of law. Even the Baron's absence from young Dorne's snapshot could be accounted for. He would say that he had moved out of shot at that juncture and none of us could swear he hadn't.

'Giovanni? Giovanni had been double-crossed and milched and threatened by the unspeakable Sweet. He was and is greedy to get his own back upon Sweet alive or dead and he grabbed at the chance to concoct his tarradiddle about Sweet's agitation and suspicious behaviour. The only bit of it that holds up is his account of Sweet standing on the rails at the middle level. Apparently he did just that.

'And the upshot? The Roman police force will present a file in which the available evidence will point to Sweet. I haven't held anything back from them. I haven't shoved my own reading of the case under their noses. They are an able body of men and the affair is their affair. I've got the information I was sent to get and will be closeted with the Interpol chap tomorrow. Mailer and Sweet were both wanted in England and if they had lived I would have applied for extradition and brought them back.

'I shall always think of the Baron as an antique person in a sudden antique rage, falling upon his enemy like lightning. His consort and his union had been threatened and that was his answer. When in Rome he did as the ancient Romans. I am afraid he does not in the least regret it and I'm afraid I really can't say that I do.

'The Embassy here has offered to send my report back in the Diplomatic Bag. I'll enclose this with it. And so, my dear love . . .'

II

'What will you do?' Barnaby Grant asked Sophy Jason, 'now that it's all over? Will you pick up your guide book and go on your way rejoicing?'

'Go on my way – yes, I think so.'

'To Florence?'

'To Perugia first.'

'And you will receive visitors in Perugia if they should happen to appear?'

'I'm not going into purdah in Perugia.'

'The odd thing is, Sophy, that I'm booked in at the Rosetta from next Monday.'

'Are you, now? Since when?'

'Well – since we danced together in Rome.'

Sophy said, 'It will be lovely to meet you again in Perugia.'

'You don't mind?'

'No. I shall look forward to it.'

'Don't be so brisk. Can't you throw me a nice, equivocal leer? Can't you stint like Juliet and say aye?'

She burst out laughing.

'Sophy, I think I love you.'

'Do you, Barnaby? Don't let's say anything about it until you're sure.'

'Look,' he said, 'isn't Rome lovely? The bells ring, the swallows rush about, the saints look down and the fountains play.'

'And in the Villa Giulia the Etruscans smile.'

'And the gardens smell of jasmine. Isn't Rome lovely?'

'Lovely!' she agreed. 'But all the same, strange things can happen under her skin.'

'And always have,' said Barnaby.

Tied Up in Tinsel

For my Godson, Nicholas Dacres-Mannings
when he grows up

Contents

Cast of Characters

Hilary Bill-Tasman	*Of Halberds Manor,*
	Landed proprietor

Staff at Halberds

Cuthbert	*Steward*
Mervyn	*Head houseman*
Nigel	*Second houseman*
Wilfred (Kittiwee)	*Cook*
Vincent	*Gardener-chauffeur*
Tom	*Odd boy*

Guests at Halberds

Troy Alleyn	*Celebrated painter*
Colonel Frederick Fleaton Forrester	*Hilary's uncle*
Mrs Forrester	*The Colonel's wife*
Alfred Moult	*Colonel Forrester's manservant*
Mr Bert Smith	*Authority on Antiques*
Cressida Tottenham	*Hilary's fiancée*

The Law

Major Marchbanks	*Governor at The Vale*
Superintendent Wrayburn	*Downlow Police Force*
Superintendent Roderick Alleyn	*CID*
Detective-Inspector Fox	*CID*
Detective-Sergeant Thompson	*Finger-print expert, CID*
Detective-Sergeant Bailey	*Photographer, CID*

Sundry guests and constables

CHAPTER 1

Halberds

'When my sire,' said Hilary Bill-Tasman, joining the tips of his fingers, 'was flung into penury by the Great Slump, he commenced Scrap-Merchant. You don't mind my talking?'

'Not at all.'

'Thank you. When I so describe his activities I do not indulge in *facezia*. He went into partnership in a rag-and-bone way with my Uncle Bert Smith, who was already equipped with a horse and cart and the experience of a short lifetime. "Uncle", by the way, is a courtesy title.'

'Yes?'

'You will meet him tomorrow. My sire, who was newly widowed, paid for his partnership by enlarging the business and bringing into it such items of family property as he had contrived to hide from his ravenous creditors. They included a Meissen bowl of considerable monetary though, in my opinion, little aesthetic value. My Uncle Bert, lacking expertise in the higher reaches of his profession, would no doubt have knocked off this and other heirlooms to the nearest fence. My father, however, provided him with such written authority as to clear him of any suspicion of chicanery and sent him to Bond Street, where he drove a bargain that made him blink.'

'Splendid. Could you keep your hands as they are?'

'I think so. They prospered. By the time I was five they had two carts and two horses and a tidy account in the bank. I congratulate you, by the way, upon making no allusion to Steptoe and Son. I rather judge my new acquaintances under that heading. My father

developed an unsuspected flare for trade and, taking advantage of
the Depression, bought in a low market and, after a period of acute
anxiety, sold in a high one. There came a day when, wearing his best
suit and the tie to which he had every right, he sold the last of his
family possessions at an exorbitant price to King Farouk, with whom
he was tolerably acquainted. It was a Venetian chandelier of unpar-
alleled vulgarity.'

'Fancy.'

'This transaction led to most rewarding sequels, terminated only
by His Majesty's death, at which time my father had established a
shop in South Molton Street while Uncle Bert presided over a fleet
of carts and horses, maintaining his hold on the milieu that best
suited him, but greatly increased his expertise.'

'And you?'

'I ? Until I was seven years old I lodged with my father and
adopted uncle in a two-roomed apartment in Smalls Yard, Cheapjack
Lane, E.C.4.'

'Learning the business?'

'You may say so. But also learning, after admittedly a somewhat
piecemeal fashion, an appreciation of English literature, objets d'art
and simple arithmetic. My father ordered my education. Each
morning he gave me three tasks to be executed before evening when
he and Uncle Bert returned from their labours. After supper he
advanced my studies until I fell asleep.'

'Poor little boy!'

'You think so? So did my uncle and aunt. My father's maternal
connections. They are a Colonel and Mrs Forrester. You will meet
them also tomorrow. They are called Fleaton and Bedelia Forrester
but have always been known in the family at Uncle Flea and Aunt
Bed, the facetious implication having been long forgotten.'

'They intervened in your education?'

'They did, indeed. Having got wind of my father's activities they
had themselves driven into the East End. Aunt Bed, then a vigorous
young woman, beat on my locked door with her umbrella and when
admitted gave vent to some very intemperate comments strongly
but less violently seconded by her husband. They left in a rage and
returned that evening with an offer.'

'To take over your education?'

'And me. In toto. At first my father said he'd see them damned first but in his heart he liked them very much. Since our lodging was to be demolished as an insanitary dwelling and new premises were difficult to find he yielded eventually, influenced I dare say, by threats of legal action and Child Welfare officers. Whatever the cause, I went, in the upshot, to live with Uncle Flea and Aunt Bed.'

'Did you like it there?'

'Yes. I didn't lose touch with my father. He patched up his row with the Forresters and we exchanged frequent visits. By the time I was thirteen he was extremely affluent and able to pay for my education at his own old school, at which, fortunately he had put me down at birth. This relieved us to some extent from the burden of an overpowering obligation but I retain the liveliest sense of gratitude to Flea and Bed.'

'I look forward to meeting them.'

'They are held to be eccentric. I can't see it myself, but you shall judge.'

'In what way?'

'Well – trifling departures from normal practice, perhaps. They never travel without green lined tropical umbrellas of a great age. These they open when they awake in the morning as they prefer their vernal shade to the direct light. And then they bring a great many of their valuables with them. All Aunt Bed's jewels and Uncle Flea's stocks and shares and one or two very nice objets d'art of which I wouldn't at all mind having the disposal. They also bring a considerable amount of hard cash. In Uncle Flea's old uniform case. He is on the reserve list.'

'That is perhaps a little eccentric.'

'You think so? You may be right. To resume. My education, from being conventional in form, was later expanded at my father's instance, to include an immensely thorough training in the more scholarly aspects of the trade to which I succeeded. When he died I was already accepted as a leading European authority on the great period of Chinese Ceramics. Uncle Bert and I became very rich. Everything I've touched turned to gold, as they say. In short I was a "have" and not a "have-not". To cap it all (really it was almost comical), I became a wildly successful gambler and won two quite princely non-taxable fortunes on the Pools. Uncle Bert inspired me in this instance.'

'Lovely for you.'

'Well – I like it. My wealth has enabled me to indulge my own eccentricities, which you may think as extreme as those of Uncle Flea and Aunt Bed.'

'For instance?'

'For instance, this house. And its staff. Particularly, you may think, its staff. Halberds belonged from Tudor times up to the first decade of the nineteenth century to my paternal forebears: the Bill-Tasmans. They were actually the leading family in these parts. The motto is, simply, "Unicus" which is as much as to say "peerless". My ancestors interpreted it, literally, by refusing peerages and behaving as if they were royalty. You may think me arrogant,' said Hilary, 'but I assure you that compared to my forebears I am a violet by a mossy stone.'

'Why did the family leave Halberds?'

'My dear, because they were ruined. They put everything they had into the West Indies and were ruined, very properly I dare say, by the emancipation of slaves. The house was sold off but owing to its situation nobody really fancied it and as the Historic Trust was then in the womb of time, it suffered the ravages of desertion and fell into a sort of premature ruin.'

'You bought it back?'

'Two years ago.'

'And restored it?'

'And am in process of restoring it. Yes.'

'At enormous cost?'

'Indeed. But, I hope you agree, with judgment and style?'

'Certainly. I have,' said Troy Alleyn, 'finished for the time being.'

Hilary got up and strolled round the easel to look at his portrait.

'It is, of course, extremely exciting. I'm glad you are still to some extent what I think is called a figurative painter. I wouldn't care to be reduced to a schizoid arrangement of geometrical propositions, however satisfying to the abstracted eye.'

'No?'

'No. The Royal Antiquarian Guild (The Rag as it is called) will no doubt think the portrait extremely *avant garde*. Shall we have our drinks? It's half past twelve, I see.'

'May I clean up, first?'

'By all means. You may prefer to attend to your own tools, but if not, Mervyn, who you may recollect was a signwriter before he went to gaol, would, I'm sure, be delighted to clean your brushes.'

'Lovely. In that case I shall merely clean myself.'

'Join me here, when you've done so.'

Troy removed her smock and went upstairs and along a corridor to her deliciously warm room. She scrubbed her hands in the adoining bathroom, and brushed her short hair, staring as she did so out of the window.

Beyond a piecemeal domain, still in the hands of landscape-gardeners, the moors were erected against a leaden sky. Their margins seemed to flow together under some kind of impersonal design. They bore their scrubby mantling with indifference and were, or so Troy thought, unnervingly detached. Between two dark curves the road to the prison briefly appeared. A light sleet was blown across the landscape.

Well, she thought, it lacks only the Hound of the Baskervilles, and I wouldn't put it past him to set that up if it occurs to him to do so.

Immediately beneath her window lurched the wreckage of a conservatory that at some time had extended along the outer face of the east wing. Hilary had explained that it was soon to be demolished: at the moment it was an eyesore. The tops of seedling firs poked through shattered glass. Anonymous accumulations had silted up the interior. In one part the roof had completely fallen in. Hilary said that when next she visited Halberds she would look down upon lawns and a vista through cypress trees leading to a fountain with stone dolphins. Troy wondered just how successful these improvements would be in reducing the authority of those ominous hills.

Between the garden-to-be and the moor, on a ploughed slope, a scarecrow, that outlandish, *commedia-dell'-arte*-like survival, swivelled and gesticulated in the December wind.

A man came into view down below, wheeling a barrow and tilting his head against the wind. He wore a sou'wester and an oilskin cape.

Troy thought: That's Vincent. That's the gardener-chauffeur. And what was it about Vincent? Arsenic? Yes. And I suppose this must all be true. Or must it?

The scarecrow rocked madly on its base and a wisp or two of straw flew away in the sleety wind.

II

Troy had only been at Halberds for five days but already she accepted its cockeyed grandeur. After her arrival to paint his commissioned portrait, Hilary had thrown out one or two airy hints as to the bizarre nature of his staff. At first she had thought that he was going in for a not very funny kind of leg-pulling but she soon discovered her mistake.

At luncheon they were waited upon by Cuthbert, to whom Hilary had referred as his chief steward, and by Nigel, the second houseman.

Cuthbert was a baldish man of about sixty with a loud voice, big hands and downcast eyes. He performed his duties composedly as, indeed, did his assistant, but there was something watchful and at the same time colourless in their general behaviour. They didn't shuffle, but one almost expected them to do so. One felt that it was necessary to remark that their manner was not furtive. How far these impressions were to be attributed to hindsight and how far to immediate observation, Troy was unable to determine but she reflected that after all it was a tricky business adapting oneself to a domestic staff entirely composed of murderers. Cuthbert, a head-waiter at the time, had murdered his wife's lover, a handsome young commis. Because of extenuating circumstances, the death sentence, Hilary told her, had been commuted into a lifer which exemplary behaviour had reduced to eight years. 'He is the most harmless of creatures,' Hilary had said. 'The commis called him a cuckold and spat in his face at a moment when he happened to be carving a wing-rib. He merely lashed out.'

Mervyn, the head houseman, once a signwriter, had, it emerged, been guilty of killing a burglar with a booby-trap. 'Really,' Hilary said, 'it was going much too far to gaol him. He hadn't meant to *destroy* anyone, you know, only to give an intruder pause if one should venture to break in. But he entirely misjudged the potential of an old-fashioned flat-iron balanced on a door-top. Mervyn became understandably warped by confinement and behaved so incontinently that he was transferred to The Vale.'

Two other homicides completed the indoor staff. The cook's name was Wilfred. Among his fellows he was known as Kittiwee, being a lover of cats.

'He actually trained as a chef. He is not,' Hilary had told Troy, 'one hundred per cent he-man. He was imprisoned under that heading but while serving his sentence attacked a warder who approached him when he was not in the mood. This disgusting man was known to be a cat-hater and to have practised some form of cruelty. Kittiwee's onslaught was therefore doubly energetic and most unfortunately his victim struck his head against the cell wall and was killed. He himself served a painful extension of his sentence.'

Then there was the second houseman, Nigel, who in former years had been employed in the manufacture of horses for merry-go-rounds and on the creative side of the waxworks industry until he became a religious fanatic and unreliable.

'He belonged to an extreme sect,' Hilary had explained. 'A monastic order of sorts, with some curious overtones. What with one thing and another the life put too heavy a strain upon Nigel. His wits turned and he murdered a person to whom he always refers as "a sinful lady". He was sent to Broadmoor where, believe it or not, he recovered his senses.'

'I hope he doesn't think me sinful.'

'No, no, I promise you. You are not at all the type and in any case he is now perfectly rational and composed except for weeping rather extravagantly when he remembers his crime. He has a gift for modelling. If we have a white Christmas I shall ask him to make a snowman for us.'

Finally, Hilary had continued, there was Vincent, the gardener. Later on, when the landscape specialists had completed their operations, there would be a full complement of outside staff. In the meantime there were casual labourers and Vincent.

'And really,' Hilary had said, 'it is quite improper to refer to him as a homicide. There was some ridiculous misunderstanding over a fatal accident with an arsenical preparation for the control of fungi. This was followed by a gross misdirection to a more than usually idiotic jury and after a painful interval, by a successful appeal. Vincent,' he had summed up, 'is a much wronged person.'

'How,' Troy had asked, 'did you come to engage your staff?'

'Ah! A pertinent question. You see when I bought Halberds I determined not only to restore it but to keep it up in the manner to which it had been accustomed. I had no wish to rattle dismally in Halberds with a village trot or some unpredictable Neapolitan couple who would feed me on pasta for a fortnight and then flounce off without notice. On the other hand civilized household staff, especially in this vicinity, I found to be quite unobtainable. After some thought, I made an appointment to visit my neighbour-to-be, the Governor at The Vale. He is called Major Marchbanks.

'I put my case to him. I had always understood that of all criminals, murderers are much the nicest to deal with. Murderers of a certain class, I mean. I discriminate. Thugs who shoot and bash policemen and so on are quite unsuitable and indeed would be unsafe. But your single-job man, prompted by a solitary and unprecedented upsurge of emotion under circumstances of extreme provocation, is usually well-behaved. Marchbanks supported me in this theory. After some deliberation I arranged with him that as suitable persons were released I should have the first refusal. It was, from their point of view, a form of rehabilitation. And being so rich, I can pay handsomely.'

'But was there a ready supply?'

'I had to wait for them, as it were, to fall in. For some time I lived very simply with only Cuthbert and Kittiwee, in four rooms of the east wing. But gradually the supply built up: The Vale was not the only source. The Scrubs and, in Nigel's case, Broadmoor were also productive. In passing,' Hilary had then pointed out, 'I remind you that there is nothing original in my arrangements. The idea was canvassed in Victorian times by no less a person than Charles Dickens and considerably later, on a farcical level, by Sir Arthur Wing Pinero. I have merely adopted it and carried it to its logical conclusion.'

'I think,' Troy had said, 'it's remotely possible that Rory, my husband, you know, may have been responsible for the arrest of one or even more, of your staff. Would they – ?'

'You need have no qualms. For one thing they don't know of the relationship and for another they wouldn't mind if they did. They bear no grudge as far as I can discern against the police. With the possible exception of Mervyn, the ex-signwriter, you recollect. He feels that since his booby-trap was directed against a class that the police are concerned to suppress, it was rather hard that he should suffer so grievous a penalty for removing one of them. But even he has taken against Counsel for the Prosecution and the jury rather than against the officers who arrested him.'

'Big of him, I suppose,' said Troy.

These conversations had taken place during the early sittings. Now, on the fifth day of her residence, Hilary and Troy had settled down to an oddly companionable relationship. The portrait prospered. She was working with unusual rapidity, and few misgivings. All was well.

'I'm so glad,' Hilary said, 'that it suits you to stay for Christmas. I do wish your husband could have joined us. He might have found my arrangements of some interest.'

'He's on an extradition case in Australia.'

'Your temporary loss,' said Hilary neatly, 'is my lasting gain. How shall we spend the afternoon? Another sitting? I am all yours.'

'That would be grand. About an hour while the light lasts and then I'll be under my own steam for a bit, I think.'

Troy looked at her host who was also her subject. A very rewarding subject, she thought, and one with whom it would be fatally easy to confuse interpretation with caricature. That ovoid forehead, that crest of fuzz, those astonished, light blue eyes and the mouth that was perpetually hitched up at the corners in a non-smile! But, Troy thought, isn't interpretation, of necessity, a form of caricature?

She found Hilary contemplating her as if she was the subject and he the scrutator.

'Look here,' Troy said abruptly, 'you've not by any chance been pulling my leg? About the servants and all that?'

'No.'

'No?'

'I assure you. No.'

'OK,' said Troy. 'I'm going back to work. I'll be about ten minutes fiddling and brooding and then if you'll sit again, we'll carry on.'

'But of course. I am enjoying myself,' Hilary said, 'inordinately.'

Troy returned to the library. Her brushes as usual had been cleaned in turpentine. Today they had been set out together with a nice lump of fresh rag. Her paint-encrusted smock had been carefully disposed over a chair-back. An extra table covered with paper had been brought in to supplement a makeshift bench. Mervyn again, she thought, the booby-trap chap who used to paint signs.

And as she thought of him he came in; wary-looking and dark about the jaw.

'Excuse me,' Mervyn said, and added 'madam' as if he'd just remembered to do so. 'Was there anything else?'

'Thank you *very* much,' Troy said. 'Nothing. It's all marvellous,' and felt she was being unnaturally effusive.

'I thought,' Mervyn mumbled, staring at the portrait, 'you could do with more bench space. Like. Madam.'

'Oh, rather. Yes. Thank you.'

'Like you was cramped. Sort of.'

'Well – not now.'

He said nothing but he didn't go. He continued to look at the portrait. Troy, who never could talk easily about work in progress, began to set her palette with her back to Mervyn. When she turned round it gave her quite a shock to find him close behind her.

But he was only waiting with her smock which he held as if it were a valuable top-coat and he a trained manservant. She felt no touch of his hands as he helped her into it.

'Thank you very much,' Troy repeated and hoped she sounded definitive without being disagreeable.

'Thank you, madam,' Mervyn responded and as always when this sort of exchange cropped up, she repressed an impulse to ask: 'For what?'

(For treating him like a manservant when I know he's a booby-setting manslaughterer? thought Troy).

Mervyn withdrew, delicately closing the door after him.

Soon after that, Hilary came in and for an hour Troy worked on his portrait. By then the light had begun to fail. Her host having remarked that he expected a long-distance call from London, she said she would go for a walk. They had, she felt, seen enough of each other for the time being.

III

A roughish path crossed the waste that was to become something Hilary, no doubt, would think of as a pleasance. It led past the ruined conservatory to the ploughed field she had seen from her bedroom window.

Here was the scarecrow, a straw-stuffed antic groggily anchored in a hole it had enlarged with its own gyrations, lurching extravagantly in the north wind. It was clad in the wreckage of an Edwardian frock-coat and a pair of black trousers. Its billycock hat had been pulled down over the stuffed bag which formed its head. It was extended in the classic cruciform gesture and a pair of clownish gloves, tied to the ends of the crosspiece, flapped lamentably, as did the wild remnants of something that might once have been an opera cloak. Troy felt that Hilary himself had had a hand in its creation.

He had explained in detail to what lengths, and at what enormous expense of time and money, he had gone in the accurate restoration of Halberds. Portraits had been hunted down and re-purchased, walls rehung in silk, panelling unveiled and ceilings restored by laborious stripping. Perhaps in some collection of foxed watercolours he had found a Victorian sketch of this steep field with a gesticulating scarecrow in the middle distance.

She skirted the field and climbed a steep slope. Now she was out on the moors and here at last was the sealed road. She followed it up to where it divided the hills.

She was now high above Halberds and looking down at it saw it was shaped like an E without the middle stroke and splendidly pro-portioned. An eighteenth-century picture of it hung in the library; remembering this, she was able to replace the desolation that sur-rounded the house with the terraces, walks, artificial hill, lake and vistas created, so Hilary had told her, by Capability Brown. She could make out her own room in the western façade with the hideous wreckage of a conservatory beneath it. Smoke plumed up wildly from several of the chimneys and she caught a whiff of burning wood. In the foreground Vincent, a foreshortened pigmy, trundled his barrow. In the background a bulldozer slowly laid out prelimi-naries for Hilary's restorations. Troy could see where a hillock, topped by a folly and later destroyed by a bomb, had once risen beyond an elegant little lake. That was what the bulldozer was up to: scooping out a new lake and heaping the spoil into what would become a hillock. And a 'Hilary's Folly' no doubt would ultimately crown the summit.

And no doubt, Troy thought, it will be very, very beautiful but there's an intrinsic difference between "Here it still is" and "This is how it was" and all the monstrous accumulation of his super-scrap-markets, high antiques and football pools won't do the trick for him.

She turned and took fifteen paces into the north wind.

It was as if a slide had clicked over in a projector and an entirely dissociated subject thrown on the screen. Troy now looked down into The Vale, as it was locally called, and her first thought was of the hopeless incongruity of this gentle word, for it stood not only for the valley but for the prison whose dry moats, barriers, watch-towers, yards, barracks and chimney-stacks were set out down below like a scale model of themselves for her to shudder at. Her husband some-times referred to The Vale as 'Heartbreak House'.

The wind was now fitfully laced with sleet and this steel-engraving of a view was shot across with slantwise drifts that were blown out as fast as they appeared.

Facing Troy was a road sign.

STEEP DESCENT
DANGEROUS CORNERS
ICE
CHANGE DOWN

As if to illustrate the warning, a covered van laboured up the road from Halberds, stopped beside her, clanked into bottom gear and ground its way down into The Vale. It disappeared round the first bend and was replaced by a man in a heavy macintosh and tweed hat, climbing towards her. He looked up and she saw a reddened face, a white moustache and blue eyes.

She had already decided to turn back but an obscure notion that it would be awkward to do so at once, made her pause. The man came up with her, raised his hat, gave her a conventional 'Good evening' and then hesitated. 'Coming up rough,' he said. He had a pleasant voice.

'Yes,' Troy said. 'I'll beat a retreat, I think. I've come up from Halberds.'

'Stiffish climb, isn't it, but not as stiff as mine. Please forgive me, but you must be Hilary Bill-Tasman's celebrated guest, mustn't you? My name's Marchbanks.'

'Oh, yes. He told me – '

'I come as far as this most evenings for the good of my wind and legs. To get out of the valley, you know.'

'I can imagine.'

'Yes,' said Major Marchbanks, 'it's rather a grim proposition, isn't it? But I shouldn't keep you standing about in this beastly wind. We'll meet again, I hope, at the Christmas tree.'

'I hope so, too,' said Troy.

'Rather a rum set-up at Halberds I expect you think, don't you?'

'Unusual, at least.'

'Quite. Oh,' Major Marchbanks said as if answering an unspoken query; 'I'm all for it, you know. All for it.'

He lifted his wet hat again, flourished his stick and made off by the way he had come. Somewhere down in the prison a bell clanged.

Troy returned to Halberds.

She and Hilary had tea very cosily before a cedar-wood fire in a little room which, he said, had been his five-times-great-grandmother's boudoir. Her portrait hung above the fire: a mischievous-looking old lady with a discernible resemblance to Hilary himself. The room was hung in apple-green watered silk with rose-embroidered curtains. It contained an exquisite screen, a French ormolu desk, some elegant chairs and a certain lavishness of porcelain amoretti.

'I dare say,' Hilary said through a mouthful of hot buttered muffin, 'you think it an effeminate setting for a bachelor. It awaits its chatelaine.'

'Really?'

'Really. She is called Cressida Tottenham and she too arrives tomorrow. We think of announcing our engagement.'

'What is she like?' Troy asked. She had found that Hilary relished the direct approach.

'Well – let me see. If one could taste her she would be salty with a faint rumour of citron.'

'You make her sound like a grilled sole.'

'All I can say to that is: she doesn't look like one.'

'What *does* she look like?'

'Like somebody whom I hope you will very much want to paint.'

'Oh-ho,' said Troy. 'Sits the wind in that quarter!'

'Yes, it does and it's blowing steady and strong. Wait until you see her and then tell me if you'll accept another Bill-Tasman commission and a much more delectable one. Did you notice an empty panel in the north wall of the dining-room?'

'Yes, I did.'

'Reserved for Cressida Tottenham by Agatha Troy.'

'I see.'

'She really is a lovely creature,' Hilary said with an obvious attempt at impartial assessment. 'You just wait. She's in the theatre, by the way. Well, I say *in*. She's only just in. She went to an academy of sorts and thence into something she calls organic-expressivism. I have tried to point out that this is a bastard and meaningless term but she doesn't seem to mind.'

'What do they do?'

'As far as I can make out they take off their clothes, which in Cressida's case can do nothing but please, and cover their faces with pale green tendrils, which (again in her case) is a ludicrous waste of basic material. Harmful to the complexion.'

'Puzzling.'

'Unhappily Aunt Bed doesn't quite approve of Cressida, who is Uncle Flea's ward. Her father was a junior officer of Uncle Flea's and was killed in occupied Germany when saving Uncle Flea's life. So Uncle Flea felt he had an obligation and brought her up.'

'I see,' Troy said again.

'You know,' he said, 'what I like about you, apart from your genius and your looks, is your lack of superfluous ornament. You are an important piece from a very good period. If it wasn't for Cressida I should probably make advances to you myself.'

'That really *would* throw me completely off my stroke,' said Troy with some emphasis.

'You prefer to maintain a detached relationship with your subjects?'

'Absolutely.'

'I see your point, of course,' said Hilary.

'Good.'

He finished his muffin, damped his napkin with hot water, cleaned his fingers and walked over to the window. The rose-embroidered curtains were closed but he parted them and peered into the dark. 'It's snowing,' he said. 'Uncle Flea and Aunt Bed will have a romantic passage over the moors.'

'Do you mean – are they coming tonight – ?'

'Ah, yes. I forgot to tell you. My long-distance call was from their housekeeper. They left before dawn and expect to arrive in time for dinner.'

'A change in plans?'

'They suddenly thought they would. They prepare themselves for a visit at least three days before the appointed time and yet they dislike the feeling of impending departure. So they resolved to cut it short. I shall take a rest. What about you?'

'My walk has made me sleepy, I think. I will, too.'

'That's the north wind. It has a soporific effect upon newcomers. I'll tell Nigel to call you at half past seven, shall I? Dinner at eight-thirty and the warning bell at a quarter past. Rest well,' said Hilary, opening the door for her.

As she passed him she became acutely aware of his height and also of his smell which was partly Harris tweed and partly something much more exotic. 'Rest well,' he repeated and she knew he watched her as she went upstairs.

IV

She found Nigel in her bedroom. He had laid out her ruby-red silk dress and everything that went with it. Troy hoped that this ensemble had not struck him as being sinful.

He was now on his knees blowing needlessly at a brightly burning fire. Nigel was so blond that Troy was glad to see his eyes were not pink behind their prolific white lashes. He got to his feet and in a muted voice asked her if there would be anything else. He gazed at the floor and not at Troy, who said there was nothing else.

'It's going to be a wild night,' Troy remarked trying to be natural but sounding, she feared, like a bit part in *The Corsican Brothers*.

'That is as Heaven decrees, Mrs Alleyn,' Nigel said severely and left her. She reminded herself of Hilary's assurances that Nigel had recovered his sanity.

She took a bath, seething deliciously in resinous vapours and wondered how demoralizing this mode of living might become if prolonged. She decided (sinfully, as no doubt Nigel would have considered) that for the time being, at least, it tended to intensify her nicer ingredients. She drowsed before her fire, half-aware of the hush that comes upon a house when snow falls in the world outside. At half past seven, Nigel tapped at her door and she roused herself to dress. There was a cheval-glass in her room and she couldn't help seeing that she looked well in her ruby dress.

Distant sounds of arrival broke the quietude. A car engine. A door slam. After a considerable interval, voices in the passage and an entry into the next room. A snappish, female voice, apparently on the threshold, shouted. 'Not at all. Fiddle! Who says anything about being tired? We won't dress. I said we won't dress.' An interval and then the voice again: 'You don't want Moult, do you? Moult! The Colonel doesn't want you. Unpack later. I said he can unpack later.'

Uncle Flea, thought Troy, is deaf.

'And don't,' shouted the voice, 'keep fussing about the beard.'

A door closed. Someone walked away down the passage.

About the *beard*? Troy wondered. Could she have said beard?

For a minute or two nothing could be heard from the next room. Troy concluded that either Colonel or Mrs Fleaton Forrester had retired into the bathroom on the far side, a theory that was borne out by a man's voice, coming as it were from behind Troy's wardrobe, exclaiming: 'B! About my beard!' and receiving no audible reply.

Soon after this the Forresters could be heard to leave their apartment.

Troy thought she would give them a little while with Hilary before she joined them and she was still staring bemusedly into her fire when the warning bell, booty, so Hilary had told her, from Henry the Eighth's sack of the monasteries, rang out in its tower over the stables. Troy wondered if it reminded Nigel of his conventual days before he had turned a little mad.

She shook herself out of her reverie and found her way downstairs and into the main hall, where Mervyn, on the look-out, directed her to the green boudoir. 'We are not disturbing the library,' Mervyn said with a meaningful smirk. 'Madam.'

'How very considerate,' said Troy. He opened the boudoir door for her and she went in.

The Forresters stood in front of the fire with Hilary, who wore a plum-coloured smoking suit and a widish tie. Colonel Forrester was a surprised-looking old man with a pink-and-white complexion and a moustache. But no beard. He wore a hearing-aid.

Mrs Forrester looked, as she had sounded, formidable. She had a blunt face with a mouth like a spring-trap, prominent eyes fortified by pebble-lenses and thin, grey hair lugged back into a bun. Her skirt varied in length from midi to maxi and she clearly wore more than one flannel petticoat. Her top half was covered by woollen garments in varying shades of dull puce. She wore a double chain of what Troy suspected were superb natural pearls and a number of old-fashioned rings in which deposits of soap had accumulated. She carried a string bag containing a piece of anonymous knitting and her handkerchief.

Hilary performed the introductions. Colonel Forrester beamed and gave Troy a little bow. Mrs Forrester sharply nodded.

'How do you find yourself?' she said. 'Cold?'

'Not at all, thank you.'

'I ask because you must spend much of your time in overheated studios painting from the Altogether, I said Painting From The Altogether.'

This habit of repetition in fortissimo, Troy discovered, was automatic with Mrs Forrester and was practised for the benefit of her husband, who now gently indicated that he wore his hearing-aid. To this she paid no attention.

'She's not painting *me* in the nude, darling Auntie,' said Hilary, who was pouring drinks.

'A pretty spectacle *that* would be.'

'I think perhaps you base your theories about painters on *Trilby* and *La Vie de Bohème*.'

'I saw Beerbohm Tree in *Trilby*,' Colonel Forrester remembered. 'He died backwards over a table. It was awfully good.'

There was a tap on the door, followed by the entrance of a man with an anxious face. Not only anxious but most distressingly disfigured, as if by some long-distant and extensive burn. The scars ran down to the mouth and dragged it askew.

'Hullo, Moult,' said Mrs Forrester.

'I beg your pardon, sir, I'm sure,' said the man to Hilary. 'It was just to put the Colonel's mind at ease, sir. It's quite all right about the beard, sir.'

'Oh good, Moult. Good. Good. Good,' said Colonel Forrester.

'Thank you, sir,' said the man and withdrew.

'What is it about your beard, Uncle Flea?' asked Hilary, to Troy's immense relief.

'*The* beard, old chap. I was afraid it might have been forgotten and then I was afraid it might have been messed up in the packing.'

'Well, it hasn't, Fred. I said it hasn't.'

'I know, so that's all right.'

'Are you going to be Father Christmas, Colonel?' Troy ventured and he beamed delightedly and looked shy.

'I knew you'd think so,' he said. 'But no, I'm a Druid. What do you make of that, now?'

'You mean – you belong – ?'

'Not,' Hilary intervened, 'to some spurious Ancient Order wearing cotton-wool beards and making fools of themselves every second Tuesday.'

'Oh, *come*, old boy,' his uncle protested. 'That's not fair.'

'Well, perhaps not. But no,' Hilary continued, addressing himself to Troy, 'at Halberds, St Nicholas or Santa Claus or whatever you like to call the Teutonic old person, is replaced by an ancient and more authentic figure: the great precursor of the Winter Solstice observances who bequeathed – consciously or not – so much of his lore to his Christian successors. The Druid, in fact.'

'And the vicar doesn't mind,' Colonel Forrester earnestly interjected. 'I promise you. The vicar doesn't mind a bit.'

'*That* doesn't surprise me,' his wife observed with a cryptic snort.

'He comes to the party even. So, you see, I shall be a Druid. I have been one each year since Hilary came to Halberds. There's a tree and a kissing-bough you know, and, of course, quantities of mistletoe. All the children come: the children on the place and at The Vale and in the neighbouring districts. It's a lovely party and I love doing it. Do you like dressing-up?'

He asked this so anxiously, like a character in *Alice*, that she hadn't the heart to give anything less than an enthusiastic assent and almost expected him to say cosily that they must dress up together one of these days.

'Uncle Flea's a brilliant performer,' Hilary said, 'and his beard is the *pièce de résistance*. He has it made by Wig Creations. It wouldn't disgrace King Lear. And then the wig itself! So different from the usual repellent falsity. You shall see.'

'We've made some changes,' said Colonel Forrester excitedly. 'They've re-dressed it. The feller said he thought it was a bit on the long side and might make me look as if I'd opted out. One can't be too careful.'

Hilary brought the drinks. Two of them were steaming and had slices of lemon in them.

'Your rum toddies, Aunt Bed,' he said. 'Tell me if there's not enough sugar.'

Mrs Forrester wrapped her handkerchief round her glass and sat down with it. 'It seems all right,' she said. 'Did you put nutmeg in your uncle's?'

'No.'

'Good.'

'You will think,' said the colonel to Troy, 'that rum toddies before dinner are funny things to drink but we make a point of putting them forward after a journey. Usually they are nightcaps.'

'They smell delicious.'

'Would you like one?' Hilary asked her. 'Instead of a White Lady.'

'I think I'll stick to the White Lady.'

'So shall I. Well, my dears,' Hilary said generally. 'We are a small house-party this year. Only Cressida and Uncle Bert to come. They both arrive tomorrow.'

'Are you still engaged to Cressida?' asked his aunt.

'Yes. The arrangement stands. I am in high hopes, Aunt Bed, that you will take more of a fancy to Cressida on second sight.'

'It's not second sight. It's fiftieth sight. Or more.'

'But you know what I mean. Second sight since we became engaged.'

'What's the odds?' she replied ambiguously.

'Well, Aunt Bed, I would have thought – ' Hilary broke off and rubbed his nose. 'Well, anyway, Aunt Bed, considering I met her in your house.'

'More's the pity. I warned your uncle. I said I warned you, Fred.'

'What about, B?'

'Your gel! The Tottenham gel. Cressida.'

'She's not *mine*, B. You put things so oddly, my dear.'

'Well, anyway,' Hilary said. 'I hope you change your mind, Auntie.'

'One can but hope,' she rejoined and turned to Troy. 'Have you met Miss Tottenham?'

'No.'

'Hilary thinks she will go with the house. We're still talking about Cressida,' Mrs Forrester bawled at her husband.

'I know you are. I heard.'

After this they sipped their drinks, Mrs Forrester making rather a noise with hers and blowing on it to cool it down.

'The arrangements for Christmas Day,' Hilary began after a pause, 'are, I think, an improvement on last year. I've thought of a new entrance for you, Uncle Flea.'

'Have you, though? Have you? Have you?'

'From outside. Through the french windows behind the tree.'

'Outside!' Mrs Forrester barked. 'Do I understand you, Hilary? Do you plan to put your uncle out on the terrace on a midwinter night – in a snowstorm. I said a snowstorm?'

'It'll only be for a moment, Aunt Bed.'

'You have not forgotten, I suppose, that your uncle suffers from a circulatory complaint.'

'I'll be all right, B.'

'I don't like it, I said – '

'But I assure you! And the undergarment is quilted.'

'Pshaw! I said – '

'No, but do listen!'

'Don't fuss, B. My boots are fur-lined. Go on, old boy. You were saying – ?'

'I've got a lovely tape-recording of sleighbells and snorting reindeer. Don't interrupt, anybody. I've done my research and I'm convinced that there's an overlap here between the Teutonic and the Druidical and if there's not,' Hilary said rapidly, 'there ought to be. So. We'll hear you shout "Whoa", Uncle Flea, outside, to the reindeer, and then you'll come in.'

'I don't shout very loud nowadays, old boy,' he said worriedly. 'Not the Pirbright note any more, I'm afraid.'

'I thought of that. I've had the "whoa" added to the bells and snorts. Cuthbert did it. He has a stentorian voice.'

'Good. Good.'

'There will be thirty-one children and about a dozen parents. And the usual assortment of county and farmers. Outside hands and, of course, the staff.'

'Warders?' asked Mrs Forrester. 'From That Place?'

'Yes. From the married quarters. Two. Wives and families.'

'Marchbanks?'

'If he can get away. They have their own commitments. The chaplain cooks up something pretty joyless. Christmas,' said Hilary acidly, 'under maximum security. I imagine one can hardly hear the carols for the alarm bells.'

'I suppose,' said his aunt after a good suck at her toddy, 'you all know what you're about. I'm sure I don't. I smell danger.'

'That's a dark saying, Auntie,' remarked Hilary.

Cuthbert came in and announced dinner. It was true that he had a very loud voice.

CHAPTER 2

Christmas Eve

Before they went to bed they listened to the regional weather report. It said that snow was expected to fall through the night and into Christmas Eve but that it was unlikely to continue until Christmas Day itself. A warm front was approaching over the Atlantic Ocean.

'I always think,' Hilary remarked, 'of a warm front as belonging to a décolleté Regency lady thrusting her opulent prow, as it were, into some consequential rout or ball and warming it up no end. The ball, I mean.'

'No doubt,' his aunt tartly rejoined, 'Cressida will fulfil that questionable role at the coming function.'

'Well, you know, darling, I rather think she may,' said Hilary and kissed his aunt goodnight.

When Troy hung her red dress in her wardrobe that night she discovered that the recess in which it had been built must be flanked by a similar recess in the Forrester's room so that the ancient wall that separated them had been in this section, removed and a thin partition separated their respective hanging cupboards.

Mrs Forrester, at this very moment, was evidently disposing of her own garments. Troy could hear the scrape of coathangers on the rail. She jumped violently when her own name was shouted, almost as it seemed, into her ear.

'*Troy!* Odd sort of Christian name.'

Distantly, Colonel Forrester could be heard to say: '. . . no . . . understand . . . famous . . .' His head, Troy thought was momentarily engulfed in some garment. Mrs Forrester sounded extremely cross.

'You know what *I* think about it,' she shouted and rattled the coathangers, 'I said you know . . .'

Troy, reprehensibly, was riveted in her wardrobe.

'. . . don't trust . . .' continued the voice. 'Never have. You know that.' A pause and a final shout: '. . . sooner it was left straight out to the murderers. Now!' A final angry clash of coathangers and a bang of wardrobe doors.

Troy went to bed in a daze but whether this condition was engendered by the Lucullan dinner Hilary and Kittiwee had provided or by the juxtaposition of unusual circumstances in which she found herself, she was quite unable to determine.

She had thought she was sleepy when she got into bed but now she lay awake, listening to small noises made by the fire in her grate as it settled into glowing oblivion and to faint sighs and occasional buffets of the night wind outside. Well, Troy thought, this *is* a rum go and no mistake.

After a period of disjointed but sharp reflections she began to fancy she heard voices somewhere out in the dark. 'I must be dozing, after all,' Troy thought. A gust of wind rumbled in the chimney followed by a silence into which there intruded the wraith of a voice, belonging nowhere and diminished as if the sound had been turned off in a television dialogue and only the ghost of itself remained.

Now, positively, it was out there below her window: a man's voice – two voices – engaged in indistinguishable talk.

Troy got out of bed and by the glow from her dying fire, went to her window and parted the curtains.

It was not as dark as she had expected. She looked out at a subject that might have inspired Jane Eyre to add another item to her portfolio. A rift had been blown in the clouds and the moon in its last quarter shone on a prospect of black shadows thrown across cadaverous passages of snow. In the background rose the moors and in the foreground, the shambles of broken glass beneath her window. Beyond this jogged two torchlights, the first of which cast a yellow circle on a white ground. The second bobbed about the side of a large wooden crate with the legend: 'Musical instrument. Handle with Extreme Care' stencilled across it. It seemed to be mounted on some kind of vehicle, a sledge, perhaps, since it made no noise.

The two men wore hooded oilskins that glinted as they moved. The leader gesticulated and pointed and then turned and leant into the wind. Troy saw that he had some kind of tow-rope over his shoulder. The second man placed his muffled hands against the rear end of the crate and braced himself. He tilted his head sideways and glanced up. For a moment she caught sight of his face. It was Nigel.

Although Troy had only had one look at Vincent, the non-poisoner-chauffeur-gardener, and that look from the top of a hill, she felt sure that the leader was he.

'Hup!' cried the disembodied voice and the ridiculous outfit moved off round the west wing in the direction of the main courtyard of Halberds. The moon was overrun by clouds.

Before she got back into bed Troy looked at a little Sèvres clock on her chimney-piece. She was greatly surprised to find that the hour was no later than ten past twelve.

At last she fell asleep and woke to the sound of opening curtains. A general pale glare was admitted.

'Good morning, Nigel,' said Troy.

'Good morning,' Nigel muttered, 'madam.'

With downcast eyes he placed her morning tea-tray at her bedside.

'Has there been a heavy fall of snow?'

'Not to say heavy,' he sighed, moving towards the door.

Troy said boldly: 'It was coming down quite hard last night, wasn't it? You must have been frozen pulling that sledge.'

He stopped. For the first time he lifted his gaze to her face. His almost colourless eyes stared through their white lashes like a doll's.

'I happened to look out,' Troy explained and wondered why on earth she should feel frightened.

He stood motionless for a few seconds and then said 'Yes?' and moved to the door. Like an actor timing an exit line he added, 'It's a surprise,' and left her.

The nature of the surprise became evident when Troy went down to breakfast.

A moderate snowfall had wrought its conventional change in a landscape that glittered in the thin sunshine. The moors had become interfolding arcs of white and blue, the trees wore their epaulettes with an obsequious air of conformity and the area under treatment by tractors was simplified as if a white dustsheet had been dropped over it.

The breakfast-room was in the west wing of Halberds. It opened off a passage that terminated in a door into the adjoining library. The library itself, being the foremost room of the west wing, commanded views on three sides.

Troy wanted to have a stare at her work. She went into the library and glowered at the portrait for some minutes, biting her thumb. Then she looked out of the windows that gave on to the courtyard. Here, already masked in snow and placed at dead centre, was a large rectangular object that Troy had no difficulty in recognizing since the stencilled legend on its side was not as yet obliterated.

And there, busy as ever, were Vincent and Nigel, shovelling snow from wheelbarrows and packing it round the case in the form of a flanking series of steps based on an under-structure of boxes and planks. Troy watched them for a moment or two and then went to the breakfast-room.

Hilary stood in the window supping porridge. He was alone.

'Hullo, Hullo!' he cried. 'Have you seen the work in progress? Isn't it exciting: the creative urge in full spate. Nigel has been inspired. I *am* so pleased, you can't think.'

'What are they making?'

'A reproduction of my many-times-great-grandfather's tomb. I've given Nigel photographs and of course he's seen the original in the parish church. It's a compliment and I couldn't be more gratified. Such a change from waxworks and horses for roundabouts. The crate will represent the catafalque, you see, and the recumbent figure will be life-size. Really it's extraordinarily nice of Nigel.'

'I saw them towing the crate round the house at midnight.'

'It appears he was suddenly inspired and roused Vincent up to assist him. The top of the crate was already beautifully covered by snow this morning. It's so *good* for Nigel to become creative again. Rejoice with me and have some kedgeree or something. Don't you adore having things to look forward to?'

Colonel and Mrs Forrester came in wearing that air of spurious domesticity peculiar to guests in a country house. The colonel was enchanted by Nigel's activities and raved about them while his porridge congealed in its bowl. His wife recalled him to himself.

'I dare say,' she said with a baleful glance at Hilary, 'it keeps them out of mischief.' Troy was unable to determine what Mrs Forrester really thought about Hilary's experiment with murderers.

'Cressida and Uncle Bert,' said Hilary, 'are coming by the three-thirty at Downlow. I'm going to meet them unless, of course, I'm required in the library.'

'Not if I may have a sitting this morning,' said Troy.

'The light will have changed, won't it? Because of the snow?'

'I expect it will. We'll just have to see.'

'What *sort* of portraits do you paint?' Mrs Forrester demanded.

'Extremely good ones,' said her nephew pretty tartly. 'You're in distinguished company, Aunt Bedelia.'

To Troy's intense amusement Mrs Forrester pulled a long, droll face and immediately afterwards tipped her a wink.

'Hoity-toity,' she said.

'Not at all,' Hilary huffily rejoined.

Troy said, 'It's hopeless asking what sort of things I paint because I'm no good at talking about my work. If you drive me into a corner I'll come out with the most awful jabberwocky.'

And in a state of astonishment at herself Troy added like a shame-faced schoolgirl, 'One paints as one must.'

After a considerable pause Hilary said: 'How generous you are.'

'Nothing of the sort,' Troy contradicted.

'Well!' Mrs Forrester said, 'we shall see what we shall see.'

Hilary snorted.

'I did some watercolours,' Colonel Forrester remembered, 'when I was at Eton. They weren't very good but I did them, at least.'

'That was something,' his wife conceded and Troy found herself adding that you couldn't say fairer than that.

They finished their breakfast in comparative silence and were about to leave the table when Cuthbert came in and bent over Hilary in a manner that recalled his own past as a head-waiter.

'Yes, Cuthbert,' Hilary asked, 'what is it?'

'The mistletoe, sir. It will be on the three-thirty and the person wonders if it could be collected at the station.'

'I'll collect it. It's for the kissing-bough. Ask Vincent to have everything ready, will you?'

'Certainly, sir.'

'Good.'

Hilary rubbed his hands with an exhilarated air and proposed to Troy that they resume their sittings. When the session was concluded, they went out into the sparkling morning to see how Nigel was getting on with his effigy.

It had advanced. The recumbent figure of a sixteenth-century Bill-Tasman was taking shape. Nigel's mittened hands worked quickly. He slapped on fistfuls of snow and manipulated them into shape with a wooden spatula: a kitchen implement, Troy supposed. There was something frenetic in his devotion to his task. He didn't so much as glance at his audience. Slap, slap, scoop, scoop, he went.

And now, for the first time, Troy encountered Wilfred, the cook, nicknamed Kittiwee.

He had come out of doors wearing his professional hat, checked trousers and snowy apron with an overcoat slung rather stylishly over his shoulders. He carried an enormous ladle and looked, Troy thought, as if he had materialized from a Happy Families playing card. Indeed, his round face, large eyes and wide mouth were comically in accord with such a notion.

When he saw Troy and Hilary he beamed upon them and raised a plump hand to his starched hat.

'*Good* morning, sir,' said Kittiwee. '*Good* morning, ladies.'

''Morning, Wilfred,' Hilary rejoined. 'Come out to lend a hand with the icing?'

Kittiwee laughed consumedly at this mildest of jokelets.

'Indeed *no*, sir,' he protested. 'I wouldn't dare. I just thought a *ladle* might assist the *artist*.'

Nigel thus indirectly appealed to merely shook his head without pausing in his task.

'All going well in your department?' Hilary asked.

'Yes, thank you, sir. We're doing nicely. The boy from Downlow is ever such a bright lad.'

'Oh. Good. Good,' Hilary said, rather hurriedly Troy thought. 'What about those mince-pies?'

'Ready for nibbles and wishes immediately after tea, sir, if you please,' cried Kittiwee, gaily.

'If they're on the same level as the other things you've been giving us to eat,' Troy said, 'they'll be the mince-pies of the century.'

It was hard to say who was the more delighted by this eulogy, Hilary or his cook.

Vincent came round the west wing wheeling another barrowful of snow. At close quarters he turned out to be a swarthy, thin man with a haggard expression in his eyes. He looked sidelong at Troy, tipped out his load and trundled off again. Kittiwee, explaining that he had only popped out for one second, embraced them all in the very widest of dimpled smiles and retired into the house.

A few minutes later Cuthbert came into the courtyard and boomingly proclaimed that luncheon was served.

II

Cressida Tottenham was blonde and extremely elegant. She was so elegant that her beauty seemed to be a second consideration: a kind of bonus, a gloss. She wore a sable hat. Sable framed her face, hung from her sleeves and topped her boots. When her outer garments were removed she appeared to be gloved rather than clad in the very ultimate of expensive simplicity.

Her eyes and her mouth slanted and she carried her head a little on one side. She was very composed and not loquacious. When she did talk she said: 'you know' with every second breath. She was not by any means the kind of subject that Troy liked to paint. This might turn out to be awkward: Hilary kept looking inquisitively at her as if to ask what she thought of Cressida.

To Mr Bert Smith, Troy took an instant fancy. He was a little man with an impertinent face, a bright eye and a strong out of date cockney habit of speech. He was smartly dressed in an aggressive countrified way. Troy judged him to be about seventy years old and in excellent health.

The encounter between the new arrivals and the Forresters was interesting. Colonel Forrester greeted Miss Tottenham with timid admiration calling her 'Cressy-dear'.

Troy thought she detected a gently avuncular air, tempered perhaps by anxiety. The colonel's meeting with Mr Smith was cordial to a degree. He shook hands with abandon. 'How are you?

How are you, my dear fellow?' he repeatedly asked and with each enquiry broke into delighted laughter.

'How's the colonel, anyway?' Mr Smith responded. 'You're look-ing lovely, I'll say that for you. Fair caution, you are and no error. What's all this they're givin' us abaht you dressing yourself up like Good King Thingummy? Wiv whiskers! *Whiskers!*' Mr Smith turned upon Mrs Forrester and suddenly bellowed: 'Blimey, 'e must be joking. At 'is age ! *Whiskers!*'

'It's my husband who's deaf, Smith,' Mrs Forrester pointed out, 'not me. You've made that mistake before, you know.'

'What *am* I thinking of,' said Mr Smith, winking at Troy and slapping Colonel Forrester on the back. 'Slip of the tongue, as the butcher said when he dropped it accidental in the tripe.'

'Uncle Bert,' Hilary said to Troy, 'is a comedian manqué. He speaks nicely when he chooses. This is his "aren't I a caution, I'm a cockney" act. He's turning it on for Uncle Flea's benefit. You always bring him out, Uncle Flea, don't you?'

Miss Tottenham caught Troy's eyes and slightly cast up her own.

'Really?' asked the enchanted colonel. 'Do I really, though?'

Mr Smith quietened down after this exchange and they all went in to tea which had been set out in the dining-room and had none of the cosiness of Troy's and Hilary's tête-à-têtes by the boudoir fire. Indeed an air of constraint hung over the party which Cressida's refusal to act as chatelaine did nothing to relieve.

'You're not asking me to do the pouring-out bit, darling, for God's sake,' Cressida said. 'It'd, you know, frankly bore the pants off me. I've got, you know, a kind of thing against it. Not my scene. You know.'

Mrs Forrester stared fixedly at Cressida for some moments and then said: 'Perhaps, Hilary, you would like me to perform.'

'Darling Auntie, please do. It will be like old times, won't it? When Uncle Bert used to come to Eaton Square after you'd made it up over my upbringing.'

'That's the ticket,' Mr Smith agreed. 'No hard feelings. Live and let live. That's the story, missus, isn't it?'

'You're a decent fellow in your own way, Smith,' Mrs Forrester conceded. 'We've learnt to understand each other, I dare say. What sort of tea do you like, Mrs Alleyn?'

Troy thought: I am among people who say what they think when they think it. Like children. This is a most unusual circumstance and might lead to anything.

She excepted Mr Smith from her blanket appraisal. Mr Smith, she considered, is a tricky little old man and what he really thinks about the company he keeps is nobody's business but his.

'How's all the villains, 'Illy?' he asked putting his head on one side and jauntily quizzing his muffin. 'Still keepin' their noses clean?'

'Certainly, Uncle Bert, but do choose your words. I wouldn't for the world Cuthbert or Mervyn heard you talking like that. One of them might walk in at any moment.'

'Oh dear,' said Mr Smith, unmoved.

'That yawning void over the fireplace,' Cressida said. 'Is that where you meant? You know, about my picture?'

'Yes, my darling,' Hilary responded. 'As a matter of fact – ' he looked anxiously at Troy ' – I've already ventured a tentative probe.'

Troy was saved the awkwardness of a reply by Cressida who said, 'I'd rather it was the drawing-room. Not all mixed in with the soup and, you know, your far from groovy ancestors.' She glanced discontentedly at a Lely, two Raeburns and a Winterhalter. 'You know,' she said.

Hilary turned rather pink: 'We'll have to see,' he said.

Mervyn came in with the cook's compliments and the mince-pies were ready when they were.

'What *is* he on about?' Cressida asked fretfully. 'On top of tea? And anyway I abhor mincemeat.'

'Darling I *know*. So, privately, do I. But it appears to be an authentic old custom. On taking one's first bite,' Hilary explained, 'one makes a wish. The ceremony is held, by tradition, in the kitchen. One need only take a token nibble. It will give him so much pleasure.'

'Are there still cats in the kitchen?' Cressida asked. 'There's my thing about cats, remember.'

'Mervyn,' Hilary said, 'ask Kittiwee to put Slyboots and Smartypants out, will you? He'll understand.'

'He'd better. I'm allergic,' Cressida told Troy. 'Cats send me. But totally. I've only got to catch the eye of a cat and I'm a psychotic wreck.' She enlarged upon her theme. It would be tedious to record how many times she said Troy knew.

'I should be pleased,' Mrs Forrester said loudly, 'to renew my acquaintance with Slyboots and Smartypants.'

'Rather you than me,' Cressida retorted, addressing herself to Mrs Forrester for the first time but not looking at her.

'I so far agree with you, Hilary,' said Mrs Forrester, 'in your views on your staff as to consider the cook was well within his rights when he attacked the person who maltreated cats. Well within his right I consider he was, I said – '

'Yes, Auntie, I know you did. Don't we all! No, darling,' Hilary said, anticipating his beloved. 'You're the adorable exception. Well, now. Shall we all go and mumble up our mince?'

In the kitchen they were received by Kittiwee with ceremony. He beamed and dimpled but Troy thought there was a look of glazed displeasure in his eyes. This impression became unmistakable when infuriated yowls broke out behind a door into the yard. Slyboots and Smartypants, thought Troy.

A red-cheeked boy sidled in through the door, shutting it quickly on a crescendo of feline indignation.

'We're sorry,' Hilary said, 'about the puss-cats, Wilfred.'

'It takes all sorts, doesn't it, sir?' Kittiwee cryptically rejoined with a sidelong glance at Miss Tottenham. The boy, who was sucking his hand, looked resentfully through the window into the yard.

The mince-pies were set out on a lordly dish in the middle of the kitchen table. Troy saw with relief that they were small. Hilary explained that they must take their first bites in turn, making a wish as they did so.

Afterwards Troy was to remember them as they stood sheepishly round the table. She was to think of those few minutes as almost the last spell of general tranquillity that she experienced at Halberds.

'You first, Auntie,' Hilary invited.

'Aloud?' his aunt demanded. Rather hurriedly he assured her that her wish need not be articulate.

'Just as well,' she said. She seized her pie and took a prodigious bite out of it. As she munched she fixed her eyes upon Cressida Tottenham and suddenly Troy was alarmed. I know what she's wishing, Troy thought. As well as if she were to bawl it out in our faces. She's wishing the engagement will be broken. I'm sure of it.

Cressida herself came next. She made a great to-do over biting off the least possible amount and swallowing it as if it was medicine.

'Did you wish?' Colonel Forrester asked anxiously.

'I forgot,' she said and then screamed at the top of her voice. Fragments of mince-pie escaped her lovely lips.

Mr Smith let out a four-letter word and they all exclaimed. Cressida was pointing at the window into the yard. Two cats, a piebald and a tabby, sat on the outer sill, their faces slightly distorted by the glass, their eyes staring and their mouths opening and shutting in concerted meows.

'My dear *girl*,' Hilary said and made no attempt to disguise his exasperation.

'My poor pussies,' Kittiwee chimed in like a sort of alto to a leading baritone.

'I can't take CATS,' Cressida positively yelled.

'In which case,' Mrs Forrester composedly observed, 'you *can* take yourself out of the kitchen.'

'No, no,' pleaded the colonel. 'No, B. No, no, no! Dear me! Look here!'

The cats now began to make excruciating noises with their claws on the window-pane. Troy, who liked cats and found them amusing, was almost sorry to see them abruptly cease this exercise, reverse themselves on the sill and disappear, tails up. Cressida, however, clapped her hands to her ears, screamed again and stamped her feet like an exotic dancer.

Mr Smith said drily: 'No trouble!'

But Colonel Forrester gently comforted Cressida with a wandering account of a brother-officer whose abhorrence of felines in some mysterious way brought about a deterioration in the lustre of his accoutrements. It was an incomprehensible narrative but Cressida sat on a kitchen chair and stared at him and became quiet.

'Never mind!' Hilary said on a note of quiet despair. 'As we were.' He appealed to Troy: 'Will you?' he asked.

Troy applied herself to a mince-pie and as she did so there came into her mind a wish so ardent that she could almost have thought she spoke it aloud. Don't, she found herself dottily wishing, let anything beastly happen. Please. She then complimented Kittiwee on his cooking.

Colonel Forrester followed Troy. 'You *would* be surprised,' he said, beaming at them, 'if you knew about *my* wish. *That* you would.' He shut his eyes and heartily attacked his pie. 'Delicious!' he said.

Mr Smith said: 'How soft can you get!' and ate the whole of his pie with evident and noisy relish.

Hilary brought up the rear and when they had thanked Kittiwee they left the kitchen. Cressida said angrily that she was going to take two aspirins and go to bed until dinner time. 'And I don't,' she added, looking at her fiancé, 'want to be disturbed.'

'You need have no misgivings, my sweet,' he rejoined and his aunt gave a laugh that might equally have been called a snort. 'Your uncle and I,' she said to Hilary, 'will take the air, as usual, for ten minutes.'

'But – Auntie – it's too late. It's dark and it may be snowing.'

'We shall confine ourselves to the main courtyard. The wind is in the east, I believe.'

'Very well,' he agreed. 'Uncle Bert, shall we have our business talk?'

'Suits me,' said Mr Smith. 'Any time.'

Troy wanted to have a glower at her work and said as much. So they went their several ways.

As she walked through the hall and along the passage that led to the library, Troy was struck by the extreme quietude that was obtained indoors at Halberds. The floor was thickly carpeted. Occasional lamps cast a subdued light on the walls but they were far apart. Whatever form of central heating had been installed was almost too effective. She felt as if she moved through a steamed-up tunnel.

Here was the door into the library. It was slightly ajar. She opened it, took two steps and while the handle was still in her grasp was hit smartly on the head.

It was a light blow and was accompanied by the reek of turpentine. She was neither hurt nor frightened but so much taken by surprise that for a moment she was bereft of reasoning. Then she remembered there was a light switch inside the door and turned it on.

There was the library: warm, silent, smelling of leather, woodfires and paint. There was the portrait on its easel and the work bench with her familiar gear.

And there, on the carpet at her feet, the tin palette-can in which she put her oil and turpentine.

And down her face trickled a pungent little stream.

The first thing Troy did after making this discovery was to find the clean rag on her bench and wipe her face. Hilary, dimly lit on her easel, fixed her with an enigmatic stare. 'And a nice party,' she muttered, *'you've* let me in for, haven't you?'

She turned back towards the door, which she found, to her surprise was now shut. A trickle of oil and turpentine made its sluggish way down the lacquer-red paint. But *would* the door swing to of its own accord? As if to answer her, it gave a little click and opened a couple of inches. She remembered that this was habitual with it. A faulty catch, she supposed.

But someone had shut it.

She waited for a moment, pulling herself together. Then she walked quickly to the door, opened it and repressed a scream. She was face to face with Mervyn.

This gave her a much greater shock than the knock on her head. She heard herself make a nightmarish little noise in her throat.

'Was there anything, madam?' he asked. His face was ashen.

'Did you shut the door? Just now?'

'No, madam.'

'Come in, please.'

She thought he was going to refuse but he did come in, taking four steps and then stopping where the can still lay on the carpet.

'It's made a mess,' Troy said.

'Allow me, madam.'

He picked it up, walked over to the bench and put it down.

'Look at the door,' Troy said.

She knew at once that he had already seen it. She knew he had come into the room while she cleaned her face and had crept out again, shutting the door behind him.

'The tin was on the top of the door,' Troy said. 'It fell on my head. A booby-trap.'

'Not a very nice thing,' he whispered.

'No. A booby-trap.'

'I never!' Mervyn burst out. 'My God, I never. My God, I swear I never.'

'I can't think – really – why you should.'

'That's right,' he agreed feverishly. 'That's dead right. Christ, why should I! Me!'

Troy began to wipe the trickle from the door. It came away cleanly, leaving hardly a trace.

Mervyn dragged a handkerchief from his pocket, dropped on his knees and violently attacked the stain on the string-coloured carpet.

'I think plain turpentine might do it,' Troy said.

He looked round wildly. She fetched him a bottle of turpentine from the bench.

'Ta,' he said and set to work again. The nape of his neck shone with sweat. He mumbled.

'What?' Troy asked. 'What did you say?'

'He'll see. He notices everything. They'll say I done it.'

'Who?'

'Everybody. That lot. Them.'

Troy heard herself saying: 'Finish it off with soap and water and put down more mats.' The carpet round her easel had, at her request, been protected by upside-down mats from the kitchen quarters.

He gazed up at her. He looked terrified and crafty like a sly child.

'You won't do me?' he asked. 'Madam? Honest? You won't grass? Not that I done it, mind. I never. I'd be barmy, woon't I? I never.'

'All right, *all right,*' Troy almost shouted. 'Don't let's have all that again. You say you didn't and I – as a matter of fact, I believe you.'

'Gor' bless you, lady.'

'Yes, well, never *mind* all that. But if you didn't,' Troy said sombrely, 'who on earth did?'

'Ah! That's different, ainnit? What say I know?'

'You *know*!'

'I got me own idea, ain' I? Trying to put one acrost me. Got it in for all of us, that sod, excuse me for mentioning it.'

'I don't know what you're talking about. It seems to me that I'm the one – '

'Do me a favour. You! Lady – you're just the mug, see? It's me it was set up for. Use your loaf, lady.'

Mervyn sat back on his heels and stared wildly at Troy. His face which had reminded her of Kittiwee's pastry now changed colour: he was blushing.

'I'm sure I don't know what you'll think of me, madam,' he said carefully. 'I forgot myself, I'm that put out.'

'That's all right,' she said. 'But I wish you'd just explain – '

He got to his feet and backed to the door, screwing the rag round his hand. 'Oh madam, madam, madam,' he implored. 'I do wish you'd just use your loaf.'

And with that he left her.

It was not until she reached her room and set about washing the turpentine and oil out of her hair that Troy remembered Mervyn had gone to gaol for murdering someone with a booby-trap.

III

If Cressida had lost any ground at all with her intended over the affair of the cats it seemed to Troy that she made it up again and more during the course of the evening. She was the last to arrive in the main drawing-room where tonight, for the first time, they assembled before dinner.

She wore a metallic trousered garment so adhesive that her body might itself have been gilded like the two Quattrocento victories that trumpeted above the chimney-piece. When she moved, her dress, recalling Herrick, seemed to melt about her as if she were clad in molten gold. She looked immensely valuable and of course tremendously lovely. Troy heard Hilary catch his breath. Even Mrs Forrester gave a slight grunt while Mr Smith, very softly, produced a wolf whistle. The colonel said: 'My dear, you are quite bewildering,' which was, Troy thought, as apt a way of putting it as any other. But still, she had no wish to paint Cressida and again she was uneasily aware of Hilary's questioning looks.

They had champagne cocktails that evening. Mervyn was in attendance under Cuthbert's supervision and Troy was careful not to look at Mervyn. She was visited by a sense of detachment as if she hovered above the scene rather than moved through it. The beautiful room, the sense of ease, of unforced luxury, of a kind of aesthetic liberation, seemed to lose substance and validity and to become – what? Sterile?

'I wonder,' said Hilary at her elbow, 'what that look means. An impertinent question, by the way, but of course you don't have to

give me an answer.' And before she could do so he went on.
'Cressida is lovely, don't you think?'

'I do indeed but you mustn't ask me to paint her.'

'I thought that was coming.'

'It would be no good.'

'How can you be so sure?'

'It would give you no pleasure.'

'Or perhaps too much,' Hilary said. 'Of a dangerous kind.'

Troy thought it better not to reply to this.

'Well,' Hilary said, 'it shall be as it must be. Already I feel the
breath of Signor Annigoni down the nape of my neck. Another
champagne cocktail? Of course you will. Cuthbert!'

He stayed beside her, rather quiet for him, watching his fiancée,
but, Troy felt, in some indefinable way, still communicating with her.

At dinner Hilary put Cressida in the chatelaine's place and Troy
thought how wonderfully she shone in it and how when they were
married Hilary would like to show her off at much grander parties
than this strange little assembly. Like a humanate version of his great
possessions, she thought, and was uncomfortable in the notion.

Stimulated perhaps by champagne, Cressida was much more
effervescent than usual. She and Hilary had a mock argument with
amorous overtones. She began to tease him about the splendour of
Halberds and then when he looked huffy added, 'Not that I don't
devour every last bit of it. It sends the Tottenham blood seething in
my veins like . . .' She stopped and looked at Mrs Forrester, who over
folded arms and with a magisterial frown steadily returned her gaze.

'Anyway,' Cressida said, waving a hand at Hilary, 'I adore it all.'

Colonel Forrester suddenly passed his elderly, veined fingers
across his eyes and mouth.

'Darling!' Hilary said and raised his glass to Cressida.

Mr Bert Smith also became a little flown with champagne. He
talked of his and Hilary's business affairs and Troy thought he
must be quite as shrewd as he gave himself out to be. It was not
at all surprising that he had got on in such a spectacular manner.
She wondered if, in the firm of 'Bill-Tasman and Smith Associates'
which was what their company seemed to be called, Mr Smith
was perhaps the engine and Hilary the exquisite bodywork and
upholstery.

Colonel Forrester listened to the high-powered talk with an air of wonderment. He was beside Troy and had asked to 'take her in' on his arm which she had found touching.

'Do you follow all this?' he asked her in a conspiratorial aside. He was wearing his hearing-aid.

'Not very well. I'm an ass at business,' she muttered and delighted him.

'So am I! I know! So am I! But we have to pretend, don't we?'

'I daren't. I'd give myself away, at once.'

'But it's awfully clever. All the brain-work, you know!' he murmured, raising his brows and gazing at Troy. 'Terrific! Phew! Don't you agree?'

She nodded and he slyly bit his lip and hunched his shoulders.

'We mustn't let on we're so muddly,' said the colonel.

Troy thought: this is how he used to talk to thoroughly nice girls when he was an ensign fifty years ago. All gay and playful with 'The Destiny Waltz' swooning away on the bandstand and an occasional flutter in the conservatory. The chaperones thought he was just the job, no doubt. And she wondered if he proposed to Aunt Bed on a balcony at a regimental ball. But what the devil was Aunt Bed like in her springtide, Troy wondered, and was at a loss. A dasher, perhaps? A fine girl? A spanker?

'. . . so I said: "Do me a favour, chum. You call it what you like: for my book you're at the fiddle!" "Distinguished and important collection!" Yeah! So's your old man! Nothing but a bunch of job-burgers, that lot.'

'I'm sure you're right, Uncle Bert,' said Hilary definitively and bent towards his aunt.

'That's a very nice grenade you're wearing, Auntie darling,' he said. 'I don't remember it, do I?'

'Silver wedding,' she said. 'Your uncle. I don't often get it out.'

It was a large diamond brooch pinned in a haphazard fashion to the black cardigan Mrs Forrester wore over her brown satin dress. Her pearls were slung about her neck and an increased complement of rings had been shoved down her fingers.

Mr Smith, his attention diverted from high finance, turned and contemplated her.

'Got 'em all on, eh?' he said. 'Very nice, too. Here! Do you still cart all your stuff round with you? Is that right? In a tin box? Is that a fact?'

'*Pas,*' Mrs Forrester said, '*devant les domestiques.*'

'How does the chorus go?'

Hilary intervened. 'No, *honestly*, Aunt B,' he protested throwing an agitated glance at Cuthbert, who was at the sideboard with his back turned.

'Hilary,' said Cressida, 'that reminds me.'

'Of what, my sweet?' Hilary asked apprehensively.

'It doesn't really matter. I was just wondering about tomorrow. The party. The tree. It's in the drawing-room isn't it? I've been wondering, what's the scene? You know? The stage-management and all that.'

It was the first time Troy had heard Cressida assume an air of authority about Halberds and she saw that Hilary was delighted. He embarked on a long explanation. The sleighbells, the tape-recorded sounds, the arrival of Colonel Forrester as a Druid through the french windows. The kissing-bough. The tree. The order of events. Colonel Forrester listened with the liveliest satisfaction.

This discussion took them through the rest of dinner. Cressida continued to fill out the role of hostess with considerable aplomb and before Mrs Forrester, who was gathering herself together, could do anything more about it, leant towards her and said: 'Shall we, Aunt B?' with a ravishing smile. It was the first time, Troy suspected, that she had ever addressed her future aunt-by-marriage in those terms. Mrs Forrester looked put out. She said: 'I was going to, anyway,' rose with alacrity and made for the door. Her husband got there first and opened it.

'We shan't stay long over our port,' he confided, looking from his wife to Troy. 'Hilary says there are any number of things to be done. The tree and the kissing-bough and all. Don't you like, awfully,' he said to Troy, 'having things to look forward to?'

When the ladies reached the drawing-room it was to find Vincent, Nigel and the apple-cheeked boy in the very act of wheeling in through the french windows a fine Christmas tree lightly powdered with snow. It was housed in a green tub and mounted on the kind of trolley garage hands lie upon when working underneath a car. At the far end of the room a green canvas sheet had been spread over Hilary's superb carpet and to the centre of this the tree was propelled.

Winter entered the room with the tree and laid its hand on their faces. Cressida cried out against it. The men shut the french windows and went away. A step-ladder and an enormous box of decorations had been left beside the tree.

From the central chandelier in the drawing-room someone – Nigel, perhaps – had hung the traditional kissing-bough, a bell-shaped structure made from mistletoe and holly with scarlet apples depending from it by tinsel cords. It was stuck about with scarlet candles. The room was filled with the heady smell of resinous greenery.

Troy was almost as keen on Christmas trees as Colonel Forrester himself and thought the evening might well be saved by their joint activities. Mrs Forrester eyed the tree with judicious approval and said there was nothing the matter with it.

'There's a Crib,' she said. 'I attend to that. I bought it in Oberammergau when Hilary was a pagan child of seven. He's still a pagan of course, but he brings it out to oblige me. Though how he reconciles it with Fred in his heathen beard and that brazen affair on the chandelier is best known to himself. Still, there is the service. Half past ten in the chapel. Did he tell you?'

'No,' Troy said. 'I didn't even know there was a chapel.'

'In the west wing. The parson from the prison takes it. High church, which Hilary likes. Do you consider him handsome?'

'No,' Troy said. 'But he's paintable.'

'Ho,' said Mrs Forrester.

Mervyn came in with the coffee and liqueurs. When he reached Troy he gave her a look of animal subservience that she found extremely disagreeable.

Cressida's onset of hostess-like responsibility seemed to have been left behind in the dining-room. She stood in front of the fire jiggling her golden slipper on her toe and leaning a superb arm along the chimney-piece. She waited restively until Mervyn had gone and then said: 'That man gives me the horrors.'

'Indeed,' said Mrs Forrester.

'He's such a *creep*. They all are, if it comes to that. Oh yes, I know all about Hilly's ideas and I grant you it's one way out of the servant problem. I mean *if* we're to keep Halberds up and all that, this lot is one way of doing it. Personally, I'd rather have Greeks or something. You know.'

'You don't see it, as Hilary says he does, from the murderer's point-of-view?' Mrs Forrester observed.

'Oh, I know he's on about all that,' Cressida said, jiggling her slipper, 'but, let's face it, gracious living is what really turns him on. Me, too. You know?'

Mrs Forrester stared at her for several seconds and then, with an emphatic movement of her torso, directed herself at Troy. 'How do *you* manage?' she asked.

'As best we can. My husband's a policeman and his hours are enough to turn any self-respecting domestic into a psychotic wreck.'

'A *policeman*?' Cressida exclaimed and added, 'Oh, yes, I forgot. Hilly told me. But he's madly high-powered and famous, isn't he?'

As there seemed to be no answer to this Troy did not attempt to make one.

'Shouldn't we be doing something about the tree?' she asked Mrs Forrester.

'Hilary likes to supervise. You should know that by now.'

'Not exactly a jet-set scene, is it?' Cressida said. 'You know. Gaol-boss. Gaol-doctor. Warders. Chaplain. To say nothing of the gaol-kids. Oh, I forgot. A groovy shower of neighbours all very county and not one under the age of seventy. Hilarious. Let the bells chime.'

'I am seventy years of age and my husband is seventy-three.'

'There I go,' Cressida said. 'You know? The bottom.' She burst out laughing and suddenly knelt at Mrs Forrester's feet. She swung back the glossy burden of her hair and put her hands together. 'I'm not as lethally awful as I make out,' she said. 'You've both been fantastic to me. Always. I'm grateful. Hilly will have to beat me like a gong. You know? Bang-bang. Then I'll behave beautifully: Sweetie-pie, Aunt B, forgive me.'

Troy thought: Aunt Bed would have to be a Medusa to freeze her, and sure enough a smile twitched at the corners of Mrs Forrester's mouth. 'I suppose you're no worse than the rest of your generation,' she conceded. 'You're clean and neat: I'll say that for you.'

'As clean as a whistle and as neat as a new pin, aren't I? Do you think I'll adorn Hilly's house, Aunt B?'

'Oh, you'll *look* nice,' said Mrs Forrester. 'You may depend upon that. See you behave yourself.'

'*Behave* myself,' Cressida repeated. There was a pause. The fire crackled. A draught from somewhere up near the ceiling caused the kissing-bough to turn a little on its cord. In the dining-room, made distant by heavy walls and doors, Hilary's laugh sounded. With a change of manner so marked as to be startling Cressida said: 'Would you call me a sinful lady, Aunt Bedelia?'

'What on earth are you talking about, child? What's the matter with you?'

'Quite a lot, it appears. Look.'

She opened her golden bag and took out a folded piece of paper. 'I found it under my door when I went up to dress. I was saving it for Hilary,' she said, 'but you two may as well see it. Go on, please. Open it up. Read it. Both of you.'

Mrs Forrester stared at her for a moment, frowned and unfolded the paper. She held it away from her so that Troy could see what was printed on it in enormous capitals.

SINFUL LADY BEWARE
AN UNCHASTE WOMAN IS AN ABOMINATION.
HE SHALL NOT SUFFER THEE TO DWELL IN
HIS HOUSE.

'What balderdash is this? Where did you get it?'

'I told you. Under my door.'

Mrs Forrester made an abrupt movement as if to crush the paper but Cressida's hand was laid over hers. 'No, don't,' Cressida said, 'I'm going to show it to Hilary. And I must say I hope it'll change his mind about his ghastly Nigel.'

IV

When Hilary was shown the paper, which was as soon as the men came into the drawing-room, he turned very quiet. For what seemed a long time he stood with it in his hands, frowning at it and saying nothing. Mr Smith walked over to him, glanced at the paper and gave out a soft, protracted whistle. Colonel Forrester looked inquiringly from Hilary to his wife who shook her head at him. He then turned away to admire the tree and the kissing-bough.

'Well, boy,' said Mrs Forrester. 'What do you make of *that*?'

'I don't know. Not, I think, what I am expected to make of it. Aunt Bed.'

'Whatever anybody makes of it,' Cressida pointed out, 'it's not the nicest kind of thing to find in one's bedroom.'

Hilary broke into a strange apologia: tender, oblique, guarded. It was a horrid, silly thing to have happened, he told Cressida and she mustn't let it trouble her. It wasn't worth a second thought. 'Look,' he said, 'up the chimney with it, vulgar little beast,' and threw it on the fire. It blackened, its preposterous legend turned white and started out in momentary prominence, it was reduced to a wraith of itself and flew out of sight. 'Gone! Gone! Gone!' chanted Hilary rather wildly and spread his arms.

'I don't think you ought to have done that,' Cressida said, 'I think we ought to have kept it.'

'That's right,' Mr Smith chimed in. 'For dabs,' he added.

This familiar departmental word startled Troy. Mr Smith grinned at her. 'That's correct,' he said. 'Innit? What your good man calls routine, that is. Dabs. You oughter kep' it, 'Illy.'

'I think, Uncle Bert, I must be allowed to manage this ridiculous little incident in my own way.'

'Hullo-ullo-ullo!'

'I'm quite sure, Cressida darling, it's merely an idiot-joke on somebody's part. *How* I detest practical jokes!' Hilary hurried on with an unconvincing return to his usual manner. He turned to Troy. 'Don't you?'

'When they're as unfunny as this. If this is one.'

'Which I don't for a moment believe,' Cressida said. 'Joke! It's a deliberate insult. Or worse.' She appealed to Mrs Forrester. 'Isn't it?' she demanded.

'I haven't the remotest idea what it may be. What do you say to all this, Fred? I said what – '

She broke off. Her husband had gone to the far end of the room and was pacing out the distance from the french windows to the tree.

'Thirteen, fourteen, fifteen – fifteen feet exactly,' he was saying. 'I shall have to walk fifteen feet. Who's going to shut the french window after me? These things need to be worked out.'

'Honestly, Hilly darling, I do *not* think it can be all shrugged off, you know, like a fun thing. When you yourself have said Nigel always refers to his victim as a sinful lady. It seems to me to be perfectly obvious he's set his sights at me and I find it terrifying. You know, terrifying.'

'But,' Hilary said, 'it isn't. I promise you, my lovely child, it's not at all terrifying. The circumstances are entirely different – '

'I should hope so, considering she was a tart.'

' – and of course I shall get to the bottom of it. It's too preposterous. I shall put it before – '

'You can't put it before anybody. You've burnt it.'

'Nigel is completely recovered.'

''Ere,' Mr Smith said. 'What say one of that lot's got it in for 'im? What say it's been done to discredit 'im? Planted? Spiteful, like?'

'But they get on very well together.'

'Not with the colonel's chap. Not with Moult they don't. No love lost there, I'll take a fiver on it. I seen the way they look at 'im. And 'im at them.'

'Nonsense, Smith,' said Mrs Forrester. 'You don't know what you're talking about. Moult's been with us for twenty years.'

'What's that got to do with it?'

'Oh *Lord*!' Cressida said loudly and dropped into an armchair.

' – and who's going to read out the names?' the colonel speculated. 'I can't wear my specs. They'd look silly.'

'*Fred!*'

'What, B?'

'Come over here, I said come over here.'

'Why? I'm working things out.'

'You're over-exciting yourself. Come here. It's about Moult. I said it's – '

The colonel, for him almost crossly, said: 'You've interrupted my train of thought, B. What about Moult?'

As if in response to a heavily contrived cue and a shove from off-stage, the door opened and in came Moult himself, carrying a salver.

'Beg pardon, sir,' Moult said to Hilary, 'but I thought perhaps this might be urgent, sir. For the colonel, sir.'

'What *is* it, Moult?' the colonel asked quite testily.

Moult advanced the salver in his employer's direction. Upon it lay an envelope addressed in capitals: 'COL FORRESTER.'

'It was on the floor of your room, sir. By the door, sir. I thought it might be urgent,' said Moult.

CHAPTER 3

Happy Christmas

When Colonel Forrester read the message on the paper he behaved in much the same way as his nephew before him. That is to say for some seconds he made no move and gave no sign of any particular emotion. Then he turned rather pink and said to Hilary: 'Can I have a word with you, old boy?' He folded the paper and his hands were unsteady.

'Yes, of course – ' Hilary began when his aunt loudly interjected. 'No!'

'B, you must let me – '

'No. If you've been made An Object,' she said, 'I want to know how, I said – '

'I heard you. No, B. No, my dear. It's not suitable.'

'Nonsense. Fred, I insist – ' She broke off and in a completely changed voice said: 'Sit down, Fred. Hilary!'

Hilary went quickly to his uncle. They helped him to the nearest chair. Mrs Forrester put her hand in his breast pocket and took out a small phial. 'Brandy,' she said and Hilary fetched it from the tray Mervyn had left in the room.

Mr Smith said to Troy: 'It's 'is ticker. He takes turns.'

He went to the far end of the room and opened a window. The North itself returned, stirring the tree and turning the kissing-bough.

Colonel Forrester sat with his eyes closed, his hair ruffled and his breath coming short. 'I'm perfectly all right,' he whispered. 'No need to fuss.'

'Nobody's fussing,' his wife said. 'You can shut that window, if you please, Smith.'

468

Cressida gave an elaborate and prolonged shiver. 'Thank God for that, at least,' she muttered to Troy who ignored her.

'Better,' said the colonel without opening his eyes. The others stood back.

The group printed an indelible image across Troy's field of observation: an old man with closed eyes, fetching his breath short, Hilary, elegant in plum-coloured velvet and looking perturbed, Cressida lounging discontentedly and beautifully in a golden chair, Mrs Forrester, with folded arms a step or two removed from her husband and watchful of him. And coming round the Christmas tree, a little old cockney in a grand smoking jacket.

In its affluent setting and its air of dated formality the group might have served as subject-matter for some Edwardian problem-painter: Orchardson or, better still, the Hon. John Collier. And the title? 'The Letter'. For there it lay where the colonel had dropped it, in exactly the right position on the carpet, the focal-point of the composition.

To complete the organization of this hopelessly obsolete canvas Mr Smith stopped short in his tracks, while Mrs Forrester, Hilary and Cressida turned their heads and looked, as he did, at the white paper on the carpet.

And then the still picture animated. The colonel opened his eyes. Mrs Forrester took five steps across the carpet and picked up the paper.

'Aunt Bed – !' Hilary protested but she shut him up with one of her looks.

The paper had fallen on its face. She reversed it and read and – a phenomenon that is distressing in the elderly – blushed to the roots of her hair.

'Aunt Bed – ?'

Her mouth shut like a trap. An extraordinary expression came into her face. Fury? Troy wondered. Fury certainly but something else? Could it possibly be some faint hint of gratification? Without a word she handed the paper to her nephew.

As Hilary read it his eyebrows rose. He opened his mouth, shut it, re-read the message, and then, to Troy's utter amazement, made a stifled sound and covered his mouth. He stared wildly at her, seemed to pull himself together and in a trembling voice said: 'This is – no – I mean – this is preposterous. My dear Aunt Bed!'

'Don't call me THAT!' shouted his aunt.

'I'm most dreadfully sorry. I always do – oh! Oh! I see.'

'Fred. Are you better?'

'I'm all right now, thank you, B. It was just one of my little goes. It wasn't – that thing that brought it on, I do assure you. Hilly's quite right, my dear. It *is* preposterous. I'm very angry, of course, on your account, but it *is* rather ridiculous, you know.'

'I *don't* know. Outrageous, yes. Ridiculous, no. This person should be horsewhipped.'

'Yes, indeed. But I'm not quite up to horsewhipping, B, and in any case one doesn't know who to whip.'

'One can find out, I hope.'

'Yes, well, that's another story. Hilly and I must have a good talk.'

'What you must do is go to bed,' she said.

'Well – perhaps. I do want to be all right for tomorrow, don't I? And yet – we were going to do the tree and I love that.'

'Don't be a fool, Fred. We'll ring for Moult. Hilary and he can – '

'I don't want Hilary and Moult. There's no need. I'll go upstairs backwards if you like. Don't fuss, B.' Colonel Forrester stood up. He made Troy a little bow. 'I am so awfully sorry,' he said, 'for being such a bore.'

'You're nothing of the sort.'

'Sweet of you. Goodnight. Goodnight, Cressida, my dear. Goodnight, Bert. Ready, B?'

He's the boss, after all, Troy thought as he left on his wife's arm. Hilary followed them out.

'What a turn-up for the books,' Mr Smith remarked. 'Oh dear!'

Cressida dragged herself out of her chair. 'Everybody's on about the Forrester bit,' she complained. 'Nobody seems to remember *I've* been insulted. We're not allowed to know what this one said. You know. What was written. They could hardly call Aunt B a sinful lady, could they? Or could they?'

'Not,' said Mr Smith, 'with any marketing potential they couldn't.'

'I'm going to bed,' Cressida said, trailing about the room. 'I want a word with Hilary. I'll find him upstairs, I suppose. Goodnight, Mrs Alleyn.'

'Do we just abandon all this – the tree and so on?'

'I dare say he'll do it when he comes down. It's not late, after all, is it? Goodnight, Mr Smith.'

'Night-night, Beautiful,' said Mr Smith. 'Not to worry. It's a funny old world but we don't care, do we?'

'I must say I do, rather. You know?' said Cressida and left them.

'Marvellous!' Mr Smith observed and poured himself a drink. 'Can I offer you anything, Mrs A?'

'Not at the moment, thank you. Do *you* think this is all a rather objectionable practical joke?'

'Ah! That's talking. Do I? Not to say practical joke, exactly, I don't. But in a manner of speaking – '

He broke off and looked pretty sharply at Troy. 'Upset your apple-cart a bit, has it?'

'Well . . .'

'Here! *You* haven't been favoured yourself? Have you?'

'Not with a message.'

'With something, though?'

'Nothing that matters,' said Troy, remembering her promise to Mervyn and wishing Mr Smith was not quite so sharp.

'Keeping it to yourself?' he said. 'Your privilege, of course, but whatever it is if I was you I'd tell 'Illy. Oh, well. It's been a long day and all. I wouldn't say no to a bit of kip, myself.' He sipped his drink. 'Very nice,' he said, 'but the best's to come.'

'The best?'

'My nightcap. Know what it is? Barley water. Fact. Barleywater with a squeeze of lemon. Take it every night of my life. Keeps me regular and suits my fancy. 'Illy tells that permanent spectre of his to set it up for me in my room.'

'Nigel?'

'That's right. The bloodless wonder.'

'What's your opinion of the entourage, Mr Smith?'

'Come again?'

'The set-up. At Halberds.'

'Ah. I get you. Well, now: it's peculiar. Look at it any way you like it's eccentric. But then in a manner of speaking, so's 'Illy. It suits him. Mind, if he'd set 'imself up with a bunch of smashers and grabbers or job-buyers or mags-men or any of that lot, I'd of spoke up very strong against. But murderers – when they're oncers, that is – they're different.'

'My husband agrees with you.'

'And *he* ought to know, didn't 'e? Now, you won't find Alf Moult agreeing with that verdict. Far from it.'

'You think he mistrusts the staff?'

'Hates their guts if you'll pardon me. He comes of a class that likes things to be done very, very regular and respectable, does Alf Moult. Soldier-servant. Super-snob. I know. I come from the one below, myself: not up to his mark he'd think but near enough to know how he ticks. Scum of the earth, he calls them. If it wasn't that he can't seem to detect any difference between the colonel and Almighty God, he'd refuse to demean hisself by coming here and consorting with them.'

Mr Smith put down his empty glass, wiped his fingers across his mouth and twinkled. 'Very nice,' he said. 'You better come and see my place one of these days. Get 'Illy to bring you. I got one or two works might interest you. We do quite a lot in the old master lark ourselves. Every now and then I see something I fancy and I buy it in. What's your opinion of Blake?'

'Blake?'

'William. Tiger, tiger.'

'Superb.'

'I got one of 'is drawings.'

'Have you, now!'

'Come and take a butcher's.'

'Love to,' said Troy. 'Thank you.'

Hilary came in overflowing with apologies. 'What you must think of us!' he exclaimed. 'One nuisance treads upon another's heels. Judge of my mortification.'

'What's the story up to date, then?' asked Mr Smith.

'Nothing more, really, except that Cressida has been very much disturbed.'

'What a shame. But she's on the road to recovery, I see.'

'What do you see?'

'It was worse when they favoured the blood red touch. Still and all, you better wipe it off.'

'What a really dreadful old man you are, Uncle Bert,' said Hilary, without rancour but blushing and using his handkerchief.

'I'm on me way to me virtuous couch. If I find a dirty message under the door I'll scream. Goodnight all.'

They heard him whistling as he went upstairs.

'You're not going just yet, are you?' Hilary said to Troy. 'Please don't or I'll be quite sure you've taken umbrage.'

'In that case I'll stay.'

'How heavenly cool you are. It's awfully soothing. Will you have a drink? No? I shall. I need one.' As he helped himself Hilary said: 'Do you madly long to know what was in Uncle Flea's note?'

'I'm afraid I do.'

'It's not really so frightful.'

'It can't be since you seemed inclined to laugh.'

'You *are* a sharp one, aren't you? As a matter of fact it said quite shortly that Uncle Flea's a cuckold spelt with three Ks. It was the thought of Aunt Bed living up to her pet name that almost did for me. Who with, one asks oneself? Moult?'

'No wonder she was enraged.'

'My dear, she wasn't. Not really. Basically she was as pleased as Punch. Didn't you notice how snappy she got when Uncle Flea said it was ridiculous?'

'I don't believe you.'

'You may as well, I promise you.'

Troy giggled.

'Of course she'd love it if Uncle Flea did go into action with a horsewhip. I can never understand how it's managed, can you? It would be so easy to run away and leave the horsewhipper laying about him like a ringmaster without a circus.'

'I don't think it's that kind of horsewhip. It's one of the short jobs like a jockey's. You have to break it in two when you've finished and contemptuously throw the pieces at the victim.'

'You're wonderfully well-informed, aren't you?'

'It's only guesswork.'

'All the same, you know, it's no joke, this business. It's upset my lovely Cressida. *She* really *is* cross. You see, she's never taken to the staff. She was prepared to put up with them because they do function quite well, don't you think? But unfortunately she's heard of the entire entourage of a Greek millionaire who died the other day, all wanting to come to England because of the Colonels. And now she's convinced it was Nigel who did her message and she's dead set on making a change.'

'You don't think it was Nigel?'

'No. I don't think he'd be such an ass.'

'But if – I'm sorry but you did say he was transferred to Broadmoor.'

'He's as sane as sane can be. A complete cure. Oh, I know the message to Cressida is rather in his style but I consider that's merely a blind.'

'*Do* you!' Troy said thoughtfully.

'Yes, I do. Just as – well – Uncle Flea's message is rather in Cuthbert's vein. You remember Cuthbert slashed out at the handsome commis who had overpersuaded his wife. Well, it came out in evidence that Cuthbert made a great to-do about being a cuckold. The word cropped up all over his statements.'

'How does he spell it?'

'I've no idea.'

'What is your explanation?'

'To begin with, I don't countenance any notion that both Nigel and Cuthbert were inspired, independently, to write poison-pen notes on the same sort of paper, (it's out of the library) in the same sort of capital letters.'

(Or, thought Troy, that Mervyn was moved at the same time, to set a booby-trap.)

'Or, equally,' Hilary went on, 'that one of the staff wrote the messages to implicate the other two. They get on extremely well together, all of them.'

'Well, then?'

'What is one left with? Somebody's doing it. It's not me and I don't suppose it's you.'

'No.'

'No. So we run into a *reductio ad absurdum*, don't we? We're left with a most improbable field. Flea. Bed. Cressida. Uncle Bert.'

'And Moult?'

'Good heavens,' said Hilary. 'Uncle Bert's fancy! I forgot about Moult. Moult, now. *Moult.*'

'Mr Smith seems to think – '

'Yes, I dare say.' Hilary glanced uneasily at Troy and began to walk about the room as if he were uncertain what to say next. 'Uncle

Bert,' he began at last, 'is an oddity. He's not a simple character. Not at all.'

'No?'

'No. For instance there's his sardonic-East-End-character-act. "I'm so artful, you know, I'm a cockney." He *is* a cockney, of course. Vintage barrow-boy. But he's put himself in inverted commas and comes out of them whenever it suits him. You should hear him at the conference table. He's as articulate as the next man and, in his way, more civilized than most.'

'Interesting.'

'Yes. He's got a very individual sense of humour, has Uncle Bert.'

'Tending towards Black Comedy?'

'He might have invented the term. All the same,' Hilary said, 'he's an astute judge of character and I – I can't pretend he isn't, although – '

He left this observation unfinished. 'I think I'll do the tree,' he said. 'It settles one's nerves.'

He opened the lid of the packing case that had been placed near the tree.

Mr Smith had left ajar the double-doors into the great hall, whence there now came sounds of commotion. Somebody was stumbling rapidly downstairs and making ambiguous noises as he came. A slither was followed by an oath and an irregular progress across the hall. The doors burst wide open and in plunged Mr Smith: an appalling sight.

He was dressed in pyjamas and a florid dressing-gown. One foot was bare, the other slippered. His sparse hair was disordered. His eyes protruded. And from his open mouth issued dollops of foam.

He retched, gesticulated and contrived to speak.

'Poisoned!' he mouthed. 'I been poisoned.'

An iridescent bubble was released from his lips. It floated towards the tree, seemed to hang for a moment like an ornament from one of the boughs and then burst.

II

'Soap,' Hilary said. 'It's soap, Uncle Bert. Calm yourself, for heaven's sake, and wash your mouth out. Go to a downstairs cloakroom, I implore you.'

Mr Smith incontinently bolted.

'Hadn't you better see to him?' Troy asked.

'What next, what next! How inexpressibly distasteful. However.'

Hilary went. There followed a considerable interval, after which Troy heard them pass through the hall on their way upstairs. Soon afterwards Hilary returned looking deeply put-out.

'In his barley water,' he said. 'The strongest possible solution of soap. Carnation. He's been hideously sick. This settles it.'

'Settles – ?'

'It's some revolting practical joker. No, but it's too bad! And in the pocket of his pyjama jacket another of these filthy notes. "What price Arsnic." He might have died of fright.'

'How is he, in fact?'

'Wan but recovering. In a mounting rage.'

'Small blame to him.'

'Somebody shall smart for this,' Hilary threatened.

'I suppose it couldn't be the new boy in the kitchen?'

'I don't see it. He doesn't know their backgrounds. This is some-body who knows about Nigel's sinful lady and Cuthbert being a cuckold and Vincent's slip over the arsenical weed-killer.'

'And Mervyn's booby-trap,' Troy said before she could stop herself.

Hilary stared at her.

'You're not going to tell me – ? *You are!*'

'I promised I wouldn't. I suppose these other jobs sort of let me out but – all right, there was an incident. I'm sure he had nothing to do with it. Don't corner me.'

Hilary was silent for some time after this. Then he began taking boxes of Christmas tree baubles out of the packing case.

'I'm going to ignore the whole thing,' he said. 'I'm going to main-tain a masterly inactivity. Somebody wants me to make a big scene and I won't. I won't upset my staff. I won't have my Christmas ruined. Sucks-boo to whoever it may be. It's only ten to eleven, believe it or not. Come on, let's do the tree.'

They did the tree. Hilary had planned a golden colour scheme. They hung golden glass baubles, big in the lower branches and tapering to minuscule ones at the top, where they mounted a golden angel. There were festoons of glittering gold tinsel and masses of gilded candles. Golden stars shone in and out of the foliage. It was a most fabulous tree.

'And I've even gilded the people in the crib,' he said. 'I hope Aunt Bed won't object. And just you wait till the candles are lit.'

'What about the presents? I suppose there are presents?'

'The children's will be in golden boxes brought in by Uncle Flea, one for each family. And ours, suitably wrapped, on a side table. Everybody finds his own because Uncle Flea can't read the labels without his specs. He merely tows in the boxes in a little golden car on runners.'

'From outside? Suppose it's a rough night?'

'If it's too bad we'll have to bring the presents in from the hall.'

'But the colonel will still come out of the storm?'

'He wouldn't dream of doing anything else.'

With some hesitation Troy suggested that Colonel Forrester didn't seem very robust and was ill-suited to a passage, however brief, through the rigours of a mid-winter storm, clad, she understood, in gold lamé. Hilary said he could wear gloves. Noticing, perhaps, that she was not persuaded, he said Vincent would hold an umbrella over the colonel and that in any case it wouldn't do for his wig and crown of mistletoe to get wet although, he added, a sprinkling of snow would be pretty. 'But of course it would melt,' he added. 'And that could be disastrous.'

Hilary was perched on the top of the step-ladder. He looked down through green foliage and golden baubles at Troy.

'You don't approve,' he said. 'You think I'm effete and heartless and have lost my sense of spiritual values.'

This came uncomfortably near to what in fact Troy had been thinking.

'You may be right,' he went on before she could produce an answer. 'But at least I don't pretend. For instance, I'm a snob. I set a lot of importance on my being of ancient lineage. I wouldn't have proposed to my lovely, lovely Cressida if she'd had a tatty origin. I value family trees even more than Christmas trees. And I love being rich and able to have a truly golden tree.'

'Oh,' Troy said, 'I've nothing but praise for the golden tree.'

'I understand you perfectly. You must pray for me in the chapel tomorrow.'

'I'm not qualified.'

Hilary said: 'Never mind about all that. I've been keeping the chapel as a surprise. It really is quite lovely.'

'Are you a Christian?'

'In the context,' said Hilary, 'it doesn't arise. Be an angel and hand up a bauble.'

It was midnight when they had completed their work. They stood at the other end of the long room before the dying fire and admired it.

'There will be no light but the candles,' Hilary said. 'It will be perfectly magical. A dream-tree. I hope the children will be enchanted, don't you?'

'They can't fail. I shall go to bed, now, I think.'

'How nice it's been, doing it with you,' he said, linking his arm in hers and leading her down the room. 'It has quite taken away all that other beastly nonsense. Thank you so much. Have you admired Nigel's kissing-bough?'

They were under it. Troy looked up and was kissed.

'Happy Christmas,' said Hilary.

She left him there and went up to her room.

When she opened her wardrobe she was surprised to hear a murmur of voices in the Forresters' room. It was distant and quite indistinguishable but as she hung up her dress she heard footsteps tread towards her and the colonel's voice, close at hand, said very loudly and most decisively: 'No, my dear, that is absolutely final. And if you don't, I will.'

A door slammed. Troy had a picture of Mrs Forrester banging her way into their bathroom but a moment later had to reverse this impression into one of her banging her way back into the bedroom. Her voice rose briefly and indistinctly. The colonel's footfall receded. Troy hastily shut the wardrobe door and went to bed.

III

Christmas Day came in with a wan glint of sunshine. The view from Troy's bedroom might have been framed by robins, tinsel and holly. Snow took the sting out of a landscape that could have been set up for Hilary's satisfaction.

As she dressed Troy could hear the Forresters shouting to each other next door and concluded that the colonel was back on his usual form. When she opened her wardrobe she heard the now familiar jangle of coathangers on the other side.

'Good morning!' Troy shouted. She tapped on the common wall. 'Happy Christmas!' she cried.

A man's voice said: 'Thank you, madam. I'll tell the Colonel and Mrs Forrester.'

Moult.

She heard him go away. There was a distant conjunction of voices and then he returned, discreetly tapping on the wall.

'The Colonel and Mrs Forrester's compliments, madam, and they would be very happy if you would look in.'

'In five minutes,' Troy shouted. 'Thank you.'

When she made her call she found Colonel and Mrs Forrester in bed and bolt upright under a green-lined umbrella of the sort associated with Victorian missionaries and Empire builders. The wintry sun lay across their counterpane. Each wore a scarlet dressing-gown, the skirts of which were deployed round the wearer like some monstrous calyx. They resembled gods of a sort.

In unison they wished Troy a Happy Christmas and invited her to sit down.

'Being an artist,' Mrs Forrester said, 'you will not find it out of the way to be informally received.'

At the far end of the room a door into their bathroom stood open and beyond that a second door into a dressing-room where Moult could be seen brushing a suit.

'I had heard,' said Troy, 'about the umbrella.'

'We don't care for the sun in our eyes. I wonder,' said Mrs Forrester, 'if I might ask you to shut the bathroom door. Thank you very much. Moult has certain prejudices which we prefer not to arouse. Fred, put in your aid. I said put in your aid.'

Colonel Forrester who had smiled and nodded a great deal without seeming to hear anything much, found his hearing-aid on his bedside table and fitted it into his ear.

'It's a wonderful invention,' he said. 'I'm a little worried about wearing it tonight, though. But, after all, the wig's awfully long. A Druid with a visible hearing-aid would be *too* absurd, don't you think?'

'First of all,' Mrs Forrester began, 'were there any developments after we went to bed?'

'We're dying to know,' said the colonel.

Troy told them about Mr Smith and the soap. Mrs Forrester rubbed her nose vexedly. 'That's very tiresome,' she said. 'It upsets my theory, Fred, it upsets my theory.'

'Sickening for you, B.'

'And yet, does it? I'm not so sure. It might be a ruse, you know I said . . .'

'I'm wearing my aid, B.'

'What,' Troy asked, 'is your theory?'

'I was persuaded that Smith wrote the letters.'

'But surely . . .'

'He's a good creature in many ways but his sense of humour is coarse and he dislikes Cressida Tottenham.'

'B, my dear, I'm sure you're mistaken.'

'No you're not. You're afraid I'm right. He doesn't think she's good enough for Hilary. Nor do I.'

'Be that as it may, B.'

'Be that as it is, you mean. Don't confuse me, Fred.'

' – Bert Smith would certainly not write that disgraceful message to me. About you.'

'I don't agree. He'd think it funny.'

The colonel looked miserable. 'But it's not,' he said.

'Hilary thought it funny,' Mrs Forrester said indignantly and turned to Troy. 'Did *you*? I suppose Hilary told you what it said.'

'In general terms.'

'Well? Funny?'

Troy said: 'At the risk of making myself equally objectionable I'm afraid I've got to confess that . . .'

'Very well. You need go no further.' Mrs Forrester looked at her husband and remarked, astoundingly, 'Impertinent, yes. Unfounded, of course. Preposterous, not so far-fetched as you may suppose.'

A reminiscent gleam, Troy could have sworn, came into Mrs Forrester's eye.

'I don't believe Bert would make himself sick,' the colonel urged.

'I wouldn't put it past him,' Mrs Forrester said darkly. 'However,' she continued with a wave of her hand, 'that is unimportant. What

I wished to talk to you about, Mrs Alleyn, is the line I hope we shall all take in this matter. Fred and I have decided to ignore it. To dismiss it – ' she swept her arm across the colonel who blinked and drew back ' – entirely. As if it had never been. We refuse to give the perpetrator of these insults, the satisfaction of paying them the slightest attention. We hope you will join us in this stand.'

'*Because*,' her husband added, 'it would only spoil everything – the tree and so on. We're having a rehearsal after church and one must give one's full attention.'

'And you're quite recovered, Colonel?'

'Yes, yes, quite, thank you. It's my old ticker, you know. A leaky valve or some nonsense of that sort, the quacks tell me. Nothing to fuss about.'

'Well,' Troy said, getting up. 'I'll agree – mum's the word.'

'Good. That settles that. I don't know how this girl of yours is going to behave herself, Fred.'

'She's *not mine*, B.'

'She was your responsibility.'

'Not now, though.' The colonel turned towards Troy but did not look at her. His face was pink. He spoke rapidly as if he had memorized his observations and wished to get rid of them. 'Cressida,' he explained, 'is the daughter of a young fellow in my regiment. Germany. 1950. We were on an exercise and my jeep overturned.' Here the colonel's eyes filled with tears. 'And do you know this dear fellow got me out? I was pinned face down in the mud and he got me out and then the most dreadful things happened. Collapse. Petrol. And I promised him I'd keep an eye on the child.'

'Luckily,' said Mrs Forrester, 'she was well provided for. School in Switzerland and all that. I say nothing of the result.'

'Her mother died, poor thing. In childbirth.'

'And now,' said Mrs Forrester suddenly shutting up their umbrella with a definitive snap, 'now she's in some sort of actressy business.'

'She's an awfully pretty girl, don't you think?'

'Lovely,' said Troy warmly and went down to breakfast.

Hilary was busy during the morning but Troy did a certain amount of work on the portrait before making herself ready for church.

When she looked through the library windows that gave on the great courtyard she got quite a shock. Nigel had completed his effigy. The packing case was mantled in frozen snow and on top of it, sharply carved and really quite impressive in his glittering iciness lay Hilary's Bill-Tasman ancestor, his hands crossed, rather like flat-fish, on his breast.

At half past ten the monk's bell rang fast and exuberantly in its tower as if the operator was a bit above himself. Troy made her way downstairs and across the hall and, following instructions, turned right into the corridor which served the library, the breakfast-room, the boudoir, Hilary's study and, as it now transpired, the chapel.

It was a superb chapel. It was full, but by no means too full, of treasures. Its furniture included monstrance, candlesticks, Quattrocento confessional – the lot: all in impeccable taste and no doubt, awfully valuable.

Troy experienced a frightful desire to hang crinkly paper garlands on some insipid plaster saint.

Cuthbert, Mervyn, Nigel, Vincent, Kittiwee and the boy were already seated. They were supplemented by a cluster of odd bodies whom she supposed to be outside workers at Halberds and their wives and children. Hilary and Cressida were in the front pew. The rest of the house-party soon assembled and the service went through with High Church decorum. The prison chaplain gave a short, civilized sermon. Colonel Forrester, to Troy's surprise and pleasure, played the lovely little organ for the seasonable hymns. Hilary read the gospel and, Mr Smith, with surprising aplomb and the full complement of aitches, the epistle.

At three o'clock that afternoon the ceremony of the tree was rehearsed.

It was all very thoroughly planned. The guests would assemble in the library, Troy's portrait and impedimenta having been removed for the occasion to Hilary's study. Vincent, with umbrella and a charming little baroque car on runners, loaded with Christmas boxes, would be stationed outside the drawing-room windows. At eight o'clock recorded joybells would usher in the proceedings. The children would march in procession two-by-two from the library across the hall to the drawing-room, where they would find the golden tree blazing in the dark. The adults would follow.

These manœuvres executed, Colonel Forrester, fully accoutred as a Druid, would emerge from the little cloakroom next the drawing-room where Cressida had helped to make him up. He would slip through a door into the entrance porch and from there into the wintry courtyard. Here he would effect a liaison with Vincent. The recorded music, sleighbells, snorts and cries of 'Whoa!' would be released. The french windows, flung open from within by Cuthbert and Mervyn, would admit the colonel towing his gilded car. To a fan-fare ('of trumpets also and shawms,' Hilary said) he would encircle the tree and then, abandoning his load, would bow to his audience, make one or two esoteric gestures and retire to the limbo whence he had come. He would then pick up his skirts and bolt back through the hall and into the cloakroom, where with Cressida's help he would remove his beard, moustache and eyebrows, his wig, his boots and his golden gown. In due course he would appear in his native guise among the guests.

The rehearsals did not go through without incidents, most of which were caused by the extreme excitability of the colonel him-self. Troy became very anxious about him and Mrs Forrester, whose presence he had feebly tried to prevent, finally put her foot down and told Hilary that if he wanted his uncle to perform that evening he must stop making him run about like a madman. She would not be answerable for the consequences, she said, if he did not. She then removed her husband to rest in his room, obliging him, to his mild annoyance, to ascend the stairs backwards and stop for ten seconds at every fifth step.

Cressida, who seemed to be extremely unsettled, drifted up to Troy and watched this protracted exit.

The colonel begged them not to wait and at Cressida's suggestion they went together to the boudoir.

'There are moments,' Cressida said, 'when I catch myself wonder-ing if this house is not a loony-bin. Well, I mean, look at it. It's like one of those really trendy jobs. You know, the Happening thing. We did them in Organic-Expressivists.'

'What *are* Organic-Expressivists?' Troy asked.

'You can't really *explain* O-E. You know. You can't say it's "about" that or the other thing. An O-E Exposure is one thing for each of *us* and another for each of the *audience*. One simply hopes there will be

a spontaneous emotional release,' Cressida rapidly explained. 'Zell –
our director – well, *not* a director in the establishment sense – he's
our *source* – he puts enormous stress on spontaneity.'

'Are you rejoining the group?'

'No. Well, Hilary and I are probably getting married in May, so if
we do there wouldn't really be much point, would there? And
anyway the O-E's in recess at the moment. No lolly.'

'What did you yourself do in the performances?'

'At first I just moved about getting myself released and then Zell
thought I ought to develop the Yin-Yang bit if that's what it's called.
You know, the male-female bit. So I did. I wore a kind of net trouser-
token on my left leg and I had long green crêpe-hair pieces stuck to
my left jaw. I must say I hated the spirit-gum. You know, on your
skin? But it had an erotic-seaweed connotation that seemed to communicate rather successfully.'

'What else did you wear?'

'Nothing else. The audiences met me. You know? Terribly well.
It's because of my experience with crêpe-hair that I'm doing Uncle
Fred's beard. It's all ready-made and only has to be stuck on.'

'I do hope he'll be all right.'

'So do I. He's all up-tight about it, though. He's fantastic, isn't he?
Not true. I'm way up there over him and Auntie B. I think he's the
mostest. You know? Only I don't exactly send Auntie B, I'm afraid.'

She moved gracefully and irritably about the beautiful little room.
She picked up an ornament and put it down again with the half-
attention of an idle shopper.

'There's been a row in the kitchen,' she said. 'Did you know? This
morning?'

'Not I.'

'About me, in a sort of way. Kittiwee was on about me and
his ghastly cats and the others laughed at him and – I don't know
exactly – but it all got a bit out of hand. Moult was mixed up in it.
They all hate Moult like poison.'

'How do you know about it?'

'I heard. Hilly asked me to look at the flowers that have been
sent. The flower-room's next the Servants' Hall, only we're meant
to call it the staff common-room. They were at it hammer-
and-tongs. You know. Yelling. I was just wondering whether I

ought to tell Hilly when I heard Moult come into the passage. He was shouting back at the others. He said: "You lot! You're no more than a bloody squad of bloody thugs," and a good deal more. And Cuthbert roared like a bull for Moult to get out before one of them did him over. And I've told Hilly. I thought he might have told you, he likes you so much.'

'No.'

'Well, anyway let's face it I'm not prepared to marry into a permanent punch-up. I mean it's just crazy. It's not my scene. If you'd heard! Do you know what Cuthbert said? He said: "One more crack out of you and I'll bloody block your light."'

'What do you suppose that means?'

'I know what it sounded like,' Cressida said. 'It sounded like murder. And I mean that. Murder.'

IV

It was at this point that Troy began to feel really disturbed. She began to see herself as if she was another person, alone among strangers in an isolated and falsely luxurious house and attended by murderers. That, she thought, like it or lump it, is the situation. And she wished with all her heart she was out of it and spending her Christmas alone in London or with any one of the unexceptionable friends who had so warmly invited her.

The portrait was almost finished. Perhaps quite finished. She was not sure it hadn't reached the state when somebody with wisdom should forcibly remove her from it and put it out of her reach. Her husband had been known to perform this service but he was twelve thousand miles away and unless, as sometimes happened, his job in the Antipodes came to a quick end, would not be home for a week. The portrait was not dry enough to pack. She could arrange for it to be sent to the framers and she could tell Hilary she would leave – when? Tomorrow? He would think that very odd. He would smell a rat. He would conclude that she was afraid and he would be dead right. She was.

Mr Smith had said that he intended returning to London the day after tomorrow. Perhaps she could leave with him. At this point Troy saw that she would have to take a sharp look at herself. It was an occasion for what Cressida would probably call maintaining her cool.

In the first place she must remember that she was often overcome, in other people's houses, by an overpowering desire to escape, a tyrannical restlessness as inexplicable as it was embarrassing. Every nerve in her body would suddenly telegraph 'I must get out of this.' It could happen, even in a restaurant where, if the waiter was slow with the bill, Troy suffered agonies of frustration. Was her present most ardent desire to be gone no more than the familiar attack exacerbated by the not inconsiderable alarms and eccentricities of life at Halberds? Perhaps Hilary's domestics were, after all, as harmless as he insisted. Had Cressida blown up a servants' squabble into a display of homicidal fury?

She reminded herself of the relatively calm reaction to the incidents of the Forresters and, until the soap episode, of Mr Smith. She took herself to task, tied her head in a scarf, put on her overcoat and went for a short walk.

The late afternoon was icily cold and still, the darkening sky was clear and the landscape glittered. She looked more closely at Nigel's catafalque which was now frozen as hard as its marble progenitor in the chapel. Really Nigel had been very clever with his kitchen instruments. He had achieved a sharpness and precision far removed from the blurred clumsiness of the usual snow effigy. Only the northern aspect, Troy thought, had been partly defaced by the wind and occasional drifts of rain and even there it was the snow-covered box steps that had suffered rather than the effigy itself. Somebody should photograph it, she thought, before the thaw comes.

She walked as far as the scarecrow. It was tilted sideways, stupid and motionless, at the impossible angle in which the wind had left it. A disconsolate thrush sat on its billycock hat.

By the time she had returned, tingling, to the warm house, Troy had so far got over her impulsive itch as to postpone any decision until the next day. She even began to feel a reasonable interest in the party.

And indeed Halberds simmered with expectation. In the enormous hall with its two flights of stairs, giant swags of fir, mistletoe and holly caught up with scarlet tassels hung in classic loops from the gallery and picture rails. Heroic logs blazed and crackled in two enormous fireplaces. The smell was superb.

Hilary was there, with a written timetable in his hand issuing final instructions to his staff. He waved gaily to Troy and invited her to stay and listen.

'Now! Cuthbert! To go over it once more,' Hilary was saying. 'You will make sure the drawing-room door is locked. Otherwise we shall have children screaming in before they should. When everybody is here (you've got your guest list), check to make sure Vincent is ready with the sledge. You wait until half past seven when the first recorded bells will be played and Colonel Forrester will come downstairs and go into the cloakroom near the drawing-room where Miss Tottenham will put on his beard.'

'Choose your words, sweetie,' Cressida remarked. 'I'd look a proper Charlie, wouldn't I?'

Kittiwee sniggered.

'Miss Tottenham,' Hilary said, raising his voice, 'will help the colonel with his beard. You now check that Nigel is at hand to play his part and at a quarter to eight you tap the door of the cloakroom near the drawing-room to let Colonel Forrester and Miss Tottenham know we are ready. Yes?'

'Yes, sir. Very good, sir.'

'You and Nigel then light the candles on the tree and the kissing-bough. That's going to take a little time. Be sure you get rid of the step-ladder and turn off all the lights. *Most* important. Very well. That done, you tell Nigel to return to the record-player in the hall here. Nigel: at five to eight precisely, you increase the *indoor* recording of the bells. Plenty of volume, remember. We want the house to be *full* of bells. Now! Mervyn! When you hear the bells, unlock the drawing-room doors and, I implore you, be sure you have the key to hand.'

'I've got it on me, sir.'

'Good. Very well. You, Cuthbert, come to the library and announce the tree. Full voice, you know, Cuthbert. Give it everything, won't you?'

'Sir.'

'You and Mervyn, having thrown open the drawing-room doors, go right through the room to the french windows. Check that the colonel is ready outside. Vincent will by this time be with him and will flash his torch. Wait by the windows. Now, then. The crucial moment,' Hilary excitedly continued, 'has arrived. *When* everybody has come in

and settled in their places – I shall see to that and I dare say Mrs Alleyn
will be very kind and help me – you, Cuthbert, stand in the window
where Vincent can see you and give his signal. Vincent, be ready for
this. You must keep out of sight with the sleigh, until the last moment.
When the inside bells stop, bring the sleigh into the courtyard, where
you will join the colonel. And when you get your signal, the sound
effects for the entrance will be turned on. The loud-speakers,' Hilary
explained to Troy, 'are outside for greater verisimilitude. And now,
now, Cuthbert! Keep your heads, you and Mervyn, I implore you.
Coolness is all. Coolness and co-ordination. *Wait* for your own voice
shouting "Whoa" on the loud-speakers, *wait* for the final cascade of
sleighbells and then, and *only* then – fling wide the french windows
and admit the colonel with his sledge. Vincent, you must watch the
colonel like a lynx for fear that in his zeal he tries to effect an entrance
before we are ready for him. Make certain he removes his gloves. Take
them off him at the last moment. He has to wear them because of
chilblains. See he's well *en train* beforehand with the tow-ropes of his
sledge over his shoulders. He may show a hideous tendency to tie
himself up in them like a parcel. Calm him.'

'Do my best, sir,' said Vincent, 'but he does show the whites of his
eyes, like, when he gets up to the starting cage.'

'I know. I depend on your tact, Vincent. Miss Tottenham will see
him out of the cloakroom and you take over in the courtyard. After
that he's all yours.'

'Thank you, sir,' said Vincent dubiously.

'Those,' said Hilary, surveying his troops, 'are my final words to
you. That is all. Thank you.' He turned to Troy. 'Come and have tea,'
he said. 'It's in the boudoir. We help ourselves. Rather like the
Passover with all our loins, such as they are, girded up. I do hope
you're excited. Are you?'

'Why – yes,' she agreed, surprised to find that it was so, 'I am. I'm
very excited.'

'You won't be disappointed, I promise. Who knows, said Hilary,
'but what you won't look back on tonight as a unique experience.
There, now!'

'I dare say I shall,' Troy said, humouring him.

CHAPTER 4

The Tree And The Druid

Bells everywhere, the house sang with their arbitrary clamour: it might have been the interior of some preposterous belfry. Nigel was giving zealous attention to his employer's desire for volume.

'Whang-whang-whang-*whang*,' yelled an over-stimulated little boy making extravagant gestures and grimaces. Sycophantic little girls screamed their admiration in his face. All the children leapt to their feet and were pounced upon by their parents assisted by Hilary and Troy. Three of the parents who were also warders at The Vale began to walk purposefully about the room and with slightly menacing authority soon reformed the childish rabble into a mercurial crocodile.

'Bells, bells, bells, *bells*!' shouted the children like infant prodigies at grips with Edgar Allen Poe.

Cuthbert entered, contemplated his audience, fetched a deep breath and bellowed: 'The Tree, sir.'

An instant quiet was secured. The bells having given a definitive concerted crash hummed into silence. All the clocks in the house and the clock in the stable tower struck eight and then, after a second or two, the bells began again, very sweetly, with the tune of St Clement Danes.

'Come along,' said Hilary.

With the chanciness of their species the children suddenly became angelic. Their eyes grew as round as saucers, their lips parted like rosebuds, they held hands and looked enchanting. Even the over-stimulated little boy calmed down.

Hilary, astonishingly, began to sing. He had a vibrant alto voice and everybody listened to him.

'Oranges and lemons, say the Bells of St Clement's
You owe me five farthings, say the Bells of St Martin's.'

Two and two they walked, out of the library, into the passage, through the great hall now illuminated only by firelight, and, since the double-doors of the drawing-room stood wide open, into the enchantment that Hilary had prepared for them.

And really, Troy thought, it was an enchantment. It was breathtaking. At the far end of this long room, suspended in darkness, blazed the golden Christmas tree alive with flames, stars and a company of angels. It quivered with its own brilliance and was the most beautiful tree in all the world.

'When will you pay me? say the Bells of Old Bailey,
When I grow rich, say the Bells of Shoreditch.'

The children sat on the floor in the light of the tree. Their elders – guests and the household staff – moved to the far end of the room and were lost in shadow.

Troy thought: This is Uncle Flea's big thing and here, in a moment, will come Uncle Flea.

Hilary, standing before the children, raised his hands for quiet and got it. From outside in the night came sounds that might have been made by insubstantial flutes piping in the north wind. Electronic music, Troy thought, and really almost *too* effective: it raised goose-pimples: it turned one a little cold. But through this music came the jingle of approaching sleighbells. Closer and closer, to an insistent rhythm, until they were outside the french windows. Nothing could be seen beyond the tree but Hilary in his cunning had created an arrival. Now came the stamp of hooves, the snorts, the splendid cries of 'Whoa.' Troy didn't so much as think of Cuthbert.

The windows were opened.

The tree danced in the cold air: everything stirred and glittered: the candle flames wavered, the baubles tinkled.

The windows were shut.

And round the tree, tugging his golden car on its runners, came The Druid.

Well, Troy thought, it may be a shameless concoction of anachronisms and Hilary's cockeyed sense of fantasy, but it works.

The Druid's robe, stiff, wide-sleeved and enveloping, was of gold lamé. His golden hair hung about his face in formal strands and his golden beard spread like a fan across his chest. A great crown of mistletoe shaded his eyes, which were spangled and glinted in the dark. He was not a comic figure. He was strange. It was as if King Lear had been turned into O-Luk-Oie the Dream God. He circled the tree three times to the sound of trumpets and pipes.

Then he dropped the golden cords of his car. He raised his arms, made beckoning gestures and bowed with extended hands.

Unfortunately he had forgotten to remove his gloves which were of the sensible knitted kind.

'*Fred. Your gloves I said –* '

But he was gone. He had returned whence he came. A further incursion of cold air, the windows were shut, the bells receded.

He was gone.

II

The joyful pandemonium that now broke out among the children was kept within reasonable bounds by Hilary and Troy, who had become a sort of ADC to the action. The names of the families were emblazoned in glitter on the boxes and the children broke into groups, found, delved and exclaimed.

Mervyn stood by the tree with an extinguisher, watching the candles. Hilary signalled to Nigel, who switched on the lights by a wall table where the grown-up presents were assembled. Troy found herself alongside Mrs Forrester.

'He was splendid,' Troy cried. 'He was really splendid.'

'Forgot his gloves. I knew he would.'

'It didn't matter. It didn't matter in the least.'

'It will to Fred,' said Mrs Forrester. And after a moment: 'I'm going to see him.' Or Troy thought that was what she said. The din was such that even Mrs Forrester's well-projected observations were hard to hear. Hilary's adult visitors and the household staff were now opening their presents. Nigel had begun to circulate with champagne cocktails. To Troy they seemed to be unusually potent.

Cressida was edging her way towards them. At Hilary's request she wore her dress of the previous night, the glittering trouser suit that went so admirably with his colour scheme. She raised her arm and signalled to Mrs Forrester over the heads of the intervening guests. Something slightly less lackadaisical than usual in her manner held Troy's attention. She watched the two women meet in the crowd. Cressida stooped her head. The heavy swag of her pale hair swung across her face and hid it but Mrs Forrester was caught by the wall light. Troy saw her frown and set her mouth. She hurried to the door, unceremoniously shoving herself through groups of visitors.

Cressida made for Troy.

'I say,' she said, 'was he all right? I tried to see but I couldn't get a good look.'

'He was splendid.'

'Good. You spotted him, of course?'

'What?'

'Spotted him, I said – Great Grief!' Cressida exclaimed, 'I'm beginning to talk like Aunt Bed. You *saw*, didn't you?'

'Saw? What?'

'Him.'

'Who?'

'Moult.'

'*Moult?*'

'You don't tell me,' Cressida bawled, 'that you didn't realize? Sharp as you are and all.'

'I don't know what you mean.'

'It wasn't – ' An upsurge of laughter among the guests drowned Cressida's next phrase but she advanced her lovely face towards Troy's and screamed: '*It was Moult. The Druid was Moult.*'

'*Moult!*'

'Uncle Flea's had a turn. Moult went on for the part.'

'Good Lord! Is he all right?'

'Who?'

'Uncle – Colonel Forrester?'

'I haven't seen him. Aunt B's gone up. I expect so. It seems he got over-excited again.'

'Oh!' Troy cried out. 'I *am* so sorry.'

'I know. Still,' Cressida shouted, 'just one of those things. You know.'

Nigel appeared before them with his champagne cocktails.

'Drink up,' Cressida said, 'and have another with me. I need it. Do.'

'All right. But I think there's rather a lot of brandy in them, don't you?'

'There'd better be.'

Hilary broke through the crowd to thank Troy for her present: it was a wash-drawing she had made of the scarecrow field from her bedroom window. He was, she could see, as pleased as Punch: indistinguishable thanks poured out of him. Troy watched his odd hitched-up mouth (like a camel's, she thought) gabbling away ecstatically.

At last he said: 'It all went off nicely, don't you think, except for Uncle Flea's gloves? How he could!'

Troy and Cressida, one on each side of him, screamed their intelligence. Hilary seemed greatly put out and bewildered. 'Oh *no*!' he said. 'You *don't* tell me! *Moult*!' And then after further exclamations, 'I must say he managed very creditably. Dear me, I must thank him. Where is he?'

The over-stimulated little boy appeared before them. He struck an attitude and blew a self-elongating paper squeaker into Hilary's face. Toy trumpets, drums and whistles were now extremely prevalent.

'Come here,' Hilary said. He took Cressida and Troy by their arms and piloted them into the hall, shutting the doors behind them. The children's supper was laid out in great splendour on a long trestle table. Kittiwee, the boy and some extra female helps were putting final touches.

'That's better,' Hilary said. 'I must go and see Uncle Flea. He'll be cut to the quick over this. But first tell me, Cressida darling, what exactly happened?'

'Well, I went to the cloakroom as arranged, to do his make-up. Moult was there already, all dressed up for the part. It seems he went to their rooms to help Uncle Fred and found him having a turn. Moult gave him whatever he has but it was as clear as clear he couldn't go on for the show. He was in a great taking-on. You know? So they cooked it up that Moult would do it. He'd heard all about it over and over again, of course and he'd seen the rehearsals and knew the business. So when Uncle Fred had simmered down and had put his boots up and all that (he wouldn't let Moult get Aunt B), Moult put on the robe and wig and came down. And I slapped on his whiskers and crown and out he went into the courtyard to liaise with Vincent.'

'He really did manage all right, didn't he? I came in for his entrance. I couldn't see him awfully well because of being at the back but he seemed to do all the things. And then when he eggzitted I returned to the cloakroom and helped him clean up. He was in a fuss to get back to Uncle Fred and I said I'd tell Aunt B. Which I did.'

'Darling, too wonderful of you. Everybody has clearly behaved with the greatest expedition and aplomb. Now, I must fly to poorest Flea and comfort him.'

He turned to Troy. '*What* a thing!' he exclaimed. 'Look! Both you darlings continue in your angelic ways like loves and herd the children in here to their supper. Get Cuthbert to bellow at them. As soon as they're settled under the eyes of these splendid ladies, Cuthbert and the staff will be ready for us in the dining-room. He'll sound the gong. If I'm late don't wait for me. Get the grown-ups into the dining-room. There are place-cards but it's all very informal, really. And ask Cuthbert to start the champagne at once. *Au revoir, au 'voir 'voir,'* cried Hilary running upstairs and wagging his hand above his head as he went.

'All jolly fine,' Cressida grumbled. 'I'm worn to a frazzle. But still. Come on.'

She and Troy carried out Hilary's instructions and presently the adult party was seated round the dinner-table. Troy found herself next to her acquaintance of the moors, Major Marchbanks, who said politely that this was a piece of luck for him.

'I was too shy to say so when we met the other afternoon,' he said, 'but I'm a great admirer of your work. I've actually got one of your pictures and who do you suppose gave it to me?'

'I can't imagine.'

'Can't you? Your husband.'

'Rory!'

'We are old friends. And associates. He gave it to me on the occasion of my marriage. And long before yours, I expect. He may not have even met you then.'

'I don't paint in the same way now.'

'But it's been a development, I venture? Not an abandonment?'

'Well,' said Troy, liking him, 'I choose to think so.'

Mr Smith was on her other side. He had heard about Moult's gallant effort and was greatly intrigued. Troy could feel him there at her left elbow, waiting to pounce. Several times he made a rather sly exclamation of 'Oi,' but as Major Marchbanks was talking she disregarded it. When she was free she turned and found Mr Smith with his thumbs in his armholes and his head on one side, contemplating her. He gave her a sideways chuck of his head and a click of his tongue. 'Oi,' he repeated. Troy had taken a certain amount of champagne. 'Oi, yourself,' she replied.

'Turn up for the books, Alf Moult making like he was Nebuchadnezzar in a bathrobe.'

Troy stared at him. 'You know, you're right,' she said. 'There was something distinctly Blakian. Disallowing the bathrobe.'

'Where's he got to?'

'He's up with the colonel, I think.'

''E's meant to be doling out mince-pies to the little angels.'

'That's as it may be,' Troy said darkly and drank some more champagne.

Hilary had arrived and had sat down beside a lady on Major Marchbanks's left. He looked slightly put out. Mr Smith called up the table to him. ''Ow's the colonel?' and he said: 'Better, thank you,' rather shortly.

'The old lady's keeping him company, then?'

'Yes.' Hilary added some appropriate general remarks about his uncle's disappointment and signalled to Cuthbert, who bent over him with a major-domo's air. None of the servants, Troy thought, seemed to be at all put out by the presence of so many of Her Majesty's penal servants. Perhaps they enjoyed displaying for them in their new roles.

Hilary spoke quietly to Cuthbert but Cuthbert, who seemed incapable of quiet utterance, boomingly replied: 'He's not there, sir,' and after a further question: 'I couldn't say, sir. Shall I enquire?'

'Do,' said Hilary.

Cuthbert made a slight, majestic signal to Mervyn, who left the room.

'That's peculiar,' said Mr Smith. 'Where's Alf gone to hide 'is blushes?'

'How do you know it's Moult they're talking about?'

'They said so, di'n they?'

'I didn't hear them.'

'It's peculiar,' Mr Smith repeated. He leant back in his chair and fixed his beady regard upon Hilary. He did not pick his teeth. Troy felt that this was due to some accidental neglect in his interpretation of the role for which he so inscrutably cast himself.

She drank some more champagne. 'Tell me, Mr Smith,' she began recklessly, 'Why do you – or do you – '

But Mr Smith was paying no attention to Troy. His attention was fixed upon Mervyn, who had returned and was speaking to Cuthbert. Cuthbert again bent over his employer.

'Moult, sir,' he intoned, 'is not on duty in the hall.'

'Why the devil not!' Hilary snapped quite loudly.

'I'm sure I can't say, sir. He received instructions, sir. Very clear.'

'All right, well, *find* him, Cuthbert. He's wanted with the colonel. Mrs Forrester won't leave the colonel by himself. Go *on*, Cuthbert. Find him. Go yourself.'

Cuthbert's eyebrows mounted his forehead. He inclined, returned to Mervyn and raised a finger at Nigel with whom he finally left the dining-room. Mervyn remained in sole command.

Hilary looked round his table and said, laughingly, and in French, something about the tyranny of one's dependents which, Troy imagined, was incomprehensible to all but a fraction of his guests.

She turned to Major Marchbanks. She was now fairly certain within herself that she would be showing great strength of character if she were to refuse any more champagne. She looked severely at her glass and found it was full. This struck her as being exquisitely funny but she decided not to interfere with it.

'Who,' asked Major Marchbanks, 'is Moult?'

Troy was glad to find that she was able to give him a coherent answer. 'Do you,' she asked, 'find this party very extraordinary?'

'Oh, but completely fantastic,' he said, 'when one looks at it objectively. I mean four hours ago I was doing the honours at The Vale Christmas feast and here I am with three of my warders, drinking Bill-Tasman's champagne and waited upon by a company of you know what.'

'One of them – Cuthbert, I think – was actually at The Vale, wasn't he?'

'Oh yes. He's an old boy. I recommended him. With appropriate warnings, you know. I really think he rather likes displaying his waiter's expertise for us Vale persons. He was at the top of his profession was Cuthbert.'

'He's given me a morsel too much to drink,' Troy said carefully.

Major Marchbanks looked at her and burst out laughing. 'You don't tell me you're tiddly?'

'That would be going too far, which is what I hope I haven't. Gone,' Troy added with dignity.

'You seem all right to me.'

'Good.'

'I say,' Hilary said leaning towards Troy and speaking across the intervening guests, 'isn't it too boring about Moult? Aunt Bed won't budge until he relieves her.'

'What can he be doing?'

'Flown with success, I dare say, and celebrating it. Here's to your bright eyes,' Hilary added and raised his glass to her.

Troy said. 'Look. I'll nip up and relieve Mrs Forrester. Do let me.'

'I can't possibly – '

'Yes, you can. I've finished my lovely dinner. Don't stir, please, anybody,' said Troy and was up and away with a celerity that greatly pleased her. At least, she thought, I'm all right on my pins.

In the hall the children's supper party was breaking up and they were being drafted back into the drawing-room. Here they would collect their presents, move to the library and gradually be put in order for departure. On their account the party would be an early one.

At the foot of the stairs Troy encountered Cuthbert.

'Have you found Moult?' she asked.

'No, madam,' Cuthbert said making a sour face. 'I don't understand it at all, madam. It's very peculiar behaviour.'

(So, Troy irrelevantly thought, is killing a commis while you're carving a wing-rib.)

She said: 'I'm going up to relieve Mrs Forrester.'

'Very kind, I'm sure, madam. And too bad, if I may say so, that you should be put upon.'

'Not a bit of it,' said Troy lightly.

'*Moult!*' Cuthbert said. He actually spoke softly but with such a wealth of venom that Troy was quite taken aback. She continued upstairs, and finding herself a bit swimmy in the head, went first to her own room. There she took two aspirins, put a cold sponge on the back of her neck, opened her window, stuck her head out and gasped.

Two snow flakes touched her face: like the Ice Maiden's fingers in Hans Andersen. She paused for one moment to look at the deadened landscape and then shut her window, drew her curtains and went to call on the Forresters.

III

Colonel Forrester was in bed and awake. He was propped up by pillows and had the look of a well-washed patient in a children's ward. Mrs Forrester sat before the fire, knitting ferociously.

'Thought you might be Moult,' she said.

Troy explained her errand. At first it looked as if Mrs Forrester was going to turn her down flat. She didn't want any dinner, she announced, and in the same breath said they could send up a tray.

'Do go, B,' her husband said. 'I'm perfectly well. You only fuss me, my dear. Sitting angrily about.'

'I don't believe for a moment they've really looked for him, I said – '

'All right, then. *You* look. Go and stir everybody up. I bet if you go, they'll find him.'

If this was cunning on the part of the colonel it was effective. Mrs Forrester rammed her knitting into a magenta bag and rose.

'It's very kind of you,' she snarled at Troy. 'More than that yellow doll of Hilary's thought of offering. Thank you. I shall not be long.'

When she had gone the colonel bit his underlip, hunched his shoulders and made big eyes at Troy. She made the same sort of face back at him and he gave a little giggle.

'I do so hate fusses,' he said, 'Don't you ?'

'Yes, I do rather. Are you really feeling better?'

'Truly. And I'm *beginning* to get over my disappointment, though you must admit it *was* provoking for me, wasn't it?'

'Absolutely maddening.'

'I hoped you'd understand. But I'm glad Moult did it nicely.'

'When did you decide to let him?'

'Oh – at the last moment. I was actually in the dressing-room, putting on my robe. I got a bit stuck inside it as one can, you know, with one's arms above one's head and one's mouth full of material and I rather panicked and had a turn. Bad show. It was a crisis and there had to be a quick decision. So I told him to carry on,' said the colonel as if he described a tight corner in a military engagement, 'and he did. He put me in here and made me lie down and then he went back to the dressing-room to put on the robe. And carried on. Efficiently, you thought?'

'Very. But it's odd of him not to come back, isn't it?'

'Of course it is. He should have reported at once. Very poor show indeed,' said the colonel, drawing himself up in bed and frowning.

'You don't think he could have gone straight to your dressing-room to take off the robe? There's a door from the passage into the dressing-room, isn't there?'

'Yes. But he should have made his report. There's no excuse.'

'Would you mind if I just looked in the dressing-room? To see if the robe is there?'

'Do, do, do, do,' said the colonel.

But there was no golden robe in the dressing-room which, as far as Troy could judge, was in perfect order. A little crimson room it was, with a red flock wall-paper and early Victorian furniture. Heavy red curtains on brass rings were drawn across the windows. It might have been a room in Bleak House and no doubt that was exactly the impression Hilary had intended it to make. She looked in the cupboards and drawers and even under the bed, where she found a rather battered tin box with 'Col. F. Forrester' painted in white letters on it. Remembering Hilary's remarks upon their normal luggage, she supposed this must contain the Forresters' valuables.

Somewhere, a long way off, a car door slammed. She thought she could hear voices.

She half opened the curtains and heard more doors slam and engines start up. The guests were leaving. Rays from invisible head-lamps played across the snowy prospect, horns sounded, voices called.

Troy rattled the curtains shut and returned to the colonel.

'Not there,' she said. 'I suppose he left it in the cloakroom downstairs. I must ask Cressida – she'll know. She took his whiskers off.'

'Well, I'm jolly furious with Moult,' said the colonel, rather drowsily. 'I shall have to discipline him, I can see that.'

'Did he show himself to you. In the robe? Before he went downstairs?'

'Eh? Did he now? Well, yes, but – well, in point of fact I dozed off after my turn. I do that, you know,' said the colonel, his voice trailing away into a drone. 'After my turns. I do doze off.'

He did so now, gently puffing his cheeks in and out and making little noises that reminded Troy of a baby.

It was very quiet in the bedroom. The last car had left and Troy imagined the house-party standing round the drawing-room fire talking over the evening. Or perhaps, she thought, they are having a sort of hunt-for-Moult game. Or perhaps he's been found sleeping it off in some forgotten corner.

The colonel himself now slept very soundly and peacefully and Troy thought there was really no need for her to stay any longer. She turned off all the lights except the bedside lamp and went downstairs.

She found a sort of public meeting going on in the hall. The entire staff were assembled in a tight, apprehensive group being addressed by Hilary. Mrs Forrester balefully sat beside him as if she was in the chair. Mr Smith smoking a cigar stood on the outskirts like a heckler. Cressida, looking exhausted, was stretched in a porter's chair with her arms dangling and her feet half out of her golden sandals.

' – and all I have to tell you,' Hilary was saying, 'is that he must be *found*. He must be somewhere and he must be *found*. I know you've got a lot to do and I'm sorry and really it's too ridiculous but there it is. I don't know if any of you have suggestions to make. If you have I'd be glad to hear them.'

From her place on the stairs Troy looked at Hilary's audience. Cuthbert. Mervyn. Nigel. Vincent. Kittiwee. The boy. Standing farther back, a clutch of extra helpers, male and female, brought in for the occasion. Of these last, one could only say that they looked tired and puzzled.

But the impression was very different when she considered the regular staff. Troy was sure she hadn't concocted this impression and she didn't think it stemmed from pre-knowledge. If she hadn't known anything about their past, she believed, she would still have thought that in some indefinable way the staff had closed their ranks and that fear had inspired them to do so. If they had picked up death-masks of their faces and clapped them over their own, they could scarcely have been less communicative. This extravagant notion was given a kind of validity by the fact that – surely – they were all most uncommonly pale? They stared straight in front of themselves as if they were on parade.

'Well,' Hilary said, 'Cuthbert? You're the chief of staff. Any ideas?'

'I'm afraid not, sir. We have made, I think I may say, sir, a thorough search of the premises. Very thorough, sir.'

'Who,' Mrs Forrester snapped out, 'saw him last?'

'Yes. All right. Certainly, Aunt Bed. Good question,' said Hilary who was clearly flustered.

There was a considerable pause before Cressida said: 'Well, I've *said*, sweeties, haven't I? When he eggzitted after his thing I went back as arranged to the cloakroom and he came in from the outside porch and I took off his robe, wig and make-up and he said he'd go and report to Uncle Fred and I went back to the party.'

'Leaving him there?' Hilary and Mrs Forrester asked in unison.

'Like I said, for heaven's sake. Leaving him there.'

Nobody had paid any attention to Troy. She sat down on the stairs and wondered what her husband would make of the proceedings.

'All right. Yes. Good. All right,' said poor Hilary. 'So far so good. Now then. Darling, you therefore came into the hall, here, didn't you, on your way to the drawing-room?'

'I didn't do an Uncle Tom's Cabin, darling, and take to the snow.'

'Of course not. Ha-ha. And – let me see – the people in charge of the children's supper were here, weren't they?' Hilary looked appealingly in their direction. 'Kitti – er – Cook – and all his helpers?' he wheedled.

'That's right,' said Cressida. 'Busy as bees.' She closed her eyes.

'And I expect,' Hilary said, 'some of you remember Miss Tottenham coming into the hall, don't you?'

Kittiwee said huffily: 'Well, sir, I'm sure we were very busy round the supper table at the far end of the hall and, personally speaking, I didn't take notice to anything but my work. However, sir, I do call the incident to mind because of a remark that was passed.'

'Oh?' Hilary glanced at Cressida who didn't open her eyes.

'I asked him,' she said, 'if his bloody cats were shut up.'

'Yes, I see.'

Mrs Forrester adjusted her thick-lensed spectacles to look at Cressida.

'The thing is,' Hilary hurried on, 'did any of you happen to notice Moult when he came out of the cloakroom there? After Miss Tottenham. Because he must have come out and he ought to have gone up the right-hand flight of the stairs to the colonel's room and then returned to help with the children.'

Hilary's reference to the stairs caused his audience to shift their attention to them and discover Troy. Mrs Forrester exclaimed: 'Has he – ?' and Troy said quickly: 'No. Not a sign. The colonel's quite all right and fast asleep.'

Nobody, it transpired, had seen Moult come out of the cloakroom or go anywhere. Kittiwee again pointed out that the hall was large and dark and they were all very busy. When asked if they hadn't wondered why Moult didn't turn up to do his job, they intimated with unmistakable spitefulness that this didn't surprise them in the least.

'Why?' Mrs Forrester barked.

Kittiwee simpered and Cuthbert was silent. One of the women tittered.

Mr Smith removed his cigar from his mouth. 'Was 'e sozzled?' he asked of nobody in particular and as there was no response added: 'What I mean, did 'e take a couple to celebrate 'is triumph?'

'That's a point,' Cressida conceded. She opened her eyes. 'He was in a tizzy about going on for the part. It was pretty silly, really, because after all – no dialogue. Round the tree, business with arms, and off. Still, he was nervous. And when I fixed his whiskers I must say it was through a pretty thick scotch mist.'

'There y'are,' said Mr Smith.

'Aunt Bed – does Moult sometimes – ?'

'Occasionally,' said Mrs Forrester.

'I think he had it on him,' Cressida said. 'That's only my idea, mind. But he sort of patted himself – you know?'

Hilary said: 'He was already wearing the robe when you went in to make him up, wasn't he?'

'That's right. He put it on upstairs, he said, for Uncle Fred to see.'

'Which he didn't,' Troy said. 'He'd gone to sleep.'

'Moult didn't say anything about that. Though, mind you,' Cressida added, 'I was only with him for a matter of a minute. There was nothing to fixing his beard: a couple of spots of spirit-gum and Bob was your uncle. But I did notice he was all up-tight. He was in no end of a taking-on. Shaking like a leaf he was.'

'Vincent!' Hilary suddenly exclaimed and Vincent gave a perceptible start. 'Why didn't I think of you! You saw Moult outside when he left the drawing-room, didn't you? After his performance?'

Vincent, almost indistinguishably, acknowledged that he did.

'Well – what about it? Did he say anything or – or – look anything – or do anything? Come *on*, Vincent?'

But no. It appeared that Vincent had not even noticed it was Moult. His manner suggested that he and Moult were not on such terms that the latter would have divulged his secret. He had emerged from his triumph into the icy cold, hunched his shoulders against the wind and bolted from the courtyard into the porch. Vincent saw him enter the little cloakroom.

'Which gets us nowhere,' Mrs Forrester said with a kind of stony triumph.

'I don't know why there's all the carry-on, 'Illy,' said Mr Smith. 'Alf Moult's sleeping it off.'

'Where?' Mrs Forrester demanded.

'Where, where, where! Anywhere. You don't tell me there's not plenty of lay-bys for a spot of kip where nobody's thought of looking! 'Ow about the chapel?'

'My dear Uncle Bert – surely – '

'Or all them old stables and what-'ave-you at the back. Come orf it!'

'Have you – ?' Hilary asked his staff.

'I looked in the chapel,' Mrs Forrester announced.

'Has anybody looked – well – outside. The laundries and so on?'

It appeared not. Vincent was dispatched to do this. 'If 'e's there,' Troy heard him mutter, ''e'll 'ave froze.'

'What about the top storey? The attics?' Mr Smith asked.

'No, sir. We've looked,' said Cuthbert, addressing himself exclusively to Hilary. It struck Troy that the staff despised Mr Smith for the same reason that they detested Moult.

A silence followed: mulish on the part of the staff, baffled on the part of the house-party, exhausted on all counts. Hilary finally dismissed the staff. He kept up his grand seigniorial role by thanking his five murderers, congratulating them upon their management of the party and hoping, he said, that their association would continue as happily throughout the coming year. Those of the temporary helpers who lived in the district he excused from further duties.

The house-party then retired to the boudoir, it being, Hilary said, the only habitable room in the house.

Here, after a considerable amount of desultory speculation and argument, everybody but Troy, who found she detested the very sight of alcohol, had a nightcap. Hilary mixed two rum toddies and Mrs Forrester said she would take them up to her room. 'If your uncle's awake,' she said, 'he'll want one. If he isn't . . .'

'You'll polish them both off yourself, Auntie?'

'And why not?' she said. 'Goodnight, Mrs Alleyn. I am very much obliged to you. Goodnight, Hilary. Goodnight, Smith.' She looked fixedly at Cressida. 'Good night,' she said.

'What have *I* done?' Cressida demanded when Mrs Forrester had gone. 'Honestly, darling, your relations!'

'Darling, you *know* Auntie Bed, none better. One can only laugh.'

'Heh, heh, heh. Anyone'd think I'd made Moult tight and then hidden him in the boot cupboard.' Cressida stopped short and raised a finger. '*A propos,*' she said. 'Has anybody looked in the cupboards?'

'Now, my darling child, why on earth should he be in a cupboard? You talk,' said Hilary, 'as if he were A Body,' and then looked extremely perturbed.

'If you ask my opinion, which you haven't,' said Mr Smith. 'I think you're all getting yourselves in a muck sweat about nothing. Don't you lose any sleep over Alf Moult. He knows how to look after 'imself, none better. And since it's my practice to act as I speak I'll wish you goodnight. Very nice show, 'Illy, and none the worse for being a bit of a mock-up. Wouldn't of done for the pipe-and-tabor lot, would it? Bells, Druids, Holy Families and angels! What a combination! Oh dear! Still, the kids appreciated it so we don't care, do we? Well. Bye bye, all.'

When he had gone Hilary said to Troy: 'You see what I mean about Uncle Bert? In his way he's a purist.'

'Yes, I do see.'

'I think he's fantastic,' said Cressida. 'You know? There's something basic. The grass-roots thing. You *believe* in him. Like he might be out of Genet.'

'My darling girl, what dreadful nonsense you do talk! Have you so much as *read* Genet?'

'Hilly! For heaven's sake – he's where O-E *begins*.'

Hilary said with unusual acerbity: 'And I'm afraid he's where I leave off.'

'Of course I've known all along you'll never get the message.'

Troy thought: This is uncomfortable. They're going to have a row, and was about to leave them to it when Cressida suddenly laughed and wound her arms round Hilary's neck. He became very still. She drew his head down and whispered. They both laughed. Their embrace became so explicit that Troy thought on the whole she had better evaporate and proceeded to do so.

At the door she half-turned, wondering if she should throw out a jolly goodnight. Hilary, without releasing Cressida, lifted his face and gave Troy not so much a smile as the feral grimace of Hylaeus. When she had shut the door behind her she thought: that was the sort of thing one should never see.

On her way through the hall she found a great clearance had been made and could hear voices in the drawing-room. Well, she thought, Hilary certainly has it both ways. He gets all the fun of setting-up his party and none of the tedious aftermath. That's done for him by his murderers.

She reached her room, with its well-tended fire, turned-down bed and impeccably laid-out dressing-gown, pyjamas and slippers. She supposed Nigel had found time to perform these duties, and found this a disagreeable reflection.

She hung her dress in the wardrobe and could just catch the drone of the Forresters' voices joined, it seemed, in no very urgent conversation. Troy was wide awake and restless. Too much had happened and happened inconclusively over the last few days. The anonymous messages, which, she realized with astonishment, she had almost forgotten. The booby-trap. Cressida's report of the row in the staff common-room. Uncle Flea's turns. Moult as Druid. The disappearance of Moult. Should these elements, wondered Troy, who had been re-reading her Forster, connect? What would Rory think? He was fond of quoting Forster. 'Only connect. Only connect.' What would he make of all this? And now, in a flash, Troy was perfectly certain that he would think these were serious matters.

As sometimes happens in happy marriages, Troy and her husband when parted, often found that before one of them wrote or cabled or telephoned, the other was visited by an intensified awareness, a kind of expectation. She had this feeling very vividly now and was glad of it. Perhaps in the morning there would be news.

She heard midnight strike and a moment later, Cressida, humming the Bells of St Clement's, passed the door on her way to her room at the south end of the corridor.

Troy yawned. The bedroom was overheated and at last she was sleepy. She went to her window, slipped through the curtains without drawing them and opened it at the top. The north wind had risen and the rumour of its progress was abroad in the night. Flights of cloud were blown across the heavens. The moon was high now, casting a jetty shadow from the house across the snow. It was not a deserted landscape, for round the corner of the west wing came Vincent and his wheelbarrow and in the barrow the dead body of the Christmas tree denuded of its glory. He plodded on until he was beneath the Forresters' windows and then turned into the shadow and was swallowed. She heard a swish and tinkle as he tipped his load into the debris of the ruined conservatory.

Shivering and immoderately tired, she went to bed and to sleep.

CHAPTER 5

Alleyn

Troy woke next morning at the sound of Nigel's discreet attentions to her fire. He had placed her early tea-tray by her bed.

She couldn't make up her mind, at once, to speak to him but when he opened her window curtains and let in the reflected pallor of snow she wished him good morning.

He paused, blinking his white eyelashes, and returned the greeting.

'Is it still snowing?' she asked.

'Off and on, madam. There was sleet in the night but it changed to snow later.'

'Has Moult appeared?'

'I believe not, madam.'

'How very odd, isn't it?'

'Yes, madam. Will that be all, madam?'

'Yes, thank you.'

'Thank you, madam.'

But it's all phoney, Troy thought. He turns it on. He didn't talk like that when he made rocking-horses and wax effigies. Before he reached the door she said: 'I think you made a wonderful job of that catafalque.'

He stopped. 'Ta,' he said.

'I don't know how you managed to get such precision and detail with a medium like snow.'

'It was froze.'

'Even so. Have you ever sculpted? In stone?'

'It was all working from moulds, like. But I always had a fancy to carve.'

507

'I'm not surprised.'

He said: 'Ta,' again, looked directly at her and went out.

Troy bathed and dressed and took her usual look at the landscape. Everywhere except in areas close to the house, a coverlet of snow. Not a footprint to be seen. Over on the far left the canvas-covered bulldozers and their works were mantled. Every tree was a Christmas tree. Somebody had re-erected the scarecrow or perhaps with a change in the wind it had righted itself. It looked, if anything, more human than before. Quite a number of birds had settled on it.

Troy found Hilary and Mr Smith at breakfast. Hilary lost no time in introducing the Moult theme.

'No Moult! It really is beyond a joke now,' he said. 'Even Uncle Bert agrees, don't you, Uncle Bert?'

'I give you in, it's a rum go,' he conceded. 'Under existing circs, it's rather more than that. It's upsetting.'

'What do you mean by "existing circs"?'

'Ask yourself.'

'I asked you.'

Mervyn came in with a fresh supply of toast.

'*Pas devant les domestiques,*' quoted Mr Smith.

Mervyn withdrew. 'Why not before them?' Hilary asked crossly.

'Use your loaf, boy.'

'I don't know what you're talking about, Uncle Bert.'

'No? Ah. Fancy.'

'Oh, *blast* everything!' said Hilary. He turned to Troy. 'He really *isn't* on the premises,' he said. 'Not in the house or the outbuildings. If he wandered into the grounds somewhere he didn't go off the drive or swept paths because there aren't any unaccountable foot-prints in the snow.'

'Could he have got into the back of one of the cars and gone to sleep and been driven away unnoticed?'

'He'd have woken up and declared himself by now, surely?'

'It's an idea, though,' said Mr Smith. 'What say he got into the boot of the station wagon from The Vale and come-to behind bars? That'd be a turn up for the books, wouldn't it?'

'Excessively droll,' said Hilary sourly. 'Well!' he said throwing up his hands, 'what's the next step? I don't know! The Fleas are becoming difficult, I can tell you that much. I looked in on them and found

Aunt Bed trying to valet Uncle Flea and getting it all wrong. Aunt Bed's in a rage because she can't put her jewellery away.'

'Why can't she?'

'It seems she keeps it in their locked tin box with all their securities under the bed in the dressing-room.'

'I know,' said Troy. 'I saw it.'

'Well, Moult's got the key.'

'They're potty,' said Mr Smith definitively. 'What I mean, potty. What I mean, look at it! Carts her stuff round, and it's good stuff, mind, some of it's very nice stuff. Carts it round in a flipping tin box and gives the key to a bloody disappearing act. No, what I mean, I arst you!'

'All right, Uncle Bert. All right. We all know the Fleas go their own way. That's beside the point. What we have to decide – '

The door was flung open and Mrs Forrester entered in a temper. She presented a strange front to the breakfast-table. She was attired in her usual morning apparel; a Harris tweed skirt, a blouse and three cardigans, the uppermost being puce in colour. Stuck about this ensemble at eccentric angles were any number of brooches. Round her neck hung the elaborate Victorian necklace which had been the *pièce de résistance* of her last night's toilet. She wore many rings and several bracelets. A watch, suspended from a diamond and emerald bow was pinned to her breast. She twinkled and glittered like – the comparison was inevitable – a Christmas tree.

'Look at me,' she unnecessarily demanded.

'Aunt B,' Hilary said, 'we do. With astonishment.'

'As well you might. Under the circumstances, Hilary, I feel obliged to keep my Lares and Penates about me.'

'I would hardly describe – '

'Very well. They are not kitchen utensils. That I grant you. The distinction is immaterial, however.'

'You didn't sport all that hardware last night, Mrs F,' Mr Smith suggested.

'I did not. I had it brought out and I made my choice. The rejected pieces should have been returned to their place. By Moult. They were not and I prefer, under the circumstances, to keep them about me. That, however, is not the matter at issue. Hilary!'

'Aunt Bed?'

'An attempt has been made upon our strong-box.'

'Oh my God! What do you mean?'

'There is evidence. An instrument – possibly a poker – has been introduced in an unsuccessful attempt upon the padlock.'

'It needed only this,' said Hilary and took his head between his hands.

'I am keeping it from your uncle: it would fuss him. What do you propose to do?'

'I? What can I do? Why,' asked Hilary wildly, 'do you keep it under the dressing-room bed?'

'Because it won't go under our bed which is ridiculously low.'

'What's the story, then?' Mr Smith asked. 'Did Alf Moult try to rob the till and run away in a fright when he foozled the job?'

'With the key in his pocket?' Mrs Forrester snapped. 'You're not very bright this morning, Smith.'

'It was a joke.'

'Indeed.'

Cuthbert came in. 'A telephone call, sir, for Mrs Alleyn,' he said.

'*Me?* Is it from London?'

'Yes, madam. Mr Alleyn, madam.'

'Oh how lovely!' Troy shouted before she could stop herself. She apologized and made a bolt for the telephone.

II

' – so we wound the whole thing up at ninety in the shade and here I am. A Happy Christmas, darling. When shall I see you?'

'Soon. Soon. The portrait's finished. I think. I'm not sure.'

'When in doubt, stop. Shouldn't you?'

'I dare say. I want to. But there's just one thing – '

'Troy: is anything the matter?'

'In a way. No – not with me. Here.'

'You've turned cagey. Don't you want to talk?'

'Might be better not.'

'I see. Well – when?'

'I – Rory, hold on will you? Hold on.'

'I'm holding.'

It was Hilary. He had come in unnoticed and now made deprecatory gestures and rather silly little faces at Troy. 'Please!' he said. 'May I? Do forgive me but may I?'

'Of course.'

'It's just occurred to me. So dismal for Alleyn to be in an empty house in London at Christmas. So *please*, suggest he comes to us. I know you want to fly on wings of song but you did say you might need one more sitting and anyway I should be so delighted to meet him. He might even advise about Moult or would that be anti-protocol? But – please – ?'

'I think perhaps – '

'No, you don't. You can't. You mustn't "think perhaps". Ask him. Go on, do.'

Troy gave her husband the message.

'Do you,' he said, speaking close to the receiver, 'want this? Or would you rather come home? There's something up, isn't there? Put on a carefree voice, love, and tell me. Would you like me to come? I can. I'm free at the moment.'

'Can you? Are you?'

'Then, shall I?'

'I really don't know,' Troy said and laughed, as she trusted, gaily. 'Yes. I think so.'

'When would you leave if I didn't come?'

'Well – I don't quite know,' she said and hoped she sounded playful and co-operative.

'What the hell,' her husband asked, 'is all this? Well, never mind. You can't say, obviously.'

Hilary was making modest little gestures. He pointed to himself and mouthed, 'May I?'

'Hilary,' said Troy, 'would like to have a word.'

'Turn him on,' said Alleyn. 'Or have you, by any chance, already done so?'

'Here he is,' Troy said severely. 'Rory: this is Hilary Bill-Tasman.'

She handed over the receiver and listened to Hilary. His manner was masterly: not too overtly insistent, not too effusive, but of such a nature that it made a refusal extremely difficult. I suppose, Troy thought, these are the techniques he brings to bear on his rich, complicated business. She imagined her husband's lifted eyebrow.

Presently Hilary said: 'And you *are* free, aren't you? So why not? The
portrait, if nothing else, will be your reward: it's quite superb. You
will? I couldn't be more delighted. Now: about trains – there's just
time – '

When that was settled he turned, beamingly, to Troy and held out
the receiver. 'Congratulate me!' cried Hilary and, with that charac-
teristic gesture of his, left the room, gaily wagging his hand above his
head.

Troy said: 'It's me again.'

'Good.'

'I'll come to the station.'

'Too kind.'

'So nice to see you again!'

'Always pleasant to pick up the threads.'

'Good morning.'

'Good morning.'

When Hilary announced that Vincent would put on his chauffeur's uniform and take the small car to the main line station Troy
suggested that she herself could do so. This clearly suited him very
well. She gathered that some sort of exploratory work was to be
carried out in the grounds. ('Though really,' Hilary said, 'one holds
out little hope of it,') and that Vincent's presence would be helpful.

Soon after luncheon Troy got ready for the road. She heard a
commotion under her window and looked out.

Vincent and three other men were floundering about in a half-
hearted way among broken glass and the dense thicket that invested
the site of the old conservatory. They poked and thrust with forks
and spades. But that's ridiculous, thought Troy.

She found Hilary downstairs waiting to see her off.

He stared at her. 'You look,' he said, 'as if somebody had given
you a wonderful present. Or made love to you. Or something.'

'And that's exactly how I feel,' she said.

He was silent for so long and stared so hard that she was obliged
to say: 'Is anything more the matter?'

'I suppose not,' he said slowly. 'I hope not. I was just wondering.
However! Watch out for icy patches, won't you? You can't miss the
turnings. *Bon voyage.*'

He watched her start up her engine, turned on his heel and went quickly into the house.

In her walks Troy had always taken paths that led up to the moors: 'The Land Beyond the Scarecrow,' she had called it to herself as if it belonged to a children's story. Now she drove down the long drive that was to become a grand avenue. The bulldozer men were not at work over Christmas. Their half-formed hillock and the bed for the lake that would reflect it, were covered with snow – the tractors looked ominous and dark under their tarpaulins. Farther away stood a copse of bare trees that was evidently a feature of the original estate and beyond this, fields stretching downhill, away from the moors and towards a milder and more humanized landscape. At the end of the drive she crossed a bridge over a rapid brook that Hilary had told her would be developed farther upstream, into water gardens.

A drive of some twelve miles brought her to her destination. The late afternoon sun shone bravely, there was an air of normality and self-containment about the small country town of Downlow. Troy drove along the main street to the station, parked her car and went through the office to the platform. Here, in the familiar atmosphere of paste, disinfectant and travel posters, Halberds seemed absurd and faintly distasteful.

She was early and walked up and down the platform, partly to keep warm and partly to work off her over-stimulated sense of anticipation. Strange notions came into her head. As, for instance, would Cressida in – say – ten years' time, feel more or less like this if she had been absent from Hilary for three weeks? Was Cressida much in love with Hilary? Did she passionately want to be mistress of Halberds? Judging by those representatives of county families who had rather uneasily attended the party, Cressida was unlikely to find a kindred spirit among them. Perhaps she and Hilary would spend most of their time in their SW1 flat, which Troy supposed to be on a pretty lavish scale. Would they take some of their murderers to look after them when they came up to London? Troy found that she felt uneasy about Cressida and obscurely sorry for her.

With a loud clank the signal arm jerked up. A porter and one or two other persons strolled on to the platform and from down the line came the banshee hoot of the London train.

III

'Mind? Of course I don't mind,' Alleyn said. 'I thought I should be
hanging about the flat waiting for you to come home! Instead of
which, here we are, bold as brass, driving somebody else's car
through a Christmas-tree landscape and suiting each other down to
the ground. What's wrong with that?'

'I've no complaints.'

'In that case you must now tell me what's up in the Bill-Tasman
outfit. You sounded greatly put out this morning.'

'Yes, well . . . All right. Hold on to your hat and fetch up all your
willing suspension of disbelief. You'll need it.'

'I've heard of Bill-Tasman's experiment with villains for flunkies.
Your letter seemed to suggest that it works.'

'That was early days. That was a week ago. I didn't write again
because there wasn't time. Now, listen.'

'"List, list, O list."'

'Yes, well, it's an earful.'

'"Speak, I am bound to hear."'

'Rory! Don't be a detective.'

'Oops! Sorry.'

'Here I go, then.'

Troy had got about a third of the way through her narrative when
her husband stopped her.

'I suppose,' he said. 'I have to take it that you are *not* making this
up as you go along.'

'I'm not even making the most of my raw material. Which part
do you find difficult to absorb?'

'My trouble is quantitative rather than particular but I find I jib at
Aunt Bed. I don't know why. I suppose she's not somebody in
disguise and camping it up?'

'That really would be a more appropriate theory for Mr Smith.'

'Oh,' said Alleyn. 'I know about your Mr Smith. The firm of "Bill-
Tasman and Smith" is at the top of the British if not the European
Antiquarian trade and Albert Smith, from the police angle, is as pure
as the driven snow. We've sought their opinions before now in cases
of fraud, robbery from collections and art forgeries. He started as a
barrow-boy, he had a flair, and with the aid of Bill-Tasman Senior,

he got to the top. It's not an unusual story, darling. It's merely an extreme example. Press on.'

Troy pressed on with mileage and narrative. They reached the signpost for The Vale turn-off and began to climb the lower reaches of the moors. Patches of snow appeared. In the far distance, Troy thought she recognized the high tor above The Vale.

Alleyn became quieter and quieter. Every now and then he questioned her and once or twice asked her to go over the ground again. She had got as far as the anonymous messages and the booby-trap when she interrupted herself. 'Look,' she said. 'See those plumes of smoke beyond the trees? We're nearly there. That's Halberds.'

'Could you pull up? I'd like to hear the lot while we're at it.'

'OK.'

She turned the car on to the verge of the road and stopped the engine. The sky had begun to darken, mist rose from hollows and blurred their windscreen. Rime glittered on a roadside briar.

'You must be starved with cold after Sydney in mid-summer.'

'I'm treble-sweatered and quilted. Carry on, my love.'

Ten minutes later Troy said: 'And that's it. When I left, Vincent and some chaps were tramping about with forks and spades in the ruins of the conservatory.'

'Has Bill-Tasman reported to his local police?'

'I don't think so.'

'He damn well ought to.'

'I think he's holding back for you.'

'Like hell he is!'

'For your advice.'

'Which will be to call up the local station. What else, for pity's sake? What's he *like*, Bill-Tasman? He sounded precious on the telephone.'

'He's a bit like a rather good-looking camel. Very paintable.'

'If you say so, darling.'

'He's intelligent, affected and extremely companionable.'

'I see. And what about this chap Moult? Does he drink, did you say?'

'According to Aunt Bed, occasionally.'

'Jim Marchbanks is at The Vale.'

'I forgot to tell you – we've chummed up.'

'Have you now? Nice creature, isn't he?'

They were silent for a minute or so. Presently Alleyn said his
wife's nose was as cold as an iced cherry but not as red. After a further interval she said she thought they should move on.

When they reached the turn in the drive where Halberds was
fully revealed, Alleyn said that everything had become as clear as
mud: Troy had obviously got herself into a film production, on
location, of *The Castle of Otranto* and had been written into the script
as the best way of keeping her quiet.

Cuthbert and Mervyn came out to meet them. They both seemed
to Troy to be excessively glum but their behaviour was impeccable.
Mervyn, carrying Alleyn's suitcase, led the way upstairs to a dressing-room on the far side of Troy's bathroom and connecting with it.

'Mr Bill-Tasman is in the boudoir, madam,' said Mervyn with his
back to Alleyn. He cast a rather wild glance at Troy and withdrew.

'Is that chap's name Cox?' Alleyn asked.

'I've no idea.'

'Mervyn Cox. Booby-trap. Flat-iron. Killed Warty Thompson the
cat-burglar. That's the boy.'

'Did you – '

'No. One of Fox's cases. I just remembered.'

'I'm certain he didn't rig that thing up for me.'

'You may well be right. Suspect anyone else?'

'No. Unless – '

'Unless?'

'It's so far-fetched. It's just that there does appear to have been
some sort of feud between Moult and the staff.'

'And Moult fixed the thing up to look like Mervyn's job? And
wrote the messages in the same spirit? Out of spite?'

'He doesn't seem to be particularly spiteful.'

'No?'

'He obviously adores the colonel. You know – one of those
unquestioning, dogged sort of attachments.'

'I know.'

'So what?'

'Well may you ask. What's he like to look at?'

'Oh – rather upsetting, poor chap. He's got a scarred face. Burns,
I should imagine.'

'Come here to me.'

'I think you'd better meet Hilary.'

'Blast Hilary,' said Alleyn. 'All right. I suppose so.'

It was abundantly clear to Troy, when they found Hilary alone in the boudoir that something had been added to the tale of inexplicable events. He greeted Alleyn with almost feverish enthusiasm. He gushed about the portrait (presently they would look at it) and he also gushed about Troy, who refused to catch her husband's eye. He talked more than a little wildly about Alleyn's welcome return from the Antipodes. He finally asked, with a strange and most unsuccessful attempt at off-handedness if Troy had told Alleyn of their 'little mystery'. On hearing that she had he exclaimed: 'No, but *isn't* it a bore? I do so *hate* mysteries, don't you? No, I suppose you don't as you perpetually solve them.'

'Have there been any developments?' Troy asked.

'Yes, as a matter of fact. Yes. I was leading up to them. I – I haven't made it generally known as yet. I thought I would prefer – '

Cressida came in and Hilary madly welcomed her as if they had been parted for a week. She stared at him in amazement. On being introduced to Alleyn she gave herself a second or two to run over his points and from then until the end of the affair at Halberds made a dead set at him.

Cressida was not, Troy had to admit, a gross practitioner. She kept fractionally to the right of a frontal attack. Her method embraced the attentive ear, the slight smile of understanding, the very occasional glance. She made avoidance about ninety per cent more equivocal than an accidental brush of the hands though that was not lacking either, Troy noticed, when Cressida had her cigarette lit.

Troy wondered if she always went into action when confronted with a personable man or if Alleyn had made a smash hit. Was Hilary at all affected by the manifestations? But Hilary, clearly, was fussed by other matters and his agitation increased when Mrs Forrester came in.

She, in her way, also made a dead set at Alleyn but her technique was widely different. She barely waited for the introduction.

'Just as well you've come,' she said. 'High time. Now we shall be told what to do.'

'Aunt Bed – we mustn't – '

'Nonsense, Hilary. Why else have you dragged him all this way? Not,' she added as an afterthought, 'that he's not pleased to see his wife, of course.'

'I'm delighted to see her,' said Alleyn.

'Who wouldn't be!' Hilary exclaimed. Really, Troy thought, he was showing himself in a most peculiar light.

'Well?' Mrs Forrester began on a rising inflection.

Hilary intervened. He said, with a show of firmness, that perhaps a little consultation in the study might be an idea. When his aunt tried to cut in he talked her down and as he talked he seemed to gain authority. In the upshot he took Alleyn by the elbow and, coruscating with feverish jokelets, piloted him out of the boudoir.

'Darling!' said Cressida to Troy before the door had shut, 'Your husband! You know? And I mean this. The mostest.'

The study was in the east wing next door to the boudoir. Hilary fussed about, turning on lamps and offering Alleyn tea, (which he and Troy had missed) or a drink. 'Such a mongrel time of day I always think,' he said. 'Are you sure you won't?'

Alleyn said he was sure. 'You want to talk about this business, don't you?' he asked. 'Troy's told me the whole story. I think you should call your local police.'

'She said you'd say that. I did hope you wouldn't mind if I just consulted you first.'

'Of course I don't. But it's getting on for twenty-four hours, isn't it? I really don't think you should wait any longer. It might be best to call up your provincial detective-superintendent. Do you know him?'

'Yes. *Most* uncongenial. Beastly about the staff. I really couldn't.'

'All right. Where's the nearest station? Downlow?'

'Yes. I believe so. Yes.'

'Isn't the super there a chap called Wrayburn?'

'I – I did think of consulting Marchbanks. At The Vale, you know.'

'I'm sure he'd give you the same advice.'

'Oh!' Hilary cried out. 'And I'm sure you're right but I do dislike this sort of thing. I can't expect you to understand, of course, but the staff here – they won't like it either. They'll hate it. Policemen all over the house. Asking questions. Upsetting them like anything.'

'I'm afraid they'll have to lump it, you know.'

'Oh *damn*!' Hilary said pettishly. 'All right. I'm sorry, Alleyn. I'm being disagreeable.'

'Ring Wrayburn up and get it over. After all, isn't it just possible that Moult, for some reason that hasn't appeared, simply walked down the drive and hitched a lift to the nearest station? Has anyone looked to see if his overcoat and hat and money are in his room?'

'Yes. Your wife thought of that. Nothing missing as far as we could make out.'

'Well – ring up.'

Hilary stared at him, fetched a deep sigh, sat down at his desk and opened his telephone directory.

Alleyn walked over to the window and looked out. Beyond the reflected image of the study he could distinguish a mass of wreckage – shattered glass, rubbish, trampled weeds and, rising out of them close at hand, a young fir with some of its boughs broken. Troy had shown him the view from her bedroom and he realized that this must be the sapling that grew beneath Colonel Forrester's dressing-room window. It was somewhere about here, then, that she had seen Vincent dispose of the Christmas tree at midnight. Here, too, Vincent and his helpers had been trampling about with garden forks and spades when Troy left for Downlow. Alleyn shaded the pane and moved about until he could eliminate the ghostly study and look farther into the dark ruin outside. Now he could make out the Christmas tree, lying in a confusion of glass, soil and weeds.

A fragment of tinsel still clung to one of its branches and was caught in the lamplight.

Hilary had got his connection. With his back to Alleyn he embarked on a statement to Superintendent Wrayburn of the Downlow Constabulary and, all things considered, made a pretty coherent job of it. Alleyn, in his day, had been many, many times rung up by persons in Hilary's position who had given a much less explicit account of themselves. As Troy had indicated: Hilary was full of surprises.

Now he carefully enunciated details. Names. Times. A description. Mr Wrayburn was taking notes.

'I'm much obliged to you,' Hilary said. 'There is one other point, Superintendent. I have staying with me – '

Here we go, Alleyn thought.

Hilary screwed round in his chair and made a deprecatory face at him. 'Yes,' he said. 'Yes. At his suggestion, actually. He's with me now. Would you like to speak to him? Yes, by all means.' He held out the receiver.

'Hullo,' Alleyn said, 'Mr Wrayburn?'

'Would this be Chief Superintendent Alleyn?'

'That's right.'

'Well, well, well. Long time,' said Mr Wrayburn, brightly, 'no see. When was that case? Back in 'sixty-five.'

'That's it. How are you, Jack?'

'Can't complain. I understand there's some bother up your way?'

'Looks like it.'

'What are you doing there, Chief?'

'I'm an accident. It's none of my business.'

'But you reckon we ought to take a wee look-see?'

'Your DCC would probably say so. Somebody ought to, I fancy.'

'It's a cold, cold world. I was counting on a nice quiet Christmas. So what happens? A church robbery, a suspected arson and three fatal smashes in my district and half my chaps down with flu. And now this. And look at you! You're living it up, aren't you? Seats of the Mighty?'

'You'll come up, then, Jack?'

'That's correct.'

'Good. And Jack – for your information, it's going to be a search-party job.'

'Well, ta for the tip anyway. Over and out.'

Alleyn hung up. He turned to find Hilary staring at him over his clasped hands.

'Well,' Hilary said. 'I've done it. Haven't I?'

'It really was advisable, you know.'

'You don't – you don't ask me anything. Any questions about that wretched little man. Nothing.'

'It's not my case.'

'You talk,' Hilary said crossly, 'like a doctor.'

'Do I?'

'Etiquette. Protocol.'

'We have our little observances.'

'It would have been so much pleasanter – I'd made up my mind I'd – I'd – '

'Look here,' Alleyn said. 'If you've got any kind of information that might have even a remote bearing on this business, do for heaven's sake let Wrayburn have it. You said, when we were in the other room, that there's been a development.'

'I know I did. Cressida came in.'

'Yes – well, do let Wrayburn have it. It won't go any further if it has no significance.'

'Hold on,' said Hilary. 'Wait. Wait.'

He motioned Alleyn to sit down and when he had done so, locked the door. He drew the window curtains close-shut, returned to his desk and knelt down before it.

'That's a beautiful desk,' Alleyn said. 'Hepplewhite?'

'Yes,' Hilary fished a key out of his pocket. 'It's intact. No restoration nonsense.' He reached into the back of the knee hole. Alleyn heard the key turn. Hilary seemed to recollect himself. With a curious half-sheepish glance at Alleyn, he wrapped his handkerchief about his hand. He groped. There was an interval of a few seconds and then he sat back on his heels.

'Look,' he said.

On the carpet, near Alleyn's feet, he laid down a loose crumpled newspaper package.

Alleyn leant forward. Hilary pulled back the newspaper.

He disclosed a short steel poker with an ornate handle.

Alleyn looked at it for a moment. 'Yes?' he said. 'Where did you find it?'

'That's what's so – upsetting,' Hilary gave a sideways motion of his head towards the window. 'Out there,' he said. 'Where you were looking – I saw you – just now when I was on the telephone. In the tree.'

'The Christmas tree?'

'No, no, no. The growing tree. Inside it. Lying across the branches. Caught up, sort of, by the handle.'

'When did you find it?'

'This afternoon. I was in here wondering whether, after all, I should ring up Marchbanks or the police and hating the idea of ringing up anybody because of – you understand – the staff. And I walked over to the window and looked out. *Without* looking. You know? And then I saw something catching the light in the tree. I didn't realize at once what it was. The tree's quite close to the window – almost touching it. So I opened the window and looked more carefully and finally I stepped over the ledge and got it. I'm afraid I didn't think of finger-prints at that juncture.'

Alleyn, sitting on the edge of his chair, still looked at the poker.
'You recognize it?' he said. 'Where it comes from?'

'Of course. It's part of a set. Late eighteenth-century. Probably
Welsh. There's a Welsh press to go with it.'

'Where?'

'Uncle Flea's dressing-room.'

'I see.'

'Yes, but do you? Did Troy tell you? About the Fleas' tin box?'

'Mrs Forrester says somebody had tried to force the lock?'

'Exactly! Precisely! With a poker. She actually said with a poker.
Well: *as if* with a poker. And it wasn't Moult because Moult, believe
it or not, keeps the key. So why a poker for Moult?'

'Quite.'

'And – there are dark marks on it. At the end. If you look.
Mightn't they be stains of black japanning? It's a japanned tin box.
Actually, Uncle Flea's old uniform case.'

'Have you by any chance got a lens?'

'Of course I've got a lens,' Hilary said querulously. 'One constantly
uses lenses in our business. Here. Wait a moment.'

He found one in his desk and gave it to Alleyn.

It was not very high-powered but it was good enough to show, at
the business end of the poker, a dark smear hatched across by
scratches: a slight glutinous deposit to which the needle from a
conifer adhered. Alleyn stooped lower.

Hilary said: 'Well? Anything?'

'Did you look closely at this?'

'No, I didn't, I was expecting my aunt to come in. Aunt Bed is
perpetually making entrances. She wanted to harry me and I didn't
want to add to her fury by letting her see this. So I wrapped it up and
locked it away. Just in time as it turned out. In she came with all her
hackles up. If ladies have hackles.'

'But you did notice the marks then?'

'Yes.'

'They're not made by lacquer.'

'Oh?'

'I'm afraid not.'

'Afraid? What do you mean – afraid?'

'See for yourself.'

Alleyn gave Hilary the glass. Hilary stared at him and then knelt by the crumpled paper with its trophy. Alleyn moved the desk lamp to throw a stronger light on the area. Hilary bent his body as if he performed some oriental obeisance before the poker.

'Do you see?' Alleyn said. 'It's not what you supposed, is it? Look carefully. The deposit is sticky, isn't it? There's a fir-needle stuck to it. And underneath – I think Mr Wrayburn would rather you didn't touch it – underneath, but just showing one end, there's a gold coloured thread. Do you see it?'

'I – yes. Yes, I think – yes – '

'Tell me,' Alleyn asked. 'What colour was the Druid's wig?'

IV

'Now, I tell you what,' Alleyn said to his wife. 'This thing has all the signs of becoming a top-ranking nuisance and I'm damned if I'll have you involved in it. You know what happened that other time you got stuck into a nuisance.'

'If you're thinking of bundling me off to a pub in Downlow, I'll jib.'

'What I'm thinking of is a quick return by both of us to London.'

'Before the local force get any ideas about you?'

'Exactly.'

'You're a bit late for that, darling, aren't you? Where's Mr Wrayburn?'

'In the study I imagine. I left Bill-Tasman contemplating his poker and I told him it'd be better if he saw the super alone. He didn't much like the idea, but there it is.'

'Poor Hilary!'

'I dare say. It's a bit of an earthquake under his ivory tower, isn't it?'

'Do you like him, Rory?'

Alleyn said: 'I don't know. I'm cross with him because he's being silly but – yes, I suppose if we'd met under normal conditions I'd have quite liked him. Why?'

'He's a strange one. When I was painting him I kept thinking of such incongruous things.'

'Such as?'

'Oh – fawns and camels and things.'

'Which does his portrait favour?'

'At first, the camel. But the fawn has sort of intervened – I mean the Pan job, you know, not the sweet little deer.'

'So I supposed. If he's a Pan job I'll bet he's met his match in his intended nymph.'

'She went in, boots and all, after you, didn't she?'

'If only,' Alleyn said, 'I could detect one pinch, one soupçon, of the green-eyed monster in you, my dish, I'd crow like a bloody rooster.'

'We'd better finish changing. Hilary will be expecting us. Drinks at seven. You're to meet Mr Smith and the Fleas.'

'I can wait.'

There was a tap at the door.

'You won't have to,' said Troy. 'Come in.'

It was Nigel, all downcast eyes, to present Mr Bill-Tasman's compliments to Mr Alleyn and he would be very glad if Mr Alleyn would join him in the study.

'In five minutes,' Alleyn said, and when Nigel had gone, 'Which was that?'

'The one that killed a sinful lady. Nigel.'

'I thought as much. Here I go.'

He performed one of the lightning changes to which Troy was pretty well accustomed, gave her a kiss and went downstairs.

Superintendent Wrayburn was a sandy man; big, of course, but on the bonier side. He was principally remarkable for his eyebrows which resembled those of a Scotch terrier and his complexion which, in mid-winter, was still freckled like a plover's egg.

Alleyn found him closeted with Hilary in the study. The poker, re-wrapped, lay on the desk. Before Hilary was a glass of sherry and before Mr Wrayburn, a pretty generous whisky and water from which Alleyn deduced that he hadn't definitely made up his mind what sort of job he seemed to be on. He was obviously glad to see Alleyn and said it was quite a coincidence, wasn't it?

Hilary made some elaborate explanations about drinks being served for the house-party in the drawing-room at seven but perhaps they could join the others a little later and in the meantime – surely now Alleyn would – ?

'Yes, indeed. Thank you,' Alleyn said. 'Since I'm not on duty,' he added lightly and Mr Wrayburn blushed beyond his freckles.

'Well – nor am I,' he said quickly. 'Yet. I hope. Not exactly.'

Superintendent Wrayburn, Hilary explained, had only just arrived, having been held up at the station. He'd had a cold drive. It was snowing again. He was more than pleased to have Alleyn with them. He, Hilary, was about to give Mr Wrayburn a – Hilary boggled a little at the word – a statement about the 'unfortunate mishap'.

Alleyn said 'of course' and no more than that. Mr Wrayburn produced his regulation notebook and away Hilary went, not over-coherently and yet, Alleyn fancied, with a certain degree of artful-ness. He began with Moult's last-minute substitution at the Christmas tree, and continued with Vincent's assurance that he had seen Moult (whom he thought to be the colonel) after the perform-ance, run from the courtyard into the entrance porch and thence to the dressing-room. 'Actually,' Hilary explained, 'it's a cloakroom on one's right as one comes into the house. It's in the angle of the hall and the drawing-room, which was so convenient. There's a door from it into the hall itself and another one into the entrance porch. To save muddy boots, you know, from coming into the house.'

'Quite,' said Mr Wrayburn. He gazed at his notes. 'So the last that's known of him, then, is – ?'

'Is when, having taken off his robe and make-up with Miss Tottenham's help, he presumably left the cloakroom with the avowed intention of going up to Colonel Forrester.'

'Did he leave the cloakroom by the door into the hall, sir?'

'Again – presumably. He would hardly go out into the porch and double back into the hall, would he?'

'You wouldn't think so, sir, would you? And nobody saw him go upstairs?'

'No. But there's nothing remarkable in that. The servants were getting the children's supper ready. The only light, by my express orders, was from the candles on their table. As you've seen, there are two flights of stairs leading to a gallery. The flight opposite this cloak-room door is farthest away from the children's supper-table. The staff would be unlikely to notice Moult unless he drew attention to himself. Actually Moult was – ' Hilary boggled slightly and then hurried on. 'Actually,' he said, 'Moult was supposed to help them but, of course, that was arranged before there was any thought of his substituting for Colonel Forrester.'

'Yes, sir. I appreciate the position. Are there,' Wrayburn asked, 'coats and so forth in this cloakroom, sir? Macintoshes and umbrellas and gum-boots and so on?'

Good for you, Jack, thought Alleyn.

'Yes. Yes, there are. Are you wondering,' Hilary said quickly, 'if, for some reason – ?'

'We've got to consider everything, haven't we, Mr Bill-Tasman?'

'Of course. Of course. Of course.'

'You can't think of any reason, sir, however far-fetched, like, that would lead Mr Moult to quit the premises and, if you'll excuse the expression, do a bunk?'

'No. No. I can't. And – ' Hilary looked nervously at Alleyn ' – well – there's a sequel. You've yet to hear – '

And now followed the story of the japanned uniform box at which Mr Wrayburn failed entirely to conceal his astonishment and, a stunning climax, the exhibition of the poker.

Alleyn had been waiting for this. He felt a certain amusement in Mr Wrayburn's change of manner which was instant and sharp. He became formal. He looked quickly from Hilary to the object on the desk and upon that his regard became fixed. The lens lay near at hand. Mr Wrayburn said: 'May I?' and used it with great deliberation. He then stared at Alleyn.

'I take it,' he said, 'you've seen this?'

Alleyn nodded.

Hilary now repeated his account of the finding of the poker and Mr Wrayburn peered out of the window and asked his questions and made his notes. All through this procedure he seemed in some indefinable way to invite Alleyn to enter into the discussion and to be disappointed that he remained silent.

Hilary avoided looking at the object on his desk. He turned his back, bent over the fire, made as if to stir it and, apparently disliking the feel of the study poker, dropped it with a clatter in the hearth.

Wrayburn said: 'Yes,' several times in a noncommittal voice and added that things had taken quite a little turn, hadn't they, and he must see what they could do about it. He told Hilary he'd like to take care of the poker and was there perhaps a cardboard box? Hilary offered to ring for one but Wrayburn said he wouldn't bother the staff at this stage. After some rummaging in his bureau Hilary found a long tubular carton with a number of maps in it. He took them out and Wrayburn slid the wrapped poker into it. He suggested that it might be as well not to publicize the poker and Hilary was in feverish agreement. Wrayburn thought he would like to have a wee chat with the Detective Chief-Superintendent about the turn this seemed to be taking. Hilary winced. Wrayburn then asked Alleyn if he would be kind enough to show him the cloakroom. Hilary began to say that he himself would do so but stopped short and raised his shoulders.

'I see,' he said. 'Very well.' Alleyn went to the door followed by Wrayburn carrying the carton. 'Mr Wrayburn!' Hilary said loudly.

'Sir?'

'I am sure you are going to talk about my staff.'

'I was only,' Wrayburn said in a hurry, 'going to ask as a matter of routine, for the names of your guests and the staff. We – er – we have to make these enquiries, sir.'

'Possibly. Very well, you shall have them. But I must tell you, at once, that whatever theory you may form as to the disappearance of this man, there is no question, there can never be any question, no matter what emerges, that any one of my staff, in even the remotest fashion is concerned in it. On that point,' said Hilary, 'I am and I shall remain perfectly adamant.'

'Strong,' said Mr Wrayburn.

'And meant to be,' said Hilary.

CHAPTER 6

Storm Rising

'It's a very impressive residence, this,' Superintendent Wrayburn observed.

He and Alleyn paused in the hall which was otherwise deserted. Great swags of evergreen still hung from the gallery. Fires blazed on the enormous hearths.

'What I mean is,' Superintendent Wrayburn said, 'it's impressive,' and after a moment, 'Take a look at this.'

A framed plan of Halberds hung near the entrance.

'Useful,' said Wrayburn. They studied it and then stood with their backs to the front doors getting, as Wrayburn put it, the hang of the place. Behind them lay the open courtyard, flanked east and west by projecting wings. On their left was the west wing with a corridor opening off the hall serving library, breakfast-room, boudoir, study and, at the rear angle of the house, the chapel. On their right were the drawing-room, dining-room, serveries and, at the rear corner, the kitchen. Doors under the gallery, one of them the traditional green baize swinger, led from the back of the hall, between the twin flights of stairs, into a passage which gave on the servants' quarters and various offices, including the flower-room.

Alleyn looked up at the gallery. It was dimly lit but out of the shadows there glimmered a pale greenish shape of extreme elegance. One's meant to look at that, he thought. It's a treasure.

'So what about this cloakroom, then?' Wrayburn suggested. 'Before I take any further action?'

'Why not? Here you are.'

It was in the angle between the entrance porch and the drawing-room and, as Hilary said, had a door to the hall and another to the porch. 'The plan,' Alleyn pointed out, 'shows a corresponding room on the west side. It's a symmetrical house, isn't it?'

'So when he came out,' Wrayburn mused, 'he should have walked straight ahead to the right-hand flight of stairs and up them to the gallery?'

'And along the gallery to the west corridor in the visitors' wing. Where he disappeared into thin air.'

'Alternatively – here! Let's look.'

They went into the cloakroom, shutting the door behind them and standing close together, just inside the threshold.

Alleyn was transported backstage. Here was that smell of face cream and spirit-gum. Here was the shelf with a towel laid over it and the looking-glass. Neatly spread out, fan-wise, on one side of this bench, was the Druid's golden beard and moustache and, hooked over a table lamp in lieu of a wig-block, the golden wig itself, topped by a tall crown of mistletoe.

A pair of knitted woollen gloves lay nearby.

A collection of macintoshes, gum-boots, and shooting-sticks had been shoved aside to make room for the Druid's golden robe. There was the door opening on the porch and beside it a small lavatorial compartment. The room was icy cold.

Under the make-up bench, neatly aligned, stood a pair of fur-lined boots. Their traces from the outside door to where they had been removed were still quite damp and so were they.

'We'd better keep clear of them,' Alleyn said, 'hadn't we?' From where he stood he reached over to the bench, moved the table lamp and, without touching the wig, turned its back towards them. It had been powdered, like the beard, with gold-dust. But at the place where the long hair would have overhung the nape of the neck there was a darker patch.

'Wet?' Wrayburn said pointing to it. 'Snow, would that have been? He was out in the snow, wasn't he? But the rest of the thing's only – ' he touched the mistletoe crown ' – damp.'

Alleyn flicked a long finger at the cardboard carton which Wrayburn still carried. 'Did you get a good look at it?' he asked.

'That's right,' Wrayburn said, answering a question that Alleyn had not asked. 'You're dead right. This is getting altogether different. It looks to me,' he said, 'as if we'd got a bit of a case on our hands.'

'I believe you have.'

'Well,' Wrayburn said, making small movements of his shoulders and lifting his chin, 'there'll have to be an adjustment, I mean to say in the approach, won't there?' He laid the carton on the bench as if it was made of porcelain. 'There'll need to be an analysis, of course, and a comparison. I'd better – I'd better report it to our CID. But – just let's – '

He shot a glance at Alleyn, fished in his pockets and produced a small steel rule. He introduced the end under the hair and raised it.

'Take a look,' he said. 'It's wet, of course, but d'you reckon there's a stain?'

'Might be.'

'I'm going to damn well – ' Without completing his sentence, Wrayburn lifted a strand and with a fingernail and thumb, separated a single hair and gave it a tweak. The wig tipped sideways and the crown of mistletoe fell off. Wrayburn swore.

'They make these things pretty solidly don't they?' Alleyn said. He righted the wig and held it steady. Wrayburn wound the single hair round the rule and this time jerked it free. Alleyn produced an envelope and the hair was dropped into it. Wrayburn stowed it in his tunic pocket.

'Let's have a look at the robe,' Alleyn said. He lifted it off on its coathanger and turned it round. A slide fastener ran right down the back separating the high-standing collar which showed a wet patch and was frayed.

'Cripes,' said Wrayburn, and then, 'We'll have to get this room locked up.'

'Yes.'

'Look. What seems to come out of this? I mean it's pretty obvious the hair on the poker matches this and there's not much doubt, is there, that the deposit on the poker is blood. And what about the wet patch on the wig? And the collar? That's not blood. So what? They've been cleaned. What with? Water? Wiped clear or washed. Which? Where? When?'

'You're going like a train, Jack.'

'Must have been here, after the young lady left him. Unless – well unless she did it and left him cold, in which case who got rid of him? *She* didn't. Well – did she?'

'Have you met the young lady?'

'No.'

'She's not the body-carrying type. Except her own which she carries like Cleopatra, Queen of Egypt.'

'Is that right?' Wrayburn mused. 'Is that a fact? Now, about this wig and beard and all that carry-on. To begin with, this gear's upstairs in a dressing-room. Moult supposedly puts it on, all except the whiskers, and comes down here where the young lady meets him and fixes the whiskers. She goes to the drawing-room and he goes out by that door into the porch and then into the courtyard where this Vincent liaises with him, then into the drawing-room where he does a Daddy Christmas, or what passes for it, round the tree. Then he returns the same way as he came and Vincent sees him come in here by the same door and the young lady takes off his whiskers and leaves him here. And that's the last anybody sees of him. Now. What say, somebody who knows he's here comes in from outside *with* the poker from the upstairs dressing-room and lets him have it. Say he's sitting there, nice and handy, still wearing his wig. Right. Then this character hauls him outside and dumps him, God knows where, but – Here!' Wrayburn exclaimed. 'Wait a bit! What's out there? There's a sledge out there. And there's this chap Vincent out there. Isn't there?'

'There is indeed.'

'Well!' Wrayburn said. 'It's a start, isn't it? It may not do in the finish. And I've read your book. I know what you think about drawing quick conclusions.'

'It's a start.'

'Following it up, then. This character, before he goes, sees the condition of the wig and cleans the stains off at the handbasin there and hitches it over the lamp like we found it with that blasted tiara on it. And he goes out and chucks the poker into the fir tree and disposes – God knows where – of the – if it's homicide – of the body. How about it? Come on. Prove me a fool. Come on.'

'My dear chap, I think it's a well-reasoned proposition.'

'You do?'

'There are difficulties, though.'

'There are?'

'The floor, for instance. The carpet. Clear traces of the returning wet boots but nothing else. No other boots. And nothing to suggest a body having been dragged to the door. OK, suppose it was carried out? You'd still expect some interference with the original prints and a set of new ones pointing both ways, wouldn't you?'

Wrayburn stared moodily at the string-coloured carpet with its clear damp incoming impressions. He picked up a boot and fitted it to the nearest print. 'Tallies,' he said. 'That's something. And the boot's still wet. No drying in here and it was only last night, after all. Well – what next? What's left? Alternatively – he did go upstairs and get clobbered.'

'Wearing his wig?'

'All right. Fair enough. Wearing his wig. God knows why, but wearing his wig. And goes up to the dressing-room. And gets clobbered with the dressing-room poker. And – here! Hold on! Hold on! And the clobberer throws the poker out of the window and it gets stuck in the tree?'

'It seems possible.'

'It does?'

'And the body? If he's dead?' Alleyn asked.

'Through the window too? Hang on. Don't rush me.'

'Not for the world. Is the body wearing the wig when it takes the high jump?'

Wrayburn swallowed. 'The bloody wig,' he said. 'Leave the wig for the time being. Now. I know this bunch of domestic villains are supposed to have searched the area. I know that. But what say someone – all right, one of that lot for the sake of argument – had already removed the body? In the night? Will you buy that?'

'I'll take it on approval. Removed the body and to confuse the issue returned the unmentionable wig to the cloakroom?'

'I quite like it,' said Wrayburn with a slight attempt at modesty. 'Well, anyway, it does sort of fit. It snowed up here, last night. We won't get anything from the ground, worse luck.'

'Until it thaws.'

'That's right. That's dead right.' Wrayburn cleared his throat. 'It's going to be a big one,' he said and after a considerable pause: 'Like I said, it's for our CID. I'll have to ring the Detective Chief-Super about this one and I reckon I know what he'll say. He'll say we set up a search. Look, I'll get on to this right away. You wait here. Will you?'

'Well – '

'I'd be obliged.'

'All right.'

So Wrayburn went off to telephone his Detective Chief-Superintendent and Alleyn, a prey to forebodings, was left to contemplate the cloakroom.

Wrayburn came back, full of business. 'There you are!' he said. 'Just as I thought: he's going to talk to his senior 'tecs and in the meantime I'm to carry on here. As from now. I'm to lay on a search party and ask Major Marchbanks for dogs. You'll hang on, won't you?' Alleyn promised and did so. When Wrayburn had gone he re-examined the wig, plucked a hair for himself, touched the still-damp robe and fell into an abstraction from which Mr Wrayburn's return aroused him.

'No joy,' grumbled Wrayburn. 'Breaking and entering *with* violence and Lord knows what else at the DCS's. He is calling up as many chaps as he can and the major's sending us what *he* can spare. They should be here within the hour. In the meantime – ' He broke off, glanced at Alleyn and made a fresh start. 'There'll have to be confirmation of all this stuff – statements from the party. The lot.'

'Big thing for you.'

'Are you joking? While it lasts, which will be until the CID comes waltzing in. Then back down the road smartly for me, to the drunks-in-charge. Look!' he burst out. 'I don't reckon our lot can handle it. Not on their own. Like the man said: we're understaffed and we're busy. We're fully extended. I don't mind betting the DCS'll talk to the CC before the hour's out.'

'He'll be able to call on the county for extra men.'

'He'd do better to go straight to the Yard. Now!'

Alleyn was silent.

'You know what I'm getting at, don't you?'

'I do, but I wish you wouldn't. The situation's altogether too freakish. My wife's a guest here and so am I. I'm the last person to meddle. I've told Bill-Tasman as much. Let them call in the Yard if they like, but not me. Leave me out. Get a statement from my wife, of course. You'll want to do that. And then, unless there's any good reason against it, I'll take her away and damn glad to do so. And that's final. I'll leave you to it. You'll want to lock up this place and then you can get cracking. Are there keys? Yes. There you are.'

'But – '

'My dear man, no. Not another word. Please.'

Alleyn went out, quickly, into the hall.

He encountered Hilary standing about six feet away with an air strangely compounded of diffidence flavoured with defiance.

'I don't know what you'll think of me,' said Hilary. 'I dare say you may be very cross. You see, I've been talking to our local pundit. The Detective Chief-Superintendent. And to your boss-person at the Yard.'

II

'It's just,' Hilary blandly explained, 'that I do happen to know him. Soon after I was first settled with the staff here, he paid a visit to The Vale and Marchbanks brought him over for tea. He was interested in my experiment. But we mustn't keep him waiting, must we?'

'He's still on the line?'

'Yes. He'd like to have a word with you. There's a telephone over there. I *know* you're going to forgive me,' Hilary said to Alleyn's back.

Then you know a damn sight more than's good for you, Alleyn thought. He gave himself a second or two to regain his temper and lifted the receiver. Hilary left him with ostentatious tact. Alleyn wondered if he was going to have a sly listen-in from wherever he had established the call.

The Assistant Commissioner was plaintive and slightly facetious. 'My dear Rory,' he said, 'what very odd company you keep: no holiday like a busman's, I see.'

'I assure you, sir, it's none of my seeking.'

'So I supposed. Are you alone?'

'Ostensibly.'

'Quite. Well, now your local DC Super rang me before Bill-Tasman did. It seems there's no joy down your way: big multiple stores robbery, with violence, and a near riot following some bloody sit-in.

They're sending a few chaps out but they're fully extended and can't really spare them. As far as I can gather this show of yours – '

'It's not mine.'

'Wait a minute. This show of yours looks as if it might develop into something, doesn't it?' This was the Assistant Commissioner's stock phrase for suspected homicide.

'It might, yes.'

'Yes. Your host would like you to take over.'

'But the DCS is in charge, sir. In the meantime Wrayburn the Div Super from Downlow's holding the fort.'

'Has the DCS expressed his intention of going it alone?'

'I understand he's belly-aching – '

'He is indeed. He wants the Yard.'

'But he'll have to talk to his Chief Constable, sir, before – '

'His Chief Constable is in the Bermudas.'

'Damnation!'

'This is a very bad line. What was that you said?'

Alleyn repressed an impulse to say 'You 'eard.'

'I swore,' he said.

'That won't get you anywhere, Rory.'

'Look, sir – my wife – Troy – she's a guest in the house. So am I. It's a preposterous set-up. Isn't it?'

'I've thought of that. Troy had better come back to London, don't you agree? Give her my best respects and tell her I'm sorry to visit the policeman's lot upon her.'

'But, sir, if I held the other guests I'd have to – you see what a farcical situation it is.'

'Take statements and let 'em go if you think it's OK. You've got a promising field without them, haven't you?'

'I'm not so sure. It's a rum go. It's worse than that, it's lunatic.'

'You're thinking of the homicidal domestics? An excellent if extreme example of rehabilitation. But of course you may find that somewhere among them there's a twicer. Rory,' said the AC, changing his tone, 'I'm sorry but we're uncommonly busy in the department. This job ought to be tackled at once, and it needs a man with your peculiar talents.'

'And that's an order?'

'Well, yes. I'm afraid it is.'

'Very good, sir.'

'We'll send you down Mr Fox for a treat. Would you like to speak to him?'

'I won't trouble him,' Alleyn said sourly. 'But – wait a moment.'

'Yes?'

'I believe Wrayburn has a list of the domestic staff here. I'd like to get a CRO report.'

'Of course. I'd better have a word with this super. What's his name? Wrayburn? Turn him on, will you?'

'Certainly, sir.'

'Thank you. Sorry. Good luck to you.'

Alleyn went in search of his wife. She was not in their rooms which gave evidence of her having bathed and changed. He spent a minute or two with his head through the open window, peering into the wreckage below and then went downstairs. As he crossed the hall he encountered Cuthbert with a tray of drinks and a face of stone.

'The party is in the library, sir,' Cuthbert said. 'Mr Bill-Tasman wished me to inform you. This way, if you please, sir.'

They were all there including Troy, who made a quick face at him.

Hilary was in full spate. 'My dears,' he was saying, '*what* a relief it is.' He advanced upon Alleyn with outstretched hands, took him by the biceps and gently shook him. 'My dear fellow!' Hilary gushed. 'I was just saying – I can't tell you how relieved we all are. Now do, do, do, do.' This seemed to be an invitation to drink, sit down, come to the fire or be introduced to the colonel and Mr Smith.

The colonel had already advanced. He shook hands and said there was almost no need for an introduction because Troy had been 'such a dear and so kind' and added that he was 'most awfully worried' about Moult. 'You know how it is,' he said. 'The feller's been with one, well, more years than one cares to say. One feels quite lost. And he's a nice feller. I – we – ' he hesitated, glanced at his wife and then said in a rush. 'We're very attached to him. Very. And, I do assure you, there's no harm in him. No harm at all in Moult.'

'Upsetting for you,' Alleyn said.

'It's so awful,' said the colonel, 'to think he may have got that thing, whatever it is. Be wandering about? Somewhere out there? The cold! I tell my nephew we ought to ring Marchbanks up and ask him to lay on his dogs. They must have dogs at that place. What do you say?'

Alleyn said, and meant it, that it was a good idea. He found Mr Smith bearing down upon him.

'Met before,' said Mr Smith giving him a knuckle-breaking hand-shake. 'I never caught on you was you, if you get me. When was it? Ten years ago? I gave evidence for your lot in the Blake forgery case. Remember me?'

Alleyn said he remembered Mr Smith very well.

Cressida, in a green velvet trousered garment, split down the middle and strategically caught together by an impressive brooch, waggled her fingers at Alleyn and said 'Hi, there.'

Hilary began offering Alleyn a drink and when he said he wouldn't have one was almost comically nonplussed. 'You won't?' he exclaimed.

'Not on duty, alas,' said Alleyn.

'But – no, *really*! Surely under these conditions. I mean, it's not as if you were – well, my dear man, you know what I mean.'

'Yes, I do,' Alleyn said. 'But I think we must as far as possible reduce the rather bizarre circumstances to something resembling routine police procedure.'

Hilary said: 'I know, I know but – ' and boggled. He appealed dumbly to Troy.

'It would have been lovely to have come as a visitor,' Alleyn said politely, 'but I turn out to be no such thing. I turn out to be a police-man on a job and I must try to behave accordingly.'

A complete silence followed. Hilary broke it with a slight giggle.

Mrs Forrester said: 'Very sensible,' and to her nephew: 'You can't have it both ways, Hilary, and you'd best make your mind up to it.'

'Yes. All right,' Hilary said and gulped. 'Well,' he asked Alleyn, 'what's the form, then? What would you like us to do?'

'For the moment – nothing. The first thing, of course, is to set up an organized search for the missing man. Wrayburn is bringing in people to that end as soon as they can be assembled. They'll be here within the hour. Later on I shall ask each of you for as detailed an account of the events leading up to the disappearance as you can give me. In the meantime I shall have a word with Mr Wrayburn and then, if you please, I would like to look at Moult's bedroom and at Colonel Forrester's dressing-room. After that we'll have a word with the staff. Perhaps you'd be very kind and tell them, would you.'

'Oh God,' said Hilary. 'Yes. I suppose so. Yes, of course. But you will remember, won't you, they are in a rather special position?'

'You can say that again,' Mr Smith remarked.

'I think that's all for the moment,' Alleyn said. 'So if you'll excuse me – ?'

'But you'll join us for dinner, at least?' Hilary expostulated. 'Of course you will!'

'You're very kind but I think we should press on.'

'But that's fantastic,' Cressida cried. 'You can't starve. Hilly, he can't starve.' She appealed to Troy. 'Well, can he? You know? Can he?'

Before Troy could answer Hilary began to talk rather wildly about Alleyn joining them when he could and then about game pie or at the very least, sandwiches. He rang and on the arrival of Cuthbert seemed to collect himself.

Cuthbert stood inside the door with his gaze fixed on a distant point above all their heads.

'Oh, Cuthbert,' Hilary said. 'Mr Alleyn has very kindly agreed to help us. He's going to take complete charge and we must all assist him as much as we possibly can. I know you and the staff will co-operate. Mr Alleyn may not be dining. Please arrange a cold supper, will you? Something he can take when he's free. In the dining-room.'

'Very good, sir.'

'And Cuthbert. Mr Alleyn would like, later on, to have your account, and the others' of what you've all told me. In case I've forgotten anything or got it wrong. You might just let them know, will you?'

'Certainly, sir.'

'Thank you.'

'Thank you, sir.'

When Cuthbert had gone Cressida said: 'Hilly, is it my imagination or does that man seem all up-tight to you?'

'I hope not, darling. I do hope not. Of course naturally they're a bit on edge,' Hilary pleaded. 'But nobody's going to draw any false conclusions, are they? Of course they're not. Which is why,' he added, reaching for a graceful turn of phrase, 'one is so thankful that you – ' he turned to Alleyn ' – have taken us under your wing. If you see what I mean.'

'I don't know,' Alleyn said pleasantly, 'that you've quite defined the function of an investigating officer but it's nice of you to put it that way.'

Hilary laughed extravagantly and then, with an air of elaborate and anxious solicitation, asked Alleyn if there was *anything, anything at all*, that anybody could do to help.

'Not at the moment, I think,' he said. 'Troy's given me a pretty comprehensive idea of the situation. But there is one point, as you're all here – '

'Yes? Yes?' urged Hilary, all concern.

'Nobody recognized Moult as the Druid, it seems. You did all see him, didn't you? In action?'

A general chorus of assent was followed by elaborations, from which it emerged that the house-party, with the exception of Colonel Forrester, had 'mixed' with the other guests and the children in the library and had followed the children in procession to the drawing-room. They had stood together during the tree. When the grown-ups, joined by Cressida, opened their parcels, the house-party again congealed, thanking each other and exclaiming over the gifts.

Alleyn asked if anyone, apart from his employers, had seen or spoken to Moult during the day. They all looked blank, said they might have but didn't really remember. If they had spoken it would only be to say 'Merry Christmas'.

'Right,' Alleyn said. 'Thank you. And now, if I may be excused, I'll talk to Wrayburn. By the way, may I borrow that lens of yours? It'll make me feel less of a phoney.'

'Of course, I'll – '

'Don't move. I'll get it. It's on your desk. One other thing – may I take a look at your quarters, Colonel?'

'Certainly. Certainly. If there's anything you'd like me to show you,' said Colonel Forrester with obvious keenness, 'I'll be glad – '

'No, Fred,' said his wife. 'You don't start that sort of nonsense. Rushing up and down stairs and looking for clues. I said rushing – '

'I know you did, B. It doesn't apply.'

'If I need help,' Alleyn said, 'I'll come and ask for it. May I?'

'You do that,' said the colonel warmly and threw a bold look at his wife. 'I'll be delighted. By all means. You do that.'

So Alleyn collected the lens, found Wrayburn and took him upstairs and Troy, in an extraordinary state of semi-detachment, went in with the house-party to dinner.

III

Moult's bedroom in the top storey at Halberds gave evidence, in its appointments, to Hilary's consideration for his staff. It exhibited, however, the pathological orderliness of an army barracks and had the same smell: a compound of boot-polish, leather, fag-ends, heavy cloth and an indefinable stale masculinity.

Moult's top-coat, outdoor suit and shoes, hat and gloves were all properly disposed. His empty suitcase was stowed at the back of his wardrobe. His blameless underwear lay impeccably folded in his clothes-press. Even his borderline-pornographic reading was neatly stacked on his bedside table. On the dressing-table was a pigskin case with his initials on it. Opened, it revealed two old-fashioned silver-backed brushes, a comb and a card. Alleyn showed the card to Wrayburn. 'Lt-Col. Fleaton Forrester' on one side and on the other, in a sharply pointed hand: 'A. Moult. On the twenty-fifth anniversary of a very happy association. F.F.'

When they found Moult's pocket-book in a drawer of his dressing-table it too proved to be initialled and of pigskin. The card inside, Mrs Fleaton Forrester's, said abruptly 'Moult. 1946-71. B.F.' It contained no money but a list of telephone numbers and three snapshots. The first showed the colonel in uniform, mounted on a charger, and Sergeant Moult in uniform and on foot saluting him. A round-faced man with monkey-like cheeks heavily scarred. The second showed the Colonel and Mrs Forrester gazing disconsolately at a tract of moorland and Moult gazing respectfully at them. The third was faded and altogether had the appearance of a younger Moult with one stripe up, holding by the hand an overdressed little girl of about four.

'That'll be the man himself in all three, will it?' Wrayburn speculated.

'Yes. You notice the scarred face?'

'Married? With a kid?'

'Doesn't follow as the night the day. It might be anybody's infant-phenomenon.'

'I suppose so.'

'When my chaps get here,' Alleyn said, 'we'll take dabs. And when we lay the dogs on, we'll show them one of his shoes. Did I tell you the colonel also suggested dogs from The Vale? Hullo! Listen to this!'

A hullabaloo of sorts had broken out in the chimney: a confusion of sound, thrown about and distorted, blown down and sucked back as if by some gigantic and inefficient flautist.

'That's the Nor'-west Buster getting up,' Wrayburn said. 'That's bad. That's a nuisance.'

'Why?'

'It means rain in these parts. Very heavy as a rule.'

'Snow?'

'More likely floods. Here she comes.'

The window rattled violently and was suddenly hit by a great buffet of rain.

'Lovely hunting weather,' Alleyn grunted. 'Still – you never know. It may do us more good than harm. We'll lock up here and penetrate the Forrester suite. Come on.'

They went down to the next floor and walked along the heavily carpeted corridor serving the guest rooms. It was lit by only a third of its shaded wall-lamps and very quiet. No rumour of the storm outside or of life within the house. Alleyn supposed the guests and Hilary were all in the dining-room and suddenly felt ravenous. He was about to say so but instead laid his hand on Wrayburn's arm and motioned him to be quiet. He pointed ahead. From under one of the doors a sliver of light showed on the red carpet.

Alleyn counted doors. Troy had told him which room belonged to which guest. They now approached his dressing-room linked by a bathroom with Troy's bedroom. Next came the Forresters' bedroom, bathroom and dressing-room. Beyond these were Mr Smith, and on the front corner of the west wing in a large room with its own bathroom, Cressida. Where Hilary himself slept – no doubt in some master apartment of great stateliness – Troy had no idea.

It was from under the Forresters' bedroom door that the light showed.

Alleyn listened for a moment and could hear nothing. He made a quick decision. He motioned Wrayburn to stay where he was and himself opened the door and walked straight in.

He did so to the accompaniment of a loud crash.

A man at the window turned to face him: a blond, pale man whom he had seen before, wearing dark trousers and an alpaca jacket.

'Good evening again,' Alleyn said. 'I've made a mistake. I thought this was my wife's room.'

'Next door,' the man barely articulated.

'Stupid of me. You must be Nigel, I think.'

'That's right, sir.'

'I've been admiring your work in the courtyard. It really is quite something.'

Nigel's lips moved. He was saying, inaudibly, 'Thank you very much.'

The window-pane behind him streamed with driven rain. His head, face and the front of his jacket were wet.

'You've been caught,' Alleyn said lightly.

Nigel said: 'It's come down very sudden. I was – I was closing the window, sir. It's very awkward, this window.'

'It'll ruin your snow sculpture, I'm afraid.'

Nigel suddenly said: 'It may be a judgment.'

'A judgment? On whom? For what?'

'There's a lot of sin about,' Nigel said loudly. 'One way and another. You never know.'

'Such as?'

'Heathen practices. Disguised as Christian. There's hints of blasphemy there. Touches of it. If rightly looked at.'

'You mean the Christmas tree?'

'Heathen practices round graven images. Caperings. And see what's happened to him.'

'What *has* happened to him?' asked Alleyn and wondered if he'd struck some sort of lunatic bonanza.

'He's GONE.'

'Where?'

'Ah! Where! That's what sin does for you. I know. Nobody better. Seeing what I been myself.'

Nigel's face underwent an extraordinary change. His mouth hung open, his nostrils distended, his white eyelashes fluttered and then, like a microcosm of the deluge outside, he wept most copiously.

'Now, look here – ' Alleyn began, but Nigel with an unconscionable roar fled from the room and went thudding down the corridor.

Wrayburn appeared in the doorway. 'What the hell's all that in aid of?' he asked. 'Which of them was it?'

'That was Nigel, the second houseman who once made effigies but became a religious maniac and killed a sinful lady. He is said to be cured.'

'Cured!'

'Although I believe Mr Bill-Tasman has conceded that when Nigel remembers his crime he is inclined to weep. He remembered it just now.'

'I overheard some of his remarks. The chap's certifiable. Religious maniac.'

'I wonder why he leaned out of the window.'

'He did?'

'I fancy so. He was too wet to match his story about just shutting it. And there's very little rain on the carpet. I don't believe it was open until he opened it.'

'Funny!'

'It is, rather. Let's have a look about shall we?'

They found nothing in the bedroom more remarkable than the Forresters' green-lined tropical umbrella. Nigel had turned down their bed, laid out their viyella nightwear and banked up their fire. The windows were shut.

'Wouldn't you think,' Mr Wrayburn observed, 'that they'd have heaters in these rooms? Look at the work involved! It must be dynamite.'

'He's trying to re-create the past.'

'He's lucky to have a lunatic to help him, then.'

They went through the bathroom with its soap, macintosh and hair-lotion smells. Mr Wrayburn continued to exclaim upon the appointments at Halberds: 'Bathrooms! All over the shop like an eight-star-plus hotel. You wouldn't credit it.' He was somewhat mollified to discover that in the colonel's dressing-room a radiator had been built into the grate. It had been switched on, presumably by Nigel. 'Look at that!' said Mr Wrayburn. 'What about his electrical bill! No trouble!'

'And here,' Alleyn pointed out, 'are the Welsh fire-irons. Minus the poker. Highly polished and, of course, never used. I think the relative positions of the fireplace, the bed, the window and the doors are worth noticing, Jack. If you come in from the bathroom, the window's on your right, the door into the corridor on your left and the bed, projecting from the outside wall facing you, with the fireplace beyond it in the far wall. If I were to sit on the floor on the far side of the bed and you came through the bathroom door, you wouldn't see me, would you?'

'No?' said Mr Wrayburn, expecting an elaboration but getting none. Alleyn had moved to the far side of the bed: a single high-standing Victorian four-poster unadorned with curtains. Its authentic patchwork quilt reached to the floor and showed a sharp bulge at one side. He turned it back and exposed Col. Forrester's uniform box, black-japanned, white-lettered, and quite noticeably dented and scarred about the padlock area.

'I do hate,' Alleyn said, sitting on his heels, 'this going on a job minus my kit. It makes one feel such a damned, piddling amateur. However, Fox will bring it and in the meantime I've the Bill-Tasman lens. Look here, Jack. Talk of amateurism! This isn't the handiwork of any master cracksman, is it?'

Mr Wrayburn squatted down beside him. 'Very clumsy attempt,' he agreed. 'What's he think he'd achieve? Silly.'

'Yes,' Alleyn said, using the lens, 'a bit of hanky-panky with the padlock. Something twisted in the hoop.'

'Like a poker?'

'At first glance perhaps. We'll have to take charge of this. I'll talk to the colonel.'

'What about the contents?'

'It's big enough, in all conscience, to house the crown jewels but I imagine Mrs Forrester's got the lion's share dotted about her frontage. Troy thinks they carry scrip and documents in it. And you did hear, didn't you, that Moult has charge of the key?'

Wrayburn, with a hint of desperation in his voice, said: '*I* don't know! Like the man said: you wouldn't credit it if you read it in a book. I suppose we pick the lock for them, do we?'

'Or pick it for ourselves if not for them? I'll enquire of the colonel. In the meantime they mustn't get their hands on it.'

Wrayburn pointed to the scarred area. 'By gum! I reckon it's the poker,' he said.

'Oh, for my Bailey and his dab-kit.'

'The idea being,' Wrayburn continued, following out his thought, 'that some villain unknown was surprised trying to break open the box with the poker.'

'And killed? With the poker? After a struggle? That seems to be going rather far; don't you think? And when you say "somebody" – '

'I suppose I mean Moult.'

'Who preferred taking a very inefficient whang at the box to using the key?'

'That's right – we dismiss that theory, then. It's ridiculous. How about Moult coming in after he'd done his Christmas tree act and catching the villain at it and getting knocked on the head?'

'And then – ?'

'Pushed through the window? With the poker after him?'

'In which case,' Alleyn said, 'he was transplanted before they searched. Let's have a look at the window.'

It was the same as all the others: a sash window with a snib locking the upper to the lower frame.

'We'd better not handle anything. The damn bore of it is that with this high standard of house management the whole place will have been dusted off. But if you did look down from this window, Jack, it'd be at the top of the sapling where Bill-Tasman picked up the poker. His study is directly beneath us. And if you leant out and looked to your left, it would be at the south-east corner of this wing. Hold on a jiffy. Look here.'

'What's up?'

Alleyn was moving about, close to the window. He dodged his head and peered sideways through the glass.

'Turn off the lights, Jack, will you? There's something out there – yes, near the top of the fir. It's catching a stray gleam from somewhere. Take a look.'

Mr Wrayburn shaded his eyes and peered into the night. 'I don't get anything,' he said. 'Unless you mean a little sort of shiny wriggle. You can hardly catch it.'

'That's it. Quite close. In the fir.'

'Might be anything. Bit of string.'

'Or tinsel?'

'That's right. Blowing about.'

'So what?'

'So nothing, I dare say. A passing fancy. We've still got a hell of a lot to find out. About last night's ongoings – the order of events and details of procedure and so on.'

'Mrs Alleyn will be helpful there, I make no doubt.'

'You know my views under that heading, don't you?' Alleyn said austerely.

'That was before you took over, though.'

'So it was. And now I'm in the delirious position of having to use departmental tact and make routine enquiries with my wife.'

'Perhaps,' Mr Wrayburn dimly speculated, 'she'll think it funny.'

Alleyn stared at him. 'You know,' he said at last, 'you've got something there. I wouldn't be at all surprised if she did.' He thought for a moment. 'And I dare say,' he said, 'that in a macabre sort of way she'll be, as usual, right. Come on. We'd better complete the survey. I'd like one more look at this blasted padlock, though.'

He was on his knees before it and Wrayburn was peering over his shoulder when Colonel Forrester said: 'So you *have* found it. Good. Good. Good.'

He had come in by the bathroom door behind their backs. He was a little bit breathless but his eyes were bright and he seemed to be quite excited.

'I didn't join the ladies,' he explained. 'I thought I'd just pop up and see if I could be of any use. There may be points you want to ask about. So here I am and you must pack me off if I'm a nuisance. If one wasn't so worried it would be awfully interesting to see the real thing. Oh – and by the way – your wife tells me that you're George Alleyn's brother. He was in the Brigade in my day, you know. Junior to me, of course: an ensign. In The Kiddies, I remember. Coincidence, isn't it? Do tell me: what did he do after he went on the reserve? Took to the pro-consular service I seem to remember.'

Alleyn answered this enquiry as shortly as with civility he could. The colonel sat on the bed and beamed at him, still fetching his breath rather short but apparently enjoying himself. Alleyn introduced Mr Wrayburn whom the colonel was clearly delighted to meet. 'But I oughtn't to interrupt you both,' he said. 'There you are in the thick of it with your magnifying glass and everything. Do tell me: what do you make of my box?'

'I was going to ask you about that, sir,' Alleyn said. 'It's a clumsy attempt, isn't it?'

'Clumsy? Well, yes. But one couldn't be anything else but clumsy with a thing like a poker, could one?'

'You know about the poker?'

'Oh rather! Hilary told us.'

'What exactly did he tell you?'

'That he'd found one in the fir tree out there. Now that was a pretty outlandish sort of place for it to be, wasn't it?'

'Did he describe it?'

The colonel looked steadily at Alleyn for some seconds. 'Not in detail,' he said, and after a further pause: 'But in any case when we found the marks on the box we thought: "poker", B and I, as soon as we saw them.'

'Why did you think "poker", sir?'

'I don't know. We just did. "Poker", we thought. Or B did, which comes to much the same thing. Poker.'

'Had you noticed that the one belonging to this room had disappeared?'

'Oh dear me, no. Not a bit of it. Not at the time.'

'Colonel Forrester, Troy tells me that you didn't see Moult after he had put on your Druid's robe.'

'Oh but I did,' he said opening his eyes very wide. 'I *saw* him.'

'You did?'

'Well – "saw" you may call it. I was lying down in our bedroom, you know, dozing, and he came to the bathroom door. He had the robe and the wig on and he held the beard up to show me. I think he said he'd come back before he went down. I think I reminded him about the window and then I did go to sleep and so I suppose he just looked in and went off without waking me. That's what Mrs Alleyn was referring to. I rather *fancy* although I may be wrong here, but I rather *fancy* I heard him look out.'

'Heard him? Look out?'

'Yes. I told him to look out of the dressing-room window for Vincent with the sledge at the corner. Because when Vincent was there it would be time to go down. That was how we laid it on. Dead on the stroke of half past seven it was to be, by the stable clock. And so it was.'

'What!' Alleyn exclaimed. 'You mean – ?'

'I like to run an exercise to a strict timetable and so, I'm glad to say, does Hilary. All our watches and clocks were set to synchronize. And I've just recollected: I *did* hear him open the window and I heard the stable clock strike the half-hour immediately afterwards. So, you see, at that very moment Vincent would signal from the corner and Moult would go down to have his beard put on, and – and there you are. That was, you might say, phase one of the exercise, what?'

'Yes, I see. And – forgive me for pressing it but it is important: he didn't present himself on his return?'

'No. He didn't. I'm sure he didn't,' said the colonel very doubtfully.

'I mean – could you have still been asleep?'

'Yes!' cried the colonel as if the heavens had opened upon supreme enlightenment. 'I could! Easily, I could. Of course!'

Alleyn heard Mr Wrayburn fetch a sigh.

'You see,' the colonel explained, 'I do drop off, after my turns. I think it must be something in the stuff the quack gives me.'

'Yes, I see. Tell me – those fur-lined boots. Would he have put them on up here or in the cloakroom?'

'In the cloakroom. He'd put them all ready down there for me. I wanted to dress up here because of the big looking-glass but the boots didn't matter and they're clumsy things to tramp about the house in.'

'Yes, I see.'

'You do think, don't you,' asked the colonel, 'that you'll find him?'

'I expect we will, I hope so.'

'I tell you what, Alleyn,' said the colonel and his face became as dolorous as a clown's. 'I'm afraid the poor fellow's dead.'

'Are you, sir?'

'One shouldn't say so, of course, at this stage. But – I don't know – I'm very much afraid my poor old Moult's dead. He was an awful ass in many ways but we suited each other, he and I. What do you think about it?'

'There's one possibility,' Alleyn said cautiously.

'I know what you're going to say. Amnesia. Aren't you?'

'Something, at any rate, that caused him to leave the cloakroom by the outer door and wander off into the night. Miss Tottenham says he did smell pretty strongly of liquor.'

'Did he? Did he? Yes, well, perhaps in the excitement he may have been silly. In fact – in fact, I'm afraid he was.'

'Why do you say that?'

'Because when he found me all tied up in my robe and having a turn, he helped me out and put me to bed and I must say he smelt most awfully strong of whisky. Reeked. But, if that was the way of it,' the colonel asked, 'where is he? Out on those moors like somebody in a play? On such a night, poor feller? If he's out there,' said the colonel with great energy, 'he must be found. That should come first. He must be found.'

Alleyn explained that there was a search party on the way. When he said Major Marchbanks was providing police dogs and handlers, the colonel nodded crisply, rather as if he had ordered this to be done. More and more the impression grew upon Alleyn that here was no ninny. Eccentric in his domestic arrangements Colonel Forrester might be, and unexpected in his conversation, but he hadn't said anything really foolish about the case. And now when Alleyn broached the matter of the tin box and the dressing-room the colonel cut him short.

'You'll want to lock the place up, no doubt,' he said. 'You fellers always lock places up. I'll tell Moult – ' he stopped short and made a nervous movement of his hands. 'Force of habit,' he said. 'Silly of me. I'll put my things in the bedroom.'

'Please don't bother. We'll attend to it. There's one thing, though: would you mind telling me what is in the uniform box?'

'*In* it? Well. Let me see. Papers, for one thing. My commission. Diaries. My Will.' The Colonel caught himself up. 'One of them,' he amended. 'My investments, scrip or whatever they call them.'

Again, there followed one of the colonel's brief meditations. 'Deeds,' he said. 'That kind of thing. B's money: some of it. She likes to keep a certain amount handy. Ladies do, I'm told. And the jewels she isn't wearing. Those sort of things. Yes.'

Alleyn explained that he would want to test the box for finger-prints and the colonel instantly asked if he might watch. 'It would interest me no end,' he said. 'Insufflators and latent ones and all that. I read a lot of detective stories: awful rot, but they lead you on. B reads them backwards but I won't let her tell me.'

Alleyn managed to steer him away from this theme and it was finally agreed that they would place the box, intact, in the dressing-room wardrobe pending the arrival of the party from London. The colonel's effects having been removed to the bedroom, the wardrobe and the dressing-room itself would then be locked and Alleyn would keep the keys.

Before these measures were completed Mrs Forrester came tramping in.

'I thought as much,' she said to her husband.

'I'm all right, B. It's getting jolly serious, but I'm all right. Really.'

'What are you doing with the box? Good evening,' Mrs Forrester added, nodding to Mr Wrayburn.

Alleyn explained. Mrs Forrester fixed him with an embarrassing glare but heard him through.

'I see,' she said. 'And is Moult supposed to have been interrupted trying to open it with the poker when he had the key in his pocket?'

'Of course not, B. We all agree that would be a silly idea.'

'Perhaps you think he's murdered and his body's locked up in the box.'

'Really, my dear!'

'The one notion's as silly as the other.'

'We don't entertain either of them, B. Do we, Alleyn?'

'Mrs Forrester,' Alleyn said, 'what do you think has happened? Have you a theory?'

'No,' said Mrs Forrester. 'It's not my business to have theories. Any more than it's yours, Fred,' she tossed as an aside to her husband. 'But I do throw this observation out, as a matter you may like to remember, that Moult and Hilary's murderers were at loggerheads.'

'Why?'

'Why! Why, because Moult's the sort of person to object to them. Old soldier-servant. Service in the Far East. Seen plenty of the seamy side and likes things done according to the Queen's regulations. Regimental snobbery. Goes right through the ranks. Thinks this lot a gang of riff-raff and let's them know it.'

'I tried,' said the colonel, 'to get him to take a more enlightened view but he couldn't see it, poor feller, he couldn't see it.'

'Was he married?'

'No,' they both said and Mrs Forrester added: 'Why?'

'There's a snapshot in his pocket-book – '

'*You've found him!*' she exclaimed with a violence that seemed to shock herself as well as her hearers.

Alleyn explained.

'I dare say,' the colonel said, 'it's some little girl in the married quarters. One of his brother-soldiers' children. He's fond of children.'

'Come to bed, Fred.'

'It isn't time, B.'

'Yes, it is. For you.'

Mr Wrayburn, who from the time Mrs Forrester appeared, had gone quietly about the business of removing the colonel's effects to the bedroom, now returned to say he hoped they'd find everything in order. With an air that suggested they'd better or else, Mrs Forrester withdrew her husband, leaving both doors into the bathroom open, presumably with the object of keeping herself informed of their proceedings.

Alleyn and Wrayburn lifted the box by its end handles into the wardrobe which they locked. Alleyn walked over to the window, stood on a Victorian footstool and peered for some time through Hilary's glass at the junction of the two sashes. '*This* hasn't been dusted, at least,' he muttered, 'but much good will that be to us, I don't mind betting.' He prowled disconsolately.

Colonel Forrester appeared in the bathroom door in his pyjamas and dressing-gown. He made apologetic faces at them, motioned with his head in the direction of his wife, bit his underlip, shut the door and could be heard brushing his teeth.

'He's a caution, isn't he?' Mr Wrayburn murmured.

Alleyn moved alongside his colleague and pointed to the window.

Rain still drove violently against the pane, splayed out and ran down in sheets. The frame rattled intermittently. Alleyn turned out the lights and at once the scene outside became partly visible. The top of the fir tree thrashed about dementedly against an oncoming multitude of glistening rods across which, in the distance, distorted beams of light swept and turned.

'Chaps from The Vale. Or my lot.'

'Look at that sapling fir.'

'Whipping about like mad, isn't it? That's the Buster. Boughs broken. Snow blown out of it. It's a proper shocker, the Buster is.'

'There *is* something caught up in it. A tatter of something shiny.'

'Anything might be blown into it in this gale.'

'It's on the lee-side. Still – I suppose you're right. We'd better go down. You go first, will you, Jack? I'll lock up here. By the way, they'll want that shoe of Moult's to lay the dogs on. But what a hope!'

'What about one of his fur-lined boots in the cloakroom?'

Alleyn hesitated and then said: 'Yes. All right. Yes.'

'See you downstairs then.'

'OK.'

Wrayburn went out. Alleyn pulled the curtains across the window. He waited for a moment in the dark room and was about to cross it when the door into the bathroom opened and admitted a patch of reflected light. He stood where he was. A voice, scarcely articulate, without character, breathed: 'Oh,' and the door closed.

He waited. Presently he heard a tap turned on and sundry other sounds of activity.

He locked the bathroom door, went out by the door into the corridor, locked it, pocketed both keys, took a turn to his left and was in time to see Troy going into her bedroom.

He slipped in after her and found her standing in front of her fire.

'You dodge down passages like Alice's rabbit,' he said. 'Don't look doubtfully at me. Don't worry. You aren't here, my love. We can't help this. You aren't here.'

'I know.'

'It's silly. It's ludicrous.'

'I'm falling about, laughing.'

'Troy?'

'Yes. All right. I'll expect you when I see you.'

'And that won't be – '

Troy had lifted her hand. 'What?' he asked and she pointed to her built-in wardrobe. 'You can hear the Forresters,' she said, 'if you go in there and if they've left their wardrobe door open. I don't suppose they have and I don't suppose you want to. Why should you? But you can.'

He walked over to the wardrobe and stuck his head inside. The sound of voices in tranquil conversation reached him, the colonel's near at hand, Mrs Forrester's very distant. She's still in the bathroom, Alleyn thought. Suddenly there was a rattle of coathangers and the colonel, startlingly close at hand said: ' – jolly difficult to replace – ' and a few seconds later: 'Yes, all right, I know. Don't *fuss* me.'

Silence: Alleyn turned back into the room.

'On Christmas morning,' Troy said, 'just after midnight, when I hung my dress in there, I heard them having what sounded like a row.'

'Oh?'

'Well – just one remark from the colonel. He said something was absolutely final and if *she* didn't, *he* would. He sounded very unlike himself. And then she banged a door – their bathroom door, I suppose, and I could hear her barking her way into bed. I remembered my manners with an effort and wrenched myself away.'

'Curious,' Alleyn said, and after a moment's consideration:

'I must be off.'

He was half-way across the room when Mrs Forrester screamed.

CHAPTER 7

House Work

Colonel Forrester lay in a little heap face down under the window. He looked small and accidental. His wife, in her red dressing-gown, knelt beside him and as Troy and Alleyn entered the room, was in the act of raising him to a sitting position. Alleyn helped her.

Troy said: 'He takes something doesn't he?'

'Tablets. Bedside table.'

He was leaning back in his wife's arms now, his eyes wide open and terrified and his head moving very slightly in time with his breathing. Her thin plait of hair dangled over him.

'It's not here,' Troy said.

'Must be. Pill things. Capsules. He put them there. Be quick.'

Alleyn said: 'Try his dressing-gown pocket, if you can reach it. Wait. I will.' It was empty.

'I saw them. I reminded him. You haven't looked. Fred! Fred, you're all right, old man. I'm here.'

'Truly,' said Troy. 'They're not anywhere here. How about brandy?'

'Yes. His flask's in the middle drawer. Dressing-table.'

It was there. Troy unscrewed the top and gave it to her. Alleyn began casting about the room.

'That'll be better. Won't it, Fred? Better?'

Troy brought a glass of water but was ignored. Mrs Forrester held the mouth of the flask between her husband's lips. 'Take it, Fred,' she said. 'Just a sip. Take it. You must. That's right. Another.'

Alleyn said: 'Here we are!'

He was beside them with a capsule in his palm. He held it out to Mrs Forrester. Then he took the flask from her and put it beside a glass phial on the dressing-table.

'Fred, look. Your pill. Come on, old boy.'

The delay seemed interminable. Into the silence came a tiny rhythmic sound: 'Ah – ah – ah,' of the colonel's breathing. Presently Mrs Forrester said: *'That's* better. Isn't it? *That's* better, old boy.'

He was better. The look of extreme anxiety passed. He made plaintive little noises and at last murmured something.

'What? What is it?'

'Moult,' whispered the colonel.

Mrs Forrester made an inarticulate exclamation. She brushed her husband's thin hair back and kissed his forehead.

Turn,' said the colonel, 'wasn't it?'

'Yes.'

'All right soon.'

'Of course you will be.'

'Up.'

'Not yet, Fred.'

'Yes. Get up.'

He began very feebly to scrabble with his feet on the carpet. Mrs Forrester with a look of helplessness of which Troy would have thought her totally incapable, turned to Alleyn.

'Yes, of course,' he said, answering it. 'He shouldn't lie flat, should he?'

Alleyn leant over the colonel. 'Will you let me put you to bed, sir?' he asked.

'Very kind. Shouldn't bother.'

Troy heaped up the pillows on the bed and opened it back. When she looked about her she found Alleyn with the colonel in his arms.

'Here we go,' said Alleyn and gently deposited his burden.

The colonel looked up at him. *'Collapse,'* he said, *'of Old Party,'* and the wraith of his mischievous look visited his face.

'You old fool,' said his wife.

Alleyn chuckled. 'You'll do,' he said. 'You'll do splendidly.'

'Oh yes. I expect so.'

Mrs Forrester chafed his hands between her two elderly ones.

Alleyn picked up the phial delicately between finger and thumb and held it up to the light.

'Where was it?' Troy asked.

He motioned with his head towards a lacquered leather waste-paper bin under the dressing-table. The gesture was not so slight that it escaped Mrs Forrester.

'In *there*?' she said. 'In *there*?'

'Is there something I can put the capsules in? I'd like to keep the phial if I may?'

'Anything. There's a pin box on the dressing-table. Take that.'

He did so. He spread his handkerchief out and gingerly wrapped up the phial and its stopper.

The stable door bit,' he muttered and put them in his pocket.

'What's that supposed to mean,' snapped Mrs Forrester, who was rapidly returning to form.

'It means mischief,' said Alleyn.

The colonel in a stronger voice said: 'Could there be some air?'

The curtain was not drawn across the window under which they had found him. The rain still beat against it. Alleyn said: 'Are you sure?'

Mrs Forrester said: 'We always have it open at the top. Moult does it before he goes to bed. Two inches from the top. Always.'

Alleyn found that it was unlatched. He put the heels of his hands under the top sash in the lower frame and couldn't budge it. He tried to raise it by the two brass loops at the base but with no success.

'You must push up the bottom in order to lower the top,' Mrs Forrester observed.

That's what I'm trying to do.'

'You can't be. It works perfectly well.'

'It doesn't, you know.'

'Fiddle,' said Mrs Forrester.

The exclamation was intended contemptuously but he followed it like an instruction. He fiddled. His fingers explored the catch and ran along the junction of the two sashes.

'It's wedged,' he said.

'What?'

There's a wedge between the sashes.'

'Take it out.'

'Wait a bit, Mrs Forrester,' said Alleyn. 'You just wait a bit.'

'Why?'

'Because I say,' he replied and the astounded Troy saw that Mrs Forrester relished this treatment.

'I suppose,' she snapped, 'you think you know what you're about.'

'What is it, B?' asked her husband. 'Is something wrong with the window?'

'It's being attended to.'

'It's awfully stiff. Awfully stiff.'

Alleyn returned to the bed. 'Colonel Forrester,' he said. 'Did you wrestle with the window? With your hands above your head? Straining and shoving?'

'You needn't rub it in,' said the colonel.

'Fred!' cried his wife, 'what *am* I to do with you? I said – '

'Sorry, B.'

'I'll open the other window,' Alleyn said. 'I want this one left as it is. Please. It's important. You do understand, don't you? Both of you? No touching?'

'Of course, of course, of course,' the colonel drawled. His eyes were shut. His voice was drowsy. 'When he isn't the White Knight,' Troy thought, 'he's the Dormouse.'

His wife put his hands under the bedclothes, gave him a sharp look and joined Alleyn and Troy at the far end of the room.

'What's all this about wedges?' she demanded.

'The houseman or whatever he is – '

'Yes. Very well. Nigel.'

'Nigel. He may have wedged the sashes to stop the windows rattling in the storm.'

'I dare say.'

'If so, he only wedged one.'

As if in confirmation, the second window in the Forresters' bedroom suddenly beat a tattoo.

'Ours haven't been wedged,' said Troy.

'Nor has the dressing-room. May I borrow those scissors on your table? Thank you.'

He pulled a chair up to the window, took off his shoes, stood on it and by gentle manipulation eased a closely folded cardboard wedge from between the sashes. Holding it by the extreme tip he carried it to the dressing-table.

'It looks like a chemist's carton,' he said. 'Do you recognize it? Please don't touch.'

'It's the thing his pills come in. It was a new bottle.'

Alleyn fetched an envelope from the writing-table, slid the wedge into it and pocketed it.

He put on his shoes and replaced the chair. 'Remember,' he said, 'don't touch the window and don't let Nigel touch it. Mrs Forrester, will you be all right, now? Is there anything we can do?'

She sat down at her dressing-table and leant her head on her hand. With her thin grey plait dangling and bald patches showing on her scalp she looked old and very tired.

'Thank you,' she said. 'Nothing. We shall be perfectly all right.'

'Are you sure?' Troy asked and touched her shoulder.

'Yes, my dear,' she said. 'I'm quite sure. You've been very kind.' She roused herself sufficiently to give Alleyn one of her looks. 'So have you,' she said, 'as far as that goes. Very.'

'Do you know,' he said, 'if I were you I'd turn the keys in the doors. You don't want to be disturbed do you?'

She looked steadily at him and after a moment shook her head. 'And I know perfectly well what you're thinking,' she said.

II

When Alleyn arrived downstairs it was to a scene of activity. Superintendent Wrayburn now dressed in regulation waterproofs was giving instructions to five equally waterproofed constables. Two prison warders and two dogs of super-caninely sharp aspect waited inside the main entrance. Hilary stood in front of one of the fires looking immensely perturbed.

'Ah!' he cried on seeing Alleyn. 'Here you are! We were beginning to wonder – '

Alleyn said that there had been one or two things to attend to upstairs, that the colonel had been unwell but was all right again and that he and Mrs Forrester had retired for the night.

'Oh, *Lor*!' Hilary said. 'That too! Are you sure he's all right? Poor Uncle Flea, but how awkward.'

'He's all right.'

Alleyn joined Wrayburn who made quite a thing of, as it were, presenting the troops for inspection. He then drew Alleyn aside and in a portentous murmur, said that conditions out of doors were now so appalling that an exhaustive search of the grounds was virtually impossible. He suggested however, that they should make a systematic exploration of the area surrounding the house and extend it as far beyond as seemed feasible. As for the dogs and their handlers, Wrayburn said, did Alleyn think that there was anything to be got out of laying them on with one of the boots in the cloakroom and seeing if anything came of it? Not, he added, that he could for the life of him believe that anything would.

Alleyn agreed to this. 'You've got a filthy night for it,' he said to the men. 'Make what you can of a bad job. You do understand the position, of course. The man's missing. He may be injured. He may be dead. There may be a capital charge involved: there may not. In any case it's urgent. If we could have afforded to leave it till daylight, we would have done so. As it is – do your best. Mr Wrayburn will give you your instructions. Thank you in advance for carrying out a foul assignment.'

To the handlers he made suitable acknowledgments and was at some pains to put them in the picture.

'On present evidence,' he said, 'the missing man was last seen in that cloakroom over there. He may have gone outdoors, he may have gone upstairs. We don't know where he went. Or how. Or in what state. I realize, of course, that under these conditions as far as the open ground is concerned there can be nothing for the dogs to pick up but there may be something in the entrance porch. If for instance, you can find more than two separate tracks, that would be something, and you might cast round the front and sides of the west wing, especially about the broken conservatory area. I'll join you when you do that. In the meantime Mr Wrayburn will show you the ropes. All right?'

'Very good, sir,' they said.

'All right, Jack,' Alleyn said. 'Over to you.'

Wrayburn produced the fur-lined boot – an incongruous and somehow rather piteous object – from under his cape and consulted with the handlers. The front doors were opened, letting in the uproar of the Nor'-west Buster and letting out the search parties.

Fractured torch beams zigzagged across the rain. Alleyn shut out the scene and said to Hilary: 'And now, if you please, I'll talk to the staff.'

'Yes. All right. I'll ring – '

'Are they in their own quarters – the staff common-room, you call it, don't you?'

'Yes. I think so. Yes, yes, they are.'

'I'll see them there.'

'Shall I come?'

'No need. Better not, I think.'

'Alleyn: I do beg that you won't – won't – '

'I shall talk to them exactly as I shall talk to any one of you. With no foregone conclusions and without prejudice.'

'Oh. Oh, I see. Yes. Well, good. But – look here, don't let's beat about the bush. I mean, you do think – don't you? – that there's been – violence?'

'When one finds blood and hair on the business end of a poker the thought does occur, doesn't it?'

'Oh Lord!' said Hilary. 'Oh Lord, Lord, Lord, what a *bore* it all is! What a disgusting, devastating *bore*!'

'That's one way of putting it. The staff-room's at the back through there, isn't it? I'll find my own way.'

'I'll wait in the study, then.'

'Do.'

Beyond the traditional green baize door was a passage running behind the hall, from the chapel at the rear of the west wing to the serveries and kitchen at the rear of the dining-room in the east wing. Alleyn, guided by a subdued murmur of voices, tapped on a central door and opened it.

'May I come in?' he asked.

It was a large, comfortable room with an open fire, a television and a radio. On the walls hung reproductions of post-impressionist paintings, chosen, Alleyn felt sure, by Hilary. There were book-shelves lined with reading matter that proclaimed Hilary's hopes for the intellectual stimulation of his employees. On a central table was scattered a heterogeneous company of magazines that perhaps reflected, more accurately, their natural inclination.

The apple-cheeked boy was watching television, the five members of the regular staff sat round the fire, their chairs close together. As

Alleyn came in they got to their feet with the air of men who have been caught offside. Cuthbert moved towards him and then stood still.

Alleyn said: 'I thought it would be easier if we talked this business over here where we won't be interrupted. May we sit down?'

Cuthbert, with a quick look at the others, pulled back the central chair. Alleyn thanked him and took it. The men shuffled their feet. A slightly distorted voice at the other end of the room shouted 'What you guys waitin' for? Less go.'

'Turn that off,' Cuthbert commanded in his great voice, 'and come over here.'

The rosy boy switched off the television set and slouched, blushing, towards them.

'Sit down, all of you,' Alleyn said. 'I won't keep you long.'

They sat down and he got a square look at them. At Cuthbert: once a head-waiter who had knifed his wife's lover in the hanging days and narrowly escaped the rope: swarthy, fattish, baldish and with an air of consequence about him. At Mervyn, the ex-signwriter, booby-trap expert, a dark, pale man who stooped and looked sidelong. At Wilfred, nicknamed Kittiwee, whose mouth wore the shadow of a smirk, who loved cats and had bashed a warder to death. At Slyboots and Smartypants, who lay along his ample thighs, fast asleep. At Nigel, pallid as uncooked pastry, almost an albino, possibly a lapsed religious maniac, who had done a sinful lady. Finally at Vincent now seen by Alleyn for the first time at Halberds and instantly recognized since he himself had arrested him when, as gardener to an offensive old lady, he had shut her up in a green-house heavy with arsenical spray. His appeal, based on the argument that she had been concealed by a date-palm and that he was unaware of her presence, was successful and he was released. At the time Alleyn had been rather glad of it. Vincent was a bit ferrety in the face and gnarled as to the hands.

They none of them looked at Alleyn.

'The first thing I have to say,' he said, 'is this. You know that I know who you are and that you've all been inside and what the convictions were. You,' he said to Vincent, 'may say you're in a different position from the others, having been put in the clear, but where this business is concerned and at this stage of the enquiry, you're *all* in the clear. By this I mean that your past records, as far as I can see at the moment, are of no interest and they'll go on being uninteresting unless anything crops up to make me think otherwise. A man has disappeared. We don't know why, how, when or where and we've got to find him. To use the stock phrase, alive or dead. If I say I hope one or more or all of you can help us I don't mean, repeat *don't* mean, that one or more or all of you is or are suspected of having had anything to do with his disappearance. I mean what I say: I'm here to see if you can think of anything at all, however trivial, that will give us a lead, however slight. In this respect you're on an equal footing with every other member of the household. Is that understood?'

The silence was long enough to make him wonder if there was to be no response. At last Cuthbert said: 'It's *understood*, sir, I suppose, by all of us.'

'But not necessarily believed? Is that it?'

This time the silence was unbroken. 'Well,' he said, 'I can't blame you. It's a natural reaction. I can only hope you will come to accept the proposition.'

He turned to the boy who stood apart looking guarded. 'You're a local chap, aren't you?' Alleyn said.

He extracted with some difficulty that the boy, whose name was Thomas Appleby, was a farmer's son engaged for the festive season. He had never spoken to Moult, had with the other servants come into the drawing-room for the Christmas tree, had had no idea who the Druid was, had received his present and had returned to his kitchen and outhouse duties as soon as the ceremony ended and had nothing whatever to offer in the way of information. Alleyn said he could go off to bed, an invitation he seemed to accept with some reluctance.

When he had gone Alleyn told the men what he had learnt about their movements at the time of the Christmas tree: that they too had seen the Druid, failed to recognize him, received their gifts and returned to their duties. 'I understand,' he said, 'that you, cook, with the extra women helpers, completed the arrangements for the children's supper and that you saw Miss Tottenham return to the drawing-room but didn't see anything of Moult. Is that right?'

'Yes, it is,' said Kittiwee, setting his dimples. 'And I was concerned with my own business, if I may put it that way, sir, and couldn't be expected to be anything else.'

'Quite so. And you,' Alleyn said to Vincent, 'did exactly what it had been arranged you should do in respect of the tree. At half past seven you stationed yourself round the corner of the west wing. Right?'

Vincent nodded.

'Tell me, while you were there did anyone throw open a window in the west frontage and look out? Do you remember?'

''Course I remember,' said Vincent who had an indeterminate accent and a bronchial voice. 'He did. To see if I was there like he said he would. At seven-thirty.'

'The colonel? Or Moult?'

'I wouldn't know, would I? I took him for the colonel because I expected him to be the colonel, see?'

'Was he wearing his beard?'

'I never took no notice. He was black-like against the light.'

'Did he wave or signal in any way?'

'I waved according, giving him the office to come down. According. Now they was all in the drawing-room. And he waved back, see, and I went round to the front. According.'

'Good. Your next move was to tow the sledge round the corner and across the courtyard, where you were met by Moult whom you took to be Colonel Forrester. Where exactly did you meet him?'

Behind Nigel's effigy, it appeared. There, Vincent said, he relieved the Druid of his umbrella and handed over the sledge and there he waited until the Druid returned.

'So you missed the fun?' Alleyn remarked.

'I wouldn't of bothered anyway,' said Vincent.

'You waited for him to come out and then you took over the sledge and he made off through the porch and the door into the cloakroom? Right.'

'That's what I told Mr Bill-Tasman and that's what I tell everyone else who keeps on about it, don'I?'

'Did you give him back the umbrella?'

'No. He scarpered off smartly.'

'Where were you exactly when you saw him go into the cloak-room?'

'Where was I? Where would I be? Out in the bloody snow, that's where.'

'Behind the effigy?'

'Hey!' said Vincent flaring up. 'You trying to be funny? You trying to make a monkey outa me? You said no funny business, that's what you said.'

'I'm not making the slightest attempt to be funny. I'm simply trying to get the picture.'

'How could I see him if I was be'ind the bloody statcher?'

Cuthbert, in his great voice, said: 'Choose your words,' and Kittiwee said: 'Language!'

'You could have looked round the corner, I imagine, or even peered over the top,' Alleyn suggested.

Vincent, in a tremulous sulk, finally revealed that he saw Moult go through the cloakroom door as he, Vincent, was about to conceal the sledge round the corner of the west wing.

Alleyn asked when the Christmas tree was demolished and Cuthbert said this was effected by Vincent, Nigel and the boy while the party was at dinner. The children had finished their supper and had been let loose, with their presents, in the library. The ornaments were stripped from the tree, packed into their boxes and removed. The tree itself, on its movable base, was wheeled out through the french windows, and the curtains were drawn to conceal it.

'And there it remained, I suppose. Until when?'

Another long silence.

'Well,' Alleyn said cheerfully, 'it's not there now. It's round the corner outside the study window. Who put it there? Did you, Vincent?'

He hung fire but finally conceded that he had moved the tree. 'When?' Alleyn asked, remembering Troy's midnight observation from her window. Vincent couldn't say exactly when. It emerged that after the dining-room had been cleared, the mammoth washing-up disposed of and the rest of the exhaustive chores completed, the staff, with the outside help, had sat down to a late supper. Vincent, upon whose forehead a thread of minute sweat-beads had come into being, said that he'd been ordered by Mr Bill-Tasman to clear away the tree because, Alleyn gathered, the sight of it, denuded and disreputable, would be too anti-climactic. In all the fuss Vincent had forgotten to do so until he was going to bed.

He had put on his oilskins, fetched a wheelbarrow from the woodshed, collected the tree and dumped it in the wreckage of the old conservatory.

'Why there?' Alleyn asked.

With an air strangely compounded of truculence and something that might be fear Vincent asked at large where he was expected to take it in the dead of night.

It would be shifted anyway, he said, when the bulldozers got round to making a clean sweep of all that glass and muck, which they were due to do any day now, for filling in their excavations.

Alleyn said: 'I'm sure you know, all of you, don't you, why you were asked to search the area where the tree lies? It was because it was thought that Moult might have wandered there and collapsed or even, for some reason, leant too far out of an upstairs window and fallen.'

'What an idea!' said Kittiwee and tittered nervously.

Vincent said that half a dozen bloody Moults might have fallen in that lot and he wouldn't have seen them. He had tipped the tree out and slung his hook.

'Tell me,' Alleyn said, looking round the circle, 'you must have seen quite a lot of Moult off and on? All of you?'

If they had been so many oysters and he had poked them, they couldn't have shut up more smartly. They looked anywhere but at him and they said nothing.

'Come – ' he began and was interrupted by Nigel, who suddenly proclaimed in a high nasal twang: 'He was a sinner before the Lord.'

'Shut up,' said Mervyn savagely.

'He was given to all manner of mockery and abomination.'

'Oh, *do* stop him, somebody!' Kittiwee implored. He struck out with his legs and the cats, indignant, sprang to the ground. Kittiwee made faces at Alleyn to indicate that Nigel was not in full possession of his wits.

'In what way,' Alleyn asked Nigel, 'was Moult an abomination?'

'He was filled with malice,' muttered Nigel who appeared to be at a slight loss for anathemas. 'To the brim,' he added.

'Against whom?'

'Against the righteous,' Nigel said quickly.

'Meaning you,' said Mervyn. 'Belt up, will you?'

Cuthbert said: 'That's quite enough, Nigel. You're exciting yourself and you know what it leads to.' He turned to Alleyn. 'I'm sure, sir,' he boomed, 'you can see how it is, here. We've been over-stimulated and we're a little above ourselves.'

'We're all abominations before the Lord,' Nigel suddenly announced. 'And I'm the worst of the lot.' His lips trembled. 'Sin lies bitter in my belly,' he said.

'Stuff it!' Mervyn shouted and then, with profound disgust. 'O Gawd, now he's going to cry!'

And cry poor Nigel did, noisily, into a handkerchief held to the lower half of his face like a yashmak. Over this he gazed dolorously at Alleyn through wet, white eyelashes.

'Now, look here, Nigel,' Alleyn said. 'Listen to me. No,' he added quickly anticipating a further demonstration. 'Listen. You say you're a sinner. All right. So you may be. Do you want to cleanse your bosom or your belly or whatever it is, of its burden? Well, come on, man. Do you?'

Without removing the handkerchief, Nigel nodded repeatedly.

'Very well, then. Instead of all this nonsense, how about helping us save another sinner who, for all you know, may be out there dying of exposure?'

Nigel blew his nose and dabbed at his eyes.

'Come on,' Alleyn pressed. 'How about it?'

Nigel seemed to take counsel with himself. He gazed mournfully at Alleyn for some moments and then said: 'It's a judgment.'

'On Moult? Why?'

There was no marked – there was scarcely any discernible – movement among the other four men: it was more as if they jointly held their breath and barely saved themselves from leaning forward.

'He was a wine-bibber,' Nigel shouted. 'Wine is a mocker. Strong drink is raging.'

And now there was a distinct reaction: an easing of tension, a shifting of feet, a leaning back in chairs, a clearing of throats.

'Is that the case?' Alleyn asked at large. 'What do you say? Cuthbert? Do you agree?'

'Allowing for the extravagant style of expression, sir,' Cuthbert conceded, 'I would say it is the case.'

'He tippled?'

'He did, sir, yes. Heavily.'

'Have you any reason to think, any of you, that he had taken more than was good for him yesterday afternoon?'

Suddenly they were loquacious. Moult, they said, had undoubtedly been tippling all day. Mervyn volunteered that he had seen Moult sneak out of the dining-room and had subsequently discovered that the whisky decanter on the sideboard which he had only lately filled had been half emptied. Kittiwee had an unclear story about the total disappearance of a bottle of cooking brandy from the pantry. Vincent unpersuasively recollected that when Moult met him, in the Druidical array, he had smelt very strongly of alcohol. Cuthbert adopted a patronizing and Olympic attitude. He said that while this abrupt spate of witness to Mr Moult's inebriety was substantially correct he thought it only proper to add that while Mr Moult habitually took rather more than was good for him, yesterday's excesses were abnormal.

'Do you think,' Alleyn said, 'that Colonel and Mrs Forrester know of this failing?'

'Oh, really, sir,' Cuthbert said with a confidential deference that clearly derived from his head-waiter days, 'you know how it is. If I may say so, the colonel is a very unworldly gentleman.'

'And Mrs Forrester?'

Cuthbert spread his hands and smirked. 'Well, sir,' he said. 'The ladies!' which seemed to suggest, if it suggested anything, that the ladies were quicker at spotting secret drinkers than the gentlemen.

'While I think of it,' Alleyn said. 'Colonel Forrester has had another attack. Something to do with his heart, I understand. It seems he really brought it upon himself trying to open their bedroom window. He didn't,' Alleyn said to Nigel who had left off crying, 'notice the wedge and tried to force it. He's better but it was a severe attack.'

Nigel's lips formed the word 'wedge'. He looked utterly bewildered.

'Didn't you wedge it, then? To stop it rattling in the storm? When you shut up their room for the night?'

He shook his head. 'I never!' he said. 'I shut it, but I never used no wedge.' He seemed in two minds whether to cut up rough again or go into an aimless stare. 'You seen me,' he muttered, 'when you come in.'

'So I did. You were wet. The window came down with a crash, didn't it, as I walked in.'

Nigel stared at him and nodded.

'Why?' Alleyn asked.

Again, a feeling of general consternation.

Nigel said: 'To see.'

'To see what?'

'They don't tell me anything!' Nigel burst out. 'I seen them talking, I heard.'

'What?'

'Things,' he said and became sulky and uncommunicative.

'Odd!' Alleyn said without emphasis. 'I suppose none of you knows who wedged the colonel's window? No? Ah, well, it'll no doubt emerge in due course. There's only one other thing I'd like to ask you. All of you. And before I ask it I want to remind you of what I said at the beginning. I do most earnestly beg you not to think I'm setting a trap for you, not to believe I'm influenced in the smallest degree by your past histories. All right. Now, I expect you all know about the booby-trap that was set for my wife. Did you tell them about it, Cox?'

After a considerable pause, Mervyn said: 'I mentioned it, sir,' and then burst out: 'Madam knows I didn't do it. Madam believes me. I wouldn't of done it, not to her, I wouldn't. What would I do it to her for? You ask madam, sir. She'll tell you.'

'All right, all right, nobody's said you did it. But if you didn't, and I accept for the sake of argument that you didn't, who did? Any ideas?'

Before Mervyn could reply, Nigel came roaring back into action.

'With malice aforethought, he done it,' Nigel shouted.

'Who?'

The other four men all began to talk at once: their object very clearly being to shut Nigel up. They raised quite a clamour between them. Alleyn stopped it by standing up: if he had yelled at the top of his voice it would have been less effective.

'Who,' he asked Nigel, 'did it with malice aforethought?'

'You leave me alone. Come not between the avenger and his wrath, or it'll be the worse for all of us.'

'Nobody's interrupting you,' Alleyn said and indeed it was true. They were turned off like taps.

'Come on, Nigel,' Alleyn said. 'Who was it?'

'Him. Him that the wrath of the Almighty has removed from the midst.'

'Moult?'

'That's perfectly correct,' said Nigel with one of his plummet-like descents into the commonplace.

From this point, the interview took on a different complexion. Nigel withdrew into a sort of omniscient gloom, the others into a mulish determination to dissociate themselves from any opinion upon any matter that Alleyn might raise. Cuthbert, emerging as a reluctant spokesman, said there was proof – and he emphasized the word – that Moult had set the booby-trap and upon Nigel uttering in a loud voice the word 'Spite', merely repeated his former pantomime to indicate Nigel's total irresponsibility. Alleyn asked if Moult was, in fact, a spiteful or vindictive character and they all behaved as if they didn't know what he was talking about. He decided to take a risk. He said that no doubt they all knew about the anonymous and insulting messages that had been left in the Forresters' and Cressida Tottenham's rooms and the lacing of Mr Smith's barley water with soap.

They would have liked, he thought, to deny all knowledge of these matters but he pressed them and gradually collected that Cressida had talked within hearing of Blore, that Mr Smith had roundly tackled Nigel and that Moult himself had 'mentioned' the incidents.

'When?' Alleyn asked.

Nobody seemed exactly to remember when.

'Where?'

They were uncertain where.

'Was it here, in the staff common-room, yesterday morning?'

This, he saw, had alarmed and bewildered them. Nigel said 'How – ?' and stopped short. They glared at him.

'How did I know, were you going to say?' said Alleyn. 'It seems the conversation was rather noisy. It was overheard. And Moult was seen leaving by that door over there. You'd accused him, hadn't you, of playing these tricks with the deliberate intention of getting you into trouble?'

'We've no call to answer that,' Vincent said. 'That's what you say. It's not what we say. We don't say nothing.'

'Come,' Alleyn said, 'you all disliked him, didn't you? It was perfectly apparent. You disliked him and his general attitude gave you some cause to do so.'

'Be that as it may, sir,' said Cuthbert, 'it is no reason for supposing the staff had anything to do with – ' His enormous voice trembled. He made a violent dismissive gesture ' – with whatever he's done or wherever he's gone.'

'I agree. It doesn't follow.'

'We went our way, sir, and Mr Moult went his.'

'Quite. Where to? What was Mr Moult's way and where did it take him? That's the question, isn't it?'

'If you'll excuse the liberty,' Kittiwee said, 'that's your business, sir. Not ours.'

'Of course it's my business,' Alleyn cheerfully rejoined. 'Otherwise, you know, I shouldn't waste half an hour butting my head against a concrete wall. To sum up. None of you knows anything about or is prepared to discuss, the matter of the insulting messages, booby-trap, soapy barley water or wedged window. Nor is anyone prepared to enlarge upon the row that took place in this room yesterday morning. Apart from Nigel's view that Moult was steeped in sin and, more specifically, alcohol (which you all support), you've nothing to offer. You've no theories about his disappearance and you don't appear to care whether he's alive or dead. Correct?'

Silence.

'Right. Not only is this all my eye and Betty Martin but it's extremely damaging to what I'd hoped would be a sensible relationship between us. And on top of all that it's so bloody silly that I wonder you've got the faces to go on with it. Goodnight to you.'

III

Mr Wrayburn was in the hall, pregnant with intelligence of police dogs and fur-lined boots. The dog Buck who sat grinning competently beside his handler had picked up two separate tracks from the cloakroom and across the sheltered porch, agreeing in direction with the Druidical progress. 'There and back,' said Wrayburn, 'I suppose.'

But there had been no other rewarding scents. An attempt within doors had been unproductive owing, Alleyn supposed, to a sort of canine *embarras de richesse*. All that could be taken from this, Mr Wrayburn complained, was the fact, known already, that Moult left the cloakroom and returned to it and that unless he was carried out or changed his boots, he didn't leave by the porch door a second time.

Alleyn said: 'Try one of the slippers from Moult's room: see what comes of that.'

'I don't get you.'

Alleyn explained. Wrayburn stared at him. 'I see,' he said. 'Yes, I see.'

The slipper was fetched and introduced to the dog Buck, who made a dutiful response. He was then taken to the porch and court-yard where he nosed to and fro swinging his tail but obviously at a loss. The second dog, Mack, was equally uninterested. When taken to the cloakroom, however, they both produced positive and energetic reaction over the main area but ignored the fellow of the fur-lined boot and the floor under the make-up bench.

'Well,' Wrayburn said, 'we know he was in here, don't we? Not only when he was being got up for the party but earlier when he was fixing the room, for the colonel. Still – it looks as if you're right, by gum it does. What next?'

'I'm afraid we'll have to tackle that mess that was once a conser-vatory, Jack. How's the search over the grounds going?'

'As badly as could be expected under these conditions. The chaps are doing their best but if he's lying out in that lot they could miss him over and over again. Didn't this bunch of homicides have a go at the conservatory wreckage?'

'So we're told. With forks and spades. Thundering over the terrain like a herd of dinosaurs, I dare say. I think we must have a go. After all, we can't rule out the possibility that he was hit on the head and stunned.'

'And wandered away? And collapsed?'

'You name it! Hold on while I get my macintosh.'

'You'll need gum-boots.'

'See if there are any stray pairs in the other cloakroom, will you? I won't be long.'

When Alleyn had collected his macintosh and a futile hat from his dressing-room he called on his wife.

He was surprised and not over-delighted to find Cressida Tottenham there, clothed in a sea-green garment that stuck to her like a limpet where it was most explicit and elsewhere erupted in superfluous frills.

'Look who's here!' Cressida said, raising her arm to a vertical position and flapping her hand. 'My Favourite Man! Hullo, Heart-throb!'

'Hullo, Liar,' he mildly returned.

'*Rory!*' Troy protested.

'Sorry.'

'*Manners,* Jungle Cat,' said Cressida. 'Not that I object. It all ties in with the groovy image. The ruder they are, the nearer your undoing.'

Troy burst out laughing. 'Do you often,' she asked, 'make these frontal attacks?'

'Darling: only when roused by a Gorgeous Brute. Do you mind?'

'Not a bit.'

Alleyn said: 'Gorgeous Brute or not, I'm on the wing, Troy.'

'So I see.'

'Think nothing of it if you notice a commotion under your windows.'

'Right.'

'We've been brushing our hair,' Cressida offered, 'and emptying our bosoms. Ever so cosy.'

'Have you, indeed. By the way, Miss Tottenham, while I think of it: what did you wear on your feet when you made Moult up in the cloakroom?'

'On my *feet*?' she asked and showed him one of them in a bejewelled slipper. 'I wore golden open-toed sandals, Mr Alleyn, and golden toenails to go with my handsome gold dress.'

'Chilly,' he remarked.

'My dear – arctic! So much so, I may tell you, that I thrust my ten little pigs into Uncle Flea's fur-lined trotters.'

'Damn!'

'Really? But why?' She reflected for a moment. 'My dear!' Cressida repeated, making eyes at Troy, 'it's the smell! Isn't it? Those wolfish dogs! I've mucked up poor Mr Moult's footwork for them. Admit!'

'Presumably you swapped for the performance?'

'But of course. And I'm sure his feet will have triumphed over mine or does my skin scent beat him to the post?'

Ignoring this, Alleyn made for the door and then stopped short. 'I almost forgot,' he said. 'When did you come upstairs?'

Cressida blew out her cheeks and pushed up the tip of her nose with one finger. The effect was of an extremely cheeky zephyr.

'Come on,' Alleyn said. 'When? How long ago?'

'*Well. Now.* When did I?'

'You came in here ten minutes ago, if it's any guide,' Troy said. 'I'd just wound my watch.'

'And you'd been in your room,' Alleyn said. 'How long?' He glanced at her. 'Long enough to change your clothes.'

'Which is no slight matter,' Cressida said. 'Say twenty minutes. It was getting a bit of a drag in the library. Hilly's lost his cool over the sleuthing scene and Uncle Bert Smith doesn't exactly send one. So I came up.'

'Did you meet anybody on the way?'

'I certainly did. I met that ass Nigel at the head of the stairs, bellowing away about sin. I suppose you've heard how he pushed a sexy note under my door? About me being a sinful lady?'

'You feel certain he wrote it?'

'Who else would?' Cressida reasoned. 'Whatever they might think. It's his theme-song, isn't it – the sinful lady bit?'

'Very much so. When did you go down to dinner?'

'I don't know. Last, as usual, I expect.'

'Did you at any stage meet anybody going into or coming out of the Forresters' rooms?'

Cressida helplessly flapped her arms. 'Yes,' she said. 'Nigel again. Coming out. He'd been doing his turning down the bed lot. This time he only shrank back against the wall as if I had infective hepatitis.'

'Thank you,' Alleyn said. 'I must be off.' He looked at his wife. 'All right?' he asked.

'All right.'

When he had gone Cressida said. 'Let's face it, darling. I'm wasting my powder.'

CHAPTER 8

Moult

Before he went out into the night, Alleyn visited the study and found it deserted. He turned on all the lights, opened the window curtains, and left, locking the door behind him and putting the key in his pocket. He listened for a moment or two outside the library door and heard the drone of two male voices topped by Mr Smith's characteristic short bark of laughter. Then he joined Wrayburn, who waited in the great porch with four of his men and the two handlers with their dogs. They moved out into the open courtyard.

'Rain's lifted,' Wrayburn shouted. It had spun itself into a thin, stinging drive. The noise out of doors was immense: a roar without definition as if all the trees at Halberds had been given voices with which to send themselves frantic. A confused sound of water mingled with this. There were whistles and occasional clashes as of metal objects that had been blown out of their places and clattered about wildly on their own account.

Nigel's monument was dissolving into oblivion. The recumbent figure, still recognizable, was horridly mutilated.

They rounded the front of the west wing, and turned into the full venom of the wind.

The library windows were curtained and emitted only thin blades of light and the breakfast-room was in darkness. But from the study a flood of lamplight caught the sapling fir, lashing itself to and fro distractedly, and the heaps of indeterminate rubble that surrounded it. Broken glass, cleaned by the rain, refracted the light confusedly.

Their faces were whipped by the wind, intermittent shafts of rain and pieces of blown litter. The men had powerful search-lamps and played them over the area. They met on the discarded Christmas tree and searched the great heaps of rubble and patches of nettle and docks. They found, all over the place, evidence of Hilary's men with their forks and shovels and trampling boots. They explored the sapling fir and remained, focused on it, while Alleyn with his back to the wind peered up into the branches. He saw, as he had already seen from the dressing-room window, that the tender ones were bent into uncouth positions. He actually found in a patch of loamy earth beneath the study window, prints of Hilary's smart shoes where he had climbed over the sill to retrieve the poker.

He took a light, moved up to the tree and searched its inward parts. After a minute or two he called to one of the men and asked him to hold the light steady as it was. He had to yell into the man's ear so boisterous was the roar of the wind.

The man took the light and Alleyn began to climb the tree. He kept as close as he could to the trunk where the young boughs were strongest. Wet pine needles brushed his face. Cascades of snow fell about his neck and shoulders. Branches slapped at him and he felt resin sticking to his hands. As he climbed, the tree swayed, he with it, and the light moved. He shifted round the trunk and hauled himself upward.

Suddenly an oblong sliver of fresh light appeared below and to his right. There was Hilary Bill-Tasman's face, upturned and staring at Alleyn. He had come to the library window.

Cursing, Alleyn grasped the now slender trunk with his left hand, leant outward and looked up. Dislodged snow fell into his face.

There it was. He reached up with his right hand, touched it, made a final effort and secured it. His fingers were so cold that he could scarcely feel sure of his capture. He put it in his mouth and, slithering, swaying and scrambling, came down to earth.

He moved round until the tree was between him and the library window and warmed his hands at the lamp. Wrayburn, standing close by said something Alleyn could not catch and jerked his thumb in the direction of the library. Alleyn nodded, groped in his mouth and extracted a slender strip of metallic gold. He opened his macintosh and tucked it away in the breast pocket of his jacket.

'Come indoors,' he signalled.

They had moved away and were heading back to the front of the house when they were caught in the beams of two lights. Above the general racket and clamour they heard themselves hailed.

The lights jerked, swayed and intensified as they approached. The men behind them suddenly plunged into the group. Alleyn shone his torch into their excited faces.

'What's up?' Wrayburn shouted. 'Here? What's all the excitement?'

'We've found 'im, Mr Wrayburn, we've seen 'im! We've got 'im.'

'Where?'

'Laying on the hillside, up yonder. I left my mate to see to 'im.'

'Which hillside?' Alleyn bawled.

'Acrost there, sir. On the way to The Vale Road.'

'Come on, then,' said Wrayburn excitedly.

The whole party set off along the cinder path that Troy so often had taken on her afternoon walks.

They had not gone far before they saw a stationary light and a recumbent figure clearly visible spread-eagled and face down in the snow. Someone was stooping over it. As they drew near, the stooping figure rose and began to kick the recumbent one.

'My God!' Wrayburn roared out, 'what's he doing! My *God*! Is he mad! Stop him.'

He turned to Alleyn and found him doubled up.

The man on the hillside, caught in his own torchlight, gave two or three more tentative kicks to the prostrate form and then with an obvious effort, administered a brief and mighty punt that sent it careering into the gale. It gesticulated wildly and disintegrated. Wisps of rank, wet straw were blown into their faces.

Hilary would have to find another scarecrow.

II

A further ill-tempered, protracted and exhaustive search turned out to be useless and at five minutes past twelve they returned to the house.

The rest of the search party had come in with nothing to report. They all piled up a shining heap of wet gear and lamps in the porch, left the two dogs in the unfurnished west wing cloakroom and, in their stockinged feet entered the hall. The over-efficient central heating of Halberds received them like a Turkish bath.

Hilary, under a hard drive of hospitality, came fussing out from the direction of the library. He was full of commiseration and gazed anxiously into one frozen face after another, constantly turning to Alleyn as if to call witness to his own distress.

'Into the dining-room! Everybody. Do, do, do, do,' cried Hilary, dodging about like a sheepdog. And, rather sheepishly, the search party allowed itself to be mustered.

The dining-room table displayed a cold collation that would have done honour to Dingley Dell. On a side table was ranked an assembly of bottles: whisky, rum, brandy, Alleyn saw, and a steaming kettle. If Hilary had known how, Alleyn felt, he would have set about brewing a punch bowl. As it was he implored Wrayburn to superintend the drinks and set himself to piling up a wild selection of cold meats on plates.

None of the servants appeared at this feast.

Mr Smith came in, however, and looked on with his customary air of sardonic amusement and sharp appraisal. Particularly, Alleyn thought, did Mr Smith observe his adopted nephew. What did he make of Hilary and his antics? Was there a kind of ironic affection, an exasperation at Hilary's mannerisms and – surely? – an underlying anxiety? Hilary made a particularly effusive foray upon Wrayburn and a group of disconcerted subordinates who stopped chewing and stared at their socks. Mr Smith caught Alleyn's eye and winked.

The dining-room became redolent of exotic smells.

Presently Wrayburn made his way to Alleyn.

'Will it be all right, now,' he asked, 'if I get these chaps moving? The stream's coming down very fresh and we don't want to be marooned, do we?'

'Of course you don't. I hope my lot get through all right.'

'When do you expect them?'

'I should think by daylight. They're driving through the night. They'll look in at the station.'

'If they're short on waders,' said Wrayburn, 'we can fix them up. They may need them.' He cleared his throat and addressed his troops: 'Well, now. Chaps.'

Hilary was effusive in farewells and at one moment seemed to totter on the brink of a speech but caught sight of Mr Smith and refrained.

Alleyn saw the men off. He thanked them for their work and told them he'd have been very happy to have carried on with their help and might even be obliged to call on them again though he was sure they hoped not. They made embarrassed but gratified noises and he watched them climb into their shining gear and file off in the direction of the vans that had brought them.

Wrayburn lingered. 'Well,' he said. 'So long, then. Been quite a pleasure.'

'Of a sort?'

'Well – '

'I'll keep in touch.'

'Hope things work out,' Wrayburn said. 'I used to think at one time of getting out of the uniformed branch but – I dunno – it didn't pan out that way. But I've enjoyed this opportunity. Know what I mean?'

'I think so.'

'Look. Before I go. Do you mind telling me what it was you fished out of that tree?'

'Of course I don't mind, Jack. There just hasn't been the opportunity.'

Alleyn reached into his breast pocket and produced, between finger and thumb, the golden strand; Wrayburn peered at it. 'We saw it from the dressing-room window,' Alleyn said.

'Metallic,' Wrayburn said. 'But not tinsel. Now what would that be? A bit of some ornamental stuff blown off the Christmas tree into the fir?'

'It was on the wrong side of the fir for that. It looks more like a shred of dress material to me.'

'It may have been there for some time.'

'Yes, of course. What does it remind you of?'

'By gum!' Wrayburn said. 'Yes – by gum. Here! Are you going to look?'

'Care to keep your troops waiting?'

'What do you think!'

'Come on, then.'

They unlocked the cloakroom door and went in. Again the smell of make-up, the wig on its improvised stand, the fur-topped boot, the marks on the carpet, the cardboard carton with the poker inside and, on its coathanger against the wall, the golden lamé robe of the Druid.

Alleyn turned it on its coathanger and once again displayed the wet and frayed back of the collar. He held his shred of material against it.

'Might be,' he said. 'It's so small one can't say. It's a laboratory job. But could be.'

He began to explore the robe, inch by inch. He hunted back and front and then turned it inside out.

'It's damp of course and wet at the bottom edge. As one would expect galloping about in the open courtyard. The hem's come unstitched here and ravelled out. Zips right down the back. Hullo! The collar's come slightly adrift. Frayed. Might be. Could be.'

'Yes, but – look, it'd be ridiculous. It doesn't add up. Not by any reckoning. The thing's *here*. In the cloakroom. When he was knocked off if he *was* knocked off, he wasn't wearing it. He couldn't have been. Unless,' said Wrayburn, 'it was taken off his body and returned to this room but that's absurd. What a muck it'd be in!'

'Yes,' Alleyn agreed absently. 'It would, wouldn't it?'

He had stooped down and was peering under the make-up bench. He pulled out a cardboard box that had been used for rubbish and put it on the bench.

'Absorbent tissues,' he said, exploring the contents. 'A chunk of rag. Wrapping paper and – hullo, what's this!'

Very gingerly he lifted out two pads of cotton wool about the shape of a medium-sized mushroom.

'Wet,' he said and bent over them. 'No smell. Pulled off that roll there by the powder-box. But what for? What the devil for?'

'Clean off the make-up?' Wrayburn hazarded.

'They're not discoloured. Only wettish. Odd!'

'I'd better not keep those chaps waiting,' Wrayburn said wistfully. 'It's been a pleasure, by and large. Made a change. Back to routine, now. Good luck, anyway.'

They shook hands and he left. Alleyn cut himself a sample of gold lamé from the hem of the robe.

He had a final look round and then locked the cloakroom. Reminded by this action of the study, he crossed the hall into the west wing corridor, unlocked the door and turned out the lights.

As he returned, the library door at the far end of the corridor opened and Mr Smith came out. He checked for a moment on seeing Alleyn and then made an arresting gesture with the palm of his hand as if he were on point duty.

Alleyn waited for him by the double-doors into the hall. Mr Smith took him by the elbow and piloted him through. The hall was lit by two dying fires and a single standard lamp below the gallery and near the foot of the right-hand stairway.

'You're up late,' Alleyn said.

'What about yourself?' he rejoined. 'Matter of fact, I thought I'd like a word with you if that's in order. 'Illy's gone up to bed. How about a nightcap?'

'Thanks very much, but no. Don't let me stop you, though.'

'I won't bother. I've had my lot and there's still my barley water to come. Though after that little how-d'ye-do the other night the mere idea tends to turn me up in advance.'

'There's been no more soap?'

'I should bloody well hope not,' said Mr Smith.

He walked up to the nearest hearth and kicked its smouldering logs together. 'Spare a moment?' he asked.

'Yes, of course.'

'If I was to ask you what's your opinion of this turn-up,' he said. 'I suppose I'd get what they call a dusty answer, would'n' I?'

'In the sense that I haven't yet formed an opinion, I suppose you would.'

'You telling me you don't know what to think?'

'Pretty much. I'm collecting.'

'What's that mean?'

'You've been a collector and a very successful one, haven't you, Mr Smith?'

'What of it?'

'There must have been times in your early days, when you had a mass of objects in stock on which you couldn't put a knowledgeable value. Some of them might be rubbish and some might be important. In all the clutter of a job lot there might be one or two authentic

TIED UP IN TINSEL

pieces. But in those days I dare say you couldn't for the life of you tell which was which.'

'All right. All right. You've made your point, chum.'

'Rather pompously, I'm afraid.'

'I wouldn't say so. But I tell you what. I pretty soon learned in my trade to take a shine on the buyer and seller even when I only had an instinct for good stuff. And I always had that, I always had a flare. You ask 'Illy. Even then I could pick if I was having a stroke pulled on me.'

Alleyn had taken out his pipe and was filling it. 'Is that what you want to tell me, Mr Smith?' he asked. 'Do you think someone's pulling a stroke on me?'

'I don't say that. They may be but I don't say so. No, my idea is that it must come in handy in your job to know what sort of characters you're dealing with. Right?'

'Are you offering,' Alleyn said lightly, 'to give me a breakdown on the inhabitants of Halberds?'

'That's your definition, not mine. All right, I'm thinking of person-alities. Like I said. Character. I'd of thought in your line character would be a big consideration.'

Alleyn fished out a glowing clinker with the fire-tongs. 'It depends,' he said, lighting his pipe. 'We deal in hard, bumpy facts and they can be stumbling-blocks in the path of apparent character. People, to coin a bromide, can be amazingly contradictory.' He looked at Mr Smith. 'All the same, if you're going to give me an expert's opinion on – ' he waved his hand ' – on the collection here assembled, I'll be very interested.'

There was no immediate answer. Alleyn looked at Mr Smith and wondered if he were to define his impression in one word, what that word would be. 'Sharp'? 'Cagey'? 'Inscrutable'? In the bald head with streaks of black hair trained across it, the small bright eyes and compressed lips, he found a predatory character. A hard man. But was that hindsight? What would he have made of Mr Smith if he'd known nothing about him?

'I assure you,' he repeated. 'I'll be very interested,' and sat down in one of two great porter's chairs that flanked the fireplace.

Mr Smith stared at him pretty fixedly. He took out his cigar-case, helped himself and sat in the other chair. To anyone coming into the hall and seeing them, they would have looked like subjects for a Christmas Annual illustration called 'Cronies'.

Mr Smith cut his cigar, removed the band, employed a gold lighter, emitted smoke and contemplated it.

'For a start,' he said. 'I was fond of Alf Moult.'

III

It was a curious little story of an odd acquaintanceship. Mr Smith knew Moult when Hilary was a young man living with the Forresters in Hans Place. The old feud had long ago died out and Mr Smith made regular visits to luncheon on Sundays. Sometimes he would arrive early before the Forresters had returned from church and Moult would show him into the colonel's study. At first Moult was very stand-offish, having a profound mistrust of persons of his own class who had hauled themselves up by their bootstraps. Gradually, however, this prejudice was watered down if never entirely obliterated, and an alliance was formed: grudging, Alleyn gathered, on Moult's part but cordial on Mr Smith's. He became somebody with whom Moult could gossip. And gossip he did, though never about the colonel to whom he was perfectly devoted.

He would talk darkly about how unnamed persons exploited the colonel, about tradesmen's perfidy and the beastliness of female servants of whom he was palpably jealous.

'By and large,' said Mr Smith, 'he *was* a jealous kind of bloke.' And waited for comment.

'Did he object to the adopted nephew under that heading?'

'To 'Illy? Well – kind of sniffy on personal lines like he made work about the place and was late for meals. That style of thing.'

'He didn't resent him?'

Mr Smith said quickly: 'No more than he did anybody else that interfered with routine. He was a caution on routine was Alf. 'Course he knew I wouldn't . . .' He hesitated.

'Wouldn't?' Alleyn prompted.

'Wouldn't listen to anything against the boy,' said Mr Smith shortly.

'How about Miss Tottenham? How did she fit in with Moult's temperament?'

'The glamour girl? I'm talking about twenty years ago. She was – what? – three? I never see 'er but they talked about 'er. She was being brought up by some posh family what was down on its uppers and needed the cash. Proper class lot. Alf used to rave about 'er and I will say the result bears 'im out.' The unelevating shadow of a leer slipped over Mr Smith's face and slid away again. 'Bit of all right,' he said.

'Has Moult ever expressed an opinion about the engagement?'

'He's human. Or was, whichever it is, poor bloke. He made out 'Illy was a very, very lucky man, and wouldn't hear a word to the contrary. That was because the colonel took an interest in 'er and nothing the colonel did was wrong in Alf's book. And it seems 'er old pot was killed saving the colonel's life, which would make 'im a bleedin' 'ero. So there you were.'

'You approve of the engagement?'

'It's not official yet, is it? Oh, yes. 'Illy's a good picker. You know. In the trade or out of it. Knows a nice piece when 'e sees one. She may be pushing the spoilt beauty bit now but he knows the answers to that one and no error. Oh, yes,' Mr Smith repeated, quizzing the tip of his cigar. 'I know about the Bill-Tasman image. Funny. Vague. Eccentric. Comes in nice and handy that lot, more ways than one. But 'e won't stand for any funny business, don't worry, in work *or* pleasure. She'll 'ave to be a good girl and I reckon she knows it.'

Alleyn waited for a moment and then said: 'I see no reason why I shouldn't tell you this. There's a theory in circulation that Moult was responsible for the practical jokes, if they can be so called.'

Mr Smith became vociferous. 'Don't give me that one, chum,' he said. 'That's just silly, that is. Alf Moult put soap in my barley water? Not on your nelly. Him and me was pals, wasn't we? Right? Well, then: arst yourself.'

'He didn't like the staff here, did he?'

''Course 'e didn't. Thought they was shockers and so they are. That lot! But that's not to say 'e'd try to put their pot on, writing silly messages and playing daft tricks. Alf Moult! Do me a favour!'

'You may not have heard,' Alleyn said, 'of all the other incidents. A booby-trap, in the Mervyn manner, set for my wife.'

'Hullo-ullo! I thought there was something there.'

'Did you? There was a much nastier performance this evening. After Nigel went his rounds and before Colonel Forrester went to bed, somebody wedged the window in their room. The strain of trying to open it brought on an attack.'

'There you are! Poor old colonel. Another turn! And *that* wasn't done by Alf Moult, was it!'

'Who would you think was responsible?'

'Nigel. Simple.'

'No. Not Nigel, Mr Smith. Nigel shut the window when I was in the room and then ran downstairs bellowing about his own troubles.'

'Came back, then.'

'I don't think so. There's too narrow a margin in time. Of course we'll want to know who was in that part of the house just then. And if anyone can – '

'"Help the police",' Mr Smith nastily suggested, '"in the execution of their duty."'

'Quite so.'

'I can't. I was in the library with 'Illy.'

'All the evening?'

'All the evening.'

'I see.'

'Look! This carry-on – notes and soap and booby-traps – brainless, innit? Nobody at home where it come from. Right? So where's the type that fits – ? Only one in this establishment and he's the one with the opportunity. Never mind the wedge. That may be different. It's obvious.'

'Nigel?'

'That's right! Must be. Mr Flippin' Nigel. In and out of the princely apart-e-mongs all day. Dropping notes and mixing soapy nightcaps.'

'We'll find out about the wedge.'

'You will?'

'Oh, yes.'

'Here! You think you know who done it? Don't you? Well – do you?'

'I've got an idea.'

'Innit marvellous?' said Mr Smith. 'Blimey, innit blinkin' marvellous!'

'Mr Smith,' Alleyn said, 'tell me something. Why do you go to such pains to preserve your original turn of speech? If it is your original style. Or, is it – I hope you'll excuse this – a sort of embellishment? To show us there's no nonsense about Bert Smith? Do forgive me – it's nothing whatever to do with the matter in hand. I've no right to ask you, but it puzzles me.'

'Look,' Mr Smith said, 'you're a peculiar kind of copper, aren't you? What's your game? What are you on about? Christ, you're peculiar!'

'There! You *are* offended. I'm sorry.'

'Who says I'm offended? I never said so, did I? All right, all right, Professor 'Iggins, you got it second time. Put it like this. I see plenty of fakes in our business, don't I? Junk tarted up to look like class? And I see plenty of characters who've got to the top same way as I did: from the bottom. But with them it's putting on the class. Talking posh. Plums in their gullets. Deceiving nobody but themselves. "Educated privately" in *Who's Who* and coming a gutser when they loose their cool and forget themselves. Not for mine. I'm me. Born Deptford. Ejjercation, where I could pick it up. Out of the gutter mostly. Me.' He waited for a moment and then, with an indescribably sly glance at Alleyn, said ruefully. 'Trouble is, I've lost touch. I'm not contemp'ry. I'm mixing with the wrong sort and it's a kind of struggle to keep the old flag flying if you can understand. P'raps I'm what they call an inverted snob. Right?'

'Yes,' Alleyn said. 'That may be it. It's an understandable foible. And we all have our affectations, don't we?'

'It's not a bloody affectation,' Mr Smith shouted and then with another of his terribly prescient glances: 'And it works,' he said. 'It rings the bell, don' it? They tell you George V took a shiner to Jimmy Thomas, don't they? Why? Because he *was* Jimmy Thomas and no beg your pardons. If 'e forgot 'imself and left an "h" in 'e went back and dropped it. Fact!' Mr Smith stood up and yawned like a chasm. 'Well, if you've finished putting the screws on me,' he said, 'I think I'll toddle. I intended going back tomorrow but if this weather keeps up I might alter me plans. So long as the telephone lines are in business, so am I.'

He moved to the foot of the stairs and looked back at Alleyn. 'Save you the trouble of keeping obbo on me, if I stay put. Right?'

'Were you ever in the Force, Mr Smith?'

'Me! A copper! Do me a favour!' said Mr Smith and went chuck-ling up to bed.

Alone, Alleyn stood for a minute or two, staring at the mori-bund fire and listening to the night-sounds of a great house. The outer doors were shut and barred and the curtains closed. The voice of the storm was transmitted only through vague soughing noises, distant rattling of shutters and an ambiguous mumbling that broke out intermittently in the chimneys. There were charac-teristic creaks and percussion-like cracks from the old woodwork and, a long way off, a sudden banging that Alleyn took to be a bout of indigestion in Hilary's central-heating system. Then a passage of quiet.

He was accustomed and conditioned to irregular hours, frustrations, changes of plan and lack of sleep but it did seem an unconscionable time since he landed in England that morning. Troy would be asleep, he expected, when he went upstairs.

Some change in the background of small noises caught his attention. A footfall in the gallery upstairs? What? He listened. Nothing. The gallery was in darkness but he remembered there was a time-button at the foot of each stairway and a number of switches controlling the lights in the hall. He moved away from the fireplace and towards the standard lamp near the right-hand flight of stairs and just under the gallery.

He paused, looking to see where the lamp could be switched off. He reached out his left arm towards it.

A totally unexpected blow can bring about a momentary disloca-tion of time. Alleyn for a split second, was a boy of sixteen, hit on the right upper arm by the edge of a cricket bat. His brother George, having lost his temper, had taken a swipe at him. The blunted thump was as familiar as it was shocking.

With his right hand clapped to his arm, he looked down and saw at his feet, shards of pale green porcelain gaily patterned.

His arm, from being numb, began to hurt abominably. He thought, no, not broken, that would be *too* much, and found that with an effort he could close and open his hand and then, very painfully, slightly flex his elbow. He peered at the shards scattered round his feet and recognized the remains of the vase that stood on a little table in the gallery: a big and, he was sure, extremely valuable vase. No joy for Bill-Tasman, thought Alleyn.

The pain was settling into a sort of rhythm, horrid but endurable. He tried supporting his forearm inside his jacket as if in a sling. That would do for the present. He moved to the foot of the stairs. Something bolted down them, brushed past him and shot into the shadows under the gallery. He heard a feline exclamation, a scratching and a thud. That was the green baize door, he thought.

A second later, from somewhere distant and above him, a woman screamed. He switched on the gallery lights and ran upstairs. His arm pounded with every step.

Cressida came galloping full tilt and flung herself at him. She grabbed his arms and he gave a yelp of pain.

'No!' Cressida babbled. 'No! I can't stand it. I won't take it! I hate it. No, no, no!'

'For the love of Mike!' he said, 'What is it? Pull yourself together.'

'Cats! They're doing it on purpose. They want to get rid of me.'

He held her off with his right hand and felt her shake as if gripped by a rigour. She laughed and cried and clung to him most desperately.

'On my bed,' she gabbled. 'It was on my bed. I woke up and touched it. By my face. They know! They hate me! You've got to help.'

He managed agonizingly to get hold of her wrists with both his hands and thought: Well, no bones broken, I suppose, if I can do this.

'All right,' he said. 'Pipe down. It's gone. It's bolted. Now, please. No!' he added as she made a sort of abortive dive at his chest. 'There isn't time and it hurts. I'm sorry but you'd better just sit on the step and get hold of yourself. Good. That's right. Now, please stay there.'

She crouched on the top step. She was clad in a short, diaphanous nightgown and looked like a pin-up girl adapted to some kind of sick comedy.

'I'm cold,' she chattered.

The check-system on the stair-lights cut out and they were in near darkness. Alleyn swore and groped for a wall-switch. At the same moment, like a well-timed cue in a French farce, the doors at the far ends of the gallery opened simultaneously, admitting a flood of light. Out came Troy, on the left hand, and Hilary on the right. A row of wall-lamps sprang to life.

'What in the name of heaven – ' Hilary began but Alleyn cut him short. 'Cover her up,' he said, indicating Cressida. 'She's cold.'

'Cressida! Darling! But what with?' Hilary cried. He sat beside his fiancée on the top step and made an ineffectual attempt to enclose her within the folds of his own dressing-gown. Troy ran back into the guest-room corridor and returned with an eiderdown counterpane. Voices and the closure of doors could be heard. Alleyn was briefly reminded of the arousing of the guests at Forres.

Mr Smith and Mrs Forrester arrived in that order, the former in trousers, shirt, braces and stockinged feet, the latter in her sensible dressing-gown and a woollen cap rather like a baby's.

'Hilary!' she said on a rising note, 'Your uncle and I are getting very tired of this sort of thing. It's bad for your uncle. You will put a stop to it.'

'Auntie Bed, I assure you – '

'Missus!' said Mr Smith, 'you're dead right. I'm with you all the way. Now! What about it, 'Illy?'

'I don't know anything,' Hilary snapped. 'I don't know what's occurred or why Cressida's sitting here in her nightie. And I don't know why you all turn on me. I don't like these upsets any more than you do. And how the devil, if you'll forgive me, Aunt Bed, you can have the cheek to expect *me* to do something about anything when everything's out of my hands, I do not comprehend.'

Upon this they all four looked indignantly at Alleyn.

They're as rum a job lot as I've picked up in many a long day's night, he thought and addressed himself to them.

'Please stay where you are,' he said. 'I shan't, I hope, keep you long. As you suggest, this incident must be cleared up, and I propose to do it. Miss Tottenham, are you feeling better? Do you want a drink?'

('Darling! *Do* you?' urged Hilary.)

Cressida shuddered and shook her head.

'Right,' Alleyn said. 'Then please tell me exactly what happened. You woke up, did you, and found a cat on your bed?'

'Its *eyes*! Two inches away! It was making that awful rumbling noise and doing its ghastly pounding bit. On me! On *me*! I smelt its fur. Like straw.'

'Yes. What did you do?'

'*Do?* I screamed.'

'After that?'

After that, it transpired, all hell was let loose. Cressida's reaction set up an equally frenzied response. Her visitor tore round her room and cursed her. At some stage she turned on her bedside lamp, and revealed the cat glaring out from under the petticoats of her dressing-table.

'Black-and-white?' Hilary asked. 'Or tabby?'

'What the hell does it matter?'

'No, of course. No. I just wondered.'

'Black-and-white.'

'Smartypants, then,' Hilary muttered.

After the confrontation, it seemed, Cressida on the verge of hysteria, had got off her bed, sidled to the door, opened it and then thrown a pillow at Smartypants, who fled from the room. Cressida, greatly shaken, slammed the door, turned back to her bed and was softly caressed round her ankles and shins.

She looked down and saw the second cat, Slyboots, the tabby, performing the tails-up brushing ceremony by which his species make themselves known.

Cressida had again screamed, this time at the top of her voice. She bolted down the corridor and into the gallery and Alleyn's reluctant embrace.

Closely wrapped in her eiderdown, inadequately solaced by the distracted Hilary, she nodded her head up and down, her eyes like great damp pansies and her teeth still inclined to chatter.

'All right,' Alleyn said. 'Two questions. How do you think the cats got into your room? When you visited Troy, did you leave your door open?'

Cressida had no idea.

'You do leave doors open, rather, my darling,' Hilary said, 'don't you?'

'That queen in the kitchen put them there. Out of spite. I know it.'

'Now, *Cressida*! Really!'

'Yes, he did! He's got a thing about me. They all have. They're jealous. They're afraid I'm going to make changes. They're trying to frighten me off.'

'Where,' Alleyn asked before Hilary could launch his protests, 'is the second cat, now? Slyboots?'

'He was walking about the corridor,' Troy began and Cressida immediately began a sort of internal fight with her eiderdown cocoon. 'It's all right,' Troy said quickly. 'He came into my room and I've shut the doors.'

'Do you swear that?'

'Yes, I do.'

'In heaven's name!' Mrs Forrester exclaimed, 'Why don't you take her to bed, Hilary?'

'Really, Aunt B! Well, all right. Well, I will.'

'Give her a pill. She takes pills, of course. They all do. Your uncle mustn't have any more upsets. I'm going back to him. Unless,' she said to Alleyn, 'you want me.'

'No, do go. I hope he's all right. *Was* he upset?'

'He woke up and said something about a fire-engine. Good morning to you all,' snorted Mrs Forrester and left them.

She had scarcely gone when Hilary himself uttered a stifled scream. He had risen and was leaning over the banister. He pointed downwards like an accusing deity at a heap of broken porcelain lying near a standard lamp.

'God damn it!' Hilary said, 'that's my K'ang Hsi vase. Who the hell's broken my K'ang Hsi vase!'

'Your K'ang Hsi vase,' Alleyn said mildly, 'missed my head by a couple of inches.'

'What do you mean? Why do you stand there saying things with your arm in your chest like Napoleon Bonaparte?'

'My arm's in my chest because the vase damn nearly broke it. It's all right,' Alleyn said, catching Troy's eye. 'It didn't.'

'Very choice piece, that,' Mr Smith observed. '*Famille verte.* You bought it from Eichlebaum, didn't you? Pity.'

'I should bloody well think it is a pity.'

'Insurance OK?'

'Naturally. And cold comfort that is, as you well know. The point is, who did it? Who knocked it over?' Hilary positively turned on his beloved. 'Did you?' he demanded.

'I did not!' she shouted. 'And don't talk to me like that. It must have been the cat.'

'The cat! How the hell – '

'I must say,' Alleyn intervened, 'a cat did come belting downstairs immediately afterwards.'

Hilary opened his mouth and shut it again. He looked at Cressida who angrily confronted him, clutching her eiderdown. 'I'm sorry,' he said. 'My darling. Forgive me. It was the shock. And it *was* one of our treasures.'

'I want to go to bed.'

'Yes, yes. Very well. I'll take you.'

They left, Cressida waddling inside her coverlet.

'Oh dear!' said Mr Smith. 'The little rift what makes the music mute,' and pulled a dolorous face.

'Your room's next to hers, isn't it?' Alleyn said. 'Did you hear any of this rumpus?'

'There's her bathroom between. She's got the class job on the north-west corner. Yes, I heard a bit of a how-d'yer-do but I thought she might be having the old slap-and-tickle with 'Illy. You know.'

'Quite.'

'But when she come screeching down the passage, I thought Hullo-ullo. So I come out. Gawd love us,' said Mr Smith, 'it's a right barmy turn-out though, and no error. Goodnight again.'

When he had gone Alleyn said: 'Come out of retirement,' and Troy emerged from the background. 'Your arm,' she said. 'Rory, I'm not interfering but your arm?'

With a creditable imitation of the colonel, Alleyn said: 'Don't fuss me, my dear,' and put his right arm round his wife. 'It's a dirty great bruise, that's all,' he said.

'Did somebody – ?'

'I'll have to look into the Pussyfoot theory and then, by heaven, come hell or high water, we'll go to bed.'

'I'll leave you to it, shall I?'

'Please, my love. Before you do, though, there's a question. From your bedroom window, after the party, and at midnight, you looked out and you saw Vincent come round the north-west corner of the house. He was wheeling a barrow and in the barrow was the Christmas tree. He dumped the tree under the colonel's dressing-room window. You saw him do it?'

'No. There was an inky-black shadow. I saw him coming, all right, along the path. It's wide, you know. More like a rough drive. The shadow didn't cover it. So along he came, clear as clear in the moonlight. Against the snowy background. And then he entered the shadow and I heard him tip the tree out. And then I came away from the window.'

'You didn't see him leave?'

'No. It was chilly. I didn't stay.'

'"Clear as clear in the moonlight". From that window you can see all those earthworks and on-goings where they're making a lake and a hillock?'

'Yes. Just out to the left.'

'Did you look, particularly, in that direction?'

'Yes. It was very beautiful. One could have abstracted something from it. The shapes were exciting.'

'Like a track across the snow leading into the distance?'

'Nothing as obvious as that. The whole field of snow – all the foreground – was quite unbroken.'

'Sure?'

'Quite sure. That's what made it good as a subject.'

'Nothing like a wheel track and footprints anywhere to be seen? For instance?'

'Certainly not. Vincent had trundled round the house by the track and that was already tramped over.'

'Did you look out of your window again in the morning?'

'Yes, darling, I did. And there were no tracks anywhere across the snow. And I may add that after our telephone conversation, I went out of doors. I had a look at Nigel's sculpture. It had been blurred by weathering, particularly on its windward side. Otherwise it was still in recognizable shape. I walked round the house past the drawing-room windows and had a look at last night's "subject" from that angle. No tracks anywhere on the snow. The paths round the house and the courtyard and driveway were trampled and muddy. The courtyard had been swept.'

'So nobody, during the night or morning, had gone near the earthworks.'

'Unless from the far side. Even then one would still have seen their tracks on the hillside.'

'And there had been no snowfall after midnight.'

'No. Only the north wind. The sky was still cloudless in the morning.'

'Yes. The Buster only blew up tonight. Thank you, my love. Leave me, now. I shan't be long.'

'There isn't – ?'

'Well?'

'I suppose there isn't anything I can do? Only stand and wait like those sickening angels?'

'I'll tell you what you can do. You can fetch my small suitcase and go downstairs and collect every last bloody bit of Bill-Tasman's *famille verte*. Don't handle it any more than you can help. Hold the pieces by the edges, put them in the case and bring them upstairs. I'll be here. Will you do that?'

'Watch me.'

When she was established at her task he went to the table in the gallery where the vase had stood. He looked down and there in aerial perspective was the top of a standard lamp, a pool of light surrounding it and within the pool, a pattern of porcelain shards, the top of Troy's head, her shoulders, her knees and her long, thin hands moving delicately about the floor. She was directly underneath him.

A little table, Chinese, elegant but solid, stood against the gallery railing. The ebony pedestal on which the vase had rested was still in position. It had brought the base of the vase up to the level of the balustrade. Alleyn guessed that Hilary wished people in the hall to look up and see his lovely piece of *famille verte* gently signalling from above. As indeed it had signalled to him, much earlier in this long night. Before, he thought, it had hit him on the arm and then killed itself.

He turned on all the lights in the gallery and used a pocket torch that Wrayburn had lent him. He inspected the table, inch by inch, so meticulously that he was still at it when Troy, having finished her task, switched off the downstairs lamp and joined him.

'I suppose,' she said, 'you're looking for claw-marks.'

'Yes.'

'Found any?'

'Not yet. You go along. I've almost finished here. I'll bring the case.'

And when, finally, just after Troy heard the stable clock strike one, he came to her, she knew it was not advisable to ask him if he had found any traces of Smartypants's claws on the Chinese table.

Because clearly he had not.

IV

Alleyn obeyed his own instructions to wake at three. He left Troy fast asleep and found his way through their bedroom, darkling, to his dressing-room, where he shaved and dipped his head in cold water. He looked out of his window. The moon was down but there were stars to be seen, raked across by flying cloud. The wind was still high but there was no rain. The Buster was clearing. He dressed painfully, dragging on thick sweaters and stuffing a cloth cap in his pocket.

He found his way by torchlight along the corridor, out to the gallery and downstairs. The hall was a lightless void except for widely separated red eyes where embers still glowed on the twin hearths. He moved from the foot of the stairs to the opening into the west wing corridor and, turning left, walked along it till he came to the library.

The library, too, was virtually in darkness. The familiar reek of oil and turpentine made Alleyn feel as if he had walked into his wife's studio. Had the portrait been taken out of seclusion and returned to the library?

He moved away from the door and was startled, as Troy had been before him, by the click of the latch as it reopened itself. He shut it again and gave it a hard shove.

His torchlight dodged about the room. Books, lamps, chair-backs, pictures, ornaments showed up and vanished. Then he found the work bench and at last, near it, Troy's easel.

And now, Hilary started up out of the dark and stared at him.

As he came nearer to the portrait his beam of torchlight intensified and so did the liveliness of the painting. Troy was far from being a 'representational' portrait-painter. Rather she abstracted the essence of her subjects as if, Alleyn thought, she had worked with the elements of Hilary's personality for her raw material and laid them out directly on the canvas.

What were those elements? What had she seen?

Well, of course, there was the slightly supercilious air which she had compared to that of a 'good-looking camel'. And in addition elegance, fastidiousness, a certain insolence, a certain quirkiness. But, unexpectedly, in the emphasis on a groove running from his nostrils to the corners of his faunish mouth and in the surprising heaviness of the mouth itself, Troy had unveiled a hedonist in Hilary.

The library was the foremost room in the west wing and had three outside walls. Its windows on the left as one entered it, looked on to the great courtyard. Alleyn made his way to them. He knew they were curtained and shuttered.

He opened the curtains, exposed a window and opened that. It crossed his mind that windows played a major role in whatever drama was unfolding at Halberds. Now his torchlight shone on the inside aspect of the shutters. This was the lee-side of the west wing but they rattled slightly and let in blades of cold air. Not strong enough, he thought, to make a great disturbance in the room but he returned to the easel and gingerly pushed it into a sheltered position.

Then he operated the sliding mechanism in the shutters. The louvres turned and admitted the outside world, its noise and its cold. Alleyn peered through one of the slits. There were no clouds left in the sky. Starlight made a non-darkness of the great courtyard and he could discern, quite close at hand, Nigel's catafalque, denuded of all but a fragment of its effigy, a thin pock-marked mantle of snow.

He put on his cap, turned up the double collar of his sweater, like a beaver, over his mouth and ears, settled himself on the window-seat and put out his torch.

Keeping obbo, he thought and wondered if Fox and his lot were well on their way. He could have done with a radio link. They might arrive at precisely the wrong moment. Not that, ultimately, it would make any difference.

When did the staff get up at Halberds? Sixish? Was he completely, ludicrously at fault? Waiting, as so often on the job, for a non-event?

After all, his theory, if it could be called a theory, was based on a single tenuous thread of evidence. Guesswork, almost. And he could have proved it right or wrong as soon as it entered his head. But then – no confrontation, no surprise element.

He went over the whole field of information as he had received it piecemeal from Troy, from the guests, from Hilary and from the staff. As far as motive went, a clotted mess of *non-sequiturs*, he thought. But as far as procedure went: that was another story. And the evidence in hand? A collection of imbecile pranks that might be threats. A disappearance. A man in a wig. A hair of the wig and probably the blood of the man on a poker. A scrap of gold in a fir sapling. A silly attempt upon a padlock. A wedge in a window sash. A broken vase of great price and his own left arm biceps now thrumming away like fun. Mr Smith's junk yard in his horse-and-barrow days could scarcely have offered a more heterogeneous collection, thought Alleyn.

He reversed his position, turned up the collar of his jacket and continued to peer through the open louvre. Icy blades of air made his eyes stream.

Over years of that soul-destroying non-activity known to the Force as keeping obbo, when the facility for razor-sharp perception must cut through the drag of bodily discomfort and boredom, Alleyn had developed a technique of self-discipline. He hunted through his memory for odd bits from his favourite author that, in however cockeyed a fashion, could be said to refer to his job. As: 'O me! what eyes hath Love put in my head Which have no correspondence with true sight.' And: 'Mad slanderers by mad ears believed he.' And: 'Hence, thou suborn'd informer', which came in very handy when some unreliable snout let the police-side down.

This frivolous pastime had led indirectly to the memorizing of certain sonnets. Now, when with his eyes streaming and his arm giving him hell, he had embarked upon 'The expense of spirit in a waste of shame' he saw, through his peephole, a faint light.

It came jouncing across the courtyard and darted like a moth about the catafalque of Nigel's fancy.

Here, after all, we go, thought Alleyn.

For a split second the light shone directly into his eyes and made him feel ludicrously exposed. It darted away to its original object and then to a slowly oncoming group out of some genre picture that had become blacked almost to oblivion by time. Two figures bent against the wind dragging at an invisible load.

It was a sledge. The torchlight concentrated on the ground beside the catafalque and into this area gloved hands and heavy boots shoved and manœuvred a large, flat-topped sledge.

Alleyn changed his position on the window-seat. He squatted. He slid up the fastening device on the shutters and held them against the wind almost together but leaving a gap for observation.

Three men. The wind still made a great to-do, howling about the courtyard, but he could catch the sound of their voices. The torch, apparently with some bother, was planted where it shone on the side of the packing case. A figure moved across in the field of light: a man with a long-handled shovel.

Two pairs of hands grasped the top of the packingcase. A voice said: 'Heave.'

Alleyn let go the shutters. They swung in the wind and banged open against the outside wall. He stepped over the sill and flashed his own light.

Into the faces of Kittiwee and Mervyn and, across the top of the packingcase – Vincent.

'You're early to work,' said Alleyn.

There was no answer and no human movement. It was as if the living men were held inanimate at the centre of a boisterous void.

Kittiwee's alto voice was heard. 'Vince,' it said, 'asked us to give him a hand, like. To clear.'

Silence. 'That's right,' said Vincent at last.

Mervyn said: 'It's no good now. Sir. Ruined. By the storm.'

'Quite an eyesore,' said Kittiwee.

'Nigel's not giving a hand?' Alleyn said.

'We didn't want to upset him,' Mervyn explained. 'He's easy upset.'

They had to shout these ridiculous observations against the noise of the gale. Alleyn moved round the group until he gently collided with something he recognized as one of the pillars supporting the entrance porch. He remembered that when Wrayburn's men collected their gear from the porch, one of them had switched on the converted lanterns that adorned the pillars.

Alleyn kept his torchlight on the men. They turned to follow his progress, screwing up their eyes and sticking close together. His hand reached out to the end pillar and groped round it. He backed away and felt for the wall of the house.

'Why,' he called out, 'didn't you wait for the light for this job?'

They all began to shout at once and very confusedly. Scraps of unlikely information were offered: Hilary's dislike of litter, Nigel's extreme sensitivity about the fate of his masterpiece. It petered out.

Vince said, 'Come on. Get moving,' and the pairs of gloved hands returned to the packing case.

Alleyn had found a switch. Suddenly the porch and the courtyard were there to be seen: all lit up as they had been for Hilary's party.

The drama of darkness, flashing lights and half-seen ambiguous figures was gone. Three heavily clad men stood round a packing case and glowered at a fourth man.

Alleyn said: 'Before you take it away I want to see inside that thing.'

'There's nothing in it,' Kittiwee shrilly announced, and at the same time Vincent said: 'It's nailed up. You can't.'

Mervyn said: 'It's just an old packing case, sir. The pianner come in it. It's got a lot of rubbish inside thrown out for disposal.'

'Fair enough,' Alleyn said. 'I want to look at it, if you please.'

He walked up to them. The three men crowded together in front of the case. God! he thought. How irremediably pitiable and squalid.

He saw that each of them was using the others, hopelessly, as some sort of protection for himself. They had a need to touch each other, to lose their separate identities, to congeal.

He said: 'This is no good, you know. You'll only harm yourselves if you take this line. I must see inside the case.'

Like a frightened child making a show of defiance, Kittiwee said: 'We won't let you. We're three to one. You better watch out.'

Mervyn said: 'Look, sir, *don't*. It won't do you any good. Don't.'

And Vincent, visibly trembling, 'You're asking for trouble. You better not. You didn't ought to take us on.' His voice skipped a register. 'I'm warning you,' he squeaked. 'See? I'm warning you.'

'Vince!' Kittiwee said. 'Shut up.'

Alleyn walked up to them and in unison they bent their knees and hunched their shoulders in a travesty of squaring up to him.

'The very worst thing you could do,' he said, 'would be to attack me. Think!'

'O Gawd!' Kittiwee said. 'O Gawd, Gawd, Gawd.'

'Stand aside, now. And if you knock me over the head and try the same game with another job you'll come to worse grief. You must know that. Come, now.'

Vincent made an indeterminate gesture with his shovel. Alleyn took three steps forward and ducked. The shovel whistled over his head and was transfixed in the side of the packing case.

Vincent stared at him with his mouth open and his fingers at his lips. 'My oath, you're quick!' he said.

'Lucky for you, I am,' Alleyn said. 'You bloody fool, man! Why do you want to pile up trouble for yourself? Now stand away, the lot of you. Go on, stand back.'

'*Vincey!*' Kittiwee said in scandalized tones. 'You might of cut his head off!'

'I'm that upset.'

'Come on,' Mervyn ordered them. 'Do like 'e says. It's no good.' They stood clear.

The case was not nailed up. It was hinged at the foot and fastened with hook-and-eye catches at the top. They were stiff and Alleyn could use only one hand. He wrenched the shovel from its anchorage and saying: 'Don't try that again,' dropped it to the ground at his feet.

He forced open the first two catches and the side gaped a little, putting a strain on the remaining one. He struck at it with the heel of his hand. It resisted and then flew up.

The side of the case fell against him. He stepped back and it crashed on the paved courtyard.

Moult, having lain against it, rolled over and turned his sightless gaze on Alleyn.

CHAPTER 9

Post Mortem

Moult, dead on the flagstones, seemed by his grotesque entry to inject a spasm of activity into his audience.

For a second or two after he rolled into view, the three servants were motionless. And then, without a word, they bolted. They ran out of the courtyard and were swallowed up by the night.

Alleyn had taken half a dozen steps after them when they returned as wildly as they had gone, running and waving their arms like characters in some kind of extravaganza. To make the resemblance more vivid, they were now bathed in light as if from an off-stage spot. As it intensified they turned to face it, made prohibitive gestures, shielded their eyes, and huddled together.

The field of light contracted and intensified as a police car moved into the courtyard and stopped. Vincent turned and ran straight into Alleyn's arms. His companions dithered too long, made as if to bolt and were taken by four large men who had quitted the car with remarkable expertise.

They were Detective-Sergeants Bailey and Thompson, finger-print and photography experts, respectively; the driver, and Detective-Inspector Fox.

'Now then!' said Mr Fox, the largest of the four men, 'what's all the hurry?'

Kittiwee burst into tears.

'All right, all right,' Alleyn said. 'Pipe down the lot of you. Where d'you think you're going? Over the hill to The Vale? Good morning, Fox.'

' 'Morning, Mr Alleyn. You've been busy.'

'As you see.'

'What do we do with this lot?'

'Well may you ask! They've been making a disgusting nuisance of themselves.'

'We never done a thing. We never touched him,' Kittiwee bawled. 'It's all a bloody misunderstanding.'

Alleyn, whose arm had been excruciatingly stirred up by Vincent, jerked his head towards the packing case. 'Him,' he said.

'Well, well!' Fox observed. 'A body, eh?'

'A body.'

'Would this be the missing individual?'

'It would.'

'Do we charge these chaps, then?'

'We get them indoors, for heaven's sake,' said Alleyn crossly: 'Bring them in. It'll have to be through the window over there. I'll go ahead and switch on the lights. They'd better be taken to their own quarters. And *keep quiet* all of you. We don't want to rouse the household. Cook – what's your name? – Kittiwee – for the love of decency – *shut up*.'

Fox said: 'What about the remains?'

'One thing at a time. Before he's moved the divisional surgeon will have to take a look. Bailey – Thompson.'

'Sir?'

'You get cracking with this set-up. As it lies. Dabs. Outside and inside the packing case. The sledge. All surfaces. And the body of course. Complete job.' Alleyn walked to the body and stooped over it. It was rigid and all askew. It lay on its back, the head at a grotesque angle to the trunk. One arm was raised. The eyes and the mouth were open. Old, ugly, scars on jaw and fattish cheek and across the upper lip started out lividly.

But the beard and moustache and wig would have covered those, Alleyn thought. There's nothing in that.

His hands were busy for a moment. He extracted an empty flat half-pint bottle from a jacket in the coat and sniffed at it. Whisky. From the waistcoat pocket he took a key. Finding nothing more, he then turned away from the body and contemplated Vincent and his associates.

'Are you lot coming quietly?' he asked. 'You'll be mad if you don't.'

They made affirmative noises.

'Good. You,' Alleyn said to the driver of the police car, 'come with us. You,' to Bailey and Thompson, 'get on with it. I'll call up the Div Surgeon. When you've all finished wait for instructions. Where's your second car, Fox?'

'Puncture. They'll be here.'

'When they come,' Alleyn said to Bailey, 'stick them along the entrances. We don't want people barging out of the house before you've cleared up here. It's getting on for six. Come on, Fox. Come on, you lot.'

Alleyn led the way through the library window, down the corridor, across the hall, through the green baize door and into the servants' common-room. Here they surprised the boy in the act of lighting the fire. Alleyn sent him with his compliments to Cuthbert whom he would be pleased to see. 'Is Nigel up?' he asked. The boy, all eyes, nodded. Nigel, it appeared, was getting out early morning tea-trays in the servery.

'Tell him we're using this room and don't want to be disturbed for the moment. Got that? All right. Chuck some coal on the fire and then off you cut, there's a good chap.'

When the boy had gone Alleyn rang up Wrayburn on the staff telephone, told him of the discovery and asked him to lay on the divisional surgeon as soon as possible. He then returned to the common-room where he nodded to the Yard car-driver who took up a position in front of the door.

Mervyn, Kittiwee and Vincent stood in a wet, dismal and shivering group in the middle of the room. Kittiwee mopped his great dimpled face and every now and then, like a baby, caught his breath in a belated sob.

'Now then,' Alleyn said. 'I suppose you three know what you've done, don't you? You've tried to obstruct the police in the execution of their duty which is an extremely serious offence.'

They broke into a concerted gabble.

'Pipe down,' he said, 'stop telling me you didn't do him. Nobody's said anything to the contrary. So far. You could be charged with accessories after the fact if you know what that means.'

Mervyn, with some show of dignity, said: 'Naturally.'

'All right. In the meantime I'm going to tell you what I think is the answer to your cockeyed behaviour. Get in front of the fire, for pity's sake. I don't want to talk to a set of castanets.'

They moved to the hearthrug. Pools formed round their boots and presently they began to smell and steam. They were a strongly contrasted group: Kittiwee with his fat, as it were, gone soggy; Vincent ferret-like, with the weathered hide of his calling, and Mervyn, dark about the jaws, black-browed and white-faced. They looked at nobody. They waited.

Alleyn eased his throbbing arm a little farther into his chest and sat on the edge of the table. Mr Fox cleared his throat, retired into a sort of self-made obscurity and produced a notebook.

'If I've got this all wrong,' Alleyn said, 'the best thing you can do is to put me right, whatever the result. And I mean that. Really. You won't believe me, but *really*. Best for yourselves on all counts. Now. Go back to the Christmas tree. The party. The end of the evening. At about midnight, you,' – he looked at Vincent ' – wheeled the dismantled tree in a barrow to the glasshouse wreckage under the west wing. You tipped it off under Colonel Forrester's dressing-room window near a sapling fir. Right?'

Vincent's lips moved inaudibly.

'You made a discovery. Moult's body, lying at the foot of the tree. I can only guess at your first reaction. I don't know how closely you examined it but I think you saw enough to convince you he'd been murdered. You panicked in a big way. Then and there, or later, after you'd consulted your mates – '

There was an involuntary shuffling movement, instantly repressed.

'I see,' Alleyn said. 'All right. You came indoors and told Cuthbert and these two what you'd found. Right?'

Vincent ran his tongue round his lips and spoke.

'What say I did? I'm not giving the OK to nothing. I'm not concurring, mind. But what say I did? That'd be c'rrect procedure, wouldn't it? Report what I seen? Wouldn't it?'

'Certainly. It's the subsequent on-goings that are not so hot.'

'A chap reports what he seen to the authorities. Over to them.'

'Wouldn't you call Mr Bill-Tasman the authority in this case?'

'A chap puts it through the right channels. *If. If.* See? I'm not saying – '

'I think we've all taken the point about what you're not saying. Let's press on, shall we, and arrive at what you *do* say. Let's suppose you did come indoors and report your find to Cuthbert. And to these two. But not to Nigel, he being a bit tricky in his reactions. Let's suppose you four came to a joint decision. Here was the body of a man you all heartily disliked and whom you had jointly threatened and abused that very morning. It looked as if he'd been done to death. This you felt to be an acute embarrassment. For several reasons. Because of your records. And because of singular incidents occurring over the last few days: booby-traps, anonymous messages, soap in the barley water and so on. And all in your several styles.'

'We never – ' Mervyn began.

'I don't for a moment suggest you did. I do suggest you all believed Moult had perpetrated these unlovely tricks in order to discredit you and you thought that this circumstance, too, when it came to light, would incriminate you. So I suggest you panicked and decided to get rid of the corpse.'

At this juncture Cuthbert came in. He wore a lush dressing-gown over silk pyjamas. So would he have looked, Alleyn thought, if nocturnally disturbed in his restaurant period before the advent of the amorous commis.

'I understand,' he said to Alleyn, 'sir, that you wished to see me.'

'I did and do,' Alleyn rejoined. 'For your information, Cuthbert, Alfred Moult's body has been found in the packing case supporting Nigel's version of the Bill-Tasman effigy. These men were about to remove the whole shooting box on a sledge. The idea, I think, was to transfer it to an appropriate sphere of activity where, with the unwitting aid of bulldozers, it would help to form an artificial hillock overlooking an artificial lake. End result, an artefact known, appropriately, as a Folly. I've been trying to persuade them that their best course – and yours, by the way – is to give me a factual account of the whole affair.'

Cuthbert looked fixedly at the men who did not look at him.

'So: first,' Alleyn said, 'did Vincent come to you and report his finding of the body on Christmas night? Or, rather, at about ten past midnight, yesterday morning?'

Cuthbert dragged at his jaw and was silent.

Vincent suddenly blurted out. 'We never said a thing, Cuthbert. Not a thing.'

'You did, too, Vince,' Kittiwee burst out. 'You opened your great silly trap. Didn't he, Merv?'

'I never. I said "if".'

'If what?' Cuthbert asked.

'I said supposing. Supposing what he says was right it'd be the c'rrect and proper procedure. To report to you. Which I done. I mean – '

'Shut up,' Mervyn and Kittiwee said in unison.

'My contention,' Alleyn said to Cuthbert, 'is that you decided, among you, to transfer the body to the packing case there and then. You couldn't take it straight to the dumping ground because in doing so you would leave your tracks over a field of unbroken snow for all to see in the morning and also because any effort you made to cover it at the earthworks would be extremely difficult in the dark and would stand out like a sore thumb by the light of day.

'So one of you was taken with the very bright notion of transferring it to the packing case which was destined for the earthworks anyway. I suppose Vincent wheeled it round in his barrow and one or more of you gave him a hand to remove the built-up box steps, to open the side of the case, stow away the body and replace and re-cover the steps. It was noticed next morning that the northern aspect appeared to have been damaged by wind and rain but there had been a further fall of snow which did something to restore them.'

Alleyn waited for a moment. Kittiwee heaved a deep sigh. His associates shuffled their feet.

'I really think we'd all better sit down,' Alleyn said. 'Don't you?'

They sat in the same order as in yesterday's assembly. Mr Fox, after his habit remained unobtrusively in the background and the driver kept his station in front of the door.

'I wonder,' Alleyn said, 'why you decided to shift the case at five o'clock this morning? Had you lost your collective nerve? Had its presence out there become a bit more than some of you could take? Couldn't you quite face the prospect of dragging it away in the full light of morning and leaving it to the bulldozers to cover. What were you going to do with it? Has the storm produced some morass in the earthworks or the lake site into which it could be depended upon to sink out of sight?'

They shifted their feet and darted sidelong glances at him and at each other. 'I see. That's it. Come,' Alleyn said quietly, 'don't you think you'd better face up to the situation? It looks like a fair cop, doesn't it? There you were and there's the body. You may not believe me when I tell you I don't think any of you killed him but I certainly don't intend, at this point, to charge any of you with doing so. You've conspired to defeat the ends of justice, though, and whether you'll have to face that one is another matter. Our immediate concern is to find the killer. If you're helpful rather than obstructive and behave sensibly we'll take it into consideration. I'm not offering you a bribe,' Alleyn said. 'I'm trying to put the situation in perspective. If you all want a word together in private you may have it but you'll be silly if you use the opportunity to cook up a dish of codswallop. What do you say? Cuthbert?'

Cuthbert tilted his head and stared into the fire. His right hand, thick and darkly hirsute, hung between his knees. Alleyn reflected that it had once wielded a lethal carving knife.

Cuthbert heaved a sigh. 'I don't know,' he boomed in his great voice, 'that it will serve any purpose to talk. I don't know, I'm sure.'

None of his friends seemed inclined to help him in his predicament.

'You don't by any chance feel,' Alleyn said, 'that you rather owe it to Mr Bill-Tasman to clear things up? After all, he's done quite a lot for you, hasn't he?'

Kittiwee suddenly revealed himself as a person of intelligence.

'Mr Bill-Tasman,' he said, 'suited himself. He'd never have persuaded the kind of staff he wanted to come to this dump. Not in the ordinary way. He's got what he wanted. He's got value and he knows it. If he likes to talk a lot of crap about rehabilitation that's his affair. If we hadn't given the service you wouldn't have heard so much about rehabilitation.'

The shadow of a grin visited all their faces.

'*Owe* it to him!' Kittiwee said and his moon face still blotted with tears dimpled into its widest smile. 'You'll be saying next we ought to show our gratitude. We're always being told we ought to be grateful. Grateful for what? Fair payment for fair services? After eleven years in stir, Mr Alleyn, you get funny ideas under that heading.'

Alleyn said: 'Yes. Yes, I've no doubt you do.' He looked round the group. 'The truth is,' he said, 'that when you come out of stir it's to another kind of prison and it's heavy going for the outsider who tries to break in.'

They looked at him with something like astonishment.

'It's no good keeping on about this,' he said, 'I've a job to do and so have you. If you agree with the account I've put to you about your part in this affair, it'll be satisfactory to me and I believe the best thing for you. But I can't wait any longer for the answer. You must please yourselves.'

A long pause.

Mervyn got to his feet, moved to the fireplace and savagely kicked a log into the flames.

'We got no choice,' he said. 'All right. Like you said.'

'Speak for yourself,' Vincent mumbled but without much conviction.

Cuthbert said: 'People don't think.'

'How do you mean?'

'They don't know. For us, each of us, it was what you might call an isolated act. Like a single outbreak – an abscess that doesn't spread. Comes to a head and bursts and that's it. It's out of the system. We're no more likely to go violent than anyone else. Less. We know what it's like afterwards. We're oncers. People don't think.'

'Is that true of Nigel?'

They looked quickly at each other.

'He's a bit touched,' Cuthbert said. 'He gets put out. He doesn't understand.'

'Is he dangerous?'

'I'll go with what you've put to us, sir,' Cuthbert said, exactly as if he hadn't heard Alleyn's question. 'I'll agree it's substantially the case. Vince found the body and came in and told us and we reached a decision. I dare say it was stupid but the way we looked at it we couldn't afford for him to be found.'

'Who actually moved the body into the packing case?'

Cuthbert said: 'I don't think we'll go into details,' and Mervyn and Vincent looked eloquently relieved.

'And Nigel knows nothing about it?'

'That's right. He's settled that Mr Moult was struck down by a sense of sin for mocking us and went off somewhere to repent.'

'I see.' Alleyn glanced at Fox who put up his notebook and cleared his throat. 'I'll have a short statement written out and will ask you all to sign it if you find it correct.'

'We haven't said we'll sign anything,' Cuthbert interjected in a hurry and the others made sounds of agreement.

'Quite so,' Alleyn said. 'It'll be your decision.'

He walked out followed by Fox and the driver.

'Do you reckon,' Fox asked, 'there'll be any attempt to scarper?'

'I don't think so. They're not a stupid lot: the stowing of the body was idiotic but they'd panicked.'

Fox said heavily: 'This type of chap: you know, the oncer. He always bothers me. There's something in what they said: you can't really call him a villain. Not in the accepted sense. He's funny.' Fox meditated. 'That flabby job. The cook. What was it you called him?'

'"Kittiwee".'

'I thought that was what you said.'

'He's keen on cats. *A propos*, cats come into my complicated story. I'd better put you in the picture, Br'er Fox. Step into the hall.'

II

Alleyn finished his recital to which Mr Fox had listened with his customary air: raised brows, pursed lips and a hint of catarrhal breathing. He made an occasional note and when Alleyn had finished remarked that the case was 'unusual' as if a new sartorial feature had been introduced by a conservative tailor.

All this took a considerable time. When it was over seven o'clock had struck. Curtains were still drawn across the hall windows but on looking through Alleyn found that they were guarded on the outside by Fox's reinforcements and that Bailey and Thompson held powerful lights to the body of Albert Moult while a heavily overcoated person stooped over it.

'The div surgeon,' Alleyn said. 'Here's the key of the cloakroom, Fox. Have a shiner at it while I talk to him. Go easy. We'll want the full treatment in there.'

The divisional surgeon, Dr Moore, said that Moult had either been stunned or killed outright by a blow on the nape of the neck and that the neck had subsequently been broken, presumably by a fall. When Alleyn fetched the poker and they laid it by the horrid wound, the stained portion was found to coincide and the phenomenon duly photographed. Dr Moore, a weathered man with a good keen eye, was then taken to see the wig and in the wet patch Alleyn found a tiny skein of hair that had not been washed perfectly clean. It was agreed that this and the poker should be subjected to the sophisticated attention of the Yard's pathological experts.

'He's been thumped all right,' said Dr Moore. 'I suppose you'll talk to Sir James.' Sir James Curtis was consultant pathologist to the Yard. 'I wouldn't think,' Dr Moore added, 'there'd be much point in leaving the body there. It's been rolled about all over the shop, it seems, since he was thumped. But thumped he was.'

And he drove himself back to Downlow where he practised. The time was now seven-thirty.

Alleyn said: 'He's about right, you know, Fox. I'll get through to Curtis but I think he'll say we can move the body. There are some empty rooms in the stables under the clock tower. You chaps can take him round in the car. Lay him out decently, of course. Colonel Forrester will have to identify.'

Alleyn telephoned Sir James Curtis and was given rather grudging permission to remove Moult from Hilary's doorstep. Sir James liked bodies to be *in situ* but conceded that as this one had been as he put it, rattled about like dice in a box, the objection was academic. Alleyn rejoined Fox in the hall. 'We can't leave Bill-Tasman uninformed much longer,' he said, 'I suppose. Worse luck. I must say I don't relish the prospect of coming reactions.'

'If we exclude the servants and I take it we do, we've got a limited field of possibilities, haven't we, Mr Alleyn?'

'Six, if you also exclude thirty-odd guests and Troy.'

'A point being,' said Mr Fox, pursuing, after his fashion, his own line of thought, 'whether or not it was a case of mistaken identity. Taking into consideration the wig and whiskers.'

'Quite so. In which case the field is reduced to five.'

'Anyone with a scunner on the colonel, would you say?'

'I'd have thought it a psychological impossibility. He's walked straight out of Winnie-the-Pooh.'

'Anybody profit by his demise?'

'I've no idea. I understand his Will's in the tin box.'

'Is that a fact?'

'Together with the crown jewels and various personal documents. We'll have to see.'

'What beats me,' said Mr Fox, 'on what you've told me, is this. The man Moult finishes his act. He comes back to the cloakroom. The young lady takes off his wig and whiskers and leaves him there. She takes them *off*. Unless,' Fox said carefully, 'she's lying, of course. But suppose she is? Where does that lead you?'

'All right, Br'er Fox, where does it lead you?'

'To a nonsense,' Fox said warmly. 'That's where. To some sort of notion that she went upstairs and got the poker and came back and hit him with it Gawd knows why, and then dragged him upstairs under the noses of the servants and kids and all and removed the wig and pitched him and the poker out of the window. Or walked upstairs with him alive when we know the servants saw her go through this hall on her own and into the drawing-room and anyway there wasn't time and – well,' said Fox, 'why go on with it? It's silly.'

'Very.'

'Rule her out, then. So we're left with – what? This bit of material from his robe, now. If that's what it was. That was caught up in the tree? So he was wearing the robe when he pitched out of the window. So why isn't it torn and wet and generally mucked up and who put it back in the cloakroom?'

'Don't you rather feel that the scrap of material might have been stuck to the poker. Which *was* in the tree.'

'Damn!' said Fox. 'Yes. Damn. All right. Well now. Some time or another he falls out of the upstairs window, having been hit on the back of his head with the upstairs poker. *Wearing the wig?*'

'Go on, Br'er Fox.'

'Well – presumably wearing the wig. On evidence, wearing the wig. We don't know about the whiskers.'

'No.'

'No. So we waive them. Never mind the whiskers. But the wig – the wig turns up in the cloakroom same as the robe just where they left it only with all the signs of having been washed where the blow fell and not so efficiently but that there's a trace of something that might be blood. So what do we get? The corpse falling through the window, replacing the wig, washing it and the robe clean and going back and lying down again.'

'A droll concept.'

'All right. And where does it leave us? With Mr Bill-Tasman, the colonel and his lady and this Bert Smith. Can we eliminate any of them?'

'I think we can.'

'You tell me how. Now, then.'

'In response to your cordial invitation, Br'er Fox, I shall attempt to do so.'

III

The men outside having been given the office, lifted the frozen body of Alfred Moult into their car and drove away to the rear of the great house. The effigy of Hilary Bill-Tasman's ancestor reduced to a ghastly storm-pocked wraith dwindled on the top of the packing case. And Alleyn, watching through the windows, laid out for Fox, piece by piece, his assemblage of events fitting each into each until a picture was completed.

When he had done his colleague drew one of his heavy sighs and wiped his great hand across his mouth.

'That's startling and it's clever,' he said. 'It's very clever indeed. It'll be a job to make a dead bird of it, though.'

'Yes.'

'No motive, you see. That's always awkward. Well – no apparent motive. Unless there's one locked up somewhere behind the evidence.'

Alleyn felt in his breast pocket, drew out his handkerchief, unfolded it and exposed a key: a commonplace barrel-key such as would fit a commonplace padlock.

'This may help us,' he said, 'to break in.'

'I only need one guess,' said Mr Fox.

Before Alleyn went to tell Hilary of the latest development he and Fox visited Nigel in the servery where they found him sitting in an apparent trance with an assembly of early morning tea-trays as his background. Troy would have found this a paintable subject, thought Alleyn.

At first when told that Moult was dead Nigel looked sideways at Alleyn as if he thought he might be lying. But finally he nodded portentously several times. 'Vengeance is mine, saith the Lord,' he said.

'Not in this instance,' Alleyn remarked. 'He's been murdered.'

Nigel put his head on one side and stared at Alleyn through his white eyelashes. Alleyn began to wonder if his wits had quite turned or if, by any chance, he was putting it on.

'How?' Nigel asked.

'He was hit with a poker.'

Nigel sighed heavily: Like Fox, Alleyn thought irrelevantly.

'Everywhere you turn,' Nigel generalized, 'sinful ongoings! Fornication galore. Such is the vice and depravity of these licentious times.'

'The body,' Alleyn pressed on, 'was found in the packing case under your effigy.'

'Well,' Nigel snapped, 'if you think I put it there you're making a very big mistake.' He gazed at Alleyn for some seconds. 'Though it's well known to the Lord God of Hosts,' he added in a rising voice, 'that I'm a sinner. A sinner!' he repeated loudly and now he really did look demented. 'I smote a shameless lady in the face of the heavens and they opened and poured down their vials of wrath upon me. Because such had not been their intention. My mistake.' And as usual when recalling his crime, he burst into tears.

Alleyn and Fox withdrew into the hall.

'That chap's certifiable,' said Fox, looking very put out. 'I mean to say, he's certifiable.'

'I'm told he only cuts up rough occasionally.'

'Does he cart those trays round the bedrooms?'

'At eight-thirty, Troy says.'

'I wouldn't fancy the tea.'

'Troy says it's all right. It's Vincent who's the arsenic expert, remember, not Nigel.'

'I don't like it,' Fox said.

'Damn it all, Br'er Fox, nor do I. I don't like Troy being within a hundred miles of a case as you very well know. I don't like – well, never mind all that. Look. Here are the keys of Colonel Forrester's dressing-room. I want Thompson and Bailey to give it the full treatment. Window sashes. All surfaces and objects. That's the wardrobe key. It's highly probable that there are duplicates of the whole lot but never mind. In the wardrobe, standing on its end, is this damned tin uniform box. Particular attention to that. Tell him to report to me when they've finished. I'm going to stir up Bill-Tasman.'

'*For God's sake!*' cried Hilary from the top of the stairs, '*What now!*'

He was leaning over the gallery in his crimson dressing-gown. His hair rose in a crest above his startled countenance. He was extremely pale.

'What's happening in the stable yard?' he demanded. 'What are they doing? You've found him? Haven't you? You've found him.'

'Yes,' said Alleyn. 'I'm on my way to tell you. Will you wait? Join us, Fox, when you're free.'

Hilary waited, biting his knuckles. 'I should have been told,' he began as soon as Alleyn reached him. 'I should have been told at once.'

'Can we go somewhere private?'

'Yes, yes, yes. All right. Come to my room. I don't like all this. One should be told.'

He led the way round the gallery to his bedroom, a magnificent affair in the east wing corresponding, Alleyn supposed, with that occupied by Cressida in the west wing. It overlooked on one side the courtyard, on the other the approach from the main road and in front, the parklands-to-be. A door stood open into a dressing-room and beyond that into a bathroom. The dominant feature was a four-poster on a dais, sumptuously canopied and counterpaned.

'I'm sorry,' Hilary said, 'if I was cross but really the domestic scene in this house becomes positively Quattrocento. I glance through my window – ' he gestured to the one that overlooked the courtyard ' – and see something quite unspeakable being pushed into a car. I glance through the opposite window and the car is being driven round the house. I go to the far end of the corridor and look into the stable yard and there they are, at it again, extricating their hideous find. No!' Hilary cried. 'It's too much. Admit. It's too much.'

There was a tap on the door. Hilary answered it and disclosed Mr Fox. 'How do you do,' Hilary said angrily.

Alleyn introduced them and proceeded, painstakingly, to rehearse the circumstances leading to the discovery of Moult. Hilary interrupted the recital with petulant interjections.

'Well, now you've found it,' he said when he had allowed Alleyn to finish, 'what happens? What is expected of me? My servants will no doubt be in an advanced state of hysteria and I wouldn't be surprised if one and all they gave me notice. But command me. What must I do?'

Alleyn said: 'I know what a bore it all is for you but it really can't be helped. Can it? We'll trouble you as little as possible and, after all, if you don't mind a glimpse of the obvious, it's been an even greater bore for Moult.'

Hilary turned slightly pink. 'Now you're making me feel shabby,' he said. 'What an alarming man you are. One doesn't know where to have you. Well – what shall I do?'

'Colonel Forrester must be told that Moult has been found, that he's dead, that he's been murdered and that we shall ask the colonel to identify the body.'

'Oh *no*!' Hilary shouted. 'How beastly for him! Poorest Uncle Flea! Well, I can't tell him. I'll come with you if you do,' he added. 'I mean if you tell him. Oh all *right*, then, I'll tell him but I'd like you to come.'

He walked about the room, muttering disconsolately.

Alleyn said: 'But of course I'll come. I'd rather be there.'

'On the watch!' Hilary pounced. 'That's it, isn't it? Looking out for the way we all behave?'

'See here,' Alleyn said. 'You manœuvred me into taking this case. For more than one reason I tried to get out of it but here, in the event, I am and very largely by your doing. Having played for me and got me, I'm afraid you'll have to lump me and that's the long and the short of it.'

Hilary stared at him for some seconds and then the odd face broke into a smile.

'How you do cut one down to size!' he said. 'And of course you're right. I'm behaving badly. My dear man, do believe me, really I'm quite ashamed of myself and I *am*, indeed I am, more than thankful we are in your hands. *Peccavi, peccavi*,' cried Hilary, putting his hands together and after a moment, with a decisive air,

'Well! The sooner it's over the better, no doubt. Shall we seek out Uncle Flea?'

But there was no need to seek him out. He was coming agitatedly along the corridor with his wife at his heels, both wearing their dressing-gowns.

'There you are!' he said. 'They've found him, haven't they? They've found poor Moult.'

'Come in, Uncle,' Hilary said. 'Auntie – come in.'

They came in, paused at the sight of Alleyn and Fox, said, 'Good morning,' and turned simultaneously on Hilary. 'Speak up, do,' said Mrs Forrester. 'He's been found?'

'How did you know? Yes,' said Hilary. 'He has.'

'Is he – ?'

'Yes, Uncle Flea, I'm afraid so. I'm awfully sorry.'

'You'd better sit down, Fred. Hilary, your uncle had better sit down.'

Colonel Forrester turned to Alleyn. 'Please tell me exactly what has happened,' he said. 'I should like a full report.'

'Shall we obey orders and sit down, sir? It'll take a little time.'

The colonel made a slight impatient gesture but he took the chair Hilary pushed forward. Mrs Forrester walked over to the windows, folded her arms and throughout Alleyn's recital stared out at the landscape. Hilary sat on his grand bed and Fox performed his usual feat of self-effacement.

Alleyn gave a full account of the finding of Moult's body and, in answer to some surprisingly succinct and relevant questions from the colonel, of the events that led up to it. As he went on he sensed a growing tension in his audience: in their stillness, in Mrs Forrester's withdrawal, in her husband's extreme quietude and in Hilary's painful concentration.

When he had finished there was a long silence. And then, without turning away from the window or, indeed, making any movement, Mrs Forrester said: 'Well, Hilary, your experiment has ended as might have been predicted. In disaster.'

Alleyn waited for an expostulation, if not from the colonel, at least from Hilary. But Hilary sat mum on his magnificent bed and the colonel, after a long pause, turned to look at him and said: 'Sorry, old boy. But there it is. Bad luck. My poor old Moult,' said the colonel with a break in his voice. 'Well – there it is.'

Alleyn said: 'Do I take it that you all suppose one of the servants is responsible?'

They moved just enough to look at him.

'We mustn't lose our common sense, you know, Alleyn,' said the colonel. 'A man's record is always the best guide. You may depend upon it.'

'Uncle Flea, I wish I could think you're wrong,'

'I know, old boy, I know you do.'

'The question is,' said Mrs Forrester. 'Which?'

Hilary threw up his hands and then buried his face in them.

'Nonsense!' said his aunt glancing at him. 'Don't play-act, Hilary.'

'No, B! Not fair: he's not play-acting. It's a disappointment.'

'A bitter one,' said Hilary.

'Although,' his aunt went on, pursuing her own line of thought, 'it's more a matter of which *isn't* guilty. Personally, I would think it's a conspiracy involving the lot with the possible exception of the madman.' She turned her head slightly. 'Is that the view of the police?' she asked, over her shoulder.

'No,' Alleyn said mildly.

'No! What do you mean, "No"?'

'No, I don't think the servants conspired to murder Moult. I think that with the exception of Nigel they conspired to get rid of the body because they knew they would be suspected. It seems they were not far wrong. But of course it was an idiotic thing to do.'

'May I ask,' said Mrs Forrester very loudly, 'if you realize what this extraordinary theory implies? May I ask you that?'

'But of course,' Alleyn said politely. 'Do, please. Ask.'

'It implies – ' she began on a high note and then appeared to boggle.

'There's no need to spell it out, Aunt B.'

' – something perfectly ridiculous,' she barked. 'I said something perfectly ridiculous.'

Alleyn said: 'I'm sorry to have to ask you this, sir, but there's the matter of formal identification.'

Colonel Forrester said: 'What? Oh! Oh, yes, of course. You – you want me to – to – '

'Unless there is a member of his family within call? There will presumably be relations who should be informed. Perhaps you can help us there? Who is the next of kin, do you know?'

This produced a strange reaction. For a moment Alleyn wondered if Colonel Forrester was going to have one of his 'turns'. He became white and then red in the face. He looked everywhere but at Alleyn. He opened his mouth and then shut it again, half rose and sank back in his chair.

'He had no people,' he said at last, 'that I know of. He – he has told me. There are none.'

'I see. Then, as his employer – '

'I'll just get dressed,' the colonel said and rose to his feet.

'No!' Mrs Forrester interjected. She left the window and joined him. 'You can't, Fred. It'll upset you. I can do it, I said I can do it.'

'Certainly not,' he said with an edge to his voice that evidently startled his wife and Hilary. 'Please don't interfere, B. I shall be ready in ten minutes, Alleyn.'

'Thank you very much, sir. I'll join you in the hall.'

He opened the door for the colonel who squared his shoulders, lifted his chin and walked out.

Alleyn said to Mrs Forrester. 'It can wait a little. There's no need for him to come at once. If you think it will really upset him – '

'It doesn't in the least matter what I think. He's made up his mind,' she said and followed him out.

IV

They hadn't been able to make what Mr Fox called a nice job of Moult's body owing to its being in an advanced state of rigor mortis. They had borrowed a sheet to cover it and had put it on a table in an old harness room. When Alleyn turned back the sheet Moult seemed to be frozen in the act of shaking his fist at the colonel and uttering a soundless scream out of the head that was so grossly misplaced on its trunk.

Colonel Forrester said: 'Yes,' and turned away. He walked past the constable on duty, into the yard and blew his nose. Alleyn gave him a few moments and then joined him.

'Long time,' said the colonel. 'Twenty-five years. Quarter of a century. Long time.'

'Yes,' Alleyn said. 'It's a rather special relationship – the officer/ soldier-servant one – isn't it?'

'He had his faults but we understood each other's ways. We suited each other very well.'

'Come indoors, sir. It's cold.'

'Thank you.'

Alleyn took him to the library where a fire had now been lit and sat him down by it.

'No need for it, really,' said the colonel, making tremulous conversation, 'with all this central heating Hilly's put in but it's cheerful, of course.' He held his elderly veined hands to the fire and finding them unsteady, rubbed them together.

'Shall I get you a drink?'

'What? No, no. No, thanks. I'm perfectly all right. It's just – seeing him. Might have been killed in action. They often looked like that. Bit upsetting.'

'Yes.'

'I – there'll be things to see to. I mean – you'll want – formalities and all that.'

'I'm afraid so. There'll be an inquest of course.'

'Of course.'

'Do you happen to know if he left a Will ?'

The hands were still and then, with a sudden jerk, the colonel crossed his knees and clasped them in a travesty of ease.

'A Will?' he said. 'Not a great deal to leave, I dare say.'

'Still – if he did.'

'Yes, of course.' He seemed to think this over very carefully.

'You don't know, then, if he did?'

'As a matter of fact,' the colonel said in a constrained voice, 'he gave me a – an envelope to keep for him. It may contain his Will.'

'I think we shall probably ask to see it, Colonel. Of course if it's irrelevant – '

'Yes, yes, yes,' he said. 'I know. I know.'

'Is it,' Alleyn asked lightly, 'perhaps in that famous uniform box?'

A long silence. 'I – rather think so. It may be,' said the colonel and then: 'He has – he had the key. I told you, didn't I? He looked after that sort of thing for us. Keys and things.'

'You placed an enormous trust in him, didn't you?'

'Oh that!' said the colonel, dismissing it with a shaky wave of his hand. 'Oh, rather, yes. Absolutely.'

'I think I've recovered the key of the padlock.'

The colonel gave Alleyn a long watery stare. 'Have you?' he said at last. 'From – him?'

'It was in his pocket.'

'May I have it, Alleyn?'

'Of course. But if you don't mind we'll do our routine nonsense with it first.'

'Finger-prints?' he asked faintly.

'Yes. It really is only routine. I expect to find none but his and your own, of course. We have to do these things.'

'Of course.'

'Colonel Forrester, what is it that's worrying you? There is something, isn't there?'

'Isn't it enough,' he cried out with a kind of suppressed violence, 'that I've lost an old and valued servant? Isn't that enough?'

'I'm sorry.'

'So am I,' said the colonel at once. 'My dear fellow, you must excuse me. I do apologize. I'm not quite myself.'

'Shall I tell Mrs Forrester you're in here?'

'No, no. No need for that. None in the world. Rather like to be by myself for a bit: that's all. Thank you very much, Alleyn. Very considerate.'

'I'll leave you, then.'

But before he could do so the door opened and in came Mr Bert Smith, dressed but not shaved.

'I been talking to 'Illy,' he said without preliminaries, 'and I don't much fancy what I hear. You found 'im, then?'

'Yes.'

'Been knocked off? Bashed? Right?'

'Right.'

'And there was three of them convicted murderers trying to make away with the corpse. Right?'

'Right.'

'And you make out they got nothing to do with it?'

'I don't think, at this stage, that it looks as if any of them killed him.'

'You got to be joking.'

'Have I?' said Alleyn.

Mr Smith made a noise suggestive of contempt and disgust and placed himself in front of the colonel who was leaning back in his chair frowning to himself.

'Glad to see you, Colonel,' said Mr Smith. 'It's time we got together for a talk. 'Illy's coming down when he's broken the news to 'is loved one and collected 'is auntie. Any objections?' he shot at Alleyn.

'Good Lord!' Alleyn said, 'What possible objections could there be and how on earth could I enforce them? You can hold meetings all over the house if you feel so disposed. I only hope a bit of hog-sense comes out of them. If it does I'll be glad if you'll pass it on. We could do with it.'

'Honestly,' said Mr Smith sourly, 'you devastate me.'

Hilary came in with Mrs Forrester and Cressida who was *en négligé* and looked beautiful but woebegone. The other two were dressed.

Mrs Forrester gave her husband a sharp look and sat beside him. He nodded as if, Alleyn thought, to reassure her and stave off any conversation. Hilary glanced unhappily at Alleyn and stood before the fire. Cressida approached Alleyn, gazed into his face, made a complicated, piteous gesture and shook her lovely head slowly from side to side after the manner of a motion-picture star attempting the ineffable in close-up.

'I can't cope,' she said. 'I mean I just can't. You know?'

'You don't really have to,' he said.

An expression that might have been the prelude to a grin dawned for a moment. 'Well, actually I don't, do I ?' said Cressida. 'Still, admit – it's all a pretty good drag, isn't it?'

She gave him another extremely matey look and then, in her usual fashion collapsed superbly into a chair.

Smith, Mrs Forrester and even Hilary stared at her with unmistakable disfavour, Colonel Forrester with a kind of tender bewilderment.

'Cressy, my dear!' he mildly protested.

And at that an astonishing change came about in Cressida. Her eyes filled with tears, her mouth quivered and she beat with her pretty clenched fists on the arms of her chair. 'All right, you lot,' she stammered. 'I know what you're thinking: how hard and mod and ghastly I'm being. All *right*. I don't drip round making sorry-he's-dead noises.

That doesn't mean I don't mind. I do. I liked him – Moult. He was nice to me. You've all seen death, haven't you? I hadn't. Not ever. Not until I looked out of my window this morning and saw them putting it in a car, face up and awful. You needn't say anything, any of you. No, Hilly, not even you – not yet. You're old, *old*, all of you and you don't *get* it. That's all. Crack ahead with your meeting for God's sake.'

They stared at each other in consternation. Cressida beat on the arms of her chair and said: 'Damn! I *won't* bloody cry. I *won't*.'

Hilary said: '*Darling* – ' but she stamped with both feet and he stopped. Smith muttered something that sounded like 'does you credit, love,' and cleared his throat.

Mrs Forrester said: 'I collect, Smith, that ludicrous as it sounds, you wish to hold some sort of meeting. Why don't you do it?'

'Give us a chance,' he said resentfully.

Alleyn said: 'I'm afraid I'm the stumbling-block. I'll leave you to it in a moment.'

Colonel Forrester, with something of an effort, got to his feet.

'Ask you to excuse me,' he said to Smith. 'I'm not much good at meetings. Never have been. If you'll allow me, Hilly, I'll just sit in your study till breakfast.'

'Fred – '

'No, B. I haven't got one of my turns. I simply would like a moment or two to myself, my dear.'

'I'll come with you.'

'*No,*' said the colonel very firmly indeed. 'Don't fuss me, B. I prefer to be alone.' He went to the door, paused and looked at Cressida. She had her hand pressed to her mouth. 'Unless,' the colonel said gently, 'you would care to join me, Cressy, presently. I think perhaps we're both duffers at meetings, don't you?'

She lifted her hand from her lips, sketched the gesture of blowing him a kiss, and contrived a smile. 'I'll come,' said Cressida. The colonel nodded and left them. Alleyn opened the door for him. Before he could shut it again Mr Fox appeared. Alleyn went out to him pulling the door to. According to its habit it clicked and opened a few inches.

Fox rumbled at some length. Isolated words reached the listeners round the fire. 'Finished . . . dressing-room . . . nothing . . . latent . . . urgent.'

Alleyn said: 'Yes. All right. Tell the men to assemble in the stable yard. I want to speak to them. Tell Bailey and Thompson to leave the box out and the dressing-room unlocked. We've finished up there. Colonel Forrester will open the box when he's ready to do so.'

'It's an urgent phone call, Mr Alleyn.'

'Yes. All right. I'll take it. Away you go.'

He started off, clapped his hand to his waistcoat and said: 'Damn, I forgot. The key of the box?'

'I've got it. Nothing for us, there.'

'Let the colonel have it, then, will you, Fox?'

'Very good, sir.'

'I'll take this call in the drawing-room. I'll probably be some time over it. Carry on, Fox, will you? Collect the men outside at the back.'

'Certainly, sir,' Fox said.

Fox shut the library door and Alleyn went into the hall.

But he didn't speak on the drawing-room, or any other telephone. He ran upstairs two steps at a time jolting discomfort to his left arm and sought out his wife in their room.

'My love,' he said. 'I want you to stay put. Here. And be a triple ape.'

'What on earth's a triple ape?'

Alleyn rapidly touched her eyes, ears and lips.

'Oh,' she said flatly. 'I see. And I don't breathe either, I suppose.'

'There's my girl. Now listen – '

He had not gone far with what he had to say before there was a knock on the door. At a nod from him, Troy called out: 'Just a second. Who is it?'

The door opened a crack.

Fox whispered. 'Me.'

Alleyn went to him. 'Well?'

'Like a lamb,' said Fox, 'to the slaughter.'

CHAPTER 10

Departure

'What I got to say,' said Mr Smith, 'is important and I'll thank you to hear me out. When I've said it, I'll welcome comment but hear me out first. It's a bit of luck for us that flipping door opens of itself. You heard. He's got a phone call and he's going to talk to his mob in the backyard. That gives us a breather. All right. He's made up his mind, Gawd knows why, that your lovely lot's out of it, 'Illy. That means – it's got to mean – 'e's settled for one of us. So what we say in the next confrontation is bloody important. No, missus, don't butt in. Your turn's coming.

'Now. We know Alf Moult was alive when 'e finished 'is act and waltzed out of the drawing-room winder. We know 'e was alive when 'e had 'is whiskers taken off. We know he was left, alive, in the cloakroom. And that's all we do know of our own observations. So. The important thing for us is to be able to account for ourselves, all of us, from the time we last see 'im. Right? A-course it's right.

'Well then. As it appears, we all can answer for the fair sex in the person of Cressy Tottenham. Matter of a minute after Alf finished his act, Cressy come in having removed his whiskers for 'im and she certainly hadn't 'ad time to do 'im in and dispose of 'is body.'

'Look here, Uncle Bert – '

'All right, all right, all right! I said she couldn't of, didn't I? So she couldn't of. This is important. From Cressy's point of view. Because she seems to of been the last to see 'im alive. Except of course, 'is slayer and that puts 'er in a special category.'

'It does nothing of the sort,' Hilary said.

'Don't be silly, Hilary,' said his aunt. 'Go on, Smith.'

'Ta. To resume. I was coming to you, missus. Cressy come in and mentioned to you it was Alf and not the colonel done the Daddy Christmas act and you lit off. Where did you go?'

'To my husband. Naturally.'

'Straight off? Direct?'

'Certainly, To our bedroom.'

'You didn't look in on the dressing-room?'

'I did not.'

'Can you prove it?'

Mrs Forrester reddened angrily. 'No,' she said.

'That's unfortunate, innit?'

'Nonsense. Don't be impertinent.'

'Ah, for Gawd's sake!'

'Aunt B, he's trying to help us.'

'When I require help I'll ask for it.'

'You require it now, you silly old bag,' said Mr Smith.

'How dare you speak to me like that!'

'Uncle Bert – *really*.'

'And what about yourself, 'Illy? We'll be coming to you in a sec Where was I? Oh, yes. With Cressy in the drawing-room. She tells you two about the job and one after another you leave the room. Where did you go?'

'I? I looked for Moult to thank him, I looked in the cloakroom and the library and I went upstairs to see if he was there. And I visited Uncle Flea and Aunt B was with him and finally I joined you all in the dining-room.'

'There you are,' said Mr Smith. 'So if Alf Moult went upstairs you or your auntie or (supposing he hadn't 'ad one of 'is turns) your uncle, *could* of done 'im in.'

'Well – my dear Uncle Bert – "could have"! Yes, I suppose so. But so could – ' Hilary stopped short.

'So could who? I couldn't of. Mrs Alleyn couldn't of. Cressy couldn't of. We was all sitting down to our Christmas dinner, good as gold as anyone will bear us out.'

Mrs Forrester said: 'Are we to take it, Smith, that your attitude is entirely altruistic? If you are persuaded that you are completely free of suspicion, why all this fuss?'

'Innit marvellous?' Mr Smith apostrophized. 'Innit bleeding marvellous? A man sees 'is friends, or what 'e thought was 'is friends, in a nasty situation and tries to give them the office. What does 'e get? You can't win, can you?'

'I'm sure,' she said, 'we're very much obliged to you, Smith. There's one aspect of this affair, however, that I think you have overlooked.'

She paused, thrust her hands up the opposite sleeves of her magenta cardigan and rested them on her stomach. 'Isn't it possible,' she said, 'that Moult was done away with much later in the evening? Your uncle, Hilary, will not care to admit it but Moult did, from time to time, indulge in drinking bouts. I think it extremely likely this was such an occasion. Cressida considers he had drink concealed about his person. He may well have taken it after his performance, hidden himself away somewhere, possibly in a car, and thus eluded the searchers and emerged later in the evening – to be murdered.'

'You've thought it all out very nice and tidy, 'aven't you?' sneered Mr Smith.

'And so, you may depend upon it, has Mr Alleyn,' she retorted.

'The search was very thorough, Aunt Bed.'

'Did they look in the cars?'

Hilary was silent.

'In which case,' Mrs Forrester said exactly as if he had answered, 'I cannot see that you, Smith, or Cressida or indeed you, Hilary, are to be excluded from the list of suspected persons.'

'What about yourself?' Smith asked.

'I?' she said with her customary spirit. 'No doubt I could have killed Moult. I had no conceivable motive for killing him but no doubt I could have done so.'

'Nothing simpler. You go up to the colonel who's on 'is bed and asleep. You hear Alf Moult in the dressing-room. You go froo the barfroom into the dressing-room, pick up the poker and Bob's your uncle. You shove the corpse out of the winder.' Mr Smith caught himself up. 'You did say Vince and Co. picked it up under the winder, didn't you, 'Illy?'

'I don't think I said anything about it. But according to Alleyn, yes, they did.'

'The *modus operandi* you have outlined, Smith, could have been used by anybody if my theory is correct. You've talked a great deal but you've proved nothing, I said you've – '

'Don't you bawl me out as if I was your old man,' Mr Smith roared. 'I been watching you, missus. You been acting very peculiar. You got something up your sleeve you're not letting on about.'

Hilary, with a wildish look, cried out: 'I won't have this sort of thing!'

'Yes, you will. You can't help yourself. You want to watch your aunt. I did. When Alleyn was talking about that marvellous tin box. You didn't like that, missus, did you?'

Mr Smith advanced upon Mrs Forrester. He jabbed at her with a fat forefinger. 'Come on,' he said. 'What's it all about? What's in the ruddy tin box?'

Mrs Forrester walked out of the room slamming the door. When she had gone it opened silently of its own accord.

II

The key fitted. It turned easily. Now. The hoop was disengaged. The hasp was more difficult, it really needed a lever but there was none to hand and at the cost of a broken fingernail in spite of a glove it was finally prised up from the staple.

The lid opened to a vertical position but tended to fall forward so that it was necessary to prop it up with the head. This was irksome.

A cash box: locked. A map-case. Canvas bags, tied at the neck with red tape. Tubular cartons. Manilla envelopes, labelled. 'Correspondence: B to F.F. F.F. to B.' He had kept all their letters.

'Receipts'. 'Correspondence, general.' 'Travel, etc.' 'Miscellaneous.' A document in a grand envelope. 'To our Trusty and Well-beloved – '

It was necessary to keep calm. To keep what Cressida called one's cool. Not to scrabble wildly in the welter of accumulated papers. To be methodical and workmanlike. Sensible.

A locked box that rattled. The jewels she hadn't taken out for the party. And at last a leather despatch-case with an envelope flap: locked.

No panic but something rather like it when somebody walked past the door. The keys had been removed so one couldn't lock the door.

The impulse to get out at once with the case and deal with it in safety was almost irresistible but it presented its own problems. If only one knew how to pick a lock! Perhaps they would think that Moult had burst it. It was a sliding mechanism with a metal hinged piece on the leather flap engaging with a lock on the case itself. Perhaps the slide could be knocked down? Or, better, force the hinged piece up? The poker, of course, had gone but there were the tongs with their little thin flat ends.

Yes. Between the metal flap and the lock there was just room. Shove. Shove hard and force it up.

There!

A diary. A large envelope. *My Will*. Not sealed. A rapid look at it. Leave that. Put it back – quick. The thing itself: a reinforced envelope and inside it the document, printed in German, filled in and signed. The statement in Colonel Forrester's hand. The final words: 'declare her to be my daughter' and the signature: 'Alfred Moult'.

Replace the despatch-case, quick, quick, quick,

Relock the tin box. Back into the wardrobe with it. Now, the envelope. She must hide it under her cardigan and away.

She stood up, breathless.

The doors opened simultaneously and before she could cry out there were men in the room and Alleyn advancing upon her.

'I'm afraid,' he said, 'this is it.'

And for the second time during their short acquaintance Cressida screamed at the top of her voice.

III

'It's been a short cut,' Alleyn said. 'We left the library door open and let it be known the coast was clear. Fox displayed the key of the pad-lock, Cressida Tottenham said she was on her way to the study and would give it to the colonel. We went upstairs, kept out of sight and walked in on her. It was a gamble and it might never have come off. In which case we would have been landed with a most exhaustive routine investigation. We are, still, of course but with the advantage of her first reaction. She was surprised and flabbergasted and she gave herself away in several most significant places.'

'Rory – when did you first – ?'

'Oh – that. Almost from the beginning, I think,' said he with a callow smirk. 'You see, there everybody was, accepting her story that Moult substituted for the colonel, which put her ostensibly in the clear and made a squinteyed nonsense of the evidence: the robe, the wig, the lot. Whereas if she had substituted for the colonel there was no confusion.

'She hit Moult on the base of his skull with the poker in the dressing-room, probably when he was leaning out of the window looking for his signal from Vincent, who, by the way, saw him and, according to plan, at once hauled his sledge round to the front. At this point the bells started up. A deafening clamour. She removed the wig and the robe which unzips completely down the back. If he was lolling over the sill, there'd be no trouble. Nor would it be all that difficult to tumble him out.

'The tricky bit, no doubt, was going downstairs but by that time, as she knew when she heard the bells, the whole household, including the staff, were assembled in the library. Even if one of the servants had seen her carrying the robe and all the other gear, they'd have thought nothing of it at the time. She went into the dressing-room, stuffed a couple of cotton-wool pads in her cheeks and put on the wig, the robe, the great golden beard and moustache and the mistletoe crown. And the fur-lined boots. *And* the colonel's woolly gloves which you all thought he'd forgotten. And away she went. She was met by the unsuspecting Vincent. She waltzed round the Christmas tree, returned to the cloakroom and offed with her lendings. In five minutes she was asking you if Moult did his act all right because she couldn't see very well from the back of the room.'

'Rory – where is she?'

'In her bedroom with a copper at the door. Why?'

'Is she – frightened?'

'When I left her she was furious. She tried to bite me. Luckily I was on my guard so she didn't repeat her success with the vase.'

Alleyn looked at his wife. 'I know, my love,' he said. 'Your capacity for pity is on the Dostoyevskian scale.' He put his arm round her. 'You are such a treat,' he said. 'Apart from being a bloody genius. I can't get over you. After all these years. Odd, isn't it?'

'Did she work it out beforehand?'

'No. Not the assault. It was an improvisation – a *toccata*. Now, she's in for the fugue.'

'But – those tricks – the booby-trap and all?'

'Designed to set Bill-Tasman against his cosy little clutch of homicides. She would have preferred a group of resentful Greeks in flight from the Colonels.'

'Poor old Hilary.'

'Well – yes. But she really is a horrid piece of work. All the same, there are extenuating circumstances. In my job one examines them, as you know, at one's peril.'

'Go on.'

'At one's peril,' he repeated and then said, 'I don't know at what stage Colonel Forrester felt he was, according to his code, obliged to step in. From the tenor of the documents in that infernal tin box one gathers that she was Moult's daughter by a German girl who died in childbirth, that it was Moult who, with great courage, saved the colonel's life and got a badly scarred face for his pains. That Moult had means comprising a tidy inheritance from a paternal tobacconist's shop, his savings, his pay and his wages. That the colonel, poor dear, felt himself to be under a lifelong debt to Moult. All right. Now Moult, like many of his class was an unrepentant snob. He wanted his natural daughter upon whom he doted to be "brought up a lady". He wanted the colonel to organize this process. He wanted to watch the process, as it were, from well back in the pit, unidentified, completely anonymous. And so it fell out. Until the whirligig of time, according to its practice, brought in its revenges. Hilary Bill-Tasman having encountered her at his uncle's and aunt's house, decided that she was just the chatelaine for Halberds and, incidentally, the desire of his heart. She seemed to fill the bill in every possible respect. "Tottenham" for instance. A damn good family.'

'Is it?' said Troy. 'Yes. Well. *Tottenham*. Why Tottenham?'

'I'll ask the colonel,' said Alleyn.

IV

'Moult,' said the colonel, 'was a keen follower of The Spurs. He chose it for that reason.'

'We didn't care for it,' said Mrs Forrester. 'After all, there are – Fred tried to suggest Bolton or Wolverhampton but he wouldn't hear of them. She is Tottenham by deed-poll.'

'How,' Alleyn asked, 'did it all come to a crisis?'

The colonel stared dolefully into space. 'You tell him, B,' he said.

'With the engagement. Fred felt – we both felt – that we couldn't let Hilary marry under false pretences. She had told him all sorts of tarradiddles – '

'Wait a bit,' Alleyn said. 'Did she know – ?'

They both cried out: no, of course she didn't. She had only been told that she had no parents, that there were no relatives.

'This was agreed upon with Moult,' said the colonel. 'She grew up from infancy in this belief. Of course, when she visited us he saw her.'

'Gloated,' Mrs Forrester interpolated. 'Took her to the zoo.'

'*Peter Pan* and all that,' her husband agreed. ''Fraid he forgot himself a bit and let her understand all sorts of fairy-tales – father's rank and all that.'

But it emerged that on her own account Cressida had built up a magnificent fantasy for herself and when she discovered that Hilary was steeped up to the teeth in armorial bearings went to all extremes to present herself in a complementary image.

'You see,' the colonel said unhappily, 'Hilary sets such store by that sort of thing. She considered, and one can't say without cause, that if he learnt that she had been embroidering he would take a grave view. I blame myself, I blame myself entirely, but when she persisted I told her that she should put all that nonsense out of her head and I'm afraid I went further than that.'

'He told her,' said his wife, 'without of course implicating Moult, that she came from a sound but not in the least grand sort of background, quite humble in fact and she – from something he said – she's quick, you know – she realized that she'd been born out of wedlock. Fred told her it wouldn't be honourable to marry Hilary letting him think all this nonsense. Fred said that if Hilary loved her the truth wouldn't stop him.'

'I – warned her – ' the colonel said and stopped.

'That if *she* didn't tell him, *you* would.'

The colonel opened his eyes as wide as saucers: 'Yes. I did. How did you know?' he said.

'I guessed,' Alleyn lied.

There was a long silence.

'Oh, yes?' said Mrs Forrester with a gimlet glance at the wardrobe door.

The colonel made a helpless gesture with his thin hands. 'What is so dreadful,' he said, 'what I cannot reconcile myself to believe is that – that she – '

He got up and walked over to the windows. Mrs Forrester made a portentous grimace at Alleyn.

' – that when she attacked Moult she mistook him for you?' Alleyn suggested.

He nodded.

'Believe me, Colonel,' Alleyn said, going to him. 'You need have no misgivings about that. She knew it was Moult. Believe me.'

The colonel gazed at him. 'But – I – of course one is relieved in a way. Of course. One can't help it? But – Moult? Why my poor Moult? Why her – ? No!' he cried out. 'No. I don't want to hear. Don't tell me.'

V

But Alleyn told Hilary.

He and Hilary and at the latter's entreaty, Troy, sat together in the study. The police, apart from Alleyn's driver had gone and so had Cressida and so, in a mortuary car, had her father, Alfred Moult.

As if to promote a kind of phoney symbolism, the sun had come out and the snow was melting.

Hilary said to Troy. 'But you see, she's so very beautiful. That's what diddled me, I suppose. I mean, all her ongoings and rather tedious conversation, for me was filtered through her loveliness. It reached me as something rather endearing – or, to be honest, didn't reach me at all.' He fell into a brief reverie. The look that Troy had secured in her painting – the faint smirk – crept into the corners of his mouth. 'It's all quite dreadful,' he said, 'and of course, in a way I'm shattered. I promise you – shattered. But – I understand from Uncle Flea and Aunt Bed, she really did tell me the most awful whoppers. I mean – "Tottenham" and so on.'

Troy said: 'She knew you minded about things like that.'

'Of course I do. I'm the last of the howling snobs. But – Moult? *Moult!* Her papa!'

'She didn't know,' Alleyn said, 'about Moult.'

Hilary pounced: 'When did she find out?' he snapped. 'Or did she? Has she – has she – confessed?'

'She's said enough,' Alleyn said sparsely. And as Hilary stared at him: 'She knew that documents relating to her parentage were in the uniform case. The colonel told her so when he said that you should know of her background. When she thought that the colonel was downstairs in the cloakroom waiting for her and when everybody else had assembled for the tree, she tried to break into the case with the dressing-room poker. Moult, who had been showing himself to the colonel in his robe and wig, returned to the dressing-room and caught her in the act. Climax. He'd taken a lot to drink, he was excited and he told her. The bells had started up downstairs, he looked out of the window for Vincent and she hit him with the poker.'

'Unpremeditated, then,' Hilary said quickly. 'Not planned? A kind of reflex thing? Yes?'

'You may say so.'

'At least one may be glad of that. And no designs upon poorest Uncle Flea. Thank heaven for *that*.'

Alleyn said nothing. There would not, he believed, be cause to produce the evidence of the wedge in the colonel's window sash nor of the concealment of his tablets.

'The defence,' he said, 'will probably seek to have the charge reduced to one of manslaughter.'

'How long – ?'

'Difficult to say. She may get off.'

Hilary looked alarmed.

'But not altogether, I fancy,' said Alleyn.

'You might almost say,' Hilary ventured after a pause, 'that my poor creatures, Vincent and Co., collaborated.'

'In a way, I suppose you might.'

'Yes,' Hilary said in a hurry, 'but it's one thing to staff one's house with – er "oncers" but quite another to – ' He stopped short and turned rather pink.

'I think we should be off, Rory,' said Troy.

Hilary was effusive in thanks, exclamations about his portrait, apologies and expressions of goodwill.

As they drove away in the thin sunshine he stood, manorially, on the steps of the great porch. Mervyn and Cuthbert, having assisted with the luggage, were in the offing. At the last moment Hilary was joined by Mr Smith and the Forresters. Troy waved to them.

'We might be going away from a jolly weekend party,' she said.

'Do you know,' her husband asked, 'what Hilary nearly said?'

'What?'

'That when she comes out she'll qualify for a job at Halberds. Not quite the one envisaged. Parlour-maid perhaps. With perks.'

'Rory!'

'I bet you anything you like,' said Alleyn.

Chapter and Verse:
The Little
Copplestone Mystery

Chapter and Verse was first published in *Ellery Queen's Mystery Magazine* (USA) in 1973.

When the telephone rang, Troy came in, sun-dazzled, from the cottage garden to answer it, hoping it would be a call from London.

'Oh,' said a strange voice uncertainly. 'May I speak to Superintendent Alleyn, if you please?'

'I'm sorry. He's away.'

'Oh, dear!' said the voice, crestfallen. 'Er – would that be – am I speaking to Mrs Alleyn?'

'Yes.'

'Oh. Yes. Well, it's Timothy Bates here, Mrs Alleyn. You don't know me,' the voice confessed wistfully, 'but I had the pleasure several years ago of meeting your husband. In New Zealand. And he did say that if I ever came home I was to get in touch, and when I heard quite by accident that you were here – well, I *was* excited. But, alas, no good after all.'

'I *am* sorry,' Troy said. 'He'll be back, I hope, on Sunday night. Perhaps – '

'Will he! Come, *that's* something! Because here I am at the Star and Garter, you see, and so – ' The voice trailed away again.

'Yes, indeed. He'll be delighted,' Troy said, hoping that he would.

'I'm a bookman,' the voice confided. 'Old books, you know. He used to come into my shop. It was always such a pleasure.'

'But, of course!' Troy exclaimed. 'I remember perfectly now. He's often talked about it.'

'*Has* he? Has he, really! Well, you see, Mrs Alleyn, I'm here on business. Not to *sell* anything, please don't think that, but on a

637

voyage of discovery; almost, one might say, of detection, and I think it might amuse him. He has such an eye for the curious. Not,' the voice hurriedly amended, 'in the trade sense. I mean curious in the sense of mysterious and unusual. But I mustn't bore you.'

Troy assured him that he was not boring her and indeed it was true. The voice was so much coloured by odd little overtones that she found herself quite drawn to its owner. 'I know where you are,' he was saying. 'Your house was pointed out to me.'

After that there was nothing to do but ask him to visit. He seemed to cheer up prodigiously. 'May I? May I, really? Now?'

'Why not?' Troy said. 'You'll be here in five minutes.'

She heard a little crow of delight before he hung up the receiver.

He turned out to be exactly like his voice – a short, middle-aged, bespectacled man, rather untidily dressed. As he came up the path she saw that with both arms he clutched to his stomach an enormous Bible. He was thrown into a fever over the difficulty of removing his cap.

'How ridiculous!' he exclaimed. 'Forgive me! One moment.'

He laid his burden tenderly on a garden seat, 'There!' he cried. 'Now! How do you do!'

Troy took him indoors and gave him a drink. He chose sherry and sat in the window seat with his Bible beside him. 'You'll wonder,' he said, 'why I've appeared with this unusual piece of baggage. I *do* trust it arouses your curiosity.'

He went into a long excitable explanation. It appeared that the Bible was an old and rare one that he had picked up in a job lot of books in New Zealand. All this time he kept it under his square little hands as if it might open of its own accord and spoil his story.

'Because,' he said, 'the *really* exciting thing to me is *not* its undoubted authenticity but – ' He made a conspiratorial face at Troy and suddenly opened the Bible. 'Look!' he invited.

He displayed the flyleaf. Troy saw that it was almost filled with entries in a minute, faded copperplate handwriting.

'The top,' Mr Bates cried. 'Top left-hand. Look at *that*.'

Troy read: '*Crabtree Farm at Little Copplestone in the County of Kent*. Why, it comes from our village!'

'Ah, ha! So it does. Now, the entries, my dear Mrs Alleyn. The entries.'

They were the recorded births and deaths of a family named Wagstaff, beginning in 1705 and ending in 1870 with the birth of William James Wagstaff. Here they broke off but were followed by three further entries, close together.

Stewart Shakespeare Hadet. Died: Tuesday, 5th April, 1779. 2nd Samuel 1.10.

Naomi Balbus Hadet. Died: Saturday, 13th August, 1779. Jeremiah 50.24.

Peter Rook Hadet. Died: Monday, 12th September, 1779. Ezekiel 7.6.

Troy looked up to find Mr Bates's gaze fixed on her. 'And what,' Mr Bates asked, 'my dear Mrs Alleyn, do you make of *that*?'

'Well,' she said cautiously, 'I know about Crabtree Farm. There's the farm itself, owned by Mr De'ath, and there's Crabtree House, belonging to Miss Hart, and – yes, I fancy I've heard they both belonged originally to a family named Wagstaff.'

'You are perfectly right. Now! What about the Hadets? What about *them*?'

'I've never heard of a family named Hadet in Little Copplestone. But – '

'Of course you haven't. For the very good reason that there never have been any Hadets in Little Copplestone.'

'Perhaps in New Zealand, then?'

'The dates, my dear Mrs Alleyn, the dates! New Zealand was not colonized in 1779. Look closer. Do you see the sequence of double dots – ditto marks – under the address? Meaning, of course, "also of Crabtree Farm at Little Copplestone in the County of Kent".'

'I suppose so.'

'Of course you do. And how right you are. Now! You have noticed that throughout there are biblical references. For the Wagstaffs they are the usual pious offerings. You need not trouble yourself with them. But consult the text awarded to the three Hadets. Just you look *them* up! I've put markers.'

He threw himself back with an air of triumph and sipped his sherry. Troy turned over the heavy bulk of pages to the first marker. 'Second of Samuel, one, ten,' Mr Bates prompted, closing his eyes.

The verse had been faintly underlined.

'*So I stood upon him,*' Troy read, '*and slew him.*'

'That's Stewart Shakespeare Hadet's valedictory,' said Mr Bates. 'Next!'

The next was at the 50th chapter of Jeremiah, verse 24: *'I have laid a snare for thee and thou are taken.'*

Troy looked at Mr Bates. His eyes were still closed and he was smiling faintly.

'That was Naomi Balbus Hadet,' he said. 'Now for Peter Rook Hadet. Ezekiel, seven, six.'

The pages flopped back to the last marker.

'An end is come, the end is come: it watcheth for thee; behold it is come.'

Troy shut the Bible.

'How very unpleasant,' she said.

'And how very intriguing, don't you think?' And when she didn't answer, 'Quite up your husband's street, it seemed to me.'

'I'm afraid,' Troy said, 'that even Rory's investigations don't go back to 1779.'

'What a pity!' Mr Bates cried gaily.

'Do I gather that you conclude from all this that there was dirty work among the Hadets in 1779?'

'I don't know, but I'm dying to find out. *Dying* to. Thank you, I should enjoy another glass. Delicious!'

He had settled down so cosily and seemed to be enjoying himself so much that Troy was constrained to ask him to stay to lunch.

'Miss Hart's coming,' she said. 'She's the one who bought Crabtree House from the Wagstaffs. If there's any gossip to be picked up in Copplestone, Miss Hart's the one for it. She's coming about a painting she wants me to donate to the Harvest Festival raffle.'

Mr Bates was greatly excited. 'Who knows!' he cried. 'A Wagstaff in the hand may be worth two Hadets in the bush. I am your slave forever, my dear Mrs Alleyn!'

Miss Hart was a lady of perhaps sixty-seven years. On meeting Mr Bates she seemed to imply that some explanation should be advanced for Troy receiving a gentleman caller in her husband's absence. When the Bible was produced, she immediately accepted it in this light, glanced with professional expertise at the inscriptions and fastened on the Wagstaffs.

'No doubt,' said Miss Hart, 'it was their family Bible and much good it did them. A most eccentric lot they were. Very unsound. Very unsound, indeed. Especially Old Jimmy.'

'Who,' Mr Bates asked greedily, 'was Old Jimmy?'

Miss Hart jabbed her forefinger at the last of the Wagstaff entries. 'William James Wagstaff. Born 1870. And died, although it doesn't say so, in April, 1921. Nobody was left to complete the entry, of course. Unless you count the niece, which I don't. Baggage, if ever I saw one.'

'The niece?'

'Fanny Wagstaff. Orphan. Old Jimmy brought her up. Dragged would be the better word. Drunken old reprobate he was and he came to a drunkard's end. They said he beat her *and* I daresay she needed it.' Miss Hart lowered her voice to a whisper and confided in Troy. 'Not a *nice* girl. You know what I mean.'

Troy, feeling it was expected of her, nodded portentously.

'A drunken end, did you say?' prompted Mr Bates.

'Certainly. On a Saturday night after Market. Fell through the top landing stair rail in his nightshirt and split his skull on the flagstoned hall.'

'And your father bought it, then, after Old Jimmy died?' Troy ventured.

'Bought the house and garden. Richard De'ath took the farm. He'd been after it for years – wanted it to round off his own place. He and Old Jimmy were at daggers drawn over *that* business. And, of course, Richard being an atheist, over the Seven Seals.'

'I beg your pardon?' Mr Bates asked.

'Blasphemous!' Miss Hart shouted. 'That's what it was, rank blasphemy. It was a sect that Wagstaff founded. If the rector had known his business he'd have had him excommunicated for it.'

Miss Hart was prevented from elaborating this theory by the appearance at the window of an enormous woman, stuffily encased in black, with a face like a full moon.

'Anybody at home?' the newcomer playfully chanted. 'Telegram for a lucky girl! Come and get it!'

It was Mrs Simpson, the village postmistress. Miss Hart said, 'Well, *really*!' and gave an acid laugh.

'Sorry, I'm sure,' said Mrs Simpson, staring at the Bible which lay under her nose on the window seat. 'I didn't realize there was company. Thought I'd pop it in as I was passing.'

Troy read the telegram while Mrs Simpson, panting, sank heavily on the window ledge and eyed Mr Bates, who had drawn back in confusion. 'I'm no good in the heat,' she told him. 'Slays me.'

'Thank you so much, Mrs Simpson,' Troy said. 'No answer.'

'Righty-ho. Cheerie-bye,' said Mrs Simpson and with another stare at Mr Bates and the Bible, and a derisive grin at Miss Hart, she waddled away.

'It's from Rory,' Troy said. 'He'll be home on Sunday evening.'

'As that woman will no doubt inform the village,' Miss Hart pronounced. 'A busybody of the first water and ought to be taught her place. Did you ever!'

She fulminated throughout luncheon and it was with difficulty that Troy and Mr Bates persuaded her to finish her story of the last of the Wagstaffs. It appeared that Old Jimmy had died intestate, his niece succeeding. She had at once announced her intention of selling everything and had left the district to pursue, Miss Hart suggested, a life of freedom, no doubt in London or even in Paris. Miss Hart wouldn't, and didn't want to, know. On the subject of the Hadets, however, she was uninformed and showed no inclination to look up the marked Bible references attached to them.

After luncheon Troy showed Miss Hart three of her paintings, any one of which would have commanded a high price at an exhibition of contemporary art, and Miss Hart chose the one that, in her own phrase, really did look like something. She insisted that Troy and Mr Bates accompany her to the parish hall where Mr Bates would meet the rector, an authority on village folklore. Troy in person must hand over her painting to be raffled.

Troy would have declined this honour if Mr Bates had not retired behind Miss Hart and made a series of beseeching gestures and grimaces. They set out therefore in Miss Hart's car which was crammed with vegetables for the Harvest Festival decorations.

'And if the woman Simpson thinks she's going to hog the lectern with *her* pumpkins,' said Miss Hart, 'she's in for a shock. Hah!'

St Cuthbert's was an ancient parish church round whose flanks the tiny village nestled. Its tower, an immensely high one, was said to be unique. Nearby was the parish hall where Miss Hart pulled up with a masterful jerk.

Troy and Mr Bates helped her unload some of her lesser marrows to be offered for sale within. They were observed by a truculent-looking man in tweeds who grinned at Miss Hart. 'Burnt offerings,' he jeered, 'for the tribal gods, I perceive.' It was Mr Richard De'ath, the atheist. Miss Hart cut him dead and led the way into the hall.

Here they found the rector, with a crimson-faced elderly man and a clutch of ladies engaged in preparing for the morrow's sale.

The rector was a thin gentle person, obviously frightened of Miss Hart and timidly delighted by Troy. On being shown the Bible he became excited and dived at once into the story of Old Jimmy Wagstaff.

'Intemperate, I'm afraid, in everything,' sighed the rector. 'Indeed, it would not be too much to say that he both preached and drank hellfire. He *did* preach, on Saturday nights at the crossroads outside the Star and Garter. Drunken, blasphemous nonsense it was and although he used to talk about his followers, the only one he could claim was his niece, Fanny, who was probably too much under his thumb to refuse him.'

'Edward Pilbrow,' Miss Hart announced, jerking her head at the elderly man who had come quite close to them. 'Drowned him with his bell. They had a fight over it. Deaf as a post,' she added, catching sight of Mr Bates's startled expression. 'He's the verger now. *And* the town crier.'

'What!' Mr Bates exclaimed.

'Oh, yes,' the rector explained. 'The village is endowed with a town crier.' He went over to Mr Pilbrow, who at once cupped his hand round his ear. The rector yelled into it.

'When did you start crying, Edward?'

'Twenty-ninth September, 'twenty-one,' Mr Pilbrow roared back. 'I thought so.'

There was something in their manner that made it difficult to remember, Troy thought, that they were talking about events that were almost fifty years back in the past. Even the year 1779 evidently seemed to them to be not so long ago, but, alas, none of them knew of any Hadets.

'By all means,' the rector invited Mr Bates, 'consult the church records, but I can assure you – no Hadets. Never any Hadets.'

Troy saw an expression of extreme obstinacy settle round Mr Bates's mouth.

The rector invited him to look at the church and as they both seemed to expect Troy to tag along, she did so. In the lane they once more encountered Mr Richard De'ath out of whose pocket protruded a paper-wrapped bottle. He touched his cap to Troy and glared at the rector, who turned pink and said, 'Afternoon, De'ath,' and hurried on.

Mr Bates whispered imploringly to Troy, '*Would* you mind? I *do* so want to have a word – ' and she was obliged to introduce him. It was not a successful encounter. Mr Bates no sooner broached the topic of his Bible, which he still carried, than Mr De'ath burst into an alcoholic diatribe against superstition, and on the mention of Old Jimmy Wagstaff, worked himself up into such a state of reminiscent fury that Mr Bates was glad to hurry away with Troy.

They overtook the rector in the churchyard, now bathed in the golden opulence of an already westering sun.

'There they all lie,' the rector said, waving a fatherly hand at the company of headstones. 'All your Wagstaffs, right back to the sixteenth century. But no Hadets, Mr Bates, I assure you.'

They stood looking up at the spire. Pigeons flew in and out of a balcony far above their heads. At their feet was a little flagged area edged by a low coping. Mr Bates stepped forward and the rector laid a hand on his arm.

'Not there,' he said. 'Do you mind?'

'Don't!' bellowed Mr Pilbrow from the rear. 'Don't you set foot on them bloody stones, Mister.' Mr Bates backed away.

'Edward's not swearing,' the rector mildly explained. 'He is to be taken, alas, literally. A sad and dreadful story, Mr Bates.'

'Indeed?' Mr Bates asked eagerly.

'Indeed, yes. Some time ago, in the very year we have been discussing – 1921, you know – one of our girls, a very beautiful girl she was, named Ruth Wall, fell from the balcony of the tower and was, of course, killed. She used to go up there to feed the pigeons and it was thought that in leaning over the low balustrade she overbalanced.'

'Ah!' Mr Pilbrow roared with considerable relish, evidently guessing the purport of the rector's speech. 'Terrible, terrible! And 'er sweetheart after 'er, too. Terrible!'

'Oh, no!' Troy protested.

The rector made a dabbing gesture to subdue Mr Pilbrow. 'I wish he wouldn't,' he said. 'Yes. It was a few days later. A lad called Simon Castle. They were to be married. People said it must be suicide but – it may have been wrong of me – I couldn't bring myself – in short, he lies beside her over there. If you would care to look.'

For a minute or two they stood before the headstones.

'Ruth Wall. Spinster of this Parish. 1903-1921. *I will extend peace to her like a river.*'

'Simon Castle. Bachelor of this Parish. 1900–1921. *And God shall wipe away all tears from their eyes.*'

The afternoon having by now worn on, and the others having excused themselves, Mr Bates remained alone in the churchyard, clutching his Bible and staring at the headstones. The light of the hunter's zeal still gleamed in his eyes.

Troy didn't see Mr Bates again until Sunday night service when, on her way up the aisle, she passed him, sitting in the rearmost pew. She was amused to observe that his gigantic Bible was under the seat.

'*We plough the fields,*' sang the choir, '*and scatter –* ' Mrs Simpson roared away on the organ, the smell of assorted greengrocery rising like some humble incense. Everybody in Little Copplestone except Mr Richard De'ath was there for the Harvest Festival. At last the rector stepped over Miss Hart's biggest pumpkin and ascended the pulpit, Edward Pilbrow switched off all the lights except one and they settled down for the sermon.

'A sower went forth to sow,' announced the rector. He spoke simply and well but somehow Troy's attention wandered. She found herself wondering where, through the centuries, the succeeding generations of Wagstaffs had sat until Old Jimmy took to his freakish practices; and whether Ruth Wall and Simon Castle, poor things, had shared the same hymn book and held hands during the sermon; and whether, after all, Stewart Shakespeare Hadet and Peter Rook Hadet had not, in 1779, occupied some dark corner of the church and been unaccountably forgotten.

Here we are, Troy thought drowsily, and there, outside in the churchyard, are all the others going back and back–

She saw a girl, bright in the evening sunlight, reach from a balcony toward a multitude of wings. She was falling – dreadfully – into nothingness. Troy woke with a sickening jerk.

' – on stony ground,' the rector was saying. Troy listened guiltily to the rest of the sermon.

Mr Bates emerged on the balcony. He laid his Bible on the coping and looked at the moonlit tree tops and the churchyard so dreadfully far below. He heard someone coming up the stairway. Torchlight danced on the door jamb.

'You were quick,' said the visitor.

'I am all eagerness and, I confess, puzzlement.'

'It had to be here, on the spot. If you *really* want to find out – '

'But I do, I do!'

'We haven't much time. You've brought the Bible?'

'You particularly asked – '

'If you open it at Ezekiel, chapter twelve. I'll shine my torch.'

Mr Bates opened the Bible.

'The thirteenth verse. There!'

Mr Bates leaned forward. The Bible tipped and moved.

'Look out!' the voice urged.

Mr Bates was scarcely aware of the thrust. He felt the page tear as the book sank under his hands. The last thing he heard was the beating of a multitude of wings.

'– and forevermore,' said the rector in a changed voice, facing east. The congregation got to its feet. He announced the last hymn. Mrs Simpson made a preliminary rumble and Troy groped in her pocket for the collection plate. Presently they all filed out into the autumnal moonlight.

It was coldish in the churchyard. People stood about in groups. One or two had already moved through the lychgate. Troy heard a voice, which she recognized as that of Mr De'ath. 'I suppose,' it jeered, 'you all know you've been assisting at a fertility rite.'

'Drunk as usual, Dick De'ath,' somebody returned without rancour. There was a general laugh.

They had all begun to move away when, from the shadows at the base of the church tower, there arose a great cry. They stood, transfixed, turned toward the voice.

Out of the shadows came the rector in his cassock. When Troy saw his face she thought he must be ill and went to him.

'No, no!' he said. 'Not a woman! Edward! Where's Edward Pilbrow?'

Behind him, at the foot of the tower, was a pool of darkness; but Troy, having come closer, could see within it a figure, broken like a puppet on the flagstones. An eddy of night air stole round the church and fluttered a page of the giant Bible that lay pinned beneath the head.

It was nine o'clock when Troy heard the car pull up outside the cottage. She saw her husband coming up the path and ran to meet him, as if they had been parted for months.

He said, 'This is mighty gratifying!' And then, 'Hullo, my love. What's the matter?'

As she tumbled out her story, filled with relief at telling him, a large man with uncommonly bright eyes came up behind them.

'Listen to this, Fox,' Roderick Alleyn said. 'We're in demand, it seems.' He put his arm through Troy's and closed his hand round hers. 'Let's go indoors, shall we? Here's Fox, darling, come for a nice bucolic rest. Can we give him a bed?'

Troy pulled herself together and greeted Inspector Fox. Presently she was able to give them a coherent account of the evening's tragedy. When she had finished, Alleyn said, 'Poor little Bates. He was a nice little bloke.' He put his hand on Troy's. 'You need a drink,' he said, 'and so, by the way, do we.'

While he was getting the drinks he asked quite casually, 'You've had a shock and a beastly one at that, but there's something else, isn't there?'

'Yes,' Troy swallowed hard, 'there is. They're all saying it's an accident.'

'Yes?'

'And, Rory, I don't think it is.'

Mr Fox cleared his throat. 'Fancy,' he said.

'Suicide?' Alleyn suggested, bringing her drink to her.

'No. Certainly not.'

'A bit of rough stuff, then?'

'You sound as if you're asking about the sort of weather we've been having.'

'Well, darling, you don't expect Fox and me to go into hysterics. Why not an accident?'

'He knew all about the other accidents, he *knew* it was dangerous. And then the oddness of it, Rory. To leave the Harvest Festival service and climb the tower in the dark, carrying that enormous Bible!'

'And he was hellbent on tracing these Hadets?'

'Yes. He kept saying you'd be interested. He actually brought a copy of the entries for you.'

'Have you got it?'

She found it for him. 'The selected texts,' he said, 'are pretty rum, aren't they, Br'er Fox?' and handed it over.

'Very vindictive,' said Mr Fox.

'Mr Bates thought it was in your line,' Troy said.

'The devil he did! What's been done about this?'

'The village policeman was in the church. They sent for the doctor. And – well, you see, Mr Bates had talked a lot about you and they hope you'll be able to tell them something about him – whom they should get in touch with and so on.'

'Have they moved him?'

'They weren't going to until the doctor had seen him.' Alleyn pulled his wife's ear and looked at Fox. 'Do you fancy a stroll through the village, Foxkin?'

'There's a lovely moon,' Fox said bitterly and got to his feet.

The moon was high in the heavens when they came to the base of the tower and it shone on a group of four men – the rector, Richard De'ath, Edward Pilbrow, and Sergeant Botting, the village constable. When they saw Alleyn and Fox, they separated and revealed a fifth, who was kneeling by the body of Timothy Bates.

'Kind of you to come,' the rector said, shaking hands with Alleyn. 'And a great relief to all of us.'

Their manner indicated that Alleyn's arrival would remove a sense of personal responsibility. 'If you'd like to have a look – ?' the doctor said.

The broken body lay huddled on its side. The head rested on the open Bible. The right hand, rigid in cadaveric spasm, clutched a torn page. Alleyn knelt and Fox came closer with the torch. At the top of the page Alleyn saw the word Ezekiel and a little farther down, Chapter 12.

Using the tip of his finger Alleyn straightened the page. 'Look,' he said, and pointed to the thirteenth verse. '*My net also will I spread upon him and he shall be taken in my snare.*'

The words had been faintly underlined in mauve.

Alleyn stood up and looked round the circle of faces.

'Well,' the doctor said, 'we'd better see about moving him.'

Alleyn said, 'I don't think he should be moved just yet.'

'Not!' the rector cried out. 'But surely – to leave him like this – I mean, after this terrible accident -'

'It has yet to be proved,' Alleyn said, 'that it was an accident.'

There was a sharp sound from Richard De'ath.

' – and I fancy,' Alleyn went on, glancing at De'ath, 'that it's going to take quite a lot of proving.'

After that, events, as Fox observed with resignation, took the course that was to be expected. The local Superintendent said that under the circumstances it would be silly not to ask Alleyn to carry on, the Chief Constable agreed, and appropriate instructions came through from Scotland Yard. The rest of the night was spent in routine procedure. The body having been photographed and the Bible set aside for fingerprinting, both were removed and arrangements put in hand for the inquest.

At dawn Alleyn and Fox climbed the tower. The winding stair brought them to an extremely narrow doorway through which they saw the countryside lying vaporous in the faint light. Fox was about to go through to the balcony when Alleyn stopped him and pointed to the door jambs. They were covered with a growth of stonecrop.

About three feet from the floor this had been brushed off over a space of perhaps four inches and fragments of the microscopic plant hung from the scars. From among these, on either side, Alleyn removed morsels of dark coloured thread. 'And here,' he sighed, 'as sure as fate, we go again. O Lord, O Lord!'

They stepped through to the balcony and there was a sudden whirr and beating of wings as a company of pigeons flew out of the tower. The balcony was narrow and the balustrade indeed very low. 'If there's any looking over,' Alleyn said, 'you, my dear Foxkin, may do it.'

Nevertheless he leaned over the balustrade and presently knelt beside it. 'Look at this. Bates rested the open Bible here – blow me down flat if he didn't! There's a powder of leather where it scraped on the stone and a fragment where it tore. It must have been moved – outward. Now, why, *why*?'

'Shoved it accidentally with his knees, then made a grab and overbalanced?'

'But why put the open Bible there? To read by moonlight? *My net also will I spread upon him and he shall be taken in my snare.* Are you going to tell me he underlined it and then dived overboard?'

'I'm not going to tell you anything,' Fox grunted and then: 'That old chap Edward Pilbrow's down below swabbing the stones. He looks like a beetle.'

'Let him look like a rhinoceros if he wants to, but for the love of Mike don't leer over the edge – you give me the willies. Here, let's pick this stuff up before it blows away.'

They salvaged the scraps of leather and put them in an envelope. Since there was nothing more to do, they went down and out through the vestry and so home to breakfast.

'Darling,' Alleyn told his wife, 'you've landed us with a snorter.'

'Then you *do* think – ?'

'There's a certain degree of fishiness. Now, see here, wouldn't *somebody* have noticed little Bates get up and go out? I know he sat all alone on the back bench, but wasn't there *someone*?'

'The rector?'

'No. I asked him. Too intent on his sermon, it seems.'

'Mrs Simpson? If she looks through her little red curtain she faces the nave.'

'We'd better call on her, Fox. I'll take the opportunity to send a couple of cables to New Zealand. She's fat, jolly, keeps the shop-cum-postoffice, and is supposed to read all the postcards. Just your cup of tea. You're dynamite with postmistresses. Away we go.'

Mrs Simpson sat behind her counter doing a crossword puzzle and refreshing herself with liquorice. She welcomed Alleyn with enthusiasm. He introduced Fox and then he retired to a corner to write out his cables.

'What a catastrophe!' Mrs Simpson said, plunging straight into the tragedy. 'Shocking! As nice a little gentleman as you'd wish to meet, Mr Fox. Typical New Zealander. Pick him a mile away and a friend of Mr Alleyn's, I'm told, and if I've said it once I've said it a hundred times, Mr Fox, they ought to have put something up to prevent it. Wire netting or a bit of ironwork; but, no, they let it go on from year to year and now see what's happened – history repeating itself and giving the village a bad name. Terrible!'

Fox bought a packet of tobacco from Mrs Simpson and paid her a number of compliments on the layout of her shop, modulating from there into an appreciation of the village. He said that one always found such pleasant company in small communities. Mrs Simpson was impressed and offered him a piece of liquorice.

'As for pleasant company,' she chuckled, 'that's as may be, though by and large I suppose I mustn't grumble. I'm a cockney and a stranger here myself, Mr Fox. Only twenty-four years and that doesn't go for anything with this lot.'

'Ah,' Fox said, 'then you wouldn't recollect the former tragedies. Though to be sure,' he added, 'you wouldn't do that in any case, being much too young, if you'll excuse the liberty, Mrs Simpson.'

After this classic opening Alleyn was not surprised to hear Mrs Simpson embark on a retrospective survey of life in Little Copplestone. She was particularly lively on Miss Hart, who, she hinted, had had her eye on Mr Richard De'ath for many a long day.

'As far back as when Old Jimmy Wagstaff died, which was why she was so set on getting the next door house; but Mr De'ath never looked at anybody except Ruth Wall, and her head-over-heels in love with young Castle, which together with her falling to her destruction when feeding pigeons led Mr De'ath to forsake religion and take to drink, which he has done something cruel ever since.

'They do say he's got a terrible temper, Mr Fox, and it's well known he give Old Jimmy Wagstaff a thrashing on account of straying cattle and threatened young Castle, saying if he couldn't have Ruth, nobody else would, but fair's fair and personally I've never seen him anything but nice-mannered, drunk or sober. Speak as you find's my motto and always has been, but these old maids, when they take a fancy they get it pitiful hard. You wouldn't know a word of nine letters meaning "pale-faced lure like a sprat in a fishy story", would you?'

Fox was speechless, but Alleyn, emerging with his cables, suggested 'whitebait'.

'Correct!' shouted Mrs Simpson. 'Fits like a glove. Although it's not a bit like a sprat and a quarter the size. Cheating, I call it. Still, it fits.' She licked her indelible pencil and triumphantly added it to her crossword.

They managed to lead her back to Timothy Bates. Fox, professing a passionate interest in organ music, was able to extract from her that when the rector began his sermon she had in fact dimly observed someone move out of the back bench and through the doors. 'He must have walked round the church and in through the vestry and little did I think he was going to his death,' Mrs Simpson said with considerable relish and a sigh like an earthquake.

'You didn't happen to hear him in the vestry?' Fox ventured, but it appeared that the door from the vestry into the organ loft was shut and Mrs Simpson, having settled herself to enjoy the sermon with, as she shamelessly admitted, a bag of chocolates, was not in a position to notice.

Alleyn gave her his two cables: the first to Timothy Bates's partner in New Zealand and the second to one of his own colleagues in that country asking for any available information about relatives of the late William James Wagstaff of Little Copplestone, Kent, possibly resident in New Zealand after 1921, and of any persons of the name of Peter Rook Hadet or Naomi Balbus Hadet.

Mrs Simpson agitatedly checked over the cables, professional etiquette and burning curiosity struggling together in her enormous bosom. She restrained herself, however, merely observing that an event of this sort set you thinking, didn't it?

'And no doubt,' Alleyn said as they walked up the lane, 'she'll be telling her customers that the next stop's bloodhounds and manacles.'

'Quite a tidy armful of lady, isn't she, Mr Alleyn?' Fox calmly rejoined.

The inquest was at 10:20 in the smoking room of the Star and Garter. With half an hour in hand, Alleyn and Fox visited the churchyard. Alleyn gave particular attention to the headstones of Old Jimmy Wagstaff, Ruth Wall, and Simon Castle. 'No mention of the month or day,' he said. And after a moment: 'I wonder. We must ask the rector.'

'No need to ask the rector,' said a voice behind them. It was Miss Hart. She must have come soundlessly across the soft turf. Her air was truculent. 'Though why,' she said, 'it should be of interest, I'm sure I don't know. Ruth Wall died on August thirteenth, 1921. It was a Saturday.'

'You've a remarkable memory,' Alleyn observed.

'Not as good as it sounds. That Saturday afternoon I came to do the flowers in the church. I found her and I'm not likely ever to forget it. Young Castle went the same way almost a month later. September twelfth. In my opinion there was never a more glaring case of suicide. I believe,' Miss Hart said harshly, 'in facing facts.'

'She was a beautiful girl, wasn't she?'

'I'm no judge of beauty. She set the men by the ears. *He* was a fine-looking young fellow. Fanny Wagstaff did her best to get *him*.'

'Had Ruth Wall,' Alleyn asked, 'other admirers?'

Miss Hart didn't answer and he turned to her. Her face was blotted with an unlovely flush. 'She ruined two men's lives, if you want to know. Castle and, Richard De'ath,' said Miss Hart. She turned on her heel and without another word marched away.

'September twelfth,' Alleyn murmured. 'That would be a Monday, Br'er Fox.'

'So it would,' Fox agreed, after a short calculation, 'so it would. Quite a coincidence.'

'Or not, as the case may be. I'm going to take a gamble on this one. Come on.'

They left the churchyard and walked down the lane, overtaking Edward Pilbrow on the way. He was wearing his town crier's coat and hat and carrying his bell by the clapper. He manifested great excitement when he saw them.

'Hey!' he shouted, 'what's this I hear? Murder's the game, is it? What a go! Come on, gents, let's have it. Did 'e fall or was 'e pushed? Hor, hor, hor! Come on.'

'Not until after the inquest,' Alleyn shouted.

'Do we get a look at the body?'

'Shut up,' Mr Fox bellowed suddenly.

'I got to know, haven't I? It'll be the smartest bit of crying I ever done, this will! I reckon I might get on the telly with this. "Town crier tells old world village death stalks the churchyard." Hor, hor, hor!'

'Let us,' Alleyn whispered, 'leave this horrible old man.'

They quickened their stride and arrived at the pub, to be met with covert glances and dead silence.

The smoking room was crowded for the inquest. Everybody was there, including Mrs Simpson who sat in the back row with her candies and her crossword puzzle. It went through very quickly. The rector deposed to finding the body. Richard De'ath, sober and less truculent than usual, was questioned as to his sojourn outside the churchyard and said he'd noticed nothing unusual apart from hearing a disturbance among the pigeons roosting in the balcony. From where he stood, he said, he couldn't see the face of the tower.

An open verdict was recorded.

Alleyn had invited the rector, Miss Hart, Mrs Simpson, Richard De'ath, and, reluctantly, Edward Pilbrow, to join him in the Bar-Parlour and had arranged with the landlord that nobody else would be admitted. The Public Bar, as a result, drove a roaring trade.

When they had all been served and the hatch closed, Alleyn walked into the middle of the room and raised his hand. It was the slightest of gestures but it secured their attention.

He said, 'I think you must all realize that we are not satisfied this was an accident. The evidence against accident has been collected piecemeal from the persons in this room and I am going to put it before you. If I go wrong I want you to correct me. I ask you to do this with absolute frankness, even if you are obliged to implicate someone who you would say was the last person in the world to be capable of a crime of violence.'

He waited. Pilbrow, who had come very close, had his ear cupped in his hand. The rector looked vaguely horrified. Richard De'ath suddenly gulped down his double whisky. Miss Hart coughed over her lemonade and Mrs Simpson avidly popped a peppermint cream in her mouth and took a swig of her port and raspberry.

Alleyn nodded to Fox, who laid Mr Bates's Bible, open at the flyleaf, on the table before him.

'The case,' Alleyn said, 'hinges on this book. You have all seen the entries. I remind you of the recorded deaths in 1779 of the three Hadets – Stewart Shakespeare, Naomi Balbus, and Peter Rook. To each of these is attached a biblical text suggesting that they met their death by violence. There have never been any Hadets in this village and the days of the week are wrong for the given dates. They are right, however, for the year 1921 and *they fit the deaths,* all by falling from a height, of William Wagstaff, Ruth Wall, and Simon Castle.

'By analogy the Christian names agree. William suggests Shakespeare. Naomi – Ruth; Balbus – a wall. Simon – Peter; and a Rook is a Castle in chess. And Hadet,' Alleyn said without emphasis, 'is an anagram of Death.'

'Balderdash!' Miss Hart cried out in an unrecognizable voice.

'No, it's not,' said Mrs Simpson. 'It's jolly good crossword stuff.'

'Wicked balderdash. Richard!'

De'ath said, 'Be quiet. Let him go on.'

'We believe,' Alleyn said, 'that these three people met their deaths by one hand. Motive is a secondary consideration, but it is present in several instances, predominantly in one. Who had cause to wish the death of these three people? Someone whom old Wagstaff had bullied and to whom he had left his money and who killed him for it. Someone who was infatuated with Simon Castle and bitterly jealous of Ruth Wall. Someone who hoped, as an heiress, to win Castle for herself and who, failing, was determined nobody else should have him. Wagstaff's orphaned niece – Fanny Wagstaff.'

There were cries of relief from all but one of his hearers. He went on. 'Fanny Wagstaff sold every thing, disappeared, and was never heard of again in the village. But twenty-four years later she returned, and has remained here ever since.'

A glass crashed to the floor and a chair overturned as the vast bulk of the postmistress rose to confront him.

'Lies! *Lies!'* screamed Mrs Simpson.

'Did you sell everything again, before leaving New Zealand?' he asked as Fox moved forward. 'Including the Bible, Miss Wagstaff?'

'But,' Troy said, 'how could you be so sure?'

'She was the only one who could leave her place in the church unobserved. She was the only one fat enough to rub her hips against the narrow door jambs. She uses an indelible pencil. We presume she arranged to meet Bates on the balcony, giving a cock-and-bull promise to tell him something nobody else knew about the Hadets. She indicated the text with her pencil, gave the Bible a shove, and, as he leaned out to grab it, tipped him over the edge.

'In talking about 1921 she forgot herself and described the events as if she had been there. She called Bates a typical New Zealander but gave herself out to be a Londoner. She said whitebait are only a quarter of the size of sprats. New Zealand whitebait are – English whitebait are about the same size.

'And as we've now discovered, she didn't send my cables. Of course she thought poor little Bates was hot on her tracks, especially when she learned that he'd come here to see me. She's got the kind of crossword-puzzle mind that would think up the biblical clues, and would get no end of a kick in writing them in. She's overwhelmingly conceited and vindictive.'

'Still – '

'I know. Not good enough if we'd played the waiting game. But good enough to try shock tactics. We caught her off her guard and she cracked up.'

'Not,' Mr Fox said, 'a nice type of woman.'

Alleyn strolled to the gate and looked up the lane to the church. The spire shone golden in the evening sun.

'The rector,' Alleyn said, 'tells me he's going to do something about the balcony.'

'Mrs Simpson, née Wagstaff,' Fox remarked, 'suggested wire netting.'

'And she ought to know,' Alleyn said and turned back to the cottage.

NGAIO MARSH

The Inspector Alleyn Mysteries, Volume 1

A MAN LAY DEAD

Sir Hubert Handesley's extravagant weekend house-parties are deservedly famous for his exciting Murder Game. But when the lights go up this time, there is a real corpse with a real dagger in the back. All seven suspects have skilful alibis – so Chief Detective Inspector Roderick Alleyn has to figure out the whodunit…

ENTER A MURDERER

The crime scene was the stage of the Unicorn Theatre, when prop gun fired a very real bullet; the victim was an actor clawing his way to stardom using bribery instead of talent; and the suspects included two unwilling girlfriends and several relieved blackmail victims. The stage is set for one of Roderick Alleyn's most baffling cases…

THE NURSING HOME MURDER

A Harley Street surgeon and his attractive nurse are almost too nervous to operate. Their patient is the Home Secretary – and they both have very good personal reasons to want him dead. The operation is a complete success – but he dies within hours, and Inspector Alleyn must find out why…

'Transforms the detective story from a mere puzzle into a novel.'   *Daily Express*

978-0-00-732869-7

NGAIO MARSH

The Inspector Alleyn Mysteries, Volume 2

DEATH IN ECSTASY

Who slipped cyanide into the ceremonial wine of ecstasy at the House of the Sacred Flame? The other initiates and the High Priest claim to be above earthly passions. But Roderick Alleyn discovers that the victim had provoked lust and jealousy, and he suspects that more evil still lurks behind the Sign of the Sacred Flame...

VINTAGE MURDER

New Zealand theatrical manager Alfred Meyer is planning a surprise for his wife's birthday – a jeroboam of champagne descending gently onto the stage after the performance. But, as Roderick Alleyn witnesses, something goes horribly wrong. Is the death the product of Maori superstitions – or something more down to earth?

ARTISTS IN CRIME

It starts as an art exercise – the knife under the drape, the pose outlined in chalk. But when Agatha Troy returns to her class, the scene has been re-enacted: the model is dead, fixed in the most dramatic pose Troy has ever seen. It's a difficult case for Chief Detective Inspector Alleyn. Is the woman he loves really a murderess...?

'As nearly flawless as makes no odds.' *Sunday Times*

978-0-00-732870-3

NGAIO MARSH

The Inspector Alleyn Mysteries, Volume 3

DEATH IN A WHITE TIE

The season has begun. Débutantes and chaperones are planning their gala dinners – and the blackmailer is planning strategies to stalk his next victim. But Chief Detective Inspector Roderick Alleyn knows that something is up and has already planted his friend Lord Gospell at the dinner. But someone else has got there first…

OVERTURE TO DEATH

It was planned as an act of charity: a new piano for the parish hall, and an amusing evening's entertainment to finance the gift. But all is doomed when Miss Campanula sits down to play. A chord is struck, a shot rings out, and Miss Campanula is dead. It seems to be a case of sinister infatuation for Roderick Alleyn…

DEATH AT THE BAR

A midsummer evening – darts night at *The Plume of Feathers*, a traditional Devonshire public house. A distinguished painter, a celebrated actor, a woman graduate, a plump lady from County Clare and a local farmer all play their parts in a fatal experiment which calls for the investigative expertise of Inspector Alleyn…

'The greatest exponent of the classical English detective story.'
Daily Telegraph

978-0-00-732871-0

NGAIO MARSH

The Inspector Alleyn Mysteries, Volume 4

SURFEIT OF LAMPREYS

The Lampreys were a peculiar family. They entertained their guests with charades – like rich Uncle Gabriel, who was always such a bore. The Lampreys thought if they jollied him up he would bail them out of poverty again. But Uncle Gabriel meets a violent end, and Chief Inspector Alleyn had to work out which of them killed him...

DEATH AND THE DANCING FOOTMAN

It begins as an entertainment: eight people, many of them adversaries, gathered for a winter weekend by a host with a love for theatre. It ends in snowbound disaster. Everyone has an alibi – and a motive as well. But Roderick Alleyn soon realizes that it all hangs on Thomas, the dancing footman...

COLOUR SCHEME

It was a horrible death – lured into a pool of boiling mud and left to die. Roderick Alleyn, far from home on a wartime quest for enemy agents, knows that any number of people could have killed him: the English exiles he'd hated, the New Zealanders he'd despised, or the Maoris he'd insulted. Even the spies he'd thwarted...

'She is astoundingly good.' *Daily Express*

978-0-00-732872-7

NGAIO MARSH

The Inspector Alleyn Mysteries, Volume 5

DIED IN THE WOOL

One summer evening in 1942 Flossie Rubrick, MP, one of the most formidable women in New Zealand, goes to her husband's wool shed to rehearse a patriotic speech – and disappears. Three weeks later she turns up at an auction – packed inside one of her own bales of wool and very, very dead...

FINAL CURTAIN

Just as Agatha Troy, the world famous painter, completes her portrait of Sir Henry Ancred, the Grand Old Man of the stage, the old actor dies. The dramatic circumstances of his death are such that Scotland Yard is called in – in the person of Troy's long-absent husband, Chief Detective Inspector Roderick Alleyn...

SWING, BROTHER, SWING

The music rises to a climax: Lord Pastern aims his revolver and fires. The figure in the spotlight falls – and the *coup-de-théatre* has become murder... Has the eccentric peer let hatred of his future son-in-law go too far? Or will a tangle of jealousies and blackmail reveal to Inspector Alleyn an altogether different murderer?

'A novelist of glittering accomplishment.'   *Sunday Times*

978-0-00-732873-4

NGAIO MARSH

The Inspector Alleyn Mysteries, Volume 6

OPENING NIGHT

Dreams of stardom lured Martyn Tarne from faraway New Zealand to a soul-destroying round of West End agents and managers in search of work. Now, driven by sheer necessity, she accepts the humble job of dresser to the Vulcan Theatre's leading lady. But the eagerly awaited opening night brings a strange turn of the wheel of fortune – and sudden unforeseen death...

SPINSTERS IN JEOPARDY

High in the mountains stands an historic Saracen fortress, home of the mysterious Mr Oberon, leader of a coven of witches. Roderick Alleyn, on holiday with his family, suspects that a huge drugs ring operates from within the castle. When someone else stumbles upon the secret, Mr Oberon decides his strange rituals require a human sacrifice...

SCALES OF JUSTICE

The inhabitants of Swevenings are stirred only by a fierce competition to catch a monster trout known to dwell in their beautiful stream. Then one of their small community is found brutally murdered; beside him is the freshly killed trout. Chief Detective Inspector Roderick Alleyn's murder investigation seems to be much more interested in the fish...

'A brilliant, vivacious teller of detective novels.'

News Chronicle

978-0-00-732874-1

NGAIO MARSH

The Inspector Alleyn Mysteries, Volume 7

OFF WITH HIS HEAD

When the pesky Anna Bünz arrives at Mardian to investigate local folk-dancing, she quickly antagonizes the villagers. But Mrs Bünz is not the only source of friction. When the sword dancers' traditional mock beheading of the Winter Solstice becomes horribly real, Superintendent Roderick Alleyn finds himself faced with a complex case of gruesome proportions...

SINGING IN THE SHROUDS

On a cold February London night, the police find a corpse on the quayside, her body covered with flower petals and pearls. The killer, who walked away singing, is known to be one of nine passengers on the cargo ship, *Cape Farewell*. Superintendent Roderick Alleyn joins the ship on the most difficult assignment of his career...

FALSE SCENT

Mary Bellamy, darling of the London stage, holds a 50th birthday party, a gala for everyone who loves her and fears her power. Then someone uses a deadly insect spray on Mary instead of the azaleas. The suspects, all very theatrically, are playing the part of mourners. Superintendent Alleyn has to find out which one played the murderer...

'Brilliant – ranks with Agatha Christie and Dorothy Sayers'
Times Literary Supplement

978-0-00-732875-8

NGAIO MARSH

The Inspector Alleyn Mysteries, Volume 8

HAND IN GLOVE

The April Fool's Day was a roaring success for all, it seemed –
except for poor Mr Cartell who ended up in the ditch – for
ever. Then there was the case of Mr Percival Pyke Period's letter of condolence, sent before the body was found – not to
mention the family squabbles. It's all a puzzling crime for
Superintendent Alleyn...

DEAD WATER

Times are good in the Cornish village of Portcarrow, as hun-
dreds flock to taste the healing waters of Pixie Falls. When Miss
Emily Pride inherits this celebrated land, she wants to put an
end to the villagers' exploitation of miracle cures, especially
Miss Elspeth Costs's gift shop. But someone puts an end to Miss
Cost, and Roderick Alleyn finds himself literally on the spot...

DEATH AT THE DOLPHIN

The bombed-out Dolphin Theatre is given to Peregrine Jay by
a mysterious oil millionaire, who also gives him a glove that
belonged to Shakespeare to display in the dockside theatre. But
then a murder takes place, a boy is attacked, and the glove is
stolen. Inspector Roderick Alleyn doesn't think oil and water
are a good mix...

'The queen of the straight crime novel – long may she reign!'
Sunday Times

978-0-00-732876-5

NGAIO MARSH

The Inspector Alleyn Mysteries, Volume 10

BLACK AS HE'S PAINTED

Called in to help with security arrangements for a presidential reception at a London embassy, Chief Superintendent Alleyn ensures the house and grounds are stiff with police. Nevertheless, an assassin strikes, and Alleyn finds no shortage of help, from Special Branch to a tribal court – and a small black cat named Lucy Lockett...

LAST DITCH

Young Rickie Alleyn has come to the Channel Islands to write, but village life seems tedious – until he finds the stablehand in a ditch, dead from an unlucky jump. But Rickie notices something strange and his father, Chief Superintendent Roderick Alleyn, is discreetly summoned to the scene, when Rickie disappears...

GRAVE MISTAKE

With two husbands dead, a daughter marrying the wrong man and a debilitating disease, it is no wonder that Sybil Foster took her own life. But Chief Superintendent Roderick Alleyn doesn't believe she was the type to kill herself – and he thinks someone else has made a very grave mistake...

'In the front rank of crime-story writers.'   *The Times*

978-0-00-732878-9

NGAIO MARSH

The Inspector Alleyn Mysteries, Volume 11

PHOTO-FINISH

The luxury mansion on New Zealand's Lake Waihoe is the ideal place for a world-famous soprano to rest after her triumphant tour. Among the other guests are Chief Superintendent Alleyn and his wife – but theirs is not a social visit. When tragedy strikes, and isolated by one of the lake's sudden storms, Alleyn faces one of his trickiest cases...

LIGHT THICKENS

Peregrine Jay, owner of the Dolphin Theatre, is putting on a magnificent production of Macbeth, the play that, superstition says, always brings bad luck. But one night the claymore swings and the dummy's head is more than real: murder behind the scene. Luckily, Chief Superintendent Roderick Alleyn is in the audience...

BLACK BEECH AND HONEYDEW

With all the insight and style her readers came to expect of her, Ngaio Marsh's autobiography captures all the joys, fears and hopes of a spirited young woman growing up in Christchurch, and charts her theatre and writing careers both in New Zealand and the UK. This sanguine, unpretentious and revealing book has been acclaimed for telling her most distinguished mystery – who was Ngaio Marsh?

'Read just one – and you've got to read them all.'   *Daily Mail*

978-0-00-732879-6